Sea Fighter

James H. Cobb

Sea Fighter

G. P. PUTNAM'S SONS
A MEMBER OF PENGUIN PUTNAM INC.
NEW YORK
2000

This is a work of fiction. Names, characters, places, and incidents
either are the product of the author's imagination or are used
fictitiously, and any resemblance to actual persons, living or dead,
business establishments, events, or locales is entirely coincidental.

G. P. Putnam's Sons
Publishers Since 1838
a member of
Penguin Putnam Inc.
375 Hudson Street
New York, NY 10014

Library of Congress Cataloging-in-Publication Data
Cobb, James H.
Sea Fighter / James H. Cobb.
p.   cm.
ISBN 0-399-14593-1
1. Women sailors—Fiction.   2. Imaginary wars and battles—Fiction.
3. Twenty-first century—Fiction.   I. Title.
PS3553.O178 S37   2000   99-051900 CIP
813'.54—dc21

Printed in the United States of America

1   3   5   7   9   10   8   6   4   2

This book is printed on acid-free paper. ∞

BOOK DESIGN BY RENATO STANISIC
MAP BY JEFFREY L. WARD

Dedication

To the men, and now the women, of the gunboat navy.
From Lake Erie to the Mekong Delta,
from Vicksburg to the Bismarck Archipelago,
frequently it has been required that they do the most with the least.

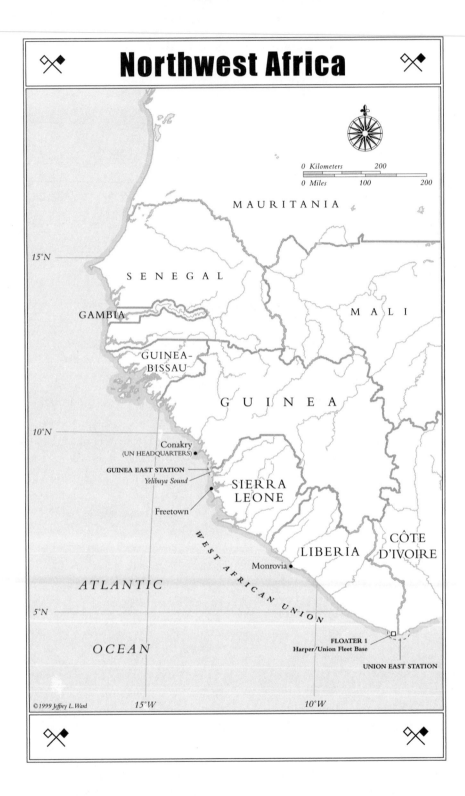

Northwest Africa

0 Kilometers 200

0 Miles 100 200

MAURITANIA

15°N

SENEGAL

GAMBIA

MALI

GUINEA-
BISSAU

GUINEA

10°N

Conakry
(UN HEADQUARTERS) ●

GUINEA EAST STATION
Yelibuya Sound

SIERRA
LEONE

Freetown

CÔTE
D'IVOIRE

LIBERIA

WEST AFRICAN UNION

Monrovia ●

ATLANTIC

5°N

FLOATER 1
Harper/Union Fleet Base

OCEAN

UNION EAST STATION

© 1999 Jeffrey L. Ward

15°W

10°W

Mobile Offshore Base, Floater 1
13.5 Miles off the African Gold Coast

2218 Hours, Zone Time; September 7, 2007

With the sun down, the small and overstressed air conditioner set in the housing module's window at last started to make headway against the equatorial heat. Still, the Marine utilities she wore, the smallest set available within the task group, felt tentlike and oppressive. Ignoring the chafing discomfort of the perspiration-damp camouflage cloth, Amanda Garrett studied the screen of her personal computer, reconsidering what she had composed.

> *Dearest Arkady:*
>
> *This is one of those special letters that we of the profession of arms find necessary to write on occasion. If you are reading it, it will mean that I am dead.*
>
> *Hopefully, I will have been lost while bringing my mission to a successful conclusion. Also hopefully, I will have died alone. As always, my prayer before action this night will be that no weakness or failing on my part will cost the lives of any more of those I command. The blood price for this operation is already far too high.*
>
> *I also regret the other costs, the personal ones we share. I wish that some of the things we dreamed of during our brief time together could have become a reality. I also wish that it could have been in me to accept all of the good things you offered. Remember that, Arkady. I thank you with all my heart for all of your selfless love, courage and companionship. Also for all the times you stood at my side when I needed someone. I will carry those memories with me on this, my last and longest voyage. In return, all I can say is that I loved you and that I'm sorry it couldn't be.*
>
> *Good-bye, love. Find happiness.*
> *Amanda*

There was no more to be said. Or there was far too much to say in the time she had remaining. Amanda initiated "File Save" and downloaded the sterile words. Two other letters, one to her father and a second to Christine Rendino, were already on the disk in her laptop. Chris would know where to find them and would see they were delivered.

This was the last task she'd set for herself. Everything was as ready as it could be made.

Amanda allowed herself a moment of quiet neutrality, staring past the screen of the personal computer to the dull white-painted wall of her quarters. Somehow, even after five months, it still didn't feel right to call it a "bulkhead" on this ship that wasn't a ship.

Hanging from hooks on that wall were the unaccustomed items of equipment she had drawn: the MOLLE load-bearing harness with the radios and flares already clipped to it, the pistol belt and ammunition pouches, the bulky Marine flak jacket, and the ballistic helmet with its camouflage-pattern cover.

She gave a start as the document on the monitor disappeared, replaced by the nautical imaging of a Navy League screensaver. Glancing at the militarily formatted clock hack in the corner of the flatscreen, she noted the time: 2221 hours.

2200 . . . had it started only seventeen hours ago? Less than three-quarters of a single day?

No. Not really. This current crisis was just the latest link in a long and tortuous chain of events. One that had been initiated long before Amanda Lee Garrett, former Commander and now Captain, U.S.N., had ever been called to duty in this strange place. Long before she had ever heard of the West African Union. Long before there had even been a West African Union of which to hear.

Origin

Liberia.

Once it had been the oldest participatory democracy on the African continent, maintaining a Constitution and Bill of Rights modeled upon that of the United States. Once its economic growth rate had been second only to that of Japan. Once its John F. Kennedy Hospital had been honored as one of the most modern and sophisticated medical research facilities in the Third World.

Once, Liberia had been a nation.

⚔

The Land Rover roared through the rank, tropic night, following the potholed pavement that climbed Mamba Point. In the darkness beyond the fan of the vehicle's headlights, there was scuttling movement. Shadowy forms sprang aside off the road, seeking deeper pools of night to hide in. Other figures huddled animal-like in the shanties and half-ruined buildings that lined the trash-strewn street.

In recent years, the citizens of Monrovia had learned that the people with the cars were also frequently the people with the guns. Likewise, they had found that those guns were often used for no more reason than to make blood spray.

Fear was not a factor restricted to pedestrians, however. The Nigerian soldier manning the Land Rover's pintle-mounted Bren gun was nervous as well. He traversed the muzzle of the weapon in short nervous arcs, covering the roadsides ahead. Death frequently walked abroad in the streets of Liberia's ruined capital. You never knew when he might step out from around a corner to greet you.

The howl of the Land Rover's engine faded to a grumble as it rolled to a halt in front of what had been Monrovia's Masonic Hall. Dismounting from the doorless 4 × 4, Captain Obe Belewa issued a short, curt command. "Keep your engine running, Corporal."

Clad in the same worn jungle camouflage as his men, the tall African army officer double-timed past the bullet-chipped statue of some long-ago Liberian Grand Master and up the marble steps to the entryway of the massive old building. The cracked Ionic columns guarding the portico glowed palely in the starlight, like part of some ancient Roman ruin.

ECOMOG (the Economic Community of West African States Military Observation Group) had taken over the building as its headquarters. A pair of lax sentries at the doorway fumbled to attention as Captain Balewa stormed past them, not bothering to reply to their hasty salutes.

A single generator-powered safety light illuminated the looted and stripped reception hall. One of the staff lieutenants attached to Headquarters Company sat at a gray metal field desk, reading a British sports magazine by its pulsing light.

"I need to talk to Colonel Eba," Balewa demanded, looming out of the shadows beyond the desk. "Now!"

Startled, the duty officer dropped his magazine, recoiling under the intensity of the speaker's words.

Broad-shouldered, hard-muscled, and grimly handsome, Belewa was an impressive figure under normal circumstances. Now, with his face set and the fires of rage burning behind his dark eyes, he was beyond impressive and well into frightening.

The duty officer knew that the Browning automatic pistol and the razor-honed jungle knife on the Captain's belt were not mere symbols of authority. They were the arms of a warrior, well-maintained and ready for instant use. The same could be said of the mechanized infantry company Belewa commanded. It was freely acknowledged to be an elite unit, the best formation of the battalion and of the Observation Group. Some dared whisper even of the entire Nigerian army.

Captain Belewa also had the reputation of being a very bad man to cross.

"The Colonel is off duty, sir," the lieutenant stammered. "He has left instructions not to be disturbed unless it is an emergency."

Belewa's fist slammed down onto the desktop with an oil-canning boom. "Then consider this an emergency! I will speak with Colonel Eba now!"

The duty officer hastily summoned a runner to guide Belewa to the Colonel's quarters. The lieutenant knew that in doing so, he would draw the eventual ire of his battalion commander down upon himself. However, at the time, that seemed the lesser of the two evils.

Belewa followed his guide up the curve of the grand stairway to another patch of generator light on the second floor of the vast old structure. Like most of Monrovia's major buildings, the Masonic Temple had long before been pillaged of everything that could be stolen, down to the doors themselves, and the illumination leaked from around a cloth curtain drawn across an empty entryway.

The sound of music and women's laughter also issued from behind the curtain.

Responding to the summons of the runner, Colonel Eba stepped out into the shadows of the hall. Belewa caught a glimpse inside the Colonel's quarters as the curtain was drawn aside. Several of the other Battalion officers lounged there, along with a couple of young Liberian women. Attractive women, clad in bright, cheap dresses, who swayed in time to the rhythmic Nigerian Afro-Pop issuing from a tape player.

Eba was a heavyset man, thickening toward a stoutness that pulled his camouflage fatigues taut. In one hand he carried a coffee mug half-filled with whiskey. "What's this about, Captain?" he demanded, scowling.

Belewa held at a rigid parade rest, his eyes focused over the head of the squat Eba. "Sir, I have received word from one of my scouting teams that the village of Simonsville, fifteen kilometers northeast of the city, is under attack by an unidentified armed force. I have sent two reports concerning this event to this headquarters."

"We thank you for your efficiency in bringing this matter to our attention, Captain," Eba replied archly. "I am sure I will be most interested in reading your reconnaissance reports in the morning."

"Sir," Belewa continued lowly, "I also dispatched two requests for the release of the Mobile Reaction Force to respond to this event. I've received no answer to either request."

"Perhaps that is because none was required." Eba took a sip of whiskey from his mug. "Simonsville is on your morning patrol route. You can check the situation out then. There's no sense in our people tearing about in the darkness chasing rumors."

"Sir, this is not a rumor! I have a scout team on a hill overlooking Simonsville now. The village is being torn to pieces! I can have my men there in twenty minutes!"

"No, Captain, no." Eba chuckled patronizingly. "You young bull officers are all the same. Always prone to charge at every little sound in the bush. That's not proper military thinking. We must not waste our strength by becoming involved in every little squabble the locals have."

The Colonel chuckled again and took another sip from his cup. "Remember, Belewa. We are here as a peacekeeping force. How would it look if we go about getting into fights all of the time."

"I thought we were here to help these people." Belewa made no effort to control the contempt in his voice.

Eba's face hardened. "You are here to obey my orders, Captain. You may investigate these events in Simonsville on your morning patrol and not one moment sooner. Do you understand?"

"Yes, sir. I understand very well."

⚹◆

The sky was barely touched with pink in the east when the column of Land Rovers and Steyr 4K-7 armored personnel carriers roared into Simonsville. But by then it was far, far too late.

There had never been much to the little village, just a small cluster of huts and shanties along a dirt track, surrounded by upland rice fields and the low scrub left behind by logging and slash-and-burn agriculture. Now only ashes remained. Ashes and a few guttering remnants of flame curling around blackened frames of buildings.

There had been people here, though. Their remnants had been left behind as well. Charred forms lay in the wreckage, twisted grotesquely, frozen in mid-writhe. The nude body of a young woman stood nailed in place against the last intact wall of the village. Given the extent of the bloodstains, she had been alive as the nails had been driven home. However, someone eventually had granted the girl as much mercy as could be found out in that scarlet night. Her head had been stricken from her shoulders with a blow from a machete.

Possibly the attackers had been part of Charles Taylor's National Patriotic Front of Liberia. Or possibly it had been one of the splinters of the United Liberation Movement of Liberia for Democracy. Or an element of "Prince" Yormie Johnson's Independent Patriotic Front, or remnants of the dead President Samuel Doe's Armed Forces. Following the Taylor-Doe civil war and the collapse of the Liberian government, a dozen different factions had sprung up to gnaw at the corpse of the fallen nation. Each was little more than a loosely organized armed rabble, hiding its inhumanity behind a high-sounding name.

Somewhere, a child cried, not with the cry of a child but with the agonized shrieks of a small, trapped animal in agony. Possibly the men who had created this carnage had a valid reason for annihilating Simonsville. More than likely, however, they didn't.

Seated in the front seat of the command Land Rover, Captain Belewa snarled his orders into his radio handset. "All elements deploy by the action plan! First Platoon—establish a security perimeter! Second Platoon—search the village for survivors! Weapons platoon, set your pickets around the vehicles and get the aid station established! Third Platoon—start a sweep beyond the village area! Look for any of the wounded or injured who may have crawled off into the bush! Move!"

Carrying their long-barreled FALN assault rifles at port arms, the Nigerian mobile troopers dismounted and streamed away on their assigned tasks. Commanding the company's headquarters section, Lieutenant Sako Atiba was kept busy for several minutes inside the Steyr communications track, notifying ECOMOG headquarters of their arrival and establishing the tactical radio net with the platoon leaders.

With those tasks accomplished, the compact and panther-lean young officer stepped down the tail ramp of the big Austrian-built APC. Walking forward along the line of parked vehicles, he went to report personally to his commanding officer, military mentor, and friend.

A faint morning breeze stirred the humid air, but it served only to stir the miasma of corruption, burnt flesh, and charred wood. This was something Atiba had long ago learned about serving in Liberia. You could never get away from the evil, sweet scent of the dead. Perhaps that was the cause of some of the savagery that had infected this land. You inhaled death with every breath. A Housa tribesman, native to Nigeria's Sahel uplands, Atiba sometimes dreamed at night of the dry, clean winds blowing in from the Sahara.

Approaching the command Land Rover, Atiba was surprised to find Captain Belewa sitting in the vehicle, looking out across the burned-out funeral pyre that was Simonsville. The tall warrior still had the radio microphone gripped in his left hand. The right, though, was clinched tightly into a pale-knuckled fist, a fist that beat slowly and deliberately against the heavy metal of the Land Rover's dashboard. Atiba was even more surprised to see the tears streaming from his company commander's eyes.

"We have got to stop doing this to ourselves, Sako," Obe Belewa murmured tightly. "We have got to stop doing this!"

Monrovia, Liberia   **0635 Hours, Zone Time; June 6, 2002**

"Ann, can you hear me?"

"Yes, Ian. Quite well."

"Very good. We have our satellite phone set up here on the roof of the Ambassador Hotel. We're still attempting to establish our video link. Not much luck yet, I'm afraid. Until then, we'll try to describe what's been going on here in Monrovia since this morning's . . . incident."

"What is happening, Ian?"

"Honestly, not a great deal that we can see. Our hotel is on the beach near the British Embassy and we are looking north toward Mamba Point and the Mamba Point Hotel, the current seat of the provisional Liberian ruling council. This appeared to be the focal point of the heavy gunfire that broke out shortly before dawn this morning. Nothing much is happening now. . . . There is a faint haze of smoke around the tall, white hotel building . . . that appears to be all."

"Have there been any other outbreaks of fighting in the area, Ian?"

"We've heard rumors of some gunfire around both the ECOMOG base outside of the city and at the Barclay Training Center, the headquarters of the Liberian Armed Forces. We have not been able to verify this, however. There is a security cordon thrown up around the hotel, and none of the press here have been able to get into the field yet today."

"Do you feel that you are in any danger, Ian?"

"No, not really. Everything seems quite calm, quite orderly, much as it has been here in Monrovia for the past couple of months. A very polite officer from the ECOMOG forces came through and assured everyone that this lock-down is only temporary and that there will be a press briefing on recent de-velopments sometime later today. . . . By the way, that sound you might be hearing is a Nigerian Army helicopter circling over the city. It has a loud-hailer system working, advising the populace to remain calm and stay off the streets. The same essential message is also being broadcast by KISS, the Monrovia ra-dio station, interspersed with the usual African pop."

"What do you think is taking place, Ian? You're our World Services man in Liberia."

"I honestly don't know, Ann. We've had a couple of extremely quiet months here. It actually looked as if the long Liberian nightmare was over. The cease-fire between the Liberian Military and ECOMOG forces and the re-maining rebel factions upcountry seemed to have been holding. There were ongoing negotiations to form a permanent representative government and to draft a new constitution. . . . Brigadier Belewa, the ECOMOG force com-mander and a most remarkable man, has been working tirelessly for a perma-nent end to this long-festering conflict. I hope this isn't a setback for the very successful and enlightened policies he's been putting into play here."

"Ian. We've been in touch with our man in Lagos. He reports that the Nigerian government has been out of communication with both the ECO-MOG garrison and the ECOWAS headquarters in Monrovia since late last night. They are apparently also in the dark about what may be happening there in Liberia."

"Ann, there is one thing I can comment on. We have seen a number of military patrols in the downtown area . . . peacekeeping patrols, I gather. They all seem to be conformed in the same way: six men, three teams of two. One of the patrols is below us in the street now. Two of the soldiers are obviously Nigerians from the ECOMOG forces, while two of the others appear to be

Liberian army. The last pair are armed but in civilian clothing . . . a rather ragged-looking couple of individuals . . . I have no idea who they may belong to. One of the lads here suggests that they might be members of one of the rebel factions. I'm not sure how that could be."

"Ian? . . . Ian?"

"Stand by, Ann. We have something here. . . . Ah, we have a development. . . . I have just been handed a flyer that was delivered to our rooms a few moments ago. It's a notification of a press conference to be held at ECOMOG headquarters this afternoon. The purpose of the conference is to, and I quote, 'clarify recent events taking place within Liberia for the world community' . . . Bloody hell!"

"What is it, Ian?"

"This document. It's signed "Brigadier Obe Belewa, Premier General of the Liberian Union.""

Freetown, Sierra Leone   0526 Hours, Zone Time; October 23, 2005

Private Jeremy Makeni yawned mightily and tried to defy the overwhelming urge to sleep. Lance Corporal Rupert, the soldier who shared the night's sentry duty at the Port Master's dock, had surrendered to sleep an hour before. Stretched out and snoring with his head propped on a coil of rope, the corporal relied on luck or Private Makeni to wake him before their relief showed up at six o'clock.

Granted that they showed up at all. The personnel of the Freetown garrison force were lax about such things, even as the fighting raged inland and on the eastern border.

Angrily, Makeni straightened and again began to pace the sentry-go he had set for himself. Was he not a soldier, even if only guarding a rickety wooden pier miles from the battle line?

When the notice had come calling him to national service, Jeremy had been overjoyed. At last, here was something better than working in his father's chophouse. At last, an opportunity to do something more than sweeping floors and washing kettles. At seventeen, a chance to be a man instead of a boy.

Pausing at the head of the pier, Jeremy looked out across the darkened waters of Kroo Bay and listened to the sluggish lap of the waves against the pilings. His father hadn't understood, of course. He couldn't see that it was time for his son to grow up. Jeremy caught him trying to pay dash to the government man to have Jeremy's name taken from the list.

He and his father had argued then. Not as father and son, but as one man with another, with men's anger and pride for the first time. They had not spoken since.

Jeremy still suspected that money had changed hands behind his back somewhere, however. Instead of being sent to the troubles up around the refugee camps or to defend against the Liberian threat, he had been assigned here after completing his month's training. To the fat and sleepy Freetown garrison.

Out in the bay, the lights of an anchored ship cast glimmering golden streaks across the oily water. It had not been there when Jeremy had come on duty. It was common for a vessel arriving in Freetown after dark to anchor in the roadstead. The pilot would go out in the morning to collect his fee and his dash, and the harbormaster, after doing the same, would clear the vessel to dock.

Jeremy turned and began to pace back down the worn planking, stepping over Corporal Rupert's sprawled legs. Damn! Why couldn't his father have left well enough alone! The fighting had begun and here he was, stuck in the city, four blocks from where he had grown up!

Jeremy's steady footsteps faltered. The fighting had begun. And maybe soon enough it would come to him. The government boasted about the victories they were winning in the field, but the rumors didn't match up. There was a battle going on out along the Kenema highway, and no one had heard anything from upcountry in days.

In such times, maybe it was not such a good thing for him and his father to also be at odds. After all, his father did remember the bad days back during the civil war. And who could blame a parent for worrying about an only son?

Jeremy Makeni grinned, his smile flashing in the darkness. After he was relieved on duty this morning, what would happen if he walked into his father's café and called for his favorite breakfast of *benchi* and bread. After arguing as two men, perhaps now they could also sit and talk and laugh as two men. Still smiling, Jeremy turned.

Abruptly, the smile left his face.

A steely smear of dawn showed in the sky, revealing a long row of shadows slinking toward the harbormaster's pier. Over the lap of the waves and Corporal Rupert's snoring, Jeremy heard the mutter of a throttled-down engine. And beyond the swampy miasma of the shoreline, he smelled the metallic exhaust of an outboard motor.

A launch of some kind, long and low and painted to match the darkness, was creeping in from the bay. Towed behind it were a string of smaller rubber boats, each loaded with a huddled mass of men. The first hint of daylight gleamed on a rifle barrel.

Jeremy yelled out a startled, wordless cry of warning as he struggled to un-sling his old bolt-action Enfield. Sleep-dazed Corporal Rupert sprang to his feet, his weapon lying forgotten on the pier decking. An instant later twin daggers of flame lanced out from the bow of the launch, the converging tracer streams shredding the noncom and flinging him aside.

Exposed for the first time to the realities of war, Jeremy Makeni froze. He was never given the instant he needed to recover. The dual-mount machine guns raked the length of the pier and something smashed into the young soldier's chest.

He fell beside Corporal Rupert, a lingering fragment of warrior's pride keeping his hand closed on the stock of his rifle. Jeremy's eyes no longer responded to the growing glow of the sun, but faintly, he heard a man speaking. For a last moment, he thought it was his father's voice.

⚓

Yelling their deep-toned battle cries, the Liberian soldiers streamed up from the pier float, ignoring the two bloodstained bodies sprawled on the upper deck. Forming into assault teams, they stormed the streets of the city, en route to their assigned objectives. It was a scene being repeated a dozen times over along the waterfront as the seizure of Sierra Leone's capital gained momentum. Over all, recorded words thundered repetitively from a bank of loudspeakers aboard the invasion transport.

"PEOPLE OF FREETOWN! STAY IN YOUR HOMES! STAY OUT OF THE STREETS! LIBERATION HAS COME! SOLDIERS OF SIERRA LEONE! LAY DOWN YOUR ARMS! YOU ARE OUR BROTHERS! WE WISH YOU NO HARM!"

Washington, D.C   **1021 Hours, Zone Time; November 20, 2005**

The indirect lighting in the White House briefing room dimmed. The two-meter-wide flatscreen set into the cherry paneling of the wall flicked on, displaying a computer graphics map of the African continent for the three people seated at the central conference table.

Secretary of State Harrison Van Lynden turned in his chair to face the man at the head of the table. "To begin, sir," the graying New Englander said, "I believe that a brief review of the situation in the crisis zone would help to put today's developments in perspective. With your permission, Mr. Dubois, our Undersecretary for African Affairs, will walk us through the recent events in the region."

Benton Childress, the forty-fourth President of the United States, nodded.

"Very well, Harry. Carry on, Mr. Dubois. Whatever you think we need to know."

"Thank you, sir." A fit-looking black man in his late thirties, Richard Dubois scowled a scholar's thoughtful scowl as he keyed a command into the wall screen control pad. The northwest quadrant of the map windowed up, filling with a view of the great West African peninsula jutting out into the Atlantic.

"West Africa, gentlemen," he began. "To say that this is an unstable and troubled region would be a cataclysmic understatement. Although potentially rich in natural resources, eight out of the world's ten most impoverished nations are located here. Although hundreds of millions of foreign-aid dollars have been expended in the region, it still contains eight out of the world's ten national populations with the shortest average life expectancy. Massive governmental corruption is rife. The military coup is the accepted method of changing administrations, and for the past two decades total anarchy has been commonplace."

Childress nodded thoughtfully. "According to my family's genealogy, some of my people may have come from over there. Only from a little farther north, near Mali."

"Many of our ancestors did, sir," Dubois agreed. "Mine came from farther east, we think from around Ghana. This region was the focus of the western Atlantic slave trade. The coastal chiefs grew rich raiding other tribes hundreds of miles inland, keeping the barracoons full for the European traders."

Van Lynden gave a brief snort of grim laughter. "If you want a touch of irony here, one of my ancestors has a connection with the area as well. He was a rather notorious Dutch sea captain who built himself something of a reputation as a blackbirder. A few centuries ago, our families might all have met under somewhat different circumstances."

Dubois touched the display control again, and once more the screen image zoomed in on the western underbelly of the peninsula. "Here is the heart of the current crisis, the neighboring coastal states of Liberia and Sierra Leone. Both nations share a unique heritage. Both were founded in the early nineteenth century by freed black African slaves from North America. Sierra Leone as a British Crown colony in the year 1808. Liberia in 1822 as an independent nation with support from abolitionist factions within the United States.

"As a result, both use English as their official language and both have a distinctive Anglo-American flavoring to their national cultures. The governments of both nations were also established around the basic principles of Western-style democracy. That, however, didn't take quite so well."

Van Lynden crossed his arms and sank deeper into the leather of his conference chair, a frown coming across his angular "down north" features. "At one time I recall that both countries were considered model states among the emerging Third World nations."

"Very true, Mr. Secretary," Dubois agreed. "Sierra Leone gained full independence from Great Britain in 1961. Both it and Liberia had stable governments, growing economies, and reasonably good civil rights records for the region. Unfortunately, things began to go wrong. Large-scale pocket-lining on the part of governmental officials and a catastrophic brush with socialism bled the life out of the regional economy. This, combined with conflicts and favoritism among the tribal factions within both nations, soon led to large-scale unrest and disaffection.

"Both countries fell into a descending spiral of coup and civil war, each new regime coming into power proving to be worse than the one it had replaced. The government of Sierra Leone managed to maintain some semblance of national order, mostly thanks to the South African mercenaries hired to put down their last wave of revolts. Liberia, however, sank into total chaos."

"That I remember," President Childress commented. "Wasn't the death of one of the Liberian presidents, Samuel Doe, I believe, videotaped and distributed by his executioners?"

"Yes, sir, in September of 1990 by the forces of the National Patriotic Front of Liberia, the Charles Taylor faction. Only, it wasn't an execution, Mr. President. President Doe was tortured to death. Mr. Taylor himself personally officiated."

"Lord, that was a bad one," Van Lynden murmured. "I remember the U.S. took some flak for not intervening at the time. Frankly, though, we couldn't find a single faction in the whole damn place that we felt we could support. In the end, we used the Marines to evacuate our embassy staff and the other foreign nationals who were in-country and then just let the chips fall where they may."

Dubois nodded. "The organization that eventually did intervene was ECOWAS, the Economic Community of West African States. In response to the crisis, ECOMOG, the ECOWAS Military Observation Group, was established. This was a body of peacekeeping troops deployed into Liberia by the ECOWAS membership with the intent of stabilizing the area and allowing the formation of a new Liberian government.

"While involving contingents from the various ECOWAS states, ECOMOG was primarily made up of Nigerian forces. Putting it bluntly, its performance was lackluster. Or at least it was until Brigadier Belewa assumed command."

Dubois called up the next preprogrammed image in the briefing system, that of a tall, powerfully built black man in camouflage fatigues and field cap. Photographed against the backdrop of a shattered building, he stood with hands on hips, stern features set as if in thought.

"Brigadier General Obe Belewa, late of the Nigerian Army," Dubois continued. "Age forty-two. Born in the city of Oyo in western Nigeria. His tribal affiliation is Yoruba. Perhaps from them he inherited his talents as an empire builder. During the precolonial age, the Yoruba ruled one of the largest and most powerful of the West African kingdoms.

"The General was educated at Sandhurst and at the University of Ibadan. A truly remarkable individual, he was considered one of the rising stars in the Nigerian military, right up until he disowned his country to take over another."

"I still wonder just how he pulled that one off," the President commented.

"By a combination of guts, will, and a feat of covert statesmanship that would have made Machiavelli proud," Dubois replied. "Belewa attended a number of service schools here in the United States, including both the Army's Special Forces course at Fort Bragg and the Command and General Staff College at Fort Leavenworth. His instructors unanimously agree that the man is a brilliant strategist and tactician.

"It must have taken him years to set up the coup. We know that he volunteered repeatedly for service with the ECOMOG garrison in Liberia. With each tour of duty he must have picked up more contacts and established more links within both the provisional Liberian government and military and the various rebel factions back in the bush. As he grew in rank, he also began to maneuver a carefully handpicked cadre of officers and NCOs into the garrison force, disaffected military personnel who owed more allegiance to Belewa personally than they did to the Nigerian government.

"Eventually, Belewa was named commander of the ECOMOG garrison. Using the power inherent in that position, he began to bring about real change within Liberia. He decisively suppressed corruption and random violence, he got food and medical aid out to the rural areas, and he restarted the national economy. In doing so, he drew the loyalty of the Liberian people, not to Nigeria or the provisional Liberian government, but to himself."

"Wasn't his being a Nigerian, an outsider, a problem?" President Childress inquired.

"No, sir," Dubois replied with a shake of his head. "Belewa turned it into an advantage. He was a man outside of all the tribal conflicts and the interfactional hatreds. He became trusted and respected because he was scrupulously honest and even-handed at all times to all the involved parties. He also never made a promise that he couldn't deliver.

"As the talks between the provisional government and the leadership of

the rebel groups wrangled on, Belewa conducted a second level of covert negotiations with the dissatisfied lower echelons of both factions. Then, roughly
three years ago, when he had all of the pieces in place, he struck.

"The leadership of both the provisional Liberian government and of the
majority of the rebel groups were wiped out in a coordinated revolt, all factions then swearing allegiance to General Belewa. The Nigerian ECOMOG
garrison also mutinied, declaring for Belewa as well. Overnight, he went from
army officer to the leader of his own nation."

Dubois deactivated the screen and turned back to face the table. "To say
the least, there was a convulsion within the ECOWAS community. Nigeria attempted a degree of saber rattling at the new Liberian regime and its leader, but
nothing much came of it. They realized that if they attempted an invasion,
they'd be looking down the gun barrels of both their own elite military units
and a large and hostile guerrilla army. Belewa's takeover became accepted as a
fait accompli."

"You know," Van Lynden said thoughtfully, "you have to admire the man's
guts."

"There's more than that to admire about the man, Mr. Secretary. He's
turned out to be an extremely resourceful, intelligent, and dynamic leader. In
only three years he has turned a total basket case of a nation into an ordered,
stable, and growing society. In many ways, he is doing exactly what needs to be
done in the region. He is suppressing corruption, he is seeing to the welfare of
the majority of his population, and he is rebuilding the economic infrastructure of Liberia. Unfortunately, he is also a hard-core military dictator with a
taste for conquest."

The wall screen flicked on once more, this time displaying a large-scale
map of Sierra Leone. "Around the first of this year, the government of Sierra
Leone began to report a sudden mass exodus of refugees coming across their
border with Liberia. This exodus eventually grew into a flood of over a quarter of a million human beings, deluging the border areas.

"The Liberian government claimed that they were disaffected individuals
who had left a number of resettlement communities being developed near the
border. The refugees said that they had been driven into Sierra Leone at bayonet point."

"Where did these refugees all come from, Rich?" Van Lynden inquired,
frowning. "I mean, from within Liberia."

"No government is ever entirely popular with all of its citizens, Mr. President. The refugees are members of the Liberian tribal groups and political factions that did not support the Belewa takeover. When they began to organize a
resistance against his regime, Belewa reacted with mass deportations from the

rebellious sectors. Entire villages and urban neighborhoods were emptied. Men, women, and children, anyone even suspected of harboring anti-Union sympathies, were swept up into the DP camps and then pushed across the border, their goods and properties being given over to Union supporters."

President Childress removed his glasses and thoughtfully began to polish the lenses. "He must have read Chairman Mao's dictum that the guerrilla is a fish swimming in an ocean of peasants. Belewa's countermove against revolution was to drain the ocean."

"Much as Milosevic attempted in Kosovo back in '99. But Belewa took things one step further. Not only did he end his internal dissension, but by releasing this human flood on the neighboring state least able to cope with it, he succeeded in weakening and disrupting that nation to an even greater extent."

Van Lynden nodded. "Again turning a negative into a positive . . . to his way of thinking, at any rate."

"That is Belewa's style," Dubois agreed. "Sierra Leone was totally unable to deal with this massive influx of refugees. They couldn't even adequately feed and house their own population. Naturally the U.N. and the International Red Cross moved in, attempting to set up and supply refugee camps in the border regions. However, simultaneously with the arrival of the refugees, there was a sudden flare-up of guerrilla activity inside of Sierra Leone. A series of attacks were launched against transport facilities, food-distribution centers, and communications lines. Everything that was needed to deal with the refugee crisis was targeted, compounding the problem."

"How convenient for certain parties," Van Lynden commented dryly.

"Did these attacks originate from some group inside of Sierra Leone, or was this an outside insurgency?" the President asked, redonning his glasses.

"No conclusive evidence was ever collected either way. The Liberian government emphatically denied any involvement. However, these guerrillas definitely were not your average band of bush bandits. They were well trained, well equipped, and working to a definite plan of action. The relief program was paralyzed. Shortly thereafter, so was the entire nation of Sierra Leone. There was famine, mob attacks on the refugee camps, mass rioting. Sierra Leone's already fragile government began to disintegrate."

"And that's when Belewa hit them openly, right when things were falling to pieces," Van Lynden stated grimly.

"Exactly. Roughly a month ago, acting on the stated grounds that Liberian citizens were being endangered in the refugee camps and that the growing civil disorder in Sierra Leone was threatening to spill across their border, the Liberians invaded. The armed forces of Sierra Leone were totally overwhelmed. Freetown fell in a little over two weeks."

President Childress shook his head. "The bold-faced son of a bitch. He creates a crisis just to give himself the opportunity to resolve it on his terms."

"Negative to positive, sir," Dubois replied. "And I believe that brings us up to today's event."

"Pretty much so, Rich." The Secretary of State swiveled his chair to fully face the head of the table. "Mr. President. This morning, an official note was delivered to the State Department by the Liberian ambassador, stating his government's intent to form a political confederation with the occupied state of Sierra Leone. As of seven A.M., Washington time, the individual states of Liberia and Sierra Leone ceased to exist. There is now only the West African Union, with its capital in Monrovia. Included in the note was a request from the Belewa regime for formal recognition of the new government, another request that we close our embassy in Freetown, and assurances that the West African Union desires only the best of relations with the United States."

"Damn! Belewa isn't wasting any time, is he?"

"He never does, Mr. President," Dubois responded. "Not when it comes to organizing and solidifying his power base."

The frown on President Childress's face deepened. "I can state this for the book right now. This administration will recognize no territorial gains by any nation brought about by military aggression. Not on any grounds. Not under any justification. You can inform the Liberian ambassador of that point, Harry. You can also inform him that our embassy in Freetown stays open."

Van Lynden nodded, giving a slight smile. "I thought you'd feel that way about it, sir."

"That stated, what else can we do about this?"

Van Lynden and Dubois exchanged glances. "Speaking frankly, sir," the Secretary of State replied, "not a whole hell of a lot. We've had an arms and tech embargo in place against the Belewa regime ever since he seized power in Liberia, and a further expansion of monetary or trade restrictions against Liber—excuse me, the West African Union—would likely hurt the general populace more than it would the government."

"Is there any potential risk to American citizens inside of Union territory?"

"There is none apparent, Mr. President," Dubois replied. "Belewa is very careful about protecting foreign nationals in-country. He wants outside investment and development in his territory. He needs the jobs and the foreign exchange."

"Harry, what about the U.N.?"

"We might be able to get a vote of censure against the Union in the United Nations, but I doubt much more," Van Lynden answered. "If Belewa can energize the economy of Sierra Leone the way he has with the Liberian, there will be more money to be made out of trading with the Union than there was with the two states individually. Beyond that, not too many people are going to give all that much of a damn."

"And the West African group, ECOWAS? Do we have any idea where they're going to stand on this?"

Dubois shook his head. "You can expect very little, Mr. President. It was an ECOWAS peacekeeping operation that put Belewa into power in the first place. The recriminations from that have left the organization nearly prostrate. Hardly anyone is talking, nobody is trusting, and there is almost no chance of anyone organizing any kind of effective countermove."

"It sounds like you both are saying we have to accept another *fait accompli*."

Van Lynden lifted his hands. "Essentially sir, yes. I don't like to see this kind of precedent set involving a flagrant armed aggression, but even I have to say that the United States has no strategic justification for a unilateral involvement at this time. As part of a U.N. or multinational effort, that would be something else. But somebody else has got to take the first step."

Across the table, the Assistant Secretary of State hesitated for a moment, then turned to face the President. "There is one thing we can do, sir," Dubois said. "West Africa is literally on the bottom of the National Security Agency's tasking list. I believe we need to focus additional intelligence-gathering assets on the region, especially on the West African Union. We need to keep an eye on Belewa, especially on where he's headed next."

"You think he's going to keep going?"

"Yes sir, Mr. President, I do. The man is an empire builder. And if he continues to take ground at the rate he has been, very soon he will be a strategic concern to the United States."

Dubois keyed the wall screen control pad again, restoring the regional map. "As you can see, Sierra Leone and Liberia, the states of the West African Union, are entirely surrounded on their landward side by two other nations, Guinea and Côte d'Ivoire. I believe that Belewa will take a year or two to stabilize his hold on Sierra Leone and then he will move against one of these two states. Probably Guinea, as it's the weaker and less stable."

"You sound like you think we might have an African Napoleon on our hands."

"Possibly, Mr. President. Or an African Hitler."

Kilimi, Near the Border of the
West African Union and Guinea

The unpaved jungle track was not made for fast driving. However, an expatriation convoy, a dozen aged and load-weary trucks and buses jammed to the limit with an unwilling human cargo, slowed the presidential command column even further. It was well after dark when the two groups of vehicles entered the perimeter of the Kilimi resettlement compound.

"Compound" was something of a misnomer. The word denotes an aspect of constructed permanence. There was nothing of permanence here. As with the other resettlement camps strung out along the Guinea border, Kilimi compound consisted of only thousands of lost and bewildered people huddled together in an area loosely defined by their patrolling guards. All that had been built were a few rude lean-tos and brush huts and a scattering of small, smoldering fires.

The previously dispossessed, some of whom had been waiting here in the forest for weeks, pressed closer to their fires, watching silently as the new arrivals were unloaded, wondering what new despairs the newcomers might be bringing with them.

Troops clustered around the refugee column, shouting, hurrying their charges out of the vehicles and herding them away into the night. One guard, impatient as an elderly man fumbled with his small bundle of possessions, lifted his rifle butt to strike.

The blow never landed. A strong hand closed on the rifle barrel and a low voice spoke out of the darkness. "Corporal. That is unnecessary."

The corporal froze in place. He knew that voice; all who lived in the new West African Union did. "Yes, General. I am sorry."

Premier General Obe Belewa released his grip on the rifle barrel. "Very good. In their way, these travelers are warriors of the Union, just as are you and I. They have a long, hard journey ahead of them. Let's not make it any harder than it has to be."

Brooding, Belewa walked on, his jungle boots scuffing the dust of the track, ignoring the cadre of guards and aides who followed at his heels. As he passed each small fire along the road, he made himself pause and study the faces revealed in the flickering light—the men, the women, the children, the old, the sick, the resigned, the angry. The people who resisted his new way and the people who supported them. He found himself wondering which among them would die.

After a time, he became aware of a hand resting on his shoulder.

"Obe, you should not do this to yourself."

"I must, Sako," he replied to Brigadier Atiba, now his chief of staff. "I must do this to remind myself how much I hate doing this."

"For the ten thousandth time, Obe, you know that we have no choice if the Union is to be built into what it should be. We must remember that we are using our enemies against our enemies. We must be strong!"

"I know, my old friend." The General straightened and squared his shoulders. "Tonight we begin the game again. We take a longer step for a greater prize."

Flashlights bobbed along the road ahead and another group of Union soldiers approached Belewa's party. Its leader snapped off a precise salute. "General, I apologize for not being present at your arrival. My border scouts are in, and I was receiving their report."

"There is never a need to apologize for doing your duty, Colonel Sinclair," Belewa replied. "What do your scouts report?"

"We have a clear border, sir. No Guinean army or police patrols noted. Given an hour to set out our guides and pickets, we can start moving the first DP parties. We can have the first wave across the line by first light."

"And the supplies for them? They have arrived?"

"As ordered, General. Each displaced person will receive a ration of flour and rice and a blanket."

"And our Special Forces teams?"

"The lead elements are preparing to move out as we speak, sir. The men would be honored if you would see them off."

"The honor would be mine, Colonel. Relay the order to all displacement compounds. Commence Operation Deluge Two as per the action plan."

❖✦

The Special Forces camp was set away from the DP compound. It, too, consisted of little more than branch-and-leaf lean-tos and smoking fire rings. But here there was a sense of order instead of bewilderment, determination instead of despair. Outlined by the campfires, figures moved swiftly. Orders were called in the darkness, and once a soldier laughed at some unheard joke by a comrade.

"Patrol, attention!"

A cluster of men sprang up from where they rested at a fireside. Their field gear, secured and ready, made hardly any clatter as they came to their feet, hitting a hard brace.

"This will be the first team across the border, General," Sinclair said.

Belewa walked down the short line of troopers, studying each one in turn by the firelight. This was better. Better by far than the ordeal of the DP camp. It always lightened his heart to get into the field with his soldiers once more, away from the grim necessities of politicking and statesmanship. He paused at the end man, who was the squad sergeant and a good representative of them all.

The soldier was of average height and lean, not with the gauntness of hunger but with the wiry sinuosity born of hard training. His eyes held none of the bloodshot muddiness of marijuana and his youthful face was confident and set.

The pattern and coloration of the camouflage he wore wasn't quite correct for the West African bush environment. Not surprisingly so, since the uniform had been purchased military surplus from the Hungarian army. Likewise, his camo cap and bush knife had come from a cut-rate Canadian sporting-goods clearinghouse, while his sandals had been made in a local village from an old truck tire.

Slung over his shoulder was a Pakistani copy of a British Sterling submachine gun, while clipped to his cheap Thai military webbing were half a dozen spare 9mm magazines and a mismatched pair of hand grenades, one a massive Russian-issue RD, the other a small, palm-size Dutch V40. A rolled jungle poncho and a small haversack containing a ration of rice and dried meat made up the rest of his kit. He wore no insignia or mark of rank. Nor did he carry any written word that might link him to the Union.

The Special Forces trooper was a patchwork warrior, painstakingly pieced together out of the discards and bargains of the world arms market. Second best in everything except dedication.

Belewa knew that it would be ludicrous to compare the equipment and training of his Special Operations units to that of the American Green Berets or the British SAS. However, he also knew that they would be decisively superior to any opponent they might meet across the line in Guinea.

"State your mission, Sergeant," Belewa barked.

"We are to cross the border and destroy the Highway Bridge at Bambafouga with dynamite charges," the team leader replied crisply. "Our secondary objective is to cut the telephone lines at Bambafouga crossing and to burn the standing crops 'round the outlying villages. Upon completing our mission, we are to return across the border for reassignment. We are to avoid contact with both the Guinean military and civilian population whenever possible, and we are to avoid causing unnecessary civilian casualties."

Belewa nodded. "Good. And why are you doing this, warrior?"

"For the Union and the future!" The trooper broke his rigid posture then, looking full into Belewa's face. "And we do it for you, General!"

Belewa smiled and shook his head. "No, my son," he said, lightly slapping the younger man on the shoulder. "Only for the Union and the future. I am not important."

The White House, Washington, D.C. 1018 hours, Zone Time; February 14, 2007

FROM: NATIONAL COMMAND AUTHORITY
TO: CHIEF OF NAVAL OPERATIONS
SUBJECT: UNITED NATIONS AFRICAN INTERDICTION FORCE

Commencing immediately, you will make all preparations required to deploy a U.S. Naval Task Group to the nation of Guinea as a possible element of the United Nations African Interdiction Force (UNAFIN) as per U.N. Resolution 26868. Said Task Group to number no more than 1800 personnel and to be suitably configured for coastal patrol and interdiction duty.

> Benton B. Childress
> President of the United States

The Pentagon, Washington, D.C. 1027 Hours, Zone Time; February 15, 2007

FROM: CNO
TO: CINCNAVSPECFORCE
SUBJECT: UNITED NATIONS AFRICAN INTERDICTION FORCE
(MISSION COMMITMENT)

Okay, Eddie Mac, this one is NAVSPECFORCE's baby. Put a Littoral Warfare package together out of your deployable assets and get it ready to go. The U.N. will be voting on the Guinea issue this Friday. The Boss wants us to be ready to move fast on this one should the interdiction motion pass. Get an estimate on your package support and logistics requirements to my Chief of Staff with all speed and I will see you get the priorities. Sorry about the force size limitations, but the President is bucking heavy congressional resistance on a U.S. involvement in West Africa. Do the best you can with what you've got.

> ADM. Jason Harwell
> Chief of Naval Operations

FROM: CINCNAVSPECFORCE
TO: CHIEF OF STAFF; PROVISIONAL UNAFIN PLANNING GROUP
SUBJECT: UNITED NATIONS AFRICAN INTERDICTION FORCE
(FORCE DEPLOYMENTS)

A: Following UNAFIN Task Force elements approved; Mobile Offshore Base 1, Patrol Gunboat-Air Cushion Squadron 1, Patrol Craft Squadron 9, TAC-NET-A Tactical Intelligence Network and all listed support elements.
B: Replace proposed SEAL detachment with a full SOC Marine Company. Trim the additional personnel slots out of LOG group as required.
C: All elements are to be placed on alert to move status for immediate forward deployment to UNAFIN Prime Base, Conakry.
Expedite.

> Vice Admiral Elliot MacIntyre
> Commander in Chief, US Naval Special Forces

Monrovia, West African Union   1431 Hours, Zone Time; April 28, 2007

United Nations Special Envoy Vavra Bey was living proof that beauty is not something reserved solely for the young. Her graduation picture from the University of Istanbul showed a rather plain, dark-haired young woman, stocky in build and sober in demeanor. For her, beauty had not come until the onset of silver hair, crow's-feet, and a double chin—the beauty born out of poise and experience, courage and confidence. Humor had come as well, but she could hold that well concealed behind her dark eyes. She was the iron-willed grandmother figure who could effortlessly invoke either adoration or stark fear as she desired. This applied not only to her children and grandchildren, but equally to the statesmen and dignitaries she confronted on the diplomatic battlegrounds of the world.

Now, seated at the end of the scarred conference table, she frowned to herself.

"What do you think, Madam Envoy?" The very formal and very young Norwegian who served as her assistant blotted at his face with a sweat-dampened handkerchief. The air-conditioning of the Mamba Point Hotel had yet to be put back in order, and the meeting room sweltered despite the windows opened to the sea breeze.

"I'm not sure, Lars. We can only hope for reason."

In her heart, Vavra Bey already knew what the answer was going to be.

Voices murmured in the corridor beyond the meeting room and the two pistol-armed sentries flanking the door snapped to attention. The envoy and the other members of the small U.N. delegation rose to their feet as Premier General Belewa returned to the room.

He was not alone. His chief of staff, Brigadier Atiba, followed him in, taking a step aside and coming to a smart parade rest near the door. A second man also followed, but he stayed close at Belewa's shoulder, as if seeking to garner an enhanced presence from the tall black warrior.

Dasheel Umamgi, the ambassador-at-large of the Algerian Revolutionary Council, wore the robes and headdress of a Muslim imam. However, Vavra Bey suspected that he had no right to the title either by education or true belief. It was just that a proclaimed religious fanaticism had been one of the better ways to achieve power in the howling chaos that had engulfed Algeria during the first years of the new century. Revolutionary Algeria had taken the place of Libya as the premier troublemaker of North Africa, and it was no surprise to find them active here.

Gray bearded and dark eyed, the mock holy man leveled a long and cold stare at Vavra. He hated her, because she too was Muslim and yet was not a true believer—in him, at any rate. She was pleased to say he had other reasons to hate her as well.

General Belewa gave an acknowledging nod to the U.N. emissaries and resumed his seat at his end of the table. Bey sank into her own chair, not speaking, allowing the General the first word.

"Madam Envoy," Belewa began slowly, "I have been in consultation with my staff and advisers and I do not know what more we can say on this matter. We flatly deny the charges leveled against us by the government of Guinea. Above and beyond our stated policy and desire for friendship with all nations, the West African Union is far too concerned with its own internal affairs to undertake this kind of . . . adventurism with its neighboring states. If Guinea is suffering from an internal rebellion, as we believe to be the case, have them look to making things right with their own discontented population. That is where the solution lies, not with accusing us of aggression."

"And yet," Bey replied, "even you must admit, General Belewa, that one of the major causes of discontent within Guinea currently stems from the massive influx of Union refugees into that nation. There are over a hundred and eighty thousand listed in the U.N. aid camps alone. We have no idea how many others are wandering and starving in the countryside."

Belewa shrugged and leaned back into his chair. "Nor do we, Madam Envoy. We have no control over this state of affairs either. These individuals have left Union territory illegally and without proper documentation. They have entered Guinea the same way. This is a criminal matter for the Guinean authorities to deal with. We have no responsibility in this matter. There is nothing we can do."

"There is, General. You can open your borders and permit these refugees to return to their homes within the Union, thus ending this crisis for both your nation and Guinea."

The tall black man shook his head decisively. "That will be impossible. As I said, there is no documentation on these individuals. How are we to know who is a true citizen of the Union and who is not? And we suspect that there may be many criminals, terrorists, and malcontents numbered among these so-called refugees. We are no better able to deal with this problem than Guinea is."

"General Belewa." Vavra Bey's voice lowered a tone. "These are citizens of the Union. The interviews we have conducted in the refugee camps all indicate the same thing, that these people were driven across the border by Union troops—we believe acting under your orders."

"We deny these charges categorically," Belewa replied flatly. "As I said, there are many malcontents among these individuals—revolutionaries, criminals, and members of the old regimes fleeing justice. People with reason to lie about the true state of affairs in the West African Union. Our borders will remain closed to these disruptive elements, and any attempt to return them to Union territory will be met by armed force."

"I see." Vavra Bey's words hung isolated in the air for a moment. "And do you also still deny that the armed forces of the West African Union have been performing acts of aggression against the nation of Guinea in preparation for an invasion and military takeover?"

"We do. The government of Guinea is seeking to shift the blame for its own failings onto the West African Union."

"The intelligence reports turned over to the United Nations by a number of major world powers indicate something quite different, General."

"Then the United Nations should look to the self-serving agendas of these world powers to learn why they wish to defame my nation!"

Vavra Bey paused for a long moment, her face immobile, her eyes lowered to the scratched tabletop, her mind seeking for any diplomatic possibility or potential not yet explored. Decades of diplomatic instinct told her they were at the point of decision and commitment. When she looked up to speak again, it would be to start them all down a precarious and potentially bloody path.

She lifted her eyes.

"General Belewa, as you are fully aware, the intent of this commission was a final effort to find a diplomatic solution to a situation that threatens to disrupt the entirety of West Africa. That solution has not been found. The West

African Union stands accused of engaging in a campaign of aggression and conquest against a neighboring state. That aggression stands self-evident. Likewise self-evident is the abuse by the West African Union of its own citizens in the face of all accepted standards of human rights and justice. Such actions are no longer acceptable to the world community."

The U.N. envoy rose to her feet, her erectness giving the impression that she was taller then she was. "A vote of censure against the West African Union, United Nations Resolution 26867, has been passed by the Security Council. A second resolution, 26868, calling for a U.N. embargo of all armaments, petroleum, and other militarily-related materials, has also been passed but placed in abeyance pending the outcome of these talks. In the meantime, U.N. forces have been moved into position to both enforce this mandate, if necessary, and to assist the government of Guinea in maintaining the security of its national borders.

"I say to you now, General Belewa, that these talks have failed. If word is not received from your government by midnight, tomorrow, that you are standing down your armed forces and ceasing your acts of aggression against the nation of Guinea, this embargo will be placed in effect."

Belewa's face was an expressionless study, his voice toneless. "As I said before, Madam Envoy, I do not know what more there is to be said on this subject."

"Apparently nothing, General."

Belewa rose abruptly. Without speaking, he turned and left the conference room. His chief of staff and the Algerian ambassador followed. The Algerian had possibly the only pleased expression in the room.

"That's it, then," Bey's aide said quietly. "My God, doesn't he realize that he will be taking on the entire world?"

"He knows, Lars," she replied quietly. "Every generation seems to spin off one or two like him who are willing to give it a try. The frightening thing is that sometimes they win."

⊗◆

General Belewa stood on the small balcony outside his private office, deeply inhaling the clean smell of the sea. He was glad he had chosen to keep the seat of the government here at what had been the Mamba Point Hotel. He liked the view. It reminded him of what the struggle was all about.

Below him, between the ridge of the point and the Mesurado River, the lights of the Union's capital city glowed in the growing tropic dusk. Not as many as there should be yet, but a few more gleamed each night as old buildings were repaired and new ones constructed.

Vehicles moved in the streets as well. Again, not as many as there should be, but they served as heralds for a resurgent economy. As Belewa watched, a truck lumbered across the ironically named United Nations Bridge, heading north, possibly to the port or maybe up the coast to the Sierra Leone provinces.

No, more than likely the port. A ship was unloading tonight. Out beyond the long artificial breakwaters of Port Monrovia, Belewa could see the yellow glare of the worklights. In his mind's eye he could visualize the tools, machinery, and armaments pouring ashore. The things he needed to make the Union strong. That cargo was more precious than ever now because it might be the last for some time.

Belewa inhaled deeply once more, drawing new strength from the night, then he returned to his responsibilities.

Sako Atiba and Ambassador Umamgi were waiting for him in the office. Belewa acknowledged the ambassador's deep salaam with a brief nod.

"Your defiance in the face of the westerners was magnificent today, General," Umamgi said as he straightened. "The Revolutionary Council salutes your courage."

"It was something that had to happen eventually, Ambassador," Belewa replied shortly, seating himself behind his desk. "Speaking frankly, I wish it could have been put off until later."

"I also wish to assure you again, General, that the Council will stand at your shoulder during the coming struggle with the colonialists. You shall have our prayers."

"A pity we couldn't have a battalion of tanks and a few surface-to-air missiles as well," Atiba interjected grimly.

Umamgi smiled without humor. "The Brigadier knows that we are a poor nation, as is your own, impoverished by our own struggle against the infidel West. However, we can promise to provide you with the long-range cargo aircraft you will need to maintain an air link with my nation and the outside world."

Atiba lifted an eyebrow sardonically. "At a price, of course."

"That's enough, Sako," Belewa interjected. "Ambassador Umamgi, you may rest assured that your alliance is held in great value by the Union. Your aid and assistance in these troubled times will be long remembered. We are most grateful for whatever assistance your nation can most generously offer."

Umamgi smiled smugly and inclined his head.

"But," Belewa went on levelly, "there are certain aspects of that aid we need to discuss, Ambassador."

"And what are they, General?"

"We are extremely grateful for the cadre of military advisers and instructors that Algeria has sent us, Ambassador. However, we find that there is a minor problem with the curriculums they are using."

"A problem?"

"Indeed." Belewa nodded. "My advisers inform me that there is a degree of . . . religious indoctrination incorporated into most of the training programs."

Umamgi smiled again, without humor. "Our troops are warriors of Islam. They only wish to share their beliefs with their comrades at arms."

Belewa returned a cold smile of his own. "And they are welcome to. In the Union, all are free to choose their own faith, be it Christianity, Islam, or the beliefs of our African forefathers. Your soldiers are free to speak of their religion in the mosques, in the streets, wherever they choose . . . except for when they are on duty in my training camps."

There was no longer even a false smile on Umamgi's face.

"You will have this matter corrected, Ambassador." Belewa's words were a command and not a question.

The clash of wills was short. Umamgi half bowed. "As you wish, General. After all, we are guests in your country."

"Thank you, Ambassador. And see to it tonight, if you please."

"At once, General. Peace be unto you."

The Algerian turned for the door, but not quite fast enough to conceal the scowl that came across his vulpine features.

After the ambassador had taken his leave, Sako Atiba donned a scowl of his own. "Damnation. Don't we have enough trouble with our enemies that we have to be saddled with friends like that?"

Belewa gave a short laugh. "Not friends, Sako, allies. And allies are like relatives—you can't choose them, you just have to accept them as they come." His features grew sober again. "The Algerians seek to use us to further their aims just as we use them to further our own. It is a thing we must live with, my friend. We shall need all the help we can get for the next few months, from whatever source."

Atiba shook his head. "This U.N. blockade. They will try to strangle the life out of us, Obe. Will they succeed?"

It was Belewa's turn to shake his head. "I don't know, my friend. This had to come sooner or later. To the Western world, it is a knee-jerk reaction to our national expansion. They don't yet understand what we are trying to do here for ourselves and for all of Africa. They cannot see beyond the military occupations and the change in the status quo."

Belewa rose from behind his desk and crossed the room to stand in front of the regional map tacked to the wall. "No, Sako. This confrontation had to come. It would have been better if we could have secured Guinea first, but we've made our preparations. We're ready to take it on now."

The Chief of Staff came to stand at his general's side. "What is our first move, Obe?"

"We attack. In any war, victory lies only in the attack. Defense is the precursor to defeat."

"And our target?"

Belewa's hand came up, his finger aimed at a point on the map "There."

Atiba's eyebrows lifted. "At Conakry? At the main U.N. base?"

"If you would kill an enemy, what better place to strike than at his heart. For a long time, Sako, they have let us alone simply because we weren't worth the trouble of bothering with. Now we must make them leave us alone by not being worth the blood price they will have to pay for interfering."

Conflict

Two craft converged on the city of Conakry.

One was an airplane, riding swift and high above the dull azure of the Atlantic. A multiengined Orion P3C turboprop, it had been built for the U.S. navy during the 1980s as a long-range antisubmarine patrol plane. Of late, however, it had undergone a change in mission. With its sleek fuselage bulged and spiked with the antennae of an extensively augmented communications array, it now served as a command-and-control aircraft, the personal ride of CINCNAVSPEFORCE, the Commander in Chief, U.S. Naval Special Forces.

The other craft was a small boat, creeping slowly west along the verdant African shoreline. It was the larger of the two classic types of Gold Coast small craft, a *pinasse*. Forty-five feet in length and narrow in beam, she had the high-bowed, long-lined sleekness of her war canoe ancestors, a grace that transcended her battered condition. With a cargo of sacked rice piled amidships and a low, tarp-roofed deck shelter astern, she held her course through the low crossing swells, a thumping two-cylinder diesel driving her on.

Each craft came from the opposing extreme of the technological spectrum as well as the opposing side of a burgeoning international conflict. They held one thing in common, however. Each was on a mission of war.

A steaming drizzle of rain streaked the louvered window of the little ad hoc office, its incessant pattering drowned out by the grumble of the overloaded air conditioner. Seated at her field desk, Christine Rendino studied the words that scrolled down the screen of her personal laptop computer.

> . . . *in the end, Chris, the powers that be decided to do considerably more to the Duke than just repair the battle damage we received in the Yangtze. We're receiving a total Block II survey. Upon completion, we'll have all of the augmented bells and whistles that have been built into the later SC-21–class hulls.*
>
> *Unfortunately, the downside is that it will mean almost another full year in the yard. We won't be ready for sea again before next October at the earliest. I'd*

hoped to take the Duke out on at least one more deployment before my tour aboard her was up, but there's not much chance of that now. Maybe I'll at least be able to get a shakedown cruise in before I have to hand her over to her next skipper.

At any rate, I'll have plenty of time to get this new crew in shape. Your transfer was just the first of many. Just about all of our old hands are gone now. The Bureau of Personnel is doling our experienced crew people to the other stealths and to the training commands as if they are pearls beyond price.

Your favorite sparring partner, Frank McKelsie, has been bumped up to Lieutenant Commander and is on his way to San Diego to become the exec on the Boyington. Dix Beltrain is just a couple of piers down from us on the Connor, helping to get her ready for sea, and Doc Golden is up at Bethesda. Chief Thomson is out of the Navy now, not that he's retiring by a long shot. He's stepped straight across into a consultant's position with Lockheed's Sea Shadow division right here in Norfolk at a pleasantly fat salary.

At the moment, it's rather like being the new kid in school again. I look around the Duke these days and all I see are a lot of faces I don't recognize. Ken Hiro is about the last of the old gang still aboard. He's having more fun than a kitten with a ball of yarn overseeing the rebuild. To tell the truth, he's doing such a good job of it that I'm feeling just a little bit redundant at the moment.

Concerning Arkady (and I'm sure you're panting to find out what's going on with him), all I can say is, not much. We've been doing our best to run a long-distance romance, but I don't think that either of us is finding it all that satisfying. However, we both have some leave coming and he's flying in from San Diego tomorrow. We're going to take the Seeadler out for a cruise and hopefully make up for some lost opportunities. Maybe we can also come to some conclusions about where the two of us are going.

You know, there's a certain irony about it all. When Arkady came aboard the Duke and we became involved, we didn't dare admit to having an affair because he was attached to the ship and under my command. However, now that he's no longer attached and an affair would be all legal and aboveboard, we haven't been able to have one to admit to.

Enough whining. I've been doing too much of that lately. I hope this new Tactical Intelligence project of yours is keeping you busy and out of trouble. I also trust that you are maintaining at least a semblance of military decorum. I doubt that Admiral MacIntyre will have nearly the patience I had with that ex-pat Valley Girl act of yours. I do envy you the job, though. Africa would be an interesting duty station. A hot one as well if things keep going the way they have. Be careful, Chris.

Love
Amanda

Christine first smiled, then frowned as she finished the e-mail. Amanda had never been one to bitch about personal problems. That she made any mention of them at all was unusual in the extreme. The wisps of discontent rising up from the letter obviously stemmed from some deeper smoldering cause.

A smile returned to the blond intelligence officer's elfin features, but a sympathetic one. She could recognize the symptoms. At the moment, Amanda Lee Garrett was a dolphin run up onto the beach. The weight and dryness of the land were starting to suffocate her.

If Christine were back in Norfolk, she could have conjured up any number of temporary cures for her old friend's condition. Among other options, she might have orchestrated a totally blowout night on the town for the two of them. Getting Amanda to well and truly let her hair down required a degree of effort, but the end results were usually interesting.

Christine checked the date on the message and found that it had been sent earlier that week. That would mean Lieutenant Vince Arkady was probably already on site. The intel's smile deepened. Probably he could turn the trick even better.

Even so, his visit would only bring about a temporary remission of the symptoms. As with that beached dolphin, the only permanent fix for Amanda Garrett would be for her to return to the sea. And at the moment, there was nothing Christine could do to bring that about.

Her yeoman appeared in the doorless office doorway. "Beg your pardon, ma'am, but Admiral MacIntyre's plane is on final approach now. You wanted to know."

"Okay, Andy. Thanks." She glanced through the window at the low gray skies and the rain-sodden tarmac beyond the naval intelligence center. "Is the Hummer around front?"

"Right outside the door, Commander."

Commander . . . Christine reached up and touched the golden oak leaves on the collar of her summer whites. The rank still sounded a little odd.

She took a deep breath and flipped the cover of the mil-spec Panasonic laptop closed. This had been her first fragment of free time for several days. It had been good to touch base with the real world for a moment. Standing up, she gave her slacks a smoothing tug. Not that it would make that much difference here on the Gold Coast. Five minutes away from an air conditioner and even the crispest set of creases would start to go limp. Donning her uniform hat, already swathed in its plastic rain cover, and taking her navy blue Windcheater from the back of her chair, she started out of the office.

Beneath the ragged scrap of canvas that sheltered the stern of the *pinasse,* her captain sat at the tiller and took careful stock of his vessel's position.

Gray walls of rain-streaked mist rose up on all sides of his little craft, merging with the low overcast. They were engulfed by one of the frequent rain squalls that haunted the African Gold Coast. The African shipmaster lacked even a compass for navigation, and yet he knew exactly where he was.

He'd held his course along the coast by steering across the regular ranks of deepwater rollers marching in from the Atlantic, maintaining his distance from the shore by throttling down his engine every few minutes to listen for the surf on his right.

On his last check, however, the sound of the breaking waves had been fading astern and the water beneath the *pinasse*'s hull had been tinged with a milky brown coloration. When a palmful of it had been tasted, a muddy organic flavor had overlain the clean bite of sea salt. They were now off the broad mouth of the Tabounsou River.

Were it not for the rain and mist, the low-set Camayenne Peninsula would have been seen to the west and extending away to the south. At the peninsula's tip would have been the city of Conakry itself, and farther south yet, Kassa Island, the closest in of the Iles de Loos group.

With the Tabounsou to starboard, their objective—the airport and the U.N. base—would be directly . . . there. On the coast and inside the river estuary easy on the starboard bow and perhaps five miles distant.

Satisfied, the captain settled back into his seat, easing the rudder over a few degrees. He pushed the throttle in a notch, slowing the chugging beat of the little engine. They had made a good landfall. Now he and his crew must arrive at their objective just as darkness was falling.

✕◆

It was a busy afternoon on the vast concrete expanse of the Conakry flight line. Half a dozen C-130 Hercules transports bearing the insignia and camouflage patterns of half a dozen nations were lined up wingtip to wingtip along one of the parking aprons, dripping in the rain and discharging relief supplies and military stores. On a second apron, a twin-engined C-160 Transall of the Armée de l'Air and a small cluster of Super Puma utility helicopters rested in between flying support missions for the Foreign Legion Advisory Group who were working with the Guinean army. In yet a third area, a U.N.-chartered 747 air freighter discharged palletized Red Cross parcels through its open bow door. A polyglot cadre of military personnel—French, British, American—and a scattering of locals worked around the grounded aircraft, struggling with mixed success to bring order out of chaos.

S E A   F I G H T E R

As Admiral MacIntyre's Orion taxied in from the main runway, Christine had more than enough time to ponder how this huge and overwhelmingly unnecessary air-base complex had come to exist.

Like any number of other Third World states, Guinea had at one time been tempted by the bright lie of communism. Swept deep within the circle of influence drawn by both the old Soviet Union and the former Red China, Guinea had, for a time, been one of the closer allies of both Moscow and Beijing on the African continent. In return for this allegiance, the Soviets had financed and constructed an international airport at Conakry.

Upon completion, the airport proved to be far too large a facility for the minimal air-transport needs of Guinea, not to mention being far too costly for the small and impoverished country to maintain. On the other hand, it did give the Russian air force a very convenient South Atlantic staging base for its huge TU-95 maritime patrol bombers, thus being the nature of foreign aid given by the late Soviet empire.

At last, the airfield was being used for the benefit of the people of Guinea. Through it poured the assistance that might yet stave off disaster for the foundering nation.

Obediently trailing the base "follow me" truck, Admiral MacIntyre's VP-3 lumbered into its parking spot, spray streaking the tarmac behind it. With a final twirling whine, its engines powered down, square-tipped propeller blades flickering into visibility.

Normally, there would have been the turnout of the base honor guard and the appropriate pomp and circumstance mandated by tradition for a flag officer's arrival. At MacIntyre's specific request, however, a squelch had been placed on the formalities. Only Christine and the commanding officers of the other two major Navy elements attached to the UNAFIN operation stood by at the base of the boarding stairs.

Since coming under his command, Christine Rendino had come to learn that the CINCNAVSPEFORCE was a man who preferred performance over ceremony by a decisive margin, especially inside a war zone. During those odd moments in his presence when she could step back from her professionalism, Christine also found herself noting that Vice Admiral Elliot "Eddie Mac" MacIntyre was a damned handsome example of an older man.

He was one of those individuals who don't age as much as they weather. The gray streaking his brown hair and the lines carved into his strong-jawed features marked where the passage of time had only been able to lightly chip at the man. Descending the stairway with his jacket collar turned up against the rain, MacIntyre moved with the quick and limber surety of a person in his prime.

"Welcome to Conakry Base, Admiral."

"Pleased to be aboard, Jim," MacIntyre replied, exchanging salutes with Captain Stottard.

Captain James Stottard was the senior American officer on the ground in Guinea, the commandant of the Conakry Base section as well as all other U.S. logistics and support forces attached to UNAFIN. A tall and bulky man with a stolid personality and humorless demeanor, the LOGBOSS was a professional bean counter and a damn good one.

The TACBOSS was present as well.

"Captain Phillip Emberly, sir!"

Phil Emberly commanded the combat elements of NAVSPECFORCE's share of the U.N. operation. Round-faced, intense, and almost radiant with self-confidence, he was a fast-tracker from Navy R & D who had overseen the final phase development of the seafighter program. As the PG-ACs were to be the core unit of the interdiction force, it had seemed appropriate that he should lead them during their operational debut.

Christine could appreciate the way Emberly had brought the experimental seafighter group up to speed. However, there were other aspects of the man she didn't appreciate quite so much.

"Pleased to meet you, Commander," MacIntyre replied. "I've heard a lot of good things about the seafighters."

The Admiral turned his attention to Christine, his fingertips coming to his brow in reply to her own salute. "Commander Rendino. It's good to see you again."

"The same here, sir."

As for herself, Christine was aware of her place in the scheme of things. Within naval intelligence circles she was becoming heir to the reputation of the brilliant and eccentric Commander Joseph Rochefort, the man who had turned the tide of the Second World War by predicting the Japanese attack on Midway Island.

With an IQ of 180, an eidetic memory, and a knack for deductive logic, she had served as intelligence officer aboard the USS *Cunningham* through America's last two major international crises. When the destroyer's crew had been dispersed, Christine had found herself snatched up by Admiral MacIntyre as his personal prize out of the Duke's treasure chest of conflict-hardened personnel. Following an early bump-up to lieutenant commander, she had been assigned to NAVSPECFORCE's operational intelligence group, commanding its first fielded Tactical Intelligence Network detachment.

"Miss Rendino, gentlemen," MacIntyre went on. "I apologize for dragging you out here in the rain when you've already got so much on your plates."

"No problem, sir," Stottard replied politely. "We were halfway hoping that you were coming in to take over the show. We still haven't gotten the word on what the final command structure is going to be down here."

MacIntyre frowned momentarily. "Not quite, Jim, although I do have some dope on that subject. We'll get into that later. For now, you can just call this a friendly tour of inspection. I want to find out what else you people need and how I can best get it for you."

"The seafighters are set to go now, sir," Emberly interjected. "Give us the word and we'll get the job done."

There was a commander's pride in the TACBOSS's words, but there was also something close to boastfulness. MacIntyre glanced in Emberly's direction. "Well, that's fine, Captain. But I think that General Belewa will be the man giving us all the word when the time comes."

A silence hung in the air for a few moments, and then MacIntyre returned his attention to the base commander. "Okay, Jim, what's the agenda?"

"We've got a series of intelligence briefings scheduled for the next couple of days, as well as a couple of planning sessions with the British and French liaisons. Commander Rendino's been setting up the program."

Christine nodded. "Yes, sir. Since we haven't been getting much formal word on how this operation is going to be structured, I figured it might be worthwhile getting some informal guidelines going."

MacIntyre nodded and tugged his cap lower over his eyes, water dripping from its visor. "Good thinking, Commander. When do we start?"

"We have a general orientation briefing scheduled for about forty-five minutes from now, sir. But if you'd like to rest up some from your flight . . ."

"Forget it. I'm not that decrepit yet. I want to be brought up to speed ASAP. We don't have much time to waste. Jim, my aide can lug my gear over to my quarters if you can provide him with some transportation. For now, I'd like to have a quick look around the base just to get my bearings. Commander Rendino here can drive me. I've got some intelligence matters I need to discuss with her."

✕◆

In spite of the rain, they left the windows of the HumVee open, the motion-breeze rendering the sodden humidity of the air a little more tolerable.

"What do you want to see first, sir?" Christine inquired.

"Nothing much in particular, really," MacIntyre replied, unzipping his jacket. "Just take us once around the field perimeter. Frankly, Commander, I want to talk to you off the record about a couple of things before we go into this first briefing."

"Sure thing, sir," Christine slued the big military 4 × 4 onto the perimeter road that circled the airfield. "What's up?"

"First, how are things with TACNET? What's your status?"

"It's coming together, sir," she replied over the muttering growl of the diesel power plant. "Some elements are already partially on line, and the rest are in theater and deploying."

"What coverage do we currently have, and how much more time will you need to be fully operational?"

The intel considered. "Floater 1 is all the way up and running. She has her aerostat streamed, and they're already flying off the smaller Eagle Eye drones. That's giving us good coverage of the central Union coast, east to about Greenville and west to the Sherbro island shadow.

"The other two 'stat carriers, the *Bravo* and the *Valiant,* have both arrived in Conakry and are replenishing from their haul across the Atlantic. They should be out on the Guinea East and Guinea West stations by this time tomorrow night, giving us full radar and signal intelligence coverage of the Guinea littoral as well."

Christine took a hand off the wheel and indicated one of the big hangars spaced along the edge of the flight line. "The Predator squadron is setting up there and the first of their birds is being assembled now. Last word I had was that they should be ready to launch by dawn tomorrow. The drone control nodes here and on Floater 1 are operational, and Abidjan should be up by midnight."

A bead of sweat trickled down the back of her neck, and she impatiently flipped her cap into the HumVee's backseat. "I'll be shifting the TACNET command and analysis nodes out to the Floater sometime during the next couple of days. Like all of the other tactical elements, we'll be running our show from out there. Barring any Murphys, we should have the whole package integrated and functional in about another twenty-four to thirty-six hours."

MacIntyre nodded. "And how about everybody else?"

"About the same status, sir. We're all getting there. The problem is that we're . . . that is, our people, the Brits and the French, are all getting there separately. It's still a stovepiped command structure. Everybody's still operating in their own little national boxes. There's almost no cross-coordination going on. Everyone's waiting for the official word about how the local chain of command is going to be set up."

MacIntyre grunted and rested his arm on the open window frame of the Hummer. "I'm bringing in a word all right, Commander. But it may not be the one anybody wants to hear. Now, I need to know something else. How's Captain Emberly doing with the Tactical Action Group?"

Christine winced inwardly, suddenly feeling thin professional ice under her skates. If it had been Amanda sitting there next to her, she knew how she would have answered. On the other hand, she was out in the real navy now. She opted for the PC response. "I don't have much input on that, sir," she said, carefully wording the reply. "I'm sure that Commander Emberly will be able to fill you in better than I can."

"Dammit, pull this thing over!"

Obediently, Christine pulled the HumVee over to the muddy roadside. Twisting around in the passenger's seat, MacIntyre fixed her with a stern stare. "Commander, when I spoke with Amanda Garrett about attaching you to my staff, she assured me of two things. One being that you are always aware of everything that's going on around you. The other was that you always can be trusted to lay the facts on the line.

"Now, I'm fully aware that Captain Emberly is the theater TACBOSS and that you are answerable to him in the chain of command. However, I am not asking you, as a junior officer, to professionally rate Captain Emberly while he's not present. I am asking you, as one of my intelligence officers, to provide me with an assessment of a critical situation affecting this operation. Now, come across with it, young lady."

Christine sighed, her hands resting on the steering wheel. "Captain Emberly has done really good work with getting the seafighters ready to go," she replied. "PG-AC 1 is working up rapidly, and the support bases for both it and Patrol Craft Group 9 have been established and are fully operational. I can't fault the job he has done with his systems and his personnel. Beyond that, I can't say, sir. I haven't had the chance to work with him very much."

"Hasn't he been working with you on a doctrine and operations plan?"

She shook her head. "No, sir, he has not. Maybe he's working on something with his own people, but he hasn't been accessing either me, TACNET, or the theater database to any great degree. I also know that he hasn't been making any medicine with anyone over at PC-9. I've had words with Lieutenant Commander Klasinski about this, and he and his Special Boat Squadron people are getting nervous over it. Mission planning doesn't seem to be a priority with Captain Emberly."

Christine hesitated for a moment, then took a deep and deliberate breath and plunged on. "I've tried to bring the subject up with the Captain, but he keeps sliding me off. His primary focus has been on getting his hardware good to go and not on what he'll be doing with it.

"The impression I get is that all he thinks he needs to do is to wave a little high tech under the Union's nose and the bad guys will all throw up their hands, scream 'Lawsy me,' and faint. Well, fa'sure it's not going to work that way, Admiral. We have a damn tricky situation developing down here, and Captain Emberly needs to realize it real fast.

"I hope that was straight enough for you, sir?" she finished apologetically.

MacIntyre nodded slowly. "Quite adequate, Commander. I was afraid of something like this. I agree. You can't find fault with the work Phil Emberly's done with the seafighter program up to this point. He's a damn good R and D man, but that's all he is. He doesn't have any combat time under his belt."

Christine shrugged her shoulders. "There aren't all that many of us that do, sir. Everybody has a first time out."

"I know. And, blast it, the seafighters are Phil's baby. Besides, he's literally the only command-rated officer we have who's qualified on combat hovercraft. Still . . ."

Silently MacIntyre grimaced and faced forward again, slouched deeper in his seat. Christine found it easy to read his mind. Do you fire a promising young officer from his first command, almost certainly ruining his career without giving him his chance? Or do you risk a crew and a mission with an overconfident greenhorn? Or do you weasel and walk the line by trying to talk a test-bed sailor into a warfighter's mind-set?

Christine promised herself that she'd get out of the uniform long before she ever reached flag rank. "Life's a bitch and then you die, sir," she said sympathetically.

MacIntyre glanced up at her and a wry smile touched his face. "Words of wisdom, Commander. Drive on. You mentioned that TACNET was starting to produce some results. Anything indicative yet?"

"Just that it's real quiet out there for the moment. Union naval operations have dropped right off the scale ever since the interdiction was declared. Hardly any action at all along the Guinea coast."

"Any chance we might have them a little intimidated?"

Christine Rendino shook her head as she popped the Hummer back into gear. "No way, sir. These guys are just lying low and scoping us out. The West African Union has a good Humint network operating inside Guinea. It's sure money that they have us under observation. Right now, they're gauging our force strengths and capacities. When they're ready, they'll start moving again."

"Do you have one of your famous prognostications on what that next move is going to be?"

"That one's easy," Christine replied. "Eighty percent probability of a direct attack against the U.N. interdiction forces. Probably right here at Conakry. Also probably very soon, before we're fully set up and ready for him."

"You seem sure Belewa is going to take us on directly?"

"Fa' certain sure, Admiral. Belewa can walk in and take Guinea anytime he wants to. He just has to kick us out of the way first."

⬦✦

Offshore, the rain had slackened and the mist had started to lift. A Guinean navy patrol launch slid past, its crew sprawled on the deck in various postures of lackadaisical unconcern. In much the same way, the crew of the *pinasse* lounged atop the cargo that filled its midships section. Only with them, it was a carefully staged pose. Alert eyes narrowed, and as they drew near their objective, each handpicked sea warrior ran his duties over in his mind.

They could see the coast now. And beyond the surf line and the beach, they could also see the approach lights of the air base glowing blue in the growing dusk.

With civil air travel at a standstill because of the unrest in-country, the U.N. military mission had taken over the old passenger terminal at Conakry International as its headquarters. Sandbag revetments and barricades of earth-filled oil drums had gone into place around the building's exterior, converting the low-set concrete structure into an ad hoc fortress. Communications antennas sprouted from the roof and diesel generators snored, supplementing the uncertain local power grid.

Inside, hastily erected partitions subdivided waiting areas and concourses into office space. The terminal restaurant was now a mess hall, serving up field ration meals around the clock, and weary members of the headquarters cadre caught an occasional fragment of sleep on the cots lining the hallways.

The airport's lounge had become the headquarters briefing center, the shelves behind the bar having been emptied out and the exterior picture windows closed off with heavy slabs of plywood. Only the frivolous split-bamboo furnishings remained, striking an incongruous note as the UNAFIN commanders gathered to speak about war.

⬦✦

"Gentlemen, forget your nerve gases, your high-energy lasers, and your genetically engineered biotoxins. This is the premier superweapon of the twenty-first century."

The picture projected onto the wall screen was one of abject deprivation. A cluster of black Africans—men, women, and children—sat hunkered in the dust. Gaunt inside their rags, disease-warped and weary beyond their years, they stared with blank-eyed incomprehension into the camera lens.

Christine Rendino paused for a moment to let the image have its impact, then she continued. "Excess population, gentlemen. There's plenty of it lying around. It's self-deploying with the occasional prod of a bayonet, and man, if you happen to be a Third World dictator, it's efficient. You can get rid of a whole bunch of people you don't like by burying them alive under a whole bunch of people who don't like you."

She had a small audience; only half a dozen other officers sat in the semi-darkness. However, even this little group was further divided. Emberly and Stottard sat at one table, while the two British liaisons were at another. Lieutenant Mark Traynor from the Royal Navy's minehunter group looked cool and very old empire in the white socks and shorts of his tropical uniform. However, Squadron Leader Evan Dane, his counterpart from the Provisional patrol helicopter group, denied the heat in the gray Nomex flight suit of a naval aviator.

Spare and wary, Lieutenant Commander Trochard, from the French navy's offshore patrol, sat alone at yet a third table. The barriers dividing the representatives of the different military missions were invisible but decidedly present. Admiral MacIntyre leaned against the wall at the back of the room. Scowling, he looked on as Christine doggedly continued.

"Using an artificially created flood of refugees to destabilize a neighbor state has been a proven and accepted battle tactic in Africa since before Zaire turned back into the Congo. The Serbs tried it in the Balkans as well. You just have to have a certain . . . pragmatic attitude to employ the doctrine."

The voice of Squadron Leader Dane came out of the shadows. "It seems to me that by herding all of your enemies in one place, you'd just be making it easier for them to unite against you, Commander."

"You're forgetting the Africa factor, the sheer poverty and lack of available resources. If you're a subsistence farmer in the Guinea backcountry who's being deluged by starving Union refugees, the refugees themselves present a far more immediate threat to your survival than the government initiating the problem. Once the food riots begin and the blood feuds get going, you can't get the factions to work together. How do you organize an army to fight a common enemy when your soldiers are all busy fighting each other for the last handful of rice in the bowl?"

Christine swept her pointer across the screen again. "Multiply this picture fifty thousand times over and you have what the government of Guinea and the U.N. aid agencies are having to deal with right now on a daily basis. Comparatively speaking, our problems are a little simpler, but just comparatively."

She clicked the projector controller in her left hand and the image on the screen shifted to one of the Premier of the West African Union. Clad in worn bush fatigues and with the cap pulled low and shading his face, he stood in front of a camouflaged armored vehicle.

"This gentleman is General Obe Belewa, career army officer and professional military dictator. Unlike certain other Africans who have aspired to this office, such as the late and unlamented Idi Amin and Muammar Qaddafi, this guy actually knows what he's doing."

Christine crossed her arms and leaned back against the wall beside the screen. "If you want an example, consider this. His first major action upon reorganizing his military after the Liberian takeover was to establish a joint army-navy NCO training academy staffed by the best of the old lifer sergeants from his ECOMOG garrison force."

Christine was pleased to see that she'd gotten some attention with that statement. Frequently a straight line could be drawn from point A to point B; good noncommissioned officers meant a good fighting unit.

"That's the way Belewa works," she continued. "He puts his resources into training, logistics, and combat support. He will not acquire any weapons system unless he can also acquire an adequate technical base to service it. If you check out the West African Union's Table of Organization, you won't find a bunch of complex and expensive jet fighters and main battle tanks sitting around rusting because they can't be maintained. What you will find are a lot of very basic infantry weapons: machine guns, rocket and grenade launchers, mortars, and recoilless rifles. However, these weapons will be in good working order, they will have plenty of ammunition, and they will be manned by people who know how to use them."

⚒◆

Offshore, the day was dying out beyond the Camayenne Peninsula. The crew of the *pinasse* used the last trace of the brief equatorial twilight to seek for the marker they had been told would be waiting for them.

They found it. A tree branch bobbing upright in the low oily swells. A totally undistinguished bit of flotsam, it would have taken several minutes of careful observation to note anything unusual about it at all. Specifically, that it wasn't drifting with the sluggish tidal currents. It had been anchored a carefully calculated number of yards offshore.

The captain cut the engine and more anchors splashed down, heavy stones linked by rope to the bow and stern of the little craft, holding it broadside to the shore . . . and directly in line with the lights of the buildings strung out beside the Conakry airfield runway.

The briefing continued.

"Belewa may be an army puke, but he also understands sea power and how to use it. While he's been waging guerrilla warfare against Guinea by land, he's also launched a parallel campaign off their coast. Fishing villages have been raided and coastal shipping has been shot up. In addition, every navigational aid along the Guinea coast has been taken out and the harbor approaches mined.

"Major damage is being done here. By hitting the fishing villages, they're cutting off a desperately needed food source. They're also driving the villagers inland to further inflame the refugee problem. Disruption of coastal shipping is putting a further strain on the ground transport network, which isn't all that much to begin with, and the mining threatens to isolate Guinea from both international aid and overseas commerce. Part of the UNAFIN blockading mission will be to prevent these incursions into Guinea's coastal waters."

"A question, Commander." Trochard, the French navy liaison, spoke in mildly accented English. "What kind of mines are we speaking of? What models? Where is their origin?"

Christine glanced over at the British mine warfare officer. "You want to answer that one, Lieutenant Traynor?"

The Englishman nodded. "So far, we've seen a very basic but effective moored contact mine of local manufacture. The West African Union has apparently set up a production line to build these weapons to a set standard. It's rather clever really. They're using old hot-water tanks as mine hulls."

There was a brief snort of laughter from Commander Emberly. Traynor only lifted an eyebrow. "It's not all that funny, Commander. These mines carry a sixty-five-pound charge of civilian blasting gelatin, more than adequate to sink a patrol boat or put a hole in a freighter hull. A Dutch ore carrier has been badly damaged, and two coastal ferries have been sunk with a heavy loss of life. To date we've located and swept seven more of these damn things in the approaches to Conakry and Rio Nunez. Every one of them has detonated as advertised."

The American TACBOSS gave a noncommittal grunt and looked away.

"What has the Guinea military been doing through all this, Commander?" MacIntyre inquired from the back of the room.

"Pretty much what you'd expect," Christine replied, "with the expected outcome. When the Union started hitting the coastal areas with their two- and three-gunboat raids, Guinea stepped up their naval cutter and police launch patrols and deployed platoon-size army garrisons to some of the coastal villages.

The Union waited until the patrols and garrisons were in place, then swarmed the coast with a series of ten- and twelve-boat search-and-destroy sweeps. They shot hell out of the navy patrols and totally flattened several of the garrisoned villages. The local military was handed a decisive defeat and the Conakry government lost a heck of a lot of face with the coastal tribes."

"It strikes me that what we're seeing here is Mao's classic guerrilla warfare doctrine applied in a maritime environment."

"Exactly, Admiral." Christine changed screen images again. This time the photograph was of a sleek and low-riding speedboat, perhaps forty feet long, and painted in a mottled gray and green camouflage. Its hull was open from bow to stern except for a small, enclosed helm station amidships. Driven by a pair of powerful outboard motors, it carried a brace of Russian-made 14.5mm KPV heavy machine guns in a twin mount forward. Hardpoints for other automatic weapons were spaced along the Fiberglas bulwarks. Its crew, half a dozen fit and wiry Africans, clad only in ragged shorts, looked up belligerently at the aircraft taking the picture. They were a considerable contrast to the refugees seen earlier in the briefing.

"This is the Union's weapon of choice for littoral warfare. I'm sure you all recognize this little guy from the Good Old Days in the Persian Gulf. It's a Boghammer gunboat, Sweden's gift to the maritime terrorist. Cheap, fast, easy to maintain, and great for work in shallow coastal water. The Union has about forty of them in commission, operating in four ten-boat squadrons. Two squadrons, the guys giving Guinea grief, base out of Yelibuya Sound in what was Sierra Leone. The other two operate over Frenchside, covering the coastal smuggling pipelines in from Côte d'Ivoire.

Christine palmed the projector controller again. "The Union navy also has a single squadron of larger vessels."

Click. Thumbing the key, she called up the first of the next sequence of images.

"This is the *Unity,* formerly the *Moa* of the Sierra Leone navy. One hundred twenty-seven feet in length, 135 tons displacement. A Chinese-built Shanghai II–class patrol boat. Primary armament consists of six 25mm autocannon in three twin mounts."

Click.

"This is the *Allegiance,* a Swift-class patrol cutter. A hundred and five feet, 103 tons, another acquisition from Sierra Leone. Currently she's carrying a bow-mounted Bofors L70 40mm cannon and an Oerlikon twin 20mm astern plus machine guns amidships. There is also evidence that both she and the *Unity* also carry shoulder-fired antiaircraft missiles, either the British Blowpipe or the Egyptian-made copy of the Russian SA-9B."

Click.

"And this is the *Promise.* The flagship of the Union fleet. Formerly, she was the minesweeper *Marabai* of the Nigerian navy. However, when General Belewa made his move in Liberia, the crew of the *Marabai* came over with him. A hundred sixty-seven feet in length. Displacement 540 tons. Her sweep gear has been unshipped and she's been rearmed as a light gun corvette with an Emerson twin thirty forward and two pairs of Russian-made ZPU 57mm pom-poms aft. And we know for sure she carries antiair missiles."

Christine tossed her pointer onto a nearby table. "This heavy squadron bases out of Monrovia. From there, it can rapidly deploy to support either the eastern or western Boghammer force. They haven't been used in action against Guinea yet, but you can bet that they're going to be out there waiting for you."

Squadron Leader Evan Dane frowned and spoke up. "Pardon me, Commander, but if the West African Union is claiming that they aren't at war with Guinea, how does their navy get off with shooting the hell out of the place?"

"Easy. The same way the Union's Special Forces get off with blowing up bridges and army barracks inland. They just stand up in the U.N. General Assembly and swear across their heart and hope to spit that they aren't doing it. The line they're peddling is that rebel factions inside of Guinea are committing these acts and that the Guinean government is using the Union as a scapegoat. You'd be surprised how many diplomats are willing to buy that line. However, out here in the real world, we all know that it's a crock."

She clicked the projector control a final time, calling up a theater map. "As you can see, the West African Littoral is an almost continuous tangle of river and creek estuaries, saltwater lagoons, and mangrove swamps, thinly inhabited and almost inaccessible in many places. Taking advantage of this, the Union navy has established a series of boat hides and supply points along the Guinea coast.

"The Boghammer strike groups infiltrate across the line from their main base at Yelibuya and stage their operations out of these hides. After a few days of raising hell, they sneak back into Union territory to rest and re-outfit. These hides also make convenient insertion and resupply points for Union Special Forces units going deep inside Guinean territory. Hopefully, once we get TAC-NET up and our interdiction patrols running, we'll be able to stop them."

"I don't think we'll have all that much trouble with this outfit, Commander." Captain Emberly spoke with a casual confidence. The dimness of the room couldn't conceal the condescendingly cocky smile on the U.S. TAC-BOSS's lips. The expression on his face and the tone in his voice grated on Christine Rendino's nerves.

"These guys have been doing pretty good so far, sir," she replied in a low voice.

"That's true, Commander. But face it, so far it's just been the locals versus the locals. When I get my people out there, I think we'll be able to get things cleaned up in pretty short order."

Christine found herself flashing back to the words of an old friend and former commanding officer: *Ships, battles, and wars have been lost because an enemy no one expected to be able to fight, could.*

There had been another part to Amanda Garrett's quote as well: *Arrogance is a weakness that I will not tolerate . . .*

"That's a damn dangerous attitude, sir," Christine found herself saying.

Emberly's smile became a mild frown of annoyance as he sat forward in his chair. "Let's keep a little grip on reality here, Commander. Beyond this trio of home-baked gunboats you've just shown us, all that we're essentially facing is an outboard motor navy."

Christine shrugged her shoulders. "And your point? If you happen to be a Guinean subsistence-level fisherman commanding a *pirogue* that's one evolutionary step above dugout canoe, a Boghammer mounting a couple of machine guns and a grenade launcher might just as well be a Kirov-class battlecruiser."

"But that is the point, Commander," the TACBOSS continued obstinately. "We aren't a bunch of subsistence-level fishermen. By African standards, these guys are probably pretty good. However, I don't see anything to match what we can bring to bear."

Christine crossed slowly to Emberly's table, the projector light blazing momentarily on her whites as she passed through the beam. "This is true, sir," she replied quietly. "The Union navy is, in fact, limited in many respects. They don't have atomic submarines or cruise missiles or aircraft carriers or stealth bombers. What they do have, though, is a valid combat doctrine that permits them to effectively utilize the resources they do possess to reach their tactical, operational, and strategic goals."

Leaning forward, she braced her arms on the tabletop and gazed balefully into Emberly's eyes. "Or, to use the short form, sir," she continued, selecting her words with care, "these guys are winning this fucking war with what they've got. They don't need anything else."

⚓◆

Shielded by the darkness, the *pinasse*'s crew started to shift cargo. Two heavy planks were lifted into place atop the cargo of rice sacks amidships and more rice sacks were used to weight the plank ends down, anchoring them into place and creating a stable, flattopped platform.

The restacking of the sacks also revealed the row of ammunition cases lined up over the boat's keel as well as the tube, base plate, and bipod of the mortar.

As the boat's captain maintained a lookout, two of the crewmen began to break out and arm the shells. The other two began assembling the weapon on its makeshift firing station.

It was a venerable old piece, a Soviet-made 82mm medium, rusty and battered from thirty years of hard use. In fact, it had been deliberately selected for this mission because of its age and worn condition. It would need to hold together only long enough to fire one last barrage.

⟡◆

MacIntyre had the final word at the briefing. Leaning with his back against the bar, he studied the half-dozen UNAFIN officers for a moment before speaking. He didn't like what he was seeing, or feeling in the room. British, French, and American, seated apart and thinking apart. The United Nations African Interdiction Force was in a hell of a lot of trouble, and the first shot hadn't even been fired yet. And what he was about to say wouldn't make things any better.

"Miss Rendino, gentlemen, I'm sure you will be interested in learning that certain decisions have finally been made by our respective governments concerning the chain of command for UNAFIN."

That had been one of the complicating factors from the start, just as it had been for so many other U.N. operations. Who got to drive the bloody train? The United States, as usual, was contributing the lion's share of the personnel, funding, and support for the mission. On the other hand, however, Guinea was an ex–French colony that still maintained strong trade and political relations with Paris. Yet again, Sierra Leone, the western half of what was now the West African Union, had been a longtime member of the British Commonwealth. And the government of Guinea naturally desired to have a say in what went on within its own territory.

There were more than enough points of national pride and honor for the diplomats to squabble over. And more than enough to put this operation at risk.

"The question has come up, sir," Lieutenant Traynor said with an ironic lift to the corner of his mouth. "I think we'd all rather like to know just who we're supposed to be answering to down here."

"We have received no word on this point from our government," Commander Trochard added. The Frenchman put a light but definite emphasis on "our government."

"All commands will be receiving formal notification presently, Commander," MacIntyre replied. "And to answer Lieutenant Traynor's question, nobody is going to be answering to anyone, at least down here. The decision has been made by the United Nations security council to block out the UNAFIN Mission assignments to the different national task forces and leave it at that.

"As per the initial UNAFIN charter, France will manage the offshore sea and air patrol and merchant boarding operations. The U.S. has the inshore surface patrol and the theater intelligence responsibilities. Great Britain will handle minesweeping and inshore patrol aviation.

"We each will remain answerable only to our respective government and command structures, and all joint operations will be formally organized through these channels. In theater, we will be answerable only to the U.N. Special Envoy for the Guinea crisis."

The only sound was the soft creaking of chairs as the room's occupants shifted their positions slightly, unobtrusively eyeing one another and considering ramifications.

MacIntyre continued, letting his voice harden a little. "This may be a suitable diplomatic solution, gentlemen, but I trust that you will all agree that it's no damn way to run a military mission. This lack of organization and 'I've got mine, too bad about yours' mind-set has turned more than one U.N. operation into a bloody fiasco, with the emphasis on 'bloody.' You may consider Somalia and Lebanon if you require examples.

"Our respective governments haven't been able to come to terms with this problem, so now we have to. We are all a long way from London and Paris and Washington, gentlemen. Putting it bluntly, if our respective governments are incapable of developing an official unified command structure for this operation, the players down here might want to consider setting up with an unofficial one. All of the different elements of UNAFIN will be facing a common foe, and you are only going to have each other to rely on.

"You have one other thing you can rely on as well. Formally, I'm here to inspect the NAVSPECFORCE elements committed to the African interdiction operation. Informally, however, I am here to assure all of you that the United States Naval Special Forces Command stands ready to provide whatever support and assistance we can to any of the national military missions involved in this operation. Either across the table or under it, as needed. Just give us the word. Beyond that, it's going to be your show."

⚔

As each ammunition case was emptied aboard the *pinasse,* it was cast into the sea. Even the little fuse wrench went overboard after the last of the twenty rounds was armed.

Now a man stood ready at the bow and stern, each with his knife hovering above an anchor line. The captain sat at the tiller, the boat's engine idling.

The gunner knelt beside the mortar, the first shell held poised over the muzzle, while his assistant stood by with the second ready in his hands.

⬦◆

The rain had passed for the moment, and a scattering of stars sweltered down through the broken overcast above the air base. The sandbag and oil drum berms around the headquarters building cut off even the faintest trace of a breeze, and MacIntyre stepped out past the sentry post at the main entrance, seeking room to think and to breathe. From the HQ's secured parking area, the Land Rovers carrying the foreign liaisons pulled away from the headquarters building. Each vehicle headed toward its respective national compound, its headlights tunneling through the humid darkness.

The Admiral didn't bother to look after them. Following the briefing, he'd spoken briefly, one on one, with the British and French UNAFIN representatives. The responses had been the same: politely worded neutrality toward the concept of a joint command and an adroit buck-passing in the direction of higher echelons. Even among the U.S. personnel, a definite "who needs them" attitude prevailed.

At least inside of NAVSPECFORCE, he could hurl a few lightning bolts at that attitude over the next couple of days. With the foreign missions, however, there wasn't anything to be done until experience taught the need for a cohesive structure within the U.N. mission.

How many people would have to die before that point was proved?

He'd paced only a few steps out toward the flight line when someone called after him. Christine Rendino overtook him a moment later. "Begging your pardon, sir, but would you mind a little company out here?"

"I wouldn't mind yours at the moment, Commander." MacIntyre matched his rangy stride to the little intel's pacing as she came to walk at his side. "I think we have some more to discuss."

"We do, sir," she replied. "Admiral, do you want me to keep up with that straight talk we were doing earlier today?"

"At all times, Commander."

"Then, sir, we have a whole hell of a lot of problems."

"You noticed too? Which ones did you spot?"

"Attitudes. Bad ones. Point one, we've already talked about, Captain Emberly. If he goes out there and tries to overawe the natives, he's going to get his head blown off. From the way I'm seeing the situation down here, our tech edge might just give us parity against the Union's superior numbers and home-ground advantage. Beyond that, the Tactical Action Group is going to need a game plan, and a damn good one. If we don't get our act together, and

SEA FIGHTER

soon, we are going to get clobbered. And Gutzon Borglum can carve that on a mountain."

MacIntyre scowled in the half-darkness. "I wish to God I didn't agree with you. Unfortunately, I do. We can't afford a disaster down here. Congressional support for UNAFIN is weak as it is. Commander Emberly has got to pay attention to the realities of the tactical situation down here. If he can't handle it, then I'm going to have to find someone that can. I'll hate having to replace him; he's done genuinely good work with the seafighter program."

"Yes, sir. But the fact is that the seafighters now need a real sea fighter. The whole interdiction force does."

MacIntyre gave an acknowledging grunt. "And what did you make out of the rest of that mess?"

"Stinkin' group dynamics, sir. What we essentially have is a bunch of very capable officers doing their jobs well. What we don't have is a team, and I doubt if one is going to gel as things stand. You don't have a single natural-born leader in the whole outfit. That is, someone who can pull these people together and make them listen and follow without the artificial support of an enforced chain of command. And that's who you're going to need to pull this U.N.-invoked can of worms together."

MacIntyre paused in his pacing and braced his hands against his hips. "You live up to your reputation, Commander. You are indeed a most insightful young woman. Tell me, do you ever make a mis-call?"

Backlit by the blue dimness of the airfield's arc lights, she gave a shrug and an ironic grin. "I suppose it could happen someday."

"Admiral MacIntyre," a voice called. "May I speak to you a moment, sir."

As if summoned up by the concerns being voiced about him, Captain Emberly emerged from the sandbagged entryway and started across the tarmac toward the Admiral and the intel. "Sir, I'd like the opportunity to explain about the briefing tonight. . . ."

They never had the chance to learn what the TACBOSS wanted to explain. MacIntyre heard a sound beyond the turbine whine of the flight line and the diesel roar of the headquarters generator, a soft fluttering whisper just on the edge of comprehension. It was a sound that he had heard only once before, on a fire- and oil-stained beach near the Kuwait–Iraq border. However, it was a sound that, once heard, was never forgotten.

Christine Rendino stood at his right, perhaps six feet away. Reacting with the ancient masculine instinct to protect the female, MacIntyre launched himself at her in a headlong dive. The sweep of his arm caught her around the hips, taking her down to the tarmac with him, his bellowed warning drowning out her startled yip.

"INCOMING!"

Shielding Christine's body as best he could with his own, MacIntyre drew in another breath. But before he could yell again, the world blazed glare-white and the steel-hard shock wave of the first shell hit bludgeoned the air from his lungs.

⊗◆

The Union mortarman was good, one of his army's best. He had four rounds in the air before the first had even impacted. He never looked up as the explosions and fire plumes danced over the U.N. air base. Instead, he focused on feeding the shells into the smoking maw of his weapon. There was no need to aim. They were aligned with the target, and with the base range set, the rolling of the boat in the low waves dispersed their fire along the full length of the flight line.

So intent was he that he didn't even count the outgoing shells. His loader had to slap him on the shoulder to advise him when the entire twenty rounds had been expended. With the fire mission completed, the mortarmen grasped the base plate of their weapon and heaved, toppling it over the side with a splash. The two support planks followed a moment later.

Fore and aft, knives flashed and the anchor lines were severed. The captain engaged the propeller clutch and opened the throttle, getting them under way once more.

They made no attempt to race from the scene, or to do anything else foolish to draw attention to themselves. They were leaving as they had come, as part of the meandering flow of small-craft traffic along the Gold Coast. There were no other weapons aboard the craft, nor any piece of military equipment or documentation. Should they be stopped and boarded by the Guinean military or police, as they probably would be before reaching home waters, there would be nothing to connect them with the Conakry attack.

With its engine chugging softly, the *pinasse* turned away to the east, steering by the stars and by the flickering glow of the fires left behind in its wake.

⊗◆

Over the ringing in his ears, MacIntyre heard Christine Rendino give a soft, grating cry of pain and protest. Rolling his weight off her, the Admiral tried to get to his feet, blindly seeking for air that wasn't tainted by dust and smoke and the acrid, sour stench of high explosives. As his hearing returned, he began to make out more of what was going on around them: the wail of an emergency vehicle siren, the belated iron honking of a Klaxon calling the base to battle stations, and the crackling roar of open flames. There were also weak calls for aid in half a dozen languages and cries of agony that could be universally understood.

"What happened?" Christine asked, dazed.

"Mortar barrage," MacIntyre replied shortly, helping the young female officer back to her feet. "Are you all right?"

"I hurt all over, but no place too specific, so I guess I'm okay. . . . Oh God!"

Together the intel and the Admiral took stock of the holocaust that had broken loose around them.

Out on the parking aprons, the French Transall had taken a direct hit. The aircraft and the fueling truck that had been servicing it were islands of incandescent wreckage in the midst of a lake of flame. The 747 air freighter was also engulfed in a haze of smoke, and the base fire trucks were converging on it in a desperate race to prevent another conflagration. Aircrews and linemen were running to the other grounded transports, checking for damage and making frantic preparations to tow or taxi the aircraft away from the spreading flames. Other blazes lit up the sky over the stores depots and in the base motor pool area.

The arc lights had gone out, either killed by the attack or deliberately extinguished to make targeting for a second strike more difficult. Even so, the flickering illumination from the fires was enough to show that the headquarters building had taken a near miss. The revetments near the entryway were torn apart and the two Guinean army sentries on duty there lay sprawled in the sand spilling from the shredded sandbags. A short distance from where MacIntyre and Christine stood, another white-clad figure also lay crumpled on the tarmac.

"Emberly?" The Admiral took a step toward the fallen man. Then, from somewhere out on the flight line, there was a secondary explosion and a sudden flare of light. At his side, MacIntyre heard Christine Rendino gave a choked moan of rising horror. Without thinking, he put his arm out to her, drawing her in and pressing her face against his chest, just as he would have tried to shield his own daughter.

Only moments before, Christine Rendino had said that if Phillip Emberly didn't take the West African Union more seriously, he'd get his head blown off. She'd meant the words as a warning, not as a prophecy.

�֍◆

Upon later reflection, Christine Rendino would grimly conclude that some good had come with the Union attack. The base sections of the different national military missions had abruptly found themselves thrown together, working to extinguish the fires and tending to the wounded. Facilities would have to be shared as the base rebuilt itself and assistance was offered and ac-

JAMES H. COBB

cepted on all sides. Lines of communication would be established, reliances developed, bonds built in the great brotherhood of "them what's been shot at."

Sometime after midnight, she found herself back in her office in the intelligence section. The window had been blown in and the glass scattered across the room, but beyond that things were intact. She sank stiffly into her chair and procured a condensation-wet can of Mountain Dew soda from the small ice chest wedged in behind her desk. Her summer whites were a bedraggled ruin, but then white was a stupid color for a military uniform anyway.

"You wouldn't have another one of those, would you, Commander?" Admiral MacIntyre stood in her doorway, looking as smoke-stained and battered as she did. Christine started to get to her feet, but he waved her back. "Oh, stay put. As Halsey said, 'The shooting's started, so we can dispense with all this damn jumping up and down business.'"

"That's good with me, Admiral," Christine replied, digging another soda out of the cooler and passing it to the suddenly very human three-star. "Here you go, sir. It's part of my private stash."

MacIntyre popped the can's tab and drank off half the contents in a single thirsty pull. "God, that might just let me get through the night. How's TAC-NET? Did your people take any damage?"

"We're pretty much okay," she replied. "The drone control station lost a transceiver antenna, but they have a spare in stock. And the guys over at the Predator group had a shell drop right beside their hangar. It only put a few holes in the wall, though. No personnel injured and no damage to the drones themselves. How bad did the rest of the base get it?"

MacIntyre brushed one of the office chairs free of glass fragments and sank into it. "Seven dead, three of them ours," he replied. "Twenty-four wounded. Some losses in stores and equipment, but nothing that can't be replaced. It could have been worse, except that Jim Stottard gets a gold star for the way he's hardened this facility up. The supply depots and quartering areas are pretty well dispersed, and the revetments and blast walls he's had built contained a lot of the damage."

MacIntyre took another sip from the can. "Yeah," he continued wearily. "It could have been a lot worse."

Christine flashed back to those hellish seconds out on the tarmac. She'd been in battle often enough before aboard the *Cunningham,* but there she'd at least had the psychological protection of the ship's bulkheads around her. This night, though, she'd lain naked before the War Gods for the first time.

She suppressed a shudder. "By the way, Admiral, thank you for knocking me on my face out there."

MacIntyre shrugged. "Old instincts, Commander. Forget it."

"Whatever, sir." She managed a grin. "And if you don't mind, I answer better to Chris. I'm still just getting in to this 'Commander' jazz."

MacIntyre managed a grin of his own and an acknowledging nod. "Chris it is, then. And so, Chris, what happened out there tonight?"

"A fast mortar strike almost certainly fired from a boat holding off the south end of the runway. It slipped in on us merged with the native coastal traffic and disengaged the same way. Twenty-four hours from now, with TACNET fully operational, we could hand you this guy on a silver platter. In fact, we probably could have spotted him working in. Since it isn't, we can't and we couldn't, and he's long gone. Sorry, sir."

"Forget that too. I'm aware that you and your people have been doing your damnedest to get your systems up and running. Unfortunately, our opponents are seldom obliging enough to work out a mutually agreeable schedule with us before starting their war. The major point is that Belewa has just thrown down the gauntlet. This so-called peacekeeping mission has just gone fangs out. And while this attack has resolved one of my problems, albeit in a pretty damn lousy manner, it also presents me with a larger one."

"Who do you bring in to replace Captain Emberly."

"Exactly. Phil Emberly may have had his limitations, but he was the only command-grade officer we had available who was current on the seafighter. Whoever I bring in as TACBOSS now will have to come up to technical speed on a new core weapons system for the Tactical Action Group. They'll also need to develop an effective use doctrine for that weapons system while already deployed in an active war zone and while coordinating operations for all of the other Action Group elements. And that doesn't even touch on minor details like the restrictive rules of engagement, a fragmented U.N. command structure, a complex geopolitical scenario, and a severe manpower limitation!"

MacIntyre crumpled the soda can in his fist and tossed it into the wastebasket. "You wouldn't know of any good professional miracle workers we could pick up on short notice, would you?"

Christine found her eyes drifting toward the laptop computer on her desk and her mind drifting back to the e-mail she had read that afternoon. "Uh, well, I do happen to know of one who might be available, sir. And so do you."

She looked on expectantly, waiting for the Admiral to pick up on the hint. He did a moment later, a grin lighting his soot-grimed features.

"Yes!" MacIntyre slapped his open palm down on the corner of her desk. "Where's the communications center hidden around here, Chris? I need to talk with the Bureau of Personnel."

"It'll be the middle of the night back in Memphis, sir."

"Then find out whoever the hell it is I need to wake up."

On a long blue and gold spring day, the little Cape Cod sloop had beat steadily southward within the long sheltering arm of Cape Hatteras. Lazily she had tacked against a mellow breeze, nosing curiously into inlets and bywaters and following no particular course to anywhere.

And now, with the coming of night, she tugged lightly at her mooring buoy. Her standing rigging creaked with the shift of the low swell and her mast tip inscribed lazy eights against a zenith glittering with a million piercing stars. Around her on the water, the moorage lights of the other yachts at rest in the small anchorage glowed companionably.

"Tell me something, babe," Vince Arkady inquired softly, his breath ruffling the bangs that swept low across Amanda's brow. "Just what in the hell is a Seeadler?"

Amanda Garrett, Commander, United States Navy, in another life, smiled lazily into Arkady's rakishly handsome face. "It's German, love. It means 'sea eagle.'"

"That's a little pretentious for a twenty-four-foot cabin boat, isn't it?"

Amanda thumped her head firmly back down on her young lover's shoulder. "I like it. It has deep connections with my first great love affair."

"Ah hah. Confession from your checkered past. This I have got to hear."

Amanda chuckled softly and shifted position, the two of them flowing into a new embrace on the clumped seat cushions—breasts to chest and thigh to thigh beneath the unzipped sleeping bag. After a dinner cooked in the sloop's tiny galley, she and Arkady had lounged close in the cockpit, talking and watching the sun set. Gradually as the dusk settled, the making of conversation had segued smoothly into the making of love. As their clothing slipped away, the two had assembled this ad hoc bed on the cockpit floorboards, both of them savoring the freedom of the open sky above.

Long bouts of slow, satisfying passion had followed, the kind shared between two well-versed and familiar lovers, interspersed with drowsing naps in each other's arms and more sleepy pillow banter.

"Okay, babe." Arkady lightly kissed the bridge of her nose. "Start talking. Who was this first grand passion of yours?"

"He was an aristocrat, I'll have you know," Amanda replied, giving her head a haughty toss. "He was a genuine Prussian count, an officer and a gentleman of the old school, and I but an innocent young thing of thirteen."

"Those Prussians start early, don't they? What'd he do? Offer you a candy bar and a ride in his armored car?"

Amanda lightly bit her bedmate's shoulder. "He also died quite a few years before I was even born. His name was Captain Felix Von Luckner, also known to the Allies in World War One as 'The Sea Devil.'"

"And what did this Felix do to so arouse your passion?"

"I'll tell you. When he was thirteen, he ran away to sea, just like I desperately wanted to do. He left his father's castle, abandoning his wealth and title and everything else to rove the world over as a common sailor aboard an old Russian square-rigger."

Arkady grinned and ran a hand down her flank. "I can see how that would work for you. Where's the Sea Devil come in, and what does all this have to do with the name of your sloop?"

"Well, eventually, my hero left the merchant marine and became an officer in the Imperial German Navy. When World War One broke out, he approached the German admiralty with an insane plan. He wanted to go a-raiding in the world's last sailing frigate."

"A sailing frigate? In the First World War? You have to be kidding."

"Nope, and it was a brilliant notion in its way. Sail-powered, he had a global range because he never need to refuel. And no one would suspect a sailing ship of being a commerce raider until it dropped its gun shields and opened fire. With absolutely nothing to lose, the Imperial Navy gave Von Luckner an elderly bark-rigged Brandenburg freighter. The count mounted a couple of small, concealed deck guns on her and renamed her . . ."

"The *Seeadler.*"

"Correct, Mr. Arkady." She rewarded him with a light kiss. "At any rate, my beloved sailed away on Christmas Day, evaded the British blockade, and politely began to ravage the world's sea-lanes."

"How do you politely ravage someone?"

Amanda arched an eyebrow. "You have to ask? For all of his ferocious nickname, and in spite of being in the middle of one of the bloodiest wars in human history, the Sea Devil never took a life if he could avoid it. His technique was to sidle up alongside an Allied merchantman, put a shot across her bow, and capture her before any resistance could be offered.

"All of the delicacies and alcohol from the prize's officers' mess would be transferred to the *Seeadler,* as would the contents of the ship's safe. The crew and the male passengers would be put over the side in well-provisioned lifeboats, while the female passengers became the Count's guests aboard his vessel. The prize would be scuttled, and the Count would transmit a radio message to the nearest Allied base, informing them of the lifeboats' position. Then he would sail away to his next adventure."

Arkady was suitably impressed. "Now, that was a guy who knew how to make war."

"I agree. My count was eminently civilized. . . . Mmm. If you insist on doing that, love, do it a little bit lower. Oh yes . . . Oh yes, yes, yes." Amanda gave a squirm of appreciation for certain events taking place beneath the sleeping bag.

"And how did you tie up with this latter-day Captain Kidd?"

"Via a couple of old books by Lowell Thomas that I found in my father's library. *Count Luckner, the Sea Devil* and *The Sea Devil's Fo'c'sle.* They were full of wonderful sea stories as told by my count, some of which might even conceivably have been true. I must have read those books a dozen times over, and I fell hopelessly and desperately in love. So much so that when Dad bought me this sloop, there could be only one name for her."

"I see. And how did you get around the fact that the Sea Devil was on the other side during the Great War?"

Amanda chuckled lowly and nestled closer, tucking her head under Arkady's chin. "That was the best part of the whole love affair. I constructed this elaborate fantasy involving a beautiful young American woman, who peradventure resembled a somewhat more mature and filled-out version of myself at the time. She's captured by the dashing Count Von Luckner, and after a number of thrilling adventures together in the South Seas, she, in turn, captures the Sea Devil's heart and wins him over to the Allied cause."

Arkady exploded into helpless mirth, and Amanda retaliated with a firm pinch in a sensitive area. "Don't laugh! The Count saved my life. If I hadn't been able to escape with him to the South Pacific, I would have smothered to death in Mrs. Mendelson's fourth-period social studies class several times over."

Arkady chuckled again and eased back to his side of the cockpit. With deliberation, the aviator flipped the sleeping bag aside, laying Amanda bare to the starlight. For a long minute he studied each inch of her, the flow of tousled shoulder-length hair sheening pewter in the faint silver glow, her fine planed features highlighted by shadow, her breasts, softened by mature womanhood yet still firm and high-riding, the smoothly curved lines of her dancer's body, a strip of midnight slipping up between her thighs.

"I'll have to thank him someday, babe," he whispered. "Losing you like that would have been a tragedy."

Amanda shivered for reasons beyond the cool breeze on her bare skin, and the spark of fire in her narrowing eyes came from something beyond the stars. Arkady covered her again, first with the sleeping bag and then with himself.

Time passed. The *Seeadler* rocked cradlelike in the wake of a passing boat. Night drew on, the air chilled from cool to cold, and the first hint of the morning fog formed. Nestled warmly beside her lover, sleep should have come easily to Amanda, but didn't.

Even as the afterglow of her shared joy and passion had passed, that strange restlessness that had gnawed at her of late reasserted itself. And for the hundredth time she asked herself why.

It was a brand of self-analysis that had grown increasingly frustrating over the past weeks. At this moment, she was at the pinnacle of her career. She'd commanded the ship she'd wanted. She'd had success in her endeavors and even a degree of fame, for what that was worth. Right now, everything she could ever ask for was within her grasp: honest love, companionship, and a bright future for the asking. And yet . . .

Why not swallow the anchor? she self-argued savagely. *Hang your medals up over the fireplace and tell this sweet boy beside you that you're ready to marry. Have your child while you still have a couple of ticks left on your biological clock and then sit back in the sunshine and be content with all you've earned. Damn, damn, damn it, Amanda, what more do you want?*

And that was the rub. She didn't know, and it had been a long time since Amanda Garrett had last not known what it was that she wanted out of life. She didn't like the sensation.

Arkady was asleep, his head resting on her breast. Lightly she stroked his dark hair and stared at the sky, watching the stately march of the stars around Polaris.

⚓

The doubts of the night lingered on into the day, keeping Amanda subdued as they got the *Seeadler* under way on the reach across the sound for Powell's Point. Even the spanking breeze that put the placid little cruising sloop's rail to the water couldn't lift her spirits to their former level as they beat to the southeast.

As the morning progressed, Amanda felt Arkady's eyes resting thoughtfully upon her. He had the knack of reading her better than any man she had ever known beyond her own father. And that had its drawbacks as well as its advantages.

"Any word yet on your next duty?" the aviator asked casually from his side of the cockpit.

"Not really," she replied, easing the tiller a few degrees. "I haven't really given it much thought yet. I still have a year to go aboard the Duke. There's no rush."

Arkady lifted an eyebrow at her. "A year isn't all that long, babe. You always told us that with career planning, you had to start early to get the slot you wanted."

Amanda shrugged with more casualness than she felt. "I suppose I did, and I suppose I was right. I just haven't had the time yet. I guess I should get working on something."

"So what are you going to be looking for?" he insisted.

"I'm not sure. I'm due for a tour on the beach, I know that. But beyond that point I'm just not sure."

"Hell, you've got to have some idea." Impatience crept into Arkady's voice.

"Well, I don't!" she snapped back. "I just don't. All right?"

They both recoiled from her sudden burst of anger, and the only sound aboard the sloop for a time was the hiss of the waves and the working of the rigging.

"I'm sorry, Arkady," she said quietly after a minute. "But I really don't know what I'll be doing next. Why is it important now?"

It was the aviator's turn to shrug as he looked off at a passing cabin cruiser. "I just figured that we might want to try coordinating something. You know, so we could get the same duty station. You're a great correspondent, babe, but it would be nice to at least be able to look at you once in a while." A ghost of his old grad school grin crept back.

Amanda was grateful for the chance to smile back. "I know what you mean, love. I don't suppose finding a slot in San Diego would be that much of a challenge. Come to think of it, I've even had a couple of civilian headhunters from out that way offer me a fat consultant's contract from Lockheed Ship-building. No, come to think about it, it wouldn't be much trouble at all to get on the West Coast."

"Uh, that's just the thing, babe. I might not be out on the West Coast for much longer. Well, there's a chance of that, anyway. I've been offered a shot at the Fleet JSF Conversion Program."

"The Joint Strike Fighter Program?" Amanda fell half a dozen points off her course. "Arkady, that's fabulous!"

"Pretty neat, anyway," he agreed, nodding somberly. "It's for the operational workup of the Vertical Takeoff and Landing variant of the aircraft. The Navy and Marines both are looking for aviators who are both jet and helicopter rated, and I did finish my carrier qualifications before I transferred over to rotorwing. There aren't too many of us out here, and they seem really anxious to talk to me."

"I imagine so!" Amanda fumbled with the tiller for a moment, re-aiming the *Seeadler's* jackstay at the distant Powell's Point lighthouse and easing her off from the drive of the wind. "Arkady, this is what you've always wanted, another shot at flying fighters."

"Among other things, yeah." He tucked his hands into the pockets of his denim jacket. "But if I take the shot, it'll mean being posted to Jacksonville."

"So?"

"So, babe, Jax is an aviation station, with damn few slots available for surface-warfare specialists."

"Oh."

Arkady continued, not meeting her eyes. "If I take this JSF job, It'll mean another couple of years of us seeing each other for a week every six months. If I pass on the JSH, I figure we can at least both get something on the same side of the continent."

"No, love," Amanda said quietly. "No. You can't miss an opportunity like this."

"Sure I can," he replied simply. He slouched lower on the cockpit bench, studying her face, his own impassive. "If that's how it has to be, yeah, I can do it." He paused for a moment, then continued. "It's either that or we both try for a different deal of the deck. I've been thinking . . ."

A shrill electronic warble issued from the *Seeadler*'s cabin, startling them both.

"Damn, damn, damn! Arkady, take the helm!"

"Got it," he replied, snapping back to Navy mode. Deftly he ducked under the boom and took over the tiller. Going forward and hunkering low, Amanda reached inside the cabin hatchway and disconnected the cellular phone from the jack of the solar power charger. This was her personal work phone, the one that could not be disregarded.

"Garrett here."

"Commander Garrett," a distant and decisive voice whispered. "This is Commander Koletter, the OOD at NAVSPECFORCE Atlantic. A situation has developed that requires your presence at LANTFLEETCOM immediately. Admiral MacIntyre's orders."

"Admiral MacIntyre." All thoughts of a personal nature drained away in an instant. That carefully deliberate phrase. "A situation has developed," and Eddie Mac MacIntyre's personal brand made this a fire-alarm call. "I'm aboard my boat at the moment, Commander, just off the mouth of Albemarle Sound. I'll put in to Port Powell immediately and try and rent a car."

"That won't be necessary, Commander. Can you give us your position?"

"Affirmative." Amanda reached into the cabin again and procured the *Seeadler*'s handheld GPU. It was the work of a minute to establish and read off the fix.

"Acknowledged, Commander Garrett. Maintain those coordinates. A Coast Guard helicopter is being launched to pick you up. They will be over your location shortly. Please be ready to signal them in."

"We'll be standing by. Garrett out." She snapped the cellular phone shut, not even realizing that she had slipped into naval radio discipline.

"What's the word, Skipper?" Arkady inquired crisply.

"Something pretty hot," she replied, her own thoughts jumping ahead.

"They're sending out a helo for me. Bring her into the wind and let's get the canvas off of her. They'll be doing a sling pickup, so we'll need bare poles. While I get my gear together, you start the auxiliary and break out a marker strobe and some smoke flares. You're going to have to take her back alone . . ."

Amanda let her string of commands trail off. The bubble so carefully built the previous day and night had burst as if it had never been.

She hunted for Arkady's eyes. "Love," she said carefully, "I think you had something you wanted to say before that phone call. What was it?"

From his station at the tiller, Arkady smiled back at her. There was a degree of sadness in that smile, but his vivid blue eyes held only love and a quiet resignation. "It wasn't anything important, babe. Nothing at all."

Atlantic Fleet Command Operations Center
Norfolk, Virginia   1037 Hours, Zone Time; May 3, 2007

The Coast Guard HH-60 Jayhawk settled onto the Operations Center helipad amid the whirlwind of its own liftwash. Amanda returned her cranial helmet and life jacket to the crew chief and disembarked, ducking low to keep well clear of the still-spinning rotor blades.

A naval officer in now dust-stained Blue Bakers waited for her at the edge of the helipad. "Commander Garrett?" he called over the fading howl of the helicopter's turbines. "I'm Lieutenant Kravin, NAVSPECFORCE Atlantic Operations. Commander Koletter's compliments. We've been expecting you, ma'am."

"What's the situation?" Amanda asked.

"Can't say exactly, Commander. All I can say is that Eddie Mac—that is, Admiral MacIntyre—wants you on a secure line ASAP. The scuttlebutt is that there's big trouble with the U.N. mission in Africa."

They started across from the landing site to the Operations Center. Located in the heart of the largest naval base in the Western world, the masts of the in-port elements of the 2nd Fleet could be seen rising beyond the low windowless concrete building. Even escorted by a staff officer, it required both Amanda's identification card and a voice-print authentication to get past the steel entry doors and alert Marine sentries. From there, a short elevator ride delivered them two levels down to the underground bunker-within-a-bunker of Atlantic Fleet Signals.

A few minutes more and Amanda found herself seated alone in a small briefing room, facing the glowing screen of a live videocom link.

"Admiral MacIntyre is on line, Commander," a crisply professional voice spoke seemingly out of midair. "The channel is secure, and we are putting you through now."

The Atlantic Fleet Command test pattern on the wall screen snapped over to the grim visage of the NAVSPECFORCE C.O. From the curved bulkhead behind him Amanda surmised that he was speaking from the communications bay of his personal command-and-control aircraft. Also given the way his eyes met hers, she too was visible on a reverse visual link. Amanda became acutely aware of the frayed casualness of her jeans and sweater, and of how her hair was bound back in a shaggy amber ponytail.

MacIntyre, on the other hand, seemed to pay no note at all. "Good morning, Commander Garrett. I'm sorry I had to interrupt your leave."

"No problem, sir. I apologize for being out of uniform. I came in directly from my boat, and I haven't had the opportunity to change."

MacIntyre waved the point away. "Lord knows that's the least of my problems, Commander, or yours."

Amanda noted that the Admiral, who usually gave the impression of being as imperturbable and durable as an oaken dock piling, looked tired, a haze of unshaven beard darkening his squared jaw. "What's going on, sir?" she inquired, concerned.

"I'm speaking to you from the tarmac here at the U.N. base in Conakry. We've just had the hell shot out of us by the West African Union. We've taken casualties."

Amanda's heart froze in her chest. Christine! The Admiral knew full well that she and the little blond intel were close. And given the way MacIntyre worked, it would be very possible that he would make a death notification himself.

He must have read her expression. "Your friend Commander Rendino is all right," he said. "She was with me during the attack, and she only picked up a few cuts and bruises. Outside of that, she's fine."

MacIntyre gave Amanda a second or two to digest the welcome information before continuing. "Unfortunately, the same can't be said for Captain Emberly, our Tactical Action Group commander. He was killed in last night's mortar barrage, and his loss threatens to knock this whole damn UNAFIN operation into a cocked hat. We need a replacement for him, fast. How would you like the job?"

Amanda's heart skipped another beat. "Me, sir?" she floundered, momentarily at a loss for words. "But this UNAFIN job is a littoral operation, coastal work. I'm blue water."

MacIntyre tilted back the S.O.'s chair he was occupying. "You've had some interdiction experience working with the Coast Guard, and God knows you took the *Cunningham* in close during the China operation. Anyhow, that isn't my primary concern. And as the TACBOSS for our inshore patrol operation, I can promise that you'll be commanding all sorts of very smart and very capable young hands who can push all of the right buttons. They can teach you everything you'll need to know about any of the new technologies involved."

He looked directly into the screen and into her face. "What we really need down here is a leader who can pull a group of diverse elements into a fist and a good, innovative doctrine person who can figure out where that fist needs to be aimed. You're my first choice in both of these areas."

"I'm very flattered, sir." Amanda's reply came slowly, but her mind was racing. "Will this be a TDY assignment?"

"Think long term, Commander. The show down here is going to take a while. You'd have to be released from the command of the *Cunningham*."

Amanda's knee-jerk reaction was a decisive no. But then she paused for a moment. Was she giving up command of her ship? Or just of an office trailer parked beside a dry dock?

"What will the package entail, sir?" she asked cautiously.

"The core element of the Tactical Action Group is our new seafighter squadron, PGAC-1. That's why Phil Emberly was initially chosen for the TAC-BOSS slot. As backup, you'll have a pair of Cyclone-class Patrol Craft and eventually a Special Operations Capable Marine company for boarding and security operations. The whole package will stage off of the Mobile Offshore Base we have positioned off the coast of the West African Union."

"What are the mission parameters?"

"Twofold. To enforce the U.N. maritime embargo in place against the West African Union and to provide security for the nation of Guinea against hostile naval incursions."

Amanda called up her mental chart file of the world's oceans. "Admiral, you're talking about covering over seven hundred miles of extremely wild coastline with only five small hulls."

MacIntyre smiled without humor. "I indicated it would be a challenge, Commander. U.N. operations are not popular with Congress currently. They're holding us to an absolute bare-bones deployment. Minimal assets. The counter to that, as I see it, is to deploy a small Tactical Action Group backed by extensive intelligence assets in the hope we can get there 'firstest with the mostest.' You'll have Commander Rendino's full Tactical Intelligence Network at your direct disposal, including two reconnaissance drone squadrons and two aerostat-equipped intelligence-gathering ships.

"You will also receive a degree of assistance from the other UNAFIN assets. The French have a corvette squadron running offshore interdiction patrol, and Great Britain has a minehunter group and a patrol helicopter squadron working Guinea coastal security."

"What about my own aviation assets, sir?" Amanda inquired.

"Beyond the drones and a small composite Marine and Navy utility helicopter group for logistics and support, you don't have any."

"No strike aircraft at all?"

"Not authorized. Since the West African Union doesn't have an air force, the Security Council couldn't see why we needed one either. Don't ask—I don't pretend to understand the logic of it either."

MacIntyre leaned forward and rested his crossed arms on the console before him.

"There's your package, Commander. You will be decisively undermanned and handicapped by the rules of engagement set by the U.N. The tactical situation is fluid and deteriorating, and you will be fighting a tough, cunning, and capable enemy. We are just beginning to learn how much so. This will be hazardous duty. For you especially in more ways than one."

Amanda frowned. "What do you mean, sir? Why me?"

"I had a long talk with BUPERS before calling you in. The Bureau of Personnel was not pleased with the notion of you going to Africa. In fact, they screamed bloody murder at even the concept."

"Why?"

MacIntyre smiled wryly into the screen. "It seems that certain parties in high places have been doing some career planning for you, Commander."

"I still don't understand, sir."

"Here's the situation. It appears you have become something of a PR icon within the New Age Navy. Living proof that the gender integration within the Fleet has been a success. On completion of your tour aboard the Duke and your obtaining your fourth bar, it has been decided that you will be given a high-visibility position as military attaché to one of our major embassies overseas. Either France or Moscow—they haven't decided yet.

"Following that, as a senior captain, you've been penciled in to command a major unit within Fleet Amphib, probably a Wasp-class LHD. Beyond that point, even BUPERS gets a little vague. However, I get the impression that if you don't blot your copybook, you may very well end up as the youngest female rear admiral in the history of the United States Navy."

Amanda shook her head, a little awed. "I had no idea."

"That's the game plan as it was given to me." MacIntyre lifted an eyebrow sardonically. "Consider that copybook proviso well, Commander. If you take on this Africa job, and if it blows up in your face, as it gives every indication of doing, you could end up flushing this entire chain of events, along with the rest of your career, right down the head.

"In return, all I can offer is a drumhead promotion. This TACBOSS position calls for a four-striper. You'll be receiving the provisional rank of captain. In title only for the moment, however. You'll receive none of the pay and benefits, just the responsibilities, until we can get the rank officially on the books. You may consider that another big if and when as well."

MacIntyre lifted his hands in an apologetic gesture. "In the face of all this, Commander, please feel free to tell me to shove it where the sun doesn't shine. There will be no recriminations if you elect not to accept the assignment."

Amanda looked away from the screen. *Be careful of what you wish for, for you may receive it.* For weeks now, she'd been brooding about what her future might hold. Suddenly she had more futures than she could possibly ever hope to live. She'd whined about not being ready to give up her combat command yet. Well, here was another combat command, with a plentiful supply of real combat to go with it. She'd procrastinated about making decisions about what to do with her life. And apparently there were plenty of people more than willing to make those decisions for her.

Somewhere, the Fates were laughing themselves silly.

For Amanda Garrett, making major decisions rapidly was second nature. She looked back into the video monitor. "Yes, sir, you're right. It sounds like a challenging assignment. I'll be pleased to take it."

On the far end of the link, MacIntyre's palm slammed triumphantly down on the console top. "Ha! Rendino said you'd go for it!"

Amanda took a deep, deliberate breath. With the commitment made, she suddenly felt better than she had in a long time. For right or wrong, she had a course to steer. "I beg your pardon, sir, but there will be one proviso."

"Name it, Commander."

"If I have to leave my ship to take this job, I want to know that I'm leaving her in the best hands possible. I want my executive officer, Lieutenant Commander Ken Hiro, to get the *Cunningham*. And not just to fill out my tour. He gets a full hitch of his own."

MacIntyre scowled. "Officers generally don't move up to fill the command slot on the same ship they've served aboard as an exec."

"I'm fully aware of that, sir. But I'm also aware that the stealths are the current glamour command within the surface-warfare community. If you'll pardon my French, every swinging dick in the fleet is pulling strings and recalling favors to get a shot at an SC-21–class hull. Now, Ken Hiro is a superb officer. However, he doesn't have any Sea Daddies in his corner except for me. I know you must be cooking the books to get me transferred, so leave the oven on a few minutes more. Get Ken bumped to full bull and get him the command slot for the Duke. You can consider it a package deal."

The Admiral's scowl deepened for a moment, then a grin broke past it. "By God. Amanda Garrett, you're a provisional captain for less than thirty seconds and you've already got a handle on flag-grade politicking. Package accepted."

Amanda nodded into the screen. "Thank you, sir. I hope I can manage the job."

"I hope so too, Captain. Because if you can't, then we're all in a lot of trouble."

The Virginia Tidewater,
Somewhere Below Eastville
1421 Hours, Zone Time; May 4, 2007

As dusk started to settle, Rear Admiral Wilson Garrett, U.S.N., retired, ambled down toward the little combined pier and boat shelter on the bay shore below his gray ranch-style home. Standing on his short stretch of pebbled beach with his hands tucked into his jeans pockets, he scanned the expanse of Chesapeake Bay.

A lifetime's experience of gauging maritime courses and speeds told the weathered and white-haired little man that it should be soon. And sure enough, after a few minutes' wait he spotted the familiar white hull coming around the forested headland to the south. The *Seeadler* was running on her auxiliary engine, and there was only a single figure in her cockpit.

Wils Garrett found himself reflecting that it must have been an awfully long and lonely haul for that boy. As the sloop turned in toward his property, he crunched over to the dock to handle the mooring lines.

For a brownshoe, the lad was a good boat handler, and the sloop brushed against the pier fenders with hardly a bump. "How'd it go, son?" Garrett inquired, tying her off at the bow.

"No problem." Vince Arkady vaulted up out of the cockpit and onto the pier with the stern line. "I just brought her up on the engine. I'll leave the sailing to Amanda."

"I know what you mean," Garrett replied. "She has the touch for that kind of thing. I never really had the patience for it myself."

Garrett caught the wisp of hope that drifted across the aviator's face. "Is she here, Wils?"

Garrett shook his head. "No, son. She didn't get home until about ten last night, and she was gone by six. I expect the same tonight. She's hip deep in getting ready to hand over the Duke."

Arkady straightened abruptly from where he knelt by the mooring head. "Give up the Duke? What are you talking about?"

"Eddie Mac MacIntyre's offered her a new command. There's some trouble on the African Gold Coast and they need her out there ASAP." Admiral Garrett let his voice soften. "She's gone, son."

Garrett watched as the emotion played across Arkady's face for a moment, then the guards of stoicism slammed down. "Yeah, I guess she is."

Stiff spined, Arkady reboarded the *Seeadler* to collect his gear. Keeping his peace, Admiral Garrett crossed his arms and leaned back against one of the dock pilings, watching as the younger man stacked his shaving kit, duffel bag, and roll of dirty laundry on the pier deck. It was never too good to push someone that full of feelings until he'd cooled a little. Garrett waited until Arkady had disembarked again before speaking.

"Ready for some words of wisdom yet?"

Arkady started to snap back, then caught himself. That wry smile that Amanda had liked so much crept back across his face. "Yes, sir," he said. "I think I could really use some just now."

Garrett nodded. "Okay, then here you go. There's been a lot written about people 'sacrificing for love.' Well, let me clue you in—that's a load of bullcrap. A good thing is where two people add to each other, not take away. If either individual is lessened by the relationship, then something is wrong.

"Now, you and Amanda have been damn good for each other. You love her and she loves you. It stands out all over the two of you whenever you're in the same room together. However, I can tell you one thing right now, and this is from personal experience. While my daughter is one hell of a good naval officer, she would make one stinkin' navy wife."

Garrett straightened and hooked his thumbs into the belt loops. "I can tell you something else too, son. You have places to go and things to do yourself, for yourself. You would not be happy being a camp follower."

It went quiet on the pier, with only the slosh of the waves and the creak on the pier dolphins. "So what the hell do we do, Admiral?" Arkady asked eventually.

"Son, I don't know. That's something the two of you have to work out. And I do not envy you the job."

Arkady looked down at the pier decking, the evening breeze ruffling his hair. "It really stands out around us that much, huh?"

"Oh yeah, if you know what to look for. To tell you God's honest, I was halfways figuring and halfways afraid I'd have a son-in-law when the two of you got back from this cruise."

Arkady managed another wry smile and dig into the pocket of his jeans.

His hand emerged with a small black velvet ring box. Thumbing it open, he studied the bright gleam of gold in the fading daylight. Then he turned deliberately and threw ring and box both as far off the end of the pier as he could. There was a final glint, and then they disappeared in a small splash.

"You know," Garrett said mildly, "Amanda is a very practical young woman. She wouldn't have minded you taking it back."

"I know it," Arkady replied. "But it's like the reason they break the champagne glasses at the end of the toast. So they can never be used again for a lesser purpose."

Admiral Garrett gave an agreeing nod. "I see your point. She is worth it, isn't she?"

"Damn straight, sir." Arkady began collecting his gear from the dock. "Well, I guess I'd better be getting out of here."

"Don't you want to wait and see her again before you go?"

"Nah, I don't think so. It'll be . . . simpler if I don't."

"I guess you're right," Garrett slung Arkady's duffel bag over his own shoulder and they started up the path to the house. "But come on in for a drink first, anyway. She's not going to be back that soon."

Bridge of the USS Cunningham
Norfolk, Virginia   1354 Hours, Zone Time; May 6, 2007

All that lay before the big destroyer were the gray steel cliffs of the closed drydock doors, and the only vista that could be seen from her bridge were the waters of the Elizabeth River, sullen and murky beneath an overcast sky.

Not to Amanda Garrett, however. Sitting in the plastic shrouded captain's chair, she could see many other things and times and places. There were the steel-colored rollers of the southern Pacific thundering eternally eastward through the gap of Drake's Passage, the soul-piercingly beautiful flame of an East China Sea sunset, and the limpid blue of Mamala Bay with the snowy whiteness of the foam peeling back from the dagger-sharp bow of her ship as they headed out from Pearl.

"It's time, Skipper."

Ken Hiro's voice returned her to reality. The bridge was a gutted skeleton of itself. The console chassis stood empty, stripped of its electronics. Bunched and coiled cable ends were taped to the bulkheads, and the air stank of fresh paint and arc welding.

Amanda slid down from the elevated chair and cast a last professional look at how the rebuild was coming.

The long foredeck of the warship gaped open. All three of the Duke's Vertical Launch Systems had been unshipped. One would be replaced with the angled twin barrels of a 155mm VGAS bombardment system, the other two with augmented launcher arrays that would add to the Duke's arsenal both the navalized variant of the Army's ATACMS land attack missile and the Block IV Standard theater ABM.

Immediately below the bridge, the old 76mm Oto Melara mount was gone as well, one of the new five-inch 65 ERGM mounts to be installed in its place. Amanda still wasn't convinced that the ultra-long-range "smart shells" of the new gun systems could possibly be as dead accurate as the tech reps claimed they'd be.

But then, that would be for Ken to discover.

Her exec stood in the curtainless bridge entryway, clad as she was in full Dress Blues, white hatted, white gloved, and razor creased. The sturdy Japanese-American's demeanor was somber, even for him.

"Skipper . . ." Amanda mused. "I guess that's the last time I get called that on these decks."

"You're always going to be the skipper of the Duke, ma'am," Hiro replied. "Until they scrap her and melt down her plates."

Amanda shook her head. "That's not the way to think, Ken. I've had my time with her. She belongs to you now. Make her name shine, but make it shine your way."

It felt right to put her arms around him for one brief, fierce warrior's embrace. "Thanks for always backing me up, Ken."

Awkwardly he returned the hug, a choke coming to his voice. "Thanks for bringing me along, Captain."

⌗◆

The change-of-command ceremony was a simple one. There hadn't been time to organize elaboration. The Cunningham's new cadre of officers stood to on the helicopter deck, along with an honor guard of the ship's company.

There were a few special guests as well. Lieutenant Dix Beltrain had come down from the Conner. The Duke's old tactical officer was still as handsome as ever, but the boyishness was starting to wear off a little. It wouldn't be long before he'd be ready for his own first command. Carl Thomson, Amanda's old chief engineer, was also present, still not quite comfortable in a civilian business suit.

And her father, of course, standing in the back and giving her that half-smile and nod that had seen her through many graduations and award ceremonies. He had so often been gone from her life, and yet he always managed to be there when it really mattered.

One individual that she'd hoped for there was missing. He had gone and there was no word left for her. Amanda could only conclude that it was for the best.

The ship's bell of the *Cunningham* pealed out its piercingly clear tone. The 2nd Fleet chaplain gave a brief prayer for the ship and for her captains, coming and leaving, and Amanda spoke a few words that she could never afterward remember. Then came the reading of the orders that freed her from her treasured bondage and placed the burden of the Duke's destiny on another's shoulders.

His white-gloved fingers touched his brow with machinelike precision. "I relieve you, Captain Garrett."

Her answering salute was equally precise. "I stand relieved, Captain Hiro."

For her, the word now meant only a rank. For Ken, it became a way of life.

Amanda was pleased with the way she maintained herself throughout the remainder of the ceremony. She didn't start to crack until she was rung over the side for the last time. The sweet purity of the *Cunningham*'s bell sounding the four strokes and the quartermaster's voice over the MC-1 circuit passing the word, "Captain . . . departing," finally pierced her shields.

The tears started to come as she crossed the aluminum gangway that extended from the Duke's helideck to the dry-dock apron. Her father would be waiting for her there. With her gear already loaded in the stretch cab of his pickup, he'd be driving her to Dulles International to catch the evening flight to England, the first leg of her long journey to Guinea.

As planned, Admiral Garrett and the Ford were parked near the end of the gangway, but a second figure in Levi's and a civilian Windcheater leaned back against the front fender beside her father.

"Arkady!"

Forgetting decorum and the press of her blues, she dove into his arms, returning the embrace that closed around her. "Why didn't you come to the ceremony?" she asked, her voice muffled against his chest.

"I didn't think it would be such a good idea, babe. I remember you telling me how we had to be discreet about things."

"Oh, to hell with that. Let 'em all watch." She tilted her face up to accept the kiss, fully as prolonged and intense as the embrace.

"I'm so glad to see you," she said finally as they paused for breath. "I wanted a chance to explain. To tell you why I took this new assignment."

"There's nothing to explain, babe." Arkady gently reached up, tugging the lapels of her jacket straight. He was smiling at her, not with his grad school grin, but a man's sober smile of acceptance. "We both have things we need to do. For you, it's Africa. For me, maybe it's Jacksonville. I've put in my application for the Joint Strike Fighter program.

"You're going to make it this time, Arkady. I know you will."

"Maybe. I've been hanging around with someone who's helped me get strong enough to at least try again. We'll see how it goes. And that's how it'll be with you and me, babe. We'll just see how it goes. Maybe someday we'll get to finish that talk we started."

"Someday." The damned tears were coming again, and she hid them against his chest. She felt the firm, warm pressure of Arkady's hand travel down her spine in a farewell caress.

"Get going, babe. The Captain is needed on the bridge."

There wasn't a great deal said in the cab of the pickup for a time, and Wilson Garrett knew that to be the best. They had traversed the Hampton Roads bridge-tunnel and were northbound on Interstate 64 before he noted Amanda repairing the damage with her compact and squaring herself away.

"He's a hell of a good man, angel."

"One of the very best, Dad," she replied soberly, snapping the compact shut and returning it to her shoulder bag. "He deserves a lot better than what I gave him back there."

Garrett glanced over at his beautiful and once again reserved daughter. It bothered him sometimes that she was always so quick and so willing to assume responsibility for whatever came along. What was worse, he knew from whom she'd inherited the trait.

No man alive could be prouder of his offspring, or of what she had become. However, there were times that Wils Garrett wished Amanda could have enjoyed just a couple more years of girlhood.

"Yeah," he said, raising his voice slightly. "Definitely, that Arkady is a step up from some of those specimens you used to drag back to the house when you were in high school."

Out of the corner of his eye he saw a smile tug at Amanda's lips. His daughter recognized the old game. "Dad, I only went with nice boys back when I was in school."

"Does that include that Marty Johnson yahoo as well?"

Amanda replied with a faint snort. "Marty was sweet! And don't tell me you still hold a grudge over what happened at my senior prom."

"Damn right I still hold a grudge! And the little coward knows it! To this day, every time I happen to drop by the Ford Agency, he goes and hides in the back office. I think he's afraid I still might carry out some of those threats I made on his life, limb, and masculinity. And there are times when I'm tempted."

"Oh, Dad! None of what happened was actually Marty's fault!" For one precious second, Amanda was his little girl again, with all the happiness and defiance and frustration and joy that entailed.

"I don't know about fault, young lady! All I know is that he took my daughter out of my house at eight P.M. in a blue taffeta evening formal and brought her back at six A.M. in a stolen beach towel!"

"Father! For the past eighteen years, I have been telling you there was a perfectly logical and reasonable explanation for everything that happened that night!"

"Yeah, and for the past eighteen years I haven't believed a word of it!"

For a second he glanced away from the traffic flow to glare at her. Amanda glared back, then the laughter exploded out of them both.

Wilson Garrett encircled his daughter with his arm, gathering her in. They drove on, her head resting lightly on his shoulder.

En Route to Station

Conakry, Guinea, is one of those places you can't get to from here.

Amanda spent eight plodding hours aboard the transatlantic shuttle between Washington, D.C., and London. More than enough time for her to become refreshed on all of the reasons she loathed travel by commercial airliner.

To the good, the discomfort provided a useful counterirritant to the regrets she had about leaving both Arkady and the *Cunningham*. It inspired her to bury herself in her new assignment as the most readily available escape. Avoiding the plasticky meal service, the boring in-flight movie, and the repeated conversational ploys of her equally boring seatmate, she drained the power cells of her laptop studying the event and country files available on the West African Union.

She read until her eyes burned and she had to close them for a moment. When she opened them again, a premature dawn was breaking beyond the airliner's windows and the pilot was announcing their descent into Heathrow.

Transferring over to the RAF Transport Command base, all she saw of the United Kingdom was the lashing rain and overcast of an English spring as seen through a staff car's windshield. That and the inside of the air base NAAFI canteen as she waited though a long afternoon for her next flight. Again to the plus, however, was the opportunity to exchange the panty hose and scratchy gabardine of her Blues for the soft-worn comfort of wash khakis.

Two paperbacks and innumerable cups of tea later, the departure south to Conakry was called and a lumbering J Model Hercules of the Royal Air Force lifted off from a sodden runway.

Her second night in the air proved to be far more pleasant than the first.

As the sole passenger on board, she rode up forward in the Hercules cockpit, talking shop with the congenial RAF aircrew and watching the stars gleam beyond the windscreen.

Just after midnight, they executed a steep cowboy descent and touchdown at Gibraltar's abbreviated airstrip for refueling. Stretching her legs on the darkened tarmac with the shadowy bulk of "The Rock" looming over her in the night, Amanda felt the first touch of Africa, the brush of the warm dry winds blowing northward from the Sahara.

Airborne again, the Hercules started the long propeller-driven trudge around the curve of the African peninsula. Taking her turn in one of the narrow crew bunks, Amanda found that sleep came easily.

She was awakened by the light of the dawn sweeping across the cockpit as the aircraft turned southeast. Sipping a mug of ferocious tanker's tea, she watched as the tip of Cape Verde drifted past under the port-side wing, the land's end blazing green and gold against an azure sea. An hour later and they were in the pattern at Conakry.

Conakry Base, Guinea   1025 Hours, Zone Time; May 8, 2007

The seafighter service ramp had been established beyond the seaward end of the Conakry base runway. It was something new for Amanda, a naval station with no piers, no docks, no moorages, only a gently sloping beach stabilized by a layer of the same kind of pierced aluminum planking the Seabees used for temporary runways. This was all that was needed by the sleek war machine that lay basking on the ramp like a great sea turtle, its cadre of service vehicles drawn up around it.

Amanda dismounted from the Navy-gray HumVee that had carried her down from the headquarters building. The white flame of the sun danced off the waves in the estuary and the steambath heat and humidity struck as a physical assault. For someone fresh from a mid-Atlantic spring, the environment was going to take a little getting used to. As Amanda's driver unloaded her seabag and briefcase, she stepped into the shadow of a parked fuel tanker to get her bearings and to examine her new command.

The PGAC (Patrol Gunboat Air Cushion) had started its life as an LCAC (Landing Craft Air Cushion), a fast amphibious shuttle designed by Textron Marine Systems to rapidly move the men and equipment of a Marine landing force ashore from their transport vessels. However, the utility and effectiveness of the basic hovercraft design soon inspired American military planners to look for other applications for the technology. The PGACs, the seafighters, were one such new adaptation.

Much had been altered in the redesigning. The landing ramps and the starkly utilitarian drive-through superstructure of the landing craft had been replaced with a sleek and flattened boatlike hull, crafted with the slightly odd angles and geometrics of stealth technology.

Ninety feet in length by thirty-six in width, the hovercraft nestled down in a mass of heavy, black rubberized fabric like a gigantic deflated inner tube. The simile was apt, as these were the inflatable skirts of the plenum chamber that contained the bubble of high-pressure air that supported the vehicle when it was powered up and running.

A streamlined cockpit or cab sat atop the hull a short distance back from the bow, while two massive air intakes were fared into the deck at the midships line. Right aft, a crossbar antenna mount rose above the hull, running across the full width of the stern like the spoiler foil of a sports car. Centered on the crossbar mount was the black discus shape of a radar scanner. A second snubmast, finlike and sharply raked, rose from just behind the cockpit. At its top was the lensed sphere of a Mast Mounted Sighting System, looking like the head of some goggle-eyed robot. Below the MMS, an American flag hung limply in the still and breathless air of the equatorial afternoon.

The seafighter had been painted in a dusty gray light and dark camouflage, all but under the angle of the broad bow. There, in a touch of swashbuckling individuality, the standard camo pattern had been replaced by a snarling set of black shark's teeth that ran the full breadth of the hull. Two beady, leering eyes had been added just beneath the peak of the bow to complete the image of a lunging sea monster. Along the rounded curve of the deck rim, just below the cockpit, she wore her ID number and name in phantom lettering:

PGAC 02 USS QUEEN OF THE WEST

Amanda found herself smiling. "Hello, Your Majesty," she whispered.

Unlike Amanda, the Navy service crew working around the grounded seafighter had already adapted to their working environment. The men worked stripped to the waist, while the female ratings had stagged the sleeves from their shirts and had cut their dungaree pants down to shorts. Tanned skins gleamed with sunblock and sweat, and an ice chest loaded with bottled water stood readily at hand in the shade of another parked vehicle, a succinct one-word order—DRINK!—written on the inside of its open lid.

As she looked on, a man emerged from an overhead hatch in the top of the cockpit and made his way to the deck edge. The golden brown tone of this individual's skin had nothing to do with the sun. He was royalty caste Samoan, a stocky, powerful keg of a man, square-set and solid muscle, the rating badge of a chief petty officer on the sleeve of his unbuttoned khaki shirt. "Hey, Commander Lane," he yelled down, "we got the stores shipment secured in the center bay, and Scrounger reports we have a full load of fuel and water aboard. What's the holdup on departure?"

At ground level, another bare-chested man knelt inspecting the folds of the chamber skirt. Younger, more lightly built, and with hair and mustache sun-bleaching from brown to blond, he rose to his feet. Only the oil-stained oak-leaf insignia on his baseball cap marked him as an officer.

"We're holding on a passenger, Chief," he yelled back, looking up. "Conakry HQ says that we're going to be taking the new TACBOSS out to the Floater."

Commander Lane. Lieutenant Commander Jeffery Lane it must be. Amanda nodded to herself. This, then, would be the commanding officer of the seafighter squadron. She hadn't known quite what to expect, and she hadn't been disappointed.

"The new TACBOSS?" Another voice joined in the conversation and a third figure appeared in the open-side hatch of the seafighter. "Jeez, Steamer, why didn't you tell me?"

The newcomer was long legged and slim, with a short honey-colored ponytail drawn back at the base of her neck. She looked more like a member of a cheerleading squad than she did a combat crew member. The coppery gleam of a lieutenant junior grade's bars at her collar put the lie to that concept. Amused bewilderment tugged at the corner of Amanda's mouth. Lord, had she been that young fourteen years ago?

The hover commander grinned and looked up into the doorway. "Mostly because I only got the word about five minutes ago myself. Besides, what's the bitch? We've got the *Queen* squared away. Let him come."

"I'd have liked the chance to get myself squared away too. At least I could have borrowed a decent set of khakis from somebody."

Like the female enlisted hands, the JG had cut down her own uniform, seeking comfort over military regulation. Amanda found herself envying the younger woman's bare-armed and bare-legged freedom. Her own theoretically summer-weight uniform was beginning to feel like a steamed horse blanket.

"No sense in giving this guy any false expectations," Lane replied confidently. "He's going to have to find out about the real world sooner or later. Don't sweat it, Snowy. We'll larn him."

There was apparently a great deal Amanda was going to have to "larn," and rapidly. She stepped out of the tanker's shade and crossed the ramp to where the squadron commander stood.

"Commander Lane?"

He caught her rank as she approached and came to attention, his fingertips snapping to his brow in a salute. Amanda replied in kind and then extended her hand to shake his.

"My name is Amanda Garrett. I'm your new Tactical Action Group commander."

✕◆

The remainder of the introductions were conducted in the scant shade of the hovercraft's flank.

"Commander Garrett, this is Lieutenant Junior Grade Jillian Banks, the *Queen*'s exec and my copilot."

Amanda clasped hands with the uneasy young woman. "Snowy Banks?" she inquired smiling. "I've never heard of running names being used outside of the aviation wings before."

"We're something new, Commander," Snowy replied shyly, returning the smile. "No one's exactly decided whether a hovercraft is a truck that can drive on water, a boat that can sail on the land, or an airplane that just flies really low."

"I use a running name myself, ma'am," Lane added.

"So I've heard." Amanda nodded. "Steamer Lane. It's a great surfing beach, but the water's cold up there near San Francisco."

"And this is our Ben Tehoa, our senior chief."

"Of the boat and the squadron both?" Garrett inquired, gripping the CPO's hand.

"Yes, ma'am," the Chief replied, his dark eyes meeting hers with quiet confidence. "You're getting a real good outfit, Commander. One of the best. I guarantee."

Amanda would be willing to take the big man's word for it. She could sense the experience and wisdom accrued over years of service and a multitude of cruises. Senior Chief Petty Officer Ben Tehoa was an archetype, a born sailor, one who would have no difficulty in living up to her expectations. In fact, she suspected she'd be kept on her toes living up to his.

"It's a pleasure to meet you all," she continued, studying the three sober-featured individuals who, in turn, were studying her. "I only wish it were under different circumstances. I know that Captain Emberly has left me a fine outfit, and I'll try to build on the groundwork he's set down. Unfortunately, I'm afraid I know next to nothing about hovercraft, and that includes this one."

She nodded toward the grounded machine that loomed over them. "Commander Lane, Miss Banks, Chief, I need to learn what these vehicles and this squadron can do, and fast. Consider this as the first day of Bonehead Hovercraft 101 and me as the new girl in school."

Lane, his exec, and the Chief swapped brief, sideways glances. Amanda had seen this phenomenon before. A complete nonverbal conference was taking place in a matter of a few seconds. Opinions stated, options discussed and a conclusion reached. Such things happened only within a team that had become so finely honed that it not only worked together but thought together as well.

The conclusion was apparently favorable. Maybe they found a senior officer who didn't claim automatic omnipotence refreshing.

Lane flashed a broad grin. "No problem, ma'am. You'll find there's not all that much to it. Welcome aboard."

"Thank you, Commander. How about taking me on the walkaround?"

"You got it, ma'am."

He reclaimed a ragged wash khaki shirt from the tailgate of a parked HumVee. "Hey, Slim, get Captain Garrett's gear aboard the *Queen*. On the double! Ferguson! Get your support rigs clear. We'll be firing up soon! Snowy, get topside and start the departure checklist."

"Are all three of the squadron craft named after Civil War gunboats?" Amanda inquired.

"Yes, ma'am. The *Queen* here, the *Carondelet*, and the *Manassas*. There's the *Benton*, too, but she's the class test-bed vehicle back at Camp Pendleton."

As they started aft along the seafighter's flank, Amanda caught the opening of a whispered exchange behind her.

"Jeez God, Chief! Do you know who that is?"

"I saw that *Time* magazine cover too, Miss Banks . . ."

Amanda suppressed a grin, refocusing her attention on Lane's words.

"Okay, ma'am, essentially a hovercraft is a giant air pump. Our lift fans force air into the plenum chamber under the vehicle's belly. This creates a bubble of high pressure that lifts the vehicle off the deck as the air tries to escape the confines of the chamber. This thin, friction-free film of air escaping from under the skirts is what a hovercraft rides on."

Amanda gave a nod. "I see. A while back, I was a member of a military mission to Sweden to have a look at their experimental *Smyge*-class stealth Fast Attack Craft. They're hovercraft too, aren't they?"

"A close relative, ma'am. The *Smyge* is a Surface Effects Ship. Her plenum chamber has hard sidewalls that pierce the water's surface. That makes her a pure-water vehicle, while the *Queen* here is a true hovercraft. Like the original LCACs, we're fully amphibious."

Lane aimed a kick at the folds of heavy rubberized material the hover rested upon. "Our flexible chamber sidewalls allow us to sort of flow over obstacles. We can cross seventy percent of the world's beaches and, as long as it's comparatively flat, we can run on any kind of surface: swamps, sand, ice, pavement. Heck, I've had the *Queen* as much as five miles inland on training exercises and she's taken to it like a champ."

"Aren't these soft skirts a point of vulnerability? I've heard that was a problem with the hovercraft they experimented with in Vietnam."

Lane shook his head. "The old PACVs used a nylon finger skirt that was susceptible to battle damage. We use a rubberized multiplex Kevlar. When we're up on the cushion, rifle-caliber gunfire and low-velocity antitank grenades literally bounce off."

They rounded the *Queen's* sloping stern. Here were the two huge, five-bladed drive propellers, each eleven-foot airscrew mounted within a circular duct shroud and each with a twinned set of rudders behind it. A broad ramp folded down between them, leading into the darkened interior of the vehicle.

Amanda frowned slightly. "These PGs are supposed to have a low-radar cross section, aren't they?"

"Yes, ma'am. We're stealthy. Passive stealth essentially. The only sections of the superstructure that have a lot of metal in them are the top of the plenum chamber assembly and the engine platform—what we call the raft. The raft rides very low to the water, while the rest of the superstructure is primarily made up of composite materials with a very low reflective level. The hull and all metallic structural elements have also been coated with a Macroballon-based stealth paint, and we have heavier RAM panel inserts around the engines, lift fans, and weapons bays."

"What about these big above-water airscrews? I know that a rotating propeller produces a large radar signature." Amanda's frown deepened for a moment. Arkady had taught her about that. With a shake of her head, she thrust away the momentary intrusion of her personal life.

Lane shrugged. "No sweat there. Our drive props are made out of the same thermoplastic composite they use for the propellers on the J- and K-model C-130s. They're nine-tenths radar transparent. Fully closed up, we're nothing but a bump on the sea."

Lane led her up the stern ramp into the *Queen's* interior twelve-foot-wide central bay. At the rear end of the bay, a small semirigid rubber boat sat mounted on a launching track that ran back down the extended ramp/bay door. Amanda noted the boat's powerful outboard motor and the mounting bracket for a machine gun at its bow.

Her guide slapped the little craft's inflated flank as he brushed past it. "This is our eight-man miniraider. It's a cut-down sixteen-foot variant of the big twenty-four-foot raider boats the Marines and SEALs use. Real good for landing and boarding operations."

Just forward of the boat, Lane reached up and slapped something else up in the shadows near the overhead. As Amanda's eyes adjusted to the lack of light, she could make out a long, dark coffinlike mass filling in the upper left corner of the bay. Four circular base plates were set into the rear facing of the rectangular pod and hydraulic lift gear gleamed along its sides.

"Our heavy hitters," he went on laconically. "A four-round missile cell. Harpoon Twos for antishipping or SeaSLAMs for land attack. The launchers up-angle through the top of the hull and fire forward over the bow."

Amanda was impressed. "You have a SeaSLAM control station aboard?"

"Yes, ma'am. A little farther up front. I'll show you in a second."

"What kind of a loadout do you usually carry?"

"Two and two. When we're fully rigged out for serious ship hunting, we carry a second four-round cell back here, giving us a total of eight heavy missiles. We've got our starboard launcher unshipped currently to make more room for carrying a boarding party."

A set of nylon strap and aluminum tube benches were folded up against the starboard bulkhead. Utilitarian in the extreme, Amanda found herself grateful that she wouldn't have to be riding them for any length of time.

Forward of the missile cell, the bay broke into a cross-shaped intersection, the side arms extending out to the side hatches in the hull. Narrowing, the central bay continued on toward the bow. An aluminum ladder also ran vertically to a hatch in the overhead, while a second angled forward and upward into the cockpit.

"Cockpit access and topside access," Lane affirmed. "Forward here, on the port and starboard sides, are the gun tubs for the secondary armament. Forward of them on the starboard side is our mess room and galley. That is, if you want to consider a microwave and a coffee urn a galley. On the port side we have a chemical head and a bunkroom. Four bunks. Our offboat quarters are aboard Floater 1, of course, but the onboard racks come in handy on a long patrol."

The hover commander pointed beyond the cockpit ladder. "At the head of the bay and just under the cockpit, you can see consoles of the two main fire-control stations. They're multimode—either one of them can access and direct any of the onboard weapons systems."

"What's your standard crew complement?" Amanda inquired.

"Nine. Pilot and copilot. Two gunners. Four engineers and a chief of the boat."

She frowned slightly. "That's pretty light for a vessel this complex, isn't it?"

"Oh, that's just onboard crew, ma'am. We've also got a twenty-four-man service and maintenance team assigned to each PG. Sort of like an aircraft's ground crew. Again, most of our service people are aboard the offshore base, but, as you saw, we keep a small detachment here at Conakry to assist with patrol turnarounds."

"I see. How about a look at the engines?"

"This way, Captain."

The two engine rooms flanked the central bay, their access hatches set into the rearward-facing bulkheads of the intersection side arms. Lane popped the latches of the one on the port side, swinging open the sound-insulated thermoplastic door.

If the rest of the seafighter was cramped, the engine compartment was claustrophobic—a fifty-five-foot shoe box crammed almost solid with convoluted ductwork, a massive blower assembly, and two huge turbofan engines lying nose to tail. The main power plants were inert for the moment, but the growling snore of an auxiliary diesel could be heard and the air stank of kerosene, ozone, and a whole family of lubricants.

A brown-haired female rating flowed around the bulk of an intake duct. In addition to the cut-down dungarees that passed as uniform aboard the seafighter, she wore a pair of "Mickey Mouse" ear protectors slung around her neck, such as Amanda had seen used on a carrier flight deck. She came to an easy attention in the closet-size workspace in the forward end of the engine compartment.

"Okay, Scrounge," Lane said, "this is Captain Garrett, our new TAC-BOSS. Captain, this is Gas Turbine Tech First Class Sandra Caitlin, our senior engineer aboard. In the family, she's known as 'Scrounger' because she's our best, uh, 'acquisitions specialist.'"

Amanda extended her hand to the enlisted woman. "A pleasure to meet you, Miss Caitlin. I'm impressed. In most outfits no one short of a senior CPO can acquire a rating in that specialty."

"I can manage at it, Commander," Chief Tehoa commented from the doorway. "It's just that the Scrounge here is an artist."

The turbine tech's dark eyes glinted shrewdly as she grinned back at Tehoa's comment. "I'm just good at what you call networking, ma'am."

Amanda nodded soberly. "I'll keep that in mind, Miss Caitlin. How about a quick look around your territory?"

"Sure thing, ma'am. Watch yourself, though, we're kind of cramped for space."

"Lead on."

With Amanda following, Caitlin started down the narrow access passage that flanked the engines on the inboard side. "Kind of cramped" was an understatement. It was a tight and irregular fit even for a small-framed person, and Lane and Chief Tehoa were reduced to edging sideways in many places.

"First thing you've got to remember, ma'am, is that if you ever come in the engine spaces when we're powered up, you've got to wear either one of the command headsets or a set of these ear guards." The turbine tech tapped the gray plastic earmuffs she carried around her neck. "We're practically riding these hair dryers bareback in here, and even a short direct exposure to the sound could wreck your hearing."

"Check." Amanda nodded. "Carry on."

"Okay. The propulsion modules on the gunboats are pretty much the same as they use on the standard LCAC. That is, we have four Avco Lycoming TF-40 gas turbines, two in each engine room. We have the uprated C models that put out close to four thousand shaft horsepower apiece. The forward engine in each module drives a pair of five-foot lift fans to pump the plenum chamber. The aft engine drives the propulsion airscrew."

"I know that a standard LCAC can turn fifty knots in a good sea state," Amanda commented with interest. "Can we do better than that?"

"Sure thing, Commander. We're streamlined and have a narrower beam-to-length ratio than the landing craft. Combine that with our hotter engines and five-bladed props and we can pull sixty-five easy."

"That's the squadron average, Captain," Lane added, edging along behind Amanda. "For reasons known only to the Scrounge, the *Queen* always seems to be able to turn a couple of extra knots."

The young lady in question shrugged and flashed that sly grin again. "Talent, Skipper."

Amanda ran a finger along a gasketed seam in the turbine housing, seeking and not finding any residue of oil leakage. "How about fuel consumption?"

"I have to confess she's a gas hog," Lane replied. "Roughly eight hundred gallons an hour when we're running flat out. But in that hour you've gone somewhere. Also, since we don't have to worry about transporting cargo, more of our lift capacity can be used for fuel. Our fixed tankage in the raft gives us a seven-hundred-and-fifty-mile operational radius, and if we need more, we can carry a fuel blivet in the center bay."

Amanda nodded to herself, adding the factor into the mental operations file she was developing. "That still doesn't give us a lot of on-station loiter time."

"We got what we call 'swimmer mode' for that, ma'am," Caitlin interjected promptly. "When we're off cushion and sitting in the water, we can lower a couple of electric propulsor pods below the skirt. They're a set of one-hundred-and-fifty-horsepower electric drives that run off our auxiliaries. You can only do about five knots, but you can poke around on 'em forever on just a couple of gallons of diesel. They're superquiet, too. When we're up on the cushion, you can hear us coming ten miles off. Running swimmer, you don't know we're there till we're alongside."

Between the two turbofans was another small workspace and another ladder leading up to a hatch in the overhead. A strip of canvas had been tied over the ladder and a set of hand tools were displayed in a neat array of pockets and loops.

"An idea of yours, Miss Caitlin?" Amanda inquired.

"Yes, ma'am," the rating replied proudly. "It keeps things handy but out of the way."

"Take it down immediately," Amanda said flatly, "and get these tools properly secured."

There was a moment of awkward silence in the workspace, then Amanda continued, mellowing the abrupt command. "I daresay it is handy, Miss Caitlin, but we're operating in a combat zone now. In the advent of an onboard fire or a sinking, I don't want a solitary thing between you and that escape hatch. Understood?"

The turbine tech gave a quick acknowledging nod. "Understood, ma'am. It's history."

Next on the tour was the PG's secondary armament. For that they returned to the center bay and went topside to the weather deck, Commander Lane picking up a command headset en route.

The hovercraft's broad and railless back was jacketed with antiskid to provide a degree of security for anyone standing on it. In addition to the hooded throats of the big lift fans, the grilled intake and exhaust ports for the turbines were inset in the deck. Also, two large pocket panel hatches were located side by side, just aft of the cockpit, on what would be the shoulders of the broad hull.

"Okay, Snowy," Lane spoke into the headset mike. "Open the port-side gun tub and elevate the pedestal to firing position."

The selected hatch panel slid smoothly aside and a pair of slim gun barrels elevated into sight with a hiss of hydraulics. The H-shaped weapons mount reached deck level and the twin autocannon snapped from vertical to horizontal, training outboard with a final decisive click. Amanda noted the missile-launching rail mounted above each gun and the impressive sensor and targeting array fixed between them.

"We have two of these," Lane commented. "They're a modified variant of the Boeing Avenger antiaircraft missile system. Only, instead of a single fifty-caliber machine gun mounted under the launching rails, we carry a pair of thirty-millimeter chain guns. Antisurface and antiair capable, they're the same

Hughes M230 model carried by the Apache helicopter gunship. The ammunition load is three thousand rounds, carried in the base of the pedestal. Each mount also has a one-hundred-and-sixty-degree field of fire."

Stepping forward, Amanda peered down into the cylindrical well from which the weapon had emerged. Spaced in slots around the perimeter of the well were a dozen cylindrical and rectangular ordnance pods.

"In addition to the standard four-round Stinger antiair pods the Avengers use," Lane continued, "our launchers have been modified to also accept seven-round packs of Hydra rockets and laser-guided Hellfire antitank missiles."

"What kind of targeting and fire control?"

"Take your pick. Radar, low-light television, and thermographic imaging."

Amanda whistled softly. "Impressive."

"For our displacement, we're the most heavily armed warship in existence," Lane agreed proudly. "Snowy, secure the mount."

The autocannons went vertical once more and the weapons pedestal sank obediently from sight.

"What other armament do you carry?" Amanda asked thoughtfully.

"There's a power-driven scarfring in the cockpit hatch that can take either a pair of fifty-caliber machine guns or a Mark 19 grenade launcher, if we need it."

She nodded slowly, but her thoughts were already racing ahead. "Would there be any problem with our running with the side hatches and tailgate open?"

Lane and Chief Tehoa exchanged puzzled glances. "Not in an average sea state," Lane replied. "It'd be noisy as hell and we'd take some spray inboard, but nothing that would particularly hurt us."

"Good." She turned to the CPO. "Chief, I've got a project for you. I want a set of pintle mounts rigged for the side and stern hatches of every boat in the squadron. They'll need to accept either a fifty-caliber machine gun or a grenade launcher and be designed so that we can unship them and get them out of the way in a hurry for loading and unloading operations. You'll also need to make provisions for safety webbing across the open hatchways, ammunition storage, and an intercom link for the gunners. Can do?"

Being a senior Chief, Ben Tehoa merely nodded. "You want single or twin mounts on the fifty-calibers, ma'am?"

"Twins, if we can squeeze them in. I want every ounce of firepower that will fit shoehorned into these hulls. Oh, and we might need some kind of quick-release monkey harness for the gunners so they can stay on their feet while we're maneuvering."

She smiled at her two subordinates, her hands braced on her hips. "Gentlemen, pound for pound, we may be the most heavily armed craft in commission. However, according to the historical precedents I've read, retrofitting additional weaponry is an old tradition in the gunboat navy. We always seem to end up needing a little more punch than the book says we'll require, so we might as well get a jump on the problem from the start."

Steamer Lane and Chief had another wordless, side-glance conference. They seemed pleased with the concept. "However you want it, ma'am," the hovercraft commander replied, "but where do we get the gun crews? We don't have slots for them in our table of organization."

"We'll get into that later. For now, Commander, I've held up the wheels of progress long enough. Let's get under way."

They dropped through the circular hatch in the cockpit overhead. The service trucks were pulling back from the hovercraft and Snowy Banks was in the right-hand pilot's seat, working her way down an aircraft-style checklist. The entire cockpit area had an aircraft feel to it, like the flight deck of a big military transport plane. The pilot's and copilot's stations were located behind a broad V-shaped windscreen and a bank of multimode telepanels that displayed systems status and navigational data.

A complex lever-studded control pedestal separated the pilot's seats. Amanda noted a conventional rudder-control dial centered on it, and she suspected that this might be the steering for the swimmer system, operating separately from the two half-wheel control yokes of the air rudders. However, a heavy T-grip joystick was located just below the dial controller, and she had no idea what purpose it served.

A second pair of jump seats were squeezed in behind the pilot's chairs, as well as a gunner's saddle for the hatch weapons mount. This latter was swung back against the overhead and latched marginally out of the way.

Lane slid into the left-hand pilot's seat while Amanda took the jump seat immediately behind him. Wedged in at her side was a small chart table and another set of flatscreen monitors. A button- and trigger-studded joystick suggested that this station might also be used as an auxiliary weapons control point. Amanda elected not to do any experimental button-pushing until she was a little more sure of her ground.

Chief Tehoa slammed the overhead hatch shut and locked the dogging lever. Moving with an amazing ease in the cramped confines of the cockpit, he moved aft to the ladderway and dropped down into the main hull.

"Set to crank?" Lane asked, jacking his command headset into the intercom hardlink.

"Prestart checklist complete and all boards are green. All stations report ready to get under way," Banks replied crisply. Reaching down, she hit a key on the control pedestal and a row of four red lights snapped yellow. "Auto-start sequence set. All engines ready to crank."

The hover commander nodded and thumbed the interphone button on the end of his control yoke. "All stations, stand by to move out. Snowy, light 'em up."

Another key was touched. Glowing lines crawled up the scales of tape displays as a low rising whine grew from somewhere aft. One after another, the row of yellow lights flicked green, the gas turbines coming on stream in a shrill tremolo quartet.

"Cranking . . . cranking . . . cranking . . . cranking . . . we have power!"

Pilot and copilot lifted right and left hands respectively from the controls, their palms smacking together in a high five. There was an instinctive flow to the gesture, as if it were some personal shared tag-end to the checklist.

"Put her on the pad."

The young female j.g. interlaced her fingers through the fan control levers and rolled them forward. A deeper contralto howl merged into the chorus as the lift fans spun up. Lane dropped his hand to the T-grip controller.

Once, on leave in the Canary Islands, Amanda had taken a camel ride. The rolling heave she had felt when the dromedary had gotten to its feet was similar to the sensation of the hovercraft lifting up onto its inflating skirts. Abruptly they were six feet farther off the ground and there was a slippery uncertainty to the way they were holding position.

Lane was rocking the T-grip joystick forward, and a series of explosive roaring bursts sounded from astern. "This is the puff-port controller," he said, raising his voice over the background noise. "The puff ports are a series of vents located around the top of the plenum chamber. When you trip one, it releases a jet of high-pressure air that acts like a steering thruster on a spacecraft. We use 'em for low-speed maneuvering. Right now, we're riding friction-free. If I wasn't holding us in place with the ports, we'd slide right off the beach."

He twisted the controller to the left. With an almost supernatural smoothness, the *Queen of the West* rotated in her own length until she was aimed out across the estuary. Wisps of sand whirled beyond the windshield as Lane deftly canceled out the start of her forward slide with the bow ports.

"I've been working on this project for almost two years now, ma'am," the hover commander said, grinning, "and, begging your pardon, but I still think this is just about the neatest damn shit in the world."

Peering forward around the pilot's seat, Amanda found herself agreeing. "You may have something there, Commander. Let's see what else she's got."

"Will comply, ma'am."

Steamer Lane shifted his hand from the T-grip to the rudder yoke. Snowy in turn came forward on the pitch controls and propulsion throttles.

A third voice segued into the *Queen's* bellowing song of power, the full-throated baritone roar of the twin drive propellers. The big machine surged forward down the beach, punching through the surf line in an explosion of sand and spray.

Trailing a scant white-water wake behind her, the *Queen of the West* arced across the mud-stained outflow of the Tabounsou estuary, aiming for the azure coastal waters beyond. The scattering of fishermen and coastal mariners in their *pirogues* looked up at the hovercraft's thunderous passage, lifting their hands in respectful acknowledgment. Steamer Lane replied with a double bark of the seafighter's air horns and held his course for the southeast, paralleling the verdant coastline.

Peering forward out of the windscreen, Amanda continued to acquaint herself with the decidedly odd sea feel of the air-cushion gunboat. She'd sailed fast small craft before, even competing aboard Cigarette-class open ocean racing boats on more than one occasion. None of her past experiences quite matched this, however.

Despite the flickering rapidity of the wave patterns sweeping under the hovercraft's bow, the seafighter flowed effortlessly across the ocean's surface. Riding over the swells instead of driving through them, there was none of the jolt and spank of a displacement hull running at speed.

"What's our ETA at Floater 1, Lieutenant?" she inquired.

"It's a three-hundred-mile run," Lane replied. "We'll be there in about five hours."

"Five hours?" Amanda pulled herself out of the jump seat and came to kneel between the two pilot's stations. "How fast are we going?"

"'Bout fifty knots."

Amanda felt her eyebrows lift. "Fifty knots? I had my old destroyer up close to fifty knots once, evading a wake-chaser torpedo, and she almost shook apart on me!"

Her "old destroyer." That was the first time she'd ever referred to the *Cunningham* in those terms.

Steamer Lane and Snowy Banks exchanged proud parent grins.

"This is just good cruise for us, ma'am," Snowy said. "We can do this all day."

Lane glanced at his copilot again, and Amanda sensed one of those non-verbal discussions taking place. Banks gave a minute shrug of her shoulders, a devilish glint showing momentarily in her brown eyes.

"In fact, Commander, we can do lots better," the *Queen's* commander said casually, reaching the drive throttles. "Strap in, ma'am, and we'll give you a demonstration."

Amanda did so, with alacrity. As a survivor of plebe hazing at Annapolis, plus being a holder of both a Shellback and a Bluenose certificate, she understood the mechanism of initiation into a small, tight-knit, and proud community. One could either respond with a stiff-necked resistance, weakening that bond of community, or one could submit and strengthen it. Drawing the seat belt tight, Amanda braced herself and got a firm grip on her stomach.

The digital iron log flickered upward—55 . . . 60 . . . —the roar of the airscrews growing in proportion, a deep and resonant vibration building within the vehicle frame. 65 . . . 68 . . . Scrounger Caitlin's extra knots making themselves apparent. The wave patterns blurred into a blue-steel and frost-white mosaic.

"All hands, stand by to maneuver," Land said casually over the interphone circuit.

"Hey, Skipper," Amanda heard another voice respond in her earphones. "You want some movin' music?"

"Sounds good, Danno. Give me something appropriate for goin' off the lip."

"You got it, sir."

Suddenly the driving twang and bite of California surfing music blared over the interphone link, a formidable CD deck obviously having been wired into the system. Cueing off of the music, Lane slammed the seafighter's helm hard over. The quadruple rudders dug into the blast of the airscrews and the hovercraft tore into a hard left turn. Amanda yelped, groping for the grab bar on the back of the pilot's seat as, seat belt or not, the G forces threatened to hurl her across the cockpit.

His powerfully muscled forearms holding the control yoke against its locks, Lane leaned against the lateral pull. Riding with it as well, Snowy Banks deftly trimmed the throttles and propeller controls, using the power of its raving engines to hold the *Queen of the West* into its minimum-radius turn.

She could do only so much, however. Amanda felt the stern of the hovercraft start to break loose in a wild aquatic skid, like a racing car spinning out on an icy corner. At that instant, Lane reversed rudder.

Whump! Amanda piled up against the chart table as the seafighter began to describe the second half of a foaming S-turn, the coastline a speed-smeared streak across the windscreen.

"That's interesting, Commander," she said through gritting teeth. "A major aspect of hovercraft navigation must be judging how deeply your rudders can hold you into the line of your turn at varying speeds."

"Exactly, ma'am." Lane nodded, replying over the jaunty electronic back-beat in the headset. "Another thing you'll have to get used to is that we can work in close. Real close."

The *Queen* sheared off toward the land. This stretch of the Guinea coast was open, sandy beach with a respectable, foaming shore break. Lane indeed started working in close, on the very ragged edge of blue water, skirting the line where the incoming Atlantic rollers broke into tumbling surf.

The ride was no longer smooth now. The *Queen* bucked and shuddered as she tore through the turbulent crests and depressions of the breaking waves. Spray exploded across the windscreen and Steamer Lane, his jaw set and his hands white knuckled on the control yoke, held them right on the division be-tween honest water and slop, weaving them sinuously along the contours of the coast.

This was no mere stunt. This was a maneuver carefully thought out and long drilled. Without instructions, Snowy Banks had jacked her seat up to its full height and was scanning far ahead along the surf line. "Clear . . . clear . . . clear," she chanted, allowing Lane to focus on dancing the seafighter through the white-water turbulence of the wave break.

Not only had Amanda never experienced anything close to this, she had never imagined it, either. The trembling in her body had little to do with the vibration of the vehicle frame, and the rush of adrenaline through her system rendered the experience superhumanly clear and intense. The soaring rock beat in her headset helped to merge her into the great racing warcraft, making her one with it. She yielded to the sensation as she would yield to a lover.

Then the sandbar was under their bow, a low, tan, wave-swept mound reaching out from the shore like the back of a beached whale, one of the deadly "phantom islands" of the African Gold Coast. There was no time, no chance to turn away or avoid. Amanda felt the futile warning cry well out of her and she threw her arms up in an equally futile effort to ward of the shat-tering impact that must follow.

But didn't.

There was a smooth upward surge as the *Queen* rode up and over the bar, a long moment of weightlessness as the full ninety-foot length of the hovercraft gunboat launched into the air, and then a soft and resilient *chuff* as she touched down again on her skirts. From somewhere down in the hull came the exu-berant "Yeeeeeehaaaa!" of a rebel yell.

Lane pulled away from the shoreline and came back on the throttles, bring-ing them down to good cruise once more. "And that's what we can do, ma'am."

Amanda flexed her cramped fingers and took a deep, deliberate breath, let-ting the hammering beat of her heart slow. "Very interesting, Steamer," she replied, carefully keeping her voice level. "Why don't we let Snowy take a break for awhile and you can start showing me how we go about doing it."

⚔◆

For Amanda, the remainder of the journey out to the Mobile Offshore Base didn't seem to take as long as she had expected. Following her first training session at the *Queen's* controls, she'd spent the next couple of hours systematically going over the interior of the hovercraft, getting acquainted with the rest of the small crew and further familiarizing herself with the seafighter's layout.

Eventually, the two days' worth of continuous travel caught up with her and she stretched out in one of the cramped berths in the bunkroom. Not yet adapted to the magnified vacuum cleaner howl of the *Queen's* power plants, she didn't think sleep was likely. However, she could lie with half-closed eyes and consider the potentials, possibilities and problems of this new command.

Possibly she'd acclimatized more rapidly than expected or her jet lag was more severe than she realized because a touch on her shoulder startled her awake.

"Begging your pardon, Captain," Ben Tehoa said, looming over her, "but we'll be coming in to Floater 1 soon. The Skipper figured you'd want to be in the cockpit during the approach and docking."

"Thanks, Chief," Amanda replied, rubbing her gritty eyes. "I do. I'll be right up."

⚔◆

The first indication of the Mobile Offshore Base was a silvery finned teardrop hovering high in the sun-bleached sky, the tethered Aerostat balloon that lifted the scanning head of the TACNET radar three thousand feet above the sea. Then, through the heat shimmer of the horizon, a low crenellated form rose up out of the ocean like some mystic floating fortress in an Arabian Nights fantasy.

On a more prosaic and technological level, that's exactly what it was.

Amanda had studied the history of the Mobile Offshore Basing concept back to its origins during the war in Vietnam. There, to escape shoreside harassment from communist guerillas, a series of floating strike bases or "seafloats" had been constructed for U.S. Riverine and Coastal Patrol forces. Pieced together out of artillery barges and bridging pontoons and anchored in Vietnam's rivers and coastal estuaries, these ad hoc staging platforms had served the Navy well. So well, that the Seafloat was resurrected during the Persian Gulf tanker wars of the late 1980s.

In that instance, as a sidelobe of the protracted Iran-Iraq war, the Iranian Revolutionary Guard began launching harassment attacks against tanker traffic passing through the Persian Gulf. Gulf States political leaders requested U.S. assistance in keeping the Straits open. However, in the face of Iranian saber rattling, these same Gulf statesmen had lacked the political will to permit American light naval forces to stage operations off of their soil.

As a solution, a seagoing barge platform had been anchored in international waters just inside the Straits of Hormuz. From this strike base, U.S. Navy SEALs, Special Boat Squadron flotillas and U.S. Army "Black Helicopter" flights sortied nightly to wage a secretive and ultimately successful war against the Iranian Boghammer groups.

Now, given the reduced size of the United States Navy and the shrinking number of foreign bases available to the American armed forces, the concept was being expanded upon again. A new generation of military "cities at sea" was being designed, utilizing the same technology used in the construction of offshore oil installations. Floating base complexes were on the drawing boards, artificial islands that could be towed into position anywhere in the world, each capable of supporting an entire Navy task force and an embarked Marine brigade garrison, complete with airstrips large enough to accept fighter and transport aircraft.

That was still for tomorrow, however. Floater 1 merely marked another step along that path.

The offshore base consisted of nine oceangoing superbarges, each four hundred feet in length by one hundred and fifty in width, intermoored to form one gigantic rectangular platform better than three football fields long by one and a half wide.

Elevated helipads had been constructed atop the four corner barges, the "bastions" of the fortress, each large enough to accept several helicopters or VTOL aircraft. Spaced between them were the smaller gun towers of the platform's defensive armament. A tall glass-walled structure similar to an airport control tower rose from the central barge, adjacent to a towering tripod mast studded with aerial arrays and rotating antenna.

These were the only fixed installations on the platform. A polyglot village of housing modules, trailers, and cargo containers took up the rest of the extensive deck area, a dully spectrumed patchwork of white, Navy gray, and camo pattern.

"Circle the platform once please, Steamer. I'd like to look the place over."

"Will do, ma'am."

As the range closed, Amanda noted the bustling activity aboard the facility. A Cyclone-class Patrol Craft and a pair of LCU landing craft nestled against the platform's lee side, toylike against its bulk. The little PC, as sleek and rakish as a miniaturized destroyer, took on fuel from one of the barge's internal cells while a crane methodically hoisted cargo pallets from the well decks of the LCUs. As she continued to look on, a Boeing-Textron Eagle Eye reconnaissance drone lifted off from one of the helipads. The automobile-size tilt-rotor aircraft hovered like a wary hornet for a moment before transitioning to horizontal flight mode, flashing away toward the heat-hazed green line of the coast.

"How close to the beach are we?" Amanda asked, thoughtfully eyeing the drone's destination.

"A little over thirteen miles offshore," Lane replied. "Just clear of the twelve-mile limit and hanging right on the edge of the continental shelf."

Snowy nodded soberly. "If you look off to the northwest at night, you can see the lights of Monrovia. They anchored us here because of the shallows and because this is almost the exact center of our patrol line. But boy, it does put us right in the laps of the bad guys."

Amanda nodded as well. "And what happens if General Belewa objects to our familiarity?"

"Then," Steamer replied grimly, "there is going to be one hell of a fight. We have eight Mark 96 over-and-under mounts in the gun towers. We also have RAM launchers and Stinger teams in case of an air attack and chaff launchers and ECM in the event he scares up some antiship missiles somewhere. Like I said, one way or another, it'll be one hell of a fight."

Amanda noted the curtains of Kevlar armor drawn along the sides of the barge hulls and gun towers and the sandbagged hardpoints on the deck edges. Indeed, should the Union attempt to storm the platform, "one hell of a fight" might be an understatement. This was no Arabian Nights fairy castle. A more apt comparison would be to a frontier Army post deep in Apache territory.

Backing off steadily on his throttles, Lane completed his circle of the platform. The middle barge in the downwind, or "stern," tier of the platform had been cut down and modified to provide for a two-hundred-foot ramp shallow enough for a hovercraft to climb. Lane nosed the *Queen* in toward this now, humping her up and over the ramp edge. With another consummate coordination of thruster, throttle, and rudder, he and Snowy taxied their command up-ramp to the platform deck and to the waiting reception crew.

Three large open-sided hangars were located beyond the broad turnaround pad at the head of the ramp, one of which was already occupied by another parked seafighter. "That's the PG-03," Lane commented over his shoulder, "the *Carondelet*. The *Manassas* is out on barrier patrol this afternoon."

Leaning into the air blast issuing from beneath the hovercraft, a pair of wand-wielding ground guides assisted Lane as he rotated the *Queen* around a hundred and eighty degrees, backing her into her servicing bay. Deck baffles shielded equipment and personnel alike from the howling turbulence produced by the seafighter's lift fans.

The wand men executed the crossed-arm "cut" gesture as the hovercraft was properly spotted and Lane came back on the throttles. The wail of the turbines faded and the *Queen* sank down into the nest of her deflating skirts with a protracted sigh.

"We're home, Captain."

"Thank you for the introduction, Steamer," Amanda replied, releasing her seat belt. "Now I have some idea of what I have to work with." She mused for a few moments, then smiled. "The three little PGs. The Three Little Pigs. I like them. I like them a lot."

"They can ruin you for the big ships, ma'am."

As the pilots continued their shutdown procedures, Amanda levered herself out of the jump seat. She started aft, then paused for a moment. "Oh, and by the way, Lieutenant Banks, I've been meaning to have a word with you about certain modifications you've made to your uniform."

Snowy stiffened in her seat. "Uh, yes, ma'am?"

"They make good sense in this climate. I'll have to get some of my khakis cut down like that too." She slapped the younger woman lightly on the shoulder and dropped down the ladderway into the main hull.

Her quarters were located in one of the housing modules sited near the hovercraft hangars. Utilitarian in the extreme, it was the end cabin in a stark white aluminum-sided shoe box secured to the platform deck by a foundation of scarred 4 × 4s. Plumbing connectors and electrical umbilicals drooled openly from the box's belly, vanishing down scuttles into the barge's interior. The sole luxury bestowed by rank would be that she would have the space to herself.

After her guide had set her luggage inside the door, Amanda released him to return to his duties. Standing in the center of the little cabin, she examined her new living space.

It didn't take long. Three chairs, one behind a desk, a locker, and a stripped cot with its thin mattress rolled up at its head. Two small louvered windows flanked the entryway and a second narrow door way opened into a minute combination head and shower. That was all.

The bare walls—somehow the nautical term "bulkhead" didn't feel right—were a use-dingy white, the battered linoleum on the floor, gray. The fixtures and furnishings all bore the mark of long government service.

The temperature in the room was volcanic. Amanda noticed the small air

JAMES H. COBB

conditioner mounted in one of the windows and, rather anxiously, she stepped across to it and hit the start button. To her relief, a stream of cool and comparatively dry air began to flow out of its grille after a few moments, albeit with a grinding roar.

Amanda sank down into the desk chair, relishing the chill as the perspiration on her skin began to evaporate. Her first impressions of the PG squadron were good. Oh, they were unconventional, no doubt about that. But it seemed to be the kind of unconventionality that was born out of adaptive and intelligent flexibility. These were the kind of people who carried their discipline around in their guts, not in a book of regulations. She'd be able to use that, granted she could become as adaptable as they were. Please God, let the rest of her command be as promising as well.

Amanda sighed and leaned forward, resting her elbows on the desk. That forty-eight hours in transit was catching up with her again. Yet there was that urgent drive to get going, to pull things together. But Lord, where to start?

"Hey, yo! Anyone home?" a cheerfully irreverent voice inquired.

Amanda forgot about her tiredness and even about her mission for a moment. Coming out of her chair, she embraced the small figure that had come bursting through her doorway. Christine Rendino returned the hug with equal fierceness. "Hi, boss ma'am. It's about time you came to the party!"

"I'm here now, Chris. How are you doing?" Her hands still resting on Christine's shoulders, Amanda stepped back for a moment to fondly study her closest feminine friend. Little had changed over the past few months. The same inquisitive pixie's face grinned back at her, the skin now golden tanned, the shag-cut hair sun-bleached from ash blond to near white. However, Amanda also noted that the younger woman was wearing her glasses, an old indication that Christine had been putting in a lot of hours in front of a CRT screen. Looking closer, she also noted a couple of new weariness wrinkles notched in around her friend's blue-gray eyes.

"There's nothing wrong with me that a twenty-seven-hour day couldn't fix," Christine replied. "God, but it's good to see you. It's going to be like old times, hey?"

Amanda smiled soberly. "Nope, not at all like old times, my friend. We have a whole new situation. Pull up a chair and let's talk."

As Christine did so, Amanda dropped back into her own seat. The office chair was set too high for her comfort, a pointed reminder of another officer who had sat behind this desk not too long before. "Okay, Chris, you've been out here long enough for you to get a solid handle on this operation. I need to know what I'm getting into, and I need to know fast."

Chris took a deep breath and let it trickle out in a hissing sigh. "Okay, but

I'd better warn you right now that there are no short forms available out here. Nothing is simple on this job."

"Then let's start with the basics. What do you think of the Task Group?"

"Hey, I get along with 'em great," Christine replied with a quirky grin. "They're my kind of folks."

"I had a hunch they were."

"You've got a real mixed bag of personnel out here. Special Boat people, Seabees, the hover crews, my spark heads and drone jockeys. They're all pretty much new-gen littoral warrior types. Beyond a scattering of older CPOs, you don't have very many old fleet hands at all."

"I've met one of the old hands already, Chief Tehoa."

"Oh yeah. I know about him. The PG group's senior chief is a gentleman who has his shit extremely together. Good folks, boss ma'am."

"That's how I read him," Amanda agreed. "How about the rest of the seafighter people?"

"Very young, very tough, and very hot to show their stuff. This is a NAVSPECFORCE elite unit, at least on a par with the Special Boat Squadrons. These guys and gals all volunteered for this slot. Warfighters all. Especially keep your eye on the squadron commander. Steamer Lane seems to have a good balance of brains and balls going for him."

"That's my first impression as well."

Christine tilted her chair back to the limit of safety. "Beyond the loss of their previous TACBOSS, unit morale and cohesion appear high. This whole outfit's sort of like a big pack of wolf pups, all supereager and ready to start hunting. In my expert opinion, they only need one thing to bring it all together."

"And what would that be?"

The intel grinned lazily. "Some cunning old bitch wolf to show them how it's done."

Amanda found herself grinning back. "I don't consider thirty-six old, Chris."

The warble phone on the desk suddenly cut into their conversation. Amanda scooped up the handset. "Garrett here."

"This is Commander Lane, Captain. I'm over in the operations van. We have a hot contact."

"I'm on my way." Amanda dropped the phone back into its cradle and looked across the desk at her friend. "Okay, intelligence officer. Intel me where the Operations Center is?"

Operations turned out to be located in a semitrailer van parked and lashed to the barge deck not far from Amanda's quarters module.

"How much enemy activity have you been seeing in-theater?" Amanda inquired as they hastened to it.

"Not much at all recently. The Union's naval forces have been maintaining their low profile. If this is a real hotshot call, it'll be the first time they've openly challenged us since Conakry."

"Maybe they're sending me their compliments."

Inside of the Operations van, a row of computerized workstations ran down the full left-side length of the big trailer's interior, a series of multimode flatscreen displays mounted on the bulkhead before them. The van's integral air conditioners would probably have been holding the internal temperature at a reasonably comfortable level were it not for the crowd of seafighter personnel packed in behind the system operator's seats. The word had spread that one of their own was in pursuit and all hands wanted to be in on the kill. Amanda noted that Jeff Lane and his little exec were in the center of the huddle.

"Gangway! Make a hole!" Amanda commanded, driving through the excited mob. "I want only authorized duty personnel in here along with the squadron officers and senior chief! Everyone else clear out and give us some working room! Expedite!"

As the onlookers made a hasty, shuffling departure Amanda and Christine reached Lane's side at the central screen. "Okay, Steamer, what do we have?"

"A pair of Union Boghammers just nailed a police launch off Point Matakong," he replied. Leaning forward, he aimed a finger at a numbered target hack that glowed scarlet on the computer graphics map display. Even as they watched, the target hack crawled southeastward along the coast, heading for the territorial waters of the West African Union. "The launch got off a distress call before it got clobbered, and now the Bogs are running for home."

"How are we tracking this?" Amanda demanded.

"Aerostat radar," Christine replied. "The USS *Valiant* is on barrier guard duty at Station Guinea East, here, just off the border between Guinea and the West African Union. She has her bag up and she's able to surface-search about two hundred and fifty miles of coastline."

"How did those Boghammers get inside Guinean territorial waters without our detecting them then?"

"Probably they've been there all along," the intel said, frowning. "Lying low in one of their boat hides. They can lurk around in those damn salt swamps for days if they want. When a likely target comes along, they zoom out, make their kill, and then either disappear back into the mangroves or bolt for Union waters, like these guys are doing."

"Yeah," Lane said excitedly, "only this time they aren't going to make it. Tony Marlin is out there with the *Manassas*. He's going for an intercept, and their collective asses are his!"

On the tactical display, a blue target hack labeled "PGAC 4" was converging on the fleeing Union gunboats from farther offshore, maintaining an obvious pursuit curve. Christine moved down to another workstation within the van and exchanged a few quiet words with its operator. Fingers clattered lightly on a keyboard and a second bulkhead flatscreen lit off, this one filling with a high-definition video image.

"We've also got one of our Predator drones covering the barrier station," Christine said. "Now we can get a real look at what's going on out there."

As they watched, the airborne television camera panned down across a vividly tinted coastscape: an expanse of almost emerald-green forest separated from an azure sea by a slash of white sand and surf. Pulling back, the image scanned across a broad and open bay where a pair of rivers emptied into the sea on either side of a narrow central peninsula. Two white streaks of wake could be seen cutting across the mouth of the bay, heading east. A graphics targeting box materialized around the wake tips.

"That's them," Christine commented. She glanced back toward the drone systems operator. "Close the range with the target and give us full magnification on video."

"Aye, aye, ma'am."

The television image swerved and bobbled for a moment as the reconnaissance drone came around to its new heading. Then the camera zoomed in and the targeting box windowed up to fill the entire display.

The Boghammers were a matching pair of open Fiberglas shells, outboard driven and bristling with automatic weapons and grenade launchers. Half a dozen Union sailors manned each speeding craft, their ebony skins gleaming with spray as they rode their pitching and bucking sea mounts with a consummate ease and surety.

As Amanda and her squadron officers looked on, a crewman in the seaward gunboat spotted something in the distance. An arm came up and pointed and the other members of the gunboat's crew fixed their attention on the bearing.

"That's it," Lane commented. "They've spotted the *Manassas* coming in on them."

"Let's have a look at how she's doing," Amanda replied. "Systems operator, shift to the *Manassas*."

The image on the monitor blurred into a silver shimmer as the drone's autotrack system traversed the camera turret around to bear on its new target.

It was Amanda's first opportunity to see one of the hovercraft under way from the outside. True to the impression she had received aboard the *Queen*, it skimmed effortlessly over the sea's surface, brushing over the wavetops rather than ripping through them. The seafighter also ran enclosed in a cloud of shimmering, rainbowed mist, the spray whipped up by the blast of her lift fans and drive propellers.

"The best those Bogs can do is about forty-five knots," Lane said, glancing at Amanda. "The Rebel has a twenty-knot edge on them."

"Yeah," someone else commented from the back of the little crowd. "We got these guys in the bag."

As if to emphasize the point, the panels over the hovercraft's gun tubs slid back and her weapons pedestals lifted into firing position, the autocannon and missile pods indexing around to bear on the prey she pursued.

And it was at that moment that the first phase of Amanda's campaign strategy gelled in her mind.

"Get me a radio link to the skipper of the *Manassas*. On the double!"

"Aye, aye, ma'am." One of the systems operators passed her back a headset with an attached lip microphone. Adjusting the earphones to fit, Amanda settled them over her head as they filled with the hum and hiss of an active carrier wave.

"You're up on the command frequency, Commander. Lieutenant Marlin is on line."

Amanda nodded. "*Manassas, Manassas,* this is Floater 1. Do you copy?"

"Roger, Floater! This is *Manassas*. We have the hostiles in sight! I say again, we have the hostiles in sight! We are closing the range and preparing to engage!"

A hunter's voice, taut and excited, lifted an octave by the adrenaline rush of the chase. Over the open mike and beyond the words of the hover commander, she could hear the howl of racing turbines and another voice calling out the closing range. This would have been the first blood for this crew, and she almost regretted what she had to do next.

"Lieutenant Marlin, this is Captain Amanda Lee Garrett. I'm the new Tactical Group commander. I have just arrived on station, and I have new instructions for you."

"Amanda Garrett? Uh, acknowledged, Captain. Uh, be advised that we're a little busy out here, ma'am. We are making intercept on a couple of gunboats and we're just getting set to make challenge—"

"No you are not, Lieutenant," Amanda replied firmly. "Break off the intercept and shut down."

"What? Floater 1, say again!"

"I repeat. Break off your intercept and shut down your engines. Shut down and drift! Those are orders, Lieutenant. Execute immediately!"

There wasn't a sound, either over the radio link or in the operations van.

"*Manassas,* acknowledge!"

"*Manassas* to Floater 1," the cold reply came back. "We are powering down and are off the cushion. Hostiles are escaping into Union territorial waters. Awaiting further . . . orders."

"Do you have any white-smoke candles on board, Lieutenant?"

"White-smoke candles?"

"There's no need for a readback, Lieutenant Marlin. Yes or no is adequate."

"Yes, ma'am," a gritted reply came back. "We have them aboard."

"Very good, Lieutenant. Light one off on your afterdeck. Open some of your topside access and inspection hatches as well. Make it look as if you've suffered a major engineering casualty and are dead in the water. Put on a show for the locals. Beyond that, just drift around in that bay until we can get someone out there to tow you in."

"Acknowledged, will comply." There was still anger and disappointment in the hover commander's voice, but now also a degree of intrigued curiosity. "Anything else, ma'am?"

"Yes. My apologies to you and your crew. I have no doubt you would have been able to finish the job, Lieutenant. You'll get another chance soon enough. You have my word on it. This is Floater 1, out."

Amanda slipped the headset off and turned to face the small crowd of squadron officers and CPOs who still clustered in the back of the command van. They eyed her in silent judgment, waiting. Only Christine stood by with a sly and knowing look on her face.

Amanda smiled wryly and smoothed her hair back. "Well, as you probably overheard, my name is Amanda Garrett and I am your new TACBOSS. If we could retire to somewhere with a little more elbow room, I'll officially read in my orders. I'll also endeavor to convince you all that your new C.O. is not totally, screaming out of her mind."

Transients' Mess, Conakry Base, Guinea   1207 Hours, Zone Time; May 18, 2007

"What in the heck is this?" Scrounger Caitlin asked, warily prodding the contents of her dinner tray.

Dwaine "Fryguy" Fry looked over and down critically. "Today," the lean, black missile tech said, "that is your basic White Universal Generic Vegetable Substance. Tomorrow, it will be your Yellow Universal Vegetable Substance. On Wednesday, it will be your Green Universal Generic Vegetable Substance, and on Thursday, it will be your Brown Universal Generic Vegetable Substance. Then the Brits will wait forty-eight hours and serve it on Sunday as 'meat.'"

"Thank you ever so much for sharing that with us, Mr. Fry," Scrounger replied with a withering look.

Gunner's Mate 1st Daniel "Danno" O'Roark slammed his tray onto the table and swung his feet over the bench. "Whose shit-for-brains idea was it to come up here anyway, when we know that the British cooks have the duty this week?" the burly blond Philadelphian demanded.

"Mine," Lamar Weeks, the senior turbine tech of the *Queen of the West's* starboard power room, replied grimly. "If I have to eat one more MRE, I'm going to drop to the deck and die in my own puke."

"I dunno, Lam," his partner, Machinist Mate 2nd Slim Kilgore, interjected, eyeing his dripping fork. "I'd say this is more like making the choice between the gas chamber and a hangin'."

"This is what I'm thinking, cowboy," Eddy Kresky, port-side power's number-two hand, interjected. "Am I hearing any votes here for just starving to death?"

"Maybe this will make you guys a little grateful for our own chow when we get back aboard the Floater," Chief Tehoa commented, taking his own place at the table.

"Leave us not get crazy here, Chief." Kresky sighed, returning his attention to his meal.

Located in a barn-size tent a short distance off the main flight line, the transients' mess at Conakry Base was an easy place to loathe. Its screened sides were only marginally successful at keeping the hordes of flies at bay while the African sun baked readily through the thin canvas roof. In counterpoint, the blast revetments surrounding it were most effective at sealing out the faintest trace of a breeze while the few grumbling floor fans failed to provide an adequate artificial substitute.

Here were gathered the displaced persons of the base: the Guinean security and labor troops, the French and U.N. advisers in from the field, the Red Cross personnel en route upcountry to the refugee camps, and the foreign military elements too small to maintain mess services of their own.

Lackadaisical in the heat, they straggled in to consume the bland selection of rations from a menu that compromised for all of the involved ethnic backgrounds while satisfying none.

"I'm with the Chief," Scrounger agreed. "Right now, the old Floater would look like Fort Lauderdale at spring break to me."

Danno nodded. "Yeah, that'd be good with me too. Come on, Chief. When in the hell are they letting us out of this hole?"

The big CPO answered the gunner's plea with a cool and disapproving stare. "You know the answer to that as well as I do, mister. We'll get the *Queen* off the beach just as soon as we get all of our maintenance problems licked."

"Hey, American. When will that be, American?"

As one, the crew of the *Queen* stiffened and looked around. A cluster of French Navy personnel, clad only in boots, shorts, and raffish pom-pomed berets occupied the adjacent mess table. Sun-bronzed and grinning, the Frenchmen eyed them back, especially Scrounger Caitlin as the sole female rating among the group of American sailors.

"We are from the frigate *La Fleurette,*" the spokesman of the French contingent continued. "Already we have been on station a month. Already we have stop and searched many ship. All that time we have not seen any American. Have not heard of any American Navy doing any stopping." The speaker jabbed his immediate companion, the tallest and most muscular of the group with his thumb. "My frien', he would like to know when we see you American out at sea."

Tehoa looked back balefully back over his shoulder. "You tell your friend that we'll be along by and by. As soon we get a few things sorted out."

The French seaman translated Tehoa's words, triggering a round of laughter within his party. His tall companion gave a reply, the sneering quality of his words telegraphing their meaning.

"My frien' asks when that will be, when there is no African left to fight?"

Ben Tehoa sighed . . . deeply. Pushing his tray aside, he stood up, turning to face the expectant Frenchmen. The rest of the *Queen*'s crew followed suit a moment later. The French contingent got to their feet as well.

A ripple of silence radiated outward across the mess. Had this been a classic western movie, there would have been an urgent whispered suggestion for someone to send for the sheriff. The Guinean MPs on station at the tent's entryway took a step forward, then decided that they really didn't see anything all that wrong. They returned to their station, intently studying the dusty street outside.

The Chief went face-to-face with the big French sailor, a bulldozer confronting a derrick. "You can tell your friend here," he said quietly, "that if you guys take care of your business, we'll take care of ours, and everything will be just fine."

The translation rattled off and the French sailor's grin deepened. He spoke a prolonged reply to his English-speaking partner.

"My frien' say, maybe the real reason you sit on your ass on the beach so long is you are too busy playing with the girls to want to fight the war." The translator's eyes flicked insolently at Caitlin again. "He says that maybe since you only have one girl, that's why it's taking so long."

Tehoa's massive right fist cocked back and fired forward in a single blurred motion. Crashing through the French sailor's lax defense, the blow caved in the taller man's hard-muscled stomach like a sheet of cardboard, buckling him over with an agonized grunt.

As the Frenchman folded forward, the Chief's left hand came up and clamped onto his shoulder, the fingers sinking into the flesh. Heaving his target upright, Tehoa unleashed his right fist once more, exploding the second punch full into his opponent's face.

The Frenchman crashed backward, through his line of compatriots and over the top of their mess table, piling up soup-drenched and unconscious on the ground on the other side.

"Hey, man. It's cool," the Fryguy commented to the stunned English-speaker. "I don't think you need to translate that."

⚒

"Begging your pardon, Captain Garrett, but did you get the word from Conakry?"

"I have the report from Captain Stottard on my desk. I think it's about time we get the *Queen of the West* out of there. Inform Commander Lane that he may consider himself officially repaired and that he may sortie at his convenience."

"Aye, aye, ma'am."

"Oh, and also please advise Lieutenant Clark aboard the *Carondelet* that he's scheduled to break down next."

The United Nations Building, New York   1000 Hours, Zone Time; May 22, 2007

"Good Afternoon, Admiral," Vavra Bey said graciously. "Please be seated. It is most kind of you to take the time to meet with me like this."

"It's my pleasure, Madam Envoy," Elliot MacIntyre replied, accepting a seat across from the silver-haired stateswoman. Beyond the conference table, the picture windows of the meeting room looked out across the sluggish flow of the East River and the concrete-and-asphalt beehive of Queens beyond.

"Teleconferencing is a convenience," she continued, "but I still find it difficult to develop a good working relationship with an image on a screen."

Also, it's harder to read someone off of a communications monitor, MacIntyre thought back. Given his first impressions, this matronly woman would likely be hell across a poker table. "I understand fully. I prefer working face-to-face with my own people whenever possible. Errors in communication can be more readily avoided. I presume this conference concerns the UNAFIN operation?"

"It does, Admiral MacIntyre," Bey replied. "Have you been in recent communication with the interdiction force, or at least those units under your command?"

"I receive regular situational updates on all Naval Special Forces elements,

SEA FIGHTER

Madam Envoy, especially from those operating in an active combat zone. Why? Is there some problem with the U.S. mission?"

"I was hoping you could tell me, Admiral," Vavra Bey replied, her patrician features carefully neutral. She leaned forward into the table, clasping her hands on its surface. "I have been in conference with the ambassador from Guinea. He has expressed his government's profound concerns about the developing crisis within their country.

"Union guerrilla activities are on the upswing, especially in the coastal regions. The situation is growing critical. The government of Guinea had expectations that the presence of the American naval patrol forces based on their soil would relieve the situation. To date, those . . . expectations have not been met. I have been asked to inquire if there is some technical problem or difficulty with those forces and, if so, when we might expect a rectification."

MacIntyre straightened slightly in his chair and donned his own best poker face. "Madam Envoy, I can assure you that the NAVSPECFORCE elements assigned to the African Interdiction Force are fully battle ready at this time. Also, I can assure you that operations in-theater are progressing as planned."

"Indeed, Admiral. And who has developed this plan?"

"The new commander of the Tactical Action Group, Captain Amanda Lee Garrett, one of NAVSPECFORCE's best people."

Bey nodded again and peaked her fingertips together below her chin. "I am aware of Captain Garrett's presence in Guinea. She is well known to us here at the United Nations, thanks to her involvement in both the Antarctic Treaty incident and the Chinese Civil War. She is a most striking young officer with a formidable reputation. However, this past reputation is irrelevant when one considers that she has not yet acted decisively to deal with this current situation."

A scowl brushed across MacIntyre's face. "Begging your pardon, but if Mandy Garrett hasn't made her move yet, it's because she's had a damn good reason not to."

Vavra Bey smiled a diplomat's smile. "And you would know what this reason might be, Admiral?" she probed.

"No, I wouldn't. Captain Garrett doesn't require micromanagement. Once she's been given a mission, she'll find a way to get it done. You have my personal guarantee that the situation along the Guinea coast will shortly be under control."

"I will relay that to the Guinean ambassador." The gray-haired diplomat smiled again, a true smile this time. "You have a great deal of confidence in this young woman, Admiral."

"She's earned it, Madam Envoy."

"What are the latest figures on our fuel reserves, Sako?"

"Seven to eight months at our current rate of consumption," Brigadier Atiba replied from his position across the desk from the Premier General. "Not as good as we had hoped, but I think there is still room to tighten the rationing."

"See it done." Belewa laced his fingers together across his stomach and tilted his chair back, scowling. "And the theft and wastage of gasoline and diesel are to be listed as treasonable acts under the Anti-Corruption Mandate. All offenses are to be dealt with by the Special Courts."

"I will have the formal orders written up, General." Atiba meticulously scribbled the notes into the open daybook on his lap. "We do have some good news about the fuel situation, though."

Belewa glanced sideways at his chief of staff. "And that is?"

"Our smuggling line into Côte d'Ivoire. We are already moving better than a hundred barrels a day across the frontier. Our purchasing agents believe they can easily double the deliveries over the next month as they bring in more of the local boatmen."

"There have been no problems with the Ivoire customs authorities and border patrols?"

Atiba smiled and patted the breast pocket of his uniform. "No problems. Only happy policemen who enjoy a little touch of dash."

"And the U.N. patrols?"

"Them, we don't even need to pay off. The French stay well offshore and only inspect the big ships, while Americans haven't been east of Buchanan in more than a week."

"Then where are the Americans operating?"

"When we do see one of their gunboats, it is either patrolling around the barge anchored offshore here at Monrovia or working the border over at Guinea side." Atiba shrugged offhandedly. "Mostly they seem to sit broken down on the beach at Conakry."

Belewa frowned lightly. "Have they tried to interfere with our gunboat operations?"

"Since we've resumed action along the Guinea coast, there have been two or three attempted interceptions. In each case our gunboats evaded and broke contact without much difficulty. Our intelligence agents inside the U.N. base report that the American hovercraft are suffering from severe technical problems and are operational only half of the time at best."

"Perhaps," Belewa grunted, studying the water stains on his office ceiling.

"Perhaps? Do we have reason to believe otherwise?"

"Possibly, Sako. Think. Remember when the Americans first landed in Guinea. Our intelligence reported them as being ready for battle and most formidable. Why do they suddenly have all of these problems now? If, in fact, they are having problems."

"We killed their unit commander in our raid on Conakry. We know that from the Americans' own news broadcasts."

"He has been replaced."

"Yes, by a woman." Atiba chuckled softly. "Perhaps she is finding a gunboat squadron a little more difficult to manage than a kitchen."

"No. Not this woman." General Belewa let his chair slam forward. Rising from behind his desk, he paced off a few impatient steps, his fingertips lightly drumming against the leather of his pistol holster. "I know of this woman, Sako. Every serious student of modern warfare knows about Amanda Garrett. She is someone we need to be concerned about. She is someone who concerns me."

Belewa turned on his boot heel and moved slowly back toward the desk. Pausing, he looked out beyond the sliding glass doors of the balcony and toward the distant blue line of the oceanic horizon. "She makes me think of the lion and the leopard."

"The lion and the leopard?" Atiba inquired, puzzled.

Belewa turned to look at his chief of staff. "When the lion hunts, he stands tall and lifts his head to roar at the sky, announcing to all the world that he is going out to seek his prey. When the leopard hunts, however, she lies still in the tall grass, so silent and so unmoving that you might almost step on her before you know that she is there.

"Does this make the leopard more of a coward than the lion and less of a danger? It does not. For the leopard is very patient. She waits and watches and chooses a moment that belongs only to her for the attack. She offers no warning. She gives no chance. She shows no mercy."

Belewa returned his gaze to the sea. "Something down deep in my belly is telling me that we may have a leopard out there."

Mobile Offshore Base, Floater 1   0917 Hours, Zone Time; May 23, 2007

With a ponderous delicacy, the CH 53F Sea Stallion settled onto the landing platform, the weight of the mammoth transport helicopter making the platform's supporting superbarge bobble slightly. Throttling down, the Stallion's tail ramp dropped, permitting its human payload to disembark.

"Marines, move out!" First Sergeant Tallman's bellow overrode the dying moan of the triple-turbine power plant. "Watch for the rotors! Clear the platform and form up on the main deck!"

Burdened by their seabags, weapons, and combat harness, the men of First Platoon, Fox Company, 6th Marine Regiment hunched across the landing pad to the descent ladders, helmeted heads turning as they got their first look at their new duty station.

Standing at the helicopter's tail ramp, Captain Stone Quillain didn't avail himself of the opportunity until his last man had cleared the aircraft.

Standing two inches over six feet in height, the Marine company commander was a composite of rough-hewn angles and wedges. A halfback's shoulders tapered down to a quarterback's waist and his wind-weathered face had high cheekbones, a forthright nose, and dark, rather narrow eyes that could shift from amiable to agate cold.

Stone Quillain was not a handsome man by any conventional Hollywood reckoning. However, he would have been a little surprised at the number of women who had studied him thoughtfully after noting his strong, open features and tall, rangy frame.

With the last member of the platoon on his way, Quillain took his look around at the platform and the sea and the heat-hazy horizon beyond. He gave a noncommittal grunt and slung his rucksack and flak vest over one shoulder. With his free hand, he scooped up the carrying straps of both his fully loaded seabag and the Mossburg Model 590 combat shotgun he preferred as a personal weapon. Lifting them without effort, he started for the ladderway.

A chief petty officer waited for him down on the barge's main deck. "The compliments of Commander Gueletti and the Provisional Seabee Base Support Force, sir," he said, saluting. "Welcome to Floater 1. We have your quarters ready."

"Thank you, Chief," Quillain replied, setting down his gear and returning the salute. "You can show Lieutenant DeVega here and his men where they're to be quartered. Also, I'd 'preciate it if you could have someone take care of my gear and that of my top sergeant. Yo! Tallman! Over here!"

Calvin Tallman, the Fox Company top, was a solid and stocky brick of a black man. Hailing from the hard side of Detroit, he stemmed from a background and culture decisively divergent from the rural Georgia upbringing of his company commander. However, like Quillain he acknowledged the existence of only one color: Marine Corps green.

"Tallman, you're with me while we report to the TACBOSS. Afterward, we can check out the rest of the company spaces and see what we have to work with."

"Aye, aye, Skipper."

"Want a guide to Captain Garrett's quarters, sir?" the Seabee CPO inquired. "The layout of the platform can be a little confusing until you get the hang of it."

"No, thanks, Chief. We'll manage."

The truth be told, Quillain wanted the opportunity to have a look around on his own, as well as the luxury of speaking bluntly with his own people.

✕◆

"Well, Skipper, what do you think?" Tallman asked as they strode aft through the compact village of deck modules, availing himself of the traditional openness that existed between a Marine unit commander and his top shirt.

Quillain prefaced his response with a disparaging snort. "What I think is that we're pretty much stuck up shit creek without a paddle. You heard the word back on the beach, same as I did. The Navy's tech weenies aren't having any luck getting the bells and whistles on these damn glorified landing craft of theirs to work. We're falling over patch-together 'provisional units' and 'task groups' left and right and down the middle, and the goddamn United Nations is in charge, no doubt with the entire goddamn General Assembly voting on how to make it totally goddamn impossible for us to do whatever the hell it is we're supposed to be doing!"

"And let's not forget that we got us a lady C.O. on top of it," Tallman added. "We may all be goin' to hell in a handcart, but at least we're doing it politically correct."

Quillain aimed a baleful glance at the grinning noncom. In any number of vociferous bull sessions, Quillain had argued that women had their place in the military, just not in any command position over a Marine ground combat unit.

The mere fact that his new commanding officer was the highly decorated and, in some circles, near-legendary Amanda Garrett didn't cut a great deal of slack with Quillain either. In his mind there was a vast difference between pushing buttons in the CIC of a warship and lying in the mud of an infantry battlefield.

They reached the deck space of the seafighter group and a seaman pointed the way to the officers' quarters. Shortly thereafter, the two Marines stood beside the housing module door bearing a nameplate that read, "Commander Tactical Action Force." The murmur of a feminine voice could be heard inside.

Quillain exchanged his Kevlar battle helmet for the Marine utility cover he'd carried in one of his cargo pockets. "Wait here, Top," he said lowly, slapping the cover into shape and tugging it down over his coarse, dark hair, "while I go and see just what kind of a goddamn candy-assed female we're lashed up with."

Climbing the single step to the module's doorway, he knocked.

"Come in," the muffled alto replied over the hum of the air conditioner.

Quillain flipped the door handle and entered, coming to attention in front of the desk that dominated the small living space. The precise, razor's-edge salute he aimed toward the individual seated behind that desk almost made the air crack, and he fired his words like a burst from a machine gun.

"Captain Stone Quillain, Fox Company, Second Battalion, Sixth Marine Regiment, reporting as ordered, ma'am!"

The responding salute was more casual, the responder's free hand being used to hold a telephone to her left ear. "At ease, Captain. Welcome aboard. Excuse me for a moment. I'll be right with you."

Quillain went to a parade rest that was only a nominal step down from his previous stiff-spined brace. Keeping his eyes level, he used his peripheral vision to evaluate his surroundings.

Above and beyond being an office and living quarters, the little room was also obviously being used as a planning center. An intricately Scotch-taped mosaic of maps, charts, and aerial photography covered almost every inch of wall space. Interspersed were sheets of computer printout, some of them flowing down almost to deck level, the hard copy extensively annotated and underlined with multicolored marker pen. Only the top of the neatly made bunk was completely clear, and even it had a small pile of reference books stacked near its head.

Orderly stacks of file binders sat on the desk, and a mil-spec Panasonic laptop computer sat open and ready for use beside the large and sophisticated interphone deck.

He recognized her, of course. Almost any individual who even casually followed recent world affairs would recognize America's heroine of both Drake's Passage and the China Coast: the thick, blended auburn and amber hair, the large and alert golden hazel eyes, and the striking, fine-lined features that didn't need the accent of makeup to highlight their attractiveness.

What the news bites hadn't brought out was the natural dynamic vibrancy that seemed to radiate from the woman. Quillain couldn't help but note the phenomenon, even though he'd come into the room grimly intent on not finding anything to like about his new commander. Likewise, he found himself unable to resist noting the unemphasized but definite swell of firm breasts beneath her soft uniform shirt.

Quillain savagely yanked his mental focus away from that particular image, turning it instead to the half of the telephone conversation he could overhear.

"Frankly, Lieutenant," Garrett was saying, "I don't care what our replenishment schedule is. We need an additional allocation of small-arms ammunition right now and we're going to require a lot more in the future. We've got a major live-fire training program going out here. . . . We're cross-training our service personnel to serve as auxiliary gunners aboard the PGs. . . . That's correct. We're going to be running at least three new light-weapons mounts per hull, so you can junk all of your prior expenditure projections. . . . I know I have a quarterly training allotment, Lieutenant. We've already expended it and we're burning into our operational reserves. . . . We need everything: 5.56 NATO, forty-millimeter grenade, all types, fifty-caliber, lots of fifty-caliber. And a couple of dozen more M2 barrels. We need our ammo allocations doubled all across the board."

Those golden eyes flicked in Quillain's direction. "No, cancel that. We've got our Marines here now. Triple them. . . . That's right, triple them! And we need the stuff flown in. We don't have the time to wait around for sealift."

Quillain frowned behind his fixed expression. He'd taken part in this kind of argument himself often enough, trying to pry more training ordnance out of the quartermasters. This was shooter talk.

Apparently she was still dissatisfied with the response she was receiving. Her dark brows knit together and a steely edge came to her voice. "That, I'm afraid, is your problem, Lieutenant. You can take it up with Captain Stottard and he can have a talk with Admiral MacIntyre about the situation. I don't want to have to. Get it done!"

She forcefully returned the phone to its cradle and returned her attention to Quillain, her flash of annoyance dissipating as rapidly as it had come. She stood behind the desk and extended a hand to the Marine, exchanging a firm dry-palmed handshake.

"Sorry about that, Captain. I had to clarify a few matters with our logistics people. I'm Captain Amanda Garrett, your theater TACBOSS. We're glad you and your people are here."

"Thank you, ma'am," Quillain replied stiffly. "I've just come aboard with my first platoon—"

"Is the rest of your company still on the ground at Conakry?" she interjected swiftly.

"Yes, ma'am. We'll be bringing them out—"

"Fantastic! As soon as we've finished here, get on the horn to Main Base. Go ahead and bring both of your other two rifle platoons out to the platform, but hold your weapons platoon at Conakry. I've got a special job for them."

"A special job, ma'am?" Quillain found himself falling behind the curve.

"Exactly. A pretty important one that we've got to move fast on. Let me show you what the situation is."

Garrett moved swiftly from behind her desk, crossing to a wall-mounted admiralty chart of the African Gold Coast. Brushing closely past Quillain in her intentness, she forced the Marine to take a couple of awkward steps back out of her way.

"Right," Amanda continued briskly, "we have two aerostat patrol stations established. Guinea East, here off the border of Guinea and the West African Union, and Guinea West off the border of Guinea and Guinea-Bissau."

Her fingertips swept across the expanse of the chart. "Between them, they give us a full radar coverage of the Guinea Littoral. The problem is that our aerostat carriers are converted TAGOS-class antisubmarine intelligence ships. They're slow, they're obvious, and they're working close inshore. They're also operated by the Naval Fleet Auxiliary Force, which means they're civilian manned and totally unarmed. They'd be sitting ducks for a Boghammer raid. That's where your heavy-weapons people come in."

"My people, ma'am?" Quillain asked, bewildered.

"Exactly. We'll divide your heavy-weapons platoon into two Naval Guard teams, and we'll put one aboard each of the aerostat carriers. What kind of weapons loadout do your people have?"

Quillain struggled to shift mental gears again. "My grenadier and rocket launcher squads have their standard Mark 19 chunkers and SMAWs. I didn't think we'd be needing mortars for maritime boarding and security work, so I had my mortarmen turn their sixty-millimeters in and draw Ma Deuce fifties—that is, M2 heavy machine guns, ma'am."

"Good call, Captain! That couldn't be better. We'll hold your people at Conakry until . . . oh, day after tomorrow. That'll give them a chance to rest a little and get properly outfitted for the job. Then we'll helilift them out to the 'stat carriers and fast-rope them aboard after dark. We'll pull them off again whenever the carriers go into Conakry to replenish. If we can keep the guard teams a secret, we just might be able to hand somebody a nasty surprise."

"Yes, ma'am," the Marine could only agree. Captain Garrett was apparently very good at handing out surprises.

She continued studying the chart, her hands crossed over her stomach and her lower lip lightly bitten in concentration. "That takes care of that," she continued after a moment. "Now, about your rifle platoons. I know that your men are jet-lagged and are going to need some acclimatization time, but how soon do you think you'll be ready to start operating?"

"It depends on the mission profile," Quillain replied promptly, grateful to be back on firmer ground. "What have we got?"

"A series of amphibious recon probes."

Again Garrett's hand arced gracefully across the map; this time the gesture encompassed the coasts of Sierra Leone and Liberia as well as Guinea. "Here's our problem, Captain. We have eight hundred miles of coast to cover and two missions to perform with your hundred and sixty men and my five gunboats and patrol craft. We have to simultaneously protect Guinea from Union sea raids while cutting the coastal smuggling line into the Côte d'Ivoire, the one the Union is using to breach the U.N. embargo."

She glanced at Quillain. "In effect, we have an east war and a west war, and we can't fight them both at the same time. No way do we have the assets. At least not if we try and fight conventionally."

Quillain found he was becoming intrigued in spite of himself. "What are your intentions, then, ma'am?"

"We eat the apple one bite at a time by dividing the problem into sections." Her fingernail tapped lightly against the acetate cover of the map, indicating the coast of Guinea. "Our first move will be to destroy the Union's network of coastal bases inside Guinean territory."

"The West African Union has naval bases inside Guinea?"

"Boat hides, anyway. Small, concealed moorages located in isolated areas along the coast. The Union Boghammer groups use them as rest-and-replenishment points for their raiding. We believe that Union Special Forces teams are using them for insertion and supply when they're going deep in-country. Taking out those boat hides would be a major blow to the Union's insurgency campaign. If we play it right, we can also cost the Union some equipment and personnel they can't afford to lose."

"We got these sites targeted yet?" Quillain inquired, studying the chart.

"We're getting there." Garrett smiled enigmatically. "I presume that you've heard about how we've been making fools of ourselves out here."

"Uh, I understand that the patrol force has been having some difficulty coming up to speed, ma'am," Quillain replied, with more diplomacy than he thought he could muster.

"That's good. Actually we've been working very hard for the past few weeks to make ourselves look like the biggest bunch of goobers ever commissioned by the United States Navy. We've been faking equipment breakdowns, botching intercepts, aborting patrols, anything to make us look inept to the locals and to the Union's intelligence service. And it's been paying off."

Quillain rested his hands on his hips. "How so, ma'am?" he asked, puzzled.

"The Union navy is losing its fear of us. Beyond the raid on Conakry base, the Union scaled their coastal operations way back when the U.N. blockade went into effect. Our analysis was they were trying to gauge our effectiveness before risking their forces against us. So we've been striving to make ourselves look totally ineffective. Apparently our Three Stooges act has made the proper impression, because they're ramping up their operational tempo again.

"We've got Boghammer groups back out there, marauding all up and down the Guinea coast. And every time they do, our TACNET recon drones and aerostat radars backtrack the raiders to their staging points."

She indicated a series of bloodred circles that had been drawn on the map's surface along the Guinea coastline. "We have four of the boat hides boresighted already, and we think there are just a couple more to go. That's where you and your Marines come in, Captain. I want to insert recon patrols at each of these sites. I want them to scout out the terrain, verify that these are actually the Union deep-strike bases, and deploy remote antipersonnel sensors so that we'll know when these bases are occupied, all without being detected. Can do?"

Quillain nodded decisively. "Can do, ma'am. Just say the word. What's the next move?"

"Then, Captain, we take out all of the hides in a single coordinated strike, choosing a moment that will maximize the cost to the Union in equipment, supplies, and personnel." A quiet fierceness crept into her voice as she spoke. "By all accounts, General Belewa and his people are tough, smart, and adaptable. Well, we're not going to give them a chance to adapt. We're going to smash the whole damn network in one shot and not leave them anything to rebuild."

Those were good Marine-sounding words of a kind Quillain hadn't expected to hear. "Looks like a solid package to me, ma'am," he said cautiously. "But I hadn't figured on my boys operating ashore on this cruise. Our mission briefing was sort of vague about whether or not we were authorized to operate on the ground in Guinea."

Garrett lifted an ironic eyebrow. "I've noted that vagueness myself, and I'm going to be very careful about not asking for any clarification until after we get this job done. That way, if I get called down for exceeding my authority on this mission package, I can blush prettily and say, 'Oops, I misunderstood my rules of engagement.'"

She turned away from the chart and faced Quillain, levelly meeting his gaze. "Don't worry, Captain. When we make our move, you'll be operating under my written orders. If there's any official flak coming on this operation, I'll be the one catching it. Putting it bluntly, the shit does not slide downhill in my command."

"That wasn't a concern, ma'am," Quillain replied gruffly. Damn it all entirely, he wasn't used to having a five-foot-something slip of damned attractive female assure him of her protection.

She gave him a flash of her sober smile. "I'm sure it wasn't, Captain, but I like to make clear the way I do things right from the beginning. At any rate, I know you've got a lot of work to do, so I won't keep you any longer. Take care of those immediate points we discussed and get your men squared away. We'll see you in the officers' mess for dinner and then at the Operations Group meeting this evening at 2000 hours. You and your people will get a chance to meet the rest of the task force commanders, and we can continue with the mission orientation at that time. We'll be needing your input."

"Yes, ma'am. Thank you, ma'am."

⚑◆

Sergeant Tallman straightened from his leaning posture against the side of the quarters module as Quillain exited from its door. He noted that his company commander had a slightly stunned yet thoughtful expression on his face.

"How bad is it, Skipper?" Tallman asked.

"Top, I can tell you two things right now," Quillain replied after a moment's consideration. "One is that we're in for one hell of an interesting cruise. And as for the other"—he aimed a thumb back at the office doorway—"that ain't no candy-assed female."

Mobile Offshore Base, Floater 1   0632 Hours, Zone Time; June 4, 2007

"Clearly what we're seeing in Guinea is another example of the Pentagon's overdependence on high-tech gadgetry. They've put another conglomeration of complex and fragile technical systems out in the field in the hands of a bunch of undertrained and undisciplined high school kids, and now they wonder why they can't get them to work."

The program was CNN's *Defense Today* video newsmagazine, and the speaker was an elderly ex–Army Special Forces officer who had built a second career as a journalist sniping at U.S. military policy.

"And so, Colonel," the moderator took up smoothly, "you put stock in the stories coming out of Conakry concerning the effectiveness and reliability of the Navy's new seafighter squadron?"

"I could have told you from the start that these Buck Rogers hovercraft were going to turn into another expensive Navy boondoggle. The Navy knows it and they're running scared. That's why they attached their current wonder woman, Amanda Garrett, to the seafighter group, in the hope of drumming up some kind of favorable PR out of this fiasco. But even she's going to have a hard time making a good show out of this . . ."

Amanda clicked the television remote, killing the taped satellite broadcast. "Good work, ladies and gentlemen. Over the past couple of weeks, that's what we've managed to get the pundits saying about us. Unfortunately for him,

General Belewa has been listening to these people. Now it's our turn to make them all look like fools."

A chuckle rippled around the interior of the briefing module. The narrow space was filled with the tactical officers of the Tactical Action Group, the captains and execs of the seafighters and the Cyclone Patrol Craft, Stone Quillain and his Marines, and the senior S.O.s of the TACNET system. Some sat at the narrow central table; others leaned against the walls; all were attentive and waiting.

Amanda turned from the wall-mounted flatscreen to the old-fashioned blackboard beside it. Swiftly, she chalked a series of words upon it.

```
POWER PROJECTION
MAINTAIN SEA LINES OF COMMUNICATION
MAINTAIN FLEET IN BEING
```

"These are the three classic maritime missions currently being performed by the navy of the West African Union," she continued, speaking over her shoulder. "Taking the fight to the enemy via power projection, keeping open the Union's sea lines of communication, and maintaining a fleet to serve as a strategic threat. As soon as we eliminate the Union's ability to perform these three missions, we get to go home. Tonight we're taking the first step . . . here."

Decisively, she drew a line through the words POWER PROJECTION.

Using the remote once more, Amanda called up the mission chart on the wall screen. She turned back to face the room, her hands on her hips.

"You all know the setup, ladies and gentlemen. TACNET and our Marine recon probes have verified the existence and location of six Union boat hides along the coast of Guinea, three of them large, three of them small. We're taking them out. All of them."

The briefing program progressed on the wall screen, graphics targeting blocks blinking into existence around each objective. "Of the three larger hides, the two westernmost, L1 at Rio Compony and L2 at Cape Varga, will be taken out by the *Sirocco* and *Santana,* each PC carrying a full Marine assault platoon. The three smaller hides, S1 at Conflict Reef, S2 at Margot de Avisos, and S3 at Reviere Morebaya, will be taken out by the PGs, each carrying a single Marine squad.

"This first wave of strikes will be coordinated to go in simultaneously, or at least as close to simultaneous as the tactical situation will permit. The two Cyclones will sortie from Floater 1 at 0900 Hours. The PGs will follow this afternoon at 1500. All units will make landfall after dark and will be at their point of assault by 2200. The landing forces will take departure at that time.

"We won't have enough recon to provide full real-time coverage for all of the assaults. However, all L Sites will have a Predator on station overhead, and everybody gets at least one drone pass over their objective within an hour of their scheduled assault time.

"Following the initial assault wave, the seafighters will recover their assault squads, regroup, and proceed to the final objective, L3 at Reviere Forecariah, taking it out at first light. For final operational details, check your onboard mission data modules and your briefing hard copy. Any questions?"

"Yes, ma'am," a Georgia-accented baritone sounded. Amanda wasn't surprised when Stone Quillain straightened from his leaning posture against the rear wall. The Marine officers had stayed on their feet during the briefing, a dark jungle-camouflaged cluster in the rear of the room.

"I'd like to point out to the Commander that L3 is the easternmost of the hides, only 'bout thirty miles west from the border between Guinea and the West African Union. If one of the other hides gets a warning off, the L3 garrison stands a pretty good chance of bugging out and escaping. If we take out L3 in the first wave and leave one of the other hides for the follow-up, any Union bolters would not only have farther to go, but we'd have forces between them and the border, positioned to intercept. I believe I mentioned that during the mission planning."

Amanda met the Marine's gaze levelly. "You did, Captain. That was a very valid point."

She let the silence hold for a moment, almost to a point of its becoming uncomfortable, then widened her attention to include the other officers in the briefing space. "Thanks to the remote ground sensors planted by our Marines, we know that there will be Union personnel present at at least four of these boat hides. This is good."

Amanda allowed her voice to rise slightly. "Every time we engage the enemy, we need to make him pay heavily for the privilege in manpower and matériel. We need to make the Union understand that every time they take us on, it will cost them more than they can afford to lose. We need to hit the enemy hard in every way that we can, at every opportunity he provides. We need to make them fear us! Now, let's get it done!"

Reviere Morbaya Tidal Estuary   2247 Hours, Zone Time; June 4, 2007

There is a trick to walking quietly through water. First, one must stay at least waist deep, so there is no sloshing as the legs swing. Then one must move very deliberately. The steps are kept small and the body's weight centered, never trusting the placement of the advancing foot until one is sure about the surface it rests upon.

Such things are second nature to an SOC Marine.

Captain Stone Quillain paused for a moment. Lifting the night-bright visor from his eyes, he took a look around at the real world.

Black. As black as you can only get under a jungle canopy at midnight. Black so palpable that it almost had texture. There was supposed to be a campfire burning somewhere not too far away, but Quillain couldn't testify to it yet. He lowered the visor and settled it over his eyes once more.

Now he could see again, albeit only in shades of glowing green. The cascade circuits of his AI2 (Advanced Image Intensifier) night-vision system magnified the traces of starlight filtering down through the overhead cover to a useful intensity. The image was fuzzy and yet more than adequate to make out the sluggish tidewater channel and the looming, gnarled trunks of the salt mangroves overgrowing it.

Quillain glanced back at the ten men of the assault squad who trailed behind him. Strung out at five-yard intervals and wading slowly ahead, each Marine held his weapon ready at high port.

A brightly glowing ball of greenish-white light rode on the right shoulder of each man, as if he had acquired a Tinkerbell-class fairy to escort him through the swamp. These were IFF (Identification Friend or Foe) sticks, a filtered chemical light worn clipped to the load-bearing harness to prevent "blue on blue" friendly-fire accidents in a night battle. Invisible to the naked eye, their infrared emissions were readily discernible to an AI2 visor.

Each Marine also hunched under a burden of body armor and ammunition and equipment. Quillain's own loadout was typical: the Mossberg 590 with a four-round shell carrier strapped to its stock, ten pounds of Interceptor flak vest and camouflaged K-pot helmet. MOLLE load-bearing harness with a full drinking water reservoir, three sixteen-round shotgun shell pouches, equally divided between slug loads and flechettes, an M9 Beretta pistol with four spare fifteen-round clips, an M7 bayonet, Ka-Bar knife, first-aid pouch, spare batteries, four hand grenades, and an assortment of pyrotechnic and smoke flares.

No rations or field shelter. They were traveling light tonight.

Then there were the electronics. In addition to his night-vision visor, Quillain carried a cigarette-pack-size tactical radio clipped to his helmet. The little AN/PRC 6725F unit linked him in to a squad communications band via an earphone and boom-mounted whisper mike.

A second radio, a SINCGARS (Single Channel Ground Air Radio System) PRC 6745 Leprechaun, was attached to his harness and jacked into the same headset. This larger three-pound set linked him in with the seafighter command channels.

Radio discipline was strict. The only sounds on the squad circuit were the softly hissing exhalations of a dozen taut and wary men.

Quillain faced forward again and resumed his advance. Random fragments of thought bounced and jittered in the back of his mind, an ignored backdrop to his focus on the mission.

Damn, but these new AI2 visors are a hell of an improvement over the old NVG series. Not so heavy, more range, and a lot wider field of vision. Still, it'd be nice to have a look around with real light and just plain old eyes.

Right foot . . . pause . . . left foot . . . pause . . . *Watch out for the damn mangrove roots! Don't trust 'em. Stick to the bottom mud, even if you have to move out deeper into the channel. Look ahead after the squad sergeant and his point man. Watch them for hand signals. Listen for the whispered warning of a pothole.*

Right foot . . . pause . . . left foot . . . pause . . . *This is salt water, so we shouldn't have to worry about that bilharzia bug they warned us about in the environmental briefing. What about leeches? Can the leeches hereabouts live in salt water? Hell! I should have taped up my boot tops and fly. Too late to worry about it now.*

Right foot . . . *Easy! Slick patch!* Pause . . . Left foot. *Shoulders aching. This damn old shotgun's getting heavy. Maybe I should stop being such a goddamn individualist and start packing an M-4 like everybody else. To hell with that now too. Focus on your patrol overwatch sector. Look alive, Stone. We're gettin' close.*

The patrol sergeant lifted a hand, signaling a halt. He looked back at Quillain, the broad glassy visor beneath his helmet rim giving him the appearance of an insectoid robot in a man's clothes. Quillain moved to his side. With helmets nearly touching, they exchanged whispers.

"How far?"

The patrol sergeant and his squad had been here before. They had been the team that had reconned this boat hide and its environs.

"Another hundred meters up this channel, Skipper. Then about half a klick overland to the east."

"Right. So far, so good."

At that moment, twenty feet away on the far side of the muddy channel, a beached log looked up and started to crawl toward them.

"Shit!"

It's entirely possible to scream in a whisper.

Twice the length of a tall man, the crocodile pushed off from the bank, mucky water rippling over the jaggedly ranked scales on its back. Its eyes glowed with white ghostfire in the visual spectrum of the Marine's nightvision goggles.

The patrol sergeant whipped his weapon, a silenced Heckler and Koch MP-5 submachine gun to his shoulder. Quillain started to do the same with the 590, then realized that the unsuppressed roar of the shotgun would resound through the swamp like a thunderclap. Juggling the Mossberg in his left hand, he tore his Ka-Bar out of its sheath with his right.

For a very long moment, the little group of amphibious predators eyed one another. Then, apparently deciding that the odds weren't in its favor, the crocodile turned in his own length and slithered back into the mangrove knees, disappearing from sight.

Quillain and the squad leader carefully and quietly released a couple of imprisoned breaths.

"You Tarzan, Skipper?" The noncom whispered, grinning into the night.

Quillain returned the knife to his harness. "Fuck Tarzan," he replied darkly. "Me Cheetah."

⧫

"*Carondelet* advises they have Hide S1 at Conflict Reef secured," Christine Rendino reported over the link from Floater 1. "Site unoccupied as per intel projections. No contact with hostiles reported. Rations, light military stores, and fifty gallons of gasoline captured. Miscellaneous documents recovered. Lieutenant Clark is standing by for further orders."

"That was the easy one," Amanda replied, speaking softly into her headset mike. "Have the *Carondelet*'s landing team document the hide on video and then destroy it."

She had no real reason for keeping her voice low. The seafighter was station-keeping in the shallows five hundred yards off the coastal mangrove line. Still, instinct was strong.

"Have the *Carondelet* team extract and reposition to support the *Queen* and the *Manassas,*" she continued. "Tell Clark to expedite. He's our force reserve now."

"Roger. Will comply."

Amanda sat at the small navigator's station in the *Queen of the West*'s cockpit, striving to maintain a situational awareness of both her flagship's mission and that of the task force as a whole.

All cockpit lights and telescreen gains had been turned down to bare minimum and the blackness beyond the windscreen had a steamed velvet tangibility. Up forward, she could barely make out the silhouettes of Steamer Lane and Snowy Banks. Bulked out by K-pot helmets and by the composite foam and Kevlar battle vests that could serve as life preserver and body armor both, they sat silently ready at their control stations. Overhead, Chief Tehoa manned the cockpit weapons mount, positioned behind a massive pair of Browning heavy

S E A   F I G H T E R

machine guns. A blessed trickle of comparatively cooler night air leaked past him through the open hatch.

"What's the situation with *Santana* at Rio Compony?"

"Hide L1 is now also secure," a faint trace of jubilation crept into Christine's voice. "And *Santana* has scored! No gunboats, but a garrison was present on site. Three guerrillas captured and one dropped in a short firefight. No casualties our side. Four hundred gallons of gasoline, a stack of documents and large stocks of rations, equipment and armament have been captured. The assault team leader reports at least enough to outfit a full platoon. He has a perimeter established and he wants to stay on the beach until daylight and have another look around for more supply caches in the area."

"I concur, Chris. This one's a keeper. Have *Santana* and her Marines hold on station until Guinean government forces can relieve them. What about the *Sirocco* and *Manassas* teams?"

"Still positioning. Should be ready to move soon. No unusual activity indicated in any of the hides we have drone coverage over. No atypical radio traffic. We're still looking good, boss ma'am. The penny hasn't dropped yet."

"Acknowledged, Floater. Maintain operations as per the mission plan."

"Roger. Floater is out and on the side."

Christine dropped off link.

Almost immediately, however, another transceiver ID number blinked on the communications telepanel. A digital electronic hail was being received from another transceiver integrated into the command net.

Amanda captured the channel hack with her joystick controller and opened it with a blip of the thumb button. "This is Royalty. Go, Mudskipper."

"At estimated channel departure point. Turning inland. Request position verification."

Captain Quillain's voice was husky and sibilant, a whisper amplified by the com system's automatic gain control.

"Stand by, Mudskipper. Verifying now." Amanda turned her attention to the tactical display screen.

From their prior reconnaissance, they had learned of two conventional lanes of approach to the Union boat hide. One was from the sea, a narrow tidal channel running almost a full kilometer back into the coastal mangrove swamp. At that moment, the *Queen of the West* was standing off the mouth of that channel.

From the landward side, a single narrow, snaking trail ran in along a natural causeway through the tangle of marshy rain forest to an area of higher ground at the head of the inlet.

The last few yards of that approach were covered by both claymore mines and a machine-gun emplacement.

The plan developed by the *Queen*'s raider force had been to take advantage of a second, smaller tidal channel that ran parallel to, but some 500 yards to the west of, the first inlet. Going ashore at the mouth of the second channel, Quillain and his men would follow it to a point directly opposite the Union boat hide. From there they would brush-bust across through the mangroves, taking the camp from its undefended flank.

Stone Quillain's SINCGARS radio had an integral Global Positioning Unit in addition to its communications circuits. Now Amanda accessed that unit via an encrypted datalink microburst, acquiring a download of the landing team's position. A few moments later, a friendly unit hack blipped into being on her tactical display, the *Queen*'s navigational system integrating the Marines' position into its operational database.

The hack was at the proper point on the graphics map. Quillain and his men were where they needed to be.

"Mudskipper, your position is verified," Amanda replied over the voice circuit, relishing the commander's luxury of knowing the exact location of her deployed forces. "Bearing to objective is zero eight seven true. I say again, zero eight seven true. Range to objective four niner zero meters."

"Acknowledged, Royalty. Movin' out."

"Good luck, Mudskipper."

There was no verbal response, just a double click on the transmitter key.

Amanda leaned forward and touched Steamer Lane's shoulder. "We're starting final approach. Take us in."

The hover commander nodded. He rolled forward on the propulsor pod throttle and shifted his hand to the dial of the steering controller. The *Queen of the West* ghosted ahead on her silent electric drives, her blunt bow aimed at the mouth of the tidal channel.

Snowy Banks spoke lowly into her headset mike, a hoarseness to the normally light and true tone of her voice.

"All stations. We are proceeding upchannel. All gunners, we are guns hot. I say again, all gunners, we are guns hot."

Overhead, Chief Tehoa yanked back the cocking levers of his twin Brownings, the lead shells in his ammunition belts jacking into the firing chambers. Releasing the levers, he allowed the bolts to slam forward again. The metallic *chuck-chang!* of the cocking machine guns rang in the tepid darkness.

⊗◆

It can be startling how quietly a body of well-trained and heavily armed men can move through heavy undergrowth. All equipment is buckled tight and taped down; nothing is left loose to snag and catch. Rifle barrels probe ahead, carefully bending and brushing aside branches and vines without breaking them. Boots are lowered in millimeter increments, sensitive to even the faintest touch of resistance from a cocked twig lying on the ground. And, of course, there is absolutely no acknowledgment of clawing thorns, clinging insects, or the sticky-slimy caress of the jungle.

The coin paid for such silence is exhaustion. In muscle strain and nervous tension, a few hundred yards of such brush-creeping can be the equivalent of a five-mile road march.

◇✗◆

Stone Quillain noted that the trees and ground cover were thinning out and that his men now had solid ground underfoot instead of the slushy morass of mud and mangrove roots that had made up the floor of the tidal swamp. They had reached their target area, the small island that held the Union boat.

The range of their night-vision visors increased as more ambient light leaked down from the sky overhead. More illumination issued a second new source, a dancing flicker of white through the trees. A fire.

The enemy.

The squad leader required no instructions. He breathed commands into his lip mike, calling in his flankers and redeploying his column of men into a skirmish line. One of the squad's three four-man fire teams sheered off, heading for the gun emplacement that covered the land-side approach to the island. Using sand maps and computer displays, the raiders had already worked through these actions a dozen times over. Now it was real thing.

Stay low! Use the cover. Hunker down and duckwalk from one brush clump to the next. Snake forward on your belly. Round in the chamber. Safety off. Keep your finger off the trigger.

Scan! Watch for sentries. Watch for fox or spider holes. Watch for the telltale, unnaturally straight line of a gun barrel protruding from a bunker.

Look down! Brush the ground ahead of you with your fingertips. Ever so lightly feel for the monofilament trip wire of a booby trap or a ground flare, or for the prongs of a land mine.

Look up! Watch the trees. The gnarled bolls of the mangroves could hide a sniper.

Breathe! Recharge your senses and flush the fatigue poisons out of your body with deep, silent, and deliberate breaths, then sidle on.

◇✗◆

Quillain and the squad leader moved up behind a waist-high mound on the forest floor, the interwoven plastic ribbons and netting of a camouflage tarp becoming apparent as they drew closer. Quillain slipped his hand beneath it and felt the metal of a row of stockpiled five-gallon jerricans. A whiff of petroleum escaped from beneath the tarp. Gasoline.

They moved on. A few yards more and the heart of Union camp was in sight.

As a military installation, it didn't look all that impressive. A cluster of small lean-tos half circled around a small firepit. Its strength lay in the caches of stores and equipment dispersed in the forest around it and in what it meant to the Union soldiers and seamen who rested and resupplied here. The hide served as a haven, a place where a warrior could let down his guard for a little while among friendly faces.

Unfortunately for them, the Union guerrillas had let down their guard a little too much. They'd gone unchallenged in their coastal strongholds for so long that they had stopped conceiving of a threat creeping in on them from the night. They would pay for that conceit.

Eight men clustered around the fire, some in ragged jungle camouflage, the others in the sun-faded khakis of the Union navy. Assault rifles and sub-machine guns leaned against log seats and a tea billy hung suspended over a low, smoldering flame that served as a mosquito smudge rather than a source of warmth. An outboard motor had been carried into the circle of firelight as well and stood half disassembled on a makeshift wooden stand, two of the navy hands working over it. Tools and tin cups clinked, and there was a low murmur of conversation interspersed by an occasional burst of laughter.

Quillain's AI2 visor adapted to the higher illumination levels, the low flames of the smudge sparkling with a clear and crystalline light. Glancing aside, he could see the IFF lights bobbing close to the ground as the fire teams established position on either flank. Suddenly, a dazzling pencil point of bright-ness appeared within his field of vision, swinging toward the cluster of men around the fire. A second followed, a third, more. Small, clear-cut dots of light converged on the Union guerrillas, seeking out and fixing on heads and chests.

Peering through a conventional set of gunsights while wearing a night-vision visor was not an easy task. Instead, each Marine had a small helium-neon infrared laser clipped to the lower grab rail of his M4 carbine or MP-5 subma-chine gun, the laser carefully dialed in to focus at the weapon's point of impact at short range. Where the laser would touch, the bullet would strike.

The AN/PAQ-5 laser sight was a mated system to the AI2 night visor, its targeting beam filtered to be visible to the wearer of the vision system but in-visible to the naked eye. The Union guerrillas were unaware of the death dots dancing across their bodies.

The range was about fifty yards, and Quillain had a discarding sabot slug load in the breech of his shotgun. Coming up on one knee, he rested the side of the Mossberg's barrel against the coarse bark of a small mangrove. Picking his man, a tall, gaunt soldier who had kept a hand resting on his FALN rifle as he sat in the smoke plume of the smudge, Quillain pressed the laser actuator with his thumb. He could swear that the Union jungle warrior looked up for a moment as the beam touched him.

"Team Red to Mudskipper," the words of the detached fire team leader leaked into his awareness through the radio earpiece. "We are in behind the gun emplacement. Emplacement is manned. Two-man crew with Bren gun."

"Roger, Red. Can you make capture or execute a quiet takedown?"

"Negative. Two-man bunker. Both men inside. No line of fire. Grenade."

"Acknowledged. Grenade. Get yourself set. Burn 'em on my word."

The U.N. rules of engagement issued to UNAFIN required that any potentially hostile elements encountered must first be challenged and a call to surrender issued before the use of lethal force was authorized. Quillain was quite aware of those rules of engagement, and he was also quite ready to ignore them.

Sorry, Mr. Secretary Goddamn General, but that ain't how things work in the real world.

Quillain would give as many of the Union guerrillas as much of a chance as he could afford, but not by putting his people at risk. And that brought up another problem.

In his mind's eye he sketched out the situation. The potential fire zone was roughly triangular in shape. Quillain and the bulk of the squad were at the peak of the triangle while the Union camp was at the center of the base. Off to the left point of the triangle from Quillain's perspective was the Union machine-gun emplacement, covered and set to be taken out by his detached fire team.

Off to the right, however, was the Boghammer moorage, out of night-visor range and partially screened by a scattering of trees and underbrush. The database on the Union gunboats indicated that they usually had a crew of six, and Quillain had visuals on only four Union sailors. Were the other two seamen standing watch on the gunboat, manning its weapons and covering the sea approaches?

Quillain's first instinct was to peel off a second fire team to scout out the boat moorage. However, given his limited manpower, he also recognized the danger of "detaching himself to death," losing the advantage of mass and firepower by dispersing his meager forces too widely. In addition, the longer he and his men stumbled around out here in the dark, the greater their chance of being spotted.

Much as he disliked the thought, he was going to have to rely on somebody. He dropped a hand to the "Press to Talk" pad on the Leprechaun transceiver. "Royalty, Royalty, this is Mudskipper . . ."

⚡

The *Queen of the West* crept upchannel, the ripples of her wake breaking along the root-lined banks being the only sound of her passage. Her stern ramp and side hatches were open and the leveled barrels of her new weapons mounts probed at the night like questing insect antennae.

The gunners leaned in their harnesses and longed for a chance to lift their night-vision visors and wipe the stinging sweat from their eyes, for an opportunity to flex their aching forearms, for a second to ask for a drink of water.

They were not official gunners' mates or fire-control operators. According to their ratings badges, they were mechanics and technicians, cooks and clerks. However, when Captain Garrett had put out the call for auxiliary gun crews, they had volunteered, despite the certainty of long hours of extra duty and the probability of increased risk.

They hadn't asked to come to this war, but they were part of it now. And, to quote General George S. Patton, they didn't intend to go home saying that all they had done was to "shovel shit in Louisiana."

⚡

" Captain, if we go in much farther, we're going to lose our turning radius in this channel."

Lane had a good point. More than one overhanging branch had brushed along the *Queen's* flank during the last couple of minutes of the approach. Amanda keyed the laser rangefinder and bounced a microsecond-long burst of light off the head of the inlet. Two hundred yards. That would be about right. Just out of range of any low-grade night-bright optics the hostiles might have.

"All right, Steamer. All stop. Hold us here."

Accessing the Mast Mounted Sighting System, Amanda panned the low-light television across the head of the inlet. Trees, a tangle of undergrowth along the shore, and, a distance inland, a small fire. Nothing that overtly looked like a moored Boghammer. However, one patch of shaggy vegetation did protrude into the channel in a somewhat odd manner.

Amanda dialed over to the thermographic imager using the trackball on her joystick and took a second look, this time sweeping for passive heat radiation.

There it was. The tangled branches and camouflage netting went transparent under the infrared scan. The angular metal and Fiberglas outline of the Boghammer stood out palely against the ambient thermal background of the salt swamp. The boat had been moored bow-on to the mangrove bank with enough slack to allow it to lift and settle with the tides.

"Royalty, Royalty, this is Mudskipper." Stone Quillain's rasping whisper invaded the interphone circuit. "We are on site. Ready to move in. What is your position?"

"Mudskipper, we are in midchannel two hundred yards south of the hide. We have the moorage and camp in sight." Hastily, Amanda called up another GPU fix from Quillain's SINCGARS unit. "We have a fix on you."

"Fine," Quillain shot back with a touch of impatience. "Can you see the gunboat and can you tell if it has a crew onboard?"

"Stand by, Mudskipper." Frustrated, Amanda cranked the camera crosshairs back and forth across the camouflaged Boghammer. She could make out the gunboat easily enough, but the little craft was moored almost directly in line with the camp inland. The mosquito smudge burning there threw off just enough thermal sidelobe to blur the heat image. She couldn't tell if there were any human bodies radiating aboard the small craft or not.

"Royalty. Does the goddamn gunboat have a goddamn crew on it, the world wonders?"

Amanda mashed down on her own transmitter key. "I say again, Mudskipper, stand by! We are working the problem!"

She leaned forward between the pilot's chairs. "Steamer, Snowy, can you make out anything with your night-vision goggles? Do we have a crew on that Boghammer?"

"Ma'am, I gotta take your word for it that we've even got Bog out there," Lane replied, flipping his visor up. "Check with Danno and the Fryguy on the fire-control consoles. The targeting scopes have better IR definition than the Mast Mounted Sight."

"Right."

⚔◆

Danno O'Roark and Dwaine Fry had a small edge over the auxiliary gunner at the door mounts. The weaponry of the seafighter was their primary tasking, and they'd had the official training and the long hours of drill time as the *Queen* had worked up and made herself ready for combat. However, like the door gunners, neither of them had ever fired a shot in anger.

The sweat soaking their dungarees didn't all stem from the heat.

"Fire control, check your scopes. Do we have a crew on the Boghammer?"

Wrists flicked as the two young sailors panned the death dots of their targeting screens across the gunboat.

"What do you think, Fryguy?"

"I dunno, Danno. There might be something up there near the bow. How do you call it, man?"

Senior by one ratings grade and four months' in-service, Danno tried to swallow on a suddenly dry throat. The TACBOSS was waiting for him to give her the word. The Lady herself. He suspected that there might be movement aboard the Boghammer as well. But he couldn't bring himself to say so, not unless he could be absolutely sure.

"We can't verify a crew on the gunboat, ma'am. We can't tell."

"Acknowledged, fire control," Captain Garrett replied matter-of-factly. "Stand by."

She'd left the fire-control stations in her communications loop, so the gunners overheard the next exchange with the landing force. "Mudskipper, this is Royalty. We cannot confirm or preclude the presence of a crew on the gunboat."

"Hell. Okay, Royalty. We'd better do this thing. If there is a gun crew on the Bog and if they open up on us, you're going to have to take 'em out."

"Will do, Mudskipper." *Click.* "Okay, fire control, you have the word. If we get fire from the Boghammer, you are to engage and suppress with thirty-millimeter cannon. I say again, thirty-millimeter cannon. Check your tactical displays and watch your angles. The Marines will be close to your line of fire."

"Fire control, acknowledged."

Now swallowing was an impossibility. Danno called up the port-side weapons pedestal on his panels and linked it with his controller. "I've got the mission," he said hoarsely.

"Team White. Team Blue. We are going for a capture. Hold position and fire only on my command."

A flurry of acknowledgment clicks sounded in Quillain's earpiece and he settled the butt of the Mossberg 590 more solidly against his shoulder.

"Team Red. Take out the Bren gun."

Two decisive clicks replied. Quillain visualized the movements: the hand grenade pins snicking free, the grenadier's arms sweeping back and then forward in the driving, deliberate pitch, the deadly little eggs arcing upward and then down, their safety levers flicking away with a sharp metallic ping.

. . .three . . . four . . . five.

A double flash of white light and the flat doubled slam of the grenade blasts.

Around the smudge fire, the Union guerrillas sat frozen for an instant, the surprise total.

"Nobody move!" Quillain bellowed. "This is the United States Marines! Raise your hands and move slowly away from your weapons! We've got you covered!"

No one moved. It was as if every figure inside the circle of firelight had been smitten by some paralyzing ray. Quillain was about to yell once more when, off on that critically uncovered right flank, a brace of heavy machine guns opened up on the Marine positions.

A heavy 14.5mm slug struck the tree Quillain had been leaning against, the shock throwing his sights off the man he had targeted. The Union gunner was firing blindly in the direction of Quillain's shouted challenge. The firelash of his tracer streams cut over the heads of the Marines, raining shattered branches and wood splinters down upon them. All hands instinctively dove forward, flattening against the rank island loam.

Across in the Union camp, guerrillas scattered, snatching up arms. The smudge fire was extinguished with a sweep of earth and someone emptied an FALN in the direction of the Marine line. The deliberate slam of the heavy-caliber rifle was joined an instant later by the fast, harsh *brrrriiiip* of a Sterling machine pistol.

"Marines! Return fire!"

The piercing crack of 5.56 NATO answered the bigger-bore Union weapons. Quillain took a second to send a 12-gauge slug load booming on its way toward a muzzle flash before slapping his hand onto the Leprechaun's transmitter key. "Royalty, Royalty! We got a firefight here! Get that gunboat off us!"

⚔

". . . We got a firefight here! Get that gunboat off us!" Amanda and the crew of the *Queen* didn't need the shouted radio call to tell them what had happened. They could see the flame of the Boghammer's bow mount and could hear the growing crackle of gunfire through the open side windows of the cockpit.

Chief Tehoa, manning the cockpit guns, also didn't need orders to know the proper reaction. Powering the dual Brownings around to bear on the Boghammer, he pressed the trigger bar, walking a twinned stream of tracers in on the Union gunboat.

Amanda flinched away from the cascade of hot shell casings raining down into the cockpit and yelled into her command headset. "Fire control! Guns free! Engage the Boghammer! Commence! Commence! Commence!"

At the number-one fire-control station beneath the cockpit, Danno O'Roark heard the call. He'd been holding the Boghammer dead on in the crosshairs of his targeting scope, and now, convulsively, he squeezed the joy-stick trigger.

And nothing happened.

Frantically, his eyes raked across the symbology on his ordnance status boards:

```
***PORT PEDESTAL***
1**30MM /\ GUN SAFED**
2**30MM \/ GUN SAFED**
```

Shit! He hadn't cleared the safeties!

"Fire control! Engage that Boghammer! Expedite!"

Panicking, Danno clawed at the settings of the ordnance menu. Calling up new ones, he crushed down on the trigger once more.

⚔

Up in the *Queen*'s cockpit, a second demand for covering fire was coming in over the loop. "Royalty! Royalty! We still got that damn gun on us! When're you . . . Jesus Keeerist!"

A rippling dinosaur scream tore the air and something blazed past the side windows of the cockpit. An instant later, the entire world lit up blue and orange as the forest exploded.

⚔

At his fire-control station, Danno O'Roark realized that something had gone incredibly, catastrophically wrong. His haste-inspired error glared back at him from the ordnance menu.

```
***PORT PEDESTAL***
1**2.75 RKT /\ SEQUENTIAL FIRE
2**2.75 RKT \/ SEQUENTIAL FIRE
```

His brain screamed at him to get off the trigger, but his hand remained frozen on the joystick as the rocket pods emptied out their warloads.

Two pods. Seven Hydra rockets per pod firing at one-half-second intervals. Ten pounds of high explosives per rocket; 140 pounds of high explosives delivered at point-blank range in three and a half seconds. The effect could only be called spectacular.

The rockets barely had time to arm before impacting. The camouflage around the Boghammer evaporated, leaving it outlined darkly in the glare for a split second, like a photographic negative of itself. Then the gunboat itself dissolved into a billion splintered fragments of Fiberglas.

Man-thick tree trunks shattered and century-old mangroves toppled as the rocket stream chewed its way back into the forest. Flaming limbs rained down on the *Queen*'s upperworks and Amanda, Lane, and Snowy all ducked as shrapnel pinged off the windscreen. Bellowing savage implications, Chief Tehoa tumbled down into the cockpit as well. Whether it was a deliberate dive for cover or he'd been knocked out of the gunner's saddle by concussion, even he couldn't say.

And then it was over and the only sound was a softly moaned "Oh fuck . . . oh fuck . . . oh fuck . . ." over the interphone.

"Check fire! *Check fire!* All mounts! Check fire!" Amanda snarled into the interphone.

"What in *thee* hell happened?" Lane demanded angrily, straightening in the command seat.

"I'm not sure, sir, but somebody's gonna pay for it," Tehoa growled, pulling himself up from the cockpit deck."

"Forget that for now," Amanda snapped back. "We might have walked some of those rockets into the Marines. Damn! Damn! Damn!"

An ominous silence reigned out in the darkness. The firefight hadn't resumed following the impact of the barrage, and all that could be seen beyond the windscreen was a small patch of flaming gasoline guttering on the surface of the channel.

"Mudskipper, Mudskipper, this is Royalty! Do you copy?" Amanda spoke urgently into her headset mike. "Mudskipper, report your status!"

Following a protracted and agonizing pause, a baleful voice replied from out of the night. "Think you used enough dynamite there, Butch?"

"Quillain, are you all right? Do you have any casualties?"

"Negative, negative. No casualties, but we're going to be spittin' splinters for a month! Jesus God, woman! I just asked for you to take out the gunboat! Not the whole damn island!"

Given the circumstances, Amanda elected to let Quillain's cavalier mode of address to a senior officer pass. "Sorry, Mudskipper," she replied meekly. "We, ah, had a little weapons malfunction here. We have it locked down now."

"I am pleased to hear it, Royalty. And we got Union guys coming out of the bush with their hands up. Those that can still walk, anyway."

Amanda went relief limp in her seat. "Look at it this way, Mudskipper. At least we convinced them to surrender."

The whisper mike at the other end of the circuit caught a faint but decisive snort. "Hell, two yards closer and you'd have convinced me to surrender too!"

Standing clear of the tidal channel once more, the *Queen of the West* blazed with real illumination. With her running and interior lights turned full up, she conducted a simultaneous loading and unloading operation. Her miniraider shuttled Marines, captured documentation, and Union prisoners out from the boat hide to the loitering hovercraft. There the documentation and prisoners were, in turn, winch-lifted to a hovering Marine CH-60 cargo helicopter for transport to Conakry.

The deck-to-helo transfer of unwilling individuals in total darkness was an exacting and tricky business. Even so, there was no other option. The *Queen* had other calls to make this night, and she couldn't be burdened with unnecessary passengers.

Forward, under the cockpit, Danno O'Roark sat leaning forward into his console, his face held in his hands. "I'm dead," he murmured. "I am so goddamn dead, my corpse stinks."

At his side, his cogunner and friend, the Fryguy, could only nod thoughtfully. "Yeah. That about sums it up."

Suddenly, the Lady herself hunkered down between the two fire-control stations. "All right, gentlemen," she said crisply. "Let's hear what happened."

Gritting his teeth, Danno described what had led up to the erroneous rocket firing, his gun-safety error, his fumbled miscall of the weapons menu, his buck fever and personal panic. He left nothing out and made no attempt to spare himself. He'd bitched his duty and had likely ruined any future he had in the Navy, but by God, he wasn't going to further humiliate himself by trying to make lame excuses.

Captain Garrett only nodded when he finished. "I see," she said finally. "Okay, Danno, I want you to write up a report on this event. Concentrate on what changes you think we need to make in our hardware, software and operational procedures to eliminate the possibility of this glitch happening again. Have it ready to go, oh, day after tomorrow. We'll go over it with Lieutenant Commander Lane and see what we can work out. As the *Queen's* senior gunner, we're going need your help in getting this bug worked out of the system. Can do?"

"Yes, ma'am! Can do, ma'am!"

She straightened, giving the gunner's mate a light slap on the shoulder. Turning away, Amanda Garrett left behind both an intensely relieved young man and yet another individual who would willingly charge hell at her beck and call.

"There they come," Snowy called, peering aft from her cockpit side window.

Standing up, Amanda slid open the overhead hatch. With one foot on the arm of the navigator's chair and a hand braced on the gunners' saddle, she lifted her head and shoulders up and out of the cockpit for a look around.

At forty knots, the predawn air was deliciously cool and the slipstream whipped her with her own hair, each strand a microscopic tingling lash. A few stars still glinted in the zenith, but streaks of pink and gray on the eastern horizon heralded the sunrise. In the faint ruddy light Amanda could make out two sleek, dark forms overtaking the *Queen,* each shadow riding atop a pad of pale, faintly luminescent spray.

She dropped back to the deck and reclosed the hatch, locking out the wind roar and turbine howl. Steamer Lane was already in communication with the other two hovercraft.

"Frenchman and Rebel, Frenchman and Rebel. This is Royalty. Form up on me in starboard echelon. Proceeding to objective L3."

"Very pretty rendezvous, Steamer," Amanda commented. "We're right where we're supposed to be on our time line. The Tactical Action Group has earned itself a very well done so far tonight."

"Yes, ma'am. Thank you," Lane replied. "About that time line, ma'am. If we crank up our speed a little we can get to that last Union hide while we still have some dark to work with."

Amanda settled back beside the navigator's console. "No, that's really not necessary, Steamer. Hold your current speed and conserve your fuel. Our set ETA on target will be fine."

Lane shrugged and glanced back over his shoulder at the second passenger in a "Well, I tried" manner. Stone Quillain slumped in the starboard jump seat, his flak jacket unzipped and his shotgun propped beside him. The big Marine smelled of caked mud and sweat and other organics, and his eyes glinted coldly in a face still streaked with camouflage paint.

"You know," he said after a moment, "somebody's bound to have gotten away from one of those other hides we hit."

"There's a pretty good chance of it," Amanda agreed quietly.

"They could have gotten to a radio. Got an alert out. This outfit could know we're coming."

"It's a safe bet they know something is up by now," she replied, fixing her gaze at the dawn beyond the cockpit windscreen.

Quillain sat forward. "They're going to have their security up. If we go busting in there after first light, we're going to be spotted and they'll bug out on us, sure as hell."

Amanda refused to meet the Marine's angry glare. Instead she lifted a

Styrofoam cup from her console, taking a placid sip of the tea it contained. "Probably."

"Hell, I've said all along that the L3 hide is the one we should have taken out first! It's their biggest and the closest to Union territory. From that point they have their best chance of successfully executing an escape and evasion! They only have to run south along the coast for a few miles and they're back in their home waters!"

"Quite right, Captain. As I said during the briefing, those are all very valid points."

Amanda took another deliberate sip of tea and Quillain slammed back into his seat, muttering under his breath not quite loudly enough to earn a court-martial.

Matakong Channel   **0519 Hours, Zone Time; June 5, 2007**

The fiery half ball of the sun edged above the low inland hills as the seafighter squadron stood through the straits between Matakong Island and the Guinea coast. The sky, clear except for the heat haze already building along the horizon, promised another searing equatorial day. The passengers and crew of a *pinasse* ferrying across to the mainland looked on with concern as the hover-craft formation blasted past.

"Good morrrrrning, Africa," Christine Rendino's voice issued from the cockpit's overhead loudspeaker, ebullient in spite of a night spent in front of the screens in the operations center.

"What do you have for us, Chris?" Amanda replied.

"Too much neat stuff to tell about. Currently, we have sixteen prisoners in the bag along with four confirmed hostile KIAs. We have over a hundred weapons captured, including four of those Union sea mines. The Brit mine-hunter guys are turning handsprings over that. Several tons of fuel ammo and supplies have been secured, and we have documents, documents, documents.

"I've had a quick look at some of the stuff the helos have brought in, and I can already tell you we have enough stuff to convince even a Berkeley journalist that Belewa and the West African Union are behind the Guinea insurgency."

"That's good, Chris, but what do you have for us now? We're in Matakong Channel about ten minutes out from L3 hide."

"I got ya a Predator over the hide at ten thousand feet. Real-time visual is up on your datalink."

Using the Mast Mounted Sighting System, the AQ-1 reconnaissance drone could barely be seen, circling like a distant seagull over the site of the Union boat hide. Amanda accessed the drone's datalink and a crisp digital television image filled the main monitor on her console. A secondary screen up forward on Steamer and Snowy's control panel lit off as well, showing a smaller version of the same vista.

The view showed a patch of now all-too-familiar coastal mangrove swamp, sheltered inside the hook of a narrow peninsula that extended out beyond the northern side of the Forecariah River estuary. In the center of the patch, a narrow creek mouth cracked the densely forested shoreline.

"What's happening down there?" Amanda inquired.

"We've got at least three Boghammers in the hide, and our ground sensors indicate twenty-plus people doing a lot of moving around. We've had intermittent radio traffic for the past two hours. Some commo with Union Army HQ in Freetown and a lot of attempts to contact the other boat hides. Nobody's been answering the phone, and I suspect they're starting to get nervous down there."

"I told you so," Quillain growled, peering over Amanda's shoulder at the monitor.

Amanda ignored the comment, staring intently at the image. "Anything else? Any indication that they're on the move yet?"

And suddenly there was just such an indication. A towering mushroom of scarlet flame and black smoke sprouted out of the tree cover.

"Whoa!" Christine exclaimed. "Big thermal! Big thermal! That was a gas dump blowing! Stand by! . . . Okay, Royalty, we've now got lower-grade thermal flares showing under the tree cover as well."

Amanda nodded to herself. "Okay, their observation posts have us spotted. They're torching their supply caches. Their ammo bunker should be next."

As if keyed by her words, a second, muddier mushroom cloud rose above the trees, discharging tracers sparkling around its base.

Quillain sighed in disgust. "Well, there they go. They're destroying everything before a bug-out."

"Um-hmm," Amanda replied absently. "If they were smart, they'd scuttle the Boghammers as well and escape overland to the Union border. But I don't think they will. I'm betting that they're going to try and get those gunboats out of there."

She straightened abruptly, her seatback thumping Quillain back a few inches. Something glinted in the back of her hazel eyes now, a flame long kept hidden behind layers of patience and deliberation.

"Commander Lane, sound general quarters! Bring the ship to battle stations! Miss Banks, have the squadron clear for action! Surface engagement! Captain Quillain, have your Marines stand by for boarding!"

Steamer Lane hit the general alarm bell, its clangor sounding in the central bay of the hovercraft. Gunners and loaders scrambled back to their weapons. All hands redonned their ear-shielding headsets as the side hatches slammed open and the stern gate dropped, the roar of the slipstream and the scream of the turbines flooding in.

"Fire control one and two, up! Pedestal mounts deployed. Loading surface engagement package. Hellfires and Hydras on the rails!"

"Portside 40 is up!"

"Starboard 40, standing by!"

"Stern 50's manned and ready!'

Quillain hesitated for a moment in the rear of the cockpit, pressing back out of the way as Chief Tehoa swarmed up the ladder to man the cockpit guns. "I hope you're right, Captain," he said finally before dropping down into the hull.

Amanda hoped she was as well. Turning back to the tactical displays, she queried Operations again. "Chris, what's happening in the hide now?"

"Ground search radar and FLIR indicate we have movement on the creek. Breaking tree cover soon . . . Yeah! We got three hostiles coming out! I say again, we've got three Bogs coming out of the crud. Check your visual!"

On the real-time video display, three sleek motor launches blasted out of the narrow stream channel and into open water. Running nose to tail, they punched through the low surf beyond the creek mouth and curved across the shallow bay, turning away from the onrushing PGs and heading for Union territory.

"I've got them!" Snowy called excitedly. "Steamer, they're cutting around the point just outside of the shore break!"

Lane's right hand came off the steering yoke for a fiercely emphasized thumbs-up. "Oh yeah, I see 'em, darlin'! Run, you motherfuckers! The shallows ain't going to save you now!"

"Intercept bearing, Steamer," Amanda ordered, coming forward to kneel between the two pilots. "Close until we're just outside of effective machine-gun range, then hold station on them."

Lane looked back at Amanda, his eyebrows lifted. "We're not taking this bunch out?"

"Oh, we will," Amanda smiled enigmatically, "eventually. But first I've got a few messages to send." She reached back to her console and called up the command communications loop. "This is TACBOSS to squadron. Maintain echelon formation with the flag craft. Fire only on my order. I say again, fire only on my order."

The Union gunboats howled across the width of Forecariah Bay, engines wide open and driving hard for the headlands at Passe du Nord. Streaming rooster-tails behind them, the forty-foot trimarans bucked and skipped as they cut across the troughs of the inbound ocean swells. Intermittently, a lightweight hull broke entirely free of the water on a seventh wave, soaring for an instant like a flying fish before smashing down again in an exploding welter of foam and spray.

Aboard the fleeing Boghammers, the Union seamen grimly clung to whatever handholds they could find and endured the battering. At the steering stations, the helmsmen looked back over their shoulders and pounded their throttles, trying to coax a few more revs out of the straining two-hundred-horsepower outboards.

This had been their coast. There hadn't been anything that they couldn't either kill or disdainfully outrun. They had laughed at the coming of the American hovercraft, the "big winds that couldn't blow." The Union gunboat-men weren't laughing now. Three snarling-jawed sea monsters held a rigid formation behind them, neither falling back nor closing the range, only awaiting their own pleasure and time.

Home was only a few minutes and miles farther down the coast, if those minutes and miles could somehow be bought. Boat captains yelled orders over the unmuffled roar of the engines and crewmen began flinging weapons and ammunition into the sea, trading armament for the extra turn of speed that might see them to safety.

✂◆

With the Marine detachment ready for whatever might be demanded of it, Stone Quillain returned to the *Queen's* cockpit. Shedding his helmet, he replaced it with a spare headset. "How we doing?" he inquired.

The question he wanted to ask was "What are we doing?" He knew full well that the seafighters had the speed and the reach to kill the Boghammers anytime they wanted. The big Marine couldn't see why they were hesitating. But then, this Amanda Garrett female seemed to have a disturbing ability to see any number of things that he couldn't.

"Very good, Captain," she replied cheerfully. "We've cleared Passe du Sud, and that's Point Sallatouk to port. It's not far to the border now. Excuse me, I have a little finessing to do."

She accessed the command radio loop again. Quillain switched over as well, listening in on what this "finessing" was all about.

"*Carondelet, Manassas,* this is TACBOSS. TACNET imaging indicates that the Bogs have jettisoned most of their heavy armament. We can tighten it up a little now. Close to five hundred yards. Mister Marlin, keep the *Manassas* right in their wake and keep pushing. Mr. Clark, take the *Carondelet* to seaward and work in on their flank. Keep them shouldered up against the coast. Mr. Lane, you enjoy surfing, you take the *Queen* in along the shore break. If these guys try for the beach, I want for us to be in position to cut them off."

Three crisp acknowledgments sounded over the loop. Smoothly the three seafighters accelerated, pulling into their new stations in a half-circle behind the retreating Boghammers.

Quillain stared at Amanda. "You're driving 'em!" he said, comprehension dawning. "You're herding 'em right up against the beach!"

"Exactly." She nodded in grim satisfaction. "The fishing villages along this stretch of coast have taken a lot of grief from the Union navy. I think it will do local morale some good for them to see these gentlemen being run out of Dodge."

The harried gunboats and their PG pursuers were running parallel to an extended stretch of white beach dotted with grounded *pirogues* and drying racks. On the magnified MMS display, a scattering of fishermen could be seen, preparing to trail their nets out for the morning catch. They stood and stared as the mismatched convoy tore into view. Their wives and children streamed onto the sand as well, drawn down from their coastal village by the echoing howl of the hovercraft turbines.

Wariness and fear was replaced by a growing realization that, for once, they weren't the ones having to run for their lives. Backs were slapped and fists were shaken at the Union Boghammers. Mouths opened to cheer and to shout jeers and derision after the fleeing toothless gunboats.

"It's psywar, Stone," she continued. "As I said at the briefing, if we're going to win this thing, we have to hit Belewa with whatever we can, whenever we can."

"Captain Garrett," Snowy Banks said, looking back from the copilot's station. "We're three minutes out from the Guinea border. After that, we're in Union territory."

"Very good, Lieutenant. Maintain pursuit. That's the next message we're going to send. No sanctuaries."

"I beg your pardon, ma'am," it was Lane's turn to look back over his shoulder, "but do the U.N. rules of engagement give us authorization to enter Union territorial waters under these circumstances?"

"Who said this has anything to do with the United Nations, Steamer?"

They blazed across the invisible line in the sea that put them in hostile territory. When it became clear that the seafighters were maintaining the chase, the Union gunboats started angling in toward the beach, the Boghammer crews seeking escape on land.

"Fire control. Mission to fire."

"Fire control standing by, Commander."

"Mission is 2.75 rocket, Danno, your favorites. I want to turn the Bogs away from the beach. Walk a salvo of Hydras between the Union gunboats and the shoreline."

"On the way, ma'am," a determined voice replied. "Programming launcher . . . Mission set to fire . . . Firing now!"

The *Queen's* port-side pedestal mount up-angled and vomited flame. Under precise computer control, the launch rail elevated a full degree during the half-second pause between the firing of each cell in the Hydra pod. The milky smoke trails of the rockets extended out in a smooth vertical fan across the azure sky.

Then the projectiles fell, plunging into the sea, detonating, shattering the water, and lifting a wall of spray between the Boghammers and the land. The gunboats flinched away.

"Well done, Mr. O'Roark."

"Thank you, ma'am."

"Floater to Royalty," Christine Rendino's voice cut into the loop. "I hate to spoil your fun, troops, but you have some large company coming. We've got another Union gunboat out there. One of the big guys. He's off Yelibuya Island and is heading north at four bells and a jingle. He will be a factor shortly."

"Acknowledged, Chris. This operation just keeps getting better. Stay on him and keep us posted. Royalty out."

Amanda looked up at the other occupants of the cramped cockpit. "I trust you heard that, people. It's time we stop fooling around. Snowy, inform the squadron we will either be boarding or sinking the Boghammers shortly. Have them designate Hellfire targets and stand by. Fire control, new mission to fire—2.75 rocket again. This time drop them right across the bow of the lead boat."

"Aye, aye, ma'am. Mission going out now!"

Another rocket flight salvoed and another wall of white water sprang out of the sea with a rippling roar. Seven clean columns of spray lanced into the sky, barring the path of the Union gunboats. The message was clear and concise. This is the end. Go farther and you die.

Bitterly, the Union flotilla commander looked over at his helmsman and made a slashing gesture across his throat. The helmsman closed his throttles and hit the kill buttons. The big outboards grumbled into silence and the Boghammer sank off the plane, wallowing to a halt. The other two craft in the flotilla followed suit a few moments later.

The only sound was the low swish of the waves and popping and creaking of the engines overheated by their futile thirty-mile crash run. That and the triumphant shriek of the American hovercraft as they closed in.

For the Union gunboat crews only one hope remained: the white flash of a bow wave on the southern horizon, closing fast.

✄◆

"*Carondelet,* you take the seaward boat. *Manassas,* you take the one inshore. We'll take the leader. Get your prisoners aboard and get your scuttling charges set with all possible speed."

"Rajah, lead."

"Will comply."

"Chris, what can you give me on the Union heavy unit coming in on us?"

"It's the big daddy, boss ma'am. The *Promise.* The flagship of the whole damn Union navy."

"Acknowledged. This is going to be . . . interesting."

The *Queen of the West* settled off cushion and reverted to swimmer mode, motoring up onto the drifting lead Boghammer. With the turbines stilled, the intermittent servo purr of the cockpit scarf ring could be heard as Chief Tehoa tracked the Union craft with his guns.

"We'll bring the prisoners aboard over the stern ramp," Amanda said, unplugging her headset from the interphone hardlink and jacking it into a remote belt unit. "Steamer, keep bow-on to the Union flagship as it closes with us and keep him covered with the pedestal mounts. Snowy, have the *Manassas* and *Carondelet* shift their Hellfire locks onto him as he comes into range. Open fire only if we're fired upon, and notify me when he closes to one klick. Hopefully, this guy will talk before he shoots."

"Will do." Lane nodded stolidly. The hover commander had donned a set of aviator's shades to shield his eyes from the rising sun. The mirrored lenses concealed whatever emotion he might be showing, but a thin veneer of sweat made his skin sheen in spite of the cool draft issuing from the air-conditioning ducts. "Think he might try and take us on, ma'am?"

"I don't know, Steamer," Amanda replied, starting aft for the ladderway. "We shall see, as the blind man said."

"Good luck, ma'am," Chief Tehoa called down from the gun saddle. The CPO's words, spoken from outside of the overhead hatch, had a hollow sound to them.

"Good luck to us all, Chief."

Down in the main bay, Stone Quillain had the boarding operation well in hand. As the *Queen* positioned in front of the Union boat, the hovercraft's stern guns, mounted at the head of her tailgate ramp, covered the Boghammer's crew. Two Marines augmented the grinning muzzles of the twin fifty-calibers, kneeling beside the mount with M4/M203 composite weapons leveled, a buckshot load in the grenade launcher, and a full magazine in the assault rifle.

"All personal weapons over the side!" Quillain's voice boomed out over the hovercraft's exterior loudspeakers. "Knives, everything, over the side, now!"

One minor blessing was that almost all the natives of Sierra Leone and Liberia spoke English. Sullenly, the Union men moved to obey.

"Okay, hands behind the head! Everybody! Nobody moves unless you are ordered. Now, one man move slowly to the bow and take our line. One man! Slow!"

Shortly the shovel-like bow of the Boghammer rode bumping and grating against the stern ramp.

"We're bringing you aboard one at a time! You in the bow, you first! Take it easy and nobody gets hurt! Screw around with us and you die!"

As each Union sailor came aboard, he was met by a grimly efficient processing line. Two Marines yanked the prisoner up the stern ramp. Two more spun the man around, twisted his arms behind his back, and applied a pair of disposable nylon handcuffs. The third pair conducted a brief but clinically thorough pat-down search, while the final team slammed the African down onto one of the fold-out passenger benches, securing him in place with a tightly cinched seat belt.

The transfer took only a matter of minutes.

"Looks like we're not having any problems here," Amanda commented as the last gunboatman was strapped down.

"We know our business," Quillain replied curtly. "Corporal, you ready to set the demos?"

"Aye, aye, sir." A youthful red-haired Marine stepped forward with an ominously bulging musette bag slung over one shoulder and a wad of gum cracking between his jaws.

"How you gonna rig her?"

The demolitions man shot an expert glance at the Boghammer bobbing astern. "Half a block of C4 in the bow and another under the steering station, tape a loop of det cord around the inside of the hull to fracture the flotation chambers," he said, incorporating a pop of his gum into his reply. "Use an M-60 igniter and a yard of M700 fuse to set her off. The weight of the engines'll pull her under. Five-minute job."

JAMES H. COBB

"Do it. And while you're aboard, take a look around for any papers and documents. Likely they dumped everything over the side, but you never can tell."

"Sure thing, sir."

The explosives-laden Marine took two fast steps down the stern ramp and jumped into the bow of the Boghammer, displaying the phlegmatic attitude of a day laborer bearing a lunch bucket.

"Captain," Steamer Lane's voice sounded in Amanda's headset, "the *Promise* has closed to four thousand yards and she's still standing on. We're tracking her in, and *Carondelet* and *Manassas* have her designated."

"Has she taken any hostile action?"

"Well, she's not shooting . . . yet."

"Right. I'm going topside."

"Topside, ma'am?"

"Yes. I'll have a little talking to do here presently."

Amanda climbed the midships access ladder to the *Queen's* weather deck. Making her way forward past the open gun tubs, she came up beside the cockpit, standing adjacent to Chief Tehoa in the gun ring.

The burly CPO nodded to her. "She's just about here, ma'am. Big son of a bitch, isn't she?"

"Uh-huh." Amanda nodded. "It's funny how they grow when their guns are aimed at you."

The Union flagship was less than a thousand yards away. The sea boiled under her sharp cutwater and a dense plume of diesel smoke trailed from her rakish stack.

The rising sun blasted at Amanda, and she felt the sweat gathering under her battle vest. Impatiently, she tore open the Velcro tabs of the body armor and shrugged it off, allowing it to thump to the deck behind her. She dropped her helmet on top of the pile and took a step forward, shaking out her hair and relishing the brush of the sea wind against her back. A few layers of Kevlar wouldn't be relevant against autocannon fire.

Behind her, she could hear the *whurr click, whurr click* of the pedestal mounts indexing as they tracked on target.

"I miss anything yet?" Stone Quillain inquired, coming up to stand on the other side of the cockpit dome. He'd left his shotgun below and now carried the stumpy launcher tube of a Predator antitank missile slung across his back. Apparently, if the shooting started, he did not intend to be just an onlooker.

Amanda concealed her smile. The Marine captain might carry a load of attitudes around with him, but some of them she could appreciate. "No," she replied, "but I think that the main show is about to begin."

Three hundred yards off, the *Promise* put her helm hard over, kicking her stern around. Water seethed under her aft quarters as her engines went to full reverse. Cutting across the bow of the *Queen of the West,* the corvette came to a stop broadside-on to the hovercraft. Gun tubes trained outboard as the Union ship brought her batteries to bear.

The conversion job that had turned the minesweep into a ship of the line had been crude but effective. The Emerson 30-millimeter guns forward had been part of her designed armament, while the twinned sets of Russian-made 57's aft had been add-ons. They were mounted in serviceable-looking gun tubs built into her well deck and aft superstructure, giving her a superposed field of fire astern. Union gun crews nestled behind the gun shields, and Amanda and her people were close enough to see the brassy gleam of shell clips inserted into breech mechanisms.

A voice whispered in Amanda's earphone. "Fire Control 1 to TACBOSS. If we have to cut loose on these guys, ma'am, hug the side of the cockpit and get aft of the pedestals as fast as you can. The muzzle blast of the thirties will be pretty bad where you're standing."

"Thanks for the tip, Danno," she replied into the boom mike. "You just concentrate on taking out those fifty-sevens."

"The cocksuckers are dead if they touch a trigger . . . begging your pardon, ma'am."

"I got the bow thirties, then," Tehoa commented conversationally. "What piece do you want, Captain Quillain?"

"I'll take the bridge," the Marine growled. Sinking onto one knee, he shifted the Predator launcher to his shoulder.

From across the hundred yards of water that separated the two vessels came the activating twang of a loud-hailer. "American gunboat, American gunboat, this is the captain of the warship *Promise* of the West African Union! You are violating Union Territorial waters and you are illegally holding members of the Union military prisoner. Release them immediately or we will open fire!"

Amanda dropped her hand to the communications link at her belt and accessed the *Queen's* own loudspeakers. "This is Captain Amanda Garrett, Commander of the U.S. Navy Task Group currently operating under the sanction of the United Nations African Interdiction Force. We request a clarification of the situation. Does a state of war currently exist between the West African Union and the nation of Guinea?"

There was a protracted silence. Amanda keyed the speaker access once more. "I say again. We request a clarification of the situation. Is the West African Union at war with the nation of Guinea?"

At last the reply sounded from the bridge wing of the corvette. "There is no war between the West African Union and Guinea. You are holding our sailors and naval craft illegally. You will release them at once!"

Amanda replied into her microphone, speaking the words she'd mentally rehearsed half a hundred times. "Negative, Captain. Be advised that the individuals we have taken into custody have been observed conducting hostile actions against the people and government of Guinea. We have absolute proof of this. If they have been acting under the orders of your government, then the West African Union is guilty of initiating acts of war against the nation of Guinea.

"If they have not been acting under the orders of your government, then they are pirates in the eyes of established international maritime law. As such, they are a matter of legitimate concern for all maritime nations. Again, I must ask, does a state of war exist between the West African Union and the Nation of Guinea?"

The grudging reply came back. "The Union is not at war with any nation."

Amanda took a deep breath and continued walking down her convoluted trail of justification. "Such being the case, these men are pirates under international maritime law. The United States Navy has exercised its right of hot pursuit to enter your territorial waters and place these criminals under arrest. They will be delivered to the civil authorities in Guinea for trial. We will now withdraw."

There was another pause, and then the voice called back from the Union bridge, a tinge of apprehension sounding within it. "If these criminals have been apprehended inside Union waters, this is a matter for Union law. We request that these criminals be turned over to us for judgment."

"Request denied. All further discussion on this matter should be brought up with the government of Guinea."

There was no response.

"Well now," Quillain commented quietly. "I guess it's pretty much raise or fold."

"Um-hmm." Amanda nodded, resting her hands on her hips. "If they fold, we've got our precedent established for operating inside their territorial waters. If they raise, well, then I guess we just play it out."

"This is Floater 1, cutting in," Christine's voice sounded in Amanda's headset. "Be advised that the *Promise* has just activated her main transmitter. Signal intelligence indicates that she's hailing Union Fleet Headquarters."

"Acknowledged, Floater." Amanda looked across at Tehoa and Quillain. "He doesn't like his hand. He's passing the buck."

Ben Tehoa shrugged. "Could be, ma'am, but then there's still many a damn fool who'll stick with a busted flush."

The cockpit side window at Amanda's feet slid open. "Captain, the squadron reports scuttling charges rigged aboard all the Bogs."

"Very good, Mr. Lane. Order the fuses ignited and the gunboats cast off. Have the squadron start backing away. Swimmer mode. Nice and steady."

"Aye, aye."

The deck underfoot began to vibrate softly as the *Queen*'s electric propellers cut water. The abandoned Boghammer bumped slowly down the seafighter's flank and then drifted into view, a marker in the widening gap between the hovercraft and the corvette. The larger Union vessel lay unmoving, taking no action but with her guns still leveled.

Quillain glanced at his wristwatch. "Not long now."

Abruptly, the flat crack of a small explosion sounded across the water, its echo mingling with the sound of two other nearby detonations. A puff of smoke and a spray of fragments jetted up from the Boghammer's belly. Filling in seconds, the gunboat's bow smoothly lifted into the air. As the demolitions man had predicted, the weight of its engines pulled it under the waves. The other Boghammers sank just as rapidly.

Smoke jetted from the *Promise*'s exhausts and propwash swirled behind her. The silhouette of the Union corvette narrowed as she started to come about.

Turning away to the south.

Quillain safetied the Predator round. "I guess the man just didn't have the cards," he said, getting to his feet. He slung the rocket launcher over his shoulder and glanced across at Amanda. "Not bad, ma'am," he said, giving the briefest of acknowledging nods.

"Thank you, Captain Quillain," she replied with all seriousness. "That's the nicest compliment I've had in a long time."

Inside the cockpit, Snowy Banks emitted a scream of exuberant relief and other cheers and rebel yells echoed up from inside the hull. Chief Tehoa lifted his powerful arms over his head, applauding, and Amanda stabbed her own fist into the sky in an acknowledgment of victory.

"TACBOSS to Squadron," she called into her headset. "All operational objectives completed! Close out the mission timeline! Let's go home!"

The exuberance continued to build on the voyage back to Floater 1, leaping contagiously over the radio links to the Mobile Offshore Base and to the other elements of the UNAFIN blockade force.

An EH 101 Merlin from the British Patrol Squadron and a dainty Sea Lynx from one of the French patrol frigates overflew the seafighter group as they approached Floater 1, the crew chiefs of the helicopters leaning far out of the side doors to wave a friendly acknowledgment.

Steamer Lane led his squadron mates in a high-speed flyby of their own.

Holding the tight echelon formation that was rapidly becoming their signature, the hovercraft ran a tight racetrack pattern around the Offshore Base before peeling off and heading for the ramp.

The rails of the platform itself were jammed with service personnel, waiting to greet the squadron. Backs were slapped as the hover crews and Marines disembarked, embraces were exchanged and female hands found themselves mobbed by enthusiastic male ratings moving in for a congratulatory kiss.

Amanda was granted the dignity due a squadron commander as she stepped down from the *Queen,* accepting the more reserved congratulations and handshakes from the task group officers. She was grateful for the space, suspecting that soon, when the last of the adrenaline surge wore off, she was going to be very, very tired.

There was one exception, however. Christine Rendino met her at the top of the *Queen's* ramp with a joyful hug. "Well, you pulled off another one."

"So far so good, anyway. Has Admiral MacIntyre been advised?"

"I've been feeding him regular updates throughout the operation. I don't know what time it is back in Hawaii, but he wants to talk to you as soon as you get in."

"Okay, I'll take it in my quarters. Then I'm going to get in the shower and cheat on the water rationing for ten minutes. Then I intend to lie down and pass out for about two days."

Steamer stepped forward at those words. "Begging your pardon on that, Captain, but there's a matter the squadron needs your assistance with if you don't mind. It'll just take a second."

"Of course, Steamer. What's the problem?"

"This way ma'am."

Lane led her around to the side of the hovercraft hangar. Amanda noted that the majority of PGAC-1's personnel were gathered there, a generalized expression of grinning anticipation on all hands. She also noted a tarp shrouding something on the side of the hangar.

"It's like this, ma'am," Steamer went on. "We're a new outfit, and we don't have an official squadron insignia yet. We didn't have a really good idea for one, either, until something you said on your first day with us caught the attention of Lieutenant Banks over there."

Steamer nodded in the direction of a half-excited, half-nervous Snowy. "She passed the idea around and we built on it some. Now we want you to have a look at it."

Someone yanked on the corner of the tarp, dropping it to the deck. An instant later Amanda exploded, almost doubling over with helpless laughter.

It was a unit badge, four feet tall and shield shaped. Across its crested top, it bore a double-leveled title:

```
PGAC SQUADRON 1
THE THREE LITTLE PIGS
```

The main body of the badge bore the image of three Disneyesque but ferociously tusked African warthogs surfing into a beach on the back of a *Queen*-class seafighter. All three wore white navy "Dixie cup" hats, while one also sported a piratical black eye patch and a foul-looking stogie cigar. Around the bottom of the shield ran the motto "Now, what's this about some damn wolf?"

"We didn't want to show this to you until we had at least one good operation under our belts," Lane continues. "We kind of felt we had to earn the right to it. What do you think, ma'am?"

Amanda straightened, wiping the tears from her eyes. She looked around into the faces of the task force personnel, of her people, and felt a sense of belonging to something that hadn't been there for some time. It felt good.

"I love it," she said, lifting her voice. "Badge authorized, but with one warning. The first person in this outfit who refers to me as 'The Old Sow' is in a lot of trouble."

Mamba Point Hotel
Monrovia, West African Union   1115 Hours, Zone Time; June 8, 2007

The meeting was a formality. But then, formality constitutes ninety-nine percent of the diplomatic process. Formalities, protocols, procedures, the endless dialogues that form the overburden within which rests the occasional precious nugget of progress.

Vavra Bey had little hope of finding such a treasure today.

"We protest the illegal intrusion of United Nations military units into our territorial waters." Premier General Belewa spoke the words, stone featured. "This was a rank violation of our national sovereignty and a flagrant attempt at international bullying."

"The Islamic Republic of Algeria protests this act of neocolonial barbarity as well!" Ambassador Umamgi spat. "We will not tolerate such acts of aggression against an ally!"

They were seated in a different meeting room within the hotel this day, one with a circular conference table in its center. Belewa, Bey, and the Algerian ambassador sat equidistant around the table, their staff seated against the walls behind them. So established when the U.N. team had arrived, Bey pondered the possible, subtle meaning of the talk's setting. Were the Algerians demanding a bigger role for themselves in the crisis? Or was Belewa reminding the U.N. representative that he did not stand entirely alone?

Vavra Bey honed her instincts to their finest edge.

"Gentlemen," she began, "there is no doubt that aggression has taken place. However, the question of aggression, by whom, against whom, is seen in a different light by the Security Council. It is felt by the Council that the actions of the UNAFIN force elements involved were correct and justified, given the evidence recovered. This evidence being indicative of an active military campaign launched against the nation of Guinea by the West African Union."

"We deny these allegations," Belewa growled. The big African's elbows rested on the tabletop and his fingers were interlaced in a doubled fist that half concealed the scowl on his face.

"Do you deny these, General?" Vavra Bey swept her hand over the tabletop, indicating the photographs and photocopied documents scattered across it. "Arms and military stores bearing the markings of the West African Union's armed forces, captured documents bearing the signatures of senior Union naval and army officers, battle plans and reports on insurgency operations—"

"Lies!" Umamgi exploded. Half standing, he leaned over his section of the table. "We have examined these documents and we have found them to be blatant fabrications produced by Western intelligence organizations. We refuse to acknowledge them!"

Bey noted the jump of a small muscle under the curve of Belewa's jaw and the momentary narrowing of his eyes. The African took a deliberate breath before speaking. "The Union admits the possibility that some of its citizens, even perhaps some of its military personnel, may have joined with rebel factions within Guinea in acts against that nation's government. Segments of our population have strong feelings about the corruption and injustice rampant in that country. However, I again categorically deny that my government has ordered any hostile acts performed against our neighboring state."

"And what of those men, General?" Bey asked softly. "The thirty-four Union nationals currently being held by the government of Guinea. Do you deny them as well?"

The muscle in Belewa's throat twitched again. "The West African Union is always concerned about the welfare of its citizens, wherever they may be. It is our hope that the United Nations might be able to assist us in arranging for their return. The ambassador from Guinea has been most . . . truculent in this matter."

Vavra Bey lifted her shoulders in a shrug. "General, if indeed these men are acting on their own recognizance, there is nothing I can do. As you have said, no recognized state of war exists between the Union and Guinea. Thus, these men cannot be classified as prisoners of war. Accordingly, their fate now rests in the hands of the civil courts of Guinea. Your men will stand trial for murder, piracy, and terrorism. I fear that the penalties handed down will be most severe."

Bey held Belewa's gaze with her own. "Perhaps if the West African Union would accept at least some responsibility for the actions of these individuals, grounds might be found for U.N. intervention on their behalf."

The General's eyes were brown ice. "There is nothing more to be said on this matter."

"As you wish."

Bey removed a cream-colored folder from the briefcase at her side, its cover bearing the embossed silver seal of the United Nations. Deliberately she placed it in the center of the conference table. "As you no doubt have been advised by your ambassador to the U.N., the Security Council has elected to act upon the evidence of Union aggression recovered by the United Nations African Interdiction Force. The trade embargo against the West African Union has been expanded to include all goods and materials except for food and medical stores. Also, the UNAFIN rules of engagement have been formally amended to permit operations inside of Union territorial waters at the discretion of the UNAFIN commanders, should such actions be necessary in support of the blockade."

"Any further violation of our territorial sovereignty will be met by armed force!"

"Then that will be at your discretion, General." Vavra Bey closed the latches of her briefcase with a decisive snap.

Mobile Offshore Base, Floater 1 1721 Hours, Zone Time; June 8, 2007

My dearest Arkady:

Well, we've pulled it off. The first go-round, at any rate. Upon reflection, I've decided that I was lucky to be dumped into this command in the middle of a crisis. Total immersion! Sink or swim! I never had time to think about all of the things I might be doing wrong.

I've been lucky in another area as well. As with our old team aboard the Duke, I've got another bunch of exceptionally good people to work with. I hope I can be worthy of their potential. I've just got to remember that I have to adapt to the rules of the tribe and the environment. If I can manage that, I think I'll be okay.

We've cleaned out Belewa's boat hides inside of Guinea and, surprisingly, no one's complained about the rather unorthodox way we went about it. The local government is just relieved to have the pressure off for a while. Our major concern, now that we have the Union kicked out, is with not letting them sneak back in.

We're running a barrier patrol now and I'm going out with it daily (or nightly—that seems to be when most of the action is around here). I just got back in from one a short time ago. I'll be darned if I'm going to let myself develop a "squadron commander spread" by sitting around on this barge all of the time.

Even after taking out the hide network, we're still spread awfully thin. Too few hulls to cover too many miles of coast. My Three Little PGs are fast, but not fast enough. (By the way, check the attached picture file. It's their new squadron patch. Unknowingly, I had a hand in designing it.) I'm worried about our ability to execute a fast response should anything blow out along the line.

It's a heck of a thing for a good surface-warfare officer to have to say, but I wish I had you and your helos here. And that, love, is for any number of reasons. I think about our last night together in the cockpit of the Seeadler, *usually just before I go to sleep at night. I hope you think of it as well, and I also hope that we have the chance to finish that conversation soon. We still have a great deal to say on the subject.*

Be well and be happy,
Amanda

P.S. Chris sends her regards.

Off the Guinea Coast
One Half Mile Southwest of Point Sallatouk   2330 Hours, Zone Time; June 11, 2007

There was an odd feel to the way *Queen of the West* rode the low, oily swells. Drifting off cushion and powered down, there was a slight but decided hesitation to the hovercraft's roll. Amanda idly analyzed the phenomenon and concluded it must be caused by the drag of the deflated plenum skirt beneath the hull.

Steamer Lane slouched in his command chair, staring out into the darkness, one hand resting on the propulsor pod controls. Intermittently his fingers would move and the *Queen* would tremble slightly as he poured a shot of power to the propellers, deftly holding the seafighter precisely on station.

As usual, the PGAC had the inshore post. Glancing at her tactical display, Amanda could see the Patrol Craft *Sirocco* circling slowly in her endless racetrack pattern six miles farther offshore. And six miles beyond her, the French corvette *La Fleurette* loitered out in deep water.

Odds were, though, if there was going to be any action, it would come here, creeping in along the coastline.

Amanda arose from her seat and stretched as well as she could in the cramped confines of the cockpit. "How's it looking, Snowy?" she inquired, peering up through the overhead hatch.

"It's a beautiful night out here, ma'am." Seated on the hatch rim, the hovercraft's copilot was a silhouette against the stars. She lowered her low-light binoculars and a faint flash of pale green light played across her pretty farm girl's features. "Nothing's happening except for a couple of fires over on the beach. Fishermen, I'd guess."

"You think we may have some trouble coming, Captain?" Steamer asked from the controls.

"I'm not sure." Amanda leaned forward to gaze out the windscreen, resting her elbow on the back of the pilot's chair. There was just enough skyglow to differentiate between the sea, land, and sky. "For the past couple of days, I've been expecting some kind of a move from our friend Belewa."

"I dunno. We kicked his ass pretty good back there, ma'am."

"That's just the point, Steamer. We've hurt him badly by eliminating his coastal bases inside of Guinea. He's going to want those bases back again." Amanda's eyes narrowed as she again sought for the thought patterns of her opponent. "He also knows that we're good now. But he's not sure yet just how good. I think he's bound to try at least one more probe to find out."

Amanda straightened and slapped the back of the chair. "At any rate, I'm going below for a cup of tea. Can I bring you two anything?"

"No, thanks, ma'am. I'm good to mid rats."

"Same here, Captain," Snowy called down from the hatchway.

Amanda started down the ladder into the main hull. "Okay. Yell if we have any developments."

The side hatches and stern ramp were closed against the possibility of a seventh wave, making the seafighter's interior an enclosed little world, dimly blue lit by the battle lights. A diesel auxiliary purred and air rustled in the air-conditioning ducts. Sailors and Marines, those on duty and off, kept their voices low.

In the port-side passage a cutthroat game of six-handed Spades raged quietly among the auxiliary gunners, while over by the open hatch of the port power room, Scrounger Catlin lay stretched out on the deck, her eyes closed and her head resting on a bunched life jacket, a whisper of new swing leaking from the headset of her portable CD player. In the central bay, half of a Marine rifle team intently studied an old issue of *Guns and Ammo*, while seated next to him on the fold-out bench, his partner mused over Steinbeck.

Other hands availed themselves of the opportunity to catch up on their sack time. All four bunks in the little berthing space were occupied, while back aft, dozing Marines sprawled in the inflatable miniraider.

Gunner's Mate Daniel O'Roark had the scanner's watch at the fire-control station under the cockpit. Grimly hunkering over his console, he alternated between the radar and the low-light television, systematically sweeping the horizon.

Amanda smiled. She'd sensed right about the boy. Ever since that misfire incident, he'd been pushing hard to make up for his error and to prove himself. He was going to be one of the good ones.

Circling the cockpit ladder, Amanda ducked into the little wardroom. Stone Quillain and Ben Tehoa were seated at the wedge-shaped mess table, nursing mugs of coffee. The CPO also had a pen in hand and a half-filled sheet of writing paper in front of him.

"Catching up on your correspondence, Chief?" Amanda inquired, pouring water into a mug and setting it in the microwave.

"Yes, ma'am. A letter to my daughters."

Amanda removed the steaming cup and dunked in a tea bag. She'd forgotten to lay in a stock of her preferred Earl Grey for this cruise and had been making due with PX generic. "You know we do have all-hands e-mail access on the barge."

"Oh, sure. That's how my wife and I take care of the routine stuff when I'm on deployment. But, you know, for my personal letters, I still like to use paper." The burly chief grinned self-consciously. "It makes it a little more special."

"I can understand that," Amanda replied, sliding in around the table. She still had a treasured stash of letters from her father safe in her desk at home, mementos of his days at sea. Those and a few from some of the other men who had been special in her life. Electronic communications could be convenient, but also soulless. She made a mental note to dig out some writing paper of her own next time Arkady was due a note.

"Have I ever shown you a picture of my family, Commander?"

"No, Chief. Not yet."

Tehoa dug a battered wallet out of his hip pocket. Flipping it open, he passed it to Amanda. The photograph was as worn and salt-stained as the wallet, but Amanda could make out the stocky, serene Samoan woman and the two little girls. The girls were perhaps six and eight years old, each with large, dark, and sober eyes and glossy black hair.

"They're beautiful, Chief," Amanda said with all honesty. "All three of them."

"I'm not going to argue, ma'am," Tehoa replied proudly, restoring his wallet to his pocket.

Stone Quillain had been silent over at his corner of the table. However, Amanda was aware that the Marine's eyes had been upon her throughout the exchange, studying her with that grim focus of his.

As an attractive woman, Amanda Garrett was used to being looked at by men. Given the right environment and circumstances, she could even enjoy the experience. However, she suspected that overt sensuality had little to do with Captain Quillain's consideration of her.

Ever since the Marine had joined the task force, Amanda had been aware that she was being minutely analyzed, her actions gauged and her performance as a commanding officer judged. And, as far as she was concerned, he had every right to do so, as did anyone else serving under her command. Just as she had the responsibility of trying to live up to their highest expectations.

Stone Quillain would be far from the first person to question her abilities during her career in the Navy. He'd be far from the last, as well. And having to prove yourself to someone every now and again is not necessarily a bad thing. It kept a person from getting sloppy with themselves.

Amanda took a deliberate sip of her tea.

"Begging your pardon, Commander." Quillain spoke up from across the table. "But I notice that you aren't packing an issue handgun. What kind of a piece is that, anyway?"

"A Ruger SP 101." She snapped open the retaining tab on the nylon cross-draw holster clipped to her belt and drew the small stainless-steel revolver. Thumbing the cylinder release, she flipped the little weapon open and passed it across to the Marine. "Technically, it's a five-shot .357 Magnum, but I've only used .38 Special in it."

Frowning, Quillain dumped the shells out into his hand; rolling them between his fingers, he sought for the feel of tarnished brass. Aiming the revolver at the battle light on the overhead, he spun the cylinder with his thumb, one-eyeing the chambers in an instinctive inspection for wear or dirt.

Wryly Amanda realized that she was being judged once more—this time for the ultimate Marine sin of neglecting a weapon.

"How come you went back to a wheel gun?" Quillain inquired with curiosity.

There was a yarn behind her choice. Unfortunately, it was one that still made Amanda feel like something of a ninny. The Marine looked on expectantly. She sensed he was genuinely trying to get an understanding of her through something he understood. He deserved the truth.

"It's a long story," she began, "going back about ten years to when I was still a lieutenant junior grade. The maritime drug-interdiction program was a major concern back then, involving assets from both the Navy and the Coast

JAMES H. COBB

Guard. As an aspect of this, a certain number of naval officers were given the opportunity to cross-deck over to the Coasties to serve a makee-learn cruise aboard one of their cutters. It seemed like a good way to get off the beach for a while, so I volunteered.

"At any rate, one day off the coast of Baja California, we made an intercept on what appeared to be an Ecuadorian tuna clipper. I was the duty boarding officer that watch, and so I led a four-man inspection team across in a Zodiac to give her the once-over.

"Although we didn't know it at the time, we'd hit the jackpot. The trawler was a cartel drug transport carrying several tons of raw morphine base. She was also carrying several senior cartel gunmen who were not interested in casually surrendering."

Chief Tehoa had put aside his letter and was listening as well.

"I started getting the feel of something wrong almost the second we were aboard the clipper. Nobody was on deck except for the one sailor who met us at the boarding ladder, and he was as nervous as all get-out. He kept trying to get us to go belowdecks or into the deckhouse and out of sight of our people on the cutter.

"I didn't buy it. I had two of my boarding hands cover the South American while I and the other two men started to search and clear the clipper's weather decks. I was moving pretty fast as I ducked around the corner of the deckhouse, and I practically ran into another of the cutter's crew, this one with a loaded SKS carbine.

"This brings us to my choice of side arms. At the time I was carrying an issue M9 Beretta automatic, and frankly, the damn thing intimidated the daylights out of me."

Amanda sighed and gave a deprecating shrug. "Don't get me wrong. The Beretta is a fine weapon. Only, you do have to know what you're doing with it. Now, I know my way around rifles and shotguns all right. My father taught me how to shoot while I was in grade school and he bought me a twenty-gauge Browning double barrel on my sixteenth birthday so we could go to the trap range together. However, I've never had the chance to really get good with a handgun. I had the basics at Annapolis and I shoot my qualification every month, but at the time I was, and still am, a long way from being any kind of expert.

"I yelled a warning to my backup team and shoved my pistol into the gunman's face. Unfortunately, I couldn't coerce the damn thing into going bang! I'd left the safety on. And by the time I could sort out the safety catch from all of the decocking levers and magazine releases and other assorted instrumentation on the Beretta's frame, I'd been shot."

SEA FIGHTER**153**

Quillain lifted an eyebrow. "How big a piece did you catch?"

Amanda's right hand instinctively came up to her left shoulder and the scar she could feel through the thin fabric of her shirt. "Not too bad. In and out and a broken collarbone."

"What happened next, Captain?" Tehoa inquired.

"Not much. My backup team did for the gunman with their M-16s, and they got me out of there."

Actually there had been quite a bit more. A savage firefight on the clipper's decks with the remainder of the cartel crew, an assault on the bridge of the drug transport, and several blood-soaked and agonizing minutes until help could arrive from the cutter.

However, in Amanda's opinion, none of that was really germane to the point she wished to make. "Anyway, the first thing I did after getting out of the hospital was to go out and buy the simplest, most reliable, and most totally idiot-proof side arm I could find. Some people who knew their business suggested the Ruger, and I've been carrying it ever since."

Quillain thumbed the shells back into the little revolver. Closing it, he passed the gun back across the table. "Yeah. Just about everything Ruger makes is hell for sturdy. I'll give 'em that."

The big man hesitated for a moment, then cleared his throat. "Thing is, if you figure on staying with Special Operations for a while, you might want to think about getting yourself somethin' a little heavier. Five rounds of .38 FMJ might be okay for standing a gangway watch in San Diego, but it's not going to do you much good in a serious firefight."

"That might be a good idea, Stone," Amanda replied with careful casualness, settling the revolver back in its holster. "What would you suggest?"

The Marine went thoughtful for a moment. "I'd say your best bet would an old Model 1911A Colt .45. There's still a few of them rattling around in the arsenals."

It was Amanda's turn to lift an eyebrow. "A Colt .45? Lord, I'd never be able to handle a hip howitzer like that."

"Oh hell! Yes you could! I know plenty of female shooters who can really hit a lick with the 1911." There was a growing animation in the big man's voice as his interest grew. "You don't have that big fat two-by-four grip you get with the Beretta, and the weight of the piece absorbs the recoil. And if you want to talk stopping power, that old .45 hardball round has just about as much as you're ever going to need."

"Think you could get me one to try out?" she asked.

Quillain nodded. "I'd guess so. I'll talk to my company armorer. He knows a few people here and there."

It was good enough to simply be having a genuine conversation with Quillain, but he might also be making a valid point. "Okay," Amanda conceded, "but I'm still going to need some instruction on it. Like I said, I'm no Annie Oakley, but I do know that the .45 is another expert's gun."

"Anything my top sergeant doesn't know about the 1911 Colt isn't worth knowing. When they finally made us convert all the way over to the Beretta, Tallman cried for three days, then went out and got drunk. He can set you up."

Quillain hesitated for a moment, looking down at the tabletop and his half-empty coffee cup. When he looked up, there was a wry acceptance on his angular features. "And I figure I can help you some, too, if you need it."

Amanda resisted the urge to grin. Sometimes you can win a battle when you least expect to. She nodded to the Marine. "Thank you, Stone. You've got a deal."

"Hey, Captain Garrett," Steamer Lane's voice rang down urgently from the cockpit. "Operations wants you on the horn. We got action!"

Amanda scrambled out from behind the mess table, leaving her mug abandoned at her place.

Topside, Snowy had dropped down out of the overhead hatch and was back in the copilot's seat, beginning the power-up checklists. Steamer passed back Amanda's command headset. "Tactical display indicates we have a single slow-moving target just crossing the line into Guinea's territorial waters. Operations has the dope."

"Thanks, Steamer." Amanda clamped on the earphones. "Operations, this is Royalty. What do you have for us?"

Christine Rendino was on the other end of the circuit. Somehow she always managed to be there when Amanda was out on station. "We've got that probe you've been expecting, boss ma'am. A standard Union three-boat Boghammer patrol just executed a sweep up to the Guinea border. Two of the Bogs turned back; one didn't. He's now half a klick over the line and is still northbound, tiptoeing along just outside of the surf. Estimated speed, five knots. He's not showing any lights and he's minimizing his wake. I have the barrier Predator orbiting him at Angels twenty-five, and I do not think this guy knows we've got him spotted."

"Good work, Chris! Stay on him! Steamer, sound General Quarters! Stand by to intercept!"

✕◆

"Marines, saddle up! Boarding drill!" Stone Quillain yelled the words more out of habit than of necessity. Around him, both his people and the Navy gun teams donned helmets and strapped on battle vests.

The *Queen* was under way, not howling along on her air cushion but slinking through the night on her silent auxiliaries. To port and starboard, the mid-ships hatches slammed open, the stumpy barrels of the grenade launchers training outboard. Back aft, the tail ramp dropped with a hissing moan of hydraulics, the slender barrels of the stern machine guns leveling at the night. The pool of air-conditioned cool within the hovercraft vented out into the darkness, replaced by an inrush of moist tropical heat intermingled with wisps of salt spray.

"All right, ladies and gentlemen," Amanda Garrett's quiet voice issued from the overhead speakers. "Here's the situation. We have a single Union Boghammer advancing up the coast, presumably on a reconnaissance mission. As he's heading in our direction, we're going to let him come to us. We will attempt an ambush and capture. Hopefully, we can take him without a shootout. However, stand by for any eventuality. We will keep you posted as the situation develops."

The *Queen's* Marine squad marshaled at their station, seated with their backs against the bulkhead in the main bay, their weapons ready at hand. Quillain was cognizant of the twelve helmeted heads turned in his direction, the twelve sets of eyes watching for their company commander's cue on how to react.

Quillain faked a yawn. "Looks like it's gonna be the swabbies' show for a while. Somebody give me a poke if they need us for anything."

Claiming the end seat on the bench, Quillain slouched down and shut his eyes, his K-pot helmet in his lap and the Mossberg propped against his leg. Like the yawn, the attempt at sleep was a charade. He had the light headset of his PRC radio jacked into the hovercraft's interphone system, and he maintained his situational awareness by monitoring the tense voices on the command channel.

"Bog holding course, steering three six zero. Speed still five knots. You guys have a ten-knot rate of closure. Separation two miles . . . Thanks, Chris . . . Steamer, this guy looks like he's still right off the surf line. Is that going to be a problem? . . . Depends, ma'am. You want to run him up on the beach or take him offshore? . . . Let's try and take him offshore . . . Fire Control. Do we have him on our radar? . . . Affirmative, ma'am. Range now three thousand yards, and I think I have a visual . . . Okay, Danno. Do you confirm target ID? . . . Yeah, that's him, Captain. Confirming visual. We got a Bog . . . All right. Gunners, get me Hellfire locks on this guy. If he runs, I want a fast kill on him. . . . Roger, ma'am, Hellfires on the pedestals. We got locks. We are tracking. . . . Range two thousand . . . Range one thousand five hundred . . . Let him come in, guns. . . . Aye, aye, ma'am. Range one thousand. Come to

Poppa. . . . We got position, Captain. Target bearing zero off the bow . . . Okay, Steamer. Go to station keeping. Kill our wake. Let him make final closure. . . . Roger. Range six-fifty . . . Arm flare tubes, we'll take him at five hundred. . . . Okay, a little more . . . Okay, stand by . . . Flares now!"

The flare mortars on the weather deck of the *Queen of the West* tonked hollowly, hurling a cluster of sputtering projectiles into the sky. An instant later and the wave crests beyond the stern ramp burned white, reflecting the glare of the burning magnesium charges.

"UNION GUNBOAT!" Amanda Garrett's voice was that of an angry goddess, thundering from the hovercraft's loudspeakers. "THIS IS THE UNITED STATES NAVY OPERATING UNDER UNITED NATIONS MANDATE! YOU HAVE MADE AN UNAUTHORIZED ENTRY INTO THE TERRITORIAL WATERS OF GUINEA. HEAVE TO AND PREPARE TO BE BOARDED. I SAY AGAIN, HEAVE TO AND PREPARE TO BE BOARDED! IF YOU RESIST, WE WILL OPEN FIRE!"

Quillain sat forward and donned his helmet. "Look alive, boys! We got business!" Keying the "Touch-to-Talk" pad of his headset, he spoke into the microphone. "Cockpit, this is the boarding team. How we looking?"

"The ambush appears successful," Amanda replied warily. "They've killed their engines, and they're just sitting there about four hundred yards out."

The flare launchers belched out another salvo, renewing the flickering false day outside.

"REMOVE THE AMMUNITION BELTS FROM YOUR MACHINE GUNS AND DROP ALL SMALL ARMS OVER THE SIDE. RAISE YOUR HANDS AND KEEP THEM RAISED. DO NOT RESIST AND YOU WILL NOT BE HARMED."

"Okay, Stone." Normally modulated, Amanda's voice returned to his headset. "We're moving in now. Standard procedure. We'll take them aboard over the tail ramp."

"Aye, aye, ma'am." Quillain lifted his thumb off the key. "Marines, stand by to receive prisoners! Covering team, load buckshot and take your stations! By the drill!"

The *Queen* was maneuvering again, closing in. The safety webbing across the mouth of the tailgate was dropped and the two Marine grenadiers knelt on either side of the stern gun mount, slamming juice-can-size shotgun shells into the lower breeches of their M-4/M-203 combo weapons.

The Navy gunner on the stern twin fifty looked over at Quillain. "How do you want this illuminated, sir?"

"We'll do it white light, son. Wait till the Captain gives the word, then hit 'em with your beams. Once we illuminate, you keep it right in their eyes, you hear?"

"Aye, aye, sir."

The second flight of flares sank into the sea, streaking the ocean's surface with a brief pattern of wave shadows before guttering out entirely. The *Queen* sluggishly began to come about, bringing her stern in line with the Boghammer. Quillain felt his muscles bunch. This was the moment of greatest vulnerability, with the seafighter able only to bring its stern guns and the Marine's small arms to bear on the potential threat.

A slender form in a battle vest came up beside Quillain. "How does it look?" Amanda asked.

"Let you know in a second, Captain. We clear to illuminate?'

"Light them up."

Thanks to Scrounger Caitlin's deft talents at acquisitioning, a pair of quarter-million-candlepower mercury iodide driving lights had been wired into the stern fifty-caliber mount. Now the gunner switched them on, sending twin sword blades of piercing silver light slashing through the darkness. They came to rest on the low gray-green hull of the Union gunboat.

The seafighter backed slowly toward the drifting Boghammer. As the smaller craft drew closer, more detail could be made out. The gunboat rode broadside-on. As per instruction, the belts had been removed from its heavy machine-gun mount and its twin barrels drooped down into the hull. There were no lighter weapons in sight, and the six-man Union crew sat in a grim row, their hands behind their heads and facing the American vessel.

The distance continued to lessen—fifty yards . . . forty . . .

Abruptly a warning switch tripped inside Quillain's head. "Shit! They're screwing with us!" He whipped the Mossberg up and in line, jacking a flechette round into the chamber. "I need more shooters back here!"

Marines surged to their company commander's side, Squad Automatic Weaponsmen with their light machine guns braced on their hips, riflemen with their carbines leveled. Bolts slammed back and fire selectors snapped over to full autofire. Amanda Garrett was respectfully, but firmly, brushed aside and over against Quillain as the tailgate became a solid wall of leveled firepower.

"Target up! If any of those sumbitches move, I mean if they so much as twitch, hose 'em! Captain Garrett, heave to! Stop closing with the Bog!"

Without an instant's hesitation, Amanda repeated the order into her lip mike. Seamlessly, command of the operation had passed to Stone Quillain.

The soft thrumming of the propellers stopped, and the only sound was the soft creaking of the hull and the occasional scuffling shift of a boot as a tense

Marine rode with the slow pitching of the deck. The crew of the Boghammer continued to stare into the blaze of the gun lights.

"Okay!" Quillain relied on his own drill field bellow over the seafighter's loud-hailer system. "Real easy now, drop the hand grenades over the side! Don't die stupid!"

The Union captain screamed a wordless cry. Six arms whipped back, the ugly iron spheres held concealed behind the crewmen's heads coming into view.

There was no order yelled in the *Queen's* central bay. A dozen automatic weapons simply cut loose in a single massed roar of devastation, the spray of ejecting shell casings sparkling in the glare of the muzzle blasts. The jackhammering thunder of the dual Browning heavies segued with the faster venomous snarl of the SAWs and the chopping crackle of the M-4s. The grenade launchers crashed out their antipersonnel charges. Then, with their big tubes emptied, the grenadiers flipped over to carbine mode, pouring full thirty-round magazines of 5.56mm after the handfuls of buckshot. Stone Quillain held down the trigger of the Mossberg and jacked the slide, pumping shotgun hulls through the action with a speed that nearly matched that of the full automatics, the distinctive bellow of the 12-gauge blurring into the firestorm.

The Fiberglas gunwales of the Union gunboat shattered under the impact of hundreds of projectiles, and so did its crew. The volley of hand grenades were never cast as the Union sailors writhed and crumpled under the raking storm of high-velocity metal. The hand grenades couldn't comprehend their convulsive change of destiny, however. As they fell from nerveless hands, safety levers flicked away and fuses ignited.

A crewman toppled over the low railing of the Boghammer, following the grenade he had lost over the side. An instant later, he was hurled grotesquely back into the boat, bounced off the surface of the sea by the underwater detonation of the hand bomb. The other grenades exploded in turn, gutting the gunboat from bow to stern, shredding any remnants of life left aboard. The fiery secondary blasts of the outboard fuel cells finished the job, turning the little craft into a shallow drifting dish filled with blood and fire.

The guns aboard the seafighter fell silent. Someone swore thickly as they dug a hot cartridge case out of an open shirt collar.

Quillain glanced at Amanda Garrett. She looked away from the funeral pyre blazing off the stern ramp, her eyes closed and her teeth clinched. Then, as Quillain watched, her eyes opened and she looked up again, instinct suppressed and control restored. Deliberately she stared at the sinking gunboat.

Quillain nodded slowly. If you're responsible for having it done, you'd better be able to look at it afterward.

"That didn't work out so well," she said, only the faintest trace of unsteadiness lingering in her voice. "We'll have to try a different approach next time."

"I guess so, Skipper," Quillain agreed, stripping reloads out of the shell carrier strapped to the Mossberg's buttstock. "We'll come up with something better."

She looked across at him curiously. "How did you know about the grenades?"

"Didn't know for certain-sure." Quillain paused to dunk the first round into the shotgun's magazine. "Only, if I'd been in their spot, that's what I would have tried."

Mobile Offshore Base, Floater 1   **0612 Hours, Zone Time; June 12, 2007**

With a final blast of her drive propellers, the *Queen of the West* hunched over the edge of the platform access ramp. Easing into her hangar, she sank down on her crumpled skirts with a tired metallic sigh. Leaning out of his cockpit window, Steamer Lane held up a single finger to the waiting service crew, passing the word that there would be another kill silhouette to paint.

The Marines shuffled stiffly down the stern ramp, en route first to the gun-cleaning racks and then to the showers and the bunkrooms. The stern gunners followed, lugging their heavy twin-mount .50 along stretcher-fashion. The shipboard turbine techs and gunner's mates sleepily had words with their opposite numbers in the service details, checking the PMS cards for the day's maintenance package and discussing systems glitches that had cropped up during the previous night's patrol.

As Amanda and the hover pilots disembarked, a runner waited for her at the foot of the ramp. "Captain Garrett, Commander Rendino requests your presence in the briefing center."

"Very well, I'm on my way," Amanda glanced at her companions. "Steamer, it looks like you and Snowy have to handle the postmission."

"No problem," the hover commander nodded in reply. "We'll take care of it, Skipper."

"Thanks, Steamer."

"Sure thing. A good hunt last night, Captain."

"Good hunters, Commander."

As Steamer and his exec turned away, Stone Quillain started down the stern ramp, shotgun slung over one shoulder. As he strode past, he gave Amanda a quick nod and a lessening of his usual scowl. Amanda nodded back, trying to contain her grin. The SOC Marine still wasn't exactly outgoing, but progress had been made on that front as well.

Slinging her pistol belt over her shoulder, she started for the briefing center.

Entering the trailer, Amanda found the wall flatscreens filled with charts of the border region between the West African Union and Côte d'Ivoire, what the Gold Coast Africans referred to as "Frenchside." She also found Christine Rendino and a solidly built, red-haired man in a flight suit studying the maps intently.

"Hi, boss ma'am. I don't think you've had the chance to meet Commander Evan Dane yet. He commands the 847th Provisional, the British patrol helicopter squadron supporting UNAFIN."

"No, I haven't, Chris, but I've been wanting the opportunity." Amanda set her pistol belt onto the center table and extended her hand to the British pilot. "It's always a pleasure to work with the Royal Navy, Commander."

"It's our pleasure, Captain Garrett," Dane replied, exchanged a firm handclasp. "Damn nice work you people did on those boat hides. It was about time somebody started to drive the bloody train around here."

"We were lucky things worked out as well as they did." With her hands resting on her hips, Amanda studied the map displays. "What's up?"

"A little side project Commander Dane and I have been working on," Christine replied. "While you and the Little Pigs have been trashing the Union's boat hides, we've been trying to do something about the Union's maritime smuggling line into Côte d'Ivoire."

"Can you confirm they have one established?"

"God, fa'sure! Over Frenchside, the coastal waters look like the Ventura freeway on Friday night."

Dane nodded his agreement. "I can show you hours of low-light video showing *pirogues* and *pinasses* crossing the line into Union waters after dark, mostly loaded with oil drums."

Christine nodded soberly. "The West African Union has established a network of agents alone the Côte d'Ivoire coast. They've recruited a cadre of seamen from among the fishing villages and they're financing and coordinating an organized program of petroleum smuggling with the intent of breaking the U.N. trade embargo."

"How did you pick up on this operation, Chris?"

The intel shrugged. "Through the network of agents I've set up in the coastal villages, of course."

"I should have known. How much are they moving?"

"Thousands of gallons a week, at least." Christine crossed her arms and leaned back against the table edge. "Probably not enough to meet the Union's overall needs, but fa'sure enough to stretch their reserves out for a few more months. And the volume's growing."

"I didn't think the Union would need all that much oil," Amanda mused.

"It's all relative. Probably what we burn in one L.A. rush hour would last them for a year. The thing is, they still have to have some. More than two-thirds of their electrical power production still comes from diesel generators, they have a communications and food distribution network to maintain, and Belewa has an active military campaign going against Guinea. Any kind of combat operation, even support for a low-grade insurgency, will burn gas like nobody's business."

"So this is a major point of vulnerability for Belewa?"

Christine nodded. "Oh yeah. In fact, for a lot of kinda subtle reasons above and beyond the obvious ones, this is Belewa's major point of vulnerability. We cut off his go-juice and this dude is kicked to the curb."

Amanda noted Dane's puzzled expression. "Translated from the original Californian, that means we win. All right, then, what are we doing to bring this state of affairs about?"

"Not bloody much, to date," Dane snorted.

"The Commander's right, boss ma'am," Christine said regretfully. "The original game plan was that any coastal smuggling from out of Côte d'Ivoire and into the Union would be intercepted by Ivoire's navy and customs service, supported by our TACNET recon and Commander Dane's helicopters. So far, things haven't worked out quite as we had hoped."

"How many smuggling intercepts have been made so far?"

"To date, a grand total of none."

"None!" Amanda exclaimed, her eyebrows lifting.

"That's right, Captain," Dane said dryly. "It's been a bit of a struggle, but we've managed."

"Yeah," Christine continued. "We're tracking and spotting just fine. Verified contacts all over the place. But we're not getting the intercepts out of the locals."

"Is there a problem with the Ivoire patrol boats?"

Christine held up one finger. "Patrol boat. Singular. The Côte d'Ivoire authorities have assigned one customs patrol boat to work with us Frenchside. A twenty-eight-foot cabin cruiser mounting a light machine gun that probably hasn't been fired since colonial independence."

"And damned if it isn't even around when you need it," Dane interjected bitterly. "Either it's off on some unspecified bloody mission, or it's bloody broken down, or its captain's left the bloody ignition key in his other bloody pair of pants."

"I take it, then, Belewa's people have gotten to the Ivoire authorities?"

"It's a safe call to make." The intel gestured at the West African area map. "The Union's strategic policy to date has been to kiss Côte d'Ivoire's ass while kicking Guinea's. It makes sense, given Guinea is the weaker sister of the two nations. Ivoire has a way stronger economy and military. They'll be harder to destabilize and conquer, so Belewa's left them on the back burner until he's better fixed to do the job. In the meantime, he's using them.

"He doesn't screw with the Ivoire economy, because a comparatively wealthy nation makes a better resource base for a smuggling operation. He's also made no overt threat against Ivoire, so that both that nation's government and the man on the street are willing to look the other way when it comes to a little blockade busting. Especially after a liberal application of dash in the right places."

"In other words," Amanda said slowly, "they won't openly sanction breaking the U.N. embargo, but they also aren't too concerned about how much attention their citizens pay to it."

Christine nodded. "Exactamundo. They just can't be too flagrant about it. There are too many U.N. observers on the border crossings landside to permit much POL to get through on the roads. Also, it's hard to backpack a meaningful amount of gas across through the jungle. That means it's got to be moved by sea, along the coast."

"Where theoretically we should be able to get at it."

"There's theory and there's reality, Captain." Dane took over the commentary. "Last night we had one more try with the Ivoire customs service."

Dane's ruddy complexion flushed further. "Christ! I hovered over a *pinasse* with a deckload of oil drums for forty-five minutes. I had my running lights at bright flash and I was dropping flares and marker strobes. The patrol boat was less than two miles away, and yet they still claimed that they couldn't see the target."

"I presume that protests have been filed with the government of Côte d'Ivoire concerning these incidents."

"Oh sure," the intel replied. "And their kickback is that no evidence of malfeasance has been discovered on the part of their personnel. Also, since no smuggling intercepts have been made, there is obviously no smuggling problem to be concerned about, and thus they are reducing their border coverage."

"Oh Lord." Amanda rubbed her eyes tiredly.

"We're not in Kansas anymore, boss ma'am. This can only be either Africa or the Twilight Zone."

"There's nothing more my people and I can do, Captain," Dane said earnestly. "Not without surface support. We can't fire on the smuggling boats. They're unarmed small craft crewed by civilians. And you can't conduct a boarding and seizure from a flippin' helicopter."

"Yeah," Christine agreed. "We've got to start hitting that supply line. And to do that, we've got to have a hull in the water over Frenchside. One that we can depend on. Can you give us one, Captain?"

Amanda didn't have an immediate reply. Turning away, she crossed her arms over her stomach and slowly paced the full length of the briefing trailer and back, her features set in thought. When she returned to the briefing screen and the two waiting officers, she shook her head.

"I want to say yes so badly I can taste it, but no, I can't afford to cut anyone loose."

"But look," Christine objected, "we already have somebody out there we can use."

The intel picked up the flatscreen remote and called up a force deployment overlay on the area chart. "When we took out the Union boat hides, we established the Union East surveillance station here, just off the borderline of the West African Union and Côte d'Ivoire. We have one of the aerostat carriers positioned there to give us full coverage of the Union Littoral. One of our Cyclone PCs, the *Santana,* is currently escorting her. Why not cut *Santana* loose from close escort and let her chase some smugglers. She can handle that and still provide a degree of protection for the 'stat carrier."

Again Amanda shook her head. "But then, who provides protection for the *Santana?* The Union has a strike force of almost twenty Boghammers based at Harper, right on the Ivoire border." Amanda leaned forward and tapped a point on the flatscreen with her fingernail. "They could sortie at any moment. That aerostat carrier, which one is she? The *Bravo?* She has a Marine security detail aboard her. Fisted together, she and the *Santana* probably have enough firepower to put up a fair fight. If they separate, however, one or both of them could get swarmed and cut to pieces. It would take us at least two hours to get a PG out there in support. Way too long."

Amanda glanced over at the British helo leader. "Unless maybe we could count on some air cover. What about it, Commander?"

"I'd love to oblige, Captain Garrett, but the only armament my Merlins carry is a single GPMG in the side door. My lads and I would be more than willing to back you up in a bash. I just don't know how much good we could do against the twin 14s those Bogs mount."

"Could you get some Sea Skuas?"

Dane grimaced. "I've been trying to get my antiship missiles back ever since we got here. The Foreign Office won't authorize their release into this theater. They claim offensive armament would be, and I quote, 'provocative and inappropriate for a peacekeeping mission.' I suspect we've got some silly bastard up there who's related to that silly bastard of yours who wouldn't let your chaps take their tanks into Somalia a few years ago."

Amanda sighed. "Well, that's it, then."

"God, there's got to be some way to work this," Christine insisted. "Why not put a PG over on Union East the same way we're doing on Guinea East. Maintain a standing patrol of one seafighter and one PC on each barrier line? That would give us the shooting edge."

Again Amanda shook her head. "That's no good either, Chris. The hover-craft just can't loiter offshore for a protracted period of time the way the PCs can. They aren't designed for it. We'd burn out our crews and overwear our equipment in short order. And we don't have enough hulls in the squadron to simultaneously rotate out to two patrol stations, not without intermittently leaving big holes in our coverage. Belewa will be watching for things like that."

Amanda propped her hip against the conference table. "As is, we're spread so desperately thin, one accident or engineering casualty could collapse our entire operation. We just can't take on anything more. We'll have to let the oil smuggling ride for a while."

The intel smacked her palm with her fist in frustration. "Jeez! But that's what we were sent out here to do!"

"That, and to protect the Guinea coast," Amanda replied. "We have the resources to do only one or the other. Currently, taking the pressure off the Guinea government has the immediate priority."

"But that's now. In the long run, a stalemate favors Belewa."

"I'm all too aware of that, Chris."

A metal pitcher of ice water and a stack of paper cups sat in the center of the table. Amanda paused for a moment to pour herself a cupful. "Unfortunately," she continued, sipping the cool liquid, "that doesn't alter our current tactical situation."

"Well, what do we do next?"

"Unfortunately, again we don't do anything."

"Say what?"

"The ball is back in the Union's court," Amanda replied grimly. "We've had our free shots with taking out their boat hides and by intercepting last night's recon probe. Now we're totally reactive again.

"If this were a blank-check operation, we'd go after them. We'd stay on the offensive. We'd use our superior recon capacity to pick and choose our targets and we'd whittle the Union navy down until it wasn't a factor anymore. As a

U.N. interdiction mission, however, we aren't permitted that option. All we can do is patrol and gather intelligence and wait for Belewa to make the next move."

Dane gave a noncommittal grunt. "I'm not sure if I like the sound of that, Captain."

Amanda lifted an ironic eyebrow. "I know that I don't, Commander, but I'm afraid we're stuck with it."

"And what happens when Belewa makes that move?" Christine insisted.

"Hopefully we spot it in time to block it. And then, again hopefully, it'll be our turn once more."

Mamba Point Hotel
Monrovia, West African Union   0620 Hours, Zone Time; June 12, 2007

"There is no contact, General. The reconnaissance patrol from West Squadron did not even make its first scheduled radio call. Also, our agent at Point Sallatouk reported automatic-weapons fire off the coast and the sighting of a boat on fire. We must assume the patrol is lost."

Belewa nodded slowly. "It is as I said, Sako. We do have a leopard to deal with."

The Premier General's personal operations center took up a double-room suite on the same floor as his office and living quarters, the civilian furnishings stripped away and replaced by the functional starkness of a military field headquarters. With its map boards and ranks of field telephones, it lacked the computerized sophistication of a First World command facility. However, it was adequate for Belewa's needs. The focused efficiency of the half-dozen hand-picked personnel staffing it made up for any technological failing.

"Has intelligence finished debriefing the soldiers who escaped from the boat hides?" Belewa inquired, grimly moving on to the next point in the morning's briefing.

"They have, General. Our long-range patrols recovered three survivors. In all instances they report essentially the same thing. An assault force infiltrated each hide site, apparently after a careful reconnoitering. The attackers issued a challenge, ordering the garrison personnel to surrender. If resistance was offered, the attackers returned an overwhelming volume of fire."

"And do we have a positive identification of these attackers?"

"Yes, sir." Brigadier Atiba paused for a moment to take a swallow of bitter tea from a canteen cup. "United States Marines. They identified themselves when they made their challenge."

"Hmm." Belewa drank slowly from his own cup. "So we have American troops on the ground in Guinea. What does their press have to say about that?"

"The Strategic Intelligence Bureau has monitored a press release from the White House concerning the operation, proclaiming it a victory in President Childress's African policies. There has been little reaction noted on CNN and TBN. As UNAFIN and Guinea are of small concern to the majority of the American public and as the operation was a success with no casualties listed, the incident is being treated as a nonstory by most of the American media."

Belewa's only response was to take another sip from his cup. His eyes, however, were cold and dark and focused on something far away.

"What is the status on our long-range patrols? How badly is the loss of the hides affecting our deep-penetration operations?"

"Very badly, sir." Atiba led the General over to a large-scale wall map of Guinea, well spiked with colored pins. "We have eight long-range patrols operating in the coastal areas between Conakry and the border of Guinea-Bissau. They relied on our gunboats for resupply as well as for insertion and extraction. With the hides destroyed, they have been cut off inside enemy territory."

"Do we still have radio contact with them?"

"Yes, General."

"Then bring them home, Sako. Order them to cease operations and walk out."

Atiba frowned. "That will effectively end all of our operations in western Guinea."

"I am quite aware of that. It gives Guinea a breathing space I am not happy about their having. Unfortunately, we have no choice. Starving soldiers don't fight well. To push the campaign in western Guinea any further right now would only cost us good men and hand our enemies another cheap victory. We will pull back until we can get a new supply line established."

"And when will that be, General?" Atiba demanded in frustration.

Belewa glanced at his chief of staff, holding a level gaze until the younger officer looked away flustered. "Sooner than you might think, Brigadier," Belewa said quietly. "And sooner," he gestured at the wall map with his cup, "than they might think."

Belewa drained off the last of his tea and set the metal cup on the corner of a field desk. "All right," he said, straightening. "We are going to weave ourselves a net, Sako. A net to catch a sea leopard in. I want the American coastal patrols kept under constant observation. I want to know how they are operating. I want to know their patrol patterns and strength levels, and I want to know about any changes that occur within them. Arrange for a joint conference with both the commander of the Military Intelligence Section and the director of the Strategic Intelligence Bureau on this matter. Bring the Chief of Naval Operations in on this as well.

"Also have Strategic Intelligence use their Internet access to pull in everything available on Captain Amanda Garrett of the United States Navy." The Premier General smiled grimly. "We must learn about our leopard. What she eats. When she sleeps. What she thinks and what she fears. Then, old friend, we shall see."

Mobile Offshore Base, Floater 1   0826 Hours, Zone Time; June 12, 2007

"Operations, this is Captain Garrett. I'm in quarters if you need me."

She dropped the phone back into its cradle. It had been a long . . . she couldn't call it a day, because this particular cycle of work and wakefulness had started well before the previous evening's nightfall. "Long" would just have to do.

Closing the blinds and turning up the air conditioner, she laid out a fresh set of khakis and underwear where they could be grabbed in a hurry. Then she stumbled into the cramped bathroom, peeling off her current stale and sweat-sodden uniform as she went.

The water-conserving showerhead metered out its miserly three-minute dribble of tepid water. As the task group commander, Amanda could disregard water rationing if she so desired. However, she considered that a form of cheating on her crew and she generally resisted the temptation. Instead, she was coming to appreciate one of the odder customs she had observed aboard the Offshore Base.

Many women aboard the platform had taken to carrying a small plastic envelope of shampoo around in their shirt pockets. Whenever a heavy Gold Coast rain squall would roll over Floater 1, "Shampoo Call" would sound and all female hands not on duty would swarm out onto the deck, lathering up their hair to take advantage of the brief unlimited access to fresh water.

Wringing out her own red-brown-blond mop under the last few drops from the showerhead, Amanda decided that, captain's dignity be damned, she'd best either take up the local custom or get a crew cut.

Without bothering to towel off, she collapsed bare on the bottom sheet of her cot, relishing the few moments of chill as the dampness evaporated from her skin. Burrowing into her pillow, she sought for sleep.

It was not easy to find. Too many lines of thought continued to swirl and tangle in her mind.

The essence of victory in warfare is attack. Putting it bluntly, when one is on the defensive, one is losing. And that was the situation she found herself in now, trapped in a holding pattern with the initiative in Belewa's hands. It was all well and good to talk about blocking punches, but that in itself was a tacit acknowledgment of having to accept the punch in the first place.

Amanda was far from pleased with the concept. It meant deliberately holding people, her people, at risk. And all for the sake of a set of engagement rules worked up in the rarefied atmosphere of international diplomacy. Something that might look good crossing a State Department desk, but that had no connection with how things actually worked in a real-world combat theater.

She remembered listening to the stories told by some of her father's old Navy comrades, officers who had served during the Vietnam conflict. They had been men who had lived through the warrior's hell of being ordered to do it the wrong way, of being commanded to follow a flawed doctrine. Had they ever lain awake like this?

Damn damn damn! Amanda twisted over onto her back and stared at the ceiling. *All right, then* she snapped at herself, *if you're going to waste your sleep time on thinking, then think about something constructive. You can't do anything about the R.O.E.s. You can't do anything to stop Belewa from coming after you in his own good time and on his terms. What you can do is to start planning for what happens afterward.*

How do you manipulate the Union attack into a justification for a counterattack? And where do you hit? And most important, how can you hurt Belewa badly enough to alter the basic strategic and tactical situation in your favor?

More than forty-five minutes passed before Amanda Garrett smiled.

Rising from her cot, she padded across to her desk. Dropping into the chair, she lit off her personal computer and accessed the digital communications link, tapping in the sat code that would connect her with the ordnance section at Conakry Base. Ignoring the decided military incongruity of her nude state, she began to type.

FROM: CMDRUSNTACFORCES- MOB 1 AUTHENTICATOR SWEET-WATER-TANGO-038
TO: CMDRUSNORDIV- CONAKRY
SUBJECT: ORDNANCE—SPECIAL OPERATIONS

REQUIRE TWO (2) ORDNANCE PACKAGES BE ASSEMBLED WITH ALL POSSIBLE SPEED FOR PG-AC-1. EACH PACKAGE TO CONSIST OF FULL LOADOUT (24 PODS-168 ROUNDS) OF 2.75 HYDRA ROCKET FOR EACH SQUADRON PG. ALL ROCKETS TO BE EQUIPPED WITH 17 POUND HEAVY BOMBARDMENT WARHEADS. ONE (1) ORDNANCE PACKAGE TO BE HELD AT CONAKRY BASE. THE SECOND TO BE HELD ABOARD MOB 1. ROCKETS ARE TO BE

PODDED, PALLETIZED AND READY FOR IMMEDIATE, SAY AGAIN, IMMEDIATE FUSING AND LOADING ON CALL FROM CMDRUSN-TACFORCES.

CAPT. AMANDA GARRETT, COMMANDING

Now she could sleep.

Hotel Camayenne,
Conakry, Guinea

As the U.N. military commitment had taken over Conakry's largest airport, so had the diplomatic mission engulfed the city's largest and, purely by happenstance, finest hotel. The Hotel Camayenne fronted on the western beach of the narrow urbanized peninsula from which it took its name. Besieged by both a struggling Third World economy and a burgeoning war, it struggled to maintain the pretensions of a top-class international hostelry.

Vice Admiral Elliot MacIntyre, in-country once more to touch base with his theater commanders, spent his morning there in conference with UN-AFIN's civilian administrative staffers, a necessary but not necessarily rewarding task.

He found one consolation in the duty, however. Amanda Garrett took part in the same round of briefing sessions, bringing the U.N. personnel up to speed on the abrupt change of affairs along the Guinea coast. And as a final reward for his bureaucratic labors, he asked her to be his guest at lunch. He found himself extraordinarily pleased at the acceptance of his invitation.

Seated in the palm shade of the Camayenne's outdoor restaurant, with the heat of the day held at bay by the trade winds angling in from the sea, their conversation drifted from professional topics to casual ones and back once more.

To MacIntyre, it seemed as if Amanda had adapted well to both her new rank and her new environment. Her skin glowed in a golden contrast to the frost white of her tropic uniform, a restored sea tan replacing the yard-side pallor MacIntyre had noted during his videoconference with her. Likewise her thick fall of brown-red hair was sun-streaking toward copper. There was something else different as well, beyond the mere physical. Something MacIntyre couldn't quite put his finger on. A focus, a surety . . . a contentment?

"So, speaking in generalities, what do you think of your new command so far?" he inquired as the busboy finished clearing away the meal dishes.

"I'm not sure yet," Amanda replied, frowning lightly in thought.

While it is easy for a woman to be attractive when she smiles, it's a far rarer thing to find one who can still be so when she frowns. MacIntyre's late wife had possessed the knack. He found now that Amanda Garrett did as well.

"In many ways," she continued, "I imagine Vietnam was rather like this in the early days."

"That's an ominous pronouncement if I've ever heard one."

Amanda arched an eyebrow and took a sip of her sherry and soda. "I didn't necessarily mean the strategic situation. I was referring more to the setting and the feel. The beleaguered ex–French colony. The handful of outsiders trying to make sense of things at the last second. The pockets of normalcy with an ugly little war just over the horizon."

She nodded toward the hotel's tennis courts, a mixed-doubles match in progress, and the glistening azure pool with its cadre of laughing and splashing swimmers.

The concertina wire of the security fences lay some distance beyond, partially concealed by the hotel landscaping.

MacIntyre gave a grunt. "This is a little pocket of abnormality, actually. What's happening out there in the jungle, that's the real world."

Amanda nodded at the irony. "True, it is very much a matter of perspective. I've been trying to gain a little more of that lately. I've been doing a lot of professional reading lately about brown–water naval operations during the Vietnam war, the Market Time and Game Warden patrols, that sort of thing. I daresay that's where a degree of this mind-set comes from."

"Did you catch Don Sheppard's book *Riverine*?"

Amanda gave an animated nod. "Oh yes, excellent. Both as a military study and as a darn good read. Those men faced many of the same challenges and tactical situations off the coast of Vietnam that we are now with UNAFIN. I'm hoping to learn a bit about what works and what doesn't."

"Picked up anything good yet?"

"Um, yes. A great deal. In many ways, we won the coastal war off South Vietnam. However, given the strategic situation, that alone wasn't an adequate enough victory to turn the overall tide of the conflict."

MacIntyre lifted the rye half of his own postmeal Shawn O'Farrell. "Do you think we can pull the win off here?"

"Speaking frankly, Admiral, I'm still not sure. Come back in another month, and I'll let you know."

MacIntyre felt the corner of his mouth quirk up. "You've got a date."

"Admiral MacIntyre, good afternoon, sir." Another naval officer in tropic whites paused at their table. Handsome in a lean and dark way, his voice carried a mild French accent and the uniform hat tucked under his arm a French navy cap badge.

MacIntyre felt a sudden irrational surge of irritation, both at the intrusion and at the conventionalities he was required now to obey. Masking both, he rose to shake hands.

"Commander Trochard. It's a pleasure to see you again. May I introduce Captain Amanda Garrett, my Tactical Action Group commander. Amanda, Commander Jacques Trochard, captain of the patrol corvette *Fleurette*."

"Ah, Captain Garrett," Trochard said jovially. "The legend at last!"

Amanda had risen to shake hands as well. Only, when Trochard's fingers closed around hers, the French officer smiled and bowed over her hand in a deft, flowing move of Gallic grace, his lips not quite touching its back.

MacIntyre's teeth creaked in his jaw.

If the Frenchman's flamboyant gesture was an attempt to lift a moment of blushing disconcertment from Amanda, it failed. With a tilt of her head and a light smile, she accepted the bow as her due, a queen politely acknowledging the act of a lesser courtier.

"It is a pleasure to meet you in person, Captain Garrett," the French officer murmured, straightening, "especially after our numerous telephone and radio conversations."

"You've worked together already, then?" MacIntyre inquired, he hoped, politely.

"In a way. Commander Trochard and I had a minor difficulty we had to deal with a short time ago."

"Indeed, Admiral," Trochard added. "One of the crew of her *Dinassaut* sent my best torpedoman home with a broken jaw."

"One which we both agreed he richly deserved."

"After considerable discussion, yes." Trochard threw his head back and laughed. "I will not make the politically incorrect error of saying that Captain Garrett is a formidable opponent for a woman. Rather, I will say that she is a formidable opponent *and* a woman."

"You're learning, Commander," she murmured.

Following that exchange, MacIntyre found that he didn't mind offering the French Corvette commander a seat quite so much.

"For a moment only, Admiral," he accepted, sinking into the chair. "Duty calls in a shrill unpleasant voice, and I am scheduled to fly back to the *Fleurette* shortly."

"As with me," Amanda said. "One of my seafighters is making a patrol turnaround at Conakry this afternoon, and I'll be going out with her."

"Captain Garrett and I were just discussing the situation here in theater," MacIntyre said, "comparing it with the late and unlamented conflict in Southeast Asia. You've worked these waters for a number of years, Commander. Do you see any parallels?"

"Only one." Trochard paused for a moment to order a glass of white wine. "That being that both are lost causes," he concluded.

"You believe so, Commander?" Amanda challenged quietly. "I'm not quite ready to admit that yet."

"That, my good Captain, is because you are newly come here and the sense of futility has yet to settle in. . . . And do not frown at me so, for I love *la belle Afrique* and I hope to come here to live after I retire. Granted a 'here' remains."

Trochard's drink arrived. Taking up the slender, stemmed glass, he leaned back in his chair. "Let me tell you of Africa, my friends, and of what we have done to her. All of you Americans are new here. We French, however, have been here a long time. We came with the other Europeans, back when this continent was an honest wilderness and each black tribe and kingdom held what land it could by tradition and by the strength of its spears. It was a system that worked for them, and they were content.

"We Europeans, however, had different ideas. We divided Africa up like a pie, each colonial power taking its own juicy slice. We drew lines on maps, governing those lines with colonial administrators and enforcing them with garrison bayonets. We did not care that our lines had arbitrarily been drawn across tribal territories or cultural and language groupings. Our system worked for us, and we were content.

"But the day of the colonies passed and the Europeans all went home, taking our administrators and garrisons with us. But we left behind our lines on the map. We left Africa divided into all these damn little boxes, each box inhabited by broken and separated peoples and by nervous and fragile little governments. The people do not like the way things are. The people want for things to be better. But the governments are afraid to change those little lines on the map for fear of losing what they do have."

Trochard took another sip of bitter wine. "Africa is no longer a collection of colonies. But it is not yet Africa again, either. Africa does not know what it is, and that is the problem."

"And what would you say the solution is, Commander?" MacIntyre asked.

"A solution? Here is a solution for you. Not the one Paris or Washington would propose, but the one I, Jacques Trochard, would propose. Let us all step back and let the whole bloody thing collapse—the lines, the boxes, the governments, everything. Let it all go to hell and then let the Africans pick up the pieces and put it back together to suit themselves."

"And how many people would die in that kind of collapse, Commander?" Amanda's voice held low.

"The Admiral asked for a solution, my good Captain, and I gave one. I do not say it is a good solution, it is just the only one I have."

MacIntyre gave an acknowledging grunt and picked up his beer chaser. "I have to admit I don't have any patented answers either."

"Nor do I," Amanda said, picking up her own glass. "But may I make a proposal, gentlemen? Let's try and buy Africa a little more time. Maybe somebody smarter than we are will come along."

Three glass rims rang solemnly together.

�֍

Commander Trochard's melancholy assessment lingered on after his departure.

"Do you think Trochard is right, Admiral, and that we are bucking a lost cause?"

MacIntyre shook his head. "It's hard to say, Amanda. But I do know that for every true lost cause in this world, there are half a dozen that people just gave up on too soon."

She flashed a heartening smile. "I agree. And if I have to fail, I prefer a futile but valiant struggle to an apathetic acceptance."

"Hear, hear."

A distant droning wail drifted across to the hotel from the east side of the peninsula. Amanda's head came up as she listened intently. "That's the *Queen* coming in," she said after a moment. "If you will excuse me, Admiral. I'll have to be getting back to the base."

"Of course, Captain," MacIntyre replied, suppressing a pang of regret. "My driver can take you out."

"Thank you, sir." She smiled and brushed back a lock of breeze-ruffled hair.

"No problem, Captain," he replied gruffly. "May I escort you to my car?"

"I'd be honored, sir."

✖

They were crossing the busy hotel lobby to the main entry when Amanda glanced over toward the small glass-fronted gift shop. Abruptly she came to a halt, so suddenly in fact that MacIntyre bumped into her.

"Anything wrong?" he inquired.

"No, sir." She shook her head, still peering into the shop window. "It's just

JAMES H. COBB

that they have something over there that's given me an idea . . . and, well, if you'll indulge me for a moment, I think I have to buy a hat."

⚑

"Captain Garrett's aboard, Skipper." Chief Tehoa's voice issued from the *Queen of the West*'s interphone. "She's on her way forward to the cockpit."

"Gotcha, Chief," Steamer Lane replied amiably into his headset. "Start getting her buttoned up back there. We'll be firing up in a minute."

"Aye, aye, sir. And, by the way, the Captain comes bearing gifts."

Steamer and Snowy Banks exchanged puzzled glances. As they heard footsteps clank on the cockpit ladderway, both hover pilots twisted in their seats to look aft.

"Oooh, that is so cool!" Snowy breathed.

Preening a little, her head lifted proudly, Amanda entered the cockpit. She was still clad in tropic whites, but instead of the standard women's uniform hat, she wore a rakish black beret. A silver U.S.N. lapel insignia gleamed in place as a cap badge.

"Oh, yeah, Snow." Lane grinned. "That is cool. When do we get ours, Captain?"

"Right now." Amanda handed forward a large paper sack. "I got enough for the *Queen*'s whole crew. There are smalls, mediums, and larges, and they're adjustable to fit. There are some spare cards of insignia in there as well that I picked up at the Conakry PX. They'll do until we can get a real cap badge designed."

"Are these standard now, Captain?" Snowy asked, rummaging with interest in the bag.

"They're authorized for the Tactical Action Group as a whole and for your seafighters specifically, Steamer. I've already cleared it with Admiral MacIntyre. I've also made arrangements with a shopkeeper over at the Hotel Camayenne to keep a big batch of these in stock for us. Our people can order them through him."

"All right, Captain, this is sharp." Steamer examined his own new headgear with interest. "Didn't I read somewhere about another Navy outfit that was authorized a black beret?"

Amanda nodded. "The PBR squadrons in Vietnam. We're doing very much the same kind of work they did, and I liked the thought of the continuity. We're a new outfit, and this gives us a proud history to look back and draw on. I think that's important.

"There's another reason as well," Amanda continued with an impish grin. "A far more personal one. Ever since I've joined this man's navy I have hated,

S E A   F I G H T E R

loathed, and despised that damn flat ashtray of a hat they stick you with as part of the women's uniform. I swore that should the day ever come when I would have the rank and influence to do something about it, I would. And, ladies and gentlemen, that day has arrived."

Mobile Offshore Base, Floater 1   1405 Hours, Zone Time; June 29, 2007

The sound of a seafighter spooling up to power disrupted the two-person conference in the briefing trailer. Both Amanda and Christine had learned it was an act of futility to try to speak over the wailing turbines. Patiently, they waited for the hovercraft to take its departure down the launch ramp before continuing.

"Okay, Chris," Amanda said as the moan of the PG faded to a tolerable level, "you were saying about the goody bag program?"

"Just that we have it up and running and that so far it seems to be a success." The intel tossed a resealable plastic sandwich bag onto the conference table. Beyond a printed card with the Three Little Pigs Unit badge in the corner, the watertight envelope contained a pack of chewing gum, a book of matches, a notepad and pencil, and a roll of black electrician's tape.

"This is just an example. We've got a bunch of different stuff that we put into the bags in different combinations: candy, fish hooks, coils of fishing line and wire, razor blades. Odds and ends that the local fishermen and boatmen can make use of. The card in there is printed in both English and French and explains about the UNAFIN mission and what we're trying to accomplish down here. We hand one of these out to every small craft we inspect to make up for the inconvenience of the boarding and search."

Amanda nodded her understanding. "Does it help any?"

"Seems to," Christine replied. "At least with the boatmen from Guinea-side. We've also been taking a digital photograph of every boat we stop to add to our intelligence database. We give big eight-by-twelve color printouts of the picture to every crewman and passenger aboard. Even the Union guys get a kick out of that."

"Just don't make those grab bags so good that they deliberately hang around our patrol zones, hoping to get inspected."

The intel chuckled. "We'll aim for a happy medium."

"Good enough." Amanda nodded. "As soon as we get two spare seconds to rub together, I'd like to organize a hearts and minds program with the fishing villages. Aid visits by our medical personnel, having the Seabees help with village development projects, that kind of thing. Having the coastal tribes on our side will make a big difference. . . ."

Amanda let her voice trail off. The sound of the departing seafighter patrol had faded almost to the point of inaudibility. Now, however, the familiar vacuum cleaner moan was growing in intensity again. She reached for the desk phone, but it trilled before her hand came to rest upon it.

"Garrett here."

"Captain, this is Operations. Commander Lane reports that the *Queen of the West*'s had a systems casualty. They're aborting and returning to the platform."

"Did the Commander say how much of a casualty he has?"

"He wasn't sure himself, Captain. He indicated some kind of hydraulics problem."

Amanda frowned. "Hydraulics" could cover a lot of territory aboard a vehicle as complex as a PGAC. "Very well. Operations, I'll check it out." She dropped the handset into the phone cradle and came to her feet. "Stay with me, Chris. We've got trouble."

✕◆

The *Queen* came in slowly, still on her air cushion but wavering as if she were having difficulty holding her course. As Amanda strode up to the platform rail, she could hear the sound of the seafighter's airscrews rising and falling erratically. She realized then that the *Queen*'s pilots were steering the hovercraft with the drive engines.

Some twenty yards off the lee side of Floater 1, the *Queen of the West* came off pad, powering down and settling onto the wave tops. Even as the drive propellers flickered to a halt, hatches swung open on her weather deck and figures emerged onto the hover's broad back. Scrounger Caitlin and Chief Tehoa surfaced amidships, while Steamer Lane slid down from the cockpit dome. All three made their way aft to a point near the stern antenna bar.

"Hey, Steamer." Amanda cupped her hands around her mouth. "What happened?"

"Hydraulic fade on the air rudders," he shouted back. "Lost pressure. Not sure why."

Scrounger flopped onto her belly at the deck edge. While Chief Tehoa held the belt of her dungaree shorts, she lithely reached over and down to an access panel on the side of the hovercraft's hull. She popped the release catches, and as the panel swung open, broad streaks of wine-colored hydraulic fluid flowed down the *Queen*'s side. Hanging casually inverted, she studied the interior of the systems bay for a time, then signaled to be drawn back up to the deck. She conversed with the Chief and Lane for a few moments, then yelled across to the platform.

"We either blew the pressure seal on the reservoir or we lost an actuator. Either way, it'll be about two hours for repairs, ma'am."

A subliminal warning tone sounded in the back of Amanda's mind and the faintest of shivers rippled down her spine.

"Very well," she called back after a moment's hesitation. "But get a move on with it. Expedite the job, Commander."

"Sure thing, Captain. What else?" Lane yelled back, mildly puzzled.

Amanda's internal alert bell continued to clang. Frowning, she glanced back at the hangar bay area and at the grounded *Carondelet*. The seafighter's servicing crew were in the middle of a skirt replacement job on her, a task Amanda recognized as also requiring two to three hours to complete. Her alarm level ramped up another degree.

"Chris. Let's get over to Operations."

⚔◆

Brushing past the light curtains, Amanda and Christine entered the screen-lit dimness of the Operations trailer. "Captain in the con," the quiet call went down the row of systems operators.

"At ease, all," Amanda said, moving down the line to the central display. "Lieutenant Dalgren?"

"Right here, ma'am," the duty officer replied, a shadow within the shadows. "Is there a problem?"

"Very possibly. The *Queen*'s going to be delayed in relieving Guinea East. Contact the *Manassas* and tell Lieutenant Marlin he's going to have to hang on station for at least an extra two hours."

"Uh, begging your pardon, ma'am, but we may have another problem there. *Manassas* has just called in a request for an early relief on station."

"What? Why?"

"They've declared a critically low fuel state, ma'am. Lieutenant Marlin is asking permission to break off and return to the platform."

"A low fuel state?" Amanda spun to face the big tactical display that showed the force deployments and coastal traffic around the Guinea East patrol station. "What in blazes was Marlin doing out there to run himself dry like that?"

"It's not Tony's fault, Captain. The *Santana,* the Patrol Craft we have escorting the Guinea East aerostat carrier, had to go into Conakry this morning to refuel. She won't be back on station again until this evening. *Manassas* has been diddy-bopping around out there by herself all watch, trying to keep the *Valiant* covered while still conducting boarding and search operations."

"Damn, damn, damn!" Amanda studied the computer graphics wall chart of the Union–Guinea border zone. The display revealed the friendly blue glow of only three U.N. unit hacks: the limbering aerostat carrier, a single British minehunter running an inshore sweep, and the *Manassas,* the last being the only real fighting unit in the group.

"Where is the French offshore patrol?" she asked in frustration.

"The French squadron is conducting a search and boarding over near the Côte d'Ivoire line, ma'am. At least eight hours hard steaming away."

"How about Guinea naval elements?"

"Nothing currently at sea or listed as available, ma'am."

"Damn . . ." She could feel the snowball starting to grow. She took a step back, closer to Christine, and lowered her voice. "Evaluation Chris, on Lieutenant Marlin. How close does he cut things?"

"The man is a charger, boss ma'am," the intel murmured back. "He is a macho, and he likes to operate. If he's yelling 'bingo' on you, then it probably means he's already down to his last spare Dixie cup full of gas. If you ask him to stretch it out, he'll try, but you could end up with a boat without enough fuel to either fight an engagement or get home again."

"Right." This was what Amanda had been dreading. A series of negative factors had converged and a rip had appeared in the thinly stretched coverage she had deployed over her theater of responsibility. A rip she didn't have the assets to repair.

Be that as it may, dithering over a critical decision could only make things worse. "Watch Officer. Make signal to *Manassas.* 'You are cleared for immediate return to platform. Make all speed within your fuel limitations.' Then get an advisory to both the *Valiant* and to that Brit minehunter. Tell them that they're going to be on their own for a little while. Tell them to keep their eyes open. Also pass the word to the service crews on both the *Queen* and the *Carondelet.* Push those repairs! The first hover that's ready for sea launches immediately."

"Aye, aye, Captain."

Amanda returned her attention to Christine. "Any way you cut it, we're going to have a hole in our patrol coverage of the border zone, at least two to four hours' worth. What could the Union do with that?"

The intel's silhouette shrugged. "That depends on two factors. One being if the Union spots the hole. That's a definite possibility given that the Union has a fairly sophisticated network of coastwatchers established.

"The second is the Union's reaction time. Are they specifically watching and waiting for this kind of hole to open, and do they have a strike already set up? Are they prebriefed to launch at a moment's notice? Two to four hours is not a lot of time to organize and get off an operation flat-footed. If they're set to go though, that's a whole different deal."

"Project to the worst postulate. They're ready and waiting."

"In that case, boss ma'am, we're really gonna get screwed."

The crews of the two crippled seafighters worked with the swift and focused precision of an organ transplant team, and still the two-hour repair jobs grew toward three. Amanda paced the decks of Floater 1, grim-eyed and staying silent. Neither ragging at the service hands nor hovering over the shoulders of the duty watch in operations would accomplish anything.

The *Manassas* came booming in over the western horizon, her turbines sputtering and dying while she was still a quarter of a mile off the platform. Paddling across in swimmer mode, she nestled against the lee side of the platform and accepted a fueling hose, kerosene cascading into her bone-dry bunkerage cells. Amanda stepped up her pacing, waiting for the first of her command to be ready for sea.

The *Queen of the West,* also now moored alongside the platform, won the race. Scrounger Caitlin slammed the last access panel closed. "That's it," she yelled. "Ready to crank!"

"All right!" Lane bellowed back from the cockpit side windows. "Starting engines. All hands stand by to cast off!"

"Just a second!" Amanda vaulted the platform rail and dropped down to the hovercraft's deck. "You've got a ride along tonight, Steamer."

"Welcome aboard, Captain. *Crank 'em!*"

The *Queen* blazed away to the northwest, trailing her spray plume behind her.

"All speed, Steamer," Amanda commanded. "Pour it on!"

"Got 'em to the wall, ma'am," Lane replied over his shoulder. "We'll maintain hot cruise all the way. Snowy, what's our ETA to Guinea East?"

"We'll be on station in about two hours, Captain," the hover's copilot replied from her station.

Amanda leaned back in the navigator's seat and tried to relax. Two hours before the gap in her defenses could be filled. Two hours more before she dare let her weight down. And yet there still was no reaction from the Union. Maybe they'd missed it. Maybe they weren't ready. Please God, maybe today wasn't the day for the worst-case postulate.

Snowy Banks tilted her head and lifted a hand to her earphones, listening. "Ma'am, there's a call coming in for you from TACNET. Commander Rendino on the command channel."

"Thanks, Snowy. I've got it." Amanda caught up her headset and accessed the com. "Amanda here, Chris."

"We got trouble, boss ma'am." Christine's urgent words crackled over the circuit. "Big trouble."

"What's happening?"

"We have a mass sortie from the Union Boghammer base at Yelibuya Sound."

"How many?"

"All of them! Seventeen boats! Both squadrons launched everything they have that's operational."

Amanda's heart lurched in her chest. "How long ago?"

"Within the last fifteen to twenty minutes. Our Predator made a routine pass over Yelibuya base at 1630 hours and everything looked butt normal. When it made its return sweep—bam, every pier was empty. They must have been standing by to scramble the second our RPV passed out of range."

"Do we have a track on them?"

"Yeah, the *Valiant,* out on Guinea East station, has acquired the Union formation on its surface-search radar. The Bogs are headed straight for them."

"Launch the *Carondelet* and the *Manassas* immediately! Have them follow us! Order *Valiant* to go to general quarters and have her head straight out to sea with all possible speed. Get me drone coverage over that Bog formation, then have a couple of helos prep-loaded with damage control and medical aid gear."

Amanda snapped out the string of orders like a burst of autocannon fire, then she twisted around in her seat to issue another command to the hover pilot. It was unnecessary. Steamer Lane had already smashed the drive throttles forward through the wire check stops to full war emergency power. Picking up her skirts, the *Queen of the West* hurled herself shrieking across the sea.

Mobile Offshore Base, Floater 1   1710 Hours, Zone Time: June 29, 2007

"Commander Rendino, you'd better have a look at this, ma'am." One voice lifted over the low headset babble within the TACNET command trailer. Christine hurried down the line of workstations to the Electronic Intelligence console. "What's the problem, Murphy?" she demanded, hunkering down beside the systems operator.

"Radio transmitters. A whole lot of them," the Elint specialist replied. "We knew the Union had a coastwatcher network, but according to the signal intercepts I'm getting, it's a lot more extensive than we ever imagined. Take a look."

On the Elint graphics display, an area box blinked into existence just off the Union coast, a radio transmission detected and triangulated on by TAC-NET's direction finder arrays. Flanked by a row of code letters and numerals, the target hack joined a row of three similar boxes.

"See. There goes another one. Whenever the *Queen* gets within visual range, bleep, another transmitter fires up with a position report. The set emission signatures all match the same make of Indonesian civil sideband transceiver that's standard issue for the Union coastwatcher net."

The S.O.'s finger traced the course of the hover squadron flagship down the coast. "They're tracking her damn near as well as we can, ma'am."

"Why in the hell haven't we monitored any of these outposts before?" Christine growled.

"They've been sleeper stations, ma'am. Not a single one's transmitted until today. The Union must have been holding this net layer in reserve for special operations."

"Shit! Signal intelligence," Christine lifted her voice, "what are you bringing in from the Union coastwatcher net?"

"Short transmission verbal numerics," the operator at the next console in line replied. "A station designation and a four- or five-numeral data block. Probably a target ID and a heading and speed. They're using some kind of simple tear-sheet cipher. No way to crack it."

"Right. We're not going to get anything worth anything from that. ECM controllers, bring up your countermeasures arrays! All nodes! Set frequency gates to cover the civil sideband channels. Initiate cascade jamming! Broad spectrum! Maximum output!"

The Elint operator looked up, startled. "Ma'am, if you light up all those big burners like that, we're going to kill all civil sideband traffic from here to Marrakech!"

Christine shot a single icy glance down at the S.O. "Mr. Murphy, do I look like a person who gives a howl in hell about the radio reception in Marrakech? Shut 'em down!"

From the transmitters aboard Floater 1, and the two aerostat carriers and from the TACNET land stations at Conakry and Abadjan, a focused electronic scream radiated out across the ether, burying a massive slice of the radio spectrum under a deafening blanket of white noise.

In the control center, several TACNET operators snatched off their headsets to escape the piercing jammer warble, an action no doubt being repeated at Union coastwatcher posts all up and down the Gold Coast. Christine Rendino gave a curt, satisfied nod. "And that goes for you, my pretty," she snarled under her breath, "and your little dog, too!"

"Commander Rendino," another S.O. called out urgently from the Predator control station. "We have a situational change with the Union Boghammer force."

The intel hastened down to the new crisis point. "What's happening?"

The drone pilot called up a wall screen, displaying the video output from the RPV he was holding over the Union gunboat group. On the monitor, a multitude of white wakes could be seen combing across the azure blue of the sea. As they looked on, the massive Union squadron divided, roughly half of the gunboats peeling off to assume a new heading.

"Eight Bogs maintaining an intercept vector to the *Valiant,* ma'am. Nine are now on a heading of three one zero true."

"Access tactical! What's out there on that bearing?"

"Nothing, ma'am. Wait a second . . . nothing except the HMS *Skye,* that British minesweep!"

"Oh my God! Notify Captain Garrett immediately. Then get on the horn to the Brits and tell them they're going to have company for tea!"

Guinea East Station   **1731 Hours, Zone Time; June, 29, 2007**

Lieutenant Mark Traynor, the commanding officer of Her Majesty's Sandown-class minehunter *Skye,* backhanded the scalding sweat from his eyes and lifted the binoculars once more. They were coming in line abreast, nine patches of white wake on the horizon, each with the dark dot of a Boghammer hull centered in it.

"Radar has a plot, Captain," the quartermaster called out from inside the *Skye's* wheelhouse. "Range to Union craft, three thousand meters and closing. Speed thirty-five knots."

"Very well. Maintain the plot." The young Englishman strove to keep his voice mature and steady, as he had always imagined it should be at times such as this. Likewise, he strove to suppress the tremor in his hand as he lifted the bridge-wing phone from its weatherproof case.

"Radio operator, any reply yet from Atlantic Command?"

"No response yet, sor," the Yorkshire-tinted response came back.

Traynor dropped the phone back into its cradle. Damn the admiralty and damn the tenuous two-thousand-mile long line of communications that linked him to their will. He needed instructions now.

He recalled the urgency in the communication he'd received a quarter of an hour before from the American TACBOSS:

HMS Skye. *Be advised Union gunboat group en route to your location. Believe attack on your vessel imminent! Advise you divert course immediately. Advise you proceed to seaward and close with USS* Valiant *for mutual protection! Expedite, repeat, expedite!"*

But then Traynor also had to recall the conversation he'd had with his own squadron commander. *Remember, lad, beyond all this United Nations bumph, you're still a Royal Naval officer and you're still working for us. Especially, watch yourself with this bit of fluff the Yanks have running their piece of the show down there. She's a bit of a wowser who likes to go looking for trouble. Just do your job and obey your orders and you'll be fine.*

Since arriving on station, however, it had appeared to Traynor that the aforementioned "bit of fluff" had more than amply demonstrated that she knew what she was talking about. Still, he had hesitated, banging off an advisory and a request for instructions to admiralty HQ before acting.

It had been the equivalency of yelling into a deep and echoing void. It was after five in London, and no doubt his communication was sitting on someone's empty desk. It was too late now anyway.

At least he'd been able to go to Action Stations on his own recognizance. For what that was worth, at any rate. Traynor leaned forward and yelled down over the bridge rail. "Gun crew, load and stand by."

Forward, on the forecastle, the gun team cranked their first round into the breech of the *Skye's* single 30mm autocannon. On the bridge wings, the duty machine gunners also fed belts of 7.62mm NATO into their GPMGs. The teenaged rating who shared the port-side bridge wing with Traynor fumbled for long, nervous seconds before he managed to close the breech of his weapon.

"Steady," Traynor murmured.

"Yes, sir, Captain. Do you think there'll be a fight, sir?"

"No, seaman, I think they're just running a bit off a bluff on us," Traynor replied with far more confidence than he felt. "I don't think the local lads are quite ready to tackle the Royal Navy yet."

⚔◆

Twelve miles to the southeast, the Naval Fleet Auxiliary Force aerostat carrier USS *Valiant* fled for her life. With a jade wake boiling behind her and the silver torpedo of her antenna balloon glinting high overhead, the squat, low-countered little vessel waddled desperately out to sea, running in a race she could never hope to win.

"You have the helm, Sergeant. If we can help by maneuvering, you just pass the word to the bridge."

"Thanks, Captain," Gunnery Sergeant Enrico DeVega replied into his headset. "Will do. Just keep heading out to sea for now."

DeVega stood at the aft end of the *Valiant's* superstructure, while below on the long, open winch deck, his twenty-man Marine guard detail stood to their battle stations. Ma Deuce 50s and Mark 19 grenade launchers were mounted onto their low-set tripods along the rails, while right aft, the SMAW teams laid reload rockets out on the deck for their Israeli-designed antitank weapons.

A tight, feral grin arced across the noncom's swarthy features. Ten years before, he had been a young *pachuco* living on the bad side of San Antonio. He had escaped a juvenile record by dumb luck and the grace of the Holy Mother and had graduated from high school more by intimidating teachers than by studying. But then had come the day when he had strutted into his mother's house, sporting his first gang tattoo and feeling like a man.

His uncle Jaime has been visiting, his Marine uncle with the medals from Grenada and Lebanon and Desert Storm. Without speaking a word, he had grabbed Enrico by the collar and had thrown him out into the front yard. There, Uncle Jaime had beaten him in front of the entire neighborhood until Enrico had lain on his belly and begged for mercy. "You want to join a gang!" his uncle had roared down at him. "Fine! But you're gonna join my gang, see! Then we'll find out how much of a tough guy you are!"

The next day, Uncle Jaime had marched him down to the Marine Corps enlistment office and had slammed him into the chair in front of the recruiter's desk.

What would Uncle Jaime say now if he could see his *pachuco* nephew about to command an entire naval engagement?

DeVega lifted his binoculars to his eyes, acquiring the white wake streaks closing on the *Valiant* from astern. "Gunners," he bellowed, "lock and load!"

⚓

"Union craft altering formation, Captain!"

"I can see them, Quartermaster." Traynor swept his glasses across the line of gunboats. The central group of three Boghammers were holding their course and speed dead on toward the *Skye*. The two end groups were accelerating, however, going wide around on the flanks of the minehunter, the line abreast altering into an engulfing arc.

There was something about the maneuver, something Traynor had read once in a book about Africa. *The Buffalo! My God, they're using the Buffalo!*

The Buffalo was the classic tactical maneuver of the Impis, the old Zulu battle regiments. The central group, the "chest" of the buffalo, took the direct impact of the enemy, while the flanking units, the "horns," swept around to strike from the sides. It was a doctrine that had once conquered half of Africa, and now, applied in a maritime format, it was being used against the *Skye*.

"Gunners, stand ready!"

⚓

Aboard the *Valiant*, Sergeant DeVega watched as the Union Boghammers swung in, half circling his ship just outside of accurate gunnery range. DeVega had never heard of the Buffalo or of the Zulu Empire. However, he recognized a flanking move when he saw one and he understood the intent behind it. He unslung his M-4 carbine, cradling it in his arms. He had thirty rounds of tracer in the magazine for directing the fire of his gunners and an M-203 grenade launcher clipped under the barrel should the opportunity present itself to get personally involved.

⚔◆

Somewhere someone snapped an order into a radio microphone. Outboard engines howled and the Boghammer groups lunged, the half-circle formations collapsing inward toward their prey.

Traynor and DeVega. Two good men. Two well-trained and capable warriors at a moment of crisis. Each with the same critical decision to make in the same split second, but each coming from a different school and philosophy of warfare.

"Radio operator! Challenge those gunboats! Warn them off!"

"To hell with this shit! Waste the cocksuckers!"

Right down to the last second before, Lieutenant Mark Traynor couldn't bring himself to believe that it was actually going to happen. And after, he couldn't believe that it was, indeed, happening.

Suddenly, the nine Boghammers surrounding his vessel unleashed single, synchronized blasts of automatic weapons targeted on the *Skye*'s upperworks. Eighteen heavy machine guns delivering more than three hundred rounds of armor-piercing 14mm per second.

"Warn them off." That futile command would haunt Mark Traynor for the rest of his life.

Something smashed into Traynor, something hideously wet and mangled that knocked the British officer to the deck. It was the body of the young rating that had been manning the bridge-wing machine gun, disemboweled and blasted away from the gun mount by half a dozen slug strikes.

Forward, the *Skye*'s 30mm mount crashed out a three-round burst. But there was only the one before the gunner slumped bullet-riddled in his harness, his loaders crumpling dead to the decks beside him.

The *Skye*'s thin aluminum and composite superstructure provided no shielding at all from the storm of heavy high-velocity projectiles that raked it. Men fell in the wheelhouse, in the passageways, in the engine rooms, bewildered by the sudden savagery that struck them down.

On the bridge wing, Traynor could only lie dazed and agonized in a pool of blood, partially his own, partially the young gunner's. With nothing that could be done to save either his ship or his crew, he could only pray to God for the mercy of a Union bullet.

The Boghammers circled and closed the range, the rifles and submachine guns of the Union gunboatmen coming into play along with the heavy mounts, ravaging the helpless minesweep from bow to stern. Risking the fire of its squadronmates, a single Bog darted in close alongside the *Skye*. The first hand grenade was hurled up onto the decks. Then the second. Then the third . . .

To the southeast, a very different scenario played out. There an intact and undamaged *Valiant* continued its trudge to seaward, with a battered and bewildered Boghammer group milling in her wake.

In his premission briefing, the Union squadron commander had been told that the American aerostat carriers were unarmed. That had been why his, the smaller and less intensively trained of the two gunboat groups, had received this specific tasking.

However, upon their attack, their "unarmed" objective had bared its fangs and had unleashed a broadside that would have done credit to a young battle cruiser. None of the Union Boghammers had been sunk in the initial furious volley, but the formation had been broken and the momentum of their attack had been lost. Turning away with rocket and grenade bursts spouting in their wakes, the gunboats had hastily scurried back out of range.

Now the Boghammer leader considered his options and alternatives, none of which seemed particularly attractive. Individual boats of the squadron had gingerly probed at the flanks of the American vessel, and each probe had met with the same response, an angry and concentrated storm of gunnery.

The Boghammers had attempted to return fire, but at the longer ranges the Americans had the advantage. The converted TAGOS ship was an exceptionally stable and seaworthy firing platform when compared to the bucking cockleshell hulls of the Boghammers, giving the *Valiant*'s defenders a decided edge in hit probability.

The Union naval officer forced down a dry swallow. To effectively bring the enemy to battle, the Boghammer group would have to charge in to a closer range, and in the running of that gauntlet, there were going to be casualties. Possibly many of them.

The Boghammer commander had acquitted himself well in the adrenaline-charged rush of the initial charge. However, that charge had been broken and the flame of the assault had been replaced with the cold-bellied reality of the standoff. He was a brave and dedicated young man in the conventional sense, but it requires a special and unique kind of courage to rally in the face of the unexpected and to lead into the face of assured death for your men and possibly for yourself.

"Cap'n," his helmsman said nervously. "We gettin' pretty far out to sea."

They were. The American ship had been holding a steady course south at its best speed, and the African coast was now only a streak of cloud along the northern horizon. The Boghammer commander grabbed at the thought. His boats weren't designed for the open ocean. And he was no longer receiving position updates on the American hovercraft. If his squadron was caught out in open water by one of the monsters, they'd be cut to pieces. And as for the failure of his initial attack, it had stemmed from poor intelligence. No one had known the American radar ships had been secretly armed. He couldn't be blamed for that. Nor could he be blamed for not wanting to put his squadron at excessive risk.

"You're right, helm," he replied, striving to keep the relief out of his voice. "We are too far out. We'll have to be satisfied with chasing them off for today. Come about and fire the recall flares."

⚔◆

Aboard the *Valiant,* the sweet chemical stench of gunpowder and rocket propellant dissipated in the sea wind. Spent shell casings glinted as they were swept over the side and the winch deck was crisscrossed with the sooty smears of SMAW backflashes. Up in the superstructure, an ex–San Antonio gang-banger watched in satisfaction as the line of Union gunboats retreated toward the distant coast. "Ayyyy macho!" he called after them, his voice lifting in derision.

PGAC-2, USS *Queen of the West*   **1748 Hours, Zone Time; June 29, 2007**

"Talk to me, Chris," Amanda demanded over the command circuit. "What's happening?"

"Good stuff and bad, boss ma'am," the intel replied grimly. "The good stuff first. The Union Boghammer groups are breaking off and are apparently returning to base. Also, the USS *Valiant* reports that she has successfully repelled her attackers without damage or casualties and she is returning to station."

"What about the Brit minehunter?"

"That's the bad stuff. We have lost all communication with the HMS *Skye* except for her emergency beacons. We have a radar skin track indicating that she's still afloat, but she's dead in the water. We also executed a drone pass a few minutes ago, and she looks in pretty bad shape. I've ordered medevac and rescue helos launched from both the platform and from Conakry. They are airborne and en route at this time."

"Very good, Chris. We're still about half an hour out from the *Skye's* position. What can you give me on the Boghammer groups?"

"Both squadrons have dispersed. All elements appear to be proceeding independently back to the Yelibuya Sound fleet base. Do you want an intercept bearing on the nearest Bog to your location?"

Amanda's jaw tightened. "Negative. What I want you to do is to track as many of those Boghammers as you can back to Yelibuya Sound. I want them followed every inch of the way and I want their return media-documented. Focus every available recon asset on that specific tasking. I want incontrovertible proof that those Union attack groups sortied from the Yelibuya fleet base."

"You got it, boss ma'am."

⋇◆

A smoke plume rose above the horizon, a pale banner of distress lifting over the crippled derelict of what had been a man-of-war. As the *Queen* bore closer to the listing hulk, more and more of the havoc became apparent: the upperworks charred and fire-blackened, the hull pocked with bullet and grenade strikes, the blood streaks trickling down from the scuppers.

As each grim detail became apparent, Amanda's rage grew. Not at Union for performing the attack, but at herself for allowing it to take place.

"Steamer, take us alongside."

"Aye, aye, Captain. Going in."

Her long and futile race over, the *Queen of the West* settled off pad. With her turbines and lift fans fading into silence, she nestled close to her wounded sister. Amanda slid the overhead hatch back and lifted herself up onto the hatch rim. In the growing twilight, faces peered down at her from the minehunter's rail. Shocked faces, blasted faces, marked by soot and the sudden aging that comes with exposure to war.

"Ahoy," Amanda called up through cupped hands. "Where's your captain?"

"Here," one old young man called back. "Leftenant Mark Traynor. Commanding officer of Her Majesty's ship *Skye* . . . or what's left of it."

"I'm Captain Amanda Garrett, U.S. Navy, commanding the Seafighter Task Force. I'm sorry, Leftenant. I'm sorry we couldn't get here sooner."

"And I'm sorry we failed to heed your warning, Captain," the Englishman replied with stark resolution. "The fortunes of war."

"Acknowledged, Leftenant. How many casualties?"

"Eight dead, eight wounded. We've got the fires out, but our engines are gone. All that's keeping us afloat are our handy billy pumps. It's my intention to stay with the ship and save her if we can, but could you take off our wounded?"

Amanda hesitated a moment before replying. "I'm afraid that will be impossible, Leftenant. We are committed to another operation. However, helicopters carrying medical aid and salvage equipment are on the way. They should be arriving within the next few minutes. Also, I've instructed the USS *Santana* to proceed here with all possible speed. She'll tow you in to Floater 1, and we can patch you up there. Again, I'm sorry, but there's nothing more we can do."

"Are you going after the bastards that did this to us?" Traynor inquired wearily.

"That is my intention."

"Then there is nothing more I could ask. Good luck and good hunting, Captain, and thank you."

Amanda dropped back down into the *Queen's* cockpit, drawing the hatch shut behind her. "Okay, Steamer. Light her up and get us under way."

"Aye, aye, ma'am," the hover commander replied, beginning his engine start sequence. "*Carondelet* and *Manassas* are coming up fast."

"Very good," Amanda replied, hunkering down between the pilot's seat. "Have them form up with us."

"We also received a message while you were topside, Captain," Snowy Banks added. "Direct from Admiral MacIntyre. He's on the ground at Conakry Base, and he instructs us to pursue and engage the Union Boghammer forces to the full limits of our capacity."

"Acknowledge the message," Amanda replied curtly. "Steamer, lay in a course for Conakry. Best possible speed."

"Conakry?" Lane twisted in his seat to face Amanda. "Captain, Admiral MacIntyre has just ordered us to go after those Boghammers, ma'am!"

"I am fully cognizant of the Admiral's orders, Commander! However, I will elect the manner in which those orders will be carried out! Now set course for Conakry Base! Best possible speed!"

The intensity of her words brooked no further discussion. "Aye, aye, Captain," Lane replied, turning back to the controls. "You're the boss."

"Miss Banks," Amanda continued with the same grim intensity, "contact logistics at Conakry. There's a special weapons loadout for the squadron being held in reserve there. They'll know the one I'm talking about. Tell them to have it standing by on the beach for us when we pull in, along with a full ordnance-loading crew and a set of fuel tankers. Tell them I expect . . . no, tell them I *require* the fastest mission turnaround they have ever executed."

"Yes, ma'am."

"Then contact TACNET and have them give us a data dump on the Union Fleet base at Yelibuya Sound. Everything they've got. Especially all of their latest reconnaissance imagery."

With her commands issued and the *Queen* up on the pad and under way once more, Amanda descended into the main hull. Proceeding to the fire-control stations, she rested her hands on the shoulders of both Danno O'Roark and the Fryguy.

"Gentlemen, if you could join me in the wardroom, we've got some work to do."

Conakry Base, Guinea   1935 Hours, Zone Time; June 29, 2007

Full darkness had fallen by the time the Three Little Pigs climbed the beach ramp at Conakry Base. As the seafighters powered down and sank onto their bellies, light-all generators cranked to life around the ramp perimeter, illuminating the scene with their glare. Navy deuce-and-a-half trucks lumbered out of the darkness, bearing plump fuel blivits and pallets of rocket pods. As promised, ready to load.

Fuel hoses were connected and transfer pumps purred to life. On the back of each hovercraft, the pocket panel hatches over the weapons bays slid back. Ordnance ratings lowered themselves into the magazines and commenced the delicate task of safetying and downloading the onboard missiles. Soon a new, different, and even more deadly cargo would be replacing them.

An open HumVee roared into the circle of light around the hovercraft. "Is Captain Garrett here?" the rating behind the wheel yelled over the engine and work clamor.

"Right here, sailor," Amanda yelled down from the *Queen*'s back. "What's up?"

"Admiral MacIntyre wants to see you up at headquarters," the enlisted driver called back. "Right away, ma'am." The youthful sailor displayed the nervousness appropriate to a minor functionary caught in the blast radius of an upper-echelon explosion.

Amanda smiled grimly. "Excellent," she replied. "I want to see the Admiral right away as well. I'll be right down."

"Steamer," she called back over her shoulder to the cockpit. "I should be gone no more than twenty minutes. I want the fuel and ordnance transfer completed and the squadron ready to start engines again when I get back."

"We'll be set, ma'am," the muffled voice replied.

Amanda started down the exterior ladder. "That's granted, of course," she added under her breath, "that I come back."

To say that Vice Admiral Elliot MacIntyre looked displeased would be an understatement. The craggy flag officer looked ready to hurl thunderbolts. Ushered into the small office he was using in the U.N. headquarters building, Amanda came to a parade rest before his desk, her spine straight, her features neutral and immobile.

"I presume, Captain," MacIntyre began coldly, "that since you acknowledged my orders instructing you to pursue and engage the Union Boghammer force, you did, in fact, receive them."

"I did receive them, sir."

"Then, Captain," MacIntyre's voice rose an increment, "will you kindly explain to me why you did not elect to carry them out?"

"Begging the Admiral's pardon," in contrast, Amanda lowered her own tone, "but I am in the process of carrying those orders out at this time."

One of MacIntyre's eyebrows lifted. "That's going to be quite a trick, Captain," he replied tartly, "considering our real-time intelligence indicates that every single Union gunboat has safely returned to base."

For the first time, Amanda lowered her eyes to meet MacIntyre's hard gaze full-on. "I'm cognizant of that fact, sir. And that is exactly where I want them to be."

The Admiral scowled and hesitated. "Proceed, Captain," he said after a moment. "What's your intent?"

Amanda let a little of the steel ease out of her spine. "Sir, I did not initiate an immediate pursuit of the Union Boghammer force because such a pursuit would have been an act of futility. Obedient to classic guerrilla-warfare doctrine, the Union flotillas scattered after their attack upon our vessels, each gunboat following an independent and evasive course back to base. We might have been able to hunt down two or three of them before they reached coastal cover, but we wouldn't have been able to strike any kind of decisive counterblow.

"Instead, I elected to allow the Union gunboat groups to return to their home base unmolested." Amanda crossed to the chart that was the office's sole wall decoration. Her finger stabbed at a point on the western coast of Sierra Leone. "Here, at the Union naval station on Yelibuya Sound."

She turned to face MacIntyre once more. "As you have indicated, sir, they have done so. Now, I have them all concentrated at one fixed location. The reason I brought PGAC-1 into Conakry Base at this time was to rearm with full warloads of surface-to-surface bombardment rockets. Upon taking departure, it is my intent to proceed directly to Yelibuya Sound and to wipe out both the Boghammer squadrons and the naval base they stage out of."

MacIntyre was startled out of his anger. "Good Lord, Amanda, you can't be serious?"

"I'm deadly serious, Admiral. We have an opportunity here to blow the entire western campaign wide open, and I don't intend to pass it by."

"We're authorized by our U.N. mandate to maintain the maritime exclusion zone and to act in defense of ourselves and of the nation of Guinea. Defense! We don't have any kind of authorization to take offensive action against the West African Union."

"I look on it as a matter of semantics, sir." Amanda returned to the desk, leaning against it with her hands braced on its edge. "The Union naval base at Yelibuya is the real threat to both our forces and to the Guinea coast. The Boghammers that stage out of it are just the bullets fired from the gun. Tonight Belewa shot that gun at us. Within that definition, destroying Yelibuya Base is an act of self-defense and thus is within our mandate."

"Damn it all entirely, Amanda." MacIntyre shook his head in dogged denial. "I know you're a radical operator, that's why I pulled you in for this job. But if you try this stunt, they're going to say that you deliberately stretched your rules of engagement to pick a fight with Belewa."

Amanda lifted her hands from the desk edge. "Well, of course. Because that's exactly what I am doing." She took a step back from the desk. Her arms crossed over her stomach, she began to pace the length of the dank little workspace, her head lowered. "Damn it, sir. We simply do not have the resources to fight this conflict conventionally. The attack on our aerostat carrier and that British minesweep just proves the point. If we give Belewa the advantage of choosing only his own battlegrounds and times of engagement, we are handing him the victory. I can't win a war of attrition against an enemy of Belewa's caliber. I have got to go on the offensive. If the U.N. rules of engagement block me from doing so overtly, then I have to stretch those rules when I counterpunch. That's my only remaining, valid option.

"Tonight, I have been given an opportunity to counterstrike within a broad definition of my operational mandate. I have to hit him hard enough, now, to change the basic strategic equation. I can't pass on this chance!"

MacIntyre sighed heavily and shook his head. "Lord, Amanda, I see where you're coming from. And from a purely military standpoint, I can agree with it. But there are other factors to be considered. An escalation of this nature takes us beyond the shooting war and up to the diplomatic interface."

"I am fully aware of that, sir." Amanda paused in her pacing. "And the diplomats, statesmen, and potentates are welcome to it. However, I was brought here specifically to deal with the shooting war, and I am endeavoring to do so to the best of my ability. All of my experience and all of my instincts tell me that going for the base at Yelibuya is the one best possible action we take at this time, given the current operational and strategic situation."

She sought for and met MacIntyre's gaze with her own. "Speaking frankly, sir, I wish you hadn't been on the ground here tonight. As senior tactical officer on station, I'd have kicked off a UNODIR advisory to you, then I'd have gone ahead and executed the strike and let the cards fall where they may. After all, what's one captain *pro tem* in the greater scheme of things.

"However, you are senior on site and this mess falls into your lap now. I understand fully that as CINCNAVSPECFORCE you have larger considerations and responsibilities to deal with than I do. Accordingly, you can't afford to play the game quite as fast and loose as I can. As the situation stands, though, I can only urge you in the strongest possible manner to allow me to commit the strike on Yelibuya Sound. It is what needs to be done if we are serious about bringing this conflict to a successful outcome."

MacIntyre studied the slender, tanned figure before him. "Tell me something, Captain," he said after a moment. "What happens if I elect to not carry through with the strike on Yelibuya?"

"Then, Admiral," she replied quietly, "I will formally accept responsibility for both the Union attack this evening and for PGAC-1's failure to intercept the Boghammer force following the attack. I will also formally request to be relieved of this command. I have no interest in fighting a war that I am being ordered to lose."

In his younger days, he might have taken that statement as a threat, a challenge, or a bluff. Damnation, even now he would take it as such coming from certain officers of his acquaintance. But not from this one. From Amanda Garrett, it was a simple statement of fact. Asked for and given.

The laugh was born deep inside of him, a rumbling chuckle that rose from deep in his chest. "Lord, and I asked for this," he said with a slow shake of his head. "Thank you, Captain. . . . Thank you, Amanda, for reminding me that, theoretically at least, victory is what this is all supposed to be about."

He straightened in his chair, his mirth fading to a glint of self-derision in his eyes. "And thank you for also reminding me that, in a world that is more comfortable with a muddled mediocrity, there are still certain people who do not accept the concept of compromise. You are correct on all points, Captain. Operation approved. Carry on. And forgive my momentary lapse into micromanagement. I'll mind my own business in the future, which will be dealing with those assorted diplomats, statesmen, and potentates you mentioned. In the meantime, you go on and win their war for them. Whether they like it or not."

Amanda Garrett flashed a sober smile that transcended the room's muddy incandescent lighting. "Aye, aye, sir."

Yelibuya Sound Naval Station   0121 Hours, Zone Time; June, 30 2007

The Union naval base at Yelibuya was neither a Norfolk nor a Portsmouth, but Captain Jonathan Kinsford was content with his command. As he walked slowly down to the command post bunker, he surveyed his realm by the light of a three-quarters moon.

Yelibuya Base had once been one of Sierra Leone's colonial-era palm-oil plantations. The aging, white-pillared mansion house still overlooked the estuary of the nameless little river that emptied into Yelibuya Sound. Now, however, the mansion served as a combined officers' club and billet, while the old plantation dock had become the base fueling pier, a gasoline barge moored to its downstream side. Upstream, a rank of smaller finger piers now lined the east side of the estuary channel, the Boghammers gunboat force slotted neatly in alongside them. A row of ordnance and engine maintenance sheds had been constructed behind the piers along with a boat railway for hull repair work.

Upslope from the water, beyond the mansion but still inside the forest line, were the clustered tents of the enlisted men's quarters and the small base motor pool along with the heavily sandbagged mound of the ammunition bunker. And directly downslope, between the mansion and the shore, centered in what had been the estate's broad front lawn, was a second, sandbagged emplacement, the base command post to which Kinsford was bound.

Kinsford was proud of that command post. He liked for things to be secure. That was why a quarter mile downstream at the river's mouth, he'd had two more sandbagged emplacements built and manned. One on either side of the entry channel. Each fortification mounted a Bofors L70 40mm antiaircraft cannon, positioned and ready to sweep the sea or sky approaches to the base.

The base was blacked out as per Kinsford's orders, and the only ground light to be seen was the occasional flash of a hand torch as the night watch went about their duties. Music still tinkled past the drawn curtains of the officers' club, however.

The boat commanders of the Boghammer squadrons were hard at work celebrating their victory over the U.N. interdiction force. The base commander had lingered late in the club, sharing in their triumph, and he suspected that the party would rage until dawn. However, as base commander, Kinsford knew that he needed to set a good example. He also suspected that the big bugs from Monrovia would descend upon them at first light for a debriefing, and that was something not to be faced with a hangover. Accordingly, he had waved off half a dozen offers for "just a last one, mon," and had stepped out into the night, taking this final slow stroll and look-about both to clear the beer fumes from his head and to ensure all was battened down for the night.

His jungle boots crunching on the gravel path, he strode on to the command post. He'd have a final check with the officer of the day and then turn in on the cot they had tucked away in a corner of the bunker. From the sound of it, there would be precious little sleep to be had up in officers' country.

The command bunker smelled of mildew and of the metallic two-cycle exhaust of the communications generator. "Situation, Lieutenant?" Kinsford inquired. Descending the narrow steps into the thick-walled confines of the bunker, he brushed aside the mosquito-net door screen.

"All quiet, sir," the duty officer replied, looking up from his field desk. He and the two signalmen manning the radios were the only staff on watch at this hour. "Nothing new to report."

"Any advisories on U.N. reaction to our strike yet?"

Underlit by the glow of the low-turned gas lantern resting on the floor, the watch officer shook his head. "No, sir. Nothing on the landline or the Navy channels, and the coastwatcher net is still off the air. The Americans are still buggering the sideband commo."

"Bloody marvelous." Kinsford grunted. "We'll probably have to wait for the post to arrive before we can get a clue as to what's going on."

Kinsford moved toward the blanketless cot set up on the duckboards in the corner of the bunker. "At any rate, I'm for a bit of sleep, lieutenant. They're having too much fun up at the big house to manage it there."

"Very good, Captain. You will find it most quiet down here at night."

The watch officer's words were rapidly disproven. As Kinsford unlaced a boot, one of the field telephones gave a rasping buzz. The watch officer scooped up the handset and exchanged a few rapid words with the caller.

"Captain, one of the gun positions reports an offshore sighting."

"Can they identify the target?"

"No, sir. Just what looks to be three unidentified vessels in the sound."

PGAC-02 USS *Queen of the West*   **0134 Hours, Zone Time; June 30, 2007**

The *Queen's* swimmer motors slowed, as did the flickering of the numerals on the readout of the Global Positioning Unit. "Steady as she goes," Amanda murmured "Steady . . . All stop! Initiate station keeping."

The position hack on the GPU display now exactly matched the one preset and locked in on the fire-control board.

"Station keeping, aye," Steamer Lane replied quietly. Deftly, he began to work the motor throttles and propeller controls, keeping the *Queen* stationary on her GPU fix against the tug of current, wave, and wind.

"Rebel, at firing point," Lieutenant Tony Marlin's voice issued from the overhead speaker. The word from Clark aboard the *Carondelet* followed a few moments later. "Frenchman, spotted and station keeping."

A bare mile off the bow lay the mouth of a small jungle river, glinting silver in the moonlight as it snaked back into the coastal forest. And by cranking up the magnification and light amplification of the Mast Mounted Sight, the buildings of the Yelibuya Boghammer base could be made out along its banks.

They had arrived. Now to do what they had come for.

"Little Pigs," Amanda spoke into her command mike, "this is little Pig Lead. Rig for shore bombardment."

Servos moaned and weapons pedestals elevated to firing position. Loading arms stabbed downward, acquiring and lifting rocket pods onto the mount rails.

"Frenchman, loaded and standing by."

"This is Rebel. We are hot. Datalinks open."

"Rebel and Frenchman, Little Pig Lead acknowledges." Amanda toggled over to intercraft. "Fire control, link your systems. Stand by to commence fire."

Below the cockpit, Danno O'Roark touched the key sequence that interlocked the *Queen of the West*'s fire-control system with that of her two sisters. Cybernetic whispers passed between the three craft. Targeting lists and engagement sequences were exchanged, the ones Danno and the Fryguy and Amanda Garrett had so carefully worked out on the voyage here. Weapons pedestals traversed and elevated, hunting with an almost biological eagerness for the proper angles and bearings.

"Fire-control systems have integrated, Captain. Initiating target selection and sequencing program . . . Program is up. . . . System safeties are off. All boards are green. Ready to fire."

"Proceed, Mr. O'Roark. Commence firing."

Two rocket pods per pedestal mount. Two mounts per hovercraft. Six mounts within the squadron. Twelve salvos of 2.75-inch artillery rockets hurled in a space of three and a half seconds. A rippling shriek of sound that tore the sky open and a molten gold glare on the wavecrests.

The pedestal ejectors hurled the emptied and smoldering rocket pods over the side. The weapons mounts whipped back to vertical and the loading arms slid the next flight into place. Again the pod muzzles panned and tracked.

There was no human involvement at all now. All was tasked to the onboard computers and to the meticulously detailed fire-control program that purred and clicked within them.

Seven rockets per pod. Twelve pods per weapons bay. Two bays per hovercraft. Seventy-two pods to be expended.

Lightning sprang from the sea and thunder echoed from the land. Fire trails arced across the dark zenith, the Hydra rounds, like burning coals, raining down into the little pocket of hell that had been Yelibuya fleet base.

Seventy-two pods, five hundred and four rockets, each bearing a seventeen-pound high-explosive warhead. And all arriving on target within a three-minute interval.

⊗◆

"Captain Kinsford, the unidentified vessels have opened fire! We are—" A sharp terminating crackle issued from the field telephone as the set, man, and installation at the other end of the circuit ceased to exist.

The hammering roar of the Hydra salvos destroying the 40mm battery drowned out the wavering howl of the rounds coming in on the main base. Night became day as a holocaust glared in though the observation slits of the command bunker.

By chance, Kinsford had been looking inland, toward the mansion house/officers' billet, and he saw its end. The tropics-softened wood of the aged structure offered no resistance to the initial rocket cluster. They drilled through and burst within the building's heart. The entire two-story structure seemed to lift off its foundations and float in midair for an instant before dissolving into a spray of flaming timbers and shredded sheet-metal roofing.

Concussion buffeted the command bunker and Kinsford and the men of the night watch were hurled around its interior like dice in a gaming box. Clinging to the internal braces for support, the Union base commander caught fragmentary glimpses of his installation disintegrating around him.

The boats and finger piers were next. An interlocking string of explosions walked deliberately down the edge of the estuary, kicking the piers to splinters and hurling the moored Boghammers aside like the broken toys of a child in tantrum. Marching on, the shell bursts reached the fueling pier and the old dock and its gasoline barge both were engulfed within a mushroom of blazing petroleum.

The string of interlocking detonations reversed itself, working back up the shore, devouring the maintenance sheds and the boat railway like a ravening dragon, leaving nothing—no structure, no wall, no stick or stone—unblasted.

The destruction of the boat line complete, the monster shifted objectives, springing across the ruins of the base to the ranked tents of the enlisted men's billets, smashing, shredding, enflaming. Kinsford could only pray that all hands had fled to the forest in terror.

The motor pool was last, the exploding fuel tanks of the base's few vehicles adding only a little to the devastation.

And then it was over.

The echo of the high-explosive avalanche reverberated away across the jungle, leaving only a crackle of burning wood and the pop and bang of ammunition cooking off aboard the charring hulks of the gunboats.

Dazed, Kinsford made the rounds of the observation slits, taking stock by the light of the numerous fires. Nothing was left. Or almost nothing. The only two structures left untouched were the command center and ammunition store. Recognizing that the reinforced bunkers might have been sturdy enough to survive even multiple hits by the artillery rockets, their attackers had elected to distribute their firepower to better effect elsewhere.

What good was ammunition, though, when there was nothing or no one left to fire it? And of what use was a command post with nothing and no one left to command?

The radios had toppled off of their stands and the signalmen lay beside them, one in a dazed sprawl, the other curled in a fetal position and sobbing. Crossing to them, Kinsford slapped and kicked the operators back into some form of functionality.

"Get me a channel to Fleet Headquarters in Monrovia. . . . No, wait, get me the direct channel to the Mamba Point Command Center. I must . . . I must report this."

It was the only thing left that could be done.

Mamba Point, Monrovia   0140 Hours, Zone Time; June 30, 2007

It had been a jubilant evening in the Union headquarters building, in all quarters, barring one.

"It is not good, Sako. It is not good. We failed."

"Obe, I hear you speaking," Brigadier Atiba replied patiently, leaning back against his general's desk, "but I do not understand what you say. We have won a great victory. You have won a great victory."

Belewa himself paced the centerline of his office, scowling at the floor. "That is not the point, Sako. Yes, winning a victory is a very good thing. But winning the war is what is important. Yes, disabling the British minesweeper was useful. Yes, we scored against the blockade. But no, we failed in our primary mission objective."

Belewa paused in his pacing and aimed his scowl at the wall chart of the Union coast. "If we had destroyed that radar ship, that would have been a true victory. That would have stuck a stick in the Leopard's eye. I should have known she would have arranged for some kind of onboard defense, and I should have massed and concentrated our forces against the one truly critical target. Instead I allowed myself to become greedy. I allowed myself to become distracted by a target of opportunity. General? Pah! I'm a fool!"

"Then let me buy a fool a drink." Reaching behind him, Atiba caught up the bottles of beer he had brought with him to Belewa's office. One after another, he struck the bottle caps off on the edge of the desk. Grinning, he held one of the bottles out to Belewa. "Who was it who told me? 'Sometimes you can't win every battle on the first day. Sometimes you must grit your teeth and try again tomorrow.'"

Gradually, a grudging smile crept onto Belewa's lips. "A fool who was a simple army officer at the time," he replied, accepting the beer. "I am the leader of a great nation now, Sako, and I must achieve perfection yesterday."

"To yesterday's perfection, then."

The two brown bottles clinked lightly and the two warriors drank to the toast.

"Ahh!" Obe Belewa's face relaxed for a moment, then the frown returned. "Sako, have you verified that all of the gunboats did, in fact, return from this mission?"

"For the third time, Yelibuya Sound has counted every boat home."

"No contact with the American gunboats at all?"

"None!" Atiba shook his head impatiently. "By the sacred names of God, Obe. Are you disappointed we didn't take casualties?"

"Of course not. But I have to wonder why we didn't." Belewa circled his desk and sank down into his chair. "If there was no indication of an American pursuit, it makes me wonder just what they might be up to out there."

"Isn't it conceivable that we just might have gotten lucky," Atiba asked with forbearance, coming to sit on the desk edge, "or that they might have fumbled their own operations?"

Belewa cocked an eyebrow. "No, it isn't. If the Leopard isn't nipping at our heels, then maybe she's already gotten ahead of us and is lying in ambush."

The Chief of Staff laughed shortly. "You and your Leopard, Obe. You make her sound as if she's some kind of witch doctress."

"I begin to think that she is, Sako. At times in our briefing sessions, I feel her spirit sitting on my shoulder, laughing at my follies."

"For the love of God, man. She's just a woman!"

"Hah! And how many times has 'just a woman' made a fool out of you, my friend." Belewa grinned back and took another draw from his beer bottle. "I seem to recall something about a little dancer in a club in Lagos—"

The corridor door burst open with no preliminary knock. A frightened signalman leaned in through it. "General Belewa! There has been an emergency transmission from Yelibuya Sound! Yelibuya Fleet Base has been destroyed!"

"What?" Brigadier Atiba sprang to his feet. "Who is attacking them? How badly are they hit?"

"They didn't say, sir. There was only the single transmission. And they didn't say the base was under attack. They said that they had been destroyed!"

"Get them back." Belewa rose to his feet as well. "Get some particulars of what's happened. Find out what's going on out there."

"We've tried, General. Yelibuya Base does not reply."

PGAC-02 USS *Queen of the West*   **0140 Hours, Zone Time; June 30, 2007**

The seafighters turned away from the Union coast and from the glow in the sky over Yelibuya Base. Igniting turbines, they came up on the pad for their sprint home. Yet there was still one blow left to strike. Coffin shaped, the four-round heavy missile cell elevated out of the *Queen*'s weather deck, up-angling to forty-five degrees.

"SeaSLAMs armed and spinning up for launch, Captain. Ready to initiate firing sequence."

"Very good, Danno. Launch at your discretion. Let's finish the job."

In the screenlight of the fire-control console, Danno O'Roark glanced across at Dwaine Fry. "I got number one, you got number two. Let's do it right. I don't want those clowns on the *Carondelet* to have to clean up after us."

"Just push the buttons, my man," the Fryguy replied, his slender fingers closing around his controller grip. "The rock is as good as in the hole."

⋈◆

A launching charge thudded and the plastic cap of the first missile cell shattered, the nose of a sleek torpedolike projectile bursting through. Spring-loaded swept wings extended from the midpoint of the fourteen-foot fuselage as it cleared the tube, tail fins unfolding and locking outward a microsecond later. Arcing up and clear of the seafighter, a command flashed from one of the SeaSLAM's onboard computers to the booster module at its stern. The solid-fuel rocket engine ignited and the projectile lunged skyward again.

The booster burn lasted only a few seconds, but during that time ram scoops snapped open, channeling air into the compressor blades of the small turbofan engine. As the rocket burned out and staged away, the jet power plant ignited, taking over propulsion. Guard panels also blew away at the projectile's nose, revealing the glassy lenses of a low-light camera system.

A second land attack missile followed the first out into the night a few seconds later. Running nose to tail, they leveled off at two thousand feet, briefly maintaining their launch headings. Then the tips of their razor blade wings snapped up and they reversed course, heading back for the coast and for Yelibuya Fleet Base.

The SeaSLAM ER (SEA-launched Standoff Land Attack Missile Expanded Response) was a true "smart bomb." In fact, it was as intelligent as is conceivable for any weapons system. In the fire-control bay of the *Queen of the West,* targeting screens displayed television images beamed back from the Sea-SLAM nose cameras. With hands delicately moving controllers, Danno and the Fryguy flew their robotic charges on to their final destiny.

Yelibuya Fleet Base Command Bunker 0142 Hours, Zone Time; June 30, 2007

"Captain Kinsford, we are through to Mamba Point," one of the signalmen croaked.

The air in the bunker rasped at the lungs, thick as it was with smoke and chemical taint and the stench of burning flesh. Kinsford stumbled to the partially functional radio console and caught up the hand mike. "Mamba Point. This is Captain Kinsford at Yelibuya Sound. Do you receive?"

"We receive, Yelibuya Sound." The faint and distant voice of a living world issued from the transceiver speaker. "What is your situation?"

Kinsford had to try twice before he could force the words from his parched throat. "Mamba Point. Yelibuya Fleet Base has been destroyed."

The Union captain never had the opportunity to hear the reply. Outside a piercing nasal whine grew in intensity and an explosion far greater than any that had come before took everyone in the command bunker off their feet. Support beams cracked, sand rained down from the overhead, and concussion blew the radio chassis completely away from the bunker walls.

Kinsford struggled to his feet and peered out through the distorted observation slits. The base ammunition bunker was gone. Nothing remained of it but a black and smoking crater gouged out of the ground.

Their attackers had ignored the fortified installations in their first attack. But now they were returning with a more potent armament to clean up the remnants. And if they had weapons powerful enough to kill the ammunition bunker . . .

"Out!" Kinsford bellowed. "Everyone, get out!" He threw himself at the narrow bunker door, but already that lethal, piercing whine was growing again.

Something pile-drivered vertically into the entryway. Kinsford got a split second's impression of a gray cylindrical body and crumpled fins, then the fuse relays in the SeaSLAM's five-hundred-pound warhead closed.

◇◆

"TACNET, this is Little Pig Lead."

"TACNET 'by."

"Chris, are you still maintaining drone coverage over Yelibuya Sound at this time?"

"Affirmative on that. We have a Predator on station."

"Acknowledged. We have executed our fire missions. Can you give us a poststrike assessment on the status of the Union naval base?"

"What Union naval base, boss ma'am?"

"Understood, TACNET. Operation completed. We are inbound to Floater 1."

Mobile Offshore Base, Floater 1   0310 Hours, Zone Time; June 30, 2007

One after another, the seafighters swept in from the predawn darkness. Boosting themselves up the boarding ramp, they slithered to a halt within their hangar slots, settling onto their bellies with a tired sigh of slowing fans. The waiting ground crews moved in and started unshipping service and access panels even as the personnel hatches swung open.

Amanda stepped away from the *Queen of the West,* her arm extended over her head with the fist clenched, a rallying call for the disembarking hovercrews. As they clustered around her in the scarlet worklights, she stepped up onto a toolbox to address them.

"Yesterday afternoon," she began, "the Union managed to burn us a little. But tonight, we recovered and we shoved their little win right back down their throats. Well done to all hands. The enemy will not try this again soon.

"In fact, we should send General Belewa a thank-you letter, signed by everyone in this command. For by attacking us he's given us the opportunity to go after him. And we are. After mission debriefing, I want all fighter crews to turn in and get as much rest as they can. You are going to need it. At oh twelve hundred today, there will be an O Group meeting for all officers and senior CPOs. We will be discussing new patrol zones, new operating doctrines, and new targets. There will be no more passive barrier patrols. There will be no more waiting for the other guy to start something. Ladies and gentlemen, the next time we go out, we will be on the offensive."

There was no spirited cheering as might have been incorporated into some Hollywood potboiler, but eyes flared hot in defiance of a night's worth of weariness and grim smiles tugged at a number of lips. And there was a verbal reaction of a sort, a soft, muttered growl of assent from among the assembled sea warriors.

It was the response Amanda had hoped for.

After dismissing all hands, she trudged over to her quarters module. As per her radioed request, Christine Rendino was waiting for her there with a stack of hard copy and computer media.

"Here you go, boss ma'am," the intel said. "Everything we've got on Belewa's coastal smuggling network into Côte d'Ivoire."

"Very good, Chris." Amanda hung her battle vest and pistol belt on the wall rack. Sinking down behind her desk, she yawned mightily. "What's the status on the British minehunter? Were they able to keep her afloat?"

"With the help of half a dozen spare auxiliary pumps, yes. *Santana* has her in tow, and they should be up with us sometime this morning. The Royal Navy has requested that we keep her alongside until they can survey the hulk and decide if she's worth salvaging."

"I've got no problem with that. We've got plenty of room for her crew. The survivors, anyway." Amanda yawned again and leaned over the desk, rubbing the aching back of her neck. "When *Santana* completes the tow, I'm relieving her on Guinea East station and I'm sending her across to join *Sirocco* on Union East. As I promised, Chris, your day has come. Starting right now, Belewa's smuggling pipeline is our new top priority."

"Whoa! I thought you said we couldn't afford to spare the hulls and manpower," Christine replied, dropping into the chair across from her captain.

"That was then. This is now. By taking out Yelibuya Sound and its Boghammer groups, we've not only reduced Belewa's available naval strength by one third, but we've eliminated the immediate seaborne threat to the Guinea coast. Now we get to jump on his back for a while.

"You've indicated to me that this oil-smuggling link is critical to Belewa's war effort. Okay, if we go after that link, right now, with the seafighter group and the PCs both, we not only hurt him strategically by cutting off his fuel, but we'll damage him operationally. We'll pin down his remaining sea power Frenchside, trying to defend his maritime lines of communication."

"Yeah." Christine nodded, her eyes thoughtful. "And between the aerostat radar, my recon drones, and the British patrol helicopters, we can probably spot any shift of Union naval westward in time to head them off at the pass."

"Exactly. And with the Union navy out of the way, we can turn the Guinea East barrier patrol over to the Guinean navy and Maritime police. We've got a chance now, Chris. For the first time, we've really got a chance." Reaching across to the stack of intelligence hard copy, Amanda selected and opened the first folder.

"It's going to be a whole new ball game," she continued, flipping open the file, "and we've got to develop a whole new mission profile to deal with these smugglers of yours."

Christine tilted her head and examined her friend's face. "Uh, that's all well and good, boss ma'am. But fa'sure, don't you think that getting horizontal and catching a few zees might also be in order?"

Amanda chuckled softly. "Oh, I daresay it would. But I need at least an outline of a valid search and intercept doctrine for Frenchside, and I need it by that O Group meeting this noon. I want our people out there and hunting effectively by tonight. We've given Belewa one shock already, and I intend to give him another nasty surprise just as soon as I can. You go ahead and turn in. I want to tinker with this for a while."

Christine sighed. Rising, she went to the small corner table that held Amanda's one-burner hot plate and put on water for tea. Returning to her deskside chair, she reached for a second file. "Okay, I think the place we should start is with the primary Union reception and departure points. . . ."

Outside, the first gray hint of dawn brushed at the sky.

Yelibuya Sound Fleet Base   0601 Hours, Zone Time; June 30, 2007

The Union army helicopter settled onto its skids at the edge of the wasteland. Its two passengers disembarked and carefully began picking their way into the cratered and smoldering devastation.

A scattering of others were present. Army sappers posting warning flags around unexploded munitions. Aid men carrying in bodies and pieces of bodies. Union navy survivors, shocked and trembling and not yet quite believing that they had indeed survived.

Obe Belewa and Sako Atiba paused beside the crushed and riddled hulk of a Boghammer gunboat, blown a full two hundred feet away from the water's edge.

"You were right, Obe," Atiba said quietly. "She is a witch."

Hands on hips, Belewa scanned the ruins of the naval base. "No, Sako," he replied after a few moments. "For us, she is something far, far worse. She's a warrior."

And the new war began.

A war not of guns and missiles but of guile and wile, of invention and un-conventionality, of slender dark hulls slinking through the night and a handful of vigilant and sleepless hunters.

◇◆

"Okay, Johnny Bull Lead, he's just about a quarter mile off your nose. Bearing 310 degrees true."

The *whup-whup-whup* of helicopter rotors sounded in Christine Rendino's headset, backdropping the voice of the British aviator. "Acknowledge that, Floater. We do have a young-fella-me-lad out there. Single man in a small *pirogue*. Moving in."

Seated at her workstation in the TACNET trailer, Christine shifted the aerostat radar display to tactical ranging. Contentedly munching a Milky Way bar, she watched as the transponder hack of the Royal Navy Merlin crawled closer to the anonymous blip centered in the screen.

"Over the little bugger now, Floater. I say again, single party, very small boat. Looks to be just a fisherman. If he's smuggling any petrol, he must be car-rying it in a hip flask. You sure this is the chap we're looking for?"

Christine activated a second display screen. For the past two hours she and her people had been monitoring a raft of Côte d'Ivoire fishing craft working the waters just short of the Union's territorial waters. Now she called up and replayed the recorded radar imaging from those past two hours, running it at fast forward. Among the Brownian motion of the circling fishing boats, one blip stood out. At the enhanced replay speed, it could be seen following a me-andering but intent course to the northwest and toward the borderline.

"Roger that, Johnny Bull. This is the dude we want. Are you sure there isn't anything unusual at all about that boat?"

"Now that you mention it, Floater, the chap does have a whacking big motor on that thing for the size of the craft."

"All right! Here we go! Betcha this guy is playing tugboat. Spiral slowly outward from his position and vertical search. I suspect you will find a pretty present."

"Rog, Floater. Doin' it."

Christine took another bite of her candy bar and awaited developments.

"Right you were, Floater," Dane's pleased words came back a few minutes later. "Four oil drums, ballasted to float just under the surface. We're hovering down over them now. Our lad must have cast off his tow when we popped over the horizon."

"Too bad. He's not hands-on with the stuff. We don't get to bust this guy."

"But he doesn't get to make his deliveries, either. My door gunner is preparing to open the tins now."

The sound of four short, precise machine-gun bursts leaked back over the circuit.

"Good heavens, Floater, I do believe the rude fellow is making a gesture."

⚔

"Hey, Scrounge, what did you find over there?"

"Looks like about forty jerricans of diesel under the deck boards, and a dozen cases of motor oil."

"Does the Captain have an explanation for it?"

"Yeah, Chief. He says it's all for his personal use. He says he's going up the coast to visit his mother."

"Where's his friggin' mother live? Norway?"

⚔

Lounging in the side hatch of the *Queen of the West,* Stone Quillain eyed the deck of the heavily laden *pinasse* as it drifted alongside. Cases of brown bottles jammed its narrow deck, hundreds of cases.

"Howdebody, Captain," the *pinasse's* skipper called cheerfully from the tiller station at the stern.

"Real good, son," Quillain called back. "Where you from and where you bound?"

"Half Cavalla, just short of Frenchside. Goin' up to Fishtown for the coast trade. No law against that."

"Depends on your cargo, son. What you carrying?"

"Nothin' but beer, Captain. No law against beer. We make it good beer in Half Cavalla. You want a case?"

Quillain shook his head. "Thank you kindly for the offer, but no thanks. But tell you what. Since it's a hot day out here and all, and you're working so hard and everything, why don't you drink one for us."

The Union boatman grinned back and stepped up to the rear tier of stacked cases, reaching for a bottle. However, as the bottle came up, so did Quillain's shotgun.

"Uh, not one of those, son. Why don't you take a bottle from one of them cases up forward there." Braced against the Marine's hip, the barrel of the Mossberg described an arc and pointed like a grim and insistent finger.

The grin froze on the face of the boatman. Hesitantly, he went forward and selected a bottle. As he popped the cap off, the "beer" displayed a decided lack of effervescence.

"That's it, son. You just take a big old drink now."

Resolutely, the Union boatman lifted the bottle to his lips. Bubbles appeared within the container, the boatman's cheeks bulged, and then came the explosive retch that ended the charade. He collapsed to the low rail of his craft, vomiting helplessly. The stench of gasoline and gastric distress issued across the few feet of water that separated the *pinasse* and the hovercraft.

"Now, I got to say that was a real good try, son," Quillain commented with some sympathy. "We're still going to arrest you and blow up your boat, but it was a real good try."

Mobile Offshore Base, Floater 1   1826 Hours, Zone Time; July 7, 2007

The Coke can plunked into the sea. Half filled with water ballast, it bobbed in the swells, glinting in the angled evening sun. Then the .45 roared. Two man-high jets of spray geysered up around it, making the can dance on the wave crest. The third round center-punched the red and silver container, driving it under. Stunned by the impact shock of the bullet, a small minnowlike fish floated to the surface and one of the Offshore Base's colony of semitame cormorants swooped down gratefully to receive it.

"How's that?" Amanda asked proudly, lowering the smoking automatic.

"Not good, not bad," Stone Quillain grunted. "Comin' along."

He took another empty soda can from the cardboard box sitting on the battered mess table. Plunging it into a bucket of salt water, he let it fully fill, then hurled it into the air in a high arcing parabola twenty yards out beyond the side of the platform.

His hand continued to move in a blur, scooping the M9 Beretta service pistol off the tabletop. Whipping it up and in line, the Marine fired a fast double tap. At the second sharp crack of the 9mm, the falling can exploded, aluminum confetti and water droplets raining into the sea.

Amanda cast a baleful glance at Quillain from beneath the visor of her baseball cap. "Didn't your mother ever teach you that a southern gentleman always lets the lady win?"

The ear protectors she wore made her words echo hollowly. Amanda and Quillain had established an ad hoc firing range on the port side of the barge, as well as a habit of taking some target practice after dinner on those nights when an early patrol wasn't scheduled.

Quillain laughed, a low, closed-mouthed *huh, huh, huh.* "Why, that'd be what you call sexual discrimination. It'd get this old boy in a lot of trouble."

"Yes, but it would do wonders for my sense of inferiority."

"Like I said. You're coming along." Quillain set the Beretta back on the table and slipped back his ear guards. "You doing those dry fire drills I taught you?"

"Uh, when I can find the time," Amanda replied guiltily.

It was Quillain's turn for a baleful glare. "Fifteen minutes morning and night! You can sleep after you retire!" The big Marine slipped into drill sergeant mode. "The only right way to combat-carry a Model 1911-A Colt is Condition Three: shell in the chamber, hammer cocked, and safety on!

"You have to learn to swipe that safety off with your thumb every time you draw that weapon. It's got to be instinct—there's no time to think in a gunfight! That means you repeat that draw-and-clear drill until it's automatic! That means three thousand times. And you better get it right, because it'll take ten thousand times around to unlearn it if you get it wrong!"

"Aye, aye, Captain," Amanda replied meekly, harking back to her days as an Annapolis plebe.

Quillain caught himself as well. "Yeah, well, it is kind of important, ma'am."

"I know it, and I do appreciate you showing me the ropes, Stone. What now? A couple more boxes through the pistols?"

"Naw, let's go to the M-4 for a while. You're shooting pretty good sitting and kneeling, but you need to work on your offhand."

"Okay, but we'll have to wait for a few minutes. We've got some fishermen downrange."

Half a mile out, a black silhouette ghosted along between Floater 1 and the brushfire tropic sunset. A single *pirogue* running before the wind on a mutton-chop sail.

Quillain snorted. "You don't think those guys are actually fishing, do you?"

"Of course not. When they tack about, you can see the lens glinting on their field glasses. They've got somebody out there pretty much all the time now. We know they're Union recon, but under the rules of engagement, we have to accept them at face value."

"Why is that?" Quillain grumbled, popping the clip out of his M-9 and jacking the live round out of the chamber. "I mean, every damn little tin-pot terrorist and dictator out there can do anything he likes to the United States—

blow up our embassies, torture our POWs, kill our kids in the streets—and no-body says boo. But when it comes to hitting back, man, we sure have to play by the Marquis of Queensbury, else the whole damn world screams bloody murder. Just why is that?"

"It's for the best reason in the world," Amanda replied, picking up the car-bine and adjusting its sling. "One that I wouldn't change for anything I can imagine."

Quillain's brows knit together. "What reason's that?"

She smiled back at the big Marine. "It's because we're the good guys, Stone."

Conakry Base, Guinea   1525 Hours, Zone Time; July 9, 2007

"You men are going to have to learn that while you might be stationed on the coast of Africa, you are still members of the United States Navy!"

The young ensign paced righteously in front of his field desk, his shoul-ders square and the creases of his tropic whites crisp. It was his first watch as duty officer of the day for the Conakry Shore Patrol detachment, and, as young ensigns have done since time immemorial, he was taking his job most seriously.

"There is a reason we set uniform standards," he expounded, "and a rea-son we expect them to be maintained!"

Danno and the Fryguy stood at an uneasy parade rest. The only "standard" to their own state of dress was that they were clad alike. Their sleeveless and buttonless dungaree shirts bore no ratings badges, only a "Three Little Pigs" squadron patch over the left breast. Both gunners also wore the black beret of the seafighter task force, sweat-stained and bleached dull by the sun.

"In fact, you men should be setting an exceptional standard out here. You are serving under the command of one of the most capable, most respected, and most honored officers in the fleet. I have no doubt that Captain Amanda Garrett expects her personnel to comport themselves like real man-of-wars-men and not like a bunch of cheap Rambo clones!"

At that moment, just as the ensign's tirade peaked, there came a knock at the office door.

"Enter!"

"Excuse me, Ensign. I understand you have a couple of my people here. Is there a problem?"

Amanda Garrett stood in the doorway. The eagles on the collar of her khaki shirt were sea-tarnished, and the shirt itself was oil-stained, sleeveless, and sun-faded to near white. Her slacks had been slashed short at midthigh, and a webbing belt, cut down from the quick-release strap of a MOLLE harness, rode low on her hips, supporting a Navy Mark IV survival knife and an obsolete and salt-cracked leather pistol holster. Her bare feet were slipped into a pair of native-made tire tread sandals and a frayed *Cunningham* baseball cap was tugged low over her mildly inquiring eyes.

There was a moment of profound silence in the little office.

"No, ma'am," the ensign sighed. "No problem. It was all just . . . a misunderstanding. Your men are free to go at any time."

Amanda gave a friendly nod. "I thought that might be the case. Danno and the Fryguy here are a couple of my best hands. I couldn't imagine what they could have done to get crosswise with the Shore Patrol. Thank you for taking care of things, Ensign. Gentlemen, let's be on our way."

Maintaining an appropriately sober and stoic demeanor, Danno and the Fryguy followed their captain out of the hallway. The explosion of hysterical laughter didn't occur until the door had almost closed behind them.

United Nations Kissidougu Relief Camp
Guinée Forestière Highlands,
15 Miles East of the Union–Guinea Border 1234 Hours, Zone Time: July 10, 2007

Kissidougu relief camp was a sprawling half-mile square patch of raw, muddy, and tightly packed tent rows set in the midst of the rank rain forests. Above it a thin haze of smoke hovered in the humid air, issuing from its myriad of charcoal and scrapwood fires. And below, on the ground, a mass of dispossessed humanity clogged its muddy streets—the newly nationless to whom the U.N. camp had become their sole refuge and home.

A rutted dirt road and a single spot helipad were the only links with the outside world, in and out. Cautiously, the Marine CH-60 flared out and eased down to its landing.

"How many DPs do you have here at Kissidougu, Lieutenant?" Christine Rendino asked her guide.

"Kissidougu is the smallest of the eight transit camps along the border." The Belgian army nurse wore combat fatigues and had her light brown hair bound in a bun at the back of her neck. She might have been a pretty young woman were it not for the weariness ground into her features. "And, at the moment, we have roughly eight thousand refugees in residence. An exact count is hard to come by. Every day we gain a few from across the line and lose a few to the graveyard."

"So Belewa has started to push more of his people across the border?"

"He has never stopped," the nurse replied as they clumped along the rain-slick duckboards that led to the field hospital. "We aren't seeing the big waves as we did at first. Now there are just little groups—ten, twenty, thirty. Sometimes even single families. And the Union soldiers are pushing them across through the heavy jungle and swamp areas now to avoid the Guinea patrols. The ones who reach the camps now are usually in poor condition, with much sickness, hunger, and exhaustion. We do what we can for them with the facilities we have."

Christine glanced down the overcrowded tent rows. "I thought the U.N. master plan called for these border camps to just be way stations? Aren't the DPs supposed to be moved out to the bigger cantonments along the coast?"

The nurse gave a small, bitter smile. "No one consulted with General Belewa before they drew up the plan. The highway out to Faranah has been mined . . . again. We haven't been able to get a refugee convoy out to the coast for a week. Nor have we been able to resupply. Some rations are being airlifted, of course, but we are just one helicopter away from starvation up here. God have mercy if the weather closes in."

"I brought some food up with me in my helo. Some cases of MREs, any-how." Christine found herself fumbling for words. The offering didn't seem very impressive in the looming face of famine.

The nurse found a true smile somewhere inside of herself. "Add enough hot water and one of those ration packs can be made into a soup that can keep an entire family alive for a day. Thank you. It will make a difference. Come this way, Commander. The man you wish to speak with is in this ward."

As with the living compound, the tent hospital was jammed far beyond its capacity. Every cot had long since been occupied, and now even the floor space between them was at a premium. The sick, injured, and dying occupied crude pallets on the canvas floor, and the U.N. and Guinean medical personnel made their way among them as best they could, moving with the zombielike rote of those who had worked too hard at the same task for too long.

Slowly they passed down the narrow aisle between the rows of cots and pallets. "What kind of wound profiles are you getting with the DPs?" Christine inquired, forcing herself to look to the right and left. "Any indication of systematic mistreatment by the Union forces?"

"It depends upon your definition of mistreatment, I suppose," her guide replied, frowning. "If you mean torture, beatings such as that, no. At least not among those who did not try to resist. The Union wants these people in good enough condition to walk away.

"If you mean families, old people and children, being turned out into a wilderness without adequate food, medicine, or shelter, yes. That kind of mistreatment is universal."

The nurse paused and indicated a small and very still form on one of the cots. "An example," she said, lowering her voice. "This little girl, five years old. Shortly before she and her mother were picked up by an Army sweep, she was bitten by a snake. A boomslang. There is no antivenom for a boomslang's bite. She will die sometime this afternoon."

Her face held emotionless, the nurse continued down the line. "We do get some wounds in. Frequently we see DPs who have been beaten, shot, and stabbed. But generally, that happens only after they have come across the line. The locals barely have enough food for their own families, and they look upon the DPs as a threat, a kind of two-legged locust. If a refugee is caught robbing from a field or storehouse, it goes hard for them."

They reached the end of the ward and halted at the last cot in line. "Here, Commander, I believe this is the man you wished to see. But please be brief. He is old . . . and very tired."

"I'll try and take it easy, Lieutenant. Thank you."

Christine reached up and keyed on the minirecorder in her shirt pocket, then knelt down beside the hospital cot. "Excuse me, sir," she inquired softly, "but are you Professor McAndrews? Professor Robert McAndrews?"

The man in question was thin to the point of emaciation, the whiteness of his thinning hair a stark contrast to the deep brown of his weathered skin. The eyes, though sunken deep into the fine-boned skull, were still bright and alert as they opened.

"Southern California," he said. "Am I correct?"

"That's right, sir." Christine found herself smiling. "Ventura, a Valley Girl."

"I thought so." The elderly man gave a slight nod. "I taught at UCLA for four years. A very colorful and rich dialect. Yes, I am Robert McAndrews. And you?"

"Lieutenant Commander Christine Rendino, United States Navy, currently attached to the United Nations Interdiction Force. If you wouldn't mind, Professor, I'd like to have a talk with you."

"And why not? A visit with an attractive young woman is a thing to be welcomed." McAndrews struggled weakly for a moment to roll over onto his side and face Christine. "How may I be of assistance to you, the United States Navy, and the United Nations?"

"Professor, I'm an intelligence officer gathering information about what's going on within the West African Union. And I'm hoping you can help me."

McAndrews frowned slightly. "I'm not sure how I could, Miss Rendino. If you are seeking for military secrets or troop deployments, I will be quite useless to you. I did not travel greatly in those circles."

"I didn't expect that you had, Doctor," Christine said, rearranging herself to sit cross-legged beside the cot. "I was hoping you could help me out in a much more critical area."

"And what area is that?"

"I'm hoping you can help me to understand just what is going on inside of the Union, and inside of the head of General Belewa."

The old man on the cot managed a rasping chuckle. "That will make for quite a dissertation, young lady. I hope you aren't planning to stand on one foot for it."

Christine smiled and shook her head. "Okay, then. Let's start with something simpler." She leaned forward to meet McAndrews's eyes. "Look, Professor, I've been able to learn quite a bit about you over the past few days. Your doctorates are in the fields of history and political science, and you also have a noteworthy reputation in both. You were also born and raised in Liberia. When your country started its slide into hell back in the eighties, you got out and went on to teach at some of the most prestigious universities in the world. However, when General Belewa came to power, you went home again and you were made welcome. We know you were prominently involved in the reorganization of the Union educational system, and we know you were the driving force behind the move to open the Union's first university.

"The next thing we know, however, is that you come staggering out of the jungle as one of Belewa's displaced political enemies. If you wouldn't mind talking about it, we'd like to know what happened."

McAndrews grimaced. "There is no reason not to speak about it, Miss Rendino. I made a cardinal error. I became an inefficiency."

"An inefficiency?

"Quite so. I elected to disagree. To have a differing opinion. And that brand of inefficiency is a grievous offense within the West African Union."

"Inefficiency. That's an interesting way to phrase it, Professor. Just what did you do that was so inefficient?"

McAndrew cocked one frost-colored eyebrow. "I endeavored to reintroduce politics to the West African Union. Since the establishment of the Belewa regime, we've only had 'government,' and the two are quite different affairs."

"I understand that concept. What kind of reintroduction did you try?"

The old man smiled gently. "Liberia was a democracy once. Perhaps not the best of democracies, but a democracy nonetheless. I found that I rather missed it, and so I attempted to found a political party."

"A political party?"

"Yes. Such things are outlawed currently, and that was one of the things I wished to change. I even had the opportunity to discuss the matter quite extensively with General Belewa himself on one occasion."

"What did he have to say about it?"

"I received a nod of the head and a 'someday when times are better.'" The old man's expression hardened. "I was not willing to wait for 'someday,' Miss Rendino. I felt there were issues within the Union that needed to be addressed immediately."

"Such as?"

"Oh, I think you can make a fair guess. Our acts of aggression against our neighboring states. The disenfranchisement and banishment of entire blocks of our population. Our belligerent confrontation with the United Nations. The restoration of a democracy was, in a way, the least of our concerns. Yet there were those of us who thought it might be the first step in addressing the rest of these problems."

"And so you formed your political party."

"Quite so." Another sad smile crossed McAndrews's face. "My idea was to organize the party covertly at first. When we had gathered a degree of strength, we would then go public as a 'loyal opposition,' as it were, and commence a dialogue with the Belewa government, promoting reform and a gradual integration of democratic principles into our society, as well as calling for debate upon the course our international affairs were taking.

"It was quite magnificent, really. We named ourselves the 'United Democratic Party of the Union of West Africa.' We had a signed membership of twelve people from within the educational community, a most impressive letterhead, and fully half a manifesto drawn up. . . . Then the Special Police came for us."

"That's how you became a DP."

"Indeed." Bitterness crept into McAndrews's voice. "In the Union under Belewa, you are not lined up against the wall and shot for being an enemy of the State, nor are you thrown into a dungeon or tortured. That wouldn't be 'efficient.' Instead, you are just thrown away, like a used cleansing tissue."

"And yet, Professor, you have to admit that you voluntarily went back to Liberia and that you worked with the Belewa government for a period of several years before you attempted to start this political rebellion of yours. You had to know what you were getting yourself into."

"This is very true, Miss Rendino. But you see, in my own folly, I elected to put stock in a myth."

"A myth?"

"Yes, the myth of the benevolent dictator. I have since learned that there is no such creature. There is only 'dictator,' period."

The professor lifted his head from the pillow, his eyes intently studying Christine's expression. "Now you tell me something, Miss Rendino. What do you feel about General Belewa? Not what your government's policy is, but what you, yourself, feel about him and what he has done."

The intel had to pause and consider for a moment. "Well, fa'sure he's flat-out wrong in launching a war against his neighbors and in causing all of this mass suffering on the part of the DPs. But on the other hand, I have to say it seems he's also done a lot of good."

"Exactly, Miss Rendino! And there lies the great tragedy of the West African Union and of the man who leads it. Obe Belewa has indeed done a great deal of good. Of him, it may honestly be said that he is a great man and leader. Yet each of his accomplishments is tainted by the fact that he is still an ironhanded tyrant! For each life he has made better, a myriad more have come to suffer."

"Say what you like about Mussolini," Christine murmured. "At least he made the trains run on time."

"A very apt quote, Miss Rendino. Currently General Belewa has a dream of a united, peaceful, and prosperous West Africa. No man can argue with that goal. But he made room in the Union for only his version of that dream. If anyone else has a dream of their own, they are cast out! There is only one straight line drawn. His way! His concept! His ideal! And in the end that will lead to the downfall of both Belewa and the Union."

Drained by his burst of emphatics, the elderly professor's head sank back to the pillow. "No man can be right all of the time, Miss Rendino, and a dictator has no one who can tell him when he is wrong."

Mobile Offshore Base, Floater 1   0110 Hours, Zone Time; July 12, 2007

POM! POM! POM! . . . The platform's deck Klaxons bellowed their metallic call to arms.

Blasted awake out of a rare and precious night's sleep, Amanda stared bleary eyed at the luminous hands of her wristwatch. "Not again!"

The interphone shrilled on her desk in counterpoint to the clamor outside of her quarters. Rolling off the cot, she stumbled to the desk and clawed the handset out of its cradle. "Garrett here."

"The Union Express is coming out, Captain," the platform duty officer reported. "Their heavy gunboat squadron has sortied from Port Monrovia and is closing with us at twenty-two knots. Commander Gueletti has taken the platform to battle stations as per SOP."

"I concur. Do we observe any additional activity?"

"Negative, ma'am. Just same old same old."

"Let's not take that for granted. Carry on and stay alert."

Amanda yanked on shirt, shorts, gun belt, and battle vest. Slinging a set of low-light binoculars around her neck and donning her command headset, she slipped her feet into her sandals and exited into the night.

The platform was alive with shadowy forms moving through the low bloodred deck lighting. Marines and Navy hands streamed from the housing modules, scrambling half dressed and half awake to the gun towers and bulwark emplacements. Amanda headed for Starboard 4, one of the gun towers assigned to the Little Pigs support personnel.

Scrambling up the tower access ladder, Amanda found the three-man, or rather two-man-and-one-woman, weapons crew already at their stations on the gun platform. With the nylon cover stripped from the Mark 96 over and under mount, they fed the ready-use belt of 25mm rounds into the Bushmaster autocannon and socked a fresh ammunition cassette into the stumpy 40mm grenade launcher superposed beneath it.

The gunner, an electrician's mate by the ratings badge on his dungaree shirt, activated his targeting scope and gun-mount drives, the gyrostabilizers coming on line with a mosquito whine. His loader, a signalman, hogged reload cases closer to the gun while the yeoman/talker fitted a headset over her ears. "Tower four manned and ready," she reported into the lip mike. She listened for a moment and then enunciated forcefully, "Three targets incoming . . . Bearing three . . . one . . . zero."

The gunner nestled his shoulders into the curved rests of the Bushmaster and pressed his face into the night-vision sight, the pale green light leaking from the eyepieces drawing a luminescent raccoon-mask pattern on his face. Twisting the control grips, he drifted the long, wicked-looking barrel of the autocannon onto the bearing. Amanda lifted her own glasses to her eyes and acquired the Union vessels.

There they were again: the rakish, boxy silhouette of the *Promise,* the cabin-cruiser sleekness of the *Allegiance,* and the spare minimalism of the Chinese-built *Unity.* The three big Union gunboats were running in line astern, parallel to the platform at about a two-thousand-yard range. Amanda's binoculars had enough magnification and light-gathering power to show that the gunboats had their main batteries trained outboard and leveled at the platform.

But then, they had done the same on all of the other nights as well.

A carrier clicked in Amanda's command headset and Lieutenant Tony Marlin whispered in her ear. "Captain. Do you want us to get the *Manassas* ready for launch?"

"Negative, Tony," she replied, lowering the glasses and keying her mike. "Continue with your maintenance. That's a priority. Although I'm afraid that you and your sea crew will be doing all the work tonight."

"We'll manage, Captain. But it'll sure be great to get back out on patrol again so we can get some sleep."

A sputtering streamlet of sparks arced upward from the lead gunboat, bursting in midair between the Union flotilla and the platform. A magnesium flare glared down from the sky. The gunner jerked his head back from his sights as the photomultiplier overloaded momentarily before ramping down. "Dammit all," he swore under his breath. "This is the fourth night in a row for this shit! What do these guys think they are doing out here?"

"They're trying to wear us down, Carlyle," Amanda replied. "Harassing us. Keeping us awake. Trying to make us get sloppy and careless. It's an old trick. Back during the Second World War, during the Guadalcanal campaign, the Japanese had a couple of big seaplanes that they'd fly over our positions at night. Our people nicknamed them 'Louie the Louse' and 'Washing Machine Charlie.' They'd circle for hours on end, running their engines out of synch and dropping small nuisance bombs, just to deny our people sleep."

"We going to let these guys get away with it, Captain?"

"There's nothing much we can do, except take it. We're still at fire only if fired upon. They get to make all the faces at us they like."

The gun boss muttered under his breath into his gunsights. Amanda smiled briefly. "Don't worry," she added. "They can't keep this up forever. Those gunboats burn diesel every time they come out. We can catch up on our sleep on our next leave, but there's no way for Belewa to replace that oil."

The Union warships continued their deliberate intimidating circuit, keeping their range and circling the platform. A second rocket flare arced over the platform, bursting and raining down its harsh metallic light. By it, Amanda could see the mounts atop the other gun towers tracking silently. On the roof of the PG hangar, the Marines had deployed Javelin and Stinger antitank and antiair missile launchers. Amanda recognized Stone Quillain's rangy silhouette as he hunkered beside one of the missileers.

Other navy gun parties crouched behind sandbag revetments along the platform edges, manning Mark 19s and Ma Deuce 50s. Marine fire teams warily prowled the decks as well, alert for stealthy boarding attempts. As Amanda looked on, one Marine unhooked something from his MOLLE harness. Cocking back his arm, he threw an object into the sea.

A dull thud sounded off the platform and a jet of spray shot into the air, sparkling in the fading flare light. A concussion grenade hurled to discourage any sabotage-intent combat swimmers attempting to approach the platform underwater.

Amanda keyed her headset. "Command Tower, this is Captain Garrett. Let me speak with Commander Gueletti, please."

"Gueletti here, Captain."

"Looks like it's going to be another long night, Steve. I suggest we go to a fifty percent stand-down at battle stations. Let's let our people get what rest they can."

"I concur, Captain. Going to fifty percent stand-down at battle stations. I've got the cooks working on battle rations and hot coffee as well. We'll get some out to you presently."

"Good thinking, Steve. Thank you."

Amanda glanced over at the young female talker on the gun crew. "Give me the headset, Yeoman. I'll be up here for a while, so you might as well get some rest."

"Yes, ma'am. Thank you." Amanda exchanged her light mobile headset for the heavier hardlinked earphones the young rating passed to her. The enlisted hand then curled up in a corner of the platform, using her heavy foam and Kevlar battle vest as a pillow. Over on the other side of the mount, the loader stretched out on the deck as well; Carlyle, the gunner, elected to stand to.

The TACBOSS and the electrician's mate maintained the silent watch.

The night wind brushed lightly at Amanda's cheek. Distractedly she noted that it was blowing from the northeast, an unusual point of the compass for this part of the world. The trades along the African Gold Coast usually came up from the diametric opposite, the southwest. Amanda frowned for a moment, then shrugged the puzzlement away, returning her attention to the circling gunboats.

Washed out in the glare of the falling star shells, a faint flicker backlit the clouds along the seaward horizon. Lightning stirred far away.

The Atlantic Intertropical Convergence Zone   July 2007

Beyond Amanda Garrett's awareness, a vast but subtle convulsion of nature was taking place as she kept her watch that night.

The first of a series of exceptionally strong high-pressure ridges was marching across the North Atlantic, not only initiating a series of savage winter storms in western Europe but also temporarily distorting the entire global weather pattern. The Atlantic Intertropical Convergence Zone, the perennial low-pressure belt that separated the westerly trade winds of the Northern Hemisphere from the easterlies of the Southern, was being pushed southward by almost a thousand miles. From its usual African landfall at Cape Verde, it was shifting to a point along the coast of Gabon.

While the convergence zone, once known to the world's mariners as "The Doldrums," is generally known as a region of still airs and light winds, it is also recognized as a generator of sharp and angry squall zones and raging thunderstorms. One such tropical depression began to form off the Gabonese coast. Trapped between the trade-wind zones and unable to push inland over the continent, it hovered sullenly over the equator for the next ten days, a vast clot of stagnant cloud cover, absorbing moisture and thermal energy like an overcharging battery, growing steadily in size and strength.

Then, as abruptly as it had come into being, the extensive high-pressure area over the North Atlantic dissipated and the standard global weather patterns reasserted themselves. The Atlantic convergence snapped back to its apportioned place and the southern Trades swept northward to the Gold Coast once more, shouldering the Gabon depression ahead of them.

Caught between the easterly and westerly trade winds like a pebble between two contrarotating wheels, the massive tropical depression began to collapse upon itself . . . and to spin.

Mobile Offshore Base, Floater 1   0528 Hours, Zone Time; July 22, 2007

Amanda snapped completely awake, yet she could not name the reason why. Her phone had not rung, the alarms had not sounded, and no one had knocked at her door. Her quarters, dimly lit by the hint of dawn light filtering in past the blinds, were cool and quiet beyond the white-noise rumble of the air conditioner. And yet something was indefinably but definitely wrong.

Lifting her head off the pillow, Amanda pushed her senses out in all directions, like a mother reacting to some subliminal warning about her child. And then the realization struck her. The sea. Something wasn't right with the sea.

Floater 1 was a vast and stable platform, well anchored to the ocean floor. Yet the complex of superbarges still rode the ocean's waves, pitching and rolling minutely with the surface action.

The rhythm of that movement, second nature to Amanda after her months aboard, had changed. And that disruption was profoundly disturbing.

Rising from the cot, she pulled on shirt, shorts, and sandals and stepped out on deck.

Red sky at morning. / Sailor, take warning . . .

The old poem flashed into her mind.

The air was still and sticky, with little to breathe within it. A few of the hands on morning watch lingered uneasily at the rail, feeling the same sense of disquiet as Amanda. The sky to the east flamed a bloody scarlet, and from the south a series of heavy, oil-topped rollers flowed in toward Floater 1, taking the platform almost broadside-on.

There was something disturbingly organic about those waves, as if they were being generated by the pulsing of some vast heart far out beneath the ocean. Amanda lifted her eyes to the southern horizon and studied the wispy cloud front rising above it. A cloud front that arced across the sky in a smooth, near-perfect curve.

"Damn, damn, damn!" Amanda didn't even realize she'd whispered the curse aloud. Hurrying back to her housing module, she had a look at the barometer mounted just inside the door. What she saw there made her run for the platform command tower.

Platform Commander Steven Gueletti was in the glass-walled observation deck atop the tower, and he wasn't alone. Christine Rendino and the Platform's enlisted meteorologist were there as well. Nobody looked as if they'd gotten any sleep.

"Good morning, Captain," Gueletti said grimly. "I was just about to call you. We have a situation developing here."

"So I noticed," Amanda replied, coming up the ladderway. "What's happening with our weather?"

"It's that big damn storm front we've had hovering around to the south of us. It's started to move, and it's heading in our direction."

"That doesn't feel like just a storm front to me out there, Steve," Amanda replied, crossing to the central chart table.

"It isn't," the Seabee replied. "Not anymore. The son of a bitch started to eye up on us last night. We've been sitting up with the weather sats, watching things develop."

"Why wasn't I notified?"

"There wasn't any sense to it until we knew what we were facing, and it was time to make some judgment calls," Christine interjected, joining them at the chart table. "And that time is upon us, boss ma'am. Welcome to the party."

The satcom printer in the corner started to rasp and hiss. "New satellite download coming in, sir," the meteorology rating announced.

"Let's have a look at them, Clancy."

The met rating returned from the printer and spread a sheaf of color hardcopy prints across the chart table.

"Damn, damn, damn!" This time it wasn't a curse, it was an awed whisper.

An eye thirty miles across peered up from the print, an eye surrounded by a broad, spiraling mass of white and gray cloud that almost filled the Gulf of Guinea.

"Those don't happen here," Gueletti said flatly. "Tropical storms just don't happen in these waters."

"Oh yes they do," Amanda replied. "Maybe only about twice a century, but they do. And it looks as if we've just hit the jackpot." She glanced up at the meteorologist. "What's the Beaufort projection on this thing?"

"The downloads we're getting from the Ocean Meteorology Buoys indicate Force Ten at this time, ma'am," the enlisted man replied. "Surface winds averaging fifty knots with twenty-five-foot waves. Heavy rain and spume. But she's building fast. Faster than anything I've ever seen before."

Amanda nodded. "That stands to reason. Any tropical cyclonic in these longitudes would be a mean and unpredictable freak. This is probably more like a large-scale neutercane effect than a classic hurricane."

"I concur, ma'am. She won't have legs, but she'll ramp up quick and tear the hell out of the immediate environment."

Another printer activated, spewing out a new sheet of hard copy. Christine moved to collect it. "It's an advisory from the National Hurricane Center," she reported, reading the document. "Our baby has officially been dubbed tropical storm Ivan, and they already have it red-flagged. They're projecting she'll go over the line to full hurricane status sometime tonight."

"Ivan the Terrible," Gueletti grimaced. "I see somebody back there has a sense of humor."

"Well, we know when. Now how about where?" Amanda inquired. "Do we have a projection on the point where she's coming ashore?"

"Yes, ma'am." The meteorologist moved some of the satellite photos aside to clear the chart displayed on the tabletop. "If Ivan maintains its current heading, the eye should come ashore just to the west of us, somewhere between our position and the Guinea border."

Amanda's brows lifted. "That puts us right dead on in the northeastern storm quadrant. That's the dangerous quarter north of the equator. Any chance at all for a deviation?"

The met hand shook his head. "There are no factors apparent, ma'am."

"How much time do we have?"

"The eye will come ashore about noon tomorrow. The leading edge will hit us about four hours before that. Call it 0800. We've got a little more than a day."

Amanda met Commander Gueletti's eyes. "Okay. Steve, this is the package. We have a dyed-in-the-wool hurricane bearing down on us and we are in the worst possible position to meet it. You know the capabilities of Floater 1 better than anyone else in the Navy. What options do we have?"

The Seabee officer looked grim as he replied. "Captain, the only option you ever have with a storm at sea is to get the hell out of its way. Since we can't, we're going to have to sit here and take it . . . right in the teeth."

Amanda acknowledged the statement with a nod. "Understood. Carry on, Commander. Let's do what we have to do."

Gueletti lifted an interphone from its cradle on the edge of the chart table and punched up the 1-MC circuit. "Attention, this is Platform Command."

Beyond the windows of the greenhouse, his voice boomed and rolled over Floater 1. "All hands on deck! All watches! All divisions! Lay to on the double! Set full emergency protocols. Batten down and rig for heavy weather. I say again, batten down and rig for heavy weather."

Gueletti restored the phone to its cradle. "We've got some interesting times ahead, Captain."

Amanda glanced out and across toward the Union coast. "We aren't the only ones," she replied.

Mamba Point Hotel, Monrovia   **0819 Hours, Zone Time; July 22, 2007**

"Most of our population will never have experienced anything like this storm," Belewa said with a shake of his head. "Our primary concern must be the coastal villages. Anything close to sea level is going to be inundated. We've got to get our people inland and to higher ground."

"Radio Monrovia and Radio Freetown are broadcasting continuous storm warnings and instructions to evacuate," Brigadier Atiba replied. "All village chiefs are also receiving telephone notification from the provincial councils."

"And what of the villages that do not have working radios or telephones? It's not enough, Sako. We must do more, and quickly."

Belewa's personal command center was jammed to overflowing, not only with a doubled duty watch but also with a steady stream of couriers and functionaries from the other government agencies within the building. Some were there to deliver urgently needed reports and information. The majority, however, had come to receive even more urgently needed orders and instructions. Belewa and Atiba had been on their feet since before first light, moving from desk to desk, issuing commands and motivation in equal amounts.

"I want full mobilization on all militia and labor companies. All Police and Special Police reserves as well. All cities and townships will go under full martial law at sundown tonight, and the Special Courts are authorized to conduct field trials for looters and shirkers. There will be no looting, and order will be maintained."

"Yes, sir. What about the regular army and navy?"

"Stand down from combat operations. Divert all elements to emergency services. Everything except for the Guinea border garrisons and patrols."

"As you order, General," Atiba replied, "but we should consider the fact that this storm will likely be as disruptive to the United Nations blockade as it will be to us. We may have an opportunity here to take some action."

"That is something to consider, Sako, and as soon as we have a free minute to do so, we shall. For the moment, we have a more dangerous enemy to fight."

Beyond the command suite's windows, the cloud cover could be seen building to the southward. Belewa paced slowly before those windows, his eyes half closed and his words following the flow of his thoughts. Atiba's pencil swept across the pages of his daybook, racing to keep up.

"I want foot and motorized army patrols to sweep the coastal zones. All coastal villages, or at least as many as we can reach, are to be ordered to evacuate inland immediately. Army Transport Command and the Civil Travel Commission are to dedicate all available assets to the task. Authorize the immediate dispersal of an extra week's fuel ration—"

At that moment, a signals officer entered the central room, a stunned expression on his face. Crossing swiftly to Atiba, he spoke a few quiet, urgent sentences. It was the Chief of Staff's turn then to wear the stunned expression.

"Obe . . . General Belewa, there is . . . an unusual development."

Belewa paused in his pacing. "What is it, Sako?"

"It's the satellite phone, the international diplomatic link. A woman is on it who claims that she is the commander of the American interdiction squadron. She asks to speak with you directly, Obe."

Belewa froze in place, his eyes widening as he shared in the disbelief. Then he broke the mental lock and shot a glance out of the window in the direction of both the American Offshore Base and the looming storm front.

"Tell her that I will be there presently. Brigadier Atiba, you are with me. The rest of you, carry on."

They crossed the hall to the communications center in the opposing hotel suite. The plate-size satellite dish had been set up on the balcony, and Belewa snapped his fingers, pointing to both the tape recorder and the remote speaker unit before accepting the handset. With Atiba and the commo officer listening in, he lifted the phone to his ear.

"This is Premier General Obe Belewa of the West African Union. To whom am I speaking?"

"This is Captain Amanda Lee Garrett of the United States Navy, currently commanding the U.S. elements attached to the United Nations African Interdiction Force. Thank you for accepting my call, General."

It was a good woman's voice, a strong and level alto, yet with a purring huskiness to it. The words it spoke were crisp and businesslike. Still, Belewa caught himself wondering just for a moment how that voice might sound whispering a love poem. Angrily, he shook the thought away.

"What is it you wish to speak to me about, Captain Garrett?" Somehow it never occurred to him to doubt his caller's identity.

"Matters that I suppose should be dealt with through proper diplomatic channels," the woman replied. "However, neither one of us really has the time for that at the moment. I'm sure that you are already aware of the developing weather situation?"

"The hurricane? Yes, Captain. We know of it."

"We here within the UNAFIN task force are aware of the danger this storm represents to your civilian population along the coast. We also know of the difficulties you will face in getting adequate warning to them. We wish to offer our assistance."

Belewa looked up and met the startled gaze of his officers. "Assistance?"

"That's correct, General," she replied evenly. "I have already instructed the signals stations in my net to commence broadcasting weather warnings on the civil AM radio bands, supplementing your own coverage. Also, while we know you have the standard Internet weather accesses available to you, we can feed you direct downloads from both our National Hurricane Center and from Atlantic Fleet Command's Meteorology Division. Can you provide us with a datalink?"

Damnation! What was he supposed to say to that! He could only nod and gesture affirmatively to the communications officer. *Yes, for the love of God, set it up!*

"We are arranging for the datalink, Captain," Belewa replied, his mind racing. What was she planning? What kind of trap could this be? "I . . . thank you for your consideration. This is most unexpected."

"Why should it be, General?" the level alto continued. "We are both professional military officers, involved in a confrontation between our nations. However, I believe we are both wise enough to know that there is a time and a place for such confrontation. This is not one of them. The United States and the United Nations have no conflict with the civil population of the West African Union, and they are the ones most at risk at this moment.

"Accordingly, I propose a truce, a cease-fire, beginning now and extending for a period of forty-eight hours beyond the termination of the coming hurricane, permitting us both to focus our assets on disaster relief and rescue. From what I judge, the most critical problem confronting us is the evacuation of your low-lying coastal regions prior to the storm coming ashore, and disaster assessment afterward. We are prepared to assist in both of these areas."

"In what way?" Belewa inquired cautiously.

"You are aware of our reconnaissance drones and our intelligence assessment capacity, General. I am prepared to put them at your disposal in the same way we are aiding the government of Guinea. Many of your isolated coastal communities are without radio or telephone communications. We can spot the communities that appear to be evacuating and those that are not, allowing your emergency services to concentrate their efforts on the villages that have not received a warning yet. Following the hurricane, we can pinpoint those areas along your coast that have been hardest hit, again allowing you to concentrate your efforts. If we work together on this, General, we can hold down the loss of life your nation is facing."

God, but she was right. What reason had he to refuse such an offer? Beyond personal pride or suspicion, at least.

"How do you wish to administer this truce, Captain Garrett? What guarantees do you require?"

"Your word of honor as an officer, sir," the reply came back fearlessly and without hesitation, "as I offer mine in return."

"Accepted, Captain. The truce goes into effect one hour from now until forty-eight hours after the storm's passage. I . . . thank you on behalf of the people of the Union."

"On behalf of UNAFIN, I thank you for allowing us to aid. Might I suggest we turn this matter over to our staffs at this time for the arrangement of details? I suspect we both have a great deal of work to do."

"Indeed, Captain."

Belewa restored the phone to its cradle. How very strange. How can it be that one who is your blood foe could also be one with whom you could place an instinctive and implicit trust? Obe Belewa silently made a pledge that he would look into this Amanda Garrett's eyes someday.

Granted they both survived.

From his station at Belewa's shoulder, Brigadier Atiba spoke softly. "Obe. Was this wise? To accept our enemies' handouts like this? It will look to the world as if we are not capable of taking care of our own citizens."

Belewa glanced at his chief of staff. "No, Sako, I do not know if this was a wise thing for me to do. I only know that it had to be done. Establish the links between National Emergency Services and the American offshore base. Time is short. No matter who offers it, let us not squander this gift."

Mobile Offshore Base, Floater 1   0305 Hours, Zone Time; July 23, 2007

It was a night when adrenaline and black coffee took the place of sleep. Dog it down, get it secured, strike it below. If it can't be readily moved under cover, lash it in place. And then, when you're sure it isn't going anywhere, throw an extra loop of line around it, just to be certain. You have to be certain, for the Wrath of God is rolling up from the south.

The 1-MC speakers warred with the thudding of helicopter rotors. "Status Bravo Personnel! Starboard watch! Report to Helipads Red One and Green Two for evacuation! Expedite!"

Amanda prowled through the shadows and glare of the worklights, supervising and spotting weak points with a mariner's eye. Floater 1 was like no vessel she had ever helped to see through a storm before, but there were lessons she had learned that were still applicable.

"Hey, you men on that trailer," she yelled across to one of the work parties. "Let the air out of that thing's tires and bleed the hydraulic pressure out of the jackstands before you strap it down. Reduce the wind resistance as much as you can and get the center of gravity as low as possible."

"Will do, ma'am," the senior petty officer acknowledged.

"And put about another dozen bights around that roll of sunshade. If the wind gets under that canvas, it'll tear like Kleenex."

"Aye, aye."

"Captain," another voice, this one with a British accent to it, hailed her. Lieutenant Mark Traynor hobbled across the deck on his wound-stiffened leg. "I beg your pardon, Captain Garrett, but I need to ask you for another favor."

"Ask, Leftenant. Whatever we can do." Amanda and the other U.S. personnel aboard Floater 1 had come to admire the fight the company of the HMS *Skye* had been making to save their crippled ship. A number of her crewmen, her wounded captain included, had stayed on aboard the platform to help keep the battle-damaged little minehunter afloat.

"I'd like to move the *Skye* a little more amidships along the lee side of the platform, if we may," the Englishman said apologetically. "It will give her a bit more shelter. We could use some help walking her down, if you could spare the manpower."

"No problem at all, Leftenant. I'll have Commander Gueletti authorize a work detail to assist you. I'm sorry that heavy lift ship didn't show up in time to haul you out before this blow. Do you think you're going to have any problems tomorrow?"

"Not to worry, ma'am," Traynor replied resolutely. "We'll keep the water out of her if we have to drink it."

As Traynor went on his way, an attention tone sounded in Amanda's command headset. Shifting from one crisis to the next, Amanda stepped back between a pair of Conex containers to reply. "Garrett here," she said into the lip mike, cupping her hands over the earphones to eliminate some of the deck-side clamor.

"This is Chris, boss ma'am. We're shutting down the Floater TACNET node at this time. All system operations are switching over to Conakry Base."

"What about the *Bravo* and *Valiant*?"

"Both successfully recovered their aerostats and they're beating out to sea now," the intel replied. "Those old TAGOs hulls were built to operate in the North Atlantic. They can take a little heavy weather. *Santana* is riding it out at Conakry, and *Sirocco* is heading Frenchside to Abidjan."

"Good enough. How about our data dump to Monrovia?"

"They're still accepting. We'll feed 'em weather from Conakry Base for as long as the satellite links stay up. I've had to secure the drone recon, though. We're approaching gust limits for the Predators at the higher altitudes, and we've flown all of the Eagle Eyes off the platform."

"Understood. When do you and your people haul out?"

"My guys and me go on the next shuttle flight. Hey, when we get on the beach at Conakry, how about we throw a good old-fashioned hurricane party?"

Amanda hesitated a moment before replying. "Maybe, Chris. I'll see you later."

She worked her way aft, heading for the hover hangars. Everything within the squadron area appeared well battened down for the coming tempest. Even the "Three Little Pigs" placards on the exterior bulkheads had been unshipped and placed under cover. Running lights flashing, the PGs themselves stood ready to launch, the last of the service crew scrambling aboard.

"Hey, Captain!" As Amanda stepped out onto the turning platform, Steamer Lane jogged across to her, Snowy Banks trotting at his heels. "We were looking for you, ma'am," Lane said. "We're all set to haul out. Do you need a hand getting your gear aboard?"

Amanda shook her head. "Not necessary, Steamer. I'm going to ride it out here aboard the platform."

The two hover pilots swapped startled glances. "Begging the Captain's pardon, ma'am," Snowy said carefully, "but, given the situation, are you sure that's wise?"

"I suppose it depends on your definition of 'wise,' Snowy." Amanda smiled back. "I spent two years commanding a Fleet Ocean tug in the Atlantic. I know a little bit about barge operations and heavy-weather work, and I think I can make myself useful. Commander Gueletti and his Seabees are going to have their hands full out here when that blow hits.

"And speaking of that blow," she continued, cutting off any further protest on the part of her officers. "You'd better get under way. You're tight on time, and you have a long run to Conakry Base."

"As you say, Captain," Lane responded reluctantly. "I wish you were coming with us, though."

"I'll be fine. You just watch yourselves out there tonight."

"No sweat, Captain. If the sea starts kicking up on us too bad, we can always haul out on the beach."

"Even so, be careful. I'd hate to be the first task force commander in naval history to lose a ship by having a tree fall on it."

Amanda looked on as the seafighters fired up and took their departure. One by one, they lumbered forward to the edge of the launching ramp, slipping over and slithering down to the uneasy sea. Crossing to the starboard rail, Amanda watched the running lights of the squadron fade into the murky night.

Even with a couple of hundred people remaining on the platform, Amanda felt suddenly very much alone.

"The squadron get off okay, ma'am?" A massive form moved up beside her at the rail.

Startled, Amanda looked up at Ben Tehoa. "Chief? What are you still doing here?"

"Same thing you are, Captain." The big CPO grinned back. "These Construction Battalion guys are real good at building airports and grading roads and such, but they're going to need the help of a couple of real sailors before this show's over."

Dawn found the platform's skeleton crew still hard at work, making final preparations for the oncoming storm. The sun rose in colors of dirty green and tarnished bronze, and the moisture-saturated air hung deathly still, lying on the chest like a coffin lid. The sea roiled, the wave patterns broken and irregular now, as if the waters themselves had grown fearful and were seeking escape.

Working with Chief Tehoa, Amanda supervised the deployment of a last few yards of lifeline. But suddenly she brought herself up short, her ears clicking and popping in response to a drop in barometric pressure so abrupt as to be physically sensed.

Looking up, she found that a stillness had fallen on the decks of Floater 1. Almost everyone else on the decks had paused as well, staring away to seaward.

It was as if the sea and sky to the south were coagulating, the horizon wrinkling and collapsing inward like melting cellophane. And then Amanda realized that it was no optical illusion. She was looking at the leading edge of Hurricane Ivan, sweeping down upon them like an atmospheric avalanche.

"Well," Chief Tehoa commented mildly. "Here she comes."

Mobile Offshore Base, Floater 1   1021 Hours, Zone Time; July 23, 2007

To Amanda it was an anarchistic, Wagnerian symphony played by an orchestra of insane gods. The wind instruments were the winds themselves, treble howl and base bellow and a thousand heterodyned variants between. The strings played from the platform's network of guy wires and tie-downs, thrumming and shrieking as the tempest plucked at them madly.

And the sea mastered the percussion section. Towering ranks of spume-fringed waves beat upon Floater 1. Crashing down upon the inundated decks, they drove the barge segments together with a kettledrumming boom, the impact of each comber radiating upward through the platform structure.

Gritting her teeth in a snarl of effort, Amanda drew herself forward from the core barge along one of the fore-and-aft lifelines. Her tightly laced life jacket served more as a shield against the high-velocity bite of the windblown rain than it did as a protection against a possible drowning. No one going over the side in this sea-spawned holocaust could hope to survive.

It was midmorning, yet only the dimmest tinge of gray daylight cut the murky darkness, supplementing the flickering gleam of the few surviving deck-side work arcs. And vision full into the blast of the hurricane was flatly impossible.

Twisting her left wrist into the lifeline to hold herself in place, Amanda covered her eyes with her right hand, leaving a slit parted between her fingers. The old typhoon fighter's trick worked as well here in the Atlantic as it did in the China Sea. With her sight partially shielded, she could look into the face of the storm, seeking Chief Tehoa.

The Chief and a Seabee work party were on deck doing direct battle with the hurricane. A fight Amanda feared they had no chance of winning.

As the tempest had mounted and the storm-driven waves had grown higher, the platform crew had been forced to uncouple the hard links joining the nine superbarges that made up Floater 1. Opening the hard links allowed the barges to ride with the seas more easily, and a failure to do so would have resulted in the couplings being torn bodily out of the barge hulls as the wave action exceeded their play limits.

However, even as links kept the barges together, they also served to keep them separate. Interconnected now by only a network of mooring hawsers, the massive barges slammed and jostled into each other with each oncoming wave.

Work details were forced to sortie out onto the decks in an agonizing effort to keep the platform components wedged apart.

Ben Tehoa led one such team now, working at the juncture point between four of the barges. Tethered off on their lifelines and with their water-sodden clothing whipping at their bodies, the seamen stood back and warily regarded the monster.

The cover plates that bridged the gaps between the platform sections were long gone, blown aside by the wave action. The yard-wide spaces between the barge hulls now gaped open and smashed closed, four sets of gnashing steel jaws waiting to pulp anything or anyone that might slip between them. Intermittently, as a storm comber crawled under the hulls, a sheeting geyser of seawater would explode upward through the gaps, the tearing wind shredding the curtain of ejected water away into a cloud of stinging salt mist.

Bearing a massive manila ship's fender, Tehoa and his men hunkered down against the force of the wind, awaiting the moment when the jaws would open again.

As Amanda looked on, it came, the barges lifting with the swell and the gaps opening in response. Faintly she heard Tehoa's wordless shout and the detail lunged forward, seeking to thrust the gag into the monster's mouth.

For an instant, Amanda thought they might succeed. Then the sea slumped away beneath the platform and a roaring jet of storm-compressed water and air fountained skyward, hurling the fender away and knocking the work party sprawling.

One seaman, fouled in his own lifeline and caught in the reversing rush of the seawater, was swept to the edge of the gap. As the sailor was on the verge of toppling between the barges, Tehoa lunged for the man. Catching his arm, the Chief hauled him away from death. Outraged at the loss of their prey, the steel jaws snapped shut with a reverberating crash.

Battered and beaten, the work party drew back into the windbreak of a deck module to regroup and reassess. Amanda joined them behind the shelter.

"How is it going, Chief?" she yelled into Tehoa's ear.

"Not good!" the big man bellowed back over the storm clamor. "Not good! It's hell keeping the fenders in place, and they don't help all that much when we can!"

"What about air bags?"

"Totally useless! The barges chew 'em up like bubble gum. Problem is, we're quartering into the weather! She ain't riding clean!"

Proving his point, another storm roller broke across Floater 1. Impacting on the port-side forward angle of the platform, its force twisted and jammed the barge complex together in ways it was not designed for.

The beam of a battle lantern flashed across the Chief and Amanda as another seaman collapsed into the shelter of the deck module. "Chief," the sailor raked spray-sodden hair out of a pair of frightened eyes, "we got trouble! We got water coming in!"

"Where?" Amanda demanded.

"This corner of Outboard Four. The next barge to port, ma'am."

"Let's go!"

The passage to the crisis point entailed a carefully gauged leap between the two superbarges, aided only by a wildly whipping lifeline, then a plunge down through a deck hatch. Within the massive platform segment, they were sheltered from the bite of rain and spray and the maniacal howl of the hurricane was at least muffled. Now, however, could be heard the squeal and creak of steel under stress, and the rolling crash of one barge against another reverberated like a thunderbolt.

Each barge had been compartmentalized into hundreds of smaller interconnected cells. The upper-level spaces were used for dry supply and equipment storage. Deeper in the massive hulls, below the waterline, could be found tankage for drinking water and fuel. Amanda, the Chief, and their guide descended to these decks via a series of narrow, condensation-slick ladders.

The barge's interior lighting circuits had failed on the lowest level, and they dropped into a darkness lit only by the glow of a few emergency battle lanterns. Dropping from the ladder, Amanda found herself standing calf-deep in seawater.

Ahead, down the passageway, a lantern beam blazed in her face. "Captain Garrett? Glad you're here, ma'am. We got trouble."

"So I see." Amanda sloshed toward the light, bracing herself against the moisture-slick bulkheads. "Who do we have down here, and how much of a problem do we have?"

"Petty Officer First Trevington, ma'am, Damage Control Four Delta." The battle lantern made a circle around a group of tense DC hands. "We got impact damage in the frames just forward of here."

"Let's have a look. Do we have pumps working on this water?"

"Yes, ma'am," the team leader replied, leading Amanda and Tehoa forward along the starboard quarter of the barge. "The barge pumps are on line and the drain valves are open. We're holding for now, but if it gets worse . . ."

They folded themselves through another small watertight door, entering the next passageway section. Here a solid sheet of water cascaded down the face of the outboard bulkhead. Amanda pushed a hand into the flow, gauging its intensity. "We've got a cracked weld," she said after a few seconds' study. "Do we have any vertical separation or plate fractures yet?"

"No, ma'am. So far we just got that one seam unzipping along the top of this bulkhead frame, but it's widening and getting longer. We're going to get involvement in the next compartment pretty quick."

As if to emphasis the DC hand's point, the barge shoulder-butted its neighbor, the impact striking through the heavy steel plates like a cannon discharge. Amanda found herself thrown back against the far bulkhead, her arm numbed to the shoulder by the shock.

Chief Tehoa caught her before she could go to the deck. "You okay, Captain?"

"Pretty much," she replied, trying to shake the numbness from her paralyzed limb. If she'd been leaning with her weight against that arm, bones would have shattered. "We've got to get this shored up before a plate caves in."

"Bracing and shoring team is already on the way, Captain," the DC man reported.

"Shoring's only going to be a temporary fix, ma'am," Tehoa added grimly, setting her back onto her feet. "The platform's going to open up like this at every impact point within the structure if we don't do something about the way she's riding. We can't take these quartering seas for much longer."

"I know it, Chief."

"Gangway! Make a hole!" The shout reverberated down the darkened passageway as the bracing and shoring team arrived on site. Bearing their array of sledgehammers, four-by-four timbers, and plywood panels, they sprang to the task of reinforcing the forward angle of the barge hull.

"Chief," Amanda said, sidling out of the way. "You stay here and see what you can do to get this secured. I'm going up to the tower to confer with Commander Gueletti."

"Okay, Captain. We'll do what we can. I just hope you and the Commander can come up with something."

"Me too, Chief. Me too."

If anything, the winds had grown in intensity while Amanda had been below. The transit back to the core barge could be made only thanks to the lifelines and the intermittent patches of protection afforded behind the deck modules. Entering the base of the platform control tower, she paused only long enough to press a few handfuls of water out of her sodden hair and khakis, then climbed for the command center. The erratic lurching and rolling of the core barge, noticeable enough on the weather deck, grew with each level climbed, forcing Amanda to maintain a death grip on the ladderway railings.

Emerging on the command deck, she suddenly froze at the head of the ladderway. Lord God! Down on the weather deck you were too close to it. But up here you could see!

As Amanda looked beyond the tower windows, a hypervelocity gust momentarily tore the curtain of rain away.

The sky glowed an evil and diseased verdigris, lightning crawling about in its boiling belly. And the waves, a vast curving front of gray storm-driven combers, marched in from the horizon, their arched backs hoary with wind-riven spray. As each wave reached the windward corner of the platform, it curled over to butt like an enraged bull elephant, perishing in an explosion of water that buried Floater 1's decks. Waves of compression and release could be seen radiating through the platform structure with each blow.

The next supersquall hit and a roaring wall of precipitation cut off the view. It was a very rare thing for Amanda Garrett to be afraid of the sea, but she knew fear now. Floater 1 couldn't take this kind of punishment for long. No mere man-made structure could.

In the far corner of the command deck, Commander Steve Gueletti leaned over the shoulder of one of his systems operators, fighting a desperate delaying action.

"How much room do we have in the stern bunkerage tanks of number one?" he demanded, his voice raised over the sound of the storm.

"Twelve thousand gallons, sir."

"Initiate high-speed fuel transfer from bow to stern bunkers. Twelve thousand gallons."

"Initiating transfer," the S.O. replied, her voice emotionless. Her fingers danced across her keyboard, feeding commands into the ballasting system. "Barge 1 systems acknowledging, fuel transfer initiated."

"Onboard sewage system. Purge all storage tanks to sea."

"Sewage system purge initiated. All storage tanks blowing to sea."

Concerned or not, Amanda looked on with interest. This was seamanship of a kind she was unfamiliar with.

"Barge 1 again," Gueletti continued, staring down at the tankage control displays. "Storage cells K4 and K8. Pump to sea."

The S.O. looked up. "Verify, sir. Those are drinking water storage. We have over four thousand gallons in each cell."

"I know it. And I know there won't be anyone left around to drink it if number one gets driven under. We've got to keep her leading edge up. Pump to sea!"

Using the handrail around the central chart table, Amanda made her way around to the ballast control station. "You've got more of a water problem than you know, Steve. I've just come up from number four. You've got some seams opening up down there."

"Tell me about it, Captain," the Seabee replied. "We're taking water in one and two as well, and I'm expecting flooding reports from the other barges at any time. She's starting to hammer herself to pieces. This quartering sea is killing us. We take much more of it and she's going to come apart like a soggy cardboard box."

Amanda tightened her grip on the rail as the tower swayed under the impact of another macroburst. "What can we do about it?"

"That's just it, Captain. There's not a solitary goddamn thing we can do."

"Commander," another systems operator called from his station. "The computer's finished the ride simulation. This doesn't look good, sir."

"You'd better have a look at this, Captain," Gueletti said, arming his way around to the simulation console. "I've had my people run a structural analysis and projection on the cumulative storm damage. This will give us an idea where we're going to stand in another couple of hours."

Amanda joined him at the shoulder of the sweating S.O. "Run the ride analysis," Gueletti commanded.

The systems operator hit a key sequence. A phantom outline of Floater 1 appeared on the computer monitor; nine rectangular barges in three ranks of three, afloat on a gridwork sea.

"Initiate standard projected storm action."

The gridwork ocean humped up and rolled. Arrows rezzed into existence, stabbing at the bow of the platform, indicating the impact points of wind and wave. Smoothly the interlinked raft of barges sequentially rode up and over the incoming waves.

"If we were facing into the wind and sea like this, we wouldn't be having any trouble," Gueletti elaborated. "However, when we anchored Floater 1 here, we oriented her to face to the southwest, into the normal predominant weather patterns. This storm's a freak, though. It's coming in straight from the south, and we're taking it on our port quarter rather than head-on."

The Seabee commander issued another order to the systems operator: "Alter storm bearing."

The computer-generated tempest on the monitor pivoted to match the real-world storm. Now the interconnected barges no longer rode smoothly; they twisted and jostled within the formation, as they were doing now. Red flashes pulsed on the screen, denoting collision points.

"Initiate cumulative damage program."

Small blue squares began to appear within the barges, radiating outward from the collision points. "This is cumulative sequential flooding from the storm damage. As you can see, as we take on water, the barges begin to lose stability within the platform structure. As stability is lost, the rate of damage accumulation accelerates. We can counter to a degree by shifting ballast within the barges, like I was doing when you came up, but not enough to stop the process."

The number of blue squares grew explosively and the riding of the barges grew wilder. "Eventually," Gueletti continued, "the cumulative damage becomes so severe that the structural integrity of the platform will be compromised."

On the monitor screen, the graphics model of Floater 1 broke up into its component segments, some of the barges capsizing and sinking, others being driven away before the storm.

"How long do we have until breakup?" Amanda asked, her voice only just audible above the wind.

"By this projection, about four hours, ma'am," the systems operator said almost apologetically.

"And how much longer until this storm blows over us?"

"Six." Gueletti let the single word hang in the air.

Amanda turned away from the simulations console. Gripping the handrail of the chart table, she stared out into the storm murk for almost a full minute, assessing potentials.

"We've got to turn her into the wind," she said abruptly. "That's all there is to it."

"Agreed, but how?" Gueletti said, coming to share a handgrip beside her. "Even in a dead calm, nothing short of an oceangoing tug could maneuver this thing. And we don't have a tug or a calm."

"We don't need either one," Amanda replied. She waved a hand at the storm beyond the windows. "We've got all the motive power we need right out there. She'll weathervane and turn into the wind by herself if we can give her half a chance. What kind of ground tackle are we holding with?"

"When Floater 1 was built, the idea was to keep all four rails of the platform clear for mooring and ship handling. Accordingly, each barge has a single central anchor well and capstan room, each capstan handling twelve hundred feet of chain. We've mostly got a mud-and-sand holding ground under us at this site, so we're using five-ton mushroom anchors, nine of 'em. We've got forty-five tons of iron on the bottom, and according to the GPUs, we haven't shifted an inch since the start of the blow."

Amanda nodded thoughtfully, absorbing the data and applying it to the problem. "What if we lift eight of the hooks and leave number two's down as a bottom drag. We could turn her around that?"

Gueletti shook his head. "I wouldn't like to try it except as an absolute last resort. Like I said, we primarily have a mud-and-sand holding ground under us. But our sonar survey indicates we've got some rock ledges down there too. If

JAMES H. COBB

we hooked the drag anchor on one of those, we could rip the whole damn capstan room right out through the bottom of the barge."

"Then how about an array of sea anchors? We lift all the hooks and let her drift until the sea anchors bring her head around."

Again came that decisive shake of the head. "That's out too, Captain. We're situated on a comparatively narrow bank of shallows out here with a deepwater trench to landward. If we get blown off this holding ground, the next stop is the beach at Monrovia."

Amanda lightly bit her lower lip, tasting the salt of the sea brine drying on it. *Don't get panicky, just work the problem. All the pieces you need are still here. You can feel it. You only have to put them together correctly.* She leaned over the chart table, staring at its surface without seeing.

"Steve," she said after a full minute. "What about the platform's towing tackle? Do you keep that aboard?"

"Sure. Every barge stores its own towing harness in a cable tier."

"It must be pretty heavy-gauge gear. And there must be a lot of it."

Gueletti shrugged. "The heaviest you can get. Quarter-mile lengths of four-inch steel hawser. All new stuff."

"All right," Amanda replied slowly. "All right, that's how we're going to do it. You're right about the anchor chains. We can't safely turn her on one of those. We don't have enough play. But we can turn her on one of your towing lines."

The Seabee cocked an eyebrow. "I don't see how. Our towing hawsers could hold one or maybe even two of our barges in this kind of sea state, but not the whole platform. We'd snap that wire like it was a thread."

"That's just it, Steve," Amanda replied, the excitement and surety growing in her voice. "We don't have to hold the platform with it. We just have to provide a point of resistance the platform can turn itself around. We'll shackle two of your towing cables together. Then we lift our anchors and let the platform drift a short distance, paying out one of the lengths of hawser as we go, to create our anchor harness. Then, as we start feeding out the second cable section, we apply the wildcat brake on the cable feed. We create drag on the line while still deploying cable fast enough to keep the cable below breaking tension. That point of resistance will turn us into the wind. It will be like using a drag anchor on the bottom. Except that we'll be producing the drag at the topside end."

"And we'd still have enough control on our drift to keep us from going off of the bank," Gueletti agreed, catching hold of the idea. "But what kind of hook can we put down that we can be sure won't shift?"

"A big one, Steve," Amanda replied. "A real big one."

"What do you have in mind? The biggest we have is five tons."

"No. We can do a lot better than that." Amanda pushed away from the chart table and crossed to the lee-side windows. "There's our anchor right there."

She pointed down to the blackened and battered hulk of the HMS *Skye,* moored to the sheltered downwind side of the platform.

"We run our cable aboard the *Skye* and secure it around the main engine mounts. Then we cut her loose and scuttle her with a demolition charge. She displaces almost five hundred tons. There's no way we're going to drag that around behind us."

"Captain," Gueletti said, aghast, "that's a Royal Navy man-of-war down there! We don't have the authority to order it sunk."

"Commander, that minehunter's going to be just another piece of junk washed up on a Union beach if this platform breaks up. The *Skye*'s lost, no matter what. But if we sacrifice her in this way, we may be able to save Floater 1."

The platform commander considered for a moment. "Hell, I guess you're right, ma'am. The taxpayers can buy the Brits another minesweep later."

"Exactly, Steve. Now, do you have a demolitions man who could rig a set of charges aboard the *Skye* that could put her on the bottom fast without compromising her structural integrity?"

"Ma'am, I've got a couple of master blasters in this outfit who could blow your bra off without bruising your . . . skin."

◇✦

The phrase "wooden ships and iron men" is a canard, a sly hint that the modern steel-age sailor is not the equal of his tar-and-oakum forebears. To Amanda Garrett, that concept was baseless. As a true mariner, she recognized the World Ocean as something elemental and unsubmitting. All of man's strengths and technologies, no matter of what age or level, are toylike when matched in a direct confrontation.

That night, amid the screaming madness of Hurricane Ivan, the labors of Floater 1's crew were as epic as any performed aboard the square-riggers of the past. It was "one hand for the ship and one hand for yourself" as the massive lengths of steel hawser were stricken up from below and shackled together. No plans had been made for such work when the platform had been built. No machinery was in place to perform the task.

Seabee muscle power jackassed tons of wire cable across the bucking, tempest-raked decks, feeding it through makeshift guides around the platform's perimeter to the *Skye*'s moorage. From there the far end was taken aboard the minesweep and down a passageway to be secured around a series of load-bearing hardpoints within the hull. Simultaneously, demolitions personnel worked in the flooded bilges of the little ship, grimly rigging their charges as stinking oil-tainted seawater rolled over them with each storm toss.

Six of Floater 1's barges were taking water by the time the task was done.

⚐◆

A small cluster of people huddled in the lee of a deck module: Amanda, Chief Tehoa, the demolitions team, and the remnants of the *Skye*'s crew.

Amanda cupped her hands protectively around the earpiece and microphone of the command headset she wore. Two other "weatherproof" communicator units had already shorted out on her. "Tower, we're ready to go down here," she yelled into the mike.

"Standing by here as well." The reply could be heard only faintly over the wind roar. "All capstan rooms manned and ready."

"Proceeding." Amanda lifted her eyes to the senior demo man. "Cut her loose!"

The Seabee nodded. Flipping a switch guard up on the detonator box he carried, he depressed a button.

Loops of det cord fired with a piercing crack, slicing through the *Skye*'s mooring lines and freeing the warship. The clawing talons of the storm caught at her blackened upperworks and she began to drift downwind, a tattered white ensign still flickering at her jackstaff. Steel squealed and rasped as loops of heavy towing cable trailed over the side after her, far lighter wire peeling off the reel connected to the onboard scuttling charges.

Amanda saw the bleak expressions on the faces of the British seamen as they watched the *Skye* depart on her last voyage. Especially she noted the jaw-clinching despair on the face of the minesweep's young captain.

"Leftenant Traynor," she called, "I am truly sorry we have to do this."

"It's quite all right, ma'am," he replied, suppressing the tremor in his voice. "At least she's dying for a good cause." The British officer extended a hand to the demo man. "If you please, Chief. She's my responsibility."

Amanda nodded and the Seabee passed over the demolition control box. Traynor flipped up the second switch guard. "Ship's company," he called hoarsely, "salute!"

As best they could on the unsteady deck, the men of the *Skye* came to attention, hands lifting to honor the silhouette that was fading beyond the sheeting rain and spray. Traynor's thumb stabbed down on the button and the *Skye*'s outline blazed with blue-white glory for an instant.

Then the sea avalanched through the dozen gaps blasted in her hull. In a matter of moments, the minesweep capsized, wrapping herself in the towing hawser as she settled. And then she was gone, and only the shriek of the cable going over the side marked her passage.

"Ship's company," Traynor's voice trailed away in the wind, "stand at ease."

"All right." It was Amanda's turn to lift her voice over the storm. "Let's get this thing done!"

✄◆

Amanda elected to place her command post on site at the winch station of Barge 2, the central segment of the forwardmost tier of the platform. The wire cable would be fed up from belowdecks at this point, run through the cable brake, and fed over the barge's bow. As the rest of the handling crew fell back to safety, Amanda and Tehoa hauled themselves onto the small open platform beside the cable feed. Exposed to the full force of the hundred-knot wind gusts and the buckshot patterns of rain and spray, they latched their safety belts to the railing. Chief Tehoa gave the broad horizontal wheel of the wildcat brake half a turn to test the mechanism, while Amanda activated the handheld Global Positioning Unit she carried. She acquired Floater 1's coordinates on the palm-size screen of the little unit, locking down the platform's position. With no visual reference points available in the storm murk, the GPU would serve as her drift gauge.

"Ready, Chief?" she yelled.

"Guess so, ma'am. Still think it'll work?"

"No problem, Chief. It's just like catching a thirty-pound catfish on a twenty-pound bass rig."

She caught the flash of Tehoa's grin in the glare of a lightning stroke. "I've never managed to pull that one off, ma'am."

"Neither have I." Amanda keyed her headset. "Tower, we're ready to raise anchors."

"Proceed, Captain. You are on circuit with the capstan rooms. Good Lord, ride all the way!"

Amanda wrestled another lungful of air from the torrent flowing over her. "All capstan rooms! Heave round!"

Moments later, Amanda felt the vibration. Massive electric motors engaged deep within each barge. Slime-covered steel links, each the diameter of a baseball bat, rose up out of the boiling waters of the anchor wells. Forty fathoms below, the anchors themselves, each an inverted ten-thousand-pound parasol of solid metal, started to shift and walk on the seafloor, the play coming out of their chains.

Another wave quartered onto the platform. Restrained now by her tautening ground tackle, Floater 1 moaned in agony as the waters crashed over her. Tie-downs snapped and a CONEX container toppled over the side. Then she lifted, and the sea shouldered under the platform with a prolonged, yielding shudder.

"Number four breaking ground," a thin voice cried in the headset.

"Number one breaking ground."

"Number seven breaking ground."

"Number five . . ." "Number eight . . ." "Number six . . ." Calls overrode as, one after another, the anchors tore loose from the bottom.

"All anchors aweigh, Captain!"

The position numbers on Amanda's GPU screen began to flicker and change. Floater 1 was adrift. No longer fighting the storm, the massive structure was now being driven before it.

Amanda pressed her lip mike close to her mouth. "Capstan rooms. Retract to ten fathoms! We're passing over the wreck of the *Skye*. Get clearance! Don't let her foul!"

Crack! One of the heavy nylon ropes that served as a cable guide parted like a piece of yarn. As the platform drifted back over the hulk of the British minehunter, the towing hawser peeled away from the barge railings, coming around from the lee side to align forward off the bow.

Crack! Crack! Crack! WHAM!

The last guide snapped, and the four-inch wire hawser whipped out ahead of the platform, taking half a dozen railing stanchions with it in an explosive sweep of sparks. As Amanda and the Chief looked on, cable began to feed up through the wildcat guides from belowdecks.

"Give her some slack!" Amanda yelled "Let's get some play out there!"

Tehoa nodded, hunching over the brake wheel.

Looking straight forward off the platform, Amanda could feel the wind batter at her left cheek. When she felt that wind full in her face, they would be aligned into the storm. She glanced down at the line counter on the winch station railing: 450 yards in the can and feeding rapidly as the platform gained way in its drift toward the coast.

"Stand by! . . . Set your wildcat!"

Chief Tehoa spun the braking wheel, closing the wildcat jaws. The grating shriek of metal on metal overrode the storm, and the deck plates beneath their feet trembled.

There was no immediate shift in the platform's heading. Given Floater 1's mammoth displacement, she would be slow to react to the comparatively slight tug of the anchor cable. Amanda knew that would be the trick, to bring time, cable length, and braking strain together in one perfect balanced equation. It was impossible to make a voice heard over the audial chaos, and Amanda made a palms-down feathering gesture with her hand, instructing Chief Tehoa to play the line.

A hundred yards stripped out of the cable tier without measurable effect.

Amanda frowned in to the force of the hurricane. The driving sea had the platform solidly in its jaws and didn't want to let go. They were still quartering. She couldn't feel any bearing change. Her thumb jerked upward. *Increase tension!*

Tehoa heaved on the brake wheel, taking it up another half-turn. The shriek became a piercing dentist's drill scream. A plume of sparks sluiced from the cable guides, spraying across the sea-washed deck in front of the station.

Two hundred and fifty yards left.

A seventh wave loomed above the leading edge of the platform. Amanda's thumb stabbed downward. *Slack off!* Ben Tehoa spun the wildcat wheel like a truck driver fighting a skid on an icy road.

A wall of water smashed down on the winch station. Grimly, the officer and the CPO clung to the railing and to consciousness as anchor line whipped away over the side, writhing in the cable guides like an enraged python seeking its freedom.

Amanda clawed her sodden hair out of her eyes and sought for the cable gauge in the half-light.

One hundred fifty yards remaining.

Her thumb stabbed upward repeatedly. *Take it up! Go for broke! All the way!*

Tehoa's muscles bulged under the wind-tattered remnants of his khaki shirt. Jaw set in a savage grimace, he strained at the spokes of the wheel, drawing steel down on steel, levering closed the bands of the cable brake.

Lightning blazed across the sky, momentarily illuminating the decks with a flashbulb clarity. Amanda was startled to see that both she and the big Samoan CPO seemed to be covered with blood. It took her a moment to realize that it was rust flayed off the anchor cable. Mixing with the sea spray on the decks and caught by the storm winds, it blew back upon them. She could taste the iron bite of it on her tongue.

The anchor line stretched out beyond the platform, beyond the limit of vision, still angling off to port, yet as straight as a knife's edge and as taut as a set guitar string. Its test load exceeded, the arm-thick mass of steel wire was actually stretching like a drawn rubber band. Should it snap, the broken end would whip back aboard the platform with the impact of an eight-inch shell, demolishing the winch station and anyone nearby.

And yet Amanda could only continue to sign, *Take it up!*

And then she noted the wind. At long last the wind was edging around to strike her full in the face. Floater 1 was turning into the storm.

"A little more!" she screamed, although no one but she could hear. "Come on, a little more."

Another massive sea struck the platform, only this time instead of flinching away from the impact, the barges lifted their heads and rode over it.

"Come on, you big bitch! Just a little more!"

The line counter snapped down from triple to double digits.

Amanda cupped her hands over the lip mike, a hideous thought striking at the same instant. *Dear God, what if this headset had flooded out too!*

"Drop all anchors! Drop all anchors!" She could only scream the command over and over and pray that someone would hear. And then the deck trembled under her feet and she knew they had won.

Forty-five tons of metal smashed into the Gold Coast seafloor, the massive scooplike anchors digging in, gouging trenches through the sand and bottom muck, bleeding away Floater 1's accumulated inertia and holding fast in the face of Ivan's wrath.

On the screen of Amanda's handheld GPU the position stopped flickering and held steady. The screech of the wildcat brake ground down into silence, the simple roar of the storm seeming almost quiet in comparison. Amanda glanced at the cable meter.

Fourteen yards.

"Tower, this is Garrett," she called. "I read the platform as stable by GPU fix. Do you concur?"

"We confirm that, Captain," Gueletti replied jubilantly. "Platform is stable. Well done, ma'am! We're going to make it."

They were. Oriented into the face of the storm, Floater 1 rode the weather now as she had been designed to, the big barges flowing up and over the incoming rollers sequentially, the interstructural colliding and twisting relieved.

In a lightning flicker, she grinned wearily at Tehoa, who grinned back in turn, sailor to sailor.

"Lock the brake, Chief," she called. "Let's go get some coffee."

Offshore Mobile Base, Floater 1   2010 Hours, Zone Time; July 23, 2007

Amanda started awake with the surprise of someone who hadn't realized they had been asleep. She recalled wedging herself in place in an inactive workstation up in the command tower, intending to rest just for a moment. But that had been . . . when? Her accumulation of stiff and aching muscles and vertebrae indicated it must have been some time ago.

Then she noted the stillness. The tower no longer swayed wildly with excessive wave motion. The wind no longer roared and bellowed, demanding admission.

It was over.

Outside, darkness was settling over the sea. The true darkness of evening and not the shrouded dimness of the storm. Enough light yet lingered to show an abating sea, its violence spent as if it, too, had grown weary. And far away in the west a scarlet streak glowed across the horizon.

Red sky at night. / Sailor's delight.

"Evening, Captain." Commander Gueletti stood backlit by the console screens. "Looks like the show's over."

"Looks like," Amanda agreed, standing and stretching out a multitude of kinked muscles. "Where's Chief Tehoa?"

"He's back down working with the damage-control parties. A hell of a good man, that."

"I won't argue that point. How are we standing, Commander?"

"It could have been a whole lot worse," the Seabee replied. "We haven't found any appreciable frame damage in any of the barges yet, and we didn't lose any plates. We're pumping out the flooded cells now. I think we can patch her up well enough to stay on station."

"How about our running gear?"

"It's torn up some, and we lost a couple of modules over the side. Nothing we can't fix or do without, though."

Amanda nodded, running a hand through her salt-sticky hair. Maybe a hot shower wasn't such an impossible dream after all. "Do we have damage reports in from the other bases?"

"No appreciable damage at Conakry, and Abidjan just got an extra-heavy rain squall. Our people at Conakry are already asking when we want them back."

"What do you think, Steve? Are we ready to open for business again?"

The wiry Seabee grinned back. "I can think of all sorts of jobs I could use some extra warm bodies for just now."

"Very well, then. Contact Conakry Base. Tell everyone to come on home."

Mamba Point Hotel
Monrovia, West African Union   2034 Hours, Zone Time; July 23, 2007

". . . Two deaths reported at Cape Shilling. Two more at Barlo Point. Three at Whale Bay." Standing before Belewa's desk, the staff officer read from the notebook in his hand. "That makes twelve total from the Freetown Provinces so far.

We have yet to receive the reports from the Turtle and Banana Islands, however. Communications are still down."

Obe Belewa nodded slowly. "Very good, Captain Tshombe. It could have been worse. Far, far worse."

"It was bad enough as it was, sir," the staff man replied soberly.

Hammers rang outside the Premier General's office. Sheets of plywood were being nailed over windows that had imploded under the impact of the hurricane winds. Women from a civil labor battalion worked with rags and buckets in the corridor, sopping up the rainwater that had infiltrated the government headquarters.

"How are things with the signals detachment?" Belewa inquired. "Have we any problems there?"

"We are fully operational, sir," Tshombe replied proudly. "We remained so throughout the storm."

"Very good, Captain. Give your men a well done from me for their good service." Belewa hesitated for a moment, then continued. "Are we still receiving information from the Americans?"

"They are still transmitting weather bulletins at regular intervals," the signals officer replied. "We have also received a message from them that they will be ready to start aerial reconnaissance photographs again shortly . . . that is, if the General wishes for us to continue to accept them."

Belewa lifted an eyebrow. "Did the Americans' photographs prove useful in preparing for the storm?"

"Yes, sir. They proved very useful."

"And would more such reconnaissance prove useful in our poststorm damage assessment?"

"Uh, yes, sir. I would think so."

"Then accept the photographs for as long as the Americans are willing to send them. Dismissed."

"Yes, sir. Thank you, sir!"

Belewa rubbed the back of his neck as the signals officer departed, recalling that he hadn't slept for thirty-six hours. The hurricane was past now. Why not stand down and withdraw to his apartment and to his bed? His command staff were all good people. Why not turn things over to Sako and sleep?

At even the thought, Belewa's eyes grew heavy. And yet the damage and casualty reports were not in from the coastal islands. Curtly, he shook himself awake. One hour more, perhaps. Yes, just one hour more and then he would rest.

A rap came at the door of his office.

"Yes?"

"The Algerian ambassador desires to speak with you, General. He says it is a matter of great importance."

Belewa allowed a groaning mutter to escape his lips. *A bloody hurricane, and now Umamgi as well.*

"Show the ambassador in."

There was an arch smugness to the imam's smile as he was ushered into Belewa's office. "Good evening, General," he said, coming to stand before the General's desk. "An unpleasant storm, was it not? I trust that it has not caused undue injury to your nation or your people."

"In fact, we have considerable damage to deal with, Ambassador," Belewa replied shortly, not offering the Algerian a seat. "I daresay we are going to be quite busy for a number of days with rescue and relief work. So saying, what may we do for you?"

"It is what I may do for you, General." Umamgi's smile widened. "This storm was not entirely an evil omen. It was sent by Allah to grant you victory in your just struggle with the West."

Belewa scowled. "What do you mean, Ambassador?"

"I bring you word from our embassy in Conakry. Our intelligence service has learned that the Americans were cowed by the fury of the tempest. They evacuated the majority of their fighting forces from the floating base they maintain off your coast."

Belewa lifted an eyebrow. "Our own agents in Conakry have informed us of the same thing, Ambassador. And your point?"

"Simply this, General. With the passing of the storm, the American forces will be returning. But they have not done so yet. There are only a handful of Americans present at their base. Not enough to defend it adequately, but enough to serve us well as prisoners and hostages.

"You have an opportunity to win this war in a single blow, General." Umamgi continued eagerly. "I have been speaking with your chief of staff. Your gunboat squadron at Port Monrovia has ridden out the storm without damage. It is ready to sail at your command. If you attack now you could sink the American base, or better yet, seize it. You could break the illegal blockade that binds your nation and make fools of the United States and United Nations both."

The room grew very still for a moment. Even the hammer blows from the next office seemed muted. And then Belewa smiled a humorless smile. "All you say is quite true, Ambassador. Such an operation would be quite feasible, were it not for the cease-fire that is in effect along the coast for the next forty-eight hours."

The Algerian's eyes widened in disbelief. "Cease-fire!" he exclaimed, taking a step closer to the desk. "I have heard rumors of a cease-fire. But still, you would throw away such an opportunity for . . . some . . . *piece of paper!*"

"There is no piece of paper, Ambassador," Belewa replied mildly. "There is only a verbal agreement between myself and the U.N. military commander."

"You . . ." Umamgi struggled to regain control. "Such things are meaningless!"

"They are only meaningless if the involved parties fail to give them meaning. The U.N. commander upheld her share of the bargain. She rendered assistance that possibly saved thousands of African lives. I shall abide by my part of the agreement as well."

"She is a Western woman!" Umamgi clenched a thin fist in helpless rage. "A perverted, godless, and evil creature! Did you ever think that this is why she made this mad pact with you! To draw your teeth at the one moment when you could tear the throat from your enemies!"

Belewa tilted his chair back and pondered. After a moment, he smiled again. "Speaking truthfully, Ambassador, no. I did not consider it. Nor, I think, did the Leopard. However, even if she did so, the gambit was well played. I have given my word. It will be kept. The cease-fire will be maintained."

"I will inform my government of this outrage! This insanity!" Umamgi sputtered. "They will not be pleased with an ally who throws away such a victory."

Belewa steepled his fingers over his chest, finding that he was enjoying himself for the first time in many days. "Ah, Ambassador, it is a great sadness, but it is decreed that some days we must disappoint even our closest and dearest allies. Such is life."

The Algerian spun on his heel and stalked for the office door. Belewa let him cross half the room before he reached out with a shout to stop the mock holy man.

"Umamgi!"

The Algerian cringed like a village cur and froze in place.

"A man who has no honor," Belewa continued in a quiet voice, "frequently cannot understand its value. You may go, Ambassador."

By the time Umamgi stepped back into the corridor, his lean features were stoic once more. Rage still burned brightly within the imam, but he had long since mastered the art of masking his true feelings and intentions. He wore such a mask now as he sought out Belewa's chief of staff.

Pacing with suppressed excitement, Brigadier Atiba looked up as Umamgi entered his workspace. "You told him?" Atiba demanded. "What did he say? Are we attacking?"

"I fear not, Brigadier," Umamgi replied, picking his words and emphasis with consummate care. "I outlined the opportunity to the General as I did for you. However, your leader does not think it . . . prudent to directly challenge the United Nations in this way at this time."

"What?" Atiba exclaimed. "You can't mean it? This is an opportunity that will never come again! I can't believe Obe would throw this away for no good reason." The Chief of Staff started to the door. "I'll talk to him myself. I'll change his mind."

Umamgi caught Atiba's arm. "Leave him in peace, my son," the Algerian said, metering careful overtones of sympathy and pity into his voice. "The General has made his decision and there it stands. He is . . . tired. Things have not gone well for him of late."

"Things are not going well for the entire Union, Ambassador! This is our opportunity to turn it all around."

"It was our chance, my son. It *was* our chance. Pray to Allah that there will be others. In the meantime, we must follow your general's decisions in these matters . . . must we not?"

Mobile Offshore Base, Floater 1   0751 Hours, Zone Time; August 1, 2007

Dear Dad:

It's about 0700 here and I've just completed a pretty good patrol debriefing and a pretty bad breakfast. In a little bit, I'm going to be turning in for the day. But first, I'm going to answer your last letter as a dutiful daughter should.

We're up and running again after our interlude with that hurricane. The British admiralty was indeed a little disgruntled at first over my innovative use of their minehunter, but they've agreed that under the circumstances we really didn't have much choice. At any rate, we've patched up our storm damage and we're back to conducting routine operations once more. Or at least as "routine" as it can get in a combat theater.

The campaign progresses slowly. Belewa continues to nibble at the Guinea governmental infrastructure with his guerrilla raids, and we continue to interdict his oil-smuggling line with our patrols. Chris assures me that we're winning, but we're doing it the slow way, one jerrican of gas at a time.

I don't much like that, Dad. I want to get this thing finished fast. I know about "Softly softly catchee monkey" and that "A hunter is patience," but I still don't like giving Belewa any more time to work with than I have to. This guy is good, Dad. Good enough to scare me.

I can feel him out there, just watching and waiting for me to make that one little mistake that will give him the edge back. It's almost as if I can feel him thinking about me at times. There have been nights here in my quarters when I've had the sensation of someone staring at the back of my neck. Enough so that I've turned to see if someone was there.

There wasn't, of course. No doubt it's just a minor case of the tropics.

And don't go taking that seriously, either. I'm sleeping okay, and I'm eating as well as the galley permits. I've lost a couple of pounds to the heat, but I needed to reduce a little anyway. And before you can nag me about it, Admiral Daddy sir, I promise that just as soon as the rush is over, I'll fly into Abidjan and take a couple of days' shore leave.

In the meantime, I'm hunting for ways to possibly speed this campaign up a little. I'll let you know what I come up with.

> *I love you.*
> *Your daughter,*
> *Amanda*

Mobile Offshore Base, Floater 1   0943 Hours, Zone Time; August 2, 2007

"I thought all this stuff was all weather- and environment-proof?"

"It's supposed to be, ma'am. But this Gold Coast climate is something else. Nothing's proof against it."

In the RPV repair bay, Christine Rendino crouched in front of a grounded Eagle Eye Recon drone, a technician kneeling at either side of her to point out the problem.

It was an easy one to spot. The heavy polymer skin had separated from the inner foam-and-aluminum core of the drone's composite wing, peeling back from the leading edge in limp folds.

"The constant heat and humidity's breaking down the bonding resin," the technician continued. "This seam along the leading edge takes the full force of the propwash when the drone's in horizontal flight mode. A corner of the skin lifts, the wind catches it, and zot!"

"Shucks and other comments," Christine frowned. "What can we do about this?"

"Nothing, ma'am. It's shot. We'll have to replace the whole wing and shoulder assembly to get this thing airworthy again."

"The whole assembly?"

"Yes, ma'am. This is a one-piece chunk of bonded composite."

"How long is it going to take?"

"Not long at all once we get the new assembly."

"And pray tell, when can we get one?

The two avtechs exchanged uneasy glances. "Uh, well, I understand there's one in the pipeline, Commander," the senior hand replied.

"Operative word—'when'!"

"Next month."

There was a soft smacking sound as the heel of Christine's hand impacted on her forehead. "Not an option! We don't have enough of these things to begin with. I can't afford to have a hangar queen sitting around for the next two weeks."

"I'm sorry, Commander, but there's nothing else we can do."

"Sure there is. Fix this one."

"Ma'am, I'm really sorry, but we just can't!" the young aviation hand replied earnestly. "If they had this assembly back at the factory, maybe they could apply a layer of new resin and run it through the bonding press again. We can't come close to doing anything like that out here. The book says there's just no way to repair this kind of composite material in the field."

Christine stood up abruptly. Muttering under her breath, she crossed to the bay workbench. Snatching up an industrial staple gun, she returned to the parked drone. As the aviation hands watched aghast, she pulled the polymer skin section taut over the wing and ran a row of heavy-gauge staples along its edges and deep into the honeycomb core material.

"There, God says the book's wrong. Stick some duct tape on this sucker and let's fly it."

Five Miles West of Cape Palmas
West African Union   0202 Hours, Zone Time; August 7, 2007

An enjungled shoreline beneath a black and silent sky. A broad and smooth beach washed by the faintly luminescent foam of a low sea. A tired and crumbling macadam roadway separating beach from forest. A single, smoky orange spark guttering on the sands.

And a quarter of a mile away, a clump of undergrowth that was no longer just a clump of undergrowth. Stealthily, a pair of nonreflective night lenses peered out through a narrow slit in the vegetation.

"Sleeper . . ." The Bear breathed the words into the pitch darkness beneath the Ghilly camouflage net. "Hey, Sleeper!"

A few inches away, the burly SOC Marine's lean and wiry teammate made the instant transition from deep slumber to alert wakefulness.

"What?" The ghost of a word drifted back.

"It looks like there's two blockaders out there now. 'Nother one just came in."

"Did you log it?"

"Yeah." The Bear nodded, even though the gesture would be unseen.

"And the rest of the squad's still got the OP covered?"

"Yeah."

"And there's no sign of enemy patrol activity?"

"No."

"Then why the shit are you buggin' me about it?" the Sleeper whisper-snarled.

"Because I figured you'd want to know!"

"When it's my watch on the glasses, then I'll want to know. Until then, I'm trying to get some sack time in here!"

"Ah, shove it. You prick!"

"Up yours, dork!"

The Sleeper returned to his favorite pastime, his head against his helmet pillow. The Bear returned to the night glasses.

"This all?" the transport sergeant asked.

"This all we got t'ru, and I think this be all anybody gets t'ru tonight," the smuggler replied in the soft mixed English-African patois of the coast. "The monsters be hungry."

"Too right," the second smuggler agreed. "Saw 'em takin' a *pinasse* just off the bar at Harper. Think I got past just because I was a little fish not worth keeping."

Two outboard-engined blockade runners lay drawn up on the sand, each assembled from a pair of *pirogues* lashed side by side to form a seagoing catamaran hull. Their combined cargoes, a dozen fifty-gallon drums of diesel oil, barely made a load for one of the three flatbed trucks that had been waiting at the rendezvous point.

Those oil drums had now been hogged up a plank onto the rear deck of the last truck in line and lashed upright in a double row. The enlisted men of the labor battalion were grateful for their abbreviated workload. The noncom commanding them, however, knew enough about current conditions within the Union to be concerned about what the two empty trucks meant.

"You got we dash?" the first smuggler demanded softly. "We got t' be back over the line before light."

The Union sergeant silently handed over the two sweat-stained envelopes. Stepping closer to the guttering beacon fire, the two Ivory Coast boatmen hastily counted the thick pads of small-denomination currency.

After a few moments, the first smuggler looked back at the noncom. "Okay for now. But you tell 'em next time it's more."

"You got nuthin' to bitch," the sergeant replied sullenly, knowing how the contents of the envelopes compared with his own army pay.

"We get plenty to bitch if we go down to the Big Hotel for oil running. Lot of men Frenchside already gone down. Lot of 'em from our village, too. Be gettin' too dangerous to dodge the monsters. You tell your big man, next time, more money! Else we go back to fishing."

The noncom replied with another coast English phrase, a well-corrupted form of "shove it up your ass." Kicking out the beacon fire, he turned back to his trucks. The smugglers responded obscenely in kind and started down the beach to their boats.

The transport sergeant paused to double-check the load lashings on the truck carrying the oil drums. Few as they were, he didn't want to lose any of them. His captain wasn't going to be pleased with this haul. But at least this time they were bringing in some fuel. There had been other nights recently when none had gotten through at all.

"Hey, Sleeper . . . Sleeper . . . Hey, buttfuck! Wake up, will ya!"

"Now what?"

"Something's going on. They just kicked out the fire. I think they're getting set to move out."

"Lessee."

The Bear moved the nite-brite binoculars to the point where he knew Sleeper's hand would be waiting. The second Marine accepted the glasses, and a minute smear of faint green light leaked from around the eyepieces as Sleeper keyed the photomultiplier system.

"Yeah. The boat guys are taking off."

Engines sounded over the hiss and rush of the nearby surf—the burble and buzz of two-cycle outboards and the deeper rumble of truck diesels turning over. Headlights snapped on, two twin-sets and a cyclopean single.

"Here come the trucks. They're heading this way."

"Check 'em out good, Sleeper. The Skipper and the Lady'll want the word on any cargo."

"I know, shit-for-brains. Gimme a second. . . . Okay, we got oil drums on the last truck. Only the last one. The other two are empty."

"They got a truckload through, huh? Trust the damn swabbies to screw up the job." The Bear reached for his personal weapon, a 9mm Heckler and Koch MP-5. The bulky cylinder of a silencer had been screwed to the stubby barrel of the submachine gun and a second cylindrical unit, a night-vision sniper scope, had been clipped to the grab-tight rail atop its receiver.

"Hey, Bear? What you doing?"

"Cleaning up, dude. Cleaning up," the Bear replied, keying on the nite-brite optics and setting the fire selector to semiauto.

One after another, the Union army vehicles rumbled by. Their headlights brushed over the hide where the two Marines lay concealed, revealing nothing to the sleepy men slouched in the cabs. As the third truck rolled past, the Bear came up onto his knees, flinging back the flap of the ghilly net. Bringing the MP-5 to his shoulder, he settled the sights on target. Feather-light, his finger caressed the finely tuned trigger.

There were noises, more like a series of soft explosive sneezes than anything that could be construed as a gunshot. Holes magically appeared low on the oil drums strapped to the truck's rear deck, each hole streaming a jet of oil, the Israeli Military Industries FMJ slugs punching cleanly through both rows of containers. The tinny *thunk, thunk, thunk* of sheet metal being pierced was lost in the roar of the gutted mufflers and the crash of the vehicle jouncing over the disintegrating pavement. Likewise, the smell of the spilling raw diesel merged with the exhaust fumes of the poorly tuned engine.

With the lifeblood of the Union dribbling out on the pavement behind it, the convoy went on its way. With their own mission completed to their satisfaction, the Bear and Sleeper did likewise.

Mobile Offshore Base, Floater 1   **1036 Hours, Zone Time; August 7, 2007**

Stone Quillain doffed his utility cover as he entered Amanda's quarters. "You wanted to see me, Skipper?"

"Um-hmm," Amanda replied absently from the far side of the desk, her attention still focused on the sheets of hard copy she held. "Sit down, Stone. I was just looking over the reports from the Observation Posts we had on the beach Unionside last night. I wanted to talk to you about one of them."

Quillain lifted a hand. "No need to say another word, ma'am. I know exactly what you're about to say. One of the OPs broke cover and shot up a load of smuggled oil drums. Their platoon leader and I have been tearing strips off the two men responsible all morning, and I can promise you it won't happen again."

Amanda chuckled softly "I hope you left a few shreds of meat on the bone. You see, those men of yours have given me an idea. I want to see what you might think of it."

"What y'all got, Skipper?"

Amanda tossed the patrol reports onto her cluttered desktop and tilted her chair back, thoughtfully studying the ceiling of the quarters cubicle. "Maybe a way to crank up the pressure on Belewa a little."

"That sounds like a worthy project. I'm listening."

"So far, our campaign to bleed off the Union's oil reserves has been essentially passive. We're embargoing Belewa's oil imports, but we haven't been able to do anything about the reserves he already has in-country."

"Yeah?" Quillain replied cautiously.

Amanda let her chair flip forward again. Reaching for a file folder, she passed it across the desk to the Marine. "Take a look at these."

"What are they?"

"Photo printouts. Photographs of the Wellington Creek tank farm, located in Kizzy township, just east of Freetown and inside the Sierra Leone river estuary. Formerly it belonged to the Shell Oil Company. Currently, however, it's being used by the West African Union as their primary petroleum storage and distribution center for both their western provinces and for their military campaign against Guinea."

Quillain glanced up, frowning suspiciously. "Excuse me, but just what are you thinking about, ma'am?"

Amanda leaned forward over the desk, intently meeting Quillain's gaze. "Something I want you to think about too, Stone. What if we could take out Wellington Creek? Not only would Belewa's operations against Guinea be derailed, but we could shorten this entire campaign by months at least."

"Lord A'mighty! You are serious!"

"You bet I'm serious." Amanda rose to her feet and paced off a few steps. "The target is there, it's critical, and it's vulnerable. Just by forcing the Union to shift their remaining fuel reserves around to cover its loss would take a huge bite out of whatever POL stocks they'll have left. This is a natural, Stone. This is a body blow!"

"Hell, Skipper, I'm not arguing the point," Quillain replied. "It sounds like just a hell of an idea to me. The problem will be with selling it to the Diplodinks. I don't think the Security Council would authorize a direct boots-on-the-dirt raid on Union territory, at least not without arguing about it for six months. The idea makes too much sense."

"I agree, Captain. That's why I wasn't going to ask for authorization."

"Lord . . . A . . . mighty!"

Amanda's golden hazel eyes glowed with an almost impish enthusiasm, and she arched an eyebrow at the Marine. "Like the man said, it's only illegal if we get caught."

Quillain slapped his utility cover against his knee. "Begging the Captain's pardon, but how in *thee* hell does she figure on doing that? Taking out an oil depot is going to cause talk! We pull a stunt like that and those Union boys over there are going to run screaming to the General Assembly and the Third World

254   JAMES H. COBB

media. You were able to justify that strike on Yelibuya by the skin of your teeth. You try this one and for certain-sure you're going to end up getting yourself fried for exceeding your mandate!"

"The potential definitely exists," Amanda replied, shrugging her slim shoulders. "And if it blows up in our faces, I'll just have to take the fall for exceeding my authority. So be it. But if we can pull it off . . . aborting this whole damn war and maybe preventing thousands of casualties . . . I think the risk will be worth it."

She started to pace again, slowly. "The keys to this operation are going to be no linkage and a low profile. We'll have to make it look like some sort of local vandalism or sabotage launched against the Union government by its own citizens. That means no overt U.S. presence ashore, nothing left behind that could connect our forces to the act, and most importantly, no casualties. Theirs or ours . . . Oh, and also we've got to figure out some way to eliminate a couple of thousand tons of petroleum without blowing up or burning down half of Kizzy township."

Quillain wiped a hand across his face and muttered something under his breath.

"What was that, Stone?"

"Nothing, Skipper. I was just thinking about this damn fool I knew once who went around talking about candy-assed female officers."

Wellington Creek Petroleum Depot
Kizzy Township, West African Union   0310 Hours, Zone Time; August 10, 2007

Rain poured from the night skies, the heavy, misting, blood-temperature rain of the African Gold Coast. The two middle-aged Union militiamen on sentry-go at the depot's main gate were long used to such deluges. Nonetheless, familiarity didn't make the sodden weight of their cheap cotton uniforms any easier to bear. Nor did it allow their vision to extend much beyond the feeble yellow circle of the gate arc light.

Nothing had happened during the first half of their watch except for the hourly pass of the Military Police motor patrol. Nothing ever happened around Freetown. That was why the security of the depot had been left in the hands of the local Home Defense battalion.

Propping their rifles behind them to protect them from the wet, the sentries leaned back against the corroded chain-link fencing of the gate. It was a futile gesture. The bluing had long ago been worn from their ancient Lee Enfield rifles, and rust already was setting in. Another chore to deal with before going home.

There was only one good thing about militia duty on such a night. It would be a full week before it would come around again. With half-closed eyes, the sentries stared into the darkness.

Then, gradually, the sentries became aware of voices and music growing louder over the hammering patter of the rain. Half a dozen men clad in ragged dungarees approached down Parsonage Road, one of them bearing a cheap tape player balanced on his shoulder. Afro-Pop blared from it into the night, blurring the jocular babble of their conversation, and bottles glinted in their hands.

Boatmen or oil workers, the sentries mutually decided without comment, coming from the bars and disco clubs up around Macauley Street and heading home to their shacks along the beach. A common enough thing. Common enough to be ignored.

According to the standing orders of the sentry post, anyone approaching the oil depot after dark was to be challenged and asked to present identification. However, after being told, profanely, what they could do with their identification for the hundredth time, the militiamen had abandoned the practice.

One of the raggedly clad men waved a beer bottle in the direction of the sentries, calling out the universal coast greeting of "Howdebody!"

The sentry nodded a reply, thirstily wondering if he could ask for a drink.

Then, just as the group of boatmen came opposite the sentry post, a silenced pistol whispered out a single bullet.

The arc light over the depot gate shattered and went out. The party of "boatmen" pivoted and lunged at the sentries, launching a silent, furious assault. The hard-swung tape player decked one of the militiamen, while a sand-filled sock took out the other. Neither Union soldier had the chance to cry out even a single word of warning.

Other forms materialized out of the darkness, uniformed, helmeted, armed, pushing open the gates and swarming through. Some raced toward the looming white cylinders of the oil storage tanks, while others rushed the lights of the guard shack a few yards away.

Within the guard shack, the sergeant of the security detail and his corporal sat at the shack's desk, playing cards, while the members of the off-duty sentry team sprawled asleep in the room's two bunks. When both the front and rear doors exploded open, surprise was again total. The "boatmen" stormed in and piled on, swinging callused fists and a variety of blunt instruments.

The sergeant and the two sentries went down, lunging for weapons they were not permitted to reach. The corporal tried for the telephone, another act of futility, as the phone lines had already been cut. Battered into unconsciousness, the occupants of the shack, along with the two gate sentries, were gagged and blindfolded with rags and bound with coarse locally made cord taken from a captured smuggler's *pirogue*.

With that accomplished, the leader of the "boatmen" stepped back out into the night.

"All secure, Skipper."

Stone Quillain nodded to Sergeant Tallman, rain dripping from his helmet brim. "Good enough. Now you and the rest of your guys rejoin the Marine Corps. We still got work to do."

Touching the "Press-to-Talk" pad on his Leprechaun transceiver, Quillain spoke lowly into his whisper mike. "Royalty, this is Mudskipper. Phase one complete."

Elsewhere in the darkness, hunters converged on prey. There were two other groups of Militia sentries to be dealt with, a pair of roving two-man security patrols within the confines of the tank farm itself. An Eagle Eye recon drone hovering just beneath the overcast tracked each patrol on its FLIR sensors, its systems operator coaching a Marine fire team in on each target.

Only a few of the tank farm's arc lights still burned; failing maintenance and energy rationing had extinguished the rest. The Marines had night-vision visors, the militiamen did not. Unaware of the threat converging on them through the shadows, the Union patrols walked into ambush.

Grenade launchers leveled. Invisible targeting lasers lashed out, designating impact points. Fingers contracted on triggers.

A series of soft, tinny thumps sounded in the night, the noise almost lost in the beating of the rain.

The grenade launchers had been loaded with silent-discharge shells. Rather than firing their projectiles directly from the launcher tubes, the hot gases released by the low-yield propellant charges were contained inside telescoping shell bases to vent away slowly and silently. The pistoning action of the shell bases explosively doubling in length hurled the payloads on their way.

The projectiles launched were nonlethal "beanbag" rounds, small disk-shaped envelopes filled with high-density plastic beads. They struck with the force of a .38-caliber revolver round but with the impact dispersed out over several square inches rather than at a single point.

To the targeted militiamen, the experience was similar to being slugged in the gut by an invisible heavyweight boxer. Even as they crumpled retching to the muddy ground, the Marine ambush parties charged in, finishing the job with carbine butts and sap gloves.

Binding and gagging the members of the security patrols with the same kind of coarse local cord that had been used at the guard shack, the Marines carefully dragged the unconscious Union soldiers up onto higher ground, away from the fuel storage tanks. They were also careful to seek out and recover the discharged beanbags, each round having been marked with a dollop of the same luminescent chemical used in the Marine IFF light sticks.

"Phase two complete. Patrols are down. Tank farm secured."

"Acknowledged. Proceed to phase three."

Stone Quillain looked around at the remainder of the strike force clustered behind the guard shack. Sergeant Tallman and the other black Marines who had masqueraded as the Freetown boatmen had redonned their uniforms and equipment harnesses. Padded tool rolls had been opened and heavy-duty bolt cutters and steel pipe cheater bars were being distributed.

"Okay, boys, you know the drill," Quillain said, pulling down his AI2 visor. "Corporal MacHenny, your fire team maintains gate security. Be ready to fall back to the extraction point the second you get the word. The rest of you know your objectives. Remember to watch your equipment inventories! If we brought it in, we take it back out! Let's go!"

Breaking up into two-man assault details, the Marines dispersed, Quillain and Tallman heading for the nearest of the multithousand-gallon storage tanks.

Scrambling over the pressed-earth leak-containment berm that surrounded the tank, the two men followed the feeder pipelines to its base. Christine Rendino had discreetly hacked the Shell engineering database and had acquired a set of technical schematics for the Wellington Creek installation. Thus, Quillain and Tallman knew exactly what they were looking for and where it would be located. Powering down their tactical electronics as an antispark precaution, they set to work.

The maintenance dumping valve was located on the north side of the tank and, as expected, a heavy, padlocked safety chain had been looped through the valve wheel. The bolt cutters and the brawn of the two Marines made short work of it, however. Rust provided a second line of defense, but a second application of brawn defeated that as well. Creaking, the valve opened.

Pressurized by its own weight within the tank, diesel oil burst forth. Half a dozen turns of the wheel sent a horizontal jet of fuel eight inches wide and thirty feet long spewing out on the rain-sodden ground, hundreds of precious gallons wasting away each minute.

Tallman yanked the wheel off the valve stem and spun it away into the night like a steel Frisbee, while Quillain unwound a grounding wire from the cheater bar, stamping its free end into the soil at the base of the tank. They fitted a cheater bar over the vertical shaft of the stem, and then, with muscles bulging and boots slipping in the mud and oil, the Marines strained against the length of pipe.

Slowly, the valve stem gave way, bending from the vertical to the horizontal and farther. Even after the open valve was discovered, closing it again would be no small chore.

The two Marines stood back, taking a second to catch up on their breathing. "Man," Tower commented, eyeing the rapidly spreading pool of oil. "I hope nobody smokes in bed around here."

"Yeah, the rain should help keep things damped down, though. And with the wind blowing offshore, nobody's going to notice the fumes for a while. Let's go."

They sloshed out to the containment berm, already wading through more petroleum than water. Once clear of the oil pool, Quillain reactivated his systems.

"Tank two," the first report came in from out of the darkness. "Diesel. Open."

"Tank four. Diesel. Open."

"Tank three. Gasoline. Open."

"Tank five. Dry hole."

"Tank six. Kerosene, maybe jet fuel. Open."

"Tank teams acknowledged. Tank one diesel and open. Tank teams proceed to extraction point. Establish extraction perimeter."

A volley of double clicks came back in reply. Quillain switched channels and accessed the seafighter command circuit. "Royalty, this is Mudskipper. Phase three completed. Operation successful. Standing by for extraction."

Amanda Garrett spoke no words of praise. Those could wait until the raider force was off the beach. "Acknowledged, Mudskipper. Initiating extraction. Boats are inbound."

"Roger." *Click!* Stone bounced back to the raider force commo loop. "All elements. All elements. Extract! Extract! Extract! All elements acknowledge and fall back to extraction point. Move!"

The extraction point was the tank farm's handling pier where, during better days, the Shell Oil barges had unloaded their cargoes. The other sabotage teams were already there, crouching in a wary half-circle around the foot of the pier, weapons up and scanning the darkness. Quillain stood within the half-circle, counting in his men as the security teams jogged in from the night.

"Sixteen . . . eighteen . . . twenty-two . . . twenty-four. Tallman, d'you confirm the count?"

"Twenty-four out, twenty-four back. All hands accounted for, Captain. We good to go."

"Tool count on the cheater bars and bolt cutters?"

"Six and six."

"Right. All hands! Double-check your gear! We don't leave nothin' behind. Nothin'!"

There was movement out on the Sierra Leone estuary. Three patches of shadow defined themselves into a trio of sixteen-foot miniraider Zodiacs. Ghosting in on silenced outboards, they drew alongside the pilings of the loading pier, tucking in against the floating personnel stage.

"Designated personnel for boat one, go!" Quillain called hoarsely. The billowing waves of raw petroleum fumes saturating the air were starting to rasp at his throat.

Eight Marines peeled out of the security perimeter, moving with quiet haste onto the pier and down to the landing stage. Drilled repeatedly in the boarding procedure, each man knew the order in which he'd board and his place in the little craft. The loading took only seconds and then the miniraider pushed off, the Navy coxswain opening his throttle for the run out to the recovery vessel.

"Boat one away, Captain."

"Personnel for boat two, go!"

Quillain and Tallman were the last two men aboard the last boat, Quillain's boots being the last to leave the dock.

The seafighters lay a bare two hundred yards offshore, closed up and fully stealthed with their weapons pedestals and secondary armament retracted inboard. A filtered strobe light pulsed at the head of each snub mast, flashing the identification number of the hovercraft. Visible only to the night-vision visors of the Raider coxswains, it guided each small boat home to its mother ship.

Tail ramps dropped and electric motors hummed, winching the raiders aboard, and the job was done.

⚔◆

"*Carondelet* and *Manassas* report raiders recovered, Captain," Steamer Lane advised jubilantly from the cockpit. "Threat boards are clear, and Operations reports no reaction ashore."

"We're good down here as well, Steamer," Amanda replied into the headset mike. "Close the tailgate and head us out. Maintain full stealth and swimmer mode until we clear the area."

The landing party dismounted from the raider craft, dripping with mud, oil, and water, and redolent with the good-natured giddiness of men who have just doffed the burden of tension and danger. Stone Quillain loomed over Amanda, the white flash of a broad grin breaking past the oil stains and camouflage paint smeared on his face. Amanda grinned back and held up her right hand, palm out. Quillain's own more massive paw lifted, slapped hers in a high five that cracked like a rifle shot.

"It went perfect!" the big Marine roared. "Totally, abso-goddamn-lutely perfect! Desperate Jesus! The first Special Forces operation in history to ever go down exactly as planned, and we can't tell anybody about it!"

"I guess we'll just have to save the story for our memoirs, Stone. Well done! Extremely well done!"

"Thank you kindly, Skipper. I'll pass the word along to the boys." Stone doffed his helmet and peeled off his MOLLE harness, stacking his gear against the central bay bulkhead in an oil-and-mud-sodden heap. "Lord, but a cup of coffee's going to taste good."

Amanda moved back a hasty step to avoid getting splattered. "I'll have some sent back for you. For Pete's sake, don't go forward until you clean up a little. You're dripping gunk all over the decks."

Quillain replied with a baleful glance. "Well, there you go! Never invite a woman to a poker game, a hunting camp, or a war. First thing you know, they start trying to tidy everything up."

Wellington Creek Petroleum Depot
Kizzy, West African Union   0746 Hours, Zone Time; August 10, 2007

The depot was a petroleum swamp, its tanks rising up out of a stinking, sticky morass of mud, spilled fuel, and standing water that sheened with a rainbow layer of oil contamination, all barely contained by the surrounding safety berms.

Around the berm perimeters, salvage operations were already under way. A labor group drawn from among the women and older children of Freetown were hard at work, sopping up puddled diesel with bundles of rags, then wringing them out into open-topped oil drums. All electrical power to the tank farm had been cut and a cordon of militia sentries stood to around the complex, alert for anyone bearing a lit cigarette or any other open flame.

"How much did we lose?" Belewa asked flatly.

"All of the aviation fuel," the moon-faced depot manager replied hesitantly. He was essentially a civilian administrator, and the ill-fitting militia uniform he had donned did little to give or inspire confidence. "Although there was little enough left of that. And perhaps seventy percent of the diesel and gasoline. The open valves weren't discovered for a half hour or more, and it took time to call in the technical personnel to cap them off—"

"I did not ask for excuses! I asked only for how much fuel was lost!"

The manager's words trailed off, fear catching him around the throat.

Belewa looked away, disgusted. Not with the depot manager, but with himself. Terrifying this fat and hapless little man accomplished nothing.

"I am certain you and your staff did all that was possible, Major Hawkins," he said, keeping his voice controlled. "Now it is your job to save as much as you can. Every liter is precious."

"We will do our best, General. But much of it has already soaked into the ground. And for the rest, the water, the dirt, even after it has been double-strained . . ." Again the director's voice trailed off.

"Every liter, Major," Belewa said over his shoulder, striding back toward the tank farm gates.

His chief of staff and a group of military police officers clustered near the guard shack. Beyond them, spotted in an open lot well back from the miasma of the oil spill, sat the BO105 helicopter that had carried Belewa and Atiba to the raid site. Its presence was an indicator of the disaster's scale. Fuel rationing had long since mandated that the Union's few air assets be used only in response to extreme emergency.

"Brigadier," Belewa snapped, not breaking stride as he passed the group, "do you have the security report?"

"Yes, sir," Atiba replied, looking up.

"Good. Then we will go. There is nothing more we can accomplish here."

Noting the approach of his two VIP passengers, the helicopter pilot started the spool-up of the 105's power plant. Within minutes they were airborne, flying south along the coast en route back to Monrovia.

Belewa watched the beach slip past beneath them for a time before speaking into his intercom headset. "What did the security people have to say, Sako?" he inquired over the wind roar and turbine howl flooding in through the doorless side hatches.

"It appears that this may have been an act of civil insurrection," the Chief of Staff replied. "There is no evidence of a U.N. involvement."

"Pah!"

"The gate sentries and the men in the guard shack report they were attacked by locals, by blacks," Atiba insisted.

"And there are a great many black men serving in the American Marine Corps."

"If it were the American Marines, why didn't they blow up the entire depot? Or why not simply drop one of their missiles on it?"

"Deniability, Sako! Deniability! This way, it can be said, just as you are saying, that this was an act of sabotage committed by our own people. Not only do they deprive us of our oil reserves, but it can be held up to the world as an example of how the Union is starting to collapse under the U.N. embargo. Of how our people are starting to turn against us."

"I cannot see it, General! Our ambassador at the United Nations indicates that the Security Council is maintaining a wait-and-see attitude concerning Guinea and the Union. They seem content to let the embargo take its course. There has been no discussion of a U.N. escalation that would involve aggressive acts against our territory. No sign at all. We would have received ample warning."

"This has nothing to do with the United Nations! The U.N. may be satisfied to maintain an embargo and to wait and see. She is not! She does not understand 'wait and see.' She is here to make war! On us!"

"The American commander again? Then what do we do? File a protest?"

"On what grounds? With what evidence? What kind of proof do we have?" Belewa brought his fists down on his knees in angry frustration. "And what would the Security Council do except to grin in our faces? With the Leopard fighting their battles for them, they are freed from having to make unpleasant decisions concerning us."

Belewa lifted his fists again, then caught himself. Instead, he used one hand to tiredly rub his eyes. "Remember this, my friend, for your own future battlefields. You may think and plan and prepare for a campaign and believe that you have prepared for every conceivable eventuality. But there will always be at least one random factor that you will overlook. I overlooked the Leopard, Sako. I did not consider the Leopard."

Mamba Point Hotel
Monrovia, West African Union   2121 Hours, Zone Time; August 11, 2007

The vista from his office balcony no longer gave General Belewa the pleasure it once had. The wind from the sea was as cooling and mellow as ever, but the sea itself had become an ally of his foes. And the night itself was too dark.

The generators ran only here at his headquarters and at the Monrovia fleet base and army garrison, three lonely constellations in the night. The rest of the capital underwent a rationing-mandated blackout. No streetlights burned. No vehicles moved in those streets. No buildings were illuminated save by the faint flicker of candlelight or the ruddy glow of charcoal. Even kerosene and lamp oil were precious and hard to come by now.

The people, his people, huddled in the darkness again. It was as if he had never come to this place. As if he had never tried to make a difference.

"General . . . Obe. May we speak with you?"

"Of course, Sako."

Brigadier Atiba and Ambassador Umamgi waited within, standing beside Belewa's desk. His chief of staff smiled, an eagerness and a fire flaring within his old comrade that Belewa had not seen for many days.

The Algerian mullah was smiling as well, but for him it seemed only an enhancement of the growing sardonicism he had been displaying these past weeks. Two stapled and typewritten pages in the format of an operations proposal lay on the desk blotter.

"General, I think we may have a plan."

"What kind of plan, Sako?"

"A plan to break the blockade. A way to get us the fuel we need. A way to beat the Leopard, Obe!"

Belewa dropped into his chair. Picking up the proposal, his eyes sought the first paragraph. "Is this a concept of yours, Sako?"

"No, but it looks good to me. The premise was suggested by the Algerians. Ambassador Umamgi promises his government's full support in the operation. It is all so simple, Obe. It has to work!"

Belewa scanned the first page, then the second. It was indeed simple. All so very, very simple.

"No."

There was a moment of stunned silence. The excitement drained from Atiba's face, bewilderment and anger boiling up in replacement.

"No? What do you mean, no? This will work, Obe! This plan strikes right at the heart of your Leopard. Haven't you always taught us to strike at your enemy's weaknesses? Well, this plan strikes at the weakness of the Garrett woman. It will destroy her and the stranglehold she has on us!"

"It also takes us back to places we have left behind, Sako." Belewa threw the proposal back onto the desktop. "It drives us to do things we have sworn never to do again. We will think of something else."

"Now I say no!" Atiba leaned forward, slamming his palms down onto the desktop, glaring into Belewa's face. "Obe, we are running out of time! We lost half of our oil reserves last night. Half! We have less than six weeks left! Then everything you and I have worked for is over!"

"We will find some other way to break the blockade! One that leaves our honor intact."

"Honor be damned! What other way? We are throwing away a chance to win! I want a reason for this, Obe, not talk of honor and places we've been. I want one solid reason why we should not at least try!"

"You desire a solid reason? I will give you one." Belewa rose from behind the desk, his eyes locking with Atiba's. "We will not execute this plan because I say we will not! Is that adequate, Brigadier?"

The impact of Belewa's words pushed the Chief of Staff back from the desk. For a long heartbeat the two warriors stood posed, rank and past friendship an irrelevancy. Then Atiba turned and stormed from the room.

The General and the Ambassador were alone then, and it was Umamgi who broke the silence. "There is a parable," the Algerian said quietly, "of a man who was a great king. However, this man valued his own pride more than he did his kingdom. And because of his pride, one day the king lost his kingdom. And since there was no kingdom, there was no reason for there to be a king. And since there was no longer a reason for a king, *inshalla*, there was no longer a reason for there to be a man. A thought, General."

Belewa felt his hand come to rest on the flap of his pistol holster.

"Get out!"

The mullah only smiled, nodded, and turned for the door. As it closed behind him, Belewa sank down behind his desk once more, his head coming to rest on his crossed arms.

1¼ Miles Southwest of
Point Yannoi, Côte d'Ivoire   2210 Hours, Zone Time; August 16, 2007

Deftly, Felix Akwaba brought his *pirogue* into the wind, heaving to in the easy ocean swell. Rising stiffly from the aft thwart, he lowered the patched cotton sail, letting his little craft drift. Settling back again, he held the bow into the waves with an occasional dip of the steering paddle.

The night was lit only by a half moon and the ten million and one tropic stars overhead. It mattered little to Felix, however. He'd been sailing this stretch of coast for fifty-odd years, and he knew it better than he did the inside of his own hut.

If he should glance back over his right shoulder, he would see the phosphorescent flash of the surf rolling over Biahuin Reef. If he should look over the left, it would be the flashing red warning beacon of the radio mast at Point Yannoi, a marker as good as any official lighthouse on the coast.

This was the usual place and the correct time. They would make their appearance soon.

When it happened, as always, it was a little startling, the only warning being the hiss of a razor-sharp bow cutting water. That bow loomed abruptly out of the darkness, towering over the pirogue and sweeping past as the vessel came alongside. A sweep of foredeck followed, a slender gun barrel up-angled against the sky and a rakish superstructure, the faint glowworm glow of the binnacle light in the wheelhouse the only illumination visible along the Patrol Craft's 170-foot length.

Felix heard the muffled engines now, reversing, and a moment later the wooden hull of his *pirogue* and the steel one of the newcomer bumped lightly together. Boathooks reached down, holding his craft alongside, and a dark shape extended a hand to help pull him aboard.

His helmeted and flak-jacketed guide led him silently inboard. Again as usual, the interior of the little warship was illuminated with that odd blood-red light that did not hurt Felix's night-adjusted eyes. Within the cramped ward-room, she was waiting.

"Comment allez-vous, Monsieur Akwaba. Le petit biere?"

When she had first sought him out, her French had the stiffness and for-mality of the European about it. Now, however, after only a few short months, she had the lilting flow of the African idiom down perfectly. Almost unnerv-ingly so. Because of her near-white hair and gray-blue eyes, the agents she re-cruited among the Frenchside boatmen privately referred to her as *Le Petite Phantome,* "The Little Ghost."

Felix sometimes wondered if there was more truth in that name than he knew. The white folk claimed that they had no sorcerers or sorceresses living among them. However, with this one, he wasn't so sure.

"Merci, s'il vous plait, Capitaine," Felix replied carefully, taking a seat across the table from the female American naval officer. "The night is warm."

Producing a chilled bottle of Flag lager, she filled the two water glasses waiting on the table. After waiting a moment for the foam to settle, they drank together, accomplishing the ritual of hospitality.

"How is the fishing?" she inquired, setting her glass on the table.

"Not good and not bad. Much the same as always."

"And your granddaughters away at school?"

"Ha! They write their grandpapa letters and my son-in-law reads them aloud to me and to the whole village. They make me proud."

The Little Ghost smiled. "I am pleased to hear it, my friend. And things along the coast, how are they?"

Now the pleasantries were past and it was time to get to business.

"The Union men have been around recruiting, seeking for more boatmen to haul oil Englishside."

"And are they finding many who want to try?"

"It is not as easy as it once was. You and your sea monsters, your skimmer gunboats, have taken too many. Of course, the smugglers who have been caught are only sentenced to a month or two in the prisons, less than that if their families can pay dash to the judge. But even a month in the Ivoire Bastille is not a pleasant thing. And when they return home, their boats are gone. They have nothing."

Felix took another sip of beer. "No," he said, "this time the Union men have to make big promises to get all the men they want."

"And do they want many?" Those eyes, the color of a dawn horizon at sea, narrowed just a little.

"Very many. More than ever before."

"And what promises are the Union men making to get them?"

"More money, almost twice as much for each barrel of diesel or petrol delivered. And this time the Union men are paying for the fuel themselves. And finally, a new outboard motor for every boat that dares the blockade, delivered in advance. My own wife would be tempted to smuggle for that."

The Little Ghost nodded thoughtfully. "I imagine they are getting their men with that offer."

"They are."

"I see. That is most interesting, my friend." The woman reached into her shirt pocket and produced a folded pad of paper money. West African CFA francs, used bills as always, and in small denominations, money that wouldn't attract attention. "Thank you for being my eyes and ears."

Felix stowed the francs away in the pocket of his own ragged shirt. At times he wondered about being a spy on his own people, but then, he wasn't as young a man as he once was. The fish were harder to catch than when he was a youth and his granddaughters' school was expensive.

And then, what would happen if the West African Union succeeded in eating up Guinea? At the moment, this Belewa fellow smiled at the Côte d'Ivoire. But then, so does the shark just before taking a bite.

"There is a plan as well," Felix continued. "When the engines and the fuel are delivered, each boatman is told a night and a time and a place. This time, they are not to make the run to Englishside on their own. All of the smuggling boats are to sail at once and travel together like a great school of fish."

"And the Union thinks we won't notice?" the Little Ghost asked.

"They are sure you will. But the Union men have made one last promise. This time, so they say, there will be Union gunboats waiting to escort the smugglers across the line. Many Union gunboats. This time, so they say, the sea monsters will die."

"I think it's a Hail Mary play," Christine Rendino said, cradling a half-empty coffee mug in her hands. "A desperation move. Belewa's going for broke."

Following her interview with her informant aboard the *Sirocco,* the intel had thumbed a priority ride back to Floater 1 aboard a British patrol helicopter. She'd risked the sling lift in the early-morning darkness so she could be back aboard the platform and waiting when Amanda and the other senior tactical officers returned from patrol.

Gathered in the briefing trailer, Christine, Amanda, Stone Quillain, and Steamer Lane drained the coffee urn, striving to keep sleep at bay while confronting this latest crisis.

"Do we have any other intel supporting the word you've received from your agent?" Amanda inquired, rubbing her eyes.

"It explains what we've been seeing at the naval station at Harper. The two Boghammer squadrons there have been reinforced with every available hull the Union navy can scrape together. We're estimating between twenty-two and twenty-four Bogs currently operational. These squadrons have also had their fuel restrictions lifted. For the past week they've been conducting intensive maneuver and live-fire training. Fa'sure, they're gearing up for some kind of big push."

"I don't suppose your guy could give us the word on when this show is scheduled," Steamer inquired.

Christine shrugged. "He doesn't have to. It's easy enough to figure. The Union plans on making their move at night. That makes sense. They want darkness cover. On the other hand, they're going to be herding an uncoordinated swarm of fishing boats down the coast, none of which will have night-vision systems or even rudimentary navigational equipment. They're going to need moonlight, as much of it as they can get."

"And we've got a full moon in six days," Amanda said slowly.

"Yep," Christine acknowledged. "I'd say their valid operational time frame will extend from two days before full moon to two days after. The long-range weather projection indicates that we can also expect low seas and clear weather throughout that time frame. Conditions will be as good as they get for a convoy run. If the Union misses this gate, it'll be a month before they can try again. And they don't have another month to spare."

No one spoke, and all eyes came to rest on Amanda Garrett.

She seemed to be gazing off into the distance beyond the trailer walls, her golden hazel eyes half closed and shadowed with lack of sleep. Only that slight unconscious action, that light biting of her lower lip in thought, testified to her mental focus. The adding and subtracting of a warrior's sums.

"I think we can put enough of a package together to take to the U.N. rep," Christine continued hesitantly. "She can confront the government of Côte d'Ivoire with it. This deal is going to be too big for them to sweep under the rug. They'll have to take action or run the risk of losing too much international face. If we move fast, maybe we can break this thing before it gets launched."

"No."

Amanda shook her head decisively. "We don't tell anyone ashore about this. Not even anyone at Conakry Base. I will personally brief Admiral MacIntyre on this situation. Beyond that, this information stays strictly on the platform. I don't want Union intelligence to have any chance at all to learn that we've been tipped to their plans."

She pushed back her chair and rose to her feet, pacing, the sudden surge of battle-inspired adrenaline kicking her up and moving. "If Belewa wants to come out and engage, we're going to let him. This is what we've been waiting for since Yelibuya Sound. Another chance for a stand-up fight with the Union navy within our rules of engagement, and another opportunity to take them down hard."

Steamer Lane looked grim. Stone Quillain smiled wolfishly, one fist lifting in a sharp thumbs-up. As for herself, Christine wasn't quite sure what her response should be.

"Steamer, start cooking your maintenance schedules. I want full squadron availability during this upcoming full-moon phase. Maximum effort! We're going to have all three PGs out there on station for all five nights. It means a doubled patrol schedule for all hands, but we can hack that for a little while. Pass the word to *Santana* and *Sirocco* as well. We'll be shifting both of them over to support positions on Ivory East. We'll also need to coordinate operations with the Brit helo group. Everybody gets invited to this party."

"Aye, aye, ma'am."

"Stone, I'm not quite sure what all your people are going to be doing yet, but I want all three rifle platoons regrouped here on the barge. Everyone except for our coastwatcher patrols on the eastern Liberian beaches."

"Y'all got it, Skipper."

"Christine. Can you give us a one-day jump-off warning before they make their move?"

The intel nodded slowly. "Yes, ma'am. I believe we can give you a twenty-four-hour notification of event with a reasonable accuracy level."

Amanda hesitated, meeting Christine's cool blue-gray gaze for a long moment, then turned away. "All right, let's get going on this ground work. We'll start on the details tonight. I want a special O Group meeting at 1900 hours for . . . let's call it for Operation OK Corral."

⬦◆

Twenty minutes later, Amanda sat at her desk calling up the first of a protracted series of data dumps on her laptop. A Styrofoam cup of double-steeped tea sat at her elbow. She'd learned that if she absorbed enough caffeine to get through the comparatively cool morning hours, the generalized discomfort of the full day's heat would keep her awake and operational, without having to resort to the go-pill kit. It was a useful thing to know when all hell was on the verge of breaking loose.

She was just taking her first cautious sip of the hot liquid when a sharp rap sounded at the module door.

"Come in."

Christine Rendino entered and assumed a parade rest in front of Amanda's desk, her eyes emotionless and looking somewhere beyond Amanda's shoulder. "Request permission to speak frankly with the Captain."

Amanda sighed and pushed the laptop aside. Back during the briefing, Christine had started to look and sound like a naval officer. That almost inevitably meant that the little intel was truly and royally pissed off about something and that she wanted Amanda to know about it.

"You know you always have permission, Chris. Let's hear it. What's the problem?"

The intel relaxed minutely, resting her hands on her hips. "You've been spending a lot of time with Stone Quillain lately, haven't you?"

Amanda lifted an eyebrow. "Does this concern my professional life or my personal one?"

"Both! I mean, I'm wondering here if you've been hanging around with the Marine mentality so much that maybe some of the gung ho is starting wear off on you."

The intel's words were an attack, and an angry nerve-sharpened response almost reached Amanda's lips. Almost.

Amanda caught herself in time and called the words back. Christine Rendino had been serving as her emotional Jiminy Cricket for years now, and she had come to learn it was bad joss to disregard her friend's observations.

"Sit down, Chris," she said quietly. "Pour yourself a cup of this high-octane tea and tell me what you're seeing."

After a moment, the little intel stopped bristling and accepted both the tea and the chair. "All right," she said. "What I think I'm seeing now is something

I haven't ever seen before. Amanda Garrett looking for a fight. Hey, I mean you've always done the job, but I have never, ever seen you take your people into a battle that wasn't absolutely required to do that job."

Amanda took a deliberate sip of tea. "And you don't think OK Corral is a necessary fight?"

"What I think isn't important, boss ma'am. What you think is. And what I am asking is, have you done as much thinking about this job as maybe you should have? Belewa is up against the ropes. If we can just keep the oil tap turned off for a few more weeks, he's going down.

"That's the real strategic key to this whole thing," Christine continued earnestly. "We don't have to go to guns with this guy. We can starve him to death. If we can bust up this mass smuggling run by means other than by a direct confrontation, it'll serve the same purpose. And a big bunch of Union . . . and probably American sailors will stay alive."

When applied to those most elemental equations of life and death, additional consideration was always in order. Amanda thought for a long moment before replying.

"To tell you the truth, Chris," she said finally. "I really didn't do too much deep thinking at all about the OK Corral operation before committing us to it. But then, that's become rather SOP for me lately. I'm not exactly sure why, but as this campaign has progressed, I've found myself reacting to Belewa more and more by instinct and intuition than by logic. If I were back at the Naval War College laying this scenario out as a problem in strategic analysis, I'd probably agree with you. But here and now, living it, my heart and my gut are sending me a different message."

Christine frowned. "And they're saying?"

"That this show is a long way from being over. Back in the briefing trailer, you called this bulk-smuggling operation a Hail Mary play. I disagree with that assumption. Yes, we are going into the endgame. Yes, Belewa's back is against the wall. But that only makes him more dangerous. Belewa is not going to yield passively, Chris. Not while he has a drop of fuel, or a round of ammunition, or a single man responding to orders. This I am sure of. He will only become more driven and more willing to take chances."

Amanda set her cup on the desktop and leaned back in her chair, the salt-rusted pivot squeaking. "That's what OK Corral is about, Chris. The fuel is almost secondary. This is a chance to bleed Belewa, to force him into an engagement at something close to our terms. If we can take a large block of his fighting strength out of the game now, it will leave him with that much less to work with when he finally does make his last stand."

The intel was quiet for a moment, deep in considerations of her own.

"Well," Amanda inquired. "What do you think of OK Corral now?"

"I think I liked the Kurt Russell version best. Wasn't Val Kilmer just to die for as Doc Holliday?"

Off the Coast of the West African Union
Four Miles South-Southwest
of Cape Palma   0122 Hours, Zone Time; August 22, 2007

"You called it right, Captain," Ben Tehoa commented, peering over the shoulder of his squadron commander. "They're bypassing Port Harper and continuing up the coast."

Captain Garrett nodded absently as she studied the radar display, her amber hair dull flame in the cockpit's scarlet battle lights. "Our recon indicates they have truck convoys waiting up at their usual landing points along the Grand Cess coastal highway. I've been worried that they might try and bring the smuggling fleet directly in at Harper, but I guess that would be a little too flagrant even for the Union. This was the last big maybe, Chief. OK Corral is good to go."

"You think they know we're out here, ma'am?"

"I think they're expecting us to be."

The radar sweep etched scores of glowing dots clustered between the ghostfire green of the coast and the incandescent blue of the squadron's course line. A second console screen carried a real-time download from the low-light cameras of a circling Predator drone. Upon it, dozens of straggling wakes cut across the surface of the sea, outboard engines churning the luminescence from the water.

A mismatched flotilla of small craft trudged westward beneath the full moon, each boat burdened to the point of risk with cans and drums of diesel and gasoline. On their seaward flank, a long line of Boghammer gunboats cruised warily nose to tail, a mobile wall of men and firepower fencing out the threat of U.N. intervention.

Farther yet to seaward, that intervention loitered. The Three Little Pigs padded silently along in swimmer mode, paralleling the course of the Union convoy, awaiting their time.

"Those Union gunboats look like they've got bigger crews aboard tonight," Tehoa commented.

Captain Garrett nodded again. "Um-hmm. They're running a couple of extra gunners per hull. I had the Predator make a low pass a while ago to check them out and they look like army heavy-weapons men. Every boat's also carrying a heavy ammunition load. They're here to fight. No doubt about it."

Captain Garrett looked back over her shoulder, smiling ruefully. "I can really pick 'em, can't I, Chief?"

Tehoa grinned back. "It's no fun if it's too easy, ma'am. By your leave, I'll go do a walk around in the main hull."

"Carry on. You've got about half an hour before we hit the engagement zone."

Tehoa dropped down the ladder into the *Queen*'s central bay. Methodically he began a circuit of the seafighter's battle stations, checking out systems and personnel alike, exchanging a few quiet words with the hands. Danno and Fryguy at fire control, Lamar and Slim in the starboard power room, the auxiliary gun crews at the hatch mounts.

Like the Boghammers, the *Queen* carried a couple of extra souls aboard this night—extra ammo humpers ready to feed the ravenous autoweapons during a prolonged battle. With the Marine landing team absent and with the miniraider Zodiac unshipped, there was plenty of room for them as well as for the small mountain of cartridge and grenade cases lashed down along the centerline of the bay.

"Yo, Scrounger! How's things going in here?" Tehoa called, looking in through the port-side power room hatch.

"Green boards, Chief," the brunette turbine tech replied, turning away from the silent main engines. "Everything's looking okay."

Those were her words, but her expression didn't match with them. Sandra "Scrounger" Caitlin had something on her mind and under her skin. Tehoa simply stood and looked at the young woman, waiting for the truth to come out.

"Chief," she asked hesitantly. "Do you have a second? I need to talk to you about something."

"If I don't, I'll make one. Come on, let's hit the wardroom."

With the seafighter called to quarters, the little messroom/living space was empty. Tehoa slid into one of the bench seats and waited while Scrounger took a Coke she really didn't want from the refrigerator. Patiently, he gave her the time she needed to start at her own beginning.

"Chief," she said finally, her eyes lowered to the unopened beverage can in her hands, "have you ever heard of 'The Touch'?"

"The Touch? You mean where someone gets a premonition that they're going to be killed on a mission?"

The girl nodded without lifting her eyes. "Yeah."

"I've heard the stories. I've never seen it happen myself, though. What's the word, Scrounge? You thinking that maybe you're going to buy the farm tonight?"

"I don't know, Chief," she replied, looking up, her eyes dark and troubled. "I really don't know. I just have a really funny feeling about this run. Like nothing I've ever had before."

"Scared?"

She shrugged. "Yes. . . . But not much more than usual when we're guns up. It's just . . . I don't know. I can't describe it."

The CPO studied the little turbine tech's eyes, looking deep into them and around the corner to where she kept her soul. "Why didn't you tell me about this before we launched tonight?"

She shrugged again. "I couldn't let you and the rest of the crew down, Chief," she replied softly, "even if it does mean that I'm going to die. I can't. If it comes down to a choice between being killed and not being able to live with yourself anymore, what's the difference?"

Tehoa thought for a long moment. "None, I guess, Scrounge," he replied finally. "I've never felt The Touch or anything like it. No imagination, I guess. Either that or I'm always so busy before a big show I never have the chance to notice.

"Anyhow, the way I've got it figured, when I put on the uniform, the Navy never guaranteed that I'd ever get out of it alive. They just promised that if I did die, it would be for something worth dying for. Now I don't know if this U.N. job is exactly worth taking the big fall or not. That's not for the rank and file like you or me to make the call on. I only know that I'm going to try and hold up my end of the deal."

Scrounger half-smiled and nodded her head. "Me too, Chief. I guess I only wanted to talk to somebody about it."

Tehoa gave the turbine tech a light slap on the shoulder. "Trust in your ship and your crew, and trust in being alive, Scrounge. Like I said, I've heard lots of stories about guys getting a premonition, and most of them end up with the guy still alive and well on the other side of it."

"I'm going to be fine, Chief."

"Damn right you are, sailor!"

Suddenly, the compartment's overhead speaker clicked on and Commander Lane's voice interrupted them. "All hands, we are approaching the engagement area. Close up to action stations! Fire control, arm your pedestals! Surface-engagement package! Auxiliary gunners, man your mounts! Power rooms, initiate turbine start sequences! Stand by to go on the cushion!"

"That's it, Scrounge. Let's go!"

The Chief and Caitlin slid out from behind the mess table. Realizing she still held the unopened pop can in her hand, Scrounger took a second to toss it back into the refrigerator.

Tehoa gave her a grin and a nod. "See you after the show, Scrounge."

The girl replied in kind, "Later, Chief." Then she was gone, hurrying to her station.

She'd be fine, Tehoa decided, starting for the ladder to the cockpit.

Topside, he found the command crew hard at it, Commander Lane and Ensign Banks sweeping through the prestart checklists that were now engraved permanently on their psyches. As always, their palms came up to exchange the ritual high five as the first turbine began to crank.

Chief Tehoa suddenly understood the meaning of that gesture. His pilot and copilot were making their own wordless promise to see each other alive after the battle.

Captain Garrett held her station at the navigator's console, her slim figure swaddled in the bulk of a battle vest and her fine-lined features partially concealed by her Kevlar helmet and headset. Not relaxed, but totally controlled, she focused on the tactical screens, no world existing for her beyond them.

As Tehoa watched, she inserted a CD disk into the communications deck and pushed a key. A moment later, her recorded voice issued from the radio loudspeakers, broadcasting over the Union standard military bands:

Attention, attention. This is the United States Navy, operating under the mandate of the United Nations African Interdiction Force. All craft, heave to and prepare for boarding and search. All craft, heave to and prepare for boarding and search. If we are fired upon, we will return fire. I repeat, if we are fired upon, we will return fire.

Amanda Garrett had just presented their letter of intent to the Union.

Tehoa donned his own armored vest and his helmet with the integral night-vision goggles. Unlatching and swinging back the overhead hatch, he hoisted himself up into the gunner's saddle with a grunt. God, maybe he was getting too old for this. Maybe Mary was right and he should take his twenty-and-out next year. The girls were growing so fast. Soon he would miss the whole joy of their childhood. It was something to think about.

Once in the saddle, he took a look around, his night-adapted eyes making good use of the moonlight even without the intervention of the AI2 visor. The low African coastline flowed darkly along the northern horizon, dividing the silver-tinged sea and the starblaze of the sky. Astern, the streamlined shadow forms of the *Carondelet* and the *Manassas* trailed in the *Queen*'s scant wake.

The lift fans of all three hovercraft spooled up to speed, puffs of pale spray escaping from beneath their inflating skirts as they lifted off the surface. Airscrews flickered over in a contrarotating blur of power, assuming propulsion from the retracting underwater propellers. The *Queen of the West* trembled like a nervous thoroughbred before a race, the self-generated breeze of her growing speed whipping the flag and burgee streaming from her snub mast.

Tehoa jacked in the phone link of his headset and the power lead for his night-vision visor. Then he tested the electric drive motors of the gun ring, traversing the mount a few degrees to port and starboard. He also verified that the heavy rocket flare called for in Captain Garrett's mission plan was ready within reach. Finally he pulled the Velcro tabs of the gun covers, stripping away the water- and spray-proof nylon shroud, baring the two big Browning heavy machine guns and their brassy, gleaming belts of shells.

As he stuffed the cover down into the cockpit, Tehoa felt the flow of the slipstream shift across his face. He looked up again to find the squadron turning in toward the coast, their formation shifting from a cruising line astern to their staggered combat echelon.

Aiming their stubby bows at the Union flotilla, the seafighters started to close the range. The showdown at OK Corral had begun.

Off the Coast of the West African Union
Seven Miles West-Southwest of
Cape Palma   0207 Hours, Zone Time; August 22, 2007

"Maintain speed at twenty knots until order for blow-through." On the command circuit Amanda spoke over the unmuffled squall of the turbines. "Forget the smuggling craft. Keep between the Boghammers and the coast. I say again, stay on the Bogs! I want hard kills!"

"Frenchman, acknowledging."

"Rebel, rajah."

Up forward, Steamer Lane lifted a hand in a dimly visible OK sign. He and Snowy had shifted their instrumentation lighting from standard night red to the filtered blue-green compatible with the night-vision visors they now wore.

Amanda's fingers played over the controls of her own multimode telepanels as well. Shifting the radar and tactical displays to secondary screens, she accessed fire control, a targeting recticle snapping up on her main scope. If one of the main control stations went down during the engagement, she had to be ready to assume direction of a weapons pedestal. Likewise, should the fight go long range, an extra designator might be needed for the Hellfire missiles. During their long hours on patrol, she'd had Danno O'Roark teach her the gunnery drills just for such situations. She rechecked each panel setting with careful deliberation. This time it would be no drill.

She depressed a key and a ranging laser lashed out.

"Operations, range to target six thousand yards and closing. Do we have any reaction yet?"

The Boghammers had radios; they must be hearing the challenge. At least some of the gunboats should have night-bright binoculars as well; they should be able see the American hovercraft converging on their formation.

"Acknowledged, Little Pig Lead." Christine Rendino's voice sounded stone cool in Amanda's headset, stone cool. "They've got you spotted. We are monitoring a traffic spike on the Union radio channels. . . . Be advised the Union battle line is increasing speed."

Amanda noted it as well. Wakes flashed in the moonlight as engines throttled up. Rooster tails lifting behind them, the line of gunboats accelerated, coming up onto the plane.

"Little Pig Lead!" Christine spoke sharply. "Targets are turning in on you!"

With the synchronicity of a sparrow flock, the Boghammer flotilla pivoted ninety degrees to port. The line-astern formation became a wave front, a maritime cavalry charge thundering toward the seafighter group.

"We see it, Operations," Amanda noted, pleased with the stability of her voice. "Range now five five double zero. Rate of closure forty-five knots." Her eyes flicked up from the targeting scope to the radar display. "We've given them their setup for the Buffalo. Let's see if they go for it."

"Acknowledged. Watching for it . . . Yeah! End squadrons are continuing to increase speed. We got a Buffalo. Confirm we got a Buffalo!"

On the radar screen, the Union line-abreast formation became concave, the ends curving inward toward the seafighter group, the "chest" lagging back to confront the foe, while the swiftly moving "horns" swept around to converge on the seafighter's flanks.

A grim smile tugged at the corner of her mouth. For a long time she had considered how to best evade this favored maneuver of the Union gunboatmen. In the end, however, she elected not to evade the Buffalo but to embrace it. Amanda keyed her headset mike.

"Little Pigs, power up!"

Snowy Banks leaned in over the central console. One small hand shoved the drive throttles forward, the other coming back on the propeller controls, pulling pitch from the prop blades and killing their grip on the air. Even as the turbines spooled up to their maximum output, the speed of the hovercraft increased only slightly, the augmented horsepower wasted by the futile flailing of the airscrews. A heavy vibration and an agonized metallic wailing grew from back aft. The hovercraft's power plants shuddered on their bedplates, threatening an imminent overrev.

"Little Pigs, designate targets!"

The death pips of the sighting systems crawled across the tactical display and settled on the two Boghammers directly ahead of the *Queen,* the same fire template being set simultaneously aboard both the *Manassas* and the *Carondelet.*

Others were seeking targets in the night as well. Shooting stars streaked up from the sea, converging overhead. Parachute flares burst alight over the American formation, silvery magnesium flame glaring. The seafighters stood on across a shadowless sea of shimmering mercury.

Amanda could see that the encirclement was almost complete, the hovercraft driving ever deeper into the horseshoe-shaped bucket formed by the Boghammer group. In moments, the Union gunboats would be at an effective firing range.

And yet she could not open fire, in spite of the longer range of her own force's weapons. The U.N. rules of engagement were clear. The interdiction forces were authorized to use deadly force only in self-defense. The enemy must fire the first shot, or in this instance, barrage. Be damned that none of your own people would be left alive to reply.

"Little Pigs," she snapped over the command channel. "Stand by flares!"

But then, in her own conscience, Amanda had long ago resolved that quandary. When confronted with rules of war that unnecessarily put one's own people at risk, one became tactically innovative.

Or, to put it bluntly, one cheats.

"Little Pigs, fire flares!"

The cockpit gunners aboard all three hovercraft released their illumination rounds. Only instead of firing the projectiles vertically into the air, they aimed their launch canisters horizontally, at the line of onrushing Boghammers.

Harmless though they were, the balls of multicolored flame looked most impressive streaking toward the Union gunboats. And all it required was a single nervous finger on a single trigger.

From off to starboard, a tracer stream licked out of the darkness.

"Little Pigs! We are under attack! Guns free! Guns free! Engage, engage, engage!"

Six weapons pedestals screamed hoarsely and spat rocket salvos into the sky. Six swarms of Hydra rockets arced through the night like hornets from hell and the six Boghammers at the apex of the Buffalo formation were engulfed, dying amid thunder and spray.

"Little Pigs! Execute blow-through!"

Snowy slammed the propeller controls forward. Racing prop blades shifted pitch and caught air. With one hundred percent of their propulsion power instantly onstream, the *Queen* lunged forward with a neck-snapping surge of acceleration, her sisters following suit as they raced for the gap they had blasted in the Union line of battle.

Around the perimeter, Union boat commanders bellowed futilely at their gunners and a ragged curtain of tracers swept across the kill zone mere seconds too late. The seafighters had cleared the fire stream nexus, the converging storm of autoweapons fire only chopping the water in their wakes.

At fifty knots and with their speed still increasing, the hovercraft flotilla streaked through the ruptured "chest" of the Buffalo formation and into the clear. Behind them, the "horns" began breaking up, the Union squadron's leaders confused and dismayed at the failure of their trap.

Escape and evasion for the American craft would have been a simple thing at that moment, but that wasn't why Amanda had brought them here. "Little Pigs! Echelon turn to starboard! Hard about one hundred and eighty degrees! Independent targeting! Fire as you bear! Take 'em down!"

Steamer locked the air rudders over, bringing them around in a sweeping turn to the east, reversing their course and bringing the *Queen of the West* in line with the disintegrating left horn of the Union formation. Smoothly ski jumping across the *Queen's* wake, the *Carondelet* and *Manassas* reassumed their formation slots, clearing their firing arcs. The hunted had turned and had become the hunters.

There had been no time for Danno and the FryGuy to recycle the pedestal mounts and reload with fresh rocket pods. It was all gun work now. On her tactical screen, Amanda saw the death pips of the two 30mm mounts converge on the first Boghammer in the Union line.

The autocannons raged, the *Queen's* frame shuddering with their recoil. The cockpit machine guns joined in an instant later. Chief Tehoa might have lacked the computerized fire control of the pedestal mounts, but his tracers stitched into the target with near-equal accuracy.

The Boghammer writhed, the water around it leaping and boiling. The explosive cannon shells tore away chunks of Fiberglas and flesh, while the higher-velocity machine-gun slugs simply drilled through. Fuel cells and ammunition boxes yielded to the torment, flame smeared across the surface of the sea, ending in a burgeoning explosion.

The *Carondelet* destroyed a second gunboat, the *Manassas* a third. A fourth perished as its panicking helmsman cranked his wheel over too hard in a wild effort to turn away from destruction. The Boghammer capsized, its pale belly flashing in the moonlight as it dumped its crew into the sea.

Then the free kills were over. The gunboats of the western horn came screaming across to aid their comrades in the eastern half of the Union formation. The Little Pigs turned again to face the new threat, tracer tentacles lashing and intertwining across the wavetops as the range closed. Converging at a cumulative speed of near a hundred knots, seconds-brief broadsides were exchanged as the two formations intermeshed and drove through one another once more.

In the cockpit of the *Queen*, Amanda grimly braced herself in the navigator's chair. Her part in this fight was finished for the moment. Each side had executed its carefully preplotted gambit against the other. Now the battle had dissolved into a chaos beyond all leadership and direction. Now it was in the hands of the pilots and gunners, the sole question left being who could kill the fastest and most efficiently. She was only along for the ride.

⚒◆

For Steamer Lane, the battle of Cape Palma would be a series of frozen impressions strung like beads along a central cord braided of panic and terror. There was the sound of the guns, the syncopated hammering of the 30 mikes, the sharper, angrier stutter of the machine guns, and the deliberate cough of the grenade launchers. Propellant smoke filled the cockpit like the cigarette haze in a crowded bar, thick, sweet, and powdery on the tongue. His neck ached from the weight of his helmet and vision visor as he wildly twisted his head, maintaining his situational awareness.

Lastly he would recall the face of Snowy Banks. She leaned in over the center console, her lips curled in a snarl of concentration and her eyes fixed on the movements of his hands on the main wheel and throttle. Using the puff-port controller, she augmented the air rudders, helping to hold the hovercraft into their repeated snaking turns.

The engagement became a savage two-dimensional dogfight, wakes and tracer streams tangling wildly as the two unlike forces struggled for tactical advantage. The larger seafighters had the speed and the firepower, while the smaller Union gunboats had sheer number and a tighter turning radius.

A rhythm became established within the battle, a grotesque dance of fire and destruction. A Boghammer swarm would converge on the *Queen,* striving to pen her in and pin her down like a dog pack on a bear. Steamer would firewall his throttles, breaking out of the ring, then reversing back upon his attackers. Cutting one gunboat out of the pod, he would herd the Boghammer away from the covering fire of its squadron mates, then position so that his weapons crews could smash it.

It was a new page in the history of warfare, a naval engagement such as Mahan or Yamamoto never dreamed of. And yet Steamer found himself struck by a sense of déjà vu, an overwhelming sense that he had experienced this all before.

In a free instant between maneuvers, he recognized the source. The shouts and cries of his gunners over the intercom, like the dialog of an old World War II air war movie.

"Bogs at ten o'clock!"

"Watch it! *Manassas* is out that way! Watch for her strobes. Do not blue on blue!"

"Hear ya, Chief!"

"Fuck! I'm jammed! Port-side forty is down! Somebody cover port-side!"

"This is Danno! Covering port!"

"Bog going to starboard, trending aft!"

"Starboard forty has acquired! Target still trending aft! Stern mount, take him!"

"This is stern . . . we see him! Mister Lane! Gimme rudder! Gimme left rudder! . . . I'm on him! I'm on him! God, that sucker's burning!"

As the hovercraft swerved and bucked across the sea, the ammo humpers couldn't stay on their feet down in the main hull. Rather, they dragged the ammunition cases to the door mounts on their hands and knees. Supported by their monkey harnesses, the gunners stood ankle deep amid smoldering shell casings, blessing the spray that hazed in through the open hatches. It cooled the blazing-hot gun barrels, staving off meltdown.

Then there was that other sound as well, beyond the hoarse shriek of the engines and the yammering of the weapons. A sound almost felt rather than heard, the sporadic *thunk . . . thunk . . . thunk* of high-velocity bullet strikes punching through the bulkheads. The seafighters were mostly armored against rifle-caliber gunfire, but more than rifles were being used against them this night. It was only a matter of time and failing luck.

"Royalty, Royalty, this is Frenchman! We're hit! We're hit! We've lost a power room! We're losing cushion!"

⚔◆

Amanda's head snapped up from the tactical screen. "Steamer," she yelled, "the *Carondelet* is in trouble. Steer three seven five! Converge and cover!"

"Doing it!"

She crushed her thumb down on the transmit key. "Rebel, this is Royalty. Close up with Frenchman. Cover her!"

"Already on the way, ma'am. The cavalry is charging!"

Like a school of piranha scenting blood, the surviving Boghammers also converged on the cripple, seeking vengeance against their tormentors. Setting a racetrack fire pattern around the damaged and wallowing *Carondelet*, they raked her mercilessly, blue-water Apaches circling an isolated fort.

And then the *Queen* and the *Manassas* exploded on scene, pouncing into the middle of the swarm, the hammering of their guns becoming a single continuous roar.

The *Queen* cut a flaming pinwheel arc around her wounded sister, her stern skidding outboard and her weapons spraying death into the night. As the G forces of the wild skid grew, Amanda clung to the grabrail behind the pilot's seat with her left hand, while with her right she fended off the cascade of searing shell casings raining down from the hatch guns.

"Steamer," Snowy Banks screamed. "Two of them! Coming across the bow!"

Looking up, Amanda saw a pair of Boghammers cutting directly across the path of the hovercraft. Half a dozen points of flame flickered and danced along the gunwales of the lead boat, the muzzle flashes of machine guns and automatic rifles. In the second craft, the outlines of two Union gunners could be seen, bracing a third upright as he stood in the bow, leveling a Carl Gustav rocket launcher at the cockpit of the *Queen*. For one indescribable and inescapable moment, Amanda and her crew looked down the barrel of that launcher and waited for death to emerge.

Then, from overhead, the tracer streams of Chief Tehoa's guns slashed and thrust like a saber blade, the storm of heavy slugs smashing and crumpling the living weapons mount. The barrel of the Carl Gustav sank toward the Boghammer's deck and the fist of its gunner clinched convulsively around the launcher's handgrip as death claimed him. The rest of the Bog's crew followed an instant later. The 84mm antitank round slammed into the ammunition cases lining the belly of the gunboat.

The Boghammer vanished in a blue-white fireball. The *Queen's* windscreen shattered and blew inward, bullets and shrapnel ripping through the cockpit, shorting systems and exploding telepanels. Holding its course, the surviving Union gunboat turned inside the arc being cut by the seafighter, its weapons angling back and hosing the hovercraft.

Steamer Lane tore off his night-vision visor, its lenses smeared and blinded by the blood streaming from his lacerated forehead. He had only one weapon at his immediate disposal, and he didn't hesitate to use it. Slamming the drive throttles against their stops, he locked the air rudder and puff-port controller hard over, his turn tightening into a pursuit curve.

The crew of the Union gunboat saw the nose of the seafighter come about and aim with deadly deliberation, kerosene-fired turbines shrieking. Suddenly enormous, the bow of the hovercraft loomed above the Boghammer, its broad painted shark's mouth snarling in outrage and triumph.

The *Queen's* foreskirt rode up and over their fragile shell and the sea monster ate them alive.

Amanda felt the thud and scrape of splintering Fiberglas under the *Queen's* plenum chamber and heard Steamer's short, fierce cry of victory over the intercom. "Yeah! Busted your ass!"

"Report!" she yelled into her headset over the slipstream, now howling unchecked through the cockpit. "Anyone hit? Systems status?"

"M'okay," Snowy wheezed, pulling herself upright in her seat. "Hit on the vest. Wind knocked . . . out of me. I'm okay!"

Steamer glanced across at his copilot, then dragged his attention back to his console. "Primary controls functional. Console readouts are down."

"Are we still battle worthy?" Amanda demanded.

The hover commander swiped another handful of blood out of his eyes. "We're good!"

"Steamer . . . You're bleeding!"

"Fuck that, Snow! Reboot the screens! Get me some instrumentation!"

"On it!" The young woman began working intently over the ruins of the control board.

The panels at the navigator's station were still operational. Amanda turned to the tactical display, seeking to regain track of the battle, only to find that it was over.

Only six target hacks remained in the battle area: the three blue friendlies, clustered tightly together, two circling warily about the inert third; her own craft; and the *Manassas,* guarding the crippled *Carondelet.*

To the westward, three red hostiles fled the engagement grounds—the three survivors of the Boghammer squadron. The remainder of the Union flotilla had been converted into a slowly widening debris field: scattered bits of drifting wreckage, puddles of flickering gasoline on the night sea, floating bodies, some still feebly struggling.

The convoy of oil carriers had disappeared. During the sacrifice of the gunboat force they had vanished into the network of small lagoons and salt swamps bordering this stretch of the coast.

"Frenchman, this is Royalty," she called into her lip mike. "What is your status?"

"This is Frenchman," Lieutenant Clark, the *Carondelet*'s commander, replied promptly. "Situation under control. Starboard power room knocked out by AT rocket. Two crewmen wounded. Fires are out and medevac is inbound. No loss of flotation. Weapons and sensors operational. Vessel is under way in swimmer mode."

"Roger that. Can you operate as a search-and-rescue platform?"

"Affirmative, Royalty."

"Very well. Frenchman and Rebel, initiate combat-zone search and rescue." She shifted her address to the two Patrol Craft lurking just over the horizon. "*Santana* and *Sirocco,* this is Little Pig Lead. Move into the engagement area and assist *Carondelet* and *Manassas.* We have a lot of men in the water."

The string of acknowledgments sounded in her headset. Twisting in her seat, she yelled forward to the control stations. "Steamer, come right to two seven zero! All engines ahead full! We've still got three Bogs out there, and Belewa isn't going to get them back!"

The *Queen of the West* flared about and the gale of air blasting in through the shattered windshields grew to hurricane proportion. Snowy Banks fitted her own night-vision visor over Steamer's face, then crouched low out of the slipstream beside the control pedestal, her eyes narrowed to slits against the slipstream.

Night-vision systems were almost redundant. In the cold light of the full moon, the wakes of the fleeing Boghammers could be made out with the naked eye, silver thread laced across the black sheening silk of the sea. And if the Union gunboats could be seen from the *Queen's* cockpit, so she must be visible from theirs, a shadowy, mist-shrouded revenant closing in behind them.

"Fire Control, let's finish this," Amanda directed grimly. "Load Hellfires."

Aft, behind the cockpit, the two weapons pedestals whipped vertical to loading mode. Automatic handling arms sliced downward, locking on and lifting stumpy multifinned projectiles onto the launching rails, laser-guided AGM-114 antitank missiles, navalized into small-craft killers.

"Hot birds and green boards," Danno O'Roark announced crisply. "Systems are hot. Designators are up. Port-side pedestal designating red."

A set of glowing crimson crosshairs rezzed into existence on the tactical screen, sweeping across to center on one of the surviving gunboats.

"Starboard designating green," Fryguy Fry added calmly, his sight snapping up and hunting.

"Cockpit, designating yellow." Amanda's hands played across her own keyboard, executing the systems call-ups. "I have the mast sight designator. I am assuming number-two round, starboard."

The image from the masthead video camera filled her screen, a cartwheel sight centering in it. The northernmost of the gunboats had yet to be designated, and she claimed it for her own. Guiding the camera with her joystick, she ran the death pip up the wake until she reached the dark arrowhead mass at its end. Her thumb rocked forward on the trackball atop the controller and the image zoomed in, the mass expanding until it became recognizable as a boat and crew. Her thumb pressed down and a needle beam from the infrared laser atop the snub mast lanced out, painting the target.

The designation box snapped into existence around the target, and the shrill *deedle-deedle-deedle* of the audile prompt sounded in her ears. Lock established. An invisible thread of modulated light linked her and the Boghammer now. Upon its launching, sensors in the nose of her missile would recognize the coding of that one specific point of flickering illumination and would home in on it unerringly.

"Target red designated."

"Target green designated."

"Target yellow designated," Amanda completed the litany. "Commence firing."

"Target red, on the way."

Danno squeezed his actuator trigger. One hundred pounds of hypertech destruction sprang off its launch rail. Its flame trail studded with shock wave diamonds, it arced up and over the shoulder of the hovercraft, seeking its last home.

"Target green, on the way."

A second ripping roar and orange-blue glare, the acrid, chemical fumes of rocket exhaust concentrating within the cockpit.

"Target yellow . . ."

And then the realization came to Amanda Garrett. For fully half her life she had served as one of her nation's military officers. She had been involved in numerous battles and had commanded in engagements where hundreds had died. And yet not until this moment had she ever personally aimed and triggered a weapon that would take another human life.

Downrange, two of the three surviving Boghammers blazed out of existence as the high-explosive/fragmentation warheads of the Hellfires did their job. Amanda commanded her finger to close on the joystick trigger . . . repeatedly.

"Cockpit . . ." a perplexed voice inquired over her headset. "Captain . . . do you have a hangfire? . . . Do you want us to assume the round?"

Amanda's lips parted to whisper yes.

But at the same instant, an enraged scream welled up from deep within her, directed at herself and resounding within her soul . . . *HYPOCRITE!* Amanda's hand closed convulsively and the final round of the battle howled on its way. She forced her eyes to stay open, following the dwindling fire plume away into the night until it climaxed in a white flare on the surface of the sea.

Without needing orders, Lane backed off on the hover's throttles. The battering torrent of wind pouring in through the empty windscreen frames softening to a brisk breeze. Amanda took a deep and deliberate breath. "Maintain this heading, Steamer. Let's see if there are any survivors out there we can pick up."

"Aye, aye, ma'am. That was one hell of a show."

"It's not over yet." Amanda switched the com over to base frequency. "This is Little Pig Lead to Floater 1. Bogs are down. I say again, Bogs are down. Initial phase complete. I think we got them all. Can you verify?"

"We verify, Little Pig Lead," Christine Rendino replied. "Twenty-six out. Twenty-six down. Good shootin', Tex."

"Acknowledged, Floater, and thank you. Now let's go see how the Marines are making out."

She switched back to intercraft, her nerves beginning to loosen. "Attention, all hands. This is the TACBOSS. Stand down from action stations and rig for search and rescue. Hey, Chief, it looks like we've swept the seas clean. Do we have a broom aboard we can tie to the masthead? . . . Chief?"

A sudden icy chill rippled down her spine. Twisting around in her seat, she reached up into the shadows, toward the gunner's saddle of the cockpit mount. She touched Chief Tehoa's leg and her fingers came away covered with a warm dark wetness.

"Steamer! Shut her down! The Chief's been hit!"

The hover commander slammed back his drive and lift throttles, dumping the *Queen* onto the swells with a skidding heave. Leaving the turbines idling, he and Snowy scrambled out of their seats to help Amanda ease the CPO's flaccid body down out of the gunring.

"Oh, jeez! There's blood all over the place back here!"

"He must have been hit back at the *Carondelet*! He never made a sound!"

"Snowy, bring up the cockpit lights! Hey, down in the main hull! Somebody get the medical kit up here! On the double!"

Scrounger Caitlin appeared at the head of the ladder bearing the Day-Glo-orange aid kit. Stunned and wide eyed, she looked as Lane pulled off Tehoa's helmet and tore down the zipper of his flak jacket, seeking for the wound while Amanda held the big man upright in her arms.

Lane worked for a few frantic moments more, then stopped.

"Ah, hell."

Steamer rocked back on his heels, his face a despairing mask of his own dried blood. "It's no good. He took one right in the throat, just above his body armor. He never knew what hit him."

"It must have happened back there when those two gunboats cut across our bow," Snowy said quietly. "He must have been hit right after he saved us." Without realizing herself that she was doing so, she moved closer to Steamer Lane, her shoulder lightly brushing his.

At the rear of the cockpit, Caitlin clung to the rungs of the ladder, sobbing aloud and unashamed. Amanda continued to hold Ben Tehoa, one hand coming up to lightly stroke his dark hair. "I'm sorry," she whispered to someone no longer present. "I'm sorry."

In swimmer mode once more, the *Queen of the West* inched closer to the Union coast. Standing on the weather deck beside the cockpit, Amanda watched as an awkward shadowy mass emerged from an inlet mouth, creeping crablike out to meet the PG over the moonstruck waves.

Drawing closer, it resolved itself as a big twenty-four-foot rigid inflatable raider boat, one of the type carried aboard the Cyclone-class Patrol Craft. The two *pirogues* lashed to its flanks distorted its shape, and a line trailed astern to the *pinasse* it had under tow. Outboard burbling under the strain, the RIB drew slowly alongside the *Queen*.

"How did your half go?" Amanda called down.

"Pretty fair," Stone Quillain replied, standing in the bow of his flagship. "A few smugglers got away into the swamps, but we figure we pretty much got all the boats and the gas."

This had been the other half of OK Corral. Amanda had sprung her trap immediately adjacent to an extensive stretch of isolated coastal swamp, a perfect sanctuary for a flotilla of small smuggling craft under attack. At the start of the engagement, the Union oil carriers had scattered into the protective cover with alacrity, only to find that someone else had gotten there first.

Nights prior, Stone Quillain and his Marines had stealthily infiltrated this same stretch of coastal marsh. Cramped and mosquito-chewed, yet with the patience of a pack of hunting crocodiles, they had lived under camouflage nets aboard their small raider craft, waiting for their prey to be driven into their arms.

"I'd say we still have around forty, fifty prisoners all told," Stone went on, gesturing toward a small, sullen cluster of African boatmen crouched under Marine guard amidships. "What do you want us to do with them?"

"Dump them on that little peninsula over to the west," Amanda replied shortly. "We'll let the Union worry about getting them home. We can't be bothered with them now. Any trouble?"

"Nah. Not really. One of the Bogs got past you and tried to hide up in the swamps, but our Predator teams busted him. Beyond that none of these old boys were packing any guns worth mentioning. Once we got the drop on them, they all gave it up pretty quick." Quillain's head turned, examining the bullet-scarred bow of the *Queen,* the battle damage apparent even by moonlight. "How'd you all do with the Bogs?"

"*Carondelet* was hit. Two wounded, but it looks like they'll make it. We lost Chief Tehoa, though."

"Damn!" The Marine let the single bitter exclamation hang in the air for a long moment before speaking again. "That is a forever crying shame. He was one of the good ones."

"He was," Amanda replied softly, neither sure nor caring if anyone else heard her.

"How about the gas and boats, Skipper? What do you want us to do with them?"

"Burn them. Burn them all!"

Off the Coast of the West African Union
Seven Miles West-Southwest of
Cape Palma   0516 Hours, Zone Time; August 22, 2007

The sun heralded its rising with an azure and tangerine curtain of light to the east, mare's tail clouds glowing incandescently above the horizon. Holding off the Union coast, the small U.S. squadron completed the night's tasks.

The *Sirocco* and *Santana* had arrived on scene. The former took the crippled *Carondelet* under tow for the long haul back to Floater 1, while the latter served as a transfer platform, the last of the wounded Union survivors being winched from her decks to a hovering medevac helicopter.

Closer inshore, the *Queen of the West* and the *Manassas* oversaw another duty.

Topside aboard the *Queen,* Amanda maintained a solitary lookout. The bloodstains on her shirt and on the backrest of the cockpit gun ring had dried, but there were others that were going to remain fresh for some time to come.

Lifting her binoculars to her eyes, she swept the seaward edge of the salt swamps, noting the stealthy hints of movement within the verdant undergrowth. Union army patrols were arriving on scene, seeking the fate of their navy comrades.

She lowered the glasses. Let them come. Her Marines were all safely embarked and away. The Union troops could only look on as the last act played out. Let them see and let them take word back to General Belewa that not one fragment of good would come to him from this night's work.

The twoscore-odd *pirogues and pinasses* of the smuggling fleet had been rafted together and anchored in half a dozen clusters strung parallel to the shore. The dawn's light shimmered and rainbowed on the water as petroleum slicks spread around each raft, gasoline and diesel from punctured cans and drums overflowing the sides of the low-riding boats.

Amanda heard movement on the access ladder. Glancing back, she saw Scrounger Caitlin emerging from the weather-deck hatch. The whole crew had been hit hard by the death of Chief Tehoa, but none more so than the female turbine tech. Amanda could sense a difference in the quiet and pale girl, a sudden new-grown maturity as if some grim wisdom welled up within her.

"We just got a call from the last medevac helo, ma'am. They say they've got room aboard for . . . for the Chief. They're asking if we want them to make pickup."

Amanda studied the young sailor thoughtfully. "Well, Sandra," somehow using a nickname didn't seem right at that moment, "you're our new chief of the boat, and you knew Ben just about as well as any of us. What do you think he'd want?"

Caitlin hesitated, then shook her head. "He'd want to ride back with us, ma'am," she said. "He'd want for us to bring him home."

"Then make it so."

"Thanks, Captain." The girl hesitated for a moment, looking out toward the sunrise. "I was talking to the Chief about something just before the fight. I wonder now if I'd . . ." Her voice trailed away.

"You wonder what?"

"Nothing, ma'am. Nothing that would have made any difference, I guess."

Amanda returned her attention to the anchored clusters of smuggling boats. She lifted her arm, then brought it down in a sharp chopping gesture.

Two hundred yards away, the coxswain of the *Queen*'s miniraider lifted his own arm in acknowledgment. Gunning the engine of his small craft, he started a pass down the line of rafted boats. In the bow of the small RIB, a Marine grenadier crouched with his M-4/M-203 combo weapon. As the raider passed each moorage, the Marine lobbed a flare round into the center of the cluster.

Fire blossomed on the sea, flames radiating outward, engulfing and consuming the small craft. Exploding oil drums thudded like a ragged artillery barrage and dusky smoke boiled into the sky. The separate plumes merged into a single column, trailing away in the offshore breeze as if marking a warrior's funeral pyre.

Mobile Offshore Base, Floater 1   **0516 Hours, Zone Time; August, 22, 2007**

Christine climbed into the briefing trailer to recover some notes she'd forgotten. She also took a moment to stretch and yawn, wondering if she would ever be able to restore herself to a normal human day-night biorhythm again.

Reclaiming the hard copy from the head of the conference table, she turned to go. But then she noted the words written on the blackboard beside the wallscreen. Amanda Garrett had chalked them there many long months ago at that first big mission briefing when the task force had gone on the offensive. The three strategic missions being undertaken by the Union navy:

```
POWER PROJECTION
MAINTAIN SEA LINES OF COMMUNICATION
MAINTAIN FLEET IN BEING
```

Amanda herself had drawn a line through POWER PROJECTION on the night they had destroyed the Union's boat hides along the Guinea coast. Now Christine Rendino took up the chalk and slashed decisively through the second.

Mamba Point Hotel, Monrovia, West African Union
0516 Hours, Zone Time; August 22, 2007

Brigadier Sako Atiba knocked at the door of General Belewa's office. At one time it would have been a needless formality, but of late, a formality had returned to his relationship with his commanding officer.

"Come in."

The Premier General sat at his desk, his elbows propped on the blotter, the heels of his hands pressed into his eyes as if the pressure would ease a great pain. Atiba came to attention before the desk, his hand flicking up in his morning's salute.

"The Chief of Staff reporting as ordered, sir."

Belewa did not look up. "You have been to Operations? You have heard?"

"Of the failure of the convoy, sir? Yes, sir." The temptation to emphasize the word "failure" was strong, but Atiba resisted.

"We lost them all, Sako. I lost them all. And for nothing."

Belewa dropped his arms to the desk, and for the first time Sako noticed the typewritten sheets on the desk before the General. It was the operational outline he and Umamgi had submitted those weeks ago. Belewa looked up into Sako's face and smiled a tired, saddened smile. The smile of a man weary to his soul.

"You were right, old friend. And bitter though the thought might be, so is Umamgi. A soldier cannot afford too much pride, and the leader of a nation even less."

The General tapped the operations plan with his finger. "Set up a meeting with the Algerians. Now we will talk about this."

Dear Mary and Cassy:

I know you have been told by now that your father will not be coming home. As your father's captain, I am writing to you on behalf of myself and all of his other shipmates to say how very sorry we are. I know this won't make things hurt any less, but we hope it will help for you to know we are thinking of you and your mother at this time of great sadness.

Your father was greatly liked and admired by everyone here who served with him. He was very wise, very kind, and very, very brave. He was killed saving me and the crew of his entire ship, and I am going to see that he receives a medal for his courage.

I know you are asking why this had to happen, why your father had to be taken like this when you and your mother needed him so badly. The only answer I can give is that your father was a very special kind of man. He was not greedy with his life; he wished to share it. Something inside made him go out to where there were people in trouble. Something inside made him want to help them and to make the world a better and safer place, both for his family and for everyone everywhere. We call such people heroes.

I could not bring your father home to you; his other shipmates and I have to stay here and finish the job he started. But I hope I will be able to meet you someday soon. Your father showed me your pictures often, and he was very proud of you both. You will be in my prayers, and if there is anything I can ever do for you or your mother, please get in touch with me.

> *Your friend,*
> *Amanda Garrett*
> *Capt., U.S.N.*

There were moisture marks on the paper as Amanda folded the letter. Tucking it into the envelope, she placed it in her hard mail rack to go out on the morning flight to Conakry. Wiping her eyes with the back of her hand, she crossed her arms on the desktop and let her head sink down to rest on them.

Amanda was well into her second twenty-four hours without sleep, yet still she felt as if she never wanted to sleep again. She found herself wishing for a certain bold and youthful helicopter pilot and five minutes to call her own. Just five minutes. Enough time to bury her face into a strong shoulder and be held by a pair of gentle arms. Enough time for someone to whisper those kindly, futile words. "Everything's going to be all right."

Someone thumped briskly on the door to her quarters. Straightening in her chair, she wiped the heel of her palm across her eyes again before responding to the knock. "Enter."

Stone Quillain appeared in the doorway, bearing a small battered ice chest with him. "Evening, Skipper," he said jovially. "How's it going?"

"Oh, fine, Stone. What can I do for you?"

"Oh, nothin', nothin' at all." Doffing his utility cover, he crashed down into the chair facing her across the desk. "It is just that this is beer night over at the platform exchange, and since I was just passing by, I figured I'd bring your ration over to you."

He popped the lid on the ice chest and produced a pair of Budweiser cans, condensation dripping from the chilled aluminum. With a theatrical flair he slammed them down on the desktop. As she had never even considered drawing her two-beers-a-week ration since stepping aboard Floater 1, Amanda looked on puzzled.

"Thank you, Stone," she said, "but I've really never been much of a beer person."

"Know exactly what you mean, Skipper," Quillain replied. "Although it's a hell of a thing for a good rednecked Georgia boy to admit to, neither was I for the longest time. It just didn't sit right. Sort of rasped on the way down. It took me a while to learn that I had to have a kind of a chaser with it to really enjoy a good glass of beer. Something to smooth things along, don't you know?"

"Such as?" Amanda inquired, intrigued in spite of herself.

"Well, I find that a good grade of bourbon generally works for me." His hand emerged from the cooler again, this time bearing a half-empty fifth of Jack Daniel's. "You might want to give it a shot. It could change your whole view of beer drinking."

An automatic refusal rose to Amanda's lips, but then she paused. Something in Quillain's eyes and voice, beyond his somewhat forced jocularity, hinted that the big Marine was trying to offer something more than mere alcohol. Amanda smiled. "You're right. I guess it wouldn't hurt to try it, anyway."

⋊✦

A total of four empty beer cans had been consigned to the wastebasket, and only a thin amber film remained on the bottom of the bourbon bottle. Amanda Garrett realized that she was very close to being drunk on duty. She also discovered that for once in her life she simply didn't give a damn.

She sat with her chair tilted back and her sandaled feet propped on the edge of her desk. Stone Quillain matched her slouched posture, his boon-dockers claiming a corner across from hers. Cradling his Styrofoam cup shot glass in his lap, he listened as she spoke, interjecting an occasional comment or encouraging grunt, an expression of somewhat studied sobriety on his angular features.

Amanda realized that she had been doing most of the talking for the past couple of hours. Nothing on matters of any great import and little of it par-ticularly coherent, just a rambling on a string of minor topics, the flow loos-ened by the effects of the alcohol.

And yet she also felt better for the sheer inconsequentiality of it. The razor edges of existence were softening. Amanda recognized the effect. Like a drug addict completing a cold-turkey withdrawal, she was coming out of her com-bat jag and reentering the normal world.

She tipped back the last few drops of whiskey out of her cup, able now to enjoy the warm glow of it flowing through her. This had been a bad one. "Stone," she inquired. "Have you ever taken casualties?"

The Marine didn't respond for a moment, but memories stirred behind his eyes. "Yeah. I've been lucky mostly, but I had to pay the butcher bill one time."

"Where?"

"In Yugoslavia, or what was left of it. Kosovo."

"Kosovo? I didn't hear of us losing any Marines there."

"You weren't supposed to. Hush job." Quillain took a hefty bite of the bourbon remaining in his cup. "It's been a while, so I guess it doesn't hurt to talk about it now."

"What happened?"

"It was back in the spring of '99, you know, when the ethnic Albanian majority, the Kosovars, in what had been the Kosovo Province of Yugoslavia, decided they were tired of being treated like field hands by the Serbian ruling minority. They figured it was about time for a revolution, and they threw themselves one.

"The problem was that the Kosovo Serbs were part of Slobodan Milose-vic's so-called Serbian Republic. A very mean outfit if you didn't happen to be born a Slav. He sent in his bullyboys and just ran over the place like it was a pos-sum in the road."

"An apt simile," Amanda commented. "Admiral MacIntyre's told me some stories about doing duty in the Adriatic back then. It didn't sound like a plea-sure cruise."

"Boy howdy, I'll tell the world." Quillain gestured with his cup. "This was just before NATO got into it with the bombing. We could see from air recon that things were looking nasty, but nobody knew for sure just how bad things were getting on the ground. The Serbs had chased out all the U.N. observers by that time, and the fragmentary intel we were getting from the Kosovar refugees was pretty ugly. Anyhow, NATO inserted a series of covert Long-Range Reconnaissance Patrols into the province to assess the situation.

"There were 'bout half a dozen teams all told: American Green Berets, British SAS, Marine Force Recon. I was with Recon back then, a butterbar louie fresh out of OCS with one cruise as an enlisted man behind me. Anyhow, I led a four-man fire team in on the Marine patrol."

Quillain slowly shook his head. "I hope I never see hell, but if I do, Kosovo was good acclimatization."

"That bad?"

"I couldn't begin to tell you, Skipper. The place was crawling with Serbian militia and military police, all of them hate crazy and killin' like rabid dogs. Killin' just for the sake of killin'. And then there were the refugees—Albanians, Serbs, Gypsies—all of them just trying to get away to somewhere where they could stay alive.

"We were on the ground four days. Harboring up during oh light hundred in swamps and brush piles and moving on a mile or so at night, mostly crawling on our bellies. You'd lie in a pool of your own piss all afternoon because a Serbian sentry was standing three feet away from you and you couldn't move to take a leak, and you went hungry because you didn't dare crinkle the wrapper on a ration bar.

"By day four we'd documented as much as we could, and we weren't helping anything by hanging around. Besides, I was getting leery about the Serbian security operations in our area. They were acting as if they knew somebody was in the neighborhood who shouldn't be there. I called for extraction and a recovery package launched at first light the next morning.

"Problem was, the only landing zone we could reach was near a highway. That couldn't be helped because of all the activity in our sector. We couldn't risk moving cross-country to another LZ. At any rate, we were at the extraction point by first light. The recovery helo, an Air Commando MH-53 Battlestar covered by a couple of A-10 attack bombers, was inbound and everything was looking good. Then we heard the trucks on the road."

Quillain hesitated, crumpling the empty cup in his hand. "I'll always wonder about the call I made next. Whether I should have aborted the extraction and tried to escape and evade through the woods. But hell, the helo was on final approach and I figured we could beat 'em out of there. Besides, I'll admit it, I was getting a little bit scared about then.

"The A-10s circled the area as the MH-53 set down and we started across the field to the helo. And just about then half of the Serbian army came charging out of the forest on our flank, screaming and yelling and firing AKs from the hip.

"The A-10s opened up. The door gunners on the Battlestar opened up. Me and my boys opened up. All of a sudden the whole damn world was shooting at each other. We fell back to the tail ramp of the lift ship, emptying magazines as fast as we could fit them in our weapons.

"We didn't have the little Leprechaun transceivers back then. We were still using the old backpack PRC–119s carried by a dedicated radio operator. My radioman had been sticking right with me through all of this. A real nice young Puerto Rican kid from New Jersey. Anyway, he and I stopped for a second at the foot of the ramp so I could call one of the strike aircraft in on a hot target. And all of a sudden my RT just sort of went 'uh' and folded up on me. I grabbed him by the harness and dragged him aboard the helo and we got out of there."

Stone flipped the crumpled cup into the trash basket, his expression shielded and impassive. "Our Corpsman worked on him, but it wasn't no good. The kid was dead. Caught a 7.65 round right on the zip of his flak jacket. Took his heart clean out. I can remember sort of holding his head and shoulders in my lap all the way back to Aviano and thinkin', 'I'm this boy's officer! I got to do something about this!' But there wasn't anything to do. Nothing at all."

He nodded toward the envelopes on Amanda's desk. "I didn't even get to write one of them letters. They just listed it as a training accident and sent him home."

Amanda nodded slowly, her own thoughts drifting back over times of blood and fire. "I lost two back aboard my old destroyer. One of them was in the Drake's Passage fight, a rather sweet midwestern boy who'd joined the Navy because he couldn't get a football scholarship. The other was in the Battle of the Yangtze Approaches. I didn't know him very well. He was a new hand who'd signed aboard just before we sailed on that cruise. I doubt I ever exchanged more than a dozen words with him. But he died obeying my orders."

The interior of her quarters shifted in and out of focus, and Amanda found herself having to be deliberate in the choice and forming of her words. "Funny . . . though. I can remember their faces . . . every detail. I guess it's because they keep coming back."

Quillain frowned. "How's that, Skipper?"

Amanda looked back at him owlishly, the hidden words she'd never intended to say to anyone slipping from her. "I mean, they keep coming back, Stone. At night, after lights out, when I'm alone. I mean, I don't really see anything, I guess . . . I just know they're there. I can feel them standing there in the dark . . . just watching me."

"What d'you reckon they want, Skipper?"

Hazily she considered. "I don't know. I don't think they're angry or that they blame me. That's not what it feels like. It's more like they . . . want to remind me about why I can never be wrong. About what the price is when I mess up . . ."

Her eyes were closing now, and she tried and failed to fight them open again. "Tonight . . . for the first time, there's going to be three of them. I think that's why I don't want to sleep. . . ."

"You got to, though, Skipper," Quillain said quietly. "You got to."

Funny, she hadn't noticed before how gentle the big man could make his voice. Her empty cup slipped from her hand, but she didn't hear it clatter to the floor.

Stone Quillain took his feet down off the desk and hoisted himself out of his chair. That was a job done, even though it had cost his last stash of decent sippin' liquor to do it. Stone had talked and boozed more than one C.O. back down after a tough operation, but this little gal had been a chore. She had a head on her like a steel towing butt. That, plus a whole lot more caring than was likely good for her.

Coming around Amanda's desk, Quillain found the deck seemed a little unsteady underfoot. A sea kicking up, no doubt. He hoisted the slumbering woman out of her chair and into his arms. He turned to lay her on her bed, only to discover that as he had her oriented, her feet would be at the head of the cot and vice versa.

A degree of backing and filling proved this to be an insurmountable engineering problem, so with a muttered "To hell with it" he laid her down and shifted the pillow to the appropriate end, slipping it under Amanda's head with clumsy care. Lost in sleep like an overtired child, she didn't even move.

Crossing to the door and switching off the overhead light, Quillain stepped out into the night. As darkness filled the little room behind him, he hesitated for a moment, then looked back.

"You boys go easy on the lady. You hear?" he murmured. "I reckon she's trying about as hard as she can."

✕◆

In the moonshadow of a platform gun tower, Steamer Lane leaned against the steel cable deck railing. His slashed forehead itched abominably under the butterfly sutures, and he had to fight down the urge to scratch. He found himself envying the characters in the old World War II movies he'd watched as a kid. Back then, before they'd invented lung cancer, a guy who couldn't figure out anything better to do with himself could always light up a cigarette. Flicking an imaginary butt over the side, he looked out to sea to the northwest.

One or two stars seemed to ride a little below the distant coastal horizon. An entire constellation had glowed there once, the lights of the city of Monrovia. One by one they'd been going out over the past months. But not quite fast enough.

The railing cable swayed slightly as another's weight came onto it. Snowy Banks leaned silently beside him now, her slender silhouette pale against deeper shadow. Neither spoke. They had been a team for so long, they no longer needed to fill in every little patch of silence with idle conversation.

"It's funny," she said after a time. "But back in NROTC, I can't recall them talking much about your people being killed."

"They talked about us taking casualties in the Academy enough. They even had a shrink in a few times talking about traumatic and post-traumatic shock syndrome and that kind of deal."

"I know. We had that too. Only, there's a whole wall in between 'taking casualties' and your people dying. Casualty is just a word that lies flat on a page. Your people dying is . . . Oh, damn it, Steamer, it's the Chief!"

"I know it, Snow. Even if they did try and tell you, it wouldn't do any good. It's one of those things you have to live. It can't be taught in a way that would mean anything."

The silence closed in once more, barring the lap and slosh of the waves between the barge hull and the Kevlar armor curtains. Gradually Steamer became aware of a growing patch of warmth on his shoulder. Not touch, only proximity. As still as a statue, his little exec looked off toward the distant coast, her head turned carefully away.

Steamer urgently wished for that cigarette again. Instead, he found his arm closed around Snowy's shoulders. She turned into him, burying her face in his chest. They could even embrace in silence and still say what needed to be said.

Mobile Offshore Base, Floater 1   1021 Hours, Zone Time; September 5, 2007

Fourteen days passed.

At first Amanda had been more than grateful for the lull in the action. The battle damage to the *Queen of the West* and *Carondelet* had been repaired, the backlog of maintenance accrued during the doubled patrols of the OK Corral operation had been dealt with, and her crews had been given a chance to rest and recover.

By the start of second week, however, the drop-the-other-shoe syndrome came into play. Amanda eyed her silent interphone deck more and more often, and curt, inquiring calls were made to the Intelligence and Operations Centers with growing frequency. Sleep became harder to come by and explosions of temperament easier. The death of Chief Tehoa on top of six months of continuous campaigning on the Gold Coast had taken its toll. Raw nerve endings drew taut, and all she wanted now was to finish it.

On the fourteenth day, after a morning spent restlessly prowling the decks of the platform, she sought out Christine Rendino.

The interior of the Intelligence Division's Control Node trailer was possibly the coolest place on Floater 1. The massively augmented air-conditioning mandated by the computer systems made the space chilly for someone who had just stepped out of an equatorial noonday. Likewise, Amanda's eyes had to adjust to a darkness lit only by glowing wall screens and CRTs.

The row of duty systems operators bent intently over their consoles, downloading data dumps, guiding reconnaissance drones, and performing the other esoteric tasks of the military intelligence gatherer. The cooling units rumbled softly beneath the deck and the voice of a Union Army officer issued from an overhead speaker, casually involved in a phone call to a subordinate and totally unaware that his every word was monitored.

Christine sat at the head of the trailer at her minute workstation, shaping her nails with an emery board by the light issuing from her personal monitor. She glanced up as Amanda edged down the line of S.O.s toward her. "Top of the morning, boss ma'am."

Amanda replied with a soft and noncommittal grunt. "Anything new to report?"

"Not a solitary flippin' thing. Just as it was at the 0600 briefing this morning and at the 1800 hour briefing last night. Nada. Zip. Zero. Peace has busted out all over and is growing like a dandelion in a field of cow pies."

"Agh." Amanda leaned back against the trailer's bulkhead. "Why does that make me feel so nervous?"

"Because it should." Christine blew lightly across her nails. "Because you were right and I was wrong back there before OK Corral. That convoy operation was only the warm-up act. Elvis has yet to enter the building."

"Thanks. I came in here hoping you'd convince me that I'm getting delusional in my old age, and that Belewa is, in fact, quietly turning belly up on us."

Christine shook her tousled blond head. "Not a chance. Right now, in my expert opinion, Belewa is busy 'fighting the fight of sit-down,' as the Zulus used to call it."

The intel gestured at the row of drone display monitors. "He's ramped everything way back. Insurgency operations inside Guinea have almost come to a halt. He's stopped shifting his political DPs into the border-crossing camps. He's even closed out his smuggling pipeline in Côte d'Ivoire. He's hunkering down and channeling whatever dribbles of fuel he has left into maintaining his civilian transportation and communications nets."

"That sounds more to me as if your scenario was correct. He's packing it in without a last gambit."

"Not so." Christine gestured pointedly with the emery board. "If that were the case, we'd be seeing endgame diplomacy. Belewa would be negotiating with the U.N., trying to cut the best deal he could. As is, he isn't talking with anyone, except maybe the Algerians."

"Then what is he up to, Chris?"

The little blond started on another nail. "He's established a holding pattern and he's waiting for something."

"For what?"

"That is the problem. I don't have a tenth of a percentile point of a clue. Whatever Belewa is setting up, we're not seeing it. Our drone sweeps and our Elint downloads aren't showing anything out of the ordinary. Whatever he's hitting us with is something new, and it's coming from way the heck out in left field."

"Come on, Chris, this isn't like you. There's got to be something showing."

"I'm sorry, boss ma'am. But the old crystal ball's burnt out. Belewa isn't giving me anything to work with. The only blip on the boards at all for the past two weeks has been some extra Algerian Airlines traffic into and out of Monrovia. This could be significant."

Amanda crossed her arms. "How so?"

"I suspect that the Union and the Algerians are involved in some kind of negotiations or joint planning and they're doing it all the old-fashioned way, face-to-face or by courier. They know how strong we are in signal and electronic intelligence, and they're locking us out by not using any form of telecommunications in reference to this operation.

"Probably Belewa has set up the same kind of security protocols for any briefing and preparation work taking place in-country as well. He isn't taking the chance of even a single electron leaking out about whatever it is he's planning."

"Do we have anyone working the problem from the Algerian end?" Amanda inquired

"LANTFLEETCOM and the Office of Naval intelligence are querying DIA and the National Security Agency for us on any unusual activity inside Algeria. Again so far, nothing outstanding."

"It sounds like he's got us behind the curve again, Chris."

"He does, fa'-certain-sure." Christine glanced up soberly at Amanda. "I'm sorry, Amanda. I'm letting you down. I'll keep working the problem, but I think he's going to blindside us on this one."

Amanda reached down and lightly ruffled her friend's hair.

"It's okay, Chris. I know you've given it your best shot. Besides," she went on with a wry shrug, "I always did like surprises."

Mobile Offshore Platform, Floater 1   0717 Hours, Zone Time; September 7, 2007

The big Colt roared repeatedly, its barrel tracking along the arc of the hurled Coke can. A few inches above the wavetops, the can jerked sharply sideways, one end opening out in a blossom of frazzled aluminum.

"Yes!" Amanda yelped as the remnants splashed into the sea. "Yes, yes, yes!" Slapping the empty automatic down on their mess-table shooting bench, she looked over at her instructor in triumph.

Beyond the barge's rail, the morning sun burned redly on the low wave crests, presenting its usual promise of steel-sizzling heat. Stripped to the waist and with his utility cover tugged down low over his eyes, Stone Quillain gave a single, sour shake of his head. "First time's always luck. When you can do that twice in a row, maybe then we'll be getting somewhere."

Amanda cast a sour glance of her own. "You," she said with great deliberation, "are totally insufferable."

"Hell, woman. You're supposed to be hitting what you shoot at. Don't expect any hoorah out of me because you finally got around to doing what you're supposed to. Reload those clips and let's try it again."

"You know, Stone, you're beginning to sound just like my father," Amanda grumbled, picking up a fresh box of .45 hardball.

"Captain! Captain Garrett!" The call was muffled by her ear protectors. She looked around to see Scrounger Caitlin trotting toward the shooting stage from across the platform.

"What's up, Scrounge?" she inquired, removing the headset.

"Operations sent me over when they couldn't get you on the interphone link, ma'am. We got a blockade runner."

Amanda stiffened. "Specifics?"

"The barrier patrol's intercepted an Algerian oil tanker entering the exclusion zone. It's refusing to heave to and it's running at flank speed straight for Port Monrovia. The French corvette making the intercept is calling for backup."

A cold chill trickled down Amanda's spine in spite of the growing warmth of the day. The waiting was over. "Scrounger, go find Commander Lane and inform him I want the *Queen* readied for an immediate launch."

"Aye, aye, ma'am!" The turbine tech bolted away on her new task.

Amanda glanced up at the helipads, checking to see what air assets were aboard and available. "Stone, I want two squads outfitted for boarding operations. One to come with us on the *Queen,* another rigged to fast-rope down from that CH-60 for a deck assault."

"You got 'em." He snatched his utility shirt and headed for Marine country, bellowing for Sergeant Tallman. Amanda scooped her mobile command interphone up off the shooting bench and settled the headphones over her ears.

"Operations, this is Captain Garrett. I have the word on the blockade runner. Take us to full alert. Flash Red, all task force elements! I say again, Flash Red, all task force elements!"

⚒◆

The *Queen of the West* howled southward into the open Atlantic, the Gold Coast fading to a haze line on the horizon behind her. At the navigator's station in the cockpit, Amanda worked to bring herself up to speed on the developing crisis.

"Talk to me, Chris. What do we have?"

"We've got the tanker *Bajara,* boss ma'am. Algerian registry, twenty-four thousand tons displacement. The Lloyd's database indicates she cleared Oran ten days ago with a mixed cargo of refined-petroleum products. Her listed destination was South Africa. However, I've just checked with Soucan Customs Control and with the harbor masters at both Cape Town and Durban. Nobody down there's ever heard of her or is showing any Algerian oil inbound."

"Right. Can you give me a visual on the target?"

"We have an Eagle Eye arriving over her now. Real-time imaging is up on your datalink. We are passing camera turret override control to your station."

Amanda's main monitor filled with an aerial view of the Algerian oil carrier: rust streaked, black hulled, and with a grimy buff-colored deckhouse right aft. At 24,000 tons displacement, she was far from being a supertanker, yet she dwarfed the petite 3,000-ton French corvette dogging her heels. Likewise, she carried enough fuel in her cargo cells to power the West African Union for half a year.

Amanda noted that the *Bajara* was running at nearly twenty knots. Smoke streaked thickly back from her stumpy funnel and the sea boiled beneath her stem and stern. Whoever was at the con of the Algerian tanker must be driving her until her engines lifted off the bedplates.

The Eagle Eye came to a hover over the blockade runner. Using her joystick controller, Amanda zoomed the little RPV's camera in on the tanker's decks. Stone Quillain silently leaned in over her shoulder and together they studied the image on the screen.

Not a soul was visible aboard the Algerian vessel. She might have been a ghost ship. For some reason, those empty decks and bridge wings magnified Amanda's already growing apprehensions.

"Chris," she said into her lip mike, "are you seeing this?"

"Yeah, I see it, " the intel replied, "I'm getting grody vibes off this one, boss ma'am. Grody to the max."

"Acknowledged. Are we seeing any other Union activity anywhere else?"

"Roger on that. The Predator we have circling over Port Monrovia is observing a definite ramp-up in activity. A lot more security and a line-handling crew is standing to at the oil pier. We're also monitoring an exchange of communications between the *Bajara* and Union naval headquarters. It's some kind of verbal numeric code that we can't read. Probably another one of those one-use, tear-pad ciphers."

"What about the Union's heavy gunboats? Are they moving out?"

"Not yet. They've got their crews aboard, however, and they've singled up all lines. They're ready to haul out fast. For the moment they're still alongside the docks, though."

"Keep an eye on them, Chris. If they sortie, I want to know about it. What's the status on *Manassas* and *Carondelet*?"

"They have both aborted patrol and are inbound. The *Carondelet* will be a factor in about an hour. The Manny in about two."

"Very well, Operations. Keep us posted."

Amanda glanced over her shoulder at Quillain. "Observations and suggestions, Captain?"

Quillain shook his head slowly. "Begging your pardon, ma'am, but let's not screw around with this guy. Let's take him down hard and fast. Direct-action drill."

"Are you smelling an ambush too?"

"I'm smelling something. Whatever it is, I figure the less time we give 'em to get set up, the better."

It was Amanda's turn to nod. "I concur. In the vernacular of the Corps, hey diddle diddle and straight up the middle."

"There you go, Skipper."

Steamer Lane called back from the front of the pilot's station. "Target bearing off the bow, Captain. Enemy in sight."

The sea and sky had grown crowded around the racing Algerian vessel. The *La Fleurette* hung back a quarter of a mile off the tanker's port quarter, paralleling her course. The fast motor launch carrying her thwarted boarding party held midway between their mothership and their intended target.

The French warship's dark blue Sea Lynx helicopter buzzed angrily overhead, accompanied in the sky by the flashing marker strobes of the small American Eagle Eye recon drone and the more massive CH-60 assault chopper carrying the Marine fast-rope team. Higher yet, a French Atlantique ANG patrol plane loitered, circling watchfully on its throttled-back turboprops.

The *Queen of the West* moved in on the tanker's starboard quarter, her tail ramp dropping as she launched her own boarders.

"*La Fleurette, La Fleurette,* this is Little Pig Leader. What is your situation?"

Glancing out of the windscreen, Amanda watched as the hovercraft's miniraider sheered away toward the tanker, its snarling outboard ripping a white foaming gash across the dark blue of the wavetops.

"Captain Garrett, this is Commander Trochard," the Corvette captain replied. "We have no change. We have hailed on all standard ship-to-ship radio bands for forty-five minutes. We also attempted contact via blinker and loud-hailer. We have received no reply or response of any nature. However, when we attempted to go alongside, they turned into us, trying to ram. At that point, I considered discretion the better part of valor and called for assistance."

"A wise call, Commander. It appears you've already dealt with all of the appropriate preliminaries. I propose we give him one more challenge and then we go for a forced three-point boarding. My helicopter team will go aboard at the bow and my boat team on the starboard side astern . Your people will hit port side astern. Do you concur?"

"I concur, Captain. We will go on your command. And of the warning?"

"I'll give him one last radio hail, and if we don't get an answer, I'd like for you to put a three-point-nine across his bow. If that doesn't work, I'll hit his bridge with some fifty-caliber. That should get his attention. When he heaves to, we position to cover our boarding parties and we send them in."

Behind her, Amanda was aware of Stone Quillain speaking into his own headset, already passing the word to the Marine boat and helicopter crews.

"Very good, Captain Garrett," the French officer's filtered voice came back. "We are standing by."

Amanda went off radio and back down to intercom. "Everybody get that?" she inquired.

"Aye, aye, ma'am," Steamer called back over his shoulder. "Where do you want me to keep her parked? Back here on his quarter?"

"For the moment. When he stops his engines, I want you to move us up to his midships line and hold us bow-on to him at about a hundred yards. I want to be able to put covering fire in for both the boat and helo teams."

"My boys are set," Quillain added grimly. Reaching overhead, he slid back the gun-ring hatch. Chief Tehoa's beloved twin-mount fifties belonged to him now.

"Very good, Stone. Danno, this is the cockpit."

"Fire control 'by. What can we do for you, ma'am?"

"Rig for heavy antiship. I want Hellfires on all the rails. If I pass the word, I want you to take apart this tub's bridge and deckhouse. If we're going to have trouble, that's where it's likely coming from. We're going to need precision and called shots. We've got an awful lot of gas and oil out there, and we don't want to make it mad at us."

"All you have to do is tell us which portholes you want 'em through, ma'am."

"Will do . . . and heat up the Harpoons as well. Just in case."

"Aye, aye."

Amanda ran down a fast mental checklist, seeking for any point she might have left uncovered. There didn't seem to be anything. And yet . . .

She shook her head, angry with herself for taking the counsel of her fears.

"All right, then, everyone," she said. "Here we go."

Her fingers played across the communications deck, calling up the international maritime guard frequency. "SS *Bajara,* SS *Bajara,* this is the United Nations African Interdiction Force. You are in violation of a U.N. exclusion zone. Stop your engines and prepare to be boarded. I say again, stop your engines and prepare to be boarded. This is your last warning. If you do not heave to immediately, we will open fire. I repeat, if you do not heave to immediately, we will open fire."

Her decks still eerily empty, the tanker continued on its drive for the African coast.

"That's it. She's had her chance. *La Fleurette,* this is Little Pig Lead. Put one across her bow."

A moment later, the forward gun turret of the corvette spat out a single round. The flat *crack . . . wham* of the cannon shot and shell detonation sounded over the moan of the *Queen*'s turbines and a geyser of white spray jetted out of the sea just off the bow of the Algerian tanker.

"No reaction so far," Christine Rendino reported over the link from the drone control center. "Wait a minute. . . . We're getting men on the decks. . . . We got a lot of uniformed men on the decks! They look like Union soldiers. . . . *I'm seeing missile launchers! We got launchers setting up all over the place! Get those boats and helos out of there! That thing's a Q ship!*"

Amanda's finger smashed down on her own transmitter key. *"Boarding craft sheer off! Helicopters! Evade! Evade! Evade!"*

The French Sea Lynx and the U.S. Blackhawk flared out like a pair of startled quail. Turning steeply, they dove for the wavetops, accelerating away from the threat. The *Queen*'s miniraider came hard about as well, almost capsizing as a wave broadsided it. Shaking off its burden of white water and foam, it clawed away from the Algerian vessel, opening the range.

A gout of orange flame pulsed at the tanker's rail and a shell exploded in the wake of the fleeing boat. At her stern, the green and white banner of the Algerian flag dropped away, replaced by the blue and white of the West African Union.

"Queen of the West and *La Fleurette,"* Amanda yelled into the command mike. "Target the tanker! Guns free! Engage! Engage! En—"

"No!" Christine Rendino's urgent cry overrode the order. *"Hold your fire! There are kids on that ship!"*

"Check fire! Check fire! Check fire! Damn it, Chris! What are you talking about?"

"Check your screens," Christine said despairingly. "They've got kids crawling all over that ship. They're using children as human shields."

Hastily Amanda accessed the Mast Mounted Sighting System and focused on the tanker's decks. Acquiring one of the weapons crews now on station along the tanker's rail, she zoomed the camera in.

There were three actual combatants present, the gunner of the antitank team, kneeling and shouldering a Carl-Gustav recoilless rifle, and his two assistants, standing ready to feed reloads into the weapon. Flanking the Union soldiers, however, were a half-dozen small, gaunt and raggedly clad figures. Boys, none of whom could have been more than twelve years old. Lined up at the rail, they stared uncomprehendingly into the camera lens.

"The goddamn cowards," Quillain growled. "The goddamn, shit-eating, sheep-fucking cowards. They're holding babies in front of them."

Amanda spoke carefully into her lip mike. "Chris, how many fire teams are you seeing?"

"Six AT teams on the main deck and a couple of Blowpipe antiair launchers on the bridge wings. All of them with human shields. I think they've got some more kids on the bridge itself."

"Acknowledged." She lifted her finger off the radio button. "Stone," she asked quietly. "Assessment, please. Is there any way we can get past those launcher crews and get aboard that ship without firing on it?"

The Marine shook his head. "No. No way in hell. Without covering fire, they'd cut us to pieces."

Amanda nodded and called up Fire Control. "Danno. This is Captain Garrett. Think about this one carefully. Could you take out that tanker's rudder with a Hellfire shot?"

The reply was a long time in coming back. "She's heavily laden, ma'am. Her rudder post is right down there on the water. I can't get a line of fire on it. I could try to put one into her steering engine room, but they got a bunch of kids standing on the fantail right above it. If I got a little high—"

"Okay, Danno. I understand. Stand easy."

Christine's filtered voice came back on the command circuit. "Little Pig Lead, this is Floater," she said almost apologetically. "I know you guys have enough trouble out there as is, but I have a situational change at Port Monrovia."

"Go, Chris. What's happening?"

"An army convoy has just arrived at the Port Monrovia tank farm, a refugee convoy. The soldiers are herding a couple of hundred people into the petroleum-storage area. Families, men, women, and children. It looks like they intend to hold them there for a while."

"Understood."

Amanda signed off, striving to hold back the wave of sickness welling up within her. Belewa in his pragmatism had used the rebellious portions of his population as a weapon of aggression. Why not also as a weapon of defense?

There was another burst of flame from the tanker's deck, and another AT shell gouged a chunk off the *Queen*'s nose. This time the shot was being fired across Amanda's bow, warning her off. The next one would be aimed to kill.

"Captain," Steamer called back uncertainly. "What do you want us to do, ma'am?"

"Disengage, Commander. Disengage."

It was easier after saying it for that first time. Straightening at her console, she issued the string of bitter commands. "Little Pig Lead to all elements. Disengage and fall back. Recover the boat parties. Fast-rope team, return to Floater 1 and stand down. *La Fleurette*, be advised we're letting him go. Fall back and shadow at long range. I say again, we're letting him go."

Beyond the rote acknowledgments to the commands, no one spoke in the cockpit or over the radio link. There was nothing to say. Steamer brought the hovercraft around, turning away from the tanker and steering for a rendezvous with the miniraider.

Amanda rose from behind the navigator's station. "Stand down from General Quarters. If anything new develops, I'll be in the wardroom."

"Aye, aye, ma'am."

Stone Quillain waited until Amanda had descended into the main hull before driving his fist into the bulkhead, the impact of his released rage making the cockpit frames shudder.

Down in the deserted mess space, Amanda set out to prepare herself one perfect cup of tea. By focusing totally on each minor action of heating the water and getting out the creamer, sugar, and tea bag, she kept at bay the torrent of despair, frustration and anger racing through her mind. She steeped the bag for the proper count of seconds in the water, added the exact spoonfuls of creamer and sugar, and settled herself behind the table. Only then, with the steaming cup in front of her and the first edge of her emotions dulled, did she allow herself to think.

Mobile Offshore Base, Floater 1   **0818 Hours, Zone Time; September 7, 2007**

"Get on the horn to both Conakry and Abidjan. Tell them I want every Predator we've got a control channel for in the air. Now! The same for the Eagle Eyes here on the platform. Get some more systems operators in here. Double up on all workstations. We're watch on watch until further notice! Asses and elbows, people! Asses and elbows! Move!"

Christine Rendino found herself sounding a little like Amanda Garrett, and the thought pleased her somewhat. Pacing in the cramped monitor-lit confines of the TACNET trailer, she orchestrated chaos.

"Donovan, we're going to need more working room. Take half a dozen laptops over to the briefing trailer and get them networked with us. Configure half of them for analysis section, the other half for tactical and mission planning. We're going to be crunching a lot of data over the next few hours. I want a drone remote and a communications terminal, too."

"You got it, Commander." The named subordinate sidled hastily down the row of workstations toward the door.

"Vleymann. Get on the Lloyd's database again. I want a download of everything ever recorded about the tanker *Bajara*. Who owns her? Who built her? How large a crew does she carry? I want detail! Engine-room specifications, deck plans, photographs, the works. Right down to what grade of steel they used in her and how many coats of paint are on the bulkheads. Pull everything on public file, then start hacking."

"Yes, ma'am." The young woman's fingers danced across her keyboard as she launched herself into the global infonets.

Turning to the watch operations coordinator, Christine leaned in over his shoulder. "Okay, Jerry, here's the new game plan. I want saturation coverage of everything around Monrovia out to a range of . . . oh, call it a hundred and twenty miles. Concentrate your assets and screw the rest of the theater for the time being. Primary focus will be on the Union security forces: Army, Navy, militia, police. If the Liberian Boy Scouts so much as have a cookout, I want to know what kind of wieners they're roasting."

"You got it, Commander," the senior S.O. replied. "I can give you one thing right now. Ground Scan radar has acquired four major truck convoys moving within that zone of interest. All of them started to roll within the last half hour, and all of them inbound toward Monrovia."

Christine frowned and looked up at the ground scan display on the bulkhead. "Let me guess. The points of origin were all major Union supply depots."

"You got it. And we're kicking up a lot of smaller one-, two-, and three-vehicle packages moving on the road net as well. All headed for Port Monrovia."

"I'm not at all surprised," Christine replied. "Probably every vehicle in the Union that can carry an oil drum is on the move. Belewa'll disperse that fuel as fast as he can get it off the ship. By this time day after tomorrow, it'll be scattered out to a couple of hundred little backcountry POL dumps. We'll never be able to get at it then. The Union will be good to go for another six months."

"Hell!" the S.O. shook his head in resignation. "What are we going to do, ma'am?"

"I don't know, Chief." A quirky smile came to the intel's face. "But we're going to do something about it. I'm not sure just what yet, but you can bet we are going to do something."

Abruptly, the overhead loudspeaker clicked and Amanda Garrett's voice issued forth, her words very controlled, cool, and intent. "This is Little Pig Lead to TACNET. Chris, this is Amanda. I need the answers to some questions, and I need them fast. We've got a job we need to take care of here."

"Yes!" Christine lifted a fist into the air and pumped it downward to her chest. "And we're off!"

Houston, Texas   1622 Hours, Zone Time; September 7, 2007

Frank Cochran yawned mightily at his desk and leaned back, wondering what to do with the last half hour of his workday. Not that he was finished with this Christless Spratly Island Project by any means. However, his brain had shut down on him prematurely; the schematics on his desktop screen were fuzzing into meaninglessness.

Double-saving the program on his computer, the lanky Texas-born petroleum engineer switched over to his Internet server to check his e-mail. If there wasn't anything that required his immediate attention there, maybe he'd call up Trophy Bass VI on his game file and go after that ten-pound lunker in Lake Pontchartrain again.

There wasn't anything of import in the mail file, and Cochran was about to yield to the temptations of cyberfishing when an IM notice flashed up in the corner of his screen.

MR. FRANK COCHRAN:
WOULD YOU PLEASE ACCESS THIS LINK IMMEDIATELY?
THIS IS A MATTER OF UTMOST IMPORTANCE.

A lengthy and underlined net address followed that Cochran didn't recognize. He suspected it was either an invitation to a porn site or an assault by one of the new cyberevangelists. Either way, he didn't have anything better to do at the moment. The oilman pointed and clicked.

The check light on the fastcam atop his monitor blinked on as the vision-phone circuits activated. His systems tower purred and a hiss of static issued from the computer's speakers. A test pattern flickered across his screen for a moment and Cochran suddenly found himself looking into the sober and attractive face of an auburn-haired and hazel-eyed woman. Clad in a well-worn khaki uniform, she sat outlined against what looked like the interior of some kind of aircraft cockpit.

Something was also vaguely familiar about the woman's face. Bemused, Cochran glanced over at the CD slots of his system, wondering if he might have accidentally accessed one of his more virulent computer role-playing games. Then the woman on the screen spoke and erased that possibility.

"Good afternoon. Are you Mr. Frank Cochran, the head of systems engineering for North Star Petroleum?"

"Uh, well, yes, I am," Cochran replied, intrigued. "And may I ask who you are?"

"My name is Amanda Garrett, Captain Amanda Garrett of the United States Navy. I'm speaking to you from the cockpit of the patrol gunboat USS *Queen of the West,* currently operating off the West African coast. I hope you'll excuse this rather unconventional method of contact, Mr. Cochran, but a critical situation has developed here and we urgently require your assistance."

This was no canned cyberadventure, much as it sounded like one. And this was no elaborate practical joke, either. He recognized that name and that face now. After the blowup in China last year, they'd both been in the newspapers and on the networks often enough.

Lord! This was just too insane!

"Uh, well, of course, Captain Garrett," he fumbled in reply. "However I can help. But what can I do for the Navy?"

"You are a highly respected petroleum systems engineer, Mr. Cochran. Your specialty, as we understand it, is refinery and pipeline safety systems. We urgently need the answers to some questions within your field of expertise, and we need them immediately."

Cochran nodded. "All right. What's the problem?"

"I'm going to show a series of aerial recon images of the oil-transfer facility at Port Monrovia in the West African Union. Specifically, I'm going to show you the loading dock, the tank farm, and the pipeline linking them. We need to know if that pipleline can be cut with an explosive charge without triggering a fire or a sympathetic detonation within the tank farm. Also, where would the safest place to make such a cut be?"

Cochran frowned. "Is the line carrying a load currently?"

"Not yet."

"Let's see your pictures."

As the image files transferred, Cochran split-screened his system and started calling up some of his work files. *Let's see, Shell did a lot of work down in that corner of the world. What did their standard systems package look like?*

It took him roughly five minutes to reach his conclusions.

"Captain Garrett, it shouldn't be that much of a problem. You've got sets of check and spill valves at both ends of that line that should catch any tube flash. I'd say you could blow a cut with a reasonable safety margin."

"Where would the best place be to blow the line?"

"Here." Cochran indicated a point on the screen image with his mouse. "Anywhere between the pier and this valve cluster at the center point of the pipeline. If they aren't actively transferring fuel, they should have the manuals here closed as well. That should give you a degree of extra protection against a flash toward the tank farm."

"Understood." The reconnaissance photos blinked out and Amanda Garrett's image refilled the monitor screen. "Now, a final question. How long would it take to repair a pipeline cut like that?"

"That would depend on a number of things. How big a charge was used to blow the cut. How available the repair materials are and how good the repair crew is. For our people, I'd say eight to twelve hours. For a good Third World outfit, I'd say sixteen to twenty-four."

"All right." The Garrett woman gave a thoughtful nod of her head, obviously moving on in her considerations. "That's what we needed. Thank you, Mr. Cochran. You've been of great service to us, sir. I'm not sure what remuneration we can give you beyond a letter of commendation and my personal thanks, but I can promise you that the matter will be looked into."

"Don't mention it. . . . Look, Captain . . . this is for real, isn't it? I mean, this isn't some kind of exercise or something, is it?"

She smiled back rather grimly. "It's all too real, Mr. Cochran. We're trying to end a war out here. God willing, you may have just helped us to do so."

Damn, but wasn't this going to be something to talk about over the dinner table with Amy and the kids! And then another thought occurred to him. "I suppose this is all top secret and hush hush, huh? I mean, I can't tell anyone about this, right?"

"I don't see why not, Mr. Cochran. By the time you could tell anyone about it, this part of the show is going to be over."

Port Monrovia   **0941 Hours, Zone Time; September 7, 2007**

The Ministry of Public Morale had orchestrated a greeting celebration at the oiling pier: a crowd of dignitaries and senior government staff, a local pop band to provide music, and a busload of brightly clad girl dancers from some of the city's youth groups. An Army honor guard stood at parade rest along the pierside, flower-bearing children interspersed between each soldier.

Obe Belewa knew that the concentration of the Union's young people at the oil pier wasn't for the gaiety of it alone. Using his nation's children as living shields against the U.N. put an ache and a sickness in his gut that was going to last him for a long time. Yet, as the old European saying went, "beggars can't be choosers."

"We've gotten it through," he murmured. "That's what matters."

Ambassador Umamgi thought the comment addressed to him. "We have won, General." He smiled humorlessly. "A great victory over the Western colonialists!"

As senior Algerian representative in-country and as the instigator of the plan, it was only right that he be present at the arrival as well. Yet his lurking presence grated on Belewa's nerves even more than usual. He served as another reminder of Belewa's own compromised ethics.

Belewa shook his head. "No, Ambassador. We haven't won. Not yet. But at least now we can carry on the fight for a time longer."

"Come, Obe," Sako Atiba interjected. "Let's at least celebrate today's victory for today." Standing between the soldier and the diplomat, the Chief of Staff wore a more honest grin of triumph. He had shared in this scheme of Umamgi's, and he did not seem too unduly concerned about the loss of honor involved.

Belewa grunted an acknowledgment.

Out at the mouth of the harbor, the *Bajara* edged slowly in through the entry channel. The port tug carefully shepherded her on her way and the three heavy gunboats of the Monrovia squadron trailed in her wake, ready for any last-minute intervention by the UNAFIN forces.

Port Monrovia was a man-made harbor. Two huge artificial breakwaters extended a mile and a quarter out to sea, their ends converging at the entry channel to form a triangle of protected water against the African coast. Army security patrols ranged the length of both breakwaters and a Panhard armored car sat at the end of the service road that ran the length of each causeway, its 90mm cannon aimed to seaward. Additional precautionary presences.

Hopefully, Belewa thought, such precautions were unnecessary. Perhaps he had at last beaten the Leopard. If so, it was not in the way he would have preferred. If there had been any honor in this last confrontation, it belonged to her. And yet she had backed down. And this late in the game he could not refuse any victory, no matter how it was won.

But was there, in fact, a victory to celebrate yet? Narrowing his eyes against the sun, Belewa looked skyward and caught the flash of slender white wings high in the azure zenith. An American Predator spy drone, circling like a hungry eagle.

The Leopard's gaze was still fixed upon him. What was she thinking?

Sako slapped him lightly on the shoulder. "Come, General, let's go out on the pier. You should be the first man up the gangway when the ship docks."

"Only to thank her crew and our warriors, Brigadier. Men and boys alike."

The oil-handling pier extended into the harbor from the southern breakwater, roughly seven hundred yards from the breakwater's shoreward root. Leaving the cluster of staff and command cars at the base of the pier, the Premier General and his chief of staff strode out along it, Umamgi hastening to stay close enough to share in the approbation.

The troopers of the bodyguard force moved watchfully with Belewa's party, not that the General felt much at risk this day. It had been a long time since Belewa had been able to give his people good news. They were hungry for it, and they cheered him as he passed through the waiting crowd, the deprivations and uncertainties of the past few months forgotten for the moment. Belewa waved and shook hands and found himself smiling.

Turning out of the central channel, the tanker stood in toward the oiling pier, its attendant tug nuzzling it slowly closer. A few minutes more and it would be within casting range of the mooring lines. The mixed Union and Algerian crew manning the rails joined in the cheering.

And then over the raised voices and blaring jincajou music, Belewa heard another sound, a hard-edged nasal whine growing rapidly in volume. He looked up just in time to see a winged and finned cigar shape flash a few hundred feet overhead, angling inland. A corner of Belewa's warrior's mind reacted analytically.

American SeaSLAM missile. Extended Response variant. Sea and air launched. Precision guidance. Land attack . . .

Then the missile was past and the shock wave of a powerful explosion slapped across the crowd, turning cheers to screams. A quarter of a mile away, a mushroom of smoke rose above the harbor breakwater. Belatedly, air raid sirens began to scream.

"Down!" Belewa bellowed. "Everyone get down and stay down! Brigadier Atiba! With me!" With his chief of staff and security trailing behind, Belewa ran for his staff car, sidestepping Ambassador Umamgi, who lay cowered on the pier decking.

⚔◆

The only casualties were a couple of lightly wounded members of an army security patrol, and overtly, the damage appeared minor. A shallow crater blasted in the heavy stone of the causeway, lightly damaging the access road that ran atop it. However, it was obvious that the impact point had carefully been centered on the petroleum-transfer pipelines that paralleled the access road. A twenty-foot gap had been torn out of the system, and other pipe sections above and below the target had been shrapnel riddled and wrenched out of alignment.

By the time Belewa and his entourage arrived at the scene, the port's fire brigade had extinguished the few smoldering pools of spilled residual oil. There had been only one missile launched, and only this one target struck.

"Brigadier Atiba, get the harbor fully secured," Belewa snapped as he dismounted from the Land Rover. "Get all undesignated civilians out of the area. And get the manager of the port oil facilities out here immediately!"

"He's on his way now, General," the Chief of Staff replied, pointing to a battered jeep tearing up the causeway from the tank farm.

Standing beside the staff car, Belewa gave the tank farm manager and his chief engineer an impatient five minutes to assess the damage before summoning them over. "How bad?" he demanded.

The director could only shake his head. "What is there to say, General? Both the eight-inch and the twelve-inch transfer lines are cut. We can't unload until they are repaired."

"Could we unload the fuel from the tanker directly into the disbursement convoys?"

The director considered for a moment before shaking his head again. "Something could be rigged, I suppose, but it would be like draining a lake through a straw. It would take weeks to off-load that tanker using portable pumps. It will be easier and faster to repair the transfer lines."

"How long?"

"It doesn't look too bad, General. A day. Two at the most."

"Twenty-four hours from now, those pipelines will be repaired and that tanker will be unloading. Is that understood? *Twenty-four hours!*"

The chill in Belewa's voice rendered any answer except "Yes, sir" extremely unwise.

Belewa allowed the suddenly sweating tank farm director to proceed with his urgent task. As Belewa turned away, he noted a piece of crumpled aluminum lying at his feet. Picking it up, he brushed the dust from its scorched, gray-painted surface and read the dark blue stenciling upon it: U.S. NAV.

He had been a fool to even dream of a victory. Not while the Leopard lived. He had thrown her off for a moment, yet she was already springing back upon him, her fangs still reaching for his throat.

"Brigadier Atiba! I want every man and every gun we've got available pulled back into the Monrovia defenses! Everything! Now!"

Mobile Offshore Base, Floater 1   1002 Hours, Zone Time; September 7, 2007

With her upperworks blackened by booster exhaust, the *Queen of the West* surged up Floater 1's docking ramp. Her squadron sisters, *Carondelet* and *Manassas,* were already in their hangar slots, their service crews swarming around them.

"Swarming" was an apt collective description of the entire platform. "All hands on deck" had been called, and the base complement was hard at work dealing with the intensifying barrage of orders that had been flowing in from the task force flag craft.

Amanda found the briefing trailer crowded upon her entry. As per her command, all senior officers and NCOs of the seafighter squadron, Fox company, and the platform service force were present. Videoconferencing links had also been established with the U.S. command cadre at Conakry Base. Also linked in were the captains of both the *Santana* and *Sirocco,* the two Patrol Craft already having been ordered to leave their stations and close with Floater 1 at their best possible speed.

Amanda worked her way forward to the head of the briefing table. "Good morning, ladies and gentlemen," she began quietly, turning to face her silent and intent audience. "The one thing we have the least of at this moment is time, so we'll get right to it. I know you all have been advised on the current situation. The West African Union has broken the blockade. They've gotten an oil tanker through.

"If they succeed in unloading and dispersing this tanker's cargo, we're right back to where we were six months ago. All of our efforts, all of our sacrifices, all of the blood spilled during this operation will have been for nothing. I do not intend to see this happen."

She scanned the faces of her officers, looking for any sign of a broken will or any hint of lingering distrust in her. Either could be disastrous during the next twenty-four hours. The structure she had tried to build here off the Gold Coast was about to face its ultimate test.

"On my own authority and personal responsibility, I have taken action to prevent the unloading of the tanker . . . for perhaps a day. Within that time frame, we have to develop, organize, and launch an operation to prevent the West African Union from acquiring these new oil reserves. We are not going to be able to wait around for outside help to arrive. We will have to go with the resources we have available to us right now. We will also have to launch this operation into the face of a fully alerted and mobilized enemy. You may rest assured that the Union will be waiting for us with everything they've got."

She scanned the room once more. She heard only the purr of the air conditioner and the creak of a chair. After a moment, Stone Quillain broke the silence.

"What's the game plan, Skipper?"

"The human shields deployed aboard the tanker and around the tank farm preclude a direct hard-kill attack with standoff weapons. In fact, the presence of those hostages nullifies most of the technological edge we have over the Union. Accordingly, we're going to try something old—in fact, a military evolution that, to the best of my knowledge, has not been attempted since the American Civil War."

Amanda sank into the chair at the head of the briefing table, crossing her arms on the tabletop. "How many of you have ever heard of a cutting-out expedition?"

UNAFIN Operations Area   **September 7, 2007**

Improvise, jury-rig, make it up as you go along . . .

"A ton of soap flakes?" The stores CPO looked up from his desk, flabbergasted.

"That's right," his division officer replied. "They want a ton of soap flakes or powdered soap or whatever we can find along that line out on the platform immediately."

"A ton, sir?"

"Don't ask me why, Simpson. I don't know. Just pallet up what we have in the head and galley stocks. Then send a truck into Conakry to see what we can dig up there. Oh, and keep a lookout for stereo equipment while you're about it, and no, I don't know what they want that for either."

⟡

Compromise, negotiate, prevaricate . . .

⟡

The French Corvette captain frowned from the videophone screen. "Captain Garrett, I am as displeased about these events as you are. Yet I cannot take an active role in any such action without the authorization. Maintaining a blockade is one thing. A direct involvement in a, as you say, 'shooting war' is another. I wager my superiors and my government will require a degree of consideration before making any such plunge."

"I understand your position, Commander Trochard," Amanda replied. "And yet you must also understand the time factor that we are confronted with. While your government considers the issue, our window of opportunity will close."

The French officer shook his head. "I am sorry, but we are not like you Americans. For all of our much-vaunted French *élan,* we simply do not have this kind of cowboy blood in us."

Amanda sighed. In battle, one used whatever weapons were available in the arsenal. She allowed her expression and her voice to soften. "Jacques, please, we need your help with this thing. . . . I need your help."

Trochard fought his own battle for a moment, then sighed his own sigh and smiled. "A thought does occur to me, Amanda. While we cannot stretch my operational mandate into a direct involvement in this matter, perhaps we could at least appear to be involved. . . . "

⟡

. . . Plot, plan, and prepare . . .

⟡

"Okay, Lieutenant." Sergeant Tallman passed the youthful lieutenant a stuffed manila envelope. "Here's all the dope you'll need. Mission parameters, maps, tide table, beach composition and gradients, Union force deployments in that sector and what we have on their patrol intervals. The Skipper needs your completed plan of operations by no later than 1600 hours. You and your men need to be ready to move by 1800."

"Got it, Sarge." Smiling ironically, the platoon leader accepted the envelope. "Damn. Eight months out of ROTC and I'm already planning my first invasion. It ain't a fuckin' job . . ."

". . . it's a fuckin' adventure," the Top wryly joined in, finishing the chorus.

⊗◆

. . . Adapt, alter, and expedite . . .

⊗◆

"Bloody hell, sir!" the crew chief exclaimed, aghast, studying the hand-sketched diagrams. "We're an ASW unit. We're just not supposed to be doing this kind of thing!"

Squadron leader Evan Dane only grinned and patted the aircrewman on the shoulder. "Well, then, young-sailor-me-lad, let's just say that we're going after the 1st African Royal Submarine Regiment and leave it at that."

⊗◆

. . . Analyze, assess, collect . . .

⊗◆

"*Guten Tag, Herr Zimmer.* Thank you for sparing us this time. It is greatly appreciated. We understand that in 2003, your firm reconditioned and sold an eighty-four-foot diesel harbor tug to the government of the West African Union. If possible, could we get some technical specifications on that vessel? Rated horsepower, power-plant manuals, wheelhouse and engine-room schematics, that sort of thing."

⊗◆

. . . Evaluate . . . consider . . . project . . .

⊗◆

"Just asking, boss ma'am, but have you thought about the possible environmental fallout of this little tea party we're throwing? We're on the verge of deliberately invoking our own little *Exxon Valdez* on the African Gold Coast here."

SEA FIGHTER **317**

"Not quite, Chris. That tanker is loaded with light petroleum distillates, diesel and gasoline, and not heavy crude oil. They should evaporate and disperse fairly rapidly in this hot a climate. Besides, if our friends the Marines work it right, there shouldn't be all that much left to worry about."

◇◆

. . . Designate, assign, and trust in the abilities of subordinates . . .

◇◆

"Okay, Corporal. Tankers take a hell of a lot of killing. What have you got?"

"Right over here, Cap'n." The demolitions man cracked his gum and led Stone Quillain over to the selection of munitions spread out on a patch of tarpaulin-covered deck. They included an innocuous-looking camouflaged shoulder bag, a thick and ominous gray metal disk roughly the size of a hub-cap, and a couple of quart-sized gray metal canisters each with the safety lever and pull ring of a grenade fuse screwed into its top.

"We've got kind of a package here, sir, put together with a standard Mark 138 forty-pound satchel charge, a limpet mine, and a couple of Mark 34 white phosphorus grenades."

Quillain nodded. "How'll she work?"

The demo man knelt down beside the tarp and began indicating components. "Y' see, we clip the Willie Pete grenades to the satchel charge and then rig the charge on top of one of the tanker's cargo cells. Then we link the limpet mine's detonator to the satchel charge with a long-length petroleum-proof det cord."

"With you so far, son."

"We drop the mine into the cargo cell through an inspection hatch. The mine sinks to the bottom of the tank. That sets up what you call your chain of events. When the satchel charge detonates, it'll do a whole bunch of stuff at once. It'll tear open the top of the cargo cell, set off the two white phosphorus grenades, and fire the det cord. The det cord then flashes down to the bottom of the tank and to the limpet mine, which it detonates a split second later. This not only blows a hole in the bottom of the ship, but it should sort of sneeze the contents of the cargo cell up and out of the hole in the top, where it will then have congress with all that burning white phosphorus that's lying around.

"We've got the goods for about half a dozen of these rigs and we'll target the cells loaded with gasoline and Avgas. We'll double-fuse everything with M700 and time for a five-minute delay."

The demo man popped his gum again. "Piece of cake."

"Lord A'mighty. Did our demo people at Little Creek have anything to say about this setup?"

"Yes, sir. They suggest we stand way back and take photographs."

. . . Work fast, faster, watch the clock, if you can't do all, do what you can. Night draws nigh.

Conakry Base, Guinea   1922 Hours, Zone Time; September 7, 2007

Unseen, a night rain had started to fall outside of the headquarters building. Vavra Bey could smell the mildewing wetness of it seeping in through the wall of sandbags beyond the empty window frame. She and the others of the U.N. diplomatic mission to Guinea had been pulled back inside the U.N. base compound for the duration of this latest crisis, both for personal security and to be closer to the developing situation.

Not that there appeared to be all that much that she could do.

The U.N. envoy removed her glasses and lightly rubbed her throbbing temples, wishing for a moment that she could be a grandmother again. Be damned with diplomacy and with the futility of trying to solve the problems of a world that didn't want them solved. Her joints ached in the humidity, and all she wanted for that moment was the warm, sun-baked dryness of her garden at home and the sound of her grandchildren at play.

A knock came at the door of the tiny office she had been allotted and it half opened, her aide looking around it. "Madam Envoy. Admiral MacIntyre has arrived."

"Very well, Lars. Show him in, please."

Bey slipped her glasses on once more. Thinking of her grandchildren had been a good thing. It reminded her of why she had become who she was.

It was a different Elliot MacIntyre than she had met that day at the U.N. Instead of the crisp blue uniform, the Admiral now wore a rain-dotted Nomex flight suit. His gray-streaked hair was matted from hours under a crash helmet, and a haze of beard darkened his angular chin.

"I apologize for my appearance, Madam Envoy," he said, accepting the chair across the desk from her. "I've been doing some traveling today."

"So I understand. Appearance is a matter of little consequence at the moment, Admiral," she replied. "Surely, though, you haven't come all the way from the United States?"

"Not quite. I was attending a conference on Adriatic security affairs at

NATO Southern Command headquarters in Naples when I received word of the blockade being broken. I, ah, 'borrowed' an Air Force F-22 and a pilot from Sigonella and hauled down here as fast as I could. I've made it a personal policy as commander in chief, NAVSPECFORCE, to be present if possible whenever any of my people might be seeing action."

"Ah." Bey nodded and interlaced her fingers. "That brings us to the current state of affairs."

"It does, Madam Envoy, and at this time I would like to state for the record that I stand behind and agree with the decision made by Captain Amanda Garrett this morning concerning the *Bajara*. Given the circumstances, she had no option except to refuse engagement and allow the tanker through the blockade. Humanitarian considerations gave her no choice."

"I agree, Admiral, and that shall be noted for the record as well. We could not place those children in the line of fire.

"I must say," she continued more slowly, "that I'm surprised that they were there in the first place. Belewa didn't strike me as that kind of man. . . . Well, desperation knows no bounds. The question before us now, Admiral, is what can we do about this, if anything?"

"Madam Envoy, if we permit General Belewa to off-load that tanker's cargo, everything UNAFIN has accomplished here on the Gold Coast will be erased. The crisis will be protracted. The strain on the Guinean government will be redoubled, and the West African Union's plans for territorial conquest will go back on track. We cannot allow this to stand."

"I agree," she replied. "However, diplomatically, I fear our options are nonexistent. What of the military ones?"

"The simple and direct option, that of blowing that tanker out of the water where it sits, has been blocked by the presence of the human shields aboard her. So has any bombardment of the oil-storage facility at Port Monrovia. It's been turned into a prison compound with several hundred of the Union's political dissidents being held there. Belewa has checked any direct attack against him."

"Leaving what, Admiral?"

MacIntyre took a deliberate breath before continuing. "Leaving a rather . . . audacious plan proposed by Captain Garrett. We don't blow the oil up, we steal it. Tanker and all."

"Steal it? I don't understand, Admiral." Confident as she was with the English language, Vavra Bey was certain she must have missed the true meaning of MacIntyre's words.

"Captain Garrett is proposing what in naval parlance is called a 'cutting-out' expedition. A small-boat assault to capture an enemy vessel in a hostile harbor."

Bey's eyebrows lifted. "I've never heard of such a thing."

MacIntyre gave a slight grimace. "It was once a fairly common naval evolution. At least back in Napoleonic times. Captain Garrett is proposing a modernized, uprated version of it. An escalating series of diversionary actions will draw Union attention and resources away from the Port Monrovia area while a stealthy penetration of Port facilities takes place. A Marine boarding team will go aboard the *Bajara,* eliminate the guards on board, and remove the human shields and the Algerian crew to a point of safety. Following that, the ship will be moved away from the pier and into the central channel of the port. There it will be set on fire and scuttled, destroying its cargo and blocking the port entrance.

"We kill two birds with one stone," MacIntyre finished. "Not only do we take out this oil shipment, but we make sure the Union can never try this stunt again, or least not until the hulk of that tanker is salvaged and moved out of the way."

Bey considered MacIntyre's words for a few long moments. "Something suggests to me," she said finally, "that this operation is much more complicated than your description would indicate."

The Admiral nodded. "That's a sound assumption, Madam Envoy. In fact, I'd be thinking twice about this plan myself if I didn't know the person who has developed it. She has a proven track record of accomplishing the extremely difficult, if not the impossible. That's why I brought her out here in the first place."

"So I recall." Bey half-smiled reminiscently. "I remember speaking to you about her in New York what seems to be a very long time ago. You expressed a great deal of confidence in her at that time as well."

"She's done everything we've asked her to do, ma'am. Now she's asking permission to finish the job. If you want my opinion, I say we should give her the chance."

"And what does your government say, Admiral?"

"I've spoken to our secretary of state and he's spoken with our president. The United States is willing to commit its forces within the confines of a U.N. action. I've also been in communication with my opposite numbers within both the United Kingdom and French UNAFIN contingents, and they have received similar authorizations from within their respective chains of command. We are good to go when we get word from you, Madam Envoy."

"Indeed." Again Vavra Bey lifted a hand to her temple to counter the ravages of her headache. She had not counted on having to deal with this aspect of statesmanship. In her younger and more idealistic days she had dreamed of prying warring armies apart, not in ordering them into battle. "When is it your intention to launch this operation?"

"Madam Envoy," MacIntyre replied grimly. "I need to take the go order with me when I leave this room. We must launch tonight."

Bey looked up sharply. "That's impossible. This kind of conflict escalation must be taken before the Security Council for a vote."

"We already have the Security Council's resolution to embargo all oil shipments to the West African Union," MacIntyre insisted. "What we're proposing is no more than an extension of that policy."

Bey shook her head. "Admiral, we have already stretched the envelope of that resolution to its limits. To date, the Security Council has turned a blind eye to our actions. However an open assault upon the territory of the West African Union goes far beyond any mandate UNAFIN has been issued. We are answerable to the world community here. Procedure and the rule of law must be followed."

"And how long will that take, Madam Envoy? How long?"

"I can be in communication with the Security Council tonight. I will propose this matter be brought to an immediate debate and vote. I can promise you an answer within . . . forty-eight hours."

MacIntyre shook his head decisively. "No good, Madam Envoy. This operation must be launched within the next two hours or it doesn't get launched at all. By 'stretching the envelope,' as you phrased it, Captain Garrett has delayed the unloading of that tanker by one night. That's all. Two days from now, Belewa's oil will have been off-loaded and dispersed out to his backcountry depots.

"I'm not saying that Belewa will win because of it, but I'm guaranteeing that the war in Guinea is going to stretch on for at least another half a year. In that interim, a hell of a lot of people are going to die, both on the battlefield and in those refugee camps."

MacIntyre held up his hand, thumb and forefinger separated by half an inch. "We are this close to seeing the UNAFIN operation become another international bad joke. For the sake of everything we've done here and for the sake of effective U.N. intervention in the crises that may follow, I don't want to see that happen."

"Neither do I, Admiral! But I have not the authority to unilaterally order this action!" Bey found herself holding her hands out to MacIntyre. "Every word you say is true. But I have no options here. By the sacred name of God, give me one that I can work with!"

MacIntyre looked down at the desktop for a moment, then back up into

Bey's eyes. An ironic yet sympathetic smile touched his face. "Madam Envoy, I fully understand your feelings just now. I was in this same position myself not too long ago, and it was Amanda Garrett who put me there too. All I might suggest to you now is a UNODIR."

"I do not know that word, Admiral," Bey replied, puzzled.

MacIntyre gave a grim smile. "It's not a word actually, Madam Envoy. It's one of those acronyms that we're so fond of in the United States military. It's the first-letter contraction of the phrase 'unless otherwise directed.' We use it in situations where we know we have a job that needs to be done immediately, but where we are also hopelessly hobbled by a wad of red tape.

"You draw up a nice neat operational plan and head it UNODIR. Then you kick it on upstairs to your lords and masters . . . after your operation has been launched and is beyond recall."

"Ah." Vavra Bey let the sound of understanding draw out. "And then, Admiral?"

"And then, if all goes well, your lords and masters smile approval upon you for your initiative."

"And if things do not go well?"

"We have another phrase to cover that eventuality, Madam Envoy. We call it 'falling on your sword.'"

Bey chuckled. "That is one I have heard before. To speak with utter frankness, I find myself wishing you had dispatched one of those UNODIR missives to me. Judging outcomes is always so much simpler than predicting them."

"Replying with utter frankness, Captain Garrett and I considered doing just that. However, neither the Captain nor I put much stock in military dictatorship. As officers of the United States Armed Forces, we must be answerable to a civilian authority. We may stretch that limit now and again, but there comes a point we simply can't go beyond. This must be a decision made by a designated U.N. official. Madam Envoy, we await your orders."

We await your orders. By all that was holy, she was a diplomat! Diplomats weren't supposed to give orders. Diplomats were supposed to negotiate and bargain and then step back at the appropriate moment to allow the presidents, kings, and premiers to make the blood decisions. Dear Allah, how had this come to pass?

She turned her chair so that she could look out the office's window, albeit all there was to be seen was that wall of sodden sandbags. It would be most easy to say no, and she would be right to do so. She and her career would be safe, and the war on the Gold Coast would drag on and thousands more would die. Or she could agree, and the attack could be launched and could fail. Her actions would be judged as wrong and she would face the condemnation of the Security Council and her personal ruin. And yet she would be wrong because she had attempted to bring the agony, death, and suffering to a close.

A novel puzzlement and an interesting philosophical challenge to someone distant enough to enjoy it. Yet it was a puzzle with a simple enough solution for Vavra Bey. She swiveled her chair back to face MacIntyre.

"Admiral, I believe the seizure of this oil tanker at Port Monrovia may very well prove necessary. Can your people present me with a copy of the plan for this military action? I will consider it and pass it along to the Security Council with my proposal that action be taken."

"No problem, Madam Envoy. One will be provided immediately."

"And, Admiral, how long would you suggest that I consider it before passing it along?"

"Oh, I'd say an hour and forty-eight minutes would be about right."

"And that most useful acronym again?"

"UNODIR, Madam Envoy. 'Unless otherwise directed.' "

❖◆

Upon leaving the U.N. field offices, MacIntyre proceeded directly to the headquarters communications center.

"Primary link to Floater 1," he snapped to the duty systems operator. "Direct line to Captain Garrett."

"The channel is already open, Admiral. Captain Garrett has been standing by. You can use the communications deck on the watch officer's desk, sir."

MacIntyre gave an acknowledging nod and scooped up the indicated handset. "Captain?"

"Garrett here," the well-remembered voice came back. "What's the word, sir?"

"The word is load and lock. The envoy bought the package."

A sigh of relief gusted over the phone. "Yes!"

"You can tell your people the show is go."

""I already have, sir. Our support and diversion elements are already deploying. My dread was having to call them back."

"Right." MacIntyre glanced at his wristwatch. "I'm showing about one hundred minutes until you initiate your primary time line. I've got a helicopter standing by to take me out to the platform, so I should just about be on hand when the fun starts."

"I'm very glad to hear that, sir." A guarded tone crept into Amanda's voice. "Commander Rendino will be standing by to receive you. I regret I will not be present."

"What are you talking about, Captain?"

"I'm going in with the boarding force, sir."

"What!" MacIntyre exploded. "Leading from the front is all well and good, Captain, but there are limits! The place of the task force commander is in her Combat Information Center, not an assault boat. Dammit, Amanda, you are not Captain Kirk!"

"I'm rather glad you noticed." A touch of humor tinged her voice for a moment. "Seriously, sir, I agree with you on all points, except in cases of operational necessity. A problem has cropped up with that Algerian tanker. She's steam turbine powered, and our thermographic scans indicate that her crew has shut down her boilers. Her plant is totally cold. Even if we put a full black gang aboard her, it would take us at least a full hour to get up enough steam to move her.

"We won't have that kind of time. We'll have to grab one of the harbor tugboats and tow her out. That's going to be my job. I'm the only officer in this command who has any tug-handling experience."

"That factor wasn't in the mission outlines I saw, Captain," MacIntyre said coldly.

"There was no sense in clouding the issues with minor operational details, sir." The hint of challenging jocularity that had crept into her voice trailed off again into somberness. "However, I will be grateful for your presence on the platform during the operation, sir. If something goes wrong, I . . . might not be in a position to deal with it effectively. I'm glad to know that home base will be covered."

"It will be, Captain. I'm en route now. Carry on. I'll speak with you after the mission."

"Aye, aye, sir."

"Good luck, Amanda. Good hunting."

The click of the disconnect was his only answer.

MacIntyre returned the phone to its cradle and wondered to himself for a moment. He was a "West Coast Navy" officer by nature, casual in his command style. It wasn't uncommon for him to address a subordinate by his or her first name.

Why did it feel so different, then, when he used hers?

❧

Three hundred miles away, Amanda hung up her desk phone. They were committed now, and she felt a burden lift. It was like making a dive from the high board of a swimming pool. The dread of the dare was behind you, for better or worse, and all that was left to worry about was the plunge itself.

For her, there was only one last loose end to deal with. She switched on her laptop and called up the word processing program. For perhaps five minutes she sat quietly, her fingertips resting on the keyboard. Then she began to type.

Dearest Arkady:
This is one of those special letters that we of the profession of arms find neces-
sary to write on occasion. If you are reading it, it will mean that I am dead . . .

Mobile Offshore Base, Floater 1   2228 Hours, Zone Time; September 7, 2007

Amanda struggled into her gear, taking on the unaccustomed weight and bulk of the equipment-studded load-bearing harness as well as the pistol belt and flak jacket. She considered the battle helmet as well, but decided to trust to luck instead of Kevlar. Twisting her hair up onto the top of her head, she contained it under her battered old *Cunningham* baseball cap, its tarnished gold braid concealed with black electrician's tape.

She dug a small double-ended tube of camouflage cream out of a harness pouch. Removing the caps, she stood before the little wall mirror and inexpertly started applying the dull green and black skin paints.

A sharp knock sounded on the door as she worked. "Come in," she called back over her shoulder.

Stone Quillain stepped up into her quarters. Fully geared and armed, he was a looming presence that filled the entirety of the little room.

"Boarding parties are ready to load, Skipper." The Marine's own face paint seemed to merge into the camouflage patterns of his equipment and jungle utilities, making him look as if he had been poured whole out of some stealth composite. Only the dark intentness of his narrowed eyes stood separate from the whole.

"Very good, Stone. I'll be ready myself as soon as I get my face on. Elizabeth Arden never quite prepared me for anything like this."

"Oh hell! What are you trying to do?" Stepping forward impatiently, Quillain took the tube of cream from her hand. "You aren't supposed to be finger painting, goddammit!"

Loading a couple of fingertips with the paint, he began to swipe it onto her face with brusque strokes. "You want a solid base of the green all over everything, including the back of your neck. Then you use the black here to kill the highlight points. Your chin, the cheekbones, the bridge of your nose. Keep it asymmetrical, so if anyone does make out your face it'll take him a couple seconds to figure out what it is he's looking at. That'll give you time to drop him. You get those spare .45 clips I sent over?"

"I did, Stone, and thank you," she replied somberly. "You've taught me a lot about this business, and I want you to know that I appreciate it. I can imagine that it hasn't been easy having to drag a green skimmer captain along behind you."

"Aw, well, hell," the big Marine muttered back. "I guess I've learned a few things too." He jammed the caps back on the tube and tucked it into one of her gear pouches. "Use that stuff on your hands, too, when we go in. Either that or keep your gloves on."

Quillain hesitated for a moment more. "There's something that I want you to know, Skipper. Shame the devil and tell the truth, I had some . . . problems about working under the command of a woman CO when I first came out here. But now, for what it's worth, I'd be pleased and proud to serve with you or with any other lady like you, anywhere, anytime."

Amanda smiled, tasting the oily touch of the camo paint on her lips. "And I would be pleased and proud to serve with you, Stone. Anywhere. Anytime."

She extended her hand and Quillain's callused fingers closed around it, the two exchanging a short and fierce grip.

"Carry on, Captain Quillain. I'll join you shortly."

"Aye, aye, Skipper."

As Quillain departed, Amanda turned back to her desk and the interphone, dialing up the Operations Center watch officer. "This is Captain Garrett. I'm shifting my flag to the *Queen* at this time. Is Commander Rendino there?"

The intel came on line in a moment. "Right here, boss ma'am." Despite the flippant use of Amanda's pet name, Christine sounded exceptionally sober this night.

"What's our status, Chris?"

"We are on the precommit timeline, ma'am. The air group is ready to take departure, and all other decoy elements are on station and standing by. Drone recon coverage is up and we are seeing no alteration in the Union force deployments. All boards are green. Operation Wolfrider is ready to commit."

"What's the word on Admiral MacIntyre?"

"His helo is inbound with a fifteen-minute ETA. The helipads should be clear, so we can bring him straight aboard."

"That's good, Chris. Until he gets up to speed, you'll be running the show."

A laugh with a degree of sob in it came back over the phone. "God, responsibility! It keeps creeping up on me like cheap underwear. Damn you, Amanda. This is more frothing-at-the-mouth crazy than anything you've ever done before. Don't be any more of a hero out there tonight than you absolutely have to. Okay?"

"I promise, Chris. Cross my heart. Take care of things until I get back."

"You know I will, boss ma'am".

Amanda glanced at her watch. "Commander Rendino. It is now 2245 hours. Advise all elements that we are committing to Operation Wolfrider. Initiate the primary timeline."

"Acknowledged, Captain. The primary timeline is initiated."

Amanda dropped the phone into its cradle and glanced for a last time at the recorded CD she'd left centered on her laptop lid. Then she stepped out into the night.

⚑◆

The misty rain that she'd hoped for blackened the antiskid on the decks and starred the scarlet worklights. Shadowy figures hurried through the darkness and voices shouted over the howl of turbines and the drone of rotors. Running lights pulsing against the black overcast. The helicopters of the composite U.K./U.S. air strike group were launching, three sleek British Merlins and one hulking American Sea Stallion lifting sequentially off the platform helipads.

Amanda lifted an unseen hand to Squadron Commander Dane in the lead aircraft and started aft to the hover hangars. As she made her way through the maze of deck modules, half-recognized voices called out of the shadows.

"Good luck, Captain!"

"Give 'em hell, ma'am!"

"Kick ass and take names, TACBOSS!"

She responded with a lifted thumb to each hail.

The trio of seafighters lay beneath the glare of the hangar arcs, their tail gates down and with the last few ammunition cases being hogged aboard. The PGACs were much changed from the gleaming, yard-new hulls that Amanda had first seen five months ago. Battered, patched, and sun blasted now, but also proven, like the men and women who crewed them.

Amanda studied them for a moment from her place in the shadows, and deep within her heart and soul, she cast off the last line that linked her with her past life aboard the Duke. This was her place now, and there were no more regrets.

Over at the far side of the hangar, Stone Quillain was completing his final premission inspection of the boarding parties. Taking a step back from the tightly packed ranks, he lifted his voice over the fading thunder of the departing helicopters.

"Who are ya?"

"Marines, sir!" the shouted reprise rolled back.

"I SAID WHO ARE YA?"

"MARINES, SIR!"

"DAMN RIGHT! MARINES, SADDLE UP!"

The deck plates rang under the boot heels of the assault teams as they broke formation and double-timed for the stern ramps of the hovercraft.

Amanda swung up through the *Queen of the West*'s side hatch and climbed the ladder into the cockpit. Looking back from the control stations, Steamer and Snowy exchanged acknowledging nods with her.

"Squadron status, Commander?"

"All craft report ramps coming up. Ready to start engines, ma'am."

"Make it so, Commander. Start engines and take us out."

"Very good, ma'am. Frenchman . . . Rebel . . . this is Royalty! Engine-start sequence!"

The *Queen*'s air horns blared their warning, trailed by the sound of cranking turbines. Steamer and Snowy's palms came up and met in their high five. Amanda didn't recall until later that this time their fingers interlaced for a moment in a tight handclasp.

Amanda settled a Command headset over her ears. "I'm riding up in the hatch for a while, Steamer. Take departure at your discretion."

"You got it, ma'am."

As the *Queen* came up on her cushion, Amanda slid the overhead hatch back and lifted herself up into the gunner's saddle. She jacked her headset into the intercom and looked forward.

And only then did she realize the platform was saluting the strike away.

The inboard rails of the two barges that flanked the launching ramp were lined solidly with Seabees, support hands, and seafighter base personnel. Underlit by the blue glow of the ramp guide lights, each crewman and -woman held rigidly at attention, fingertips at their brow.

Amanda had heard of airstrikes being saluted out before, but never a naval sortie. But then, there had never been a naval unit like this before. Another tradition to build on.

The *Queen*'s drive fans roared and she trundled forward toward the ramp break. Amanda's hand came up, returning the salute for the squadron. Then the seafighter pitched over the break and accelerated downramp for the sea. She hit water in an explosion of spray and powered clear into the night, the *Carondelet* and the *Manassas* following at ten-second intervals.

Spume and rain droplets stung at Amanda's face as the squadron dropped into combat echelon and worked up to speed. On the snubmast aft of the cockpit, the *Queen*'s flag and Amanda's command burgee whipped and crackled in the growing slipstream. The lights of the platform faded in the mist behind them. Somewhere ahead, the lights of Port Monrovia glowed.

Port Monrovia   2325 Hours, Zone Time; September 7, 2007

The tea had grown cold and weak, mixing with the rain. Belewa paid no mind, tossing back the last swallow in his canteen cup. He hadn't been able to stand the thought of waiting out this night back at Mamba Point. He had to be here, in the field, where he could think and breathe and do something.

Belewa set the empty cup inside the open tail ramp of the Styer command track. Unhampered by his sodden poncho, he climbed the side of the vehicle. Standing on its flat armored roof, he lifted his binoculars to his eyes.

From here he could see the battlefield-to-be.

His cluster of headquarters vehicles were assembled on the access road atop the southern harbor breakwater, close to the midpoint between the oiling pier and the tank farm. Just to shoreward, the tarpaulin-shielded arc welders of the tank farm repair crew sparked and sputtered as they raced to mend the severed pipelines.

Would God that they were finished now and the oil was flowing.

The shoreside piers and warehouse areas of the port had arc light illumination, as did the oiling pier and tank farm. Those lights blazed this night, power conservation be damned. The outer extremities of the vegetation-ridden breakwaters had no such lighting, however, save for the slow-blinking navigational beacons that marked the mouth of the entry channel.

With little night-vision gear available, the Union defenders had been forced to improvise. Log and palm oil bonfires had been spaced along the breakwaters at fifty-yard intervals, and at each bonfire, an infantry squad. Roving patrols also prowled the lengths of the causeways.

The fires burned sullenly in the rain, however, guttering and threatening to go out.

I wish we could illuminate with flares all night, but we haven't enough. Best to save what we have until they are truly needed.

At the end of each breakwater, covering the harbor mouth, a hardpoint had been established. A heavy-weapons platoon at each, backed by a cannon-armed Panhard AML armored car. The three gunboats of the Union navy's heavy squadron also lay at anchor side by side, directly across the mouth of the channel, their guns manned and their searchlights and radar sweeping the darkness.

How do I best use the gunboats? When the Americans move on us, do I counterattack and send the navy out after them? Or do I keep the cork in the bottle?

Belewa had a full regular infantry battalion covering the breakwaters and port facilities, and a Military Police company guarding the tank farm. He'd also brought in a company of the Union Mobile Action Force, his personal "Praetorian Guard" grown out of his beloved old mechanized troop. The other three companies of the mechanized battalion stood by at the Barclay Training Center, ready to move at a moment's notice as his reserve counterstroke. Other regular and militia units covered the beaches and city and harbor land approaches.

Belewa lowered his glasses. *I wait for you, Leopard. Come out of the night and let's finish this, you and I.*

There was no answer. But he could sense her moving out there, somewhere beyond the curtain of mist and shadow.

Belewa dropped down from the top of the vehicle and climbed inside through the tailgate. The command track's two radio operators hunched in front of their sets while Sako Atiba brooded over the deployed map table, his dark features hollow-cheeked in the dim map light.

"Anything new to report, Brigadier?" Belewa inquired, brushing the moisture from the front of his poncho.

"No, General. Nothing to report. The helicopter group that launched from the American base platform has turned away to the south and has dropped below our radar horizon. Track has been lost. We continue to note much small-craft activity off the immediate coastal area, but no pattern has formed yet."

"Very good, Brigadier."

Once it would have been "Obe" and "Sako," but somehow the names didn't taste right in the mouth anymore. Belewa collected his cup once more and turned to the tea urn. Sometimes things other than men die in war.

⚒

A mile and a half northwest of General Belewa's command post and a quarter mile off the northern breakwater, a cluster of small eight-man inflatable assault boats bobbed in the low rain-smoothed swells, a hood of radar and infrared absorbent material drawn over the huddled passengers in each craft.

In the stern of each tiny vessel, a sweating coxswain huddled, constantly cross-checking between the glowing palm-size screen of his GPU unit and the flickering watchfires along the breakwater. Occasionally, he twisted the throttle of his silent electric outboard motor, using a brief shot of power to hold on station, awaiting the order to move in.

In the bow of her craft, Amanda Garrett cautiously lifted the edge of the RAM hood and peered toward shore.

Soon.

Mobile Offshore Base, Floater 1   2325 Hours, Zone Time; September 7, 2007

The Admiral and the intel had elected to use the briefing trailer as their headquarters rather than to further crowd the already cramped confines of the Operations and TACNET vans. Half a dozen systems operators manning laptop workstations along the conference table linked them into the mission data flow and the big flatscreen monitors on the forward bulkhead gave them their overview of the battle zone.

"It's all pretty straightforward, sir," Christine said, her fingertip traveling down the graphics map of the Union coastline. "Union units are in red. Pink for militia. Bright red for the regulars. Red with the blue outline for the naval elements. Ours are blue. The Brits green. The French gold. Each point boxed in along the coastline indicates an area where a specific diversionary action is going to take place."

MacIntyre nodded, and leaned back against the end of the conference table. His day's worth of beard rasped lightly against the collar of his flight suit. "Where's Captain Garrett and the assault force at this moment?"

"Here, sir. Holding at Point Fathertree, off the northern port breakwater. They were inserted by the PGACs and will hold on station there until the coast is clear for the final approach and penetration of the harbor area itself."

"Are the PGs still with them?"

"No, sir." Christine indicated a spot roughly three miles off the harbor mouth. "The Three Little Pigs are moving out to Point Sun Village at this time, running in swimmer mode and fully stealthed. Sun Village is the missile-firing station for the strike against the Monrovia power and communications net. Following the strike, they'll move up to Point Blue Mountain, here about one mile off the harbor entrance. They'll hold there for the extraction call by the boarding teams."

MacIntyre gave a noncommittal grunt, studying the screen.

One of the systems operators looked up from her terminal. "Commander Rendino. We are coming up on initiation point for Diversion Treestump."

Christine glanced back. "Very well. Intelligence access, do we have any situational changes ashore?"

"Negative, Commander. Intel indicates no changes."

"Okay, then. Signals, pass the word. Initiate Treestump. Execute as planned."

Christine looked back to MacIntyre. "Now, sir, we start dazzling them with our fancy footwork".

"In theory," the Admiral replied, leaning back against the end of the table. "This is an aspect of this operation that I'm worried about. It seems like we're taking an awful lot for granted here."

"We don't have much choice, sir. Belewa knows when we're coming, he knows where we're coming from, and he knows where we're going. We have to do something to throw him off balance. Essentially what we are attempting to do, above and beyond sprinkling a lot of general confusion around, is to build a certain mind-set that will encourage Belewa into doing certain things that will let us sneak in through the door."

"I understand that, Chris," MacIntyre replied. "I also understand that trying to run your enemy by remote control can be a damn tricky thing to pull off. He might not be in an obliging mood tonight."

The intel grinned back. "You have to remember that Captain Garrett has an edge in this situation, Admiral. She's a woman, and we females have a certain knack at getting men to do what we want them to."

Diversion Point Treestump
7 Miles East-Southeast of Cape Mesurado
Between Monrovia and
King Grays Town   2331 Hours, Zone Time; September 7, 2007

The dull-black Fiberglas paddles didn't flash as they dug into the wave crests.

The half-dozen raider boats surfed onto the broad sandy beach, their passengers springing over the gunwales into the trailing foam. Catching up the nylon strap carrying handles looped around the gunwales of the small inflatable craft, the Marines lifted them from the sea and bore them up onto the beach.

Ahead, beyond the beach, lay a band of heavy brush and trees. And beyond that, the coast road. For the moment, the roughly paved stretch of highway was empty, the landing carefully timed between the intermittent Union motorized patrols.

To the north and south of the landing site, perhaps a mile in each direction, were the faint, guttering lights of fishermen's shacks. Out at sea, blacked out and circling slowly, the Patrol Craft USS *Santana* held station. She had delivered the Fox company assault platoon to its objective and, God willing, she would take them away.

Carrying their raider boats with them, the Marines hurried up the beach, the last man from each boat party blurring their tracks in the sand with a gunnysack.

The Foxmen did not want their presence known. At least not yet.

Port Monrovia Defense
Command Post   2334 Hours, Zone Time; September 7, 2007

One of the command track's radiomen looked up. "General Belewa. There is a communication from Captain Mosabe aboard the *Promise*. He wishes to speak with you, sir."

Belewa took two fast steps to the radio console and caught up a handset. "Belewa here."

"We are tracking unusual targets on our radar, General," the gunboat squadron commander's filtered voice replied. "Many of them."

"What do you mean unusual, Captain?"

"Like nothing we have ever seen before. Small surface contacts. Many of them. They seem to appear and disappear at random. Either that or they are moving at incredible speeds from point to point. Faster than we can establish a plot."

"Where are they coming from?" Belewa demanded.

"Nowhere, General. They just started to appear on our screens."

"Could this be some kind of American radar jamming?"

"It's nothing that we recognize."

"Speed, number, heading?"

"General, we cannot get an accurate count or an accurate plot! There is just a whole wave of them out there, bearing down on us."

Diversion Line Dewshine
Ten Miles off Monrovia   2334 Hours, Zone Time; September 7, 2007

One of three such craft involved in the same enterprise, the sixteen-foot navy miniraider chugged slowly along while an assembly line ran in its bow.

Two enlisted hands inflated a small weather balloon with helium while a third tied off a thirty-foot length of high-test fishing line to the balloon's hard point. The other end of the fishing line, in turn, was attached to a short length of two-by-four that would serve as a floating sea anchor.

The two-by-four was tossed over the raider's side and the balloon was released to soar upward to the full length of the fishing line, the thirty feet of tether being just enough to bring the balloon above the scan horizon of the surface-search radar at Port Monrovia.

Suspended beneath the balloon on another single strand of fishing line was a three-square-foot panel of common kitchen aluminum foil, its edges stiffened with light wire. As the balloon drifted slowly toward the Union coast, the foil panel twisted in the mild trade winds, randomly displaying first its edge and then its reflective broad side to the probing Union radar beams.

Diversion Point Leetah
Off the Mouth of the Po River,
Seven Miles Northwest of
Port Monrovia   2340 Hours, Zone Time; September 7, 2007

On the bridge of the Corvette *La Fleurette,* Commander Jacques Trochard glanced at the bulkhead chronometer. "Very well, gentlemen," he said crisply. "Let's become obvious."

Lights blazed on the decks. Running lights. Work lights. Pulsing helipad markers. Astern, the squadron mate of the little French man-of-war illuminated up as well, a constellation of glowing red, green, and white against the blackened sea.

The corvette's Sea Lynx helicopters lifted into the sky, their navigational beacons set to "bright flash." With their spotlights sweeping the wavetops, the helos led the way as the formation swept in toward the Union coast.

"What do we do next, *Capitaine*?" Trochard's exec inquired from behind the helm station.

"To my regret, Andre, nothing more," Trochard replied wistfully. "However, we shall endeavor to look most impressive while we are doing it."

⚓

"Sighting! The militia post at Po River reports enemy warships and helicopters approaching the coast. The outpost commander says that a landing attempt appears imminent. He requests reinforcements."

Belewa and his staff clustered in around the map table.

Diversion Strike Madcoil
Off the Union Coast Between
the Po and St. Paul Rivers   2342 Hours, Zone Time; September 7, 2007

Holding in a diamond formation, the flight of big helicopters thundered in toward the Union shoreline, holding so low to the sea that their rotorblast flattened troughs in the wave crests beneath them.

In the cockpit of the lead British Merlin, Squadron Commander Evan

Dane scanned the darkness ahead through the night-vision visor of his helmet. Gradually, delineated in the hazy greens of the photomultiplier system, he made out the pale sand of the beach and darker forest line beyond it.

His thumb came down on the transmit key atop his collective controller. "Squadron leader to squadron. Enemy coast ahead."

Lifting his thumb, he let the system revert to intercom mode. Chuckling softly, he spoke to his copilot. "You know what, Mick? I've always wanted to say that."

Crossing the beach, the helos lifted a meager twenty feet above the tree-tops and drove inland.

⚔◆

"Sighting report! The Klay highway motor patrol reports a formation of helicopters crossing the highway at a point eight miles northwest of the port area, proceeding inland. The patrol leader reports several heavy troop carrier–type machines flying at very low altitude."

More marks were scribbled on the acetate cover of the table map.

"It must be that flight that launched from the American platform," Belewa pondered aloud. "First they divert to break radar contact. Now they return and cross the coast above us. What could they be up to?"

"A commando landing somewhere in our rear areas, no doubt," Brigadier Atiba said decisively. "The Americans favor airmobile operations. That must be it."

A murmur of agreement drifted from the other staff officers crowded into the command track. Belewa made no further comment.

Diversion Point Scouter
Yatono Reef, Three Miles Northwest
of the St. Paul River   2347 Hours, Zone Time; September 7, 2007

The boat crew hauled the two wet-suit-clad figures over the rubber gunwale.

"You guys okay?" a whispered voice demanded.

"Yeah, yeah, take off! Take off!"

Aft, at the helm station, the coxswain opened the throttle of the Zodiac's powerful outboard. Snarling, the twenty-four-foot semirigid sheered away from the coast, trailing a broad and foaming V of wake behind it. Peering astern, the Marine swimmers and the navy boatmen counted seconds.

The numbers ran out. A blue-white glare illuminated the coastline and, in the heart of it, a frozen image of a warped ship's hull standing up on end and disintegrating. The shock wave followed through the water and the roar of the explosion through the air.

The coxswain swung the Zodiac parallel to the coast once more, backing off on her speed. "Okay, start heaving 'em over the side," she ordered.

They began to pitch the remainder of their cargo into the sea at ten-second intervals: smoke floats, flashing emergency strobes, flare buoys.

⚒◆

"Sightings! The wrecked ship off Yatono Village has just blown up!"

"What?" Brigadier Atiba demanded. "Confirm that. What wreck?"

"The old hulk grounded on Yatono Reef. Many confirmations now. All beach patrols north of the St. Paul are reporting in. It was a very large explosion."

Atiba shook his head in puzzlement. "It must be the Americans, but why in God's name would they blow up a shipwreck?"

"Not the ship, but the reef it's grounded on," the naval liaison officer exclaimed. "They must be blowing a gap in the reef line to permit the passage of amphibious assault craft. That can be the only explanation, General."

Belewa did not reply. He only gazed broodingly down upon the map table.

"More sighting reports coming in, General. Beach patrols now see lights on the water beyond Yatono reef. They hear boat engines and report what could be a smoke screen forming offshore. . . ."

Diversion Point OneEye
The St. Paul River Estuary
Two Miles Northwest of Port Monrovia   2352 Hours, Zone Time, September 7, 2007

With fans of spray flaring back from her sharp cutwater, the USS *Sirocco* charged the Union coast. In her wheelhouse, her captain grimly shifted his eyes between the computer graphics chart on the quartermaster's console and the fathometer screen, gauging how much water he had left off his bow and below his keel.

"Helm, come left to heading zero zero zero."

"Coming left to zero zero zero, sir."

The patrol craft leaned into her turn, clearing her bow and stern autocannon mounts. Gunners buried their faces into night-bright scopes and slender gun barrels indexed, the whine of the servo drives lost in the tumbling hiss of the sea along the PC's flanks.

"Bow and stern mounts report they have acquired initial target, sir," the wheelhouse talker barked. "Range six double oh meters. Mounts are tracking and are standing by to commence fire."

"Very well. Bow and stern mounts. Commence firing!"

The 25mm Bushmaster cannon began hammering out precise and deliberate three-round bursts, the tracers arcing away through the mist toward the shadowy coastline.

✕◆

"Attack report, General! The garrison at the mouth of the St. Paul River is being fired upon from the sea. They are returning fire!"

✕◆

Multiple tracer streams lashed out wildly from the shore, spraying the night. Mortars thudded and recoilless rifle backflares blazed like gigantic flash-bulbs along the beach line. Shell plumes lanced up and out the sea in the *Sirocco*'s wake. None too close, but all close enough.

"Helm! Come hard left to one nine zero! All engines ahead full! Bow mount, cease fire! Stern mount, continue to engage while you have the range!"

The PC arced away from the coast, dancing out of the reach of the destruction hurled after her. As the coast receded beyond its reach, her stern gun fell silent The shoreside weapons continued to rage, however, blazing away madly at specters seen in the darkness.

The *Surrocco*'s captain took a deep breath and flexed the taut muscles in his shoulders. They'd haul off a bit and let the Union troops waste their ammunition for as long as they had a mind to. When things quieted down again, they'd make another pass.

✕◆

"This must be the commitment to the attack, General," Atiba exclaimed. "Everything indicates a beach assault by the American marines on our northern flank. We need to start orienting our reserve forces to cover the northern land approaches to the harbor area."

"No," Belewa grunted, leaning over the map table. "We don't move anyone out of position. Not yet." For a moment it was as it had been in the old days. A tactical problem to be solved and the animosities forgotten. "This is all nothing, Sako. All smoke and lights and a big show. She wants us to think there will be a landing. She beckons to us. She tries to draw our attention. Look!"

Belewa's finger stabbed down onto the map circling the northern coastal sector above Port Monrovia. "The Po River. The St. Paul. All these diversions happening to the north of our position. And nothing to the south."

Belewa's fingertip arced across the map surface to the southern sector below Monrovia. "What is happening down here, Sako? What is it we are not seeing?"

Holding Point Fathertree,
Off the North Breakwater at
Port Monrovia   2400 Hours, Zone Time; September 7, 2007

The two raiders bumped softly together, Stone Quillain's hand catching one of the carrying loops on Amanda's craft. Beyond the faint hissing of the raindrops on the sea, the distant, sporadic gunfire of the St. Paul River garrison could be heard away to the north.

"How we doing?" Quillain inquired, lifting a corner of his boat's RAM hood.

"So far, so good," Amanda replied, doing the same. It felt good to admit a puff of comparatively cool air to the rank and humid interior of the little raft. "The northern diversions have all gone in. As we expected, Belewa is too smart to bite at them. Drone recon indicates he's standing pat."

Quillain gave an acknowledging grunt. "Yeah, but right about now he's got to be looking back over his shoulder, wonderin' just where the real crunch is coming from."

"So we hope." As per instruction, Amanda had turned the luminous dial of her watch inward to her wrist. Now she flipped the worn Lady Admiral face up for a moment to check the time. "We'll be giving him a suggestion as to where he can look in another few seconds here. The MADCOIL strike should be going in now."

Barclay Army Training Center
South of the City of Monrovia   0004 Hours, Zone Time; September 8, 2007

Most of the officers and men of the Union army's 1st Mobile Strike Force were too keyed up to linger inside their humidity-rank cinder-block barracks this night. Not with a fight in the offing.

Instead, they loitered around their combat-readied vehicles in the motor pool areas, talking the rambling inconsequential talk of soldiers caught in the inevitable military cycle of hurry up and wait. Shielded from the drizzle, cigarette tips glowed in cupped palms.

This urge to be out in the open instead of under the roofs of the camp's buildings would save many of their lives in the minutes to come.

They were given no warning beyond a soft droning in the distance, a droning that grew rapidly into a thudding roar. Men looked up, confused. The threat they had been told of lay out to sea, but this sound was coming from inland, from over Union territory.

An officer broke through the hesitation, bellowing a command. The base alarm Klaxons started their urgent metallic honking. Men scrambled for stacked weapons. Vehicle crewmen started engines and scrambled to clear the antiaircraft machine guns atop their trucks and tracks.

All too late to make a difference.

✖◆

Strike group MADCOIL had followed a devious flight path since crossing the Union coast. With a pair of Eagle Eye recon drones flying point like a pair of cavalry scouts, the helicopter formation had snaked its way inland, hugging the forest canopy to evade the minimal Union radar coverage. Swinging wide around the outlying outposts of the Monrovia defenses, they picked up the meandering track of the Mesurado River.

Here, the helos had turned west, following the track of the river channel back toward the city. Dropped even lower, the aircraft skimmed the surface of the sluggish estuary, the beating of their rotors contained between its thickly forested banks.

✖◆

In his night-vision visor, Evan Dane saw the shoreline of Bank Island loom ahead. With Bally lsland on his right hand, he banked the Merlin to starboard, trailing the curve of river around to the west-northwest.

Shore lights flickered past in the rain, all but invisible to the naked eye, yet piercingly bright in the night optics. The water shimmered two men's heights below.

Dane risked a single split-second glance down at the GPU screen. Right, still in the slot! Clearing Bank Island to port. The river turned fully to the north here, so their course now angled them across to a point on the west bank.

"On base leg to attack! All aircraft stand by! Come left to two seven zero on my mark!"

More lights dead on off the Merlin's nose. The riverbank and Capitol Hill beyond it.

"Flight break left and climb! Climb! On attack leg!"

Hard back on pitch and collective! War power to the turbines! Up and into a bank and a zoom beyond anything the big ASW helo had ever been intended for. They were over the shoreline now, the shacks and streets flashing past beneath them. Momentary images of night-wandering Africans gawking upward at the howling monster-birds that had swept in from the darkness.

Shack-street-shack-street shack . . . Clear sky and over the crest! No hellish glare in the side-view mirrors to announce the failure of a flight mate to clear the hill.

There! The stadium just off the line of flight to the right! The large open fenced area dead ahead with its neatly ranked rows of barracks, so different from the jumble of civilian housing they had just flown over. *This is it! This is where we're supposed to be!*

"Target ahead!"

They came down off the hill crest, diving balls to the wall; the airframe shuddered as the airspeed redlined. *Move, you old cow! D'you want these bastards to get a shooting line on us?*

Over the fence line. Over the objective! The door gunners opened up, hosing tracers at the scattering Union soldiers below.

Dane's finger closed convulsively on the ordnance release trigger. "Bombs gone!"

Racks designed to drop torpedoes and depth charges instead released fifty-gallon oil drums filled with a home-brewed napalm of gasoline blended with soap flakes. A doctored 40mm incendiary grenade screwed into the filler hole served adequately as a detonator.

Dane's night-vision system overloaded, and he tore the dead visor up and off of his eyes. The makeshift incendiaries sprayed across rooftops and splattered in spectacular blossoms of fire across the tarmacked car parks, exploding vehicle fuel tanks joining in the holocaust in the seconds that followed.

The helicopter formation swept across Barclay barracks, surfing on a wave of orange and white flame. Off his port side, outlined against the glare, Dane could see the big U.S. Sea Stallion riding nose high and with a steady stream of oil drums rolling out of its open tailgate like depth charges off the fantail of a World War II destroyer.

The last canister of hellfire dropped clear. Ordnance expended, the strike group raced away from the army base, racing now for the sanctuary of the sea. A scattering of tracers chased them, and Danes guts locked up for an instant as he saw the spark trail of a shoulder-launched antiaircraft missile arc into the sky.

However, like the night-vision visor, the infrared homing system of the little projectile was overwhelmed by its proximity to the inferno raging within the Union military base. After staggering drunkenly across the sky for a moment, the missile dove into the flames, minutely compounding the disaster.

Black sea flashed beneath the helicopters. They were on home ground again. Dane took a second to catch up on his breathing. "Well, I daresay they know there's a Caucasian in the woodpile now."

⬧◆

"General Belewa, attack . . . General! Barclay Barracks has been bombed!"

Belewa's head snapped up. "That's impossible! The United Nations has no attack aircraft here. Get a confirmation from Barclay headquarters."

"Both Barclay headquarters and the Mobile Force HQ Company have gone off the air. No reply on any tactical channel. I am receiving the report from South Sector Militia Command. They say the army base is in flames, sir."

Belewa hurled his canteen cup to the deck of the track and charged down the tail ramp. Once out in the night, he stared to the south. A dull-orange glow flickered off the low overcast, outlining Mamba Point.

"How did you do that?" His first response was a whisper that barely escaped his lips.

"How did you do that?" His second was a rising shout. Disregarding the staring cadre of the command group, he tore the cap from his head and slammed it to the sodden pavement at his feet. "Damn you! You don't have any bombers! How did you do that!"

⬧◆

"All right!" Christine exclaimed. "Yeah! On the money!"

She and Elliot MacIntyre watched the real-time video download from the Eagle Eye drone circling over the incandescent ruins of Barclay barracks. Remnants of the Mobile force battalion were fleeing the compound while exploding ammunition reserves took over the task of destruction started by the helibombers.

"I will be damned. Another phase of the magnificent improvisation works," the Admiral commented, nodding slowly as he studied the monitor. "So far, so good."

"Yes, sir." Christine nodded. "We've taken one of Belewa's key mobile reserve elements out of the game for a while. Hopefully, we've also got him all jazzed up and waiting for us to make our serious move. Now we feed him Diversion Treestump, the southern landing team." She took a step to the wall chart and ran a finger down the coastline to the engagement box below Monrovia. "This one is for all the cookies."

"When does it launch?"

"That's at the discretion of the Union, but probably within the next ten to fifteen minutes."

"Platoon alert! Road north. Vehicles incoming. Prepare to engage." The curt whispered commands issued from the Treestump team's little PRC-6725 tactical communicators.

Twice since their landing, the Union motorized patrol had swept past along the highway and twice the Marines had let it pass unmolested, huddling down out of sight in the undergrowth.

Not this time. Weapons were silently lifted, cleared, and aimed. Hands came up to swipe water droplets away from nite-brite optics.

"North scout here," another whisper leaked through the radio circuit. "Same outfit as before. Land Rover first. Ferret scout car second. Truck with infantry squad at tail of column. Vehicles traveling illuminated. Antennas on Land Rover. I say again, antennas on Land Rover."

The engines could be heard now, growling complaints as the little convoy lumbered along in low gear. Headlights reflected off the wet pavement and the big spotlight mounted on the turret of the armored car slashed slowly through the darkness like a blue-white sword blade probing along first one side of the road, then the other. The Marines pressed closer to the slimy mud floor beneath the brushwood tangle.

"All hands. Remember the drill," the platoon leader breathed into his lip mike. "Do not fire on the Land Rover. I repeat! Do not fire on the Land Rover! Do not take out those radios!"

Transceiver buttons clicked in dubious acknowledgment. The natural way of the Marine was that if you could see it, you could hit it. And if you hit it, you should kill it.

Unknowing, the Union patrol approached out of the night, rolling slowly into the center of the ambush zone.

The Marine platoon leader gave the order to fire with the trigger of his carbine. A single shot rang out, then thirty-seven other weapons joined into a composite roar of firepower.

The truck at the tail end of the Union patrol had no radio and thus no immunity. Half a dozen 40mm grenades slammed into it in the first second of the engagement, shredding the vehicle and its soldier cargo before they had a chance to dismount. Then a Predator missile fired at point-blank range gouged into the pavement underneath the ten-wheeler, flipping the big vehicle over on its side and detonating its diesel tanks in a smoky fireball.

Second in line, the Ferret armored car tried to turn into the threat, the light machine gun in its turret hammering a reply to the Marine barrage. A storm of 5.56mm NATO sleeted off its armor, smashing its headlights and search light mount, and smoke grenades burst around it, blinding the driver and gunner. The Ferret's front wheels slipped off the roadway into the ditch and the scout car high centered, howling and shuddering like a trapped and blinded rhino. But only for a heartbeat. A second Predator round caved in its frontal armor and sent golden flame spewing from its hatches and observation slits.

In the lead spot, the driver of the patrol leader's Land Rover knew his business. He floored his accelerator and powered clear of the ambush zone, the Rover's machine gunner wildly hosing the night behind them while the patrol commander yelled into his radio mike. All three men would escape unscathed and later attribute their survival to divine providence.

In actuality, they should have given thanks to the meticulous preplanning of Amanda Garrett.

⚔◆

Offshore, just beyond the surf line, the USS *Santana* held position, her throttled-down engines barely giving her steering way. Blacked out and with all hands at their battle stations, the PC had awaited the moment to play its next role in the growing elaboration of the deception program. The cue came with the first crackle of gunfire ashore.

The *Santana*'s skipper nodded to the electrician's mate at his breadboarded control panel. The enlisted hand in turn switched on a CD player and ran a set of gain levers up to their highest stops.

It was an old trick, a variant of something first used by Commander Douglas Fairbanks, Jr., and his "Beachjumpers" during World War II. But perhaps it was something old enough to work again. The "main battery" of loudspeakers lined up along the PC's main deck came to life, the amplifiers blasting the prerecorded turbine howl of the Three Little Pigs into the night.

Mobile Offshore Base; Floater 1   0024 Hours, Zone Time; September 8, 2007

"Word in from operations, Commander," the signals S.O. reported, looked up from her station. "Treestump has engaged. The ambush has been executed."

On the wall map, a flashing red engagement box blinked into existence around the Treestump ambush site.

"Very good. Keep us advised." Christine glanced down the table to a second operator. "Elint, talk to me. Do we have any Union transmissions from the Treestump event yet?"

"Stand by a second, Commander." The intelligence link held poised for a second, listening to the voices in his headset. "Yes, ma'am. Elint says that a contact report has been radioed in to Port Monrovia. Belewa's field headquarters is acknowledging . . . and we have an alert coming in from the militia garrison at King Grey's Town. They are reporting that their outposts hear the seafighter squadron offshore, near the engagement site."

"Yeah!" Christine slapped her palm down on the briefing table. "The *Santana* is working it! Get me the real-time video link with our drone over Port Monrovia." She spun to face the wall monitor. "Okay, big guy," she murmured. "There's the real bait. Come on and take it."

⚔

"Sako, get me confirmations!"

Brigadier Atiba looked up from his crouched station beside the track's radio console, one earphone pressed to the side of his head. "Confirmation on both reports, General. We have American Marines ashore in force in the southern beach sectors, and we have a second beach outpost in that area now reporting they can hear the engines of the American hovercraft group offshore."

Belewa's fist smashed down on the map table. "This is what they were trying to divert us from. She's down there! This is the real attack."

Atiba scowled. "General, this engagement is miles south of the port area. What could they hope to accomplish down there?"

"I'm not sure, Sako. But I do know Garrett will be at the heart of the attack and she will have the hovercraft with her! They're her single most powerful force element. This must be the primary effort! What's the status of the Mobile Force at Camp Barclay? Can they move out?"

"Heavy losses in equipment and personnel reported, sir. They are regrouping."

"Damnation!" Belewa's fist exploded onto the table once more, the pain of the impact helping to restore his focus. "We have to break this landing up now, before they can consolidate and launch the next phase of whatever she's planning. Order all Southern Sector Militia outposts to initiate reconnaissance in force toward the landing site. Engage the enemy on contact and get me their strength and intent. Detach the Mobile Force Company here at Port Monrovia and get them headed south with all speed. They are to launch an immediate spoiling attack down the coastal highway against the American beachhead. What's the status of the helicopter unit at Payne Airfield?"

"They have one night-capable gunship armed and ready to launch."

"Hold it on the ground until we have a target established." Belewa spun around to face the navy liaison huddled back in the far corner of the track's

SEA FIGHTER **345**

central compartment. "Lieutenant, contact the *Promise*. Inform Captain Mosabe that the gunboat squadron is to sortie immediately and proceed southward down the coast with all speed. Locate and engage the enemy!"

◇◆

"The armored fighting vehicles are starting to move out," MacIntyre noted, studying the low-light television imaging on the wall monitor.

"Yeah, looks like the Mobile Force Company's being redeployed," Christine agreed. "Amanda would call that chocolate frosting on sugar pie. The big question, though, is going to be the gunboats. Drone Ops, get us some coverage out over the mouth of the harbor."

"Aye, ma'am." At his workstation, the Eagle Eye pilot delicately worked his joystick and throttle gain.

Fifteen miles away, his small robotic command responded to the cybernetic impulses coming in over its datalinks, pivoting and darting across the night sky like an aluminum and composite hummingbird.

The image on the wall monitor swooped and bobbed, then stabilized again, focusing in on the trio of anchored gunboats.

"Stay on the *Promise* and zoom in on the foredeck."

"Doing it, Commander."

Half a dozen figures swarmed around the forecastle of the Union flagship.

"Does that look like a sea and anchor detail to you, Admiral?"

MacIntyre nodded. "Couldn't be anything else but. Back us off to normal range and go to thermographic imaging."

The image field expanded, encompassing all three of the Union gunboats once more and shifting from the light and dark grays of the low-light television to the more vivid black-and-white photo-negative effect of the infrared scanner. The gunboats became pale phantom vessels afloat on a shadow sea, a glowing white flame pulsing rhythmically in their midships sections and a faint luminescent mist hovering above them.

"All right," Christine exclaimed. "Exhaust plumes and engine heat. They're getting under way. Belewa's bought the package! He's committing the gunboats!"

The *Promise* began to move, pulling away from its anchorage in the channel and heading out through the gap in the breakwaters. The *Unity* followed in the corvette's wake, then the *Allegiance*. The gunboats made the turn southward as they reached deep water beyond the harbor mouth, all three pouring on speed.

"Wouldn't it have been a hell of a lot simpler to just sink those damn things at anchor?" MacIntyre grunted.

Christine shook her head. "It would have drawn too much attention back to the harbor area", she replied. "Besides, for what the boss ma'am has planned next, she can't afford to have any burning hulks drifting around lighting things up."

The intel looked back over her shoulder. "Communications. Inform Moonshade and Strongbow that the gunboats are clearing the harbor. They are go for penetration phase. Then inform the Treestump team they have company coming their way."

⚒

To the southeast, the Treestump Platoon Leader took stock. "Sergeant," he called to his Platoon top. "Casualty count?"

"Two men wounded, sir," a nearby patch of shadow replied. "Dyksra in third squad's caught it pretty bad."

"Right. Have a detail evacuate the wounded out to the *Santana* immediately. Have a second detail check for Union survivors. The rest of the platoon will reorient for area defense. Second squad will establish a centralized perimeter here, while first and third squads will reposition north and south along the highway and set up new hasty ambush sites. Deploy area denial munitions and Claymores. Make sure a clear path of retreat is maintained back into the defense line."

"Aye, aye, sir," the shadow said crisply. "Sounds like you figure we got trouble coming, Lieutenant."

"Trouble and the Union army, Guns. We're going to have to keep their attention for a while."

"No sweat, sir." The shadow faded back into the deeper blackness of the underbrush, whispering orders over the radio link.

The lieutenant swiped perspiration from his forehead. *No sweat, huh?*

Northern Breakwater. Port Monrovia   0040 Hours, Zone Time; September 8, 2007

Standing in a clump of brush beside the service road, Private Thomas Kajenko gave a profound sigh of relief and rezipped the fly of his fatigue trousers.

"Kajenko, is that you?" The hated voice of Corporal Kuti rang hoarsely out of the night, abruptly erasing the pleasure stemming from Kajenko's relieved bladder. "What the hell are you doing away from your post?"

"I had to take a piss. That is all, Corporal," Kajenko replied, not verbalizing his heartfelt wish that it might have been Kuti's face he'd been pissing into.

"Damn you, Kajenko, are you trying to make trouble for me with the patrol sergeant? Get back on lookout! We've got a job to do out here. Next time you bloody well piss in your pants before you leave your outpost."

"Yes, Corporal, at once." Kajenko slung his FALN and began to pick his way back down to the water's edge. A fat lot that hulking bully Kuti cared about any job this squad had to do. He had assigned Thomas and his friend, Robert Smith, the two junior men in the unit, as lookouts along the water's edge while he and his cronies huddled around the watchfire drinking tea. Be damned that he and Robert were soaked to the skin in the rain. Be damned that they had not been given relief for hours. Be damned to all NCOs, especially Nigerians.

Moving with caution, Kajenko worked his way down the ten-foot-high tumble of sharp-edged boulders that made up the seaward facing of the breakwater. The sullen flickering light from the bonfire atop the breakwater hindered more than it helped, serving only to deepen the shadows in the rock clefts.

"Robert? Hey, mon?"

There was no answer to Thomas's soft call except for the suck and hiss of the waves among the great stones.

"Robert?" Spray touched Kajenko's face, carrying with it a chill. He felt his way a few feet farther along the water's edge to where he was certain he had left his compatriot.

"Rob . . ." The name died off in his throat as his hand closed on wet steel. A FALN rifle like his own lay against the slimy rocks, half submerged in the surging water.

Suddenly, the sea tore open at Kajenko's feet. Powerful hands closed around his ankles and heaved, yanking his legs out from underneath him. Kajenko found himself falling. He opened his mouth to yell, but gained only a terrifying inrush of cold salt water. Steel-strong arms sheathed in rubber closed around him, dragging him deeper into the sea, dragging him deeper into the darkness that encompassed him.

The waves broke over a second lost rifle at the base of the breakwater. Then shadows trickled up and out of the sea. Black-faced, wet-suit-clad shadows wearing soft-soled coral boots. Half a dozen of them flowed silently up the face of the seawall to merge with the shaggy salt growth along its top, moving in to surround the rain-dimmed bonfire on the access road.

The shadows looked on as a four-man mobile patrol walked in out of the night to exchange a few routine words with the squad leader at the fire. The shadows had already clocked the schedule of this mobile patrol. They noted how the squad leader stirred his men into a semblance of alertness shortly before it was due to arrive and how they rapidly sank back into lax casualness after it departed. Weapons lain aside, the Union soldiers stood close to the warmth of the bonfire in the rain, staring into its flames.

The shadows moved closer. Drawn Ka-Bar knives gleamed like bared fangs.

"The Bearclaw team should have the door open for us soon," Amanda whispered from raft to raft.

"Should," Quillain growled back. "Hey, can you tell me something? Where in thee hell did we get this screwed-up list of call signs? Dewshine, Bearclaw, Fathertree, damnedest damn things I ever heard of."

"Oh, uh, Christine came up with them. I think they're out of some kind of comic book she's fond of."

"Shoulda known—" Quillain broke off, listening to a voice in his headset earpiece. "Okay. That's it," he said after a moment. "The door's open." He keyed his tactical transmitter. "This is Strongbow lead to all Strongbow and Moonshade elements. Move in. I say again, move in."

Quillain's and Amanda's raider craft cast loose from each other, both surging forward toward the breakwater in an electric motored rush. Kneeling in the bow of her boat, Amanda touched the transmit pad of her own PRC Leprechaun transceiver.

"Moonshade to Palace. Starting penetration. I say again, starting penetration."

The stealth hoods were thrown back and hastily stowed. The passengers aboard each small craft flexed and stretched cramped muscles in preparation for the explosion of exertion about to be called for. Ahead, the dim luminescence of a single, shielded glowstick marked the landing point.

This night, the assault teams were using CRRCs—Combat Rubber Raiding Craft—a fifteen-foot inflatable rubber boat with a soft bottom instead of a rigid keel and bellypan. Less seaworthy and more fragile then the RIB-class raiders, they had one decisive advantage. They were far lighter to carry, and that would become critical over the next few seconds.

Riding the low waves, the boats nosed into the side of the breakwater.

"Over the side!" the coxswain commanded in a fierce whisper.

Amanda and the others of her boat team rolled over the low bulwarks of their little craft. She plunged chest deep into the sea, her boots scrabbling for purchase through the algae slime that coated the steep-sloped rock jumble of the breakwater wall.

"Haul out!"

Like a pack of gigantic horseshoe crabs seeking haven on the shore, the boats began a many-legged crawl up the side of the seawall. Hands clutching nylon carrying loops, the Marines heaved themselves and their equipment and motor-laden burdens upslope a few agonizing inches at a time, the only sound of protest being the harsh whistle of breath through clenched teeth.

Amanda scrambled up the breakwater with her own team, straining at her own share of the burden. A muscle cramped from her long hours huddled on the wet bottom of the raider and hot agony tore up her leg from calf to thigh. She fell forward onto unyielding granite, her palm tearing open on the sharp-edged quarry stone.

She ignored both. Gathering her legs back under her again, she caught up the carry loop once more and arched her back into the next lift. At that moment she would have died without hesitation rather than push her share of the load off on the straining silent men around her.

They crested the slope and pushed through the rain-sodden brush that fringed its top, coming to a halt at the edge of the service road. The enemy was close, no more than a hundred and fifty feet away in either direction.

"Hold." The barely breathed ghost of a word drifted down the line from Stone Quillain. The nearby watch fire burned low now. No one was left to cast wood and palm oil upon it. The wet-suit-clad point men of the Bearclaw team had already hauled the last body out of sight.

Quillain waited until all five of the assault boats were aligned along the edge of the road, then he waited a moment more, granting a second of rest to let lungs recharge on oxygen and nerves steady down.

"Stand ready. . . . Step out on my mark . . . three . . . two . . . one . . . go."

Moving simultaneously, the five teams hustled their boats across the narrow roadway. An observer at the watchpost fifty yards to shoreward would see only a single, brief occulting of the next bonfire along the line, a single shadowy passage that would not be repeated. Something easily shrugged off as unimportant.

The climb down the inner side of the breakwater was only marginally easier than the pain-racked ascent of the outer wall. The rubber boats slithered smoothly onto the water as if grateful to be returning to their proper element, the raider teams scrambling back aboard with equal gratitude.

Unseen hands grasped Amanda's MOLLE harness, hauling her over the gunwale. She collapsed into her place in the bow, the water sluicing from her soaked utilities pooling in the bottom of the boat.

The power cells engaged and the electric outboards came to silent life, the tiny flotilla moving off into the rain-misted shadows of the inner harbor.

Amanda could feel the difference here, the sheltered smoothness of the water. And there was silence beyond the faint ripple of the bow wave. No gunshots. No shouts. No flares. No hooting alarm sirens. They'd done it.

She reached up once more for the touchpad of her radio. "Moonshade to Palace. Penetration successful. In harbor. I say again, in harbor."

Back atop the breakwater, the Bearclaw team settled into the rank foliage once more. Their evacuation craft waited for them offshore. However, they had one more task to accomplish here.

In approximately ten minutes, the Union foot patrol that scouted this section of the harbor rim would return to this point on their sentry-go. If they found the squad assigned to this outpost gone, an alert would be sounded. However, if the foot patrol also quietly disappeared, it would likely be at least another fifteen minutes before an alarm would be raised.

The Bearclaw Marines unwrapped their silenced autoweapons from their protective plastic covers. Nestling gunstocks to shoulders, they lay quietly and waited for the crunch of boot soles on gravel.

Inside the Port Monrovia Breakwaters   0105 Hours, Zone Time; September 8, 2007

The raider craft ghosted across to the very center of the mile-and-a-quarter triangle of dark still water.

Quillain had explained that in reality they would actually be safer after they'd entered the harbor than they'd been loitering around outside. The "psychology of the camp" would be working for the boarding force. The harbor garrison, by instinct, would focus outward, toward a perceived external threat, and not inward, toward what they would subconsciously consider as "safe" territory.

Still, Amanda felt horribly exposed in the presence of her enemies. Were it not plastered down wetly, she was certain the hair on the back of her neck would be standing up like that of a startled cat. Lifting a pair of night glasses to her eyes, she scanned the shoreline from south to north.

Quillain's objective, the tanker *Bajara* herself, lay moored outboard alongside the oiling pier, bow to the breakwater and her stern to the harbor channel. Her hull was backlit by the pier arcs and lights glowed golden around her deckhouse. With her boilers cold, she'd be drawing her power from a pierside landline, and that would be all for the better here presently.

Amanda panned the glasses across to the massive Bong Mining Company pier a mile north along the Port's shoreside. There, tied up at the far end float, she saw her target, the harbor tug *Union Banner.*

No lights on the float. Only the dim glow of what looked like cabin lights aboard the tug itself. The thermographic scans made by the recon drones indicated that a skeleton crew manned the craft at night. Also, there would be sentries and a series of dockside patrols that seemed to work to a random search pattern.

Amanda started as something bumped her boat. Quillain's CRRC had come alongside once more. "Okay," he whispered. "We're at point of separation. Everything set with you?"

Answer him! He can't see you nod! Make your damn throat work! "Yes. Ready."

"We're by the numbers, then? Ten minutes to position. Then the strike. Then we go."

"By the numbers. Carry on, Stone."

"See you after the show, Skipper."

Quillain pushed off, and his raider motored silently away. The other four CRRCs of the boarding team followed. Blackness swallowed them, and Amanda's boat drifted alone. She scooped up a palmful of salt water and rinsed the parch from her mouth with it. Spitting the water out over the side, she keyed her transceiver. "Moonshade to Palace. At point of separation. Strike in ten. I say again. At point of separation. Strike in ten."

Mobile Offshore Base, Floater 1   0105 Hours, Zone Time; September 8, 2007

The distant thump of Claymore mines and the angry clatter of autoweapons fire issued from the overhead speakers in the briefing trailer. The taut voice of the Treestump force team leader followed.

"Palace, Palace, this is Treestump! We have hostile forces advancing north along coastal highway toward our positions. Estimate company strength. Secondary ambush has been triggered. Ambush team falling back to our perimeter under fire. How long until we are cleared for extraction?"

Christine windowed up the wallscreen segment that covered the Treestump diversion mission. "Treestump, this is Palace," she replied into her command headset. "We see your situation. It looks like you are being probed by the King Grey's Town militia garrison. We project fifty to sixty light infantry, small arms only."

"Concur, concur on that. Southern ambush team is back within perimeter. They report hostile infantry probe is retreating. We're not worried about those guys, Palace, but intel indicates we have heavies coming in from the north. Request instructions, over."

"Acknowledge that, Treestump. Stand by."

Christine looked first to the wall graphics and then to the Admiral. Red target hacks marched steadily southward toward the diversion site—the gunboats offshore and the mechanized column along the coastal highway. Hands on hips, MacIntyre scowled at the graphic imaging. "The Union's moving faster than you figured, aren't they?" he commented.

"Yes, sir, they are. We counted on the Port Mech column losing more time passing through the city. It's not happening. And those gunboats are pulling a higher rate of knots than we projected as well."

She looked up at MacIntyre. "Sir, we need to get those guys out of there soon. But if we pull them out too soon, it could give Belewa time to realize that this is just another fake-out. He could reorient on the harbor area in time to bitch the boarding ops."

MacIntyre leaned forward to the map. Not bothering with the computerized scale, he used a V of fingers as a compass, gauging distances. "This extraction is going to be tight, very tight. Can we kick any of those SeaSLAMS loose to kill those Union gunboats?"

"We only have twelve cells out there, sir. Every round's committed to taking out a key node in the Monrovia power and communications net."

"Hell, and we can't sic the seafighters on them without leaving the boarding teams in the lurch. Those damn gunboats are the problem, Chris. I'm willing to risk having the Marines swap a few rounds with that Union armor, but the *Santana* is going to be out there alone with three hostiles moving in on her. If she gets driven off station before she can recover the Treestump team . . ."

MacIntyre stepped forward again, callused fingers measuring times and distances once more. The land-based armored task force had pulled ahead just slightly. MacIntyre assessed, then spoke. "Get me an open channel to Treestump lead."

Christine pointed to the signals operator and snapped her fingers. The S.O. executed the fast call-up and nodded back to the intel.

"You're up, sir."

"Palace to Treestump, do you copy?" MacIntyre spoke levelly into his lip mike.

"Treestump 'by, Palace. Standing by for instructions." The tension in the young Marine officer's voice had ramped up minutely.

"Lieutenant Southerland, I believe it is. This is Admiral Elliot MacIntyre. You've done your job, son, and I think it's time we start getting you out of there."

"Aye, sir! Whatever you say, Admiral."

"I'm going to walk you through something here, Lieutenant. We are showing that you still have an ambush group out on the highway north of your primary position. Do they have AT capacity?"

"Yes, sir. They have a couple of Predators left."

"Good. Leave that ambush in place and pull your primary perimeter back to the beach, right back to the waterline. Do it now. Get your boats ready to launch. In about four to five minutes, your northern ambush is going to see a light armored force moving in fast down the highway toward your position. Instruct them to kill the lead vehicles, then have them lay down anything they have that can cause confusion or delay—smoke, tear gas, area denials, anything and everything they've got. Then have them fall back to your beach position. At that point, extract out to *Santana*. Dedigitate expeditiously, son. You'll just have time to pull this off, but there will be none to spare for fooling around."

"Understood, sir. Will do. This is Treestump, out."

MacIntyre went off circuit and glanced at Christine, one iron-colored eyebrow lifting. "This is my improvisation, Commander. Let's sit back and see just how magnificent it is."

Diversion Point Treestump
6 Miles East-Southeast of
Cape Mesurado   0109 Hours, Zone Time; September 8, 2007

From his station behind the helm console, the signals talker called out sharply. "Captain, word in from the landing party. The northern ambush has just engaged the Union mechanized column. The ambush force is falling back and the Marines say they are beginning extraction."

"About time," the *Santana*'s skipper shouted back from the bridge wing. "Acknowledge the message and advise all hands that we are recovering the landing party. *And turn that damn noise off!*"

The electrician's mate operating the loudspeaker system hit the power switch, and the tooth-rattling howl of gas turbines and lift fans cut off abruptly. Now from landward they could hear the clatter of machine-gun fire and the crack of rifle shots.

"Radar—" The Captain started to yell over the now silent speaker system, then caught himself. "Radar, what's the position on those Union gunboats?"

"Range seven thousand yards and closing, sir. Heading one seven five. Speed ten knots. Plot established."

"It slowed them down some when we kicked in our electronic countermeasures," the Patrol Craft's exec commented.

"Uh-huh," his skipper grunted. "They don't want to run headlong into anything while they're radar blind."

"It's only a matter of time before they get a burn-through, or pick us up visually. What happens then?"

"Hopefully we'll be the hell out of here before the subject comes up. Give the gun mounts another nudge, Joey. We or the Marines may be needing them here in a second."

"Captain," the wheelhouse talker broke in once more. "The landing party reports they are off the beach."

The PC lay with her port side to the coast and her bow aimed to the south, ready to haul clear at a moment's notice. Stepping to the port-side bridge windows, her skipper and the exec lifted night-bright binoculars to their eyes.

The Marine boats had already cleared the surf line, the rhythmic trudge of the paddlemen becoming apparent as they drove their small craft closer to the mother ship. But also apparent were dark figures dashing down onto the beach the rafts had just departed—figures that dropped prone or knelt to aim weapons.

"Bow and stern mounts!" The Captain didn't bother with the intermediary of the talker. He relied on his own lungs. "Targets on the beach! Engage antipersonnel! Open fire!"

At the Mark 96 over and unders, gunners flipped their weapon and sight selectors to grenade launcher mode and depressed the butterfly triggers. The chunkers coughed out their loads and low-velocity 40mm rounds arced across to the beach. A double string of explosions walked across the sand, catching and freezing human silhouettes in the strobe flash of shell bursts—silhouettes that distorted under the impact of concussion and fragmentation.

"This is going to point us out to those Union gunboats, sir," the exec warned.

"Can't be helped, Joey. Those Marines can either shoot back or paddle, and right now we need them paddling."

Another shadow shape lunged out onto the beach, this one massive and angular, a Panhard AML armored car crashing through the scrubwood tangle from the roadway, its 90mm gun elevating and indexing for a target.

There was no need for a command to shift targets. The Navy gunners toggled over from grenade launcher to autocannon without missing a trigger pull. The hot, flat tracer streams of the 25mm Bushmasters converged on the Union fighting vehicle. White sparks danced on the Panhard's hull and turret, penetrator impacts, each spark marking a hole punched through armor plate. Unable to cope with the torment, the Panhard fireballed, the thud of its explosion echoing offshore.

"Captain," the radar operator called. "Union gunboat squadron increasing speed to twenty knots. Five thousand yards and closing!"

"How long until we're within effective firing range?"

"We're already in range, sir!"

As if in response to the operator's words, a yellow ball of flame streaked overhead from stern to bow. A 40mm tracer round fired from a Union bow chaser.

"Aft mount! Shift to surface targets astern! Engage as you bear! Fire countermeasures! Full spectrum!"

The *Santana*'s Mark 52 RBOC launchers hurled grenade clusters overhead. Bursting, they rained down radar-scrambling metallic chaff and dense streamers of multispectral smoke. Another few precious minutes of confusion and concealment gained.

Maybe enough. The rubber raiding craft were nuzzling against the side of the PC, like a row of piglets against the flank of a sow.

"Get those men aboard! For crissakes, move! Move!"

The overheating barrels of the Mark 96 mounts glowed dull red in the chemical haze. Navy hands knelt along the railings, helping to haul Marines up and over the lip of the deck. Wild rifle slugs fired from shore snapped overhead or ricocheted off topside fittings. A wheelhouse window shattered. Someone screamed in agony as a bullet found flesh.

"Range two thousand five hundred, sir! Closing fast!"

Astern, the Union gunboats fired steadily now, pumping blind shell streams into the smoke screen that blanketed the PC. Spray jetted from the sea and the night stank of fear and cordite.

"Captain. All members of the landing party are aboard, sir!"

"Confirm that!"

"Confirmed, sir. All hands present and accounted for! Recovering boats—"

"Screw the boats! Cut 'em loose! Helmsman, all engines ahead emergency! Get us out of here!"

Turbocharged diesels roared as throttles slammed forward against their stops. *Santana* lunged ahead, the water boiling beneath her settling stern as she pulled away.

"Countermeasures, fire second salvo! Helm, keep that smoke between us and the Union squadron! Radar, what are they doing back there?"

"Standing on, Captain. They're maintaining course and speed."

The Captain glanced at the iron log on the control console. Forty knots. "Let 'em."

Two minutes later, the Union gunboat group tore through the dissipating barrier of smoke and chaff. They sought their foe, but found only a drifting cluster of abandoned rafts and a dissipating wake angling out to sea.

"General! Messages from both Captain Mosabe and the commander of the Mobile Force company. The Americans have disengaged! They're retreating!"

"Retreating!" Belewa's brows lifted incredulously. "What do you mean, retreating?"

"The American landing force has withdrawn from the coast, General," the jubilant radioman replied. "Captain Mosabe reports he and his squadron are continuing pursuit of the landing ship. Reports are coming in from the northern sector that the U.N. diversionary actions are breaking off as well. All enemy forces are withdrawing from the coast."

"And what of the hovercraft? We had a fix on them in the southern sector near the landing site. Where are they now? Do we still have contact with the American hovercraft group?"

"No contact currently reported with the hovercraft group, sir."

Belewa gripped at the edge of the track's map table like a man dazed. "No," he murmured, staring unseeing at the white-painted interior bulkhead. "That isn't right."

Sako slapped his commander on the back. "What's the matter, Obe? Can't you hear the man? We've beaten them!"

"No!" Belewa's shout rang within the steel interior of the vehicle. "There is something wrong! She would have fought!" Belewa spun around. "Don't you see!" he cried, gripping his chief of staff by the shoulders. "This was too easy! If this had been the true battle, she would have fought. The Leopard would have fought us, Sako! This was another diversion!"

Outside in the night, an evil-toned whispering whine became perceptible.

"Recall the mobile force! Recall the gunboats! Immediately!"

The radio operators grabbed for their hot mikes. But before they could kick in their transmitters, the squalling wail of high-intensity cascade jamming blared from the speakers.

Firing Point Sun Village
Three Miles off the Mouth of
Port Monrovia   0118, Hours, Zone Time; September 8, 2007

Guided initially by the distant electronic impulses of an orbiting GPU satellite, the first SeaSLAM ER howled in toward the Union coast, passing over Port Monrovia and heading for the city beyond.

As the missile approached the north bank of the Mesurado River estuary, it bobbled minutely in its flight. Miles astern, aboard the *Queen,* Gunner's Mate Danno O'Roark's hand closed around the joystick of his fire-control station, overriding the missile's onboard navigational system and assuming manual control.

The SeaSLAM pushed over and dove, the thermographic imager in its nose broadcasting a video image of the terrain ahead and below back to the *Queen* and to O'Roark's targeting screen. With sweat burning in his eyes and his jaw set, O'Roark locked the crosshairs of the system's sighting grid onto a specific geometric pattern he'd been studying all afternoon in aerial recon photographs.

The geometric pattern on the ground grew and resolved into a fenced compound. High-tension towers led to and from the area and a double row of rectangular shapes clustered at its center, a bank of heavy electrical transformers. As the thermographic image of the power relay station exploded toward him, O'Roark put his heart and soul into holding the death pip centered on those insulator-horned outlines right up until his screen went blank.

The golden flash of an explosion split the African night, followed by the sharper blue-white glare of a massive electrical discharge. Sudden, total darkness engulfed Port Monrovia.

Bong Mining Company Pier, Port Monrovia

0120, Hours, Zone Time; September 8, 2007

"Go!"

Even as she issued the command, Amanda's CRRC surged forward in a silent rush for the pier. They had only moments to work with, the brief time that confusion would reign among the port's defenders. Conning his way in via night-vision visor, the coxswain steered for the *Union Banner.*

The head of the ore-loading dock loomed clifflike over the little craft and then the float and the low stern of the tug emerged out of the darkness. Bumping quietly alongside, Amanda and the coxswain grabbed for holds on the barnacle-studded truck tire fenders that shielded the flank of the harbor craft.

Unlike the other assault boats in the boarding force, Amanda's carried a split party. There was a single four-man Marine fire team plus the small prize crew for the tug; Amanda herself, a veteran boatswain's mate to handle the towing gear and a pair of enginemen who knew their way around Marine diesel plants.

The quartet of Marines swarmed over the tug's rail in a noiseless rush, their first task to deal with both the tug's night crew and any security forces aboard. Securing the raider alongside, Amanda and her people followed the Marines onto the deck a few moments later.

"Moonshade to Palace. At objective. I say again. At objective." Lifting her finger from the touchpad, she let the SINCGARS system go to receive.

"Acknowledged, Moonshade." The reply was breathed back into her earphone from Operations. "Strongbow also reports at objective. Sun Village maintaining firing sched. Operations continue nominal."

Again it was a matter of so far, so good. Standing adjacent to the bulky dark mass of the tug's towing drum, Amanda found herself momentarily at a loss for what to do next. The weight of her pistol tugged at her belt. However, she left the weapon where it was with the holster flap buttoned. Drawing it would accomplish little, and actually firing a shot could prove catastrophic. With the other Navy hands clustered warily behind her, she stood poised and listening.

Beyond the hiss of the waves around the pier pilings, she heard only a scattering of sound from the port, a yelled order, the racing of a truck engine, the crash of a warehouse door closing. In the distance came the thud of another heavy explosion. The seafighters were continuing their SLAM bombardment of the city, spacing the rounds out to provide a further diversion away from events in the port area.

From aboard the tug itself, there came other noises. A swift and stealthy rush of footfalls. A thump that could be felt through the deck underfoot. An exclamation that trailed off into a faint whimpering sob. Then silence, followed by two muffled splashes near the tug's bow.

The Marine fire team leader materialized out of the shadows. "All secure, ma'am."

"Very well," she replied softly. "Boats, check out the towing gear. Buckley, Smith, go take a look in the engine room. Get me a report on how soon we can get her under way. I'll be in the wheelhouse."

Whispered "aye ayes" came back.

Amanda followed the Marine team leader forward down the tug's starboard side. "Four men aboard all told, ma'am," he reported. "Two soldiers and two civilian crewmen. We've got the soldiers taken care of and over the side."

"And the crewmen?"

"Awaiting your call, ma'am."

Amidships they came to the entry of the tug's main cabin. A second Marine stood a silent sentry beside the half-open hatch. Inside, the last two members of the fire team guarded the prisoners.

The tug hands were a pair of lean and weathered African seamen clad only in ragged shorts. They had been shoved down onto the bench of the mess table, facing the deck entry. With their hands bound behind their backs with nylon riot cuffs and their mouths sealed by strips of camo tape, only their eyes could express their terror.

Amanda paused in the hatchway for a moment. The fear she read in the expressions of the two men were an aspect of her profession that she didn't enjoy. These two sailors were not enemies of either herself or of humanity as a whole. Nor did they have anything to do with the course being steered by Obe Belewa or the West African Union.

There was nothing to be done about it, however, except to brush them out of the way as gently as possible. "Put them under," she said.

The Marine guards dug yellow injector tubes out of their cargo pockets. Before the two Union seamen could realize what was happening, the injector tips had been socked against their thighs. Heavy-gauge, spring-loaded needles punched into flesh and a massive drug charge followed. After a few moments of struggle, the eyes of the two sailors rolled back into their heads and they collapsed against the mess table, no doubt wondering if they would ever wake up again.

They would. The injectors had originally been designed to carry doses of atropine as an emergency counter to nerve gas exposure. These, though, intended for use by Special Forces personnel, had been loaded with a carefully metered dose of barbiturate potent enough to knock an adult human unconscious and keep him so for several hours.

"Dump them on the float, Corporal," Amanda ordered, "and throw a tarp or something over them so they won't be too obvious. Then stand by to cast off all lines."

"Aye, aye, ma'am."

Alone, Amanda climbed the weather ladder to the wheelhouse atop the fore end of the superstructure. The tug's small bridge smelled of diesel, salt mildew, and stale cigarette smoke. The only illumination filtered in faintly through the wheelhouse's 360-degree sweep of windows or trickled up the interior ladderway from the cabin night-lights.

Amanda had a night-vision visor, a flashlight, and several glowsticks distributed around her harness. However, she was on the bridge of a ship now. This was her world. She didn't need vision to find her way.

Stepping carefully, she crossed to the center console, her fingertips touching, exploring, and identifying. Wheel . . . binnacle . . . throttles . . . propeller controls . . . engine-ready lights . . . auxiliary switches . . . engine-room interphone. The position of each control grafted itself into her brain.

Let's see. Panel lights. Should be this one.

Click! Green glowed behind a few of the gauges.

Okay. So far, so good. Binnacle light.

Click! Amanda nodded to herself as the compass dome lit. This tug had seen some hard usage and short maintenance, but at least the compass had been kept aligned. That wasn't much, but it was something. She lifted the battered interphone out of its cradle and squeezed the call button. It worked too. That was something else.

"Smith here."

"Smith. This is the Captain. I'm checking out the wheelhouse. How does it look down there?"

"Like they've been using a pack of goddamn orangutans for an engine-room crew." A good motor mac's honest outrage at the abuse of machinery could be heard in his voice.

"We saw her up and running this afternoon. Are the plants still in one piece?"

"I think they're pretty much all here, ma'am. It's hard to tell with some of the jack-leg patch jobs done on this thing."

A muscle jumped in Amanda's jaw. "Can you get her going?"

"I think so, ma'am. The injectors seem to work, and we got a charge of air for the starter. Uh, I'm just hoping this engine instrumentation is trashed, though."

"Why's that?"

"Because according to what I'm seeing on these gauges, we got no bunkerage. The fuel tanks read empty."

The Oil Tanker *Bajara*   1020 Hours, Zone Time; September 8, 2007

"Go!"

As the sudden curtain of total darkness swept over the southern side of the harbor basin, the primary boarding force made its move on the stern quarter of the *Bajara*. There were lookouts and sentries posted aboard the tanker, but they had been using white visible-spectrum light as their perimeter defense. Suddenly deprived of it, they went blind.

The five assault boats slid in under the curved side of the ship. Feather-weight titanium and Fiberglas boarding ladders had been assembled aboard each craft. Now the ladders swayed upward, the rubber-sheathed hooks at their upper ends silently fitting over the lip of the deck edge.

Quillain was the first man on the ladder from his boat. The ladder's structure, seemingly fragile, yet strong enough to bear several times his weight, quivered unnervingly as he clambered swiftly upward to the tanker's deck.

Yet not quite fast enough. A bewildered Union soldier peered over the rail almost at the head of Quillain's ladder, looking down full into Quillain's face. Through his night-vision visor, Quillain saw the African's eyes widen and his mouth open to yell.

The shots from the boat below were so well silenced that Quillain didn't hear their firing. He only felt the shock waves generated by the flight of the bullets brushing the back of his neck. The Union soldier attempted his yell, but only a faint sodden gasp emerged. No man can shout with a .45 hardball round driven through each lung.

Quillain lunged up the last rung of the ladder. Grabbing the cable railing with one hand, his other went for the front of the Union sentry's shirt. With an explosive heave, he launched the man outboard and over the side with enough force to clear the raider boat below.

The *Bajara*'s deckhouse lights flickered and came on again. Someone had gotten the landline disconnected and an auxiliary generator started. But it came too late to be of any use to her defenders. Like the buccaneers of old, the Marines were pouring over her rail.

Each squad and each fire team of each squad of the boarding platoon had its own specific objective or string of objectives. Dispersing outward, they began to fulfill them. The Foxmen cleared the tanker's decks with a deft and coolly professional ruthlessness, the only audible noise being the pad of foam-soled assault boots and the occasional cough or flutter of a sound-suppressed firearm.

Quillain personally led the force targeting the tanker's bridge, serving as point man for the headlong rush up the exterior superstructure ladderways. There hadn't been enough of the sound-suppressed Heckler and Koch SOC pistols and H&K-5 submachine guns available to issue a silenced firearm to every member of the boarding party, and Quillain had passed on the chance to carry one. He had a quiet killer of his own he preferred to rely on.

With the coming of the short, lightweight assault rifle, the bayonet had almost disappeared from the scheme of things on the battlefield. However, the Mossberg 590 combat shotgun was the last good bayonet mount in U.S. service, and Stone Quillain was one of the last true aficionados of this ancient martial art. Honed to a razor's edge and a needle point, an issue M-7 gleamed from the mounting lugs of his personal weapon.

Storming around the ladder stage on the second level of the deckhouse, Quillain found himself confronting a figure clad in Union army camouflage. Gaping at the Marine, the Union officer clawed for the pistol holster at his belt. Countering, Quillain exploded into the long-practiced moves of the ancient pikeman's drill. Lunge! Twist! Extract!

The Union officer folded over, clutching at his pierced belly and retching blood. Reversing his weapon, Quillain stepped in, driving the edge of the Mossberg's composite stock downward upon the juncture of spine and skull with surgical precision, shattering the first vertebra with the lethal and merciful vertical butt stroke. The dead man's body refused to fall fast enough. Quillain bulldozed it aside and continued the race upward.

⚑◆

On the *Bajara*'s bridge, Captain Moustapha Ahmed recalled nervously that he had not knelt to Mecca his five times that day. Truth be told, he had not done so even once, and should the absolute factuality be demanded, he rarely did when he was aboard ship and out of sight of the mullahs. However, this night, he deeply regretted not accommodating the demands of his faith.

The bridge windscreens faced to the south, and intermittently the flare of a powerful explosion outlined the horizon beyond the port. American cruise missiles. Something not good to think of when one was sitting atop thousands of tons of highly inflammable petroleum.

Ahmed wished fervently he'd been able to unload his cargo this day. He wished even more fervently that he might get himself and his ship out of here. Most fervently of all, he wished that he had prayed. This was not a time or place to have Allah displeased with you.

The Union Special Forces commanding officer of the ship's guard must have read Ahmed's expression. He grinned at the Algerian skipper's discomfort, sharing the smile with his lieutenant and the two sentries who also occupied the *Bajara*'s wheelhouse.

"What's the matter, Captain Ahmed?" the African officer said. "The U.N. is putting on a little fireworks show in your honor. Don't you appreciate it?"

"It is an honor I would avoid if I could," the Algerian grunted back. "What's to prevent them from attacking the harbor itself, and us?"

"Half of the Union army, Captain. But only half."

The Special Forces officer grinned again. Then his face collapsed inward into a bloody mush and the back of his head exploded, spraying brain matter across the port side of the bridge. Ahmed heard a series of soft coughing sounds behind him and felt silent deadly things hiss past. The three remaining Union soldiers also twisted and writhed in a few steps of a grotesque and ugly dance before crumpling to the deck, scarlet patches blossoming on their uniforms.

Ahmed did not want to see what was behind him. Yet he could not keep from turning around.

A second group of solders had burst in from the starboard bridge wing, tall and bulky men with pale eyes and artificially darkened skin, each bearing a far more lethal-looking accumulation of war tools than any of the Union troops had possessed. A literal giant of a man stood at their head, a massive and exotic-looking weapon held ready in his hands, blood sheening its bayonet.

SEA FIGHTER **363**

The giant looked deep into Ahmed's eyes and scowled disapprovingly, like a god who had judged a sinner and who now was deciding upon the appropriate eternal punishment.

The time was wrong. He had neither prayer rug nor the true bearing to Mecca. Yet, as he clutched at the edge of the chart table for support and felt the hot urine trickling down his leg, Captain Moustapha Ahmed prayed with a fervor he did not know he possessed.

◇✦

Belowdecks, other Algerians learned to pray as well. In the seamen's quarters, the majority of the *Bajara*'s civilian crew had been lounging in their sour-sheeted bunks, idly complaining about the lack of shore leave, women, and justice in general.

Suddenly the passageway hatch crashed open. The Arabic seamen looked up and found themselves staring at two men with green faces.

One of the two stood directly in the hatchway, a hand grenade clenched in his fist, the safety lever held down but with the pin already drawn. His cold blue eyes swept the room, and he lifted the grenade a little higher so that all in the compartment could see it. With great deliberation he shook his head, silently advising the Algerians not to try anything stupid. Beside him, the second Marine stood poised and ready to slam the watertight door in the face of any rush to escape the explosive results of an error in judgment.

Wisdom lived in the crew's quarters of the *Bajara* that night. No one moved. No one even breathed.

◇✦

Amidships on the tanker's weather deck, two Union sentries stood watch at the head of the gangway. Maintaining an easy parade rest, they shifted their weight from leg to leg as their tour on post inched past. Beyond the peak of their efficiency curve as sentinels, their attention had started to drift, random trains of thought distracting them.

Curses at the rain. More curses at the line platoon that had the pier watch. Those bastards had the undeserved shelter of the dockside sheds. Concern over the continuing thunder of the Monrovia bombardment. More concerns over the way the war and the world were going. Thoughts of women. Thoughts of home.

Their daydreaming killed them.

Sergeant Tallman came up swiftly and noiselessly behind his man. The burly Marine NCO's left arm whipped up and around the taller Union soldier's throat, the bone of the forearm smashing the carotid artery, jugular vein, and windpipe. Tallman's right arm came around in a lower arc, driving his K-Bar knife upward into the Union man's belly and through the diaphragm, then savagely across from left to right in the killing slash.

Hot blood gushed across Tallman's wrist and the Union soldier's back arched in agony. Tallman tightened the lock across his throat, bottling up the death scream. The African's rifle fell from his nerveless hands, and another camo-clad arm darted out of the shadows, catching it up before it could clatter to the deck.

The second sentry had simultaneously been taken out in the same quiet and savagely effective manner, and the bodies of both Union men collapsed back onto the deck. Hastily, Tallman and another Marine yanked off their K-Pot helmets and donned the uniform caps of the two dead soldiers. Catching up the Union-issue FALN rifles as well, the two Marines resumed the sentry stations at the head of the gangway, the distinctive silhouette of the headgear and the long-barreled rifles adequate to indicate "friend" in the misty darkness of the night. The remainder of the Marine squad fanned out on either side of the gangway, keeping low along the railing.

The guard had been relieved.

⌖

"Gangway secure."

"Forecastle secure."

"Crew's quarters secure."

"Engine room all secure."

One by one the reports came whispering in over the tactical circuit, the little PRC communicators having been frequency-set to work even through the steel of the tanker's hull.

And not a single loud round's been fired yet, Quillain mentally rejoiced. *Hallelujah and holy shit! Come on, Lord, keep it comin'!*

The paralytic tanker captain had been carried down to the main cabin to join the rest of his officers under guard, and the bodies of the dead Union troopers had been dumped out onto the bridge wing. Alone in the wheelhouse, Quillain was the master of all he surveyed. At least for the moment.

"Belowdeck teams," he called. "Any sign of those kids yet?"

"No sign."

"Negatory, Skipper."

"Negative."

"Roger that, all teams. Maintain search." *Wouldn't it be fine if they'd all just*

SEA FIGHTER **365**

been sent home to Momma? Better not expect it, though. God's been obliging so far, but even he's got to have his limits.

Quillain switched radios and went over to the command circuit. "Strongbow to Palace. Primary objective is secured. Situation nominal. Ready to receive Moonshade. I repeat, ready to receive Moonshade."

"Acknowledged, Strongbow. Moonshade has secured secondary. Operation proceeding."

Harbor Tug *Union Banner*   **0131 Hours, Zone Time; September 8, 2008**

"Palace to Moonshade. Strongbow reports primary secured. Strongbow standing by."

"Roger, Palace. Moonshade moving out. I say again, Moonshade moving out."

Amanda lifted her hand from the radio controller and glanced down at the engine-room interphone. What if those fuel gauges weren't broken? Ether way, there wasn't anything that could be done about it now. She picked up the interphone and buzzed the engine room.

"Smith. Start engines and make ready to answer bells."

Gripping the cord-wrapped wheel, she waited.

After a few moments, the hiss of a diesel air starter came from belowdecks, followed by the clanking rumble of a cold plant turning over, and finally, after a heart-stopping pause, the burbling bark of an ignition. A burst of sparks issued from one of the narrow twin stacks aft of the wheelhouse and the big medium-speed marine diesel bellowed to life, firing on all ten of its cylinders. A few moments later, its partner cranked over and joined in the hammering iron chorus.

The wheelhouse interphone rasped. "Those orangutans turned out to be pretty fair engineers, Captain. You got power and the bridge engine controls are engaged. You'd better let her warm up a second, though."

"Understood, Smith."

Amanda socked the phone back into its cradle. She'd hung her night-vision visor around her neck, switched on and ready, and now she lifted it over her eyes. The dark world outside the wheelhouse snapped into green-tinted light. The Marines of the fire team became visible, crouching down along the tug's deck railing. So did the unconscious tarp-covered forms of the tug's crew on the float and the next set of Union sentries down at the midpoint of the pier. Amanda could see them well enough to note they were looking in the tug's direction.

        J AMES H. C OBB

They couldn't afford to wait for any more of a warm-up. "On deck," she spoke into the tactical radio. "Cast off all lines."

The Marines sprang to the unaccustomed task. With a final look fore and aft, Amanda popped the tug's propeller controls into reverse and cracked the throttles wider. The tug shivered as her propellers cut water. Slowly she started to drift astern, the pier pilings edging past. There was a squeal and a thump as the tug cleared the float dolphins, and then they were clear and backing into the open harbor.

Gauging the clearance, Amanda spun the wheel hard over, kicking the stern around. She might be battered and maltreated, but the tug still answered her helm crisply and the engines seemed to be pulling strongly. *Dear Lord, let there just be a few gallons in the tanks. That's all I need.*

Amanda shifted the propeller controls to forward and opened the throttles to half ahead, aligning the bow with the deckhouse lights of the *Bajara,* the sole constellation glowing in the darkness of the harbor. With that done, she reached over to the auxiliary panel and closed a switch.

"Captain," an urgent call sounded on the tac circuit. "The running lights just came on!"

"I know, Sergeant. I just turned them on," she replied into the lip mike. "That's what the tug's real skipper would do if he'd been called out on a routine job. And we want to keep this all routine for just as long as we can."

Waypoint Sun Village   **0132 Hours, Zone Time; September 8, 2007**

The firing cell thumped back flush with the *Queen of the West*'s weather deck.

"All rounds expended," Snowy reported. "All missions launched."

"Right." Steamer nodded. He rocked the swimmer throttles forward and spoke into his headset mike. "Royalty to Palace. Fire missions complete. Proceeding to Waypoint Blue Mountain. Royalty to squadron. Taking departure now."

The acknowledgments flowed back as the seafighter gained silent way, edging closer to Port Monrovia's harbor mouth.

"Snow, what's on tactical? Where's that Union squadron?"

"They're still out there sweeping for the *Santana,*" she replied. "I don't think they caught the recall order yet. I think our jammers have 'em cut off."

"Yeah. Let's just hope they keep right on going."

"Yeah. . . . Hey, Steamer, what happens when they do get the word? What if we get caught inside when we go for the pickup?"

"Then I suspect, Snow, that there will be one hell of a fight on the way out."

Footsteps clattered up the ladderway and Scrounger Caitlin stuck her head up into the cockpit. "Eyeball verification on the launching cell, Skipper. Fully retracted and secured."

"Good deal, Scrounge. How's everybody down in the hull?"

"Hangin' in," the turbine tech replied. "How's the mission coming?"

"By the numbers so far, but I think things are going to blow pretty quick. We're moving in to the recovery point. Tell everyone to look alive."

"Yeah . . . yes, sir."

Snowy twisted in her harness and looked aft at the turbine tech. "Hey, Scrounge, you okay?"

"Yes, ma'am. I'm fine."

⚜

Sandra Caitlin hastily dropped back down the ladder. She didn't want to talk to anyone about what she felt like just at the moment. She recalled what had happened the last time she'd tried to speak to someone about this vague and formless uneasiness creeping into her guts. Pausing at the base of the ladder, she gripped the handrails, trying to control the protracted shudder that rippled through her body.

Aboard the Tanker *Bajara*   **0135 Hours, Zone Time; September 8, 2007**

"Strongbow, Strongbow, do you copy on this circuit?"

The familiar husky alto came through faintly on Quillain's tactical set. "Roger that, Moonshade, I got you."

"We are under way and inbound. What's the situation there?"

"Still green and quiet. We think we've got the guard force eliminated and the crew secure, but we're still working a compartment-by-compartment search. We haven't found those damn kids yet, either. I'm hoping they may already be over the side."

Stepping out onto the starboard-side bridge wing, Quillain looked aft. He saw the set of red and green running lights standing boldly in toward the tanker as if the craft that carried them had every right in the world to be there.

"Keep that search going until you're absolutely sure," Amanda replied. "You've got about five minutes before I come alongside. We can't risk getting a bunch of children trapped in the middle of a firefight."

At that instant, somewhere down in the superstructure, an automatic weapon emptied in a single protracted burst, an angry flurry of single shots following.

An excited voice cut into the channel. "This is Corporal Clasky, second squad. Skipper, we got trouble on deck two! We got a man down! We need a corpsman!"

"Roger that! Corpsman to deck two! All elements! We are blown! We are blown! Clasky, what have we got down there?"

"It's those goddamn kids, sir! The little bastards have guns! They're shooting at us!"

At the midships gangway, Sergeant Tallman thumbed off the FALN's safety and muttered under his breath to the men crouching along the railings. "Look alive, boys. We got business."

In response to the small-arms fire aboard the tanker, Union troops in platoon strength streamed out from the dockside shelters and double-timed for the gangway. The officer leading then yelled up a question. Tallman responded with a casual wave of his arm, the details of his equipment and uniform still lost in the deck's shadows.

"Steady, let 'em come in. Let 'em bunch up. Grenade launchers, load antipersonnel. Pick your targets." Tallman crooned softly, easing the mode selector of the FALN to full automatic. "Make the first one count, then rock and roll."

The lead elements of the Union platoon clustered at the base of the gangway and their officer set first foot upon it. That was Tallman's mark.

"Take 'em!" he yelled. Whipping the FALN to his shoulder, he held down the trigger.

The Union platoon melted under the raking storm of bullets and buckshot. Bodies crumpled to the pier decking or fell into the gap between the ship and the pilings. Other Union troopers out in the night recovered rapidly from their surprise, however. Muzzle flashes flickered back among the dockside sheds, and slugs whined off the tanker's side.

"Stay down! Stay back in the cover of the deck lip. Riflemen, set to semiauto! Grenadiers and SAW men, pick your targets! Conserve your ammo!" Tallman reached for his own M-4 lying on deck nearby, then noted the sprawled form of the Union sentry he had slain. Reaching over, he grabbed a fresh twenty-round clip of 7.62 NATO from the dead soldier's belt. "Waste not, want not," the NCO muttered, socking the reload into the FALN's magazine well.

Port Monrovia Defense HQ   **0135 Hours, Zone Time; September 8, 2007**

"What is our signals status?" Belewa demanded. "Who do we have communications with?"

"High-intensity jamming on all standard bands, General," the sweating radioman replied, frantically hunting up and down the frequency range for clear air. "Possibly we are being received elsewhere, but I can't read any acknowledgments."

"What about the main government station at Mamba Point?"

"I had burn-through with them for a moment, General. But then they dropped off the net. I cannot reestablish contact."

Belewa gritted his teeth. If the first American SLAM missile had destroyed the Port power-relay station, then the second must have targeted the transmitters on the top floor of the Mamba Point Hotel.

"The city telephone exchange is down," Sako Atiba reported from his position, crouched before the command track's bank of field phones. "We have only our tactical landlines around the harbor area. The Americans are executing their classic Baghdad strike template, using their cruise missiles to kill our communications and power."

"They've held off on their radio jamming until this moment as well," Belewa muttered. "Their primary assault is under way and we still aren't seeing it. Check all perimeter outposts. Something has to be happening out there!"

"Yes, sir."

Belewa stepped out of the fuggy interior of the Styre and stood on the lowered tail ramp. Looking up at the sky, he let the rain cool his face, wishing it could also cool the fevered thoughts in his mind. He had lost the initiative and he was losing the battle. He could sense it. Bit by bit, the Leopard was hooking away his control with deft claws. She laughed at him, taunting, dancing always just out of his reach as she worked to steal his kingdom.

Thank God for the rain. It hid the tears of frustration and rage from his men.

"General!" Atiba appeared in the rear hatch. "Northern sector reports one of their outpost squads has disappeared. Also that one of the breakwater patrols is overdue. They are investigating—"

Belewa spun around to face his chief of staff. "To hell with that! We know what's happening. They're already inside! Get through to Payne Field any way you can. Tell them to launch that gunship! Get it out here! Then order the reserve company down to the oiling pier! Reinforce the inner perimeter and get me the guard commander aboard the tanker!"

"Yes, sir!" Atiba disappeared back into the command track's interior, snapping commands to its crew. He returned after only a moment. "General, there is no response on the tanker landline!"

From the direction of the oiling pier came a sudden, muffled crackle of

JAMES H. COBB

gunshots. More weapons joined in a few moments later, sharper, more piercing discharges building in a rising crescendo of automatic fire.

"They're trying to board the tanker," Atiba exclaimed wildly, staring out into the night.

Belewa instinctively gauged the volumes and angles of the discharges. "No . . . No, they're already aboard the tanker! Sako! Fire full illumination. Then order every man we've got to converge on the oiling pier! Every man!"

Yanking the Browning Hi Power from his belt holster, Belewa ran in the direction of the growing firefight.

Harbor Tug *Union Banner*   **0138 Hours, Zone Time; September 8, 2007**

Monitoring her own end of the tactical net, Amanda heard Quillain's cry of "We are blown! We are blown!" and knew that the operation had just run out of grace time. She couldn't hear the gunfire at first over the chugging rumble of the tug's engines. But other indications of the Union response swiftly became apparent.

Flare rockets and mortar-launched star shells arced out over the harbor and burst, cracking open the night with their glare. Amanda's night-vision visor overloaded, and impatiently she yanked it away from her eyes. She also reached instinctively for the running light switch, then hesitated. There would be no cover of darkness now anyway, and perhaps the Union defenders had yet to realize that two of their vessels had been hijacked.

"Stone, do you copy?" *To hell with radio protocol now!* "What's your situation?"

"It's those goddamn kids!" Quillain snarled back. "They aren't just kids. They're a bunch of those kid soldiers you hear about down in these parts."

Indeed she had heard about them. They were an aspect of the brutal, total-war conflicts that had ravaged West Africa. Ten- and eleven-year-old boys, children barely big enough to pick up a rifle, had been drawn or thrust into the ranks of the combatants. Frequently they became some of the most savage and merciless killers. This was the advantage the child warrior had over the adult, not having lived long enough to either understand what it meant to take life or to fear death.

To Obe Belewa's credit, he had never used them in his battles. At least until now.

"They're forted up in one of the bunkrooms," Stone continued. "The little shits are hosing down anything that moves in the passageway. They've already got one man wounded."

"Can you get at them, Stone?"

"We're working on it. But even if we do, ain't no way we're going to get them or the Algerian crew down that gangway. We got a major firefight going along the pier. Union reinforcements are already movin' in on us."

"I'm coming in fast as well. Have the line-handling detail standing by. I'll be coming in under your counter in about two more minutes. Switch to alternative evacuation plan. I say again, switch to alternative evacuation plan."

"Roger that, Skipper. Line-handling detail is standing by. We'll give you all the cover we can. I'm going below to see if I can get those damn kids sorted out."

"Hurry, Stone! We don't have a lot of time here."

"You tell me about it!" The Marine clicked off circuit.

Amanda edged the tug's throttles open another notch and gave the wheel a half-spin to starboard. She would swing wide and move in from the southwest, keeping the bulk of the tanker between herself and the pier for as long as she could. Given the fight raging between the boarding party and the Union defense forces, maybe the tug would be ignored for a time longer. At least until the Union troops realized what she was attempting.

On the tug's foredeck, her own "main battery," the four Marines of the prize crew, crouched low behind the bow towing butts. They had come prepared for heavy combat, two of the men bearing Squad Automatic Weapons, the second pair M4/M203 carbine and grenade launcher combinations.

"On deck!" Amanda yelled through the glassless side panel of the windscreen. "Hold your fire until we're fired upon directly. Don't tip off anyone that there's a prize crew aboard."

The team leader responded with an acknowledging wave.

The pier and the tanker loomed ahead, the *Bajara*'s superstructure now starkly outlined by sweeping vehicle spotlights. Amanda could hear the gunfire now over the churning of the bow wave and the rumble of the *Banner*'s diesels.

Aboard the Tanker *Bajara*   0140 Hours, Zone Time: September 8, 2007

As the rifle slugs whined past, Quillain dodged to one side and hunkered closer to the deck. However, as conscious thought caught up with this actions, he realized that it was a futile gesture. The bullets had been ricochets, glancing wildly off the bulkhead at the "L" bend in the passageway ahead. He was as likely to be hit by one while standing erect as he was crawling on his belly.

Corporal Clasky's rifle team, minus their casualty, pressed back against the inner bulkhead. "What's the situation?" Quillain demanded, dropping in behind them.

"No change, sir," Clasky replied. "The little sons of bitches tried to bust out a minute or so ago, but we discouraged 'em with a couple of flashbangs. Other than that, they've just been shooting up the place like they're sitting on a truckload of ammo."

"Let me have a look." Quillain edged past the other Marines to the bend in the passageway. The fire team leader handed him a small stainless-steel mirror, and Quillain used it to peer around the corner.

He observed another short length of grimy ship's corridor with a watertight door centered in it. The door stood half open, and as Quillain looked on, a small face, dark and gaunt, peered cautiously around the rusted hatch frame.

Lord A'mighty! They hadn't been exaggerating. They were just kids, not even old enough to be looking at the girls yet.

"We got the passageway on the other side secured?" Quillain demanded.

The team leader nodded. "Yeah, we got another four men on the other side. Corporal Donovan and his guys."

"Right." Quillain nodded. "We give 'em one chance. Then we go in after 'em."

Quillain bellowed around the corner, using his best drill instructor inflection. "Listen up in there! This is the United States Marines! Surrender! Drop your weapons! Come out with your hands behind your head and nobody gets hurt!"

The first half of the reply he received consisted of a barrage of shrill, defiant, and amazingly obscene invective. Then the muzzle of a Sterling machine pistol slithered around the door frame, the weapon's clip being emptied in a single long barrel-burning burst.

"Okay, you little dickheads," Quillain muttered. "You asked for it. Corporal, pass the word to all hands belowdecks. Mask up."

Quillain doffed his helmet for a second and dug a gas mask out of its pouch on his MOLLE harness. With the other members of the firing team following suit, he popped the safety caps off the filters and settled the mask over his head, tugging the straps snug for an airtight seal.

"You boys set?" he asked over his shoulder, his voice muffled.

A string of equally muffled acknowledgments came back.

"Okay, Corporal, I want you and one other man with me. Have him put in another flashbang first. Then you and I follow it up with a couple of cans of CS. I want a fast, heavy concentration. We got to knock the fight out of these brats."

"You got it, sir."

"Okay, we go on three. One . . . two . . . three!"

The first Marine pivoted around the corner, aiming a hard-thrown flashbang grenade at the hatchway. The flashbang was a nonlethal munition that, true to its name, produced a dazzling burst of light and a loud but harmless explosion potent enough to momentarily stun an unprepared target.

The piercing C-R-A-A-A-C-K of the munition reverberating in the passageway was the signal for Quillain and the corporal to move. Yanking the pins out of the tear gas cylinders, they pitched them into the bunkroom, glancing them off the open door so they landed on the deck inside. Two softer muffled thuds followed, then a growing chorus of gags and retches.

The boy soldiers had been unprepared for the charge of riot gas. Gasping from the flashbang's concussion, they found themselves suddenly inhaling lungfuls of biting military-strength CS. A scream resounded from the bunkroom as someone tried to snatch up one of the grenades to hurl it back into the passageway. The young hero had discovered too late that the grenade's thermal antitamper charge had already heated the metal canister to a sizzling temperature.

Quillain and the two fire teams moved in to flank the bunkroom hatchway. Even through his mask, Quillain felt a coolness around his eyes, a leakage that indicated the gas concentration in the area was truly ferocious. No unprotected individual would be able to take it for long.

Sure enough, the first boy warrior came stumbling blindly out of the compartment, a warrior no longer, but a weeping, terrified child seeking escape. Quillain swatted the submachine gun out of his hands. Yanking the double-lapped cartridge belt from around his waist, Stone shoved him on down the line to the other Marines. The other youths followed, wheezing and helpless, all will to resist quashed.

"Get 'em up to the main messroom with the Algerians," Quillain commanded. "And get 'em in life jackets."

"Should we try and wash the tear gas off of 'em, Skipper?"

"Don't bother. They're going to be taking a swim here in a minute."

Port Monrovia Oiling Pier   **0145 Hours, Zone Time; September 8, 2007**

Belewa shoved aside the barrel of the Carl Gustav launcher. "No rockets!" he yelled to the weapons crew. "That's an order! No rockets! No grenades! We can't risk setting fire to that ship!"

Dropping down in the shelter of a piling head, the General studied the pierside battleground through smarting, smoke-narrowed eyes. The Americans had the position, no doubt of that. The tanker's steel sides rose a good ten feet above the dock like the wall of a medieval castle, the gap between the hull and the pier's edge serving as its moat.

The American Marines were taking full advantage of this high ground, pouring a steady hail of gunfire down from the deck edge upon anything that moved below. Other Marine marksmen raked the full length of the pier from the *Bajara*'s superstructure, the sprawled bodies of Union soldiers on the pier's decking standing testament to both their position and accuracy. Nor did the Americans have any limitations on the weapons they could employ. Marine grenadiers had demolished and ignited the dockside sheds with high explosives and white phosphorus, the spreading flames further hindering the Union counteroffensive.

If the Americans had a weakness, it had to be in the limited size of their boarding force. Belewa could see but a single chance. The gangway amidships. The "drawbridge" to the "castle." Seize that and the tanker's decks might be regained. There the Union's superior numbers would count once more.

With the clatter of treads and the bellow of an unmuffled diesel, a Steyr armored personnel carrier lumbered up to the base of the oiling dock. Too heavy to proceed out onto the pier decking, it dropped its tail ramp and discharged its rifle squad. Getting to his feet, Belewa ran to the side of the idling APC, ignoring the bullet strikes around his feet.

"Use your machine gun," he yelled up to the track commander. "Hold this position and fire on the tanker's deckhouse. Keep their heads down!"

The track commander nodded broadly in reply and swung his GPMG in line with the *Bajara*'s superstructure. As the weapon began chopping off short, aimed bursts, Belewa continued on to where the track's infantry squad had gone to ground.

"Bren gunners! Lay down covering fire! Drive them back from the rail! Riflemen, follow me! Forward!"

Harbor Tug *Union Banner*   0145 Hours, Zone Time; September 8, 2007

Amanda doused the tug's running lights as she came in on the tanker's quarter. Spinning the wheel to its port stop, she whipped the *Banner* into a tight, foaming turn. Handy as with all of her breed, the little tug came about almost within her own length, her stern coming in line with the *Bajara*'s.

Amanda flipped the propeller controls into reverse. Propwash boiled forward along the tug's flanks as it shuddered to a stop and then began to back down, sliding in toward the tanker like a car easing into a tight parking slot.

"On deck," Amanda snapped into her lip mike. "Stand by the line thrower and the towing drum. Prepare to establish the tow."

"Aye, aye."

"On deck, aboard the *Bajara*. Are you set to receive our line?"

"This is the *Bajara*. Standing by."

The sharp crackle of gunfire could be heard over the hot mike of the Marine line handler. The steel bulk of the tanker's hull and the rumble of the *Banner*'s engines muffled the sounds of battle somewhat on the tug's bridge. However, Amanda could sense the pierside engagement growing in intensity.

As yet, little of the firepower had been aimed in the direction of the *Banner*. Huddling in the tanker's shadow, the tug was still not being considered as a factor by the Union defense forces. How long this fragile immunity would continue was anyone's guess.

Playing with the throttles and propeller controls, Amanda eased the tug in as close as she dared, killing the tug's stern way with a last burst of power. The tanker's quarter loomed over them like a convex cliffside, the outlines of the Marine line team peering over her rail.

"On deck. Cast line!"

At the tug's stern, a line thrower cracked and a rippling coil of thin nylon cord trailed the throw weight up and over the tanker's rail.

"On the tug. We have the carrier."

"Second carrier on. Heave away." In the best navy tradition, the boatswain's mate on the *Banner*'s aft deck didn't bother with the radio; his own bellow overrode the sound of the gunfire.

The Marines drew up the lead end of a second, heavier nylon line, then the *Banner*'s towing drum began to clank and rumble and the rusty length of a heavy steel hawser swayed slowly toward the tanker's deck, drawn upward by the straining muscles of the line handlers.

Copper-jacketed lead ricocheted and a glass panel in the bridge windscreen exploded. Amanda flinched away from the spraying shards, her narrowed eyes focused on the inching progress of the hawser.

It seemed to take hours for the cable to extend upward. At last, the end of the hawser reached the *Bajara*'s rail and the inexperienced line handlers wrestled with its stiff metallic weight. *Oh, God, don't drop it!* Amanda pleaded mentally.

Hogged across to the central towing butt on the tanker's stern, the towline finally was hooked into place. In the flare light, Amanda saw the acknowledging wave of the line handlers.

"On deck. We have the tow established. Give me some slack—I'm running us out to set a short harness. Stand by to set your wildcat on my mark. On deck on the *Bajara*! Cast off all mooring lines. I say again, cast off all mooring lines!"

Emerging from the tanker's deckhouse, Quillain ran forward, hunkering low to stay out of the arc of fire streaming up from the pier. The volumes were building as more and more Union soldiers joined the fight. Bodies clad in Marine utilities lay sprawled along the rail, some writhing in wound agony, others deathly still.

The demolitions team crouched around an open cargo cell hatch, silently focusing on rigging one of the demolition charges. Quillain passed by without speaking. It was never a good idea to interrupt an explosives man on a job. Continuing amidships, he sought out Sergeant Tallman.

He found the company top lying prone on the deck edge amid a broad fan of empty 7.62- and 5.56-millimeter shell casings, switching off between his overheating M-4 carbine and a captured FALN.

"Situation?" Quillain yelled over the gunfire dropping down beside the noncom.

"Bad, Skipper. The locals are getting their act together."

Peering over the deck lip, Quillain saw the truth in the NCO's words. In the unsteady illumination of the dockside fires and the Union star shells he could make out shadowy figures working their way down the pier from one patch of cover to the next. Other Union troopers covered the advance with a steady, hammering barrage of small-arms fire.

"We're taking casualties, Captain, and we can't maintain this fire volume much longer. We're going through ammo like shit through a goose."

"We won't have to, Top. Captain Garrett'll be pulling us out of here in a minute."

Damn it, woman, Quillain beamed the fervent telepathic message into the night, *you are pulling us out of here, right?*

She must have heard him. Amanda's reply came back crisply over the tactical radio link. "On deck on the *Bajara*! Cast off all mooring lines! I say again, cast off all mooring lines!"

Thank you, Lord . . . and Lady!

"Cast off!" Quillain took up Amanda's call and bellowed it fore and aft. "Cast off all lines!"

A Marine lunged for one of the spring lines near the gangway, struggling to draw the heavy manila python up and off of its mooring butt. Before he could finish the task, his head snapped back and his helmet went flying. He fell backward, a thin, catlike wail escaping him.

"Corpsman," Quillain roared, "Corpsman!" He rolled and crawled down the deck to the mooring butt. Slugs tore at the deck lip, hot metal fragments raking his hands as he tore at the heavy fiber cable, horsing it off the butt and over the side.

Harbor Tug *Union Banner*   0153 Hours, Zone Time; September 8, 2007

Peering back over her shoulder, Amanda gauged the widening distance between her craft and the tanker. *All right. That's about enough for a good short tow.*

"On deck. Set your wildcats. Snub her off!"

The boatswain spun the brake wheel and the towing drum locked with a rusty shriek. On the tug's bridge, Amanda rocked the throttles forward and the diesels responded with a rising growl of power and a churning flurry of foaming wake. Slowly the massive steel hawser rose up out of the sea.

Port Monrovia Oiling Pier   0153 Hours, Zone Time; September 8, 2007

Obe Belewa saw the mooring lines falling away from the tanker's sides. Somehow they were getting the ship under way. There was no more time left. There was only now! Gun in hand, he rose to his feet and lifted his voice above the crash and chaos of the fighting.

"Soldiers of the Union! Follow me!"

The Tanker *Bajara*   0153 Hours, Zone Time; September 8, 2007

A deep roiling shout lifted simultaneously from a multitude of throats. Scores of figures rose up from behind cover along the shattered pier and charged headlong for the tanker's gangway.

"Captain," Tallman yelled, "this is it! They're starting their big push!"

"Then push 'em back!" Quillain snarled. Ignoring the saturation of hot lead in the air, Quillain came up on one knee at the edge of the deck, sweeping the Mossberg 590 to his shoulder. Then he started killing.

A computerized fire-control system might well have been operating his weapon. Reload . . . seek target . . . lock on . . . shoot! Reload . . . seek target . . . lock on . . . shoot! The slide of the pump action sang and smoking shell hulls accumulated at his side. Three . . . four . . . five . . . half a dozen Union solders fell to the slug load thunderbolts cast by Quillain's 12-gauge.

The last round in the magazine slammed into the chamber and the Mossberg's foresight traversed, seeing new prey. The ghost ring acquired another figure, a tall, running man. Brandishing an upraised pistol, he led a cluster of Union troopers toward the base of the gangway.

The calculating machine that had taken over Stone Quillain's mind analyzed for a fragment of a second. *Officer . . . priority target . . . lock on!* The Marine's finger tightened on the trigger.

Two hundred feet aft, at the *Bajara's* stern, the *Union Banner's* towing hawser snapped taut.

✠◆

The tanker's deck lurched as the shotgun roared, its muzzle bobbing slightly. The figure caught in the ghost ring fell, but not with the shock-borne decisiveness of a square hit.

"Shit! Shit! Shit!" Quillain rolled back from the deck edge, fumbling in a harness pouch for more ammunition. Then he caught himself and relaxed. It was okay. All of a sudden, one miss didn't matter. They were moving.

Port Monrovia, Oiling Pier   0154 Hours, Zone Time; September 8, 2007

Something seared across the calf of Belewa's right leg, exploding into the decking at his feet, the shock and spray of wood splinters taking him down.

Get up! Get up! Get up! he screamed at himself, forcing his half-paralyzed leg to move. He clawed the Browning from where it had fallen and staggered to his feet, forcing himself onward a few hunched steps more. Then he realized the exchange of gunfire had slackened abruptly and that the charging Union soldiers around him were stumbling to a halt.

The tanker was moving, the black wedge of water widening between her after end and the pier even as they watched. The squeal and groan of distorting metal sounded from amidships as the gangway twisted laterally and then slipped from the dock's edge to crash into the harbor. Outlined in the glare of the falling starshells, the *Bajara* slowly gained way astern, backing out toward the central channel, slipping beyond reach.

"NO!" Belewa's leg buckled beneath him again, his scream a cry of rage and denial.

Mobile Offshore Base, Floater 1   0154 Hours, Zone Time; September 8, 2007

"Moonshade to Palace." Amanda's slightly hoarse but matter-of-fact voice issued from the overhead speaker in the briefing trailer. "Tow established. We are under way."

"Acknowledged, Moonshade," Operations replied with equal matter-of-factness. "*Bajara* is under way. You are inside the time line."

S E A F I G H T E R   379

"She's done it! By God, she's done it!" MacIntyre emphasized his words with a crushing arm around Christine Rendino's shoulders. The intel's reply was a wordless, joyous squeal of relief.

Via the electronic vision of the hovering Eagle Eye, the Algerian tanker could be made out on the wall monitor, edging slowly astern, the *Union Banner* straining at the tow line like a husky attempting to drag a railway car. The enormity of the task and the tug's inching speed restored sobriety rapidly.

"How far out to the scuttling site?" MacIntyre demanded.

Christine reached back for the display controller and called up the Monrovia harbor chart. "In the main channel, out toward the harbor entrance, far enough so that they won't be able to get another deep-draft ship past her. They've got about two-thirds of a mile to go."

"Two-thirds of a mile," MacIntyre scowled. "That's one hell of a gauntlet to run at five knots. When will the seafighters be committed to cover the extraction force?"

"Amanda's tasked to make that decision, Admiral," Christine replied. "Covering the extraction, the PGs are going to burn through their ammo load awful fast. She wants to hold off committing for as long as possible to maintain a firepower reserve."

MacIntyre's brows knitted together. "So she intends to just sit out there and take it?"

"Something like, sir."

A systems operator looked up from his work station. "Commander Rendino, TACNET indicates that the Union gunboats have picked up on the attack against Port Monrovia. They've come about and are heading back to the port at full speed. We estimate they will be a factor within the next twenty-five minutes."

Port Monrovia Oiling Pier   **0157 Hours, Zone Time; September 8, 2007**

Atiba had brought the Steyr command track up to the base of the oiling pier. Its headlight glared into Belewa's eyes as he hobbled toward it, the leg of his jungle fatigues sodden with blood.

"The General's been wounded," one of the staff called out. "Get an aid man up here."

"Never mind that," Belewa yelled back over the idling engine. "Where is Brigadier Atiba? I need Atiba!"

"Here, General." The Chief of Staff swung down from the track's lowering tailgate. "Your orders, sir."

"Communications status? Where do we have contact? What have we got left to fight with?" Belewa's damaged leg refused to support him any further, and he slid down to the tarmac of the access road, his back to one of the track's bogie wheels. The summoned aid man knelt beside him, hastily tearing open his medical kit.

"We have regained communication with Roberts Field, General," Atiba replied coolly, standing over Belewa. "They are launching the gunship now. We also believe the gunboat squadron has received its recall order and is returning."

"Good." Belewa pulled himself upright. Taking the canteen from the aid man's belt pouch he took a long pull of the tepid water, clearing the dryness and smoke taint from his throat. "The damned Americans are using one of our own harbor tugs to move the tanker. Redeploy the harbor defense units along the breakwaters. Concentrate all fire on that tugboat! Sink it at all costs! Then commandeer any small craft you can find and organize a force to retake the tanker before they can get it out of the harbor."

Belewa gulped another mouthful from the canteen, then grimaced as the aid man clamped a compress over the oozing leg wound. "It will not end this way. I will not let it end this way!"

The Tanker *Bajara*   0158 Hours, Zone Time; September 8, 2007

Quillain stuck his head in through the door of the tanker's main crew's mess. "You got 'em ready to go?"

The space was jammed with a combination of the vessel's civilian officers and crew, the sniffling and red-eyed children of the human shield force and the few soldiers of the ship's guard who had managed to throw their hands up in time to surrender. All had been strapped into life jackets and all sat uneasily on the mess-room benches, their hands behind their heads. Submachine-gun-armed Marines covered them from one end of the compartment.

"Yes, sir," the guard leader replied. "Ready to move 'em out."

"Okay, we'll put 'em over the port side. We're still getting land fire to starboard. Single file! Let's go! Hurry it up!"

The grim-eyed guards herded the prisoners down a short passageway to the starboard side of the deckhouse and to a weather-deck hatch. Beyond the hatch another pair of Marine sentries stood by at a gap cut in the tanker's cable railing. First in line, the Algerian captain goggled at the cut railing and at the black waters of the harbor beyond. Frantically, he stammered what must have been a protest in Arabic.

"Pipe down and get on with it," Quillain growled. "The longer you wait, the farther you swim!" Grabbing the captain by the back strap of his life jacket, he marched the man the two steps across the deck and launched him over the side, the Algerian's despairing wail climaxing with a splash.

The other prisoners followed in short order, alternating between the children and adults until the mess room was empty and a string of blinking life-jacket beacons trailed in the wake of the tanker. The tanker crew and the boy soldiers would have to make their own way to shore. There was no more that the Marines could do.

The Union gunnery had dropped off when the *Bajara* had first pulled clear of the dock, but now the intensity of the shoreside fire was growing again. The occasional thud of a grenade launcher or the snarl of a SAW replied from the tanker's deck and upperworks.

Quillain hurried across to the starboard side, dropping down beside Tallman at the deck edge.

"What's happening?" Quillain demanded.

"The Union's starting to pour it on again, Skipper. Only this time they're not shooting at us. They're going for the tug."

"Well, we knew they weren't stupid."

Looking forward, they could see the *Union Banner* straining at the end of the towline, a blunt arrowhead at the tip of the white foam shaft of her wake. Tracer streams arced toward the little craft and a backflash flared atop the shadowy line of the breakwater. A recoilless rifle round detonated alongside the *Banner* an instant later.

"SAW teams and grenadiers," Tallman barked into his tactical mike. "Carl Gustav on the breakwater at ten o'clock. Take him out." Marine gunners responded and another series of explosions danced along the top of the breakwater, incoming this time instead of outgoing.

"That's the stuff, Top. Keep 'em off the tug."

Tallman looked across to his C.O. "That's just the thing, sir. We can't. Not for much longer. Ammo's getting real tight. We burned a whole lot of our base load holding them off at the pier. Only a few rounds of forty left, and the SAWs are eatin' M-4 clips. Another five minutes and we're gonna be down to pistols and K-Bars."

"Lord A'mighty."

Harbor Tug *Union Banner*　　　　　　　**0159 Hours, Zone Time; September 8, 2007**

The remainder of the bridge windscreen dissolved in a jagged shimmering spray as automatic-weapons fire raked the tug's upperworks. Amanda threw her arms up, shielding her face from the stinging bite of the shattered glass. Sinking to her knees beside the wheel, she hunched down, keeping under the minimal cover of the steel bulkheads below the now-empty windscreen frames.

Peering forward, she held her course, her right hand on the wheel. The *Bajara* was fighting the tow. Running stern foremost with no one at her helm, the big tanker kept falling off the line of advance, veering erratically at the end of the hawser. Amanda had to keep correcting, hauling the big sullen bitch back into the channel.

God save us all if we ground making the turn.

"Not far," she whispered aloud. "Not far now."

Again, a sleeting storm of high-velocity metal swept over the tug. With no glass left to shatter, the bullets glanced and whined off the heavier fittings and punched through the bulkheads with a dull *pock, pock, pock* sound like the opening of a string of pull-top cans.

Suddenly something smashed into Amanda's back with the impact of a sledgehammer. It hurled her forward onto the glass-covered deck, the air smashed from her lungs in a choked shriek. She lay facedown in the darkness, unbreathing, unable to breathe, a searing heat centered in her back. Dazed, she hung on to the edge of consciousness, asking a question of the Universe. *Is this death?*

The Universe answered: No . . . It was a voice on the Leprechaun circuit. Christine . . .

"Moonshade! Moonshade! Do you copy! Moonshade! You have motor launches converging on you. *Amanda, do you hear me?*"

Amanda pushed herself up to her knees. *You can die later! Move, goddamn you! Move!*

She broke the lock on her lungs and dragged in an agonizing load of oxygen while fumbling for the switch of the tactical communicator. "On deck!" She couldn't recognize the rasping croak that emerged from her throat. "Repel boarders! Repel boarders!"

"Roger," the terse response from the fire team leader snapped back. "Engaging!"

Another kind of reply raged from the *Banner's* lower deck, as the Marines opened up on the new threat. Pulling herself upright at the center console, Amanda fought to regain situational awareness.

The Port Monrovia pilot's launch had been pressed into service as an ad-hoc Boghammer. Running twenty yards off the *Banner's* port side, Bren guns flamed from its foredeck while Union soldiers packed its cockpit. Flank to flank, the two commandeered craft exchanged small-caliber broadsides like Napoleonic ships of the line.

Amanda forced her eyes to focus on the miraculously intact compass dome. *God, We're falling off course again. Helm, come right ten points!* She gave the command to herself, as she would have to a duty quartermaster. Spinning the wheel, she kicked the rudder over, ignoring the scalding pain that still radiated from her back.

"Amanda," Christine's voice sounded in her headset again, an electronic guardian angel looking down from on high. "Watch it! A second boat's coming in on your starboard side."

And the Marines were already committed. *Damn! Damn! Damn!*

She clawed the interphone out of its cradle. "Engine room! Repel boarders to starboard!" Dropping the handset, she threw herself across to the far side of the bridge.

A small outboard skiff carrying half a dozen Union soldiers was trying to come alongside. Bucking the wash that churned down the tug's flank, the soldier in the skiff's bow groped for the rail.

Amanda couldn't recall making the conscious decision to draw her weapon, but the .45 came up on target, both of her hands closing around its grips. The wavering flare light made for poor shooting, but the long hours of relentless drill under the instruction of Stone Quillain compensated. The big Colt roared as its sights came in line, the seven-round clip consumed in seconds.

Her target toppled limply over the skiff's side and the open boat staggered off course, someone aboard it rattling off a wild answering volley from a machine pistol. Then a pair of shotguns opened up from the *Banner's* engine-room hatch, lashing the small craft with a storm of buckshot. Silenced and with no living hand at its engine tiller, the skiff whirled away astern.

So did the pilot launch that had come in from the other side. The Marine grenadiers scored with multiple 40mm hits and the launch exploded into flames. In the glare of the blazing hulk, Amanda caught the silhouette of a buoy sweeping past down the port side.

The marker for the entry channel! Turn her! She got back on the helm, bringing the tug's nose around, aiming her for the gap in the breakwaters.

Easy! Easy! Not too sharp. Follow me, you big bastard!

Amanda played the wheel and engine controls, attempting to keep excessive strain off the towline as the *Bajara's* stern slowly indexed around, aligning in the channel.

All right! Well done, Helm!

The tug and its tow were almost at the dead center of the harbor now, temporarily beyond the reach of effective shore fire. Amanda attempted to take a deep breath and found that she could. The burning near her spine had faded to a mere hotness. She reached back to find a lump embedded in her flak jacket. Distorted first by its penetration of the steel bridge bulkhead and then again by its impact against the vest's ballistic plate, the machine-gun bullet popped out into the palm of her grimy hand.

She fingered the little cooling lump of death for a moment and found herself grinning a tight feral grin. *This wasn't the one.*

She held the *Banner* on course for the harbor mouth.

Mobile Offshore Base, Floater 1   **0204 Hours, Zone Time; September 8, 2007**

"Damn near there," MacIntyre muttered.

"Getting close," Christine agreed wearily. "Signals, advise the seafighter group to power up and stand by for extraction."

"Latest situational update from *Queen of the West* indicates they are already up on the pad and standing by for the word, Commander," the S.O. replied.

"Very good, Sigs. You can advise Commander Lane that he can expect the word shortly."

"Aye, aye."

Christine knew the trailer air-conditioning was already pushed to its maximum setting, but her uniform shirt was sodden with sweat. Even Admiral MacIntyre, for all his stone-faced stoicism, had darkening circles of perspiration under the arms of his flight suit.

"What else can the Union hit us with?" he demanded quietly.

The intel's temples throbbed, her thoughts thickening in her brain. *Hey, God, isn't there anybody else out here who can answer questions?*

"I think the gunboats are the Union's last hole card, Admiral," she replied.

Closing her eyes, Christine leaned back against the conference table, wishing for just one true lungful of cool dry air. *Maybe like you could get out on the Mojave in the early morning.* She let that mental image wash out reality for a moment, seeking that breath of desert breeze.

"Commander Rendino! Radar has acquired a bogey launching from Payne Field!"

The mental image exploded and Christine's eyes snapped open. "Identify!"

"Single target. Possibly a helicopter. On heading for Port area. Coming in fast."

Port Monrovia Oiling Pier   **0204 Hours, Zone Time; September 8, 2007**

"Do we have radio contact with the helicopter?" His leg hastily bandaged, Belewa pulled himself upright in the open rear door of the command track.

The numbness had gone from his torn limb, and he spoke through gritted teeth.

"Off and on, sir," the radio operator replied. "Jamming is still intense, but we are getting burn-through as he gets closer."

"There he is!" a guard yelled from outside. The whistling drone of a light helicopter echoed beneath the overcast. Belewa twisted in the hatchway and looked up just as the Messerschmitt-Bolkow BO 105 gunship swept past overhead, flare light reflecting palely from its underbelly.

"Order them to sink the tug! Sink it!"

Union Army Gunship Owl Three Five   0205 Hours, Zone Time; September 8, 2007

The attack order came in faintly over the warble of the American jamming, but plain enough to be made out by the gunship's pilot. "Owl Three Five acknowledges," he replied casually into his headset mike, not unduly concerned as to whether his reply was heard or not.

Holding his course, he angled out across the harbor area, weaving to snake through the pattern of slowly descending star shells. The target was easy to acquire. The Algerian tanker was a black cutout against the shimmering metallic silver of the harbor, the tug a smaller shadow off the tanker's stern, the silver water roiling behind it.

A simple matter. The only trick would be to get close enough to ensure that no round could wander and hit the larger vessel.

"Arm rockets. One and four," he commanded over the intercom. The BO 105 carried four Matra 68mm rocket pods on its snub wings. Two of the six-round clusters would be adequate for the task at hand.

His copilot hit the arming switches and the glowing blue rings of the cart-wheel sight materialized on the cockpit heads-up display.

Crossing the harbor, the pilot swung wide beyond the northern break-water. Coming around again, he set his attack run, pulling the little twin-turbine gunship through an unnecessarily steep bank, deftly flying by instruments and enjoying the drag of the G forces. With the latest fuel restrictions, he needed to draw every bit of pleasure he could from his limited air time.

The night swirled past beyond the rain-streaked windscreen, going level again as they lined up on the target. Smoothly, the pilot eased the helicopter over into a shallow accelerating dive, the crossbar in the center of the weapon sight resting on the tug's deck, the vertical stroke passing through the pilot-house. Now, to hold that sight picture until they reached firing range.

From what he had heard, the ground-pounders and the navy had been fumbling around with the Americans out here all night. Now it was time to put an end to this children's play. The pilot grinned tightly and flipped the thumb guard up and off the firing button on his collective lever. The arming tone squalled in his headset.

Mobile Offshore Base, Floater 1 0205 Hours, Zone Time; September 8, 2007

The silhouette of the Union gunship cut across the monitor as it passed beneath the hovering Eagle Eye.

"Where the hell did he come from?" MacIntyre exclaimed, straightening.

"The Aviation unit at Payne Field. Belewa must have been able to keep one of his night-capable helicopters operational. Shit!" Christine spun around to face the S.O. at the drone control station. "Stay on that helo!"

"Aye, aye." The systems operator's hands flew across the controls of his remote terminal as he took the RPV out of station-keeping mode. The image on the wall monitor swooped and pivoted as the robot tilt-rotor transitioned to level flight and moved out in pursuit of the manned aircraft.

MacIntyre stared at the monitor screen, his fists clinched. "How much armament can that gunship carry?" he demanded.

"Enough!"

The Admiral spun around to face the intel, his voice rising. "To hell with Captain Garrett's tasking options. Move those seafighters in now! Kill that helo!"

Christine could only shake her head wildly. "It's too late! Stinger antiair missiles weren't included in the cell load-out! Surface-to-surface armament had priority! And they'll never get within gun range in time!"

The Union helicopter completed its overflight of the port area. Centered in the Eagle Eye screen, it kicked up and around in a steep turn, coming back over the northern breakwater and diving in toward the helpless tug.

"God save us all!" MacIntyre's fist crashed down on the tabletop.

A choked sob escaped from Christine Rendino. She literally threw herself at the drone operator, knocking him aside and out of his chair. Leaning in over the drone control terminal, she grasped the joystick. Staring intently into the pilot's view monitor, she slammed the throttle scale to its highest mark.

The image on the wall monitor tilted insanely, as the drone peeled off into a screaming split-S maneuver, the Remotely Piloted Vehicle pitching into a maximum boost dive.

The recon camera automatically restabilized and recentered on the Union gunship. The image of the helicopter swelled explosively in the center of the screen as the course lines of the gunship and drone converged. In the last seconds of transmission, the low-light video imager looked down through the BO 105's rotor arc and into the canopy bubble, catching the shock and horror on the helicopter pilot's face as he looked up and opened his mouth to scream.

The wall monitor went abruptly dead.

Christine straightened and took a deep, deliberate breath. Extending a hand, she helped the startled drone operator back to his feet. "Call the flight deck and see if they can set us up another bird," she said. "I think I sort of busted this one."

MacIntyre palmed the sweat from his brow, brushing back his dampened hair. "Nice move, Commander," he said, taking a deep breath of his own. "Very nice move indeed."

"The coward's kamikaze, sir. You gotta love it."

Harbor Tug *Union Banner*   0206 Hours, Zone Time; September 8, 2007

The sky lit up, but with an orange glow instead of the harsh eye-stabbing whiteness of burning magnesium. Startled, Amanda looked up in time to see a blazing mass of wreckage rain down into the harbor a quarter mile off the tug's starboard side. She didn't have the vaguest clue as to what might have happened out there, but she suspected that someone might have just taken care of a problem for her.

If so, whoever it was, Amanda was grateful. She had enough to deal with just then.

A column of water jetted out of the sea ahead, the *WHAM CR-A-A-CK* of the shell detonation following a split instant later. Heavy weapons this time. The two armored cars, positioned like Scylla and Charybdis at the harbor's mouth, were opening fire. Aiming low, they attempted to walk their 90mm rounds in on the *Banner* without hitting the tanker behind the tug.

Amanda shot a final look to port and starboard, gauging their position against the channel buoys. This was as good as it was going to get. Reaching over, she slammed the engine throttles closed, then she touched the transmit pad on her Leprechaun transceiver. "This is Moonshade to all Wolfrider elements. Cutter, Cutter, Cutter! I say again, Cutter, Cutter, Cutter!"

"Acknowledged!" Steamer Lane's reply shot back instantly. "The word is Cutter and we are inbound!"

Another Panhard round howled in, this one exploding off the tug's port side, close enough to rain spray down onto the *Banner*'s weather decks.

It would be the last.

The Hellfire missiles that arced in from the sea had been designed to destroy the heaviest of main battle tanks. The thin-skinned Union armored cars presented no challenge at all. Plunging downward through the thin turret roofs, the Hellfires dissolved the French-built vehicles, the Panhard's ammunition stores magnifying the explosion so that both entryway hardpoints were engulfed and devastated.

And through the door thus kicked open came the Three Little Pigs, hunting for a fight.

Howling through the channel entrance, the three seafighters conducted a fleur-de-lys separation, the *Carondelet* and the *Manassas* peeling off to the left and right, paralleling the seawalls while the *Queen of the West* stood straight on for the *Banner.*

The flanker boats raced down the mile length of each breakwater, trailing fire, death, and destruction as they ran. A raking barrage spewing from their weapons mounts, they buried the Union defenses under a focused storm of rockets, grenades, and shell bursts.

"Yes!" Amanda pounded her fist down on the tug's wheel. This was why she had so carefully husbanded the fighting strength of the seafighter group until this moment. Stealth and audacity might get them in, but only the guns could get them out again. "Strongbow. Arm your charges and stand by for extraction! Let's get out of here!"

"Roger D, Roger D, Moonshade! Ready to go here and about time!" Quillain's jubilant response resounded in her headset. "Hey, you know that Moonshade's a damn pretty name after all."

"Acknowledged, Stone. We'll be alongside for you in a minute." Shifting communications modes, she grabbed up the interphone handset. "Engine room! Finished with engines. Arm your scuttling charges and get topside on the double. Our ride's here!"

"Don't have to tell us twice, ma'am! We're gone!"

Decelerating, the *Queen of the West* came around in a wide fish-hook turn, coming alongside the tug, starboard to port. With a final braking flurry from her puff ports, the hovercraft's inflated skirt bumped softly against the tug's rail, salt mist boiling up around both vessels. The PG's starboard grenade launcher mount had been swung back out of the side hatch and the *Queen's* hands stood by to help pull the tug's prize crew aboard.

"Go!" Amanda yelled over the turbine wail as she dropped down the exterior ladder from the wheelhouse. One after another the prize crew scrambled up the slippery skirt slope and into the hatch until only Amanda and the fire team leader remained, standing at the tug's open engine-room hatchway.

"Set to blow, ma'am!" the Marine yelled over the steady-state engine shriek, holding up the pistol grip of the hand igniter.

"I'll do it! Get aboard!"

"You sure, ma'am?"

"Yes. Get moving!"

"Okay, ma'am." He passed her the igniter. "Just pull the pin and squeeze."

She gave him a second to start up to the hovercraft, then turned back to the tug's engine-room hatch. They would use the *Banner* in the same way they had used the hulk of the British minehunter during the hurricane, as an anchor to hold the *Bajara* in the harbor channel. Shaped, "cookie cutter" charges of plastic explosive had been molded against the tug's hull plates to sink her.

Amanda yanked the safety pin from the top of the klacker, then hesitated for a second. The *Union Banner* had been her ship, under her command, if only for a matter of minutes. The little tug served her well, doing all that she had asked of it. The mariner in Amanda felt a pang of regret at what she must do now. She rested her free hand on the hatch frame for a moment, then squeezed the igniter.

She felt a thud under the soles of her boots as two meter-wide patches of steel were sliced out of the *Banner*'s hull. Peering down through the hatchway, Amanda caught a glimpse of water boiling up over the engine-room deck plates just before the interior lighting went out. Willing hands hauled her up into the *Queen*'s main bay as the tug's deck began to settle beneath her.

Popping the releases, Amanda let someone lift the MOLLE harness off her shoulders, not realizing until it was gone just how much of a burden its weight had become. Steamer Lane had the seafighter gaining way once more as she clambered up the ladder to the cockpit.

"Glad to have you back aboard, Captain," he called back over his shoulder.

"Glad to be back aboard," she replied, coming forward to hunker down between the pilot's seats. "What's our status?"

"*Carondelet* and *Manassas* have completed their fire-suppression runs and are converging on the *Bajara*," Lane replied as Snowy Banks passed Amanda a shipboard headset. "We'll cover for the Frenchman and Rebel while they pick up the bulk of the boarding party. Then they'll cover for us while we go in for the demolition team."

"Go with it, Steamer."

"Ma'am," Snowy interjected, "Operations advises that the Union heavy gunboat group is going to be a factor shortly."

Amanda gave another nod. "I suspect they are, Snowy. But one thing at a time. For now, let's get our Marines back."

Oil Tanker *Bajara*   **0215 hours, Zone Time; September 8, 2007**

The seafighters swept in, nestling against the rusty side of the Algerian oil carrier, staying up on the pad and holding themselves in place with snorting puff-port thrusters. Swarming up onto the PG's weather decks, navy hands stood by to assist as the evacuation got under way.

The Marine wounded went first, lowered over the tanker's rail via a snap ring clipped through their gear harness, their pain numbed by morphine or suppressed by willpower.

The Marine dead followed. None of Fox company would be left behind to burn.

Last came the uninjured. Fast ropes had been coiled and lashed on the backs of the hovercraft. With one end lifted and secured on the tanker's deck, and the other braced by the sailors below, the uninjured survivors of the boarding party slid down the heavy two-inch lines to the comparative safety of the hovercraft.

With their full loads aboard, *Carondelet* and *Manassas* sheered off to take up their covering stations, making room for the *Queen of the West* to dash in and recover the last handful of men from the doomed ship.

⊗◆

"All hands accounted for?" Quillain yelled over the idling moan of the PG's fans.

"All accounted for by the squad leaders and double-checked by me, Skipper. Everybody other'n us is over the side."

In the light of a single chemical glowstick, Quillain, Tallman, and the demolition team leader crouched on the tanker's deck. An ominous-looking web of det cord converged on them, linking to a carefully taped-down pattern of blasting caps, M700 time fuse, and M60 fuse igniters.

"Good, enough. Corporal, is this rig set?"

The demo man nodded, his jaw working his well-used chunk of gum. "All connections made, igniters armed, and ready to rock and roll. I can light her up as soon as you get clear, sir."

Quillain shook his head. "That's my job, Corporal. You and the top get over the side."

The sergeant and the demo man both started to mouth protests, but Quillain chopped them off. "Belay that noise! Both of you move out! Now!"

Two reluctant "Aye ayes" came back. Tallman gave his C.O. an unhappy last glance and started for the ship's side. The demo man hesitated a moment longer. "All that M-700 is cut from the same roll of fuse, and I time-tested samples myself, sir. You should have a solid five minutes of burn there, but I wouldn't try and set my watch by it."

"Don't worry, son. I'm not going to. I intend to light up these sparklers and then be over that rail just a-shittin' and a-flyin'."

Quillain watched the two noncoms disappear down the fast ropes. He abruptly became aware of the dark and lonely emptiness of the decks around him. *Well, a-shittin', anyway,* he thought, keying his radio. "Strongbow to Moonshade. All personnel clear. Igniting charges."

"Roger, Strongbow," Amanda Garrett's reply came back. "Standing by."

Hunkering down over the M-60s, Quillain pulled the safety pins and then sequentially yanked the pull rings of each igniter, drawing back the firing pin and allowing it to snap forward against the shotgun primer housed inside each little plastic cylinder.

The primers popped and fuse started to burn.

Quillain shot an automatic glance at his wristwatch, then touched the transmit pad. "Moonshade. Charges lit! Charges lit!" Grabbing his shotgun, he bolted for the rail and the fast rope.

He was half a dozen strides away from both when a burst of machine-gun fire flayed a shower of sparks off the deck around him.

Quillain responded by well-honed instinct, diving forward, rolling to one side, and bringing up his weapon in a single, continuous flow of motion, going to cover behind a valve bank.

The rain of Union illumination rounds had thinned out. As the current flight of flares sank toward the harbor, low-angled shadows crawled back aboard the tanker, blanketing her decks. Quillain switched on his night-vision visor. Lowering it over his eyes, he scanned for the source of the attack.

"Strongbow, we hear gunfire on deck. What's your situation?" Amanda's voice sounded sharply in his headset. "Stone, do you copy?"

"Yeah. I'm okay," he murmured back into the lip mike. "But we missed somebody. We got a shooter up in the deckhouse."

"Stone, are you pinned down? Can you get to the rail?"

"I'll let you know in a second."

Quillain nestled the stock of the Mossberg against his shoulder and flicked on the invisible beam of the targeting laser, his eyes tracking with the sweep of the death dot.

Movement! One level below the bridge. A head cautiously peered over the weather-deck rail. The death dot flicked over, acquiring the target. The sheet steel of the rail's spray guard wouldn't exist to the discarding sabot slug loads Quillain had in his weapon. He held his breath and took up the play in the trigger.

"Ah, Sweet Jesus!"

Stone hadn't realized he'd left the talk circuit open. Amanda caught his softly breathed exclamation. "Stone, what is it?"

"It's a kid, Skipper! We missed one of those goddamned kids!"

Overlooked somehow in the deck-clearing operations, one of the Union's boy warriors had come out of his hiding hole to single-handedly challenge the attackers. With his submachine gun lifted to a thin shoulder, he leaned into the railing, ready to do battle, totally unaware that in minutes this particular battleground would be an inferno.

"Stone," Amanda spoke levelly, "it's too late. There's nothing you can do. Get out of there. You only have four minutes left."

Quillain dropped down behind the shelter of the valve bank. Nothing he could do? Hell no, there wasn't anything he could do except to get off his tub! The little shit would just have to take his chances. He was old enough to pack a gun. His government figured he was old enough to fight and die for his country. The kid must figure the same. Cut it either way and it was no call or fault of Captain Stonewall Buford Quillain.

Quillain gauged the flare fall and the coming of the next patch of total darkness. Once he was over the rail and on the rope, he'd be out of the kid's arc of fire. It would just take a couple of seconds and he'd be gone.

Tough luck, kid. You should have gotten off when we gave you your chance. The flare flight struck water and flickered out, bringing on full darkness. Stone rose to his feet and bolted for the fast rope.

And then for some reason he was past the rope and running aft for the tanker's deckhouse.

He almost reached it before another flare hissed out over the harbor and lit off. With the reflexes of a striking snake, the boy warrior leaned out over the railing and opened fire, raining 9mm rounds down on Quillain.

Lunging forward, the Marine broke the line of fire, diving and rolling beyond the corner of the superstructure. Pressing back against the port-side bulkhead, he gripped at his bullet-creased shoulder and swore silently and savagely at himself.

"Stone. What's going on?" Amanda's voice prodded from his earphones. "Do you need assistance?"

"Negative, negative!" he snapped back, shaking the numbness from his damaged arm. "One goddamn fool up here is plenty!"

Circling around to the foot of the exterior ladderway, he began to climb, keeping his footfalls light but not daring to use the usual deliberate stealth called for in such situations. He couldn't, not with those fuses burning.

"Skipper, listen," he whispered into his lip mike. "I don't have time to explain what's going on, but if I'm not over the rail at one minute to detonation, you guys clear out."

"We are standing by, Stone," the quiet reply came back.

Quillain scanned the ladderway overhead as he climbed, wondering just what the hell he'd do if the child warrior suddenly appeared on the next stage up, subgun leveled.

This is stupid. He thought the litany with each step climbed. *This is stupid. This so goddamned stupid!*

He risked a glance at his wristwatch. Three minutes and a few seconds more. *Oh Lord, but this is stupid!*

As he eased off the ladder onto his objective deck the mental chant changed. *"Don't run! You want me. Come and get me. Do not run! We don't have time to play fucking hide-and-seek!"*

Pressing his back against the bulkhead, he slid forward toward the corner of the superstructure, trying to hear beyond the whistle of the *Queen*'s turbines. Just at the corner of the deckhouse, the flare light guttered out again.

Quillain froze, not even daring to flip down his vision visor again. Was that the tick of metal against metal?

He couldn't see it, but somehow, some . . . how he could sense the gun barrel easing around the corner from the other direction. Just at chest height. Just right for a kid to have shouldered. Right . . . *here!*

Quillain's left hand closed around the perforated cooling jacket of a Sterling machine pistol. Yanking it away with a single explosive heave, he sent the weapon spinning over the rail. He heard a startled gasp close by in the darkness and he aimed for it with the back of his right hand, landing a tremendous buffet against the side of someone's head.

Quillain yanked down his vision visor and found the stunned boy warrior sprawled at his feet. *Watch! Ninety seconds! Not going to make it!*

He slung the Mossberg over one shoulder and the boy over the other, racing for the ladderway and down.

"We are standing by, Stone." Amanda Garrett's voice whispered in his ear.

"I can't make it," he yelled back over the circuit. "Get clear!"

"We are standing by, Stone." That husky, cool, and deliberate voice spoke words beyond words. *We are not leaving you behind, mister. You don't get that easy an out! If you die, then we die with you, so you had just better get about staying alive!*

Boots ringing on the steel, he reached the main deck and ran forward for the fast rope. *How far? Two hundred feet? To hell with it! Move! How long? Maybe a minute? To hell with that too!*

At the fast rope, the *Queen of the West* lay nestled against the side of the tanker, her drive propellers flickering flat-pitched, her offside thrusters holding her in place. Sergeant Tallman stood holding the fast line taut. Snowy Banks stood in the cockpit hatch, ready to yell the go word to Steamer Lane, and

Amanda Garrett stood in the center of the hovercraft's back, looking up, hands on hips, standing by.

Gloves! Forgot my goddamn gloves! To hell with that entirely! Quillain swung over the rail and plummeted down the fast rope, the flesh flaying off his hands, boy and Marine piling up on the deck.

"Go! Go! Go!" Quillain's bellow was unnecessary. The *Queen's* inboard thrusters shoved her off from the side of the *Bajara,* the drive propellers blurring into a roar of power as the seafighter lunged ahead. With no time to get belowdecks, Tallman and Amanda dropped flat beside Quillain and his dazed prisoner. Steamer locked the *Queen's* rudders over, curving her away from the doomed ship, scrabbling for distance.

And then the whole world burst into flames.

A two-hundred-foot jet of fire geysered from the *Bajara's* deck. A second, a third, more sequential flaming eruptions, merging and intertwining into an eye-searing incandescent mushroom of scarlet and gold that continued to grow, lifting into the sky for three times the length of the dying tanker. The thermal plume it generated boiled even higher, ripping open the cloud cover over Port Monrovia and evaporating the rain even as it fell from the sky.

The light of it turned the harbor's night into a furnace-bright day. And the sound, not an explosion in any classic sense, but a deep and vibrant thundering, like the wrath of God rolling across the sea.

The moisture steamed from Quillain's utilities in the radiant glow. Looking across at his POW, Quillain found that the youth had regained consciousness. He also discovered that a miraculous change had taken place. Like the other boy warriors they had taken from the ship, he had reverted back into a child, bravadoless, bewildered, and now awed by the holocaust he and his captors were leaving behind.

Sprawled on the deck beyond the youth, Amanda Garrett looked back into Quillain's eyes and smiled.

Because we're the good guys . . .

PGAC-02 USS *Queen of the West*   0227 Hours, Zone Time; September 8, 2007

The slipstream tore at Amanda as she swung her legs down through the overhead cockpit hatch. Before dropping down into the control deck, she paused for a last look around Monrovia Harbor.

Carondelet and *Manassas* had re-formed combat echelon, with the *Queen* and the trio of seafighters streaking for the harbor mouth, leaving behind the death pyre of the *Bajara.* Even though the PG squadron was fully illuminated by the ruddy petroleum glare, gunfire from the breakwaters had trailed off to almost nothing, the stunned Union defenders finding they had nothing left to defend.

Arching her back, Amanda slid down into the cockpit. With the Union prisoner and Sergeant Tallman secure in the main bay, Stone Quillain followed her through the hatch. Regardless of his damaged shoulder and hands, he kicked down the gunner's saddle and assumed station at the twin-mount Browning fifties.

"Situation," Amanda demanded, dropping into the navigator's seat.

"One bitch left, Captain," Steamer replied. "The Union gunboat group's made it back! They're coming in from the southwest and they're going to be waiting for us outside of the harbor mouth. They're maneuvering to engage, ma'am."

"Fine!"

Startled, Steamer and Snowy twisted in their chair harnesses to look back at her. A part of Amanda's own mind was surprised by her explosive exclamation as well. Yet a cool flush flowed through her, a kind of battle madness or battle focus that erased the tensions and terrors accumulated during the night's action.

Along with it came a sure and certain knowledge that this fight wasn't over yet, but that it soon would be.

Amanda accessed the squadron command channel. "Little Pig Lead to Little Pigs! Enemy gunboats coming in on bearing two one zero. Maintain combat echelon and come left to engage as we clear the harbor entrance. Fire as you bear! I say again, fire as you bear! We're finishing this, now!"

"Acknowledged!"

"Rajah!"

"Doing it!"

Hellfire rounds and rocket pods slithered up out of the pedestal tubs and slammed onto firing rails. Auxiliary gunners screamed for cool barrels and reloads, and the shell humpers scrambled to respond. Accelerating to full war power, the Three Little Pigs blasted out through the narrow mouth of Port Monrovia, once designated by twin navigational beacons, now marked by the flaming hulks of the Union's armored fighting vehicles.

Skidding in their turns, the seafighters came around to face their new attackers. However, even before the turn was completed, autocannon tracers streamed in toward them.

The Union corvette *Promise* was closing the range at full speed, her two smaller sister gunboats running at her flanks. Their bow waves glinted bloodred in the light of the fire column, and their forward gun mounts raved at the

American squadron, hosing death. They had no hope of victory now, only the chance for vengeance.

"Little Pig Lead to Little Pigs! Enemy in sight! Engage! Engage! Engage!"

Mobile Offshore Base, Floater 1   0227 Hours, Zone Time; September 8, 2007

In the briefing trailer, the intel and the Admiral could only stare up at the overhead speaker. With the Eagle Eye drone knocked out, their only link to the battle was the squadron's Talk-Between-Ships command channel. Disembodied voices called out from the Little Pig cockpits, the adrenaline-wired words backed by the yammer and shriek of gunfire and missile launch.

"Hostiles turning to port! They're crossing the T on us!"

"Acknowledged, Frenchman. Target the column leader! Get on the Shanghai! Rebel, engage column trailer! We've got the corvette!"

"Rog that, Little Pig Lead, Hellfires on the way!"

"Yeah, baby, pour it on! Closing to thirty-mike range! Going to guns!"

"Frenchman, come left! You're blocking my arc, dammit!"

"Rog that. Rebel, where are you . . . ?"

"Little Pigs, break echelon. Independent maneuver!"

"Acknowledged, Lead . . . Oh yeah! We just tagged that fucker!"

"Heavy fire . . . watch the big guy! Breaking left . . . going for stern enfilade on enemy column."

"Go for it, Rebel! Steamer, drop in behind *Manassas*. *Carondelet,* follow us in. . . ."

"Frenchman executing . . . Oh Jesus! Jesus!"

"Clark, what's going on? What's happening back there?"

"Tony, they got the *Queen!* They got the *Queen!* Oh, God, they just blew the hell out of her!"

PGAC-02 USS *Queen of the West*   0230 Hours, Zone Time; September 8, 2007

The gun layer commanding the Z mount of the Union corvette *Promise* had no idea that he'd targeted the American flag craft. With two fresh clips of ammunition in the breech of his SU-57 twin mount, he'd spotted the flash of a missile launch and had acquired a dim outline silhouetted in the uncertain light of the tanker burning inside the harbor. Hastily setting his sights, he'd smashed his foot down on the firing pedal, hosing all eight rounds at the target.

Fate or misfortune decreed that the *Queen of the West* would plow headlong into the fire stream.

Three 57mm rounds caught her low in the forehull. Punching through her composite skin, the shells exploded in the forward systems compartments.

In death, Gunner's Mate 1st Class Daniel Sullivan O'Roark and Gunner's Mate 2nd (Missile) Dwaine Robert Fry performed one final service for their crewmates. Their bodies absorbed the bulk of the shrapnel blast that ripped back into the main bay. More fragmentation tore upward, through the overhead and into the cockpit

A fourth Union round struck lower, at the leading edge of the hull raft, tearing the forward end of the plenum chamber skirt loose from its mounting frame. The *Queen's* supporting air bubble collapsed and she came off pad at fifty knots, plowing and skidding across the sea like a crashing airliner.

Every hand aboard not strapped down in a seat or secured by a monkey harness was first thrown forward against the bulkheads, then deluged by water bursting in under fire hose pressure through the shell holes. Turbine compressors stalled. Power faltered. Chaos commanded.

Up in the cockpit, Amanda felt the concussion of the shell hits and was aware of the jagged shards of metal punching upward through the deck. She heard Steamer Lane yell a warning, then a wordless agonized cry from Snowy Banks. Then they hit.

The hovercraft's stern kicked upward as the bow dug in. The windscreen exploded back into the cockpit, pushed in by a wall of water. Possibly this latter event saved Amanda Garrett's life. She hadn't fastened her safety harness, and as the impact of the crash threw her forward out of the navigator's chair, she was met by the cushioning blast of the inrushing sea. Caught between two irresistible forces, she was kicked away from consciousness.

But not completely.

A fragile thread remained, linking her to the world. To awareness. To the awareness that she yet lived and there were things that had to be done. The entity that was Amanda Garrett tugged recklessly on that thread, demanding that limbs move, senses record. Demanding that the battle continue.

Survival as a consideration was past. Only the blind, wounded-creature instinct to fight on remained. The will to die with her jaws locked in her foe's throat.

Hands moved. Plexiglas shards cut. Salt water stung. She crawled, pulling herself back up to the navigator's station. The wave that had deluged the cockpit drained away into the main hull and the emergency battle lights flickered on. Power. Somewhere there was still power.

Up onto her knees. The panel. The panel was dead. The screens dark.

Lower right pane quadrant. Double row of breaker resets. You know that! You know what to do!

Focusing on it, she demanded that her hand obey. It did, coming up as she fiercely watched. She thrust her palm against the reset switches, driving them back in.

Circuits sparked and sputtered, but responded. Solid state, shock proof, and water sealed, enough key elements remained intact within the multiply redundant systems net for partial function. Automatic battle-damage switches opened, isolating destroyed and shorting components. Relays cycled, seeking and finding functional links.

The panel screens lit off, telling Amanda a tale of catastrophe in their patterns of red and yellow warning prompts, but at least speaking to her.

Beyond the *Queen*'s battered hull, the battle still raged. Around her lay the dead and wounded. But all that mattered to Amanda at that moment was the joystick in her hands and the glowing square of light marked "Fire Control Systems Access."

A weapons mount responded to her plea.

```
***STARBOARD PEDESTAL***
1**2.75 RKT /\ SINGLE FIRE
2**2.75 RKT \/ SINGLE FIRE
```

The main screen filled with the imaging of its thermographic sights, the spiderweb of the targeting grid coming up on call. Amanda's hands moved the joystick, both fists clinched around it to suppress the trembling. The pedestal elevated, traversed, seeking the enemy.

Gun Corvette Promise . . . *Navy of the West African Union* . . . *Former Nigerian Minesweeper Marabai . . . Length 167 feet . . . Armament . . .*

Armament. At the Corvette's bow and stern, muzzle flashes pulsed as she fired on the other craft of Amanda's squadron. Trying to kill them as she had killed the *Queen.*

Rage building within her, Amanda Garrett reached out and wiped her enemies away.

Click . . . Click . . . Click . . . Click . . . Click.

Her doubled fingers closed convulsively on the trigger. Somehow neither the gunfire nor the sound of the Hydra rockets screaming out of their launching tubes registered on her mind, only the soft clicking of the firing button as it depressed.

Hell walked the decks of the *Promise,* deliberately, from stern to bow, consuming the gunners at their stations, twisting and smashing the gun mounts, stoking the flames with the stacked ready-use ammunition.

The sighting crosshairs elevated minutely, backtracking. *Click . . . Click . . . Click . . . Click . . .*

The side bulkheads of the bridge caved in and damnation swept the *Promise*'s officers away. Jagged fiery rents opened in the exposed side of the superstructure, letting in the fire and the death.

Down-angle. Stern to bow again. Hold the prime horizontal gauge at the waterline. *Click . . . Click . . . Click . . . Click . . . Click . . .*

In the engine rooms and magazines, hull plates exploded into jagged, white-hot shards, tearing, rending, ricocheting, seeking, leaving behind nothing in their passage but terror and searing pain. But then the sea followed, curling in over the broken sizzling steel and mangled flesh, soothing, cooling, engulfing ship and crew both in its promise of peace.

Click . . . Click . . . Click . . . Click . . . Click . . . Click . . . Click . . .

The rocket pods were empty. Amanda suddenly realized they had been empty for a long time. And there was a hand, shaking her by the shoulder. And there was a voice.

"Skipper, c'mon, let go. Skipper, can you hear me? It's over. Let it go!"

Amanda looked away from the targeting screen. Stone Quillain knelt beside her, helmetless, blood and camo paint streaking his face. Gradually the rest of the world seeped back into her awareness.

Beyond the empty frames of the windscreen she saw the Union battle squadron, what remained of it. The gunboats *Alliance* and *Unity,* drifting and ablaze from bow to stern. And the corvette, the *Promise,* the outline of her flame-licked upperworks distorting as she slowly capsized.

The sounds of the night came back as well. The guns were silent, but Amanda heard the turbine howl of the *Carondelet* and the *Manassas* as they hurried to the side of their crippled sister and the thudding rotors of the first medevac helicopter in the distance.

Someone wept nearby. Across the cockpit, Steamer Lane cried as he cradled a small, pale, and very still form in his arms, her water-sodden fall of honey-colored hair fanned over his arm, her blood a growing dark stain on his uniform shirt.

Amanda returned her gaze to the navigator's console and to her hands, still locked around the joystick. "Stone, could you help me here, please?"

She was surprised at how normal her voice sounded.

With clumsy care, Stone helped break the grip of her frozen hands on the controller. Freed, Amanda fell away from the console and back against Quillain's chest. Her face pressed against the wet, smoke-reeking fabric of his utilities and his arm came around her shoulders. For a long minute they huddled together, not as a man and a woman, but only as two battered and bone-weary animals propping each other up. For the first time since she had come to Africa, Amanda felt cold.

"I guess we won," Quillain said in a cracked whisper. "Or at least as close as it's going to get."

Port Monrovia Oiling Pier

0245 Hours, Zone Time; September 8, 2007

A vast, roiling cloud of smoke drifted slowly inland, underlit by the burning hulk of the tanker. The *Bajara* was settling to the channel floor, her hull glowing a dull red and her superstructure collapsing in upon itself as the steel softened and buckled.

With the coming of dawn, the pall of burning petroleum would be a banner of disaster that would be seen for a hundred miles.

The defense force was coming in from the breakwaters, the uninjured helping the wounded. Those who could walk carried those who could not. Obe Belewa made himself stand out on the access road and watch as they stumbled past through the headlights of the command track.

There were things in their faces that he had never seen before. Things that he had never wanted to see in the face of his soldiers. Defeat, sullen disillusionment, despair.

They passed in silence, the only sound the scuffing of boots on the road. Muttered conversations and voices that had been lifted in anger out in the darkness, cut off abruptly as Belewa was recognized.

Obe could not blame them. He had promised them victory and now they knew him to be a liar.

Sako Atiba came up to stand at his shoulder. "General," he said coldly, "the American radio jamming has stopped. We have regained communication with all regional headquarters and with Mamba Point government center. What are your orders?"

The Premier General opened his mouth to reply, but found that he had no orders left to give.

Mobile Offshore Base, Floater One

0305 Hours, Zone Time; September 8, 2007

"We're secure here, Admiral." Amanda Garrett's voice was steady as it issued from the speaker, but the effort behind each word could be easily read. "*Sirocco* has the *Queen* under tow and we are inbound to the platform at this time. All wounded and injured have been medevaced. I am releasing *Carondelet* and *Manassas* for reservicing, and with your permission I am closing out the Wolfrider time line."

"Permission granted," MacIntyre replied over the radio link. "Wolfrider is secured. Well done, Captain."

SEA FIGHTER   **401**

"No, sir, not this time." Pain and a faint tremor touched the distant voice. "I cost you, Admiral. They hurt us. More than I like to think about."

MacIntyre grimaced into the microphone. "You know your Kipling, Captain. Remember what he had to say about the 'savage wars of peace'?"

"I do, Admiral. I've recalled that line a number of times lately."

"Very well, then. When can we expect you back on the platform?"

"Shortly after first light, sir. I'm riding back in with the *Queen* and her crew. I'll be available for debriefing at your convenience."

"Stand down and get some rest when you get aboard, Captain. The debrief can wait. MacIntyre out."

Christine keyed her own headset, relaying Amanda's orders. "Operations, the Lady says secure the Wolfrider timeline. All task force elements stand down from general quarters and resume standard operational protocols. Pass the word to all hands. Mission successful."

She looked around to the systems operators in the briefing trailer. "That includes you guys. Go get some sleep. We can knock down the workstations later. Well done, gang."

The wall screens blinked off, one after another, as the systems powered down. Stiffly, the S.O.s levered themselves out of their chairs, stretching out the kinks of too many sitting hours out of their spines. MacIntyre and the intel realized just the opposite, that they had been on their feet continuously since well before midnight. As the enlisted hands departed, the two officers doffed their headsets and sank down on opposite sides of the conference table.

Christine remained seated for only a moment, however. Rising once more, she moved to the blackboard on the trailer bulkhead and studied the blurred words printed on it.

POWER PROJECTION
MAINTAIN SEA LINES OF COMMUNICATION
MAINTAIN FLEET IN BEING

Lines had already been drawn through the first two missions. Now she picked up the chalk and drew one through the third. Then, turning to the trailer's small onboard refrigerator, she knelt down, popped open the door, and removed two cold cans of Mountain Dew soda.

"The last of a good vintage, Admiral," she said, returning to the table and placing one of the cans in front of MacIntyre. "I've been saving them for a special occasion."

"This qualifies, Chris. Thanks."

"What was that thing you mentioned with the Captain?" the intel inquired, resuming her chair. "That Kipling thing?"

"The savage wars of peace?" MacIntyre popped the pull ring on his can with his thumb. "It's just a line from a poem about the old British colonial times. Not a very politically correct piece of work these days, but one that still holds some truths." He took a long, deliberate pull of cold soda. "Evaluations, Commander. What happens next?"

Christine shrugged and sipped her drink. "This conflict, as we know it, is over, Admiral. Belewa is out of everything—seapower, fuel, time, everything. The direct threat to Guinea and Côte d'Ivoire has passed, although they're going to have a new set of problems to deal with as the West African Union breaks up."

MacIntyre cocked an eyebrow. "You think the Union will self-destruct?"

"Unless something radically changes, fa'sure. The West African Union is a very new government and a very tenuous one. It has, in essence, been a tribal union built around a one-man personality cult, that of General Obe Belewa. The people of the Union owed their allegiance to him personally and not to any concept of 'nation.'"

Christine rolled the cool side of her drink can across her forehead. "A prime example of this kind of thing is post–World War II Yugoslavia. For decades, Josip Broz Tito held a violently diverse ethnic and cultural grouping together by political savvy, personality, and force of will. However, once the 'Little White Violet of the Mountains' was removed from the equation, *plotz!*"

"The same principle applies here. As long as Belewa is a winner, as long as he can deliver the goods and make things better, his people will follow. But once he's shown up to be a mere mortal . . . Well, he's going to have to pull a real miracle out of his ass to salvage this situation."

"Well, that's his problem, and that of various kings, potentates, and diplomats," MacIntyre replied grimly. "We held up our part of the bargain, Chris. We knocked Belewa off his white horse. Now they get to figure out who climbs into the saddle next. They're welcome to the job."

The Admiral studied the brightly painted beverage container in his hand as if for the moment it had become very important. "She pulled it off for us again, didn't she? Another of her patented miracle packages."

Christine nodded. "Yeah, she did. She's real good at that kind of thing. Sometimes, though, I wonder how many more she has left in her before she hits the big one."

"The big one?"

The intel gave another sober nod. "Yeah. You know, the job that's finally going to be so tough that she's going to have to die to get it done."

MacIntyre glanced up. "You think that's going to happen to her?"

"Admiral, it's bound to, barring the sudden onset of the millennium. Amanda is the most totally 'give a damn' person I've ever met. And the 'give a damns' usually get used up pretty fast."

"That's all too true." MacIntyre crossed his arms on the tabletop and stared down at a coffee mug ring, his craggy features thoughtful. "You sound like you know Amanda Garrett pretty well, Chris."

The Intel shrugged. "I like to think I do. Why?"

"Because I think I'd like to know a little bit more about her myself. I don't suppose you could provide me with a . . . briefing on the subject, could you?"

"Why not, sir. Where do you want to start?"

Vice Admiral Elliot "Eddie Mac" MacIntyre hesitated for a long moment, then said, "What's her favorite color?"

Christine Rendino looked away to hide her grin. "Green. She really likes green a lot."

Conclusions

Crouching on the dusty floor of the long-abandoned shack, the Union Special Forces trooper peered through a gap between the warped boards nailed over the door.

He wore no uniform this day. Instead he was barefoot and clad in ragged civilian shirt and shorts. It had been carefully explained to him that this was a most secret and critical mission and that no one outside of himself and the military high command at Mamba Point must know of it.

He dug out the watch, one of the two objects he carried in his pockets, to check the time. They should be coming soon. The trooper returned to his vigil.

Outside, the crumbling macadam roadway was empty. Set midway between Monrovia and the airport, the hut was too far outside the city proper to see the passage of many foot travelers, and motor vehicles were now almost unknown. Only the government had any fuel left at all, and little enough of that.

Accordingly, when the trooper heard the sound of automobiles approaching, he knew it must be his target. Squinting out into the morning brightness, he watched as the small motorcade passed, first the Army Land Rover escort and then the battered Mercedes sedan. As the latter swept by, he caught the silhouette of the lone passenger in its rear seat. Yes! Target positively identified. All was going as planned.

As the little convoy proceeded toward the city, the trooper dug his hands into the small pile of earth and crumbling clay brick beside the hut door frame. After only a moment, he unearthed the coils of wire he had been told would be there. He removed the second object from his pocket, an electric hand detonator, and began connecting the wires to its terminals.

Another Special Forces team had preplanted the command-detonated antitank mine in the roadway late the previous night, running the concealed detonator leads back to this firing point in the shack. The trooper's task would be to explode the mine at the designated time, on the motorcade's return run from Monrovia to the airport. The young soldier did not know why the U.N.

representative was to be assassinated. However, Premier General Belewa had ordered that it be done, and that was enough.

⚓

As the small convoy made its way through the streets of the Union capital, Vavra Bey noted the changes since she had last been there, the growing disrepair, the uncompleted projects, the devitalization. The streets and markets were, for the most part, empty and left to the accumulating trash. And the few people abroad moved with a sullen lassitude instead of the burgeoning pride they had once carried.

The citizens of the Union might not be beaten, but they were rapidly forgetting what it was they had been trying to win. The U.N. representative could sense it. The stillness upon the city was a pause, like a man hesitating, wondering what he should do next.

The Mamba Point Hotel, once the tall, white citadel of Belewa's government, had been converted into a fire-scarred ruin, every window in the structure shattered and the upper floors burned out from a cruise missile hit. A missile Bey had claimed the responsibility for.

She was alone here, amid a people who had no reason to have any great love for her. And yet, for what she hoped to accomplish, she'd had to come by herself.

The elevators had all been knocked out, and the climb to General Belewa's office was a long and slow one. Maintaining his base of operations in the battered hotel had to be a monumental inconvenience, but perhaps also a last act of defiance. Either that or perhaps the man simply didn't give a damn anymore.

Bey's silent escort ushered her through the door into Belewa's office.

She observed that change had come to General Belewa as well. Somewhere during the past few months he had made the transition from "young" man to "no longer young" man. His closely trimmed hair was hazed with gray now, and the seams in his face had deepened, defining with greater clarity the bone beneath the flesh. The brightness and intensity still lingered in his eyes, but a fever heat burned behind them now.

He looked up as she entered, not rising, making no gesture of officiousness or formality. "What do you want?" he asked simply.

It was good. This was how she wished it to be, as well.

"It is time we talked, you and I," she replied, crossing to one of the chairs before the General's desk. "Not negotiate, but talk." Uninvited, she sat down and met his gaze.

Belewa suppressed a short, harsh bark of laughter. "About what? You've won. We've lost. What is there left to talk about?"

SEA FIGHTER **407**

"No one wins at war, General," Bey replied levelly. "At best, one only prevents things from getting worse. It is true, we have no more reason to speak of Guinea. That issue is resolved. But we need to speak of the Union and its people and what befalls them next."

"There is little to speak of there as well," Belewa retorted. "Hell returns, Madam Representative. Very likely, we collapse back into the chaos and mindless savagery we arose from. No, the United Nations need not concern itself about the Union much longer. As it was with Liberia and Sierra Leone, we'll soon be eating ourselves alive and you will be able to safely forget about us once again."

Bey lifted an eyebrow. "And this is what you want, Obe Belewa?"

"What I want?" Belewa stared in disbelief at the representative. "What I want?" The big African straightened and rose from his chair. Lifting both fists, he crashed them down on the desktop. "What I wanted was to end it all. I wanted to end all the suffering! All the starvation! All the killing and repression and brutality. Couldn't you see that! Couldn't any of you see that all I wanted was to end the madness that has infected this land for far too long?"

"Yes, General, some of us could see that."

"Then why couldn't you let me finish the job?" Belewa turned away, staring out of the glassless balcony doors toward the sea beyond. "Why couldn't you let me put things in order here? For decades you ignored this corner of the world, letting it go to the devil. Why pay attention now, just because someone is trying to put things right?"

"Because the day of empires and empire builders is past, General," Vavra Bey replied quietly. "As is the concept of 'the end justifies the means.' No one argues with your goals. But the precedents that would be set by their achievement would have been too high a price to pay. Conquest can no longer be permitted by the world community, not even with the best of intentions."

"Then how else am I supposed to do the job? Tell me that." Belewa spun back from the windows. "I'm a soldier! I have a soldier's skills and I know how to use a soldier's tools! What other options do I have?"

The U.N. representative nodded slowly. "You are a soldier, a brave and able one. But if you wish to reach these high goals you have set, you must undertake a battle far more challenging than any you have ever before dreamed of."

Vavra Bey did not speak as a diplomat now, but as a grandmother, that wisdom being more appropriate and stronger for this moment. "You must learn how to make war in another way, General. A slower and more difficult way. You must learn how to invade with ideas and how to conquer by example.

"You stand at a critical crossroads, Obe Belewa, one where many have stood before you. You have a choice. Out of stubbornness and pride, you may allow yourself to slide down into total defeat, taking all that you have built with you. Or you may lift your head again and begin this new and greater battle."

A grudging smile touched Belewa's face. "Someone told me once that I was a man cursed with excessive pride."

Vavra Bey smiled back as she might have at one of her own sons. "With pride, it is not a matter of too much or too little. More it is a question of how it is used."

Belewa smiled again, more freely, and returned to stand behind his desk. "Then tell me, how should I use mine?"

"By being willing to consider other options, both for the Union and for the region. You are right, General Belewa. West Africa has indeed been ignored by the world for far too long. But you have our attention now."

The U.N. representative rose to her feet. "I journeyed here this day to extend you a personal invitation, General. Let us resume formal talks to seek resolution in the Union's conflict with Guinea and in the matter of dealing with the refugee crisis. Let us end this war, so that we may begin the greater battle."

Belewa rested his hands on the back of his chair, his face impassive, his eyes downcast in thought. Vavra Bey stood by quietly, listening to the cry of the cormorants from beyond the empty patio door frame. Finally Belewa looked up.

"I hear your words, Madam Representative. You will have my answer by this time tomorrow."

⚓◆

The heat of the day had long since settled upon the little hut on the airport road. The Special Forces trooper fiercely resisted the lassitude the growing warmth carried with it. Kneeling in the dust by the boarded door, he ignored the sweat trickling down his back and peered between the slats, watching the highway. He must be ready. He would have only one chance and only a single second in which to act.

He set the detonator down and wiped his palms dry on the seat of his shorts. The mine lay fifty yards down the road beneath a pothole in the incoming lane. The powerful Italian antitank weapon was potent enough to destroy the heaviest of armored fighting vehicles. It would totally disintegrate the representative's car, but only if the vehicle was directly over the shaped charge when it was fired.

Dust rose down the road. Hastily the trooper snatched up the hand detonator. Yes, it was the motorcade! They were coming! Again the Land Rover in the lead, trailed by the Mercedes.

The detonator's safety pin pulled free with a sharp metallic click. The trooper had carefully paced off the distance to the pothole when he had come on station and had noted a stunted eucalyptus tree growing beside the road, opposite the mine. That was his mark.

The army vehicle rolled past, the limousine coming on.

The trooper found himself regretting that the limousine's driver had to die as well, but this was war. Prices had to be paid if the Union was to triumph. The shadow of the eucalyptus tree fell across the Mercedes, and the trooper's hand closed convulsively around the firing lever.

Monrovia, West African Union   2101 Hours, Zone Time; September 10, 2007

As he climbed the hotel stairway, Dasheel Umamgi silently cursed the bite of the prickly heat beneath his robes, then cursed again because he could not bring himself to scratch in the presence of his soldier escort. Admitting to such human frailties would be an act unworthy of a holy man, especially in front of these black swine.

He targeted yet a third curse at General Belewa for summoning him here at this hour and yet a fourth for the West African Union as a whole. This had been a most promising operation in the beginning. An opportunity for Algeria to establish a radicalist Islamic power base on the African Gold Coast. When the Council of Mullahs was ready to strike southward into Mali and Niger, such a base in the infidels' rear area would prove most useful.

The establishment of such a beachhead had seemed a simple matter. Take in a monkey republic general that everyone else had turned out and buy his allegiance with promises and a few shipments of obsolescent armament. Then support him in his struggles, as long as the cost was not too great, and manipulate him to Algeria's advantage.

All the while, agents could be inserted into his territory, beating the drum for Islamic radicalism. Weak points and weak men within his own government would also be sought out, preparing for the time when a puppet leader totally obedient to the Algerians could be installed.

Simple matters all, and yet it had not worked out as planned. Belewa turned out to be strong and a most unwilling subject for manipulation. The General was popular as well, and Algeria's plans for subverting the Union populace had faltered.

All was not quite lost, however. The plan for finding weak points within the Union government had at least borne some fruit. For the glory of Islam and Algeria, as well as for himself, Umamgi had pressed on, seeking to further isolate Belewa from the world and from his own people. The Union government now stood on the brink of collapse, and sometimes much can be gained out of chaos.

Yet it would pay to be cautious. Sometimes Umamgi had the uncomfortable suspicion that Belewa understood far more about Algeria's plans for the Union than the Ambassador might have liked. And today, something had gone wrong. Very wrong.

Reaching the floor that held Belewa's office, Umamgi's guide opened and held the stairwell door for the ambassador.

Just beyond the door stood Brigadier Sako Atiba, a military police escort standing watchfully at his side. One look into the Chief of Staff's face told the Algerian that indeed something had gone very, very wrong.

"Good evening, Ambassador," Atiba's escort said politely. "General Belewa wishes to meet you and the Chief of Staff."

Umamgi and Atiba were not given a chance to speak together, the guards ushering the two men down the hallway toward Belewa's suite. The floor seemed exceptionally quiet, the usual bustle of staff work suppressed. Men could be sensed behind the office doors, however, quiet men, waiting men.

With the coolness of the instinctive conspirator, Umamgi gauged the situation. Brigadier Atiba still carried his side arm. He was not yet under arrest. And he still carried a look of defiance and not fear. A confrontation was coming with Belewa, but the possible outcome was far from a foregone conclusion.

The Algerian pressed a discreet hand against the slit pocket in his robes, feeling for the outline of the silenced Beretta .22. The little automatic had served him well during his climb through the ranks of the Algerian revolutionary party. Perhaps tonight it might fire the first shot of a new revolution.

The MPs ushered them into Belewa's office, then fell back outside the door, closing it behind them.

The General waited. Sitting behind his great desk, he afforded Umamgi only a brief glance, but he studied Sako Atiba's face for long silent moments. Some large round object lay on the desktop, shrouded under a burlap sack.

Belewa let the scene drag out wordlessly for almost a full minute. Then he straightened abruptly, his left hand coming from behind the desk to sweep aside the burlap, revealing the dirt-encrusted metal bulk of a disarmed antitank mine.

"Our sappers made a surprise security sweep of the airport road at first light this morning, before Representative Bey's arrival." Belewa's voice was little more than a whisper. "And the Military Police established a stake-out on the firing point. The young soldier who was supposed to detonate this mine was very disillusioned to learn that his orders did not, in fact, come from this office. He has cooperated fully with our investigation."

Belewa leaned back in his chair, his eyes seeking Atiba's again. "Why, Sako?" he demanded. "Have you gone mad? Why would you set out to destroy the few rags of international recognition and acceptance this government has!"

"Because we have to strike back!" Atiba exploded in return. "Because we have to show the United Nations and the Americans that we are not afraid, that we will not let ourselves be defeated!"

"And we will do this by killing a helpless old woman in our streets! That would not prove we are brave! It would prove that we are rabid! She was a senior United Nations representative on a peace mission! What kind of respect could we ever hope to gain from such an act? What kind of honor?"

"Respect and honor!" the Chief of Staff spat back. "That's all you speak of anymore, Obe! What of the victories you promised! What of making things better for the people?"

"And getting our people labeled as mad dogs will make things better?"

Atiba stepped a pace closer to the desk. "At least mad dogs are feared. Under your leadership the Union has become a whipped and beaten cur chased into its kennel by the U.N. and by this Leopard of yours. We are losing, Obe!"

Belewa caught his reply, holding it back for half a dozen heartbeats. And when he did speak, his voice was low and controlled once more. "You are right, my old friend. We are losing. We are losing far more than we can afford. It is time for a change."

Atiba's reply was quiet as well. "Yes, Obe, it is." And then the Chief of Staff's hand swept back to the gun at his belt.

Atiba never completed the draw. General Belewa had been holding his own drawn automatic just below the level of the desktop. The worn Browning Hi-Power elevated, a three-round burst flaming from its silvered muzzle. Brigadier Atiba, thrown backward by the bullet impacts, crashed to the floor, face upward, unseeing eyes staring, his fingers still hooked under the flap of his pistol holster.

As was his way, Umamgi had taken a step aside when the confrontation had begun, waiting to see the trends before committing himself. However, even with a half-developed plan for assassination in mind, the sudden explosive climax to the conflict between the two men paralyzed him. Brigadier Sako Atiba, the secret card he had husbanded so carefully for so long, had been taken out of the game before his eyes. And Obe Belewa yet lived.

"Aiiiii, Sako!" The soft keening cry drifted across the room on the sea wind. The General sat unmoving, his head tilted forward, his face locked in a grimace of anguish. His eyes were closed, the automatic in his hand momentarily forgotten. Umamgi cut a look at the office door, so far away across the room, and took a silent, sidling step.

"Sako Atiba was my friend," Belewa's quiet words froze the Algerian in place, "and a good soldier."

Belewa had looked up again. His voice was almost casual, but his features were fixed and cold. "But he was not born to lead. He was always a follower."

Belewa swiveled in his chair to face the Algerian, the leveled Hi-Power in his fist coming to bear with the deliberation of a traversing tank turret. "Tell me, Ambassador," the African's voice grew softer yet, "who was he following tonight?"

Umamgi felt a scream well up within him. He clawed wildly for the Beretta. The pistol hung up as he tried to draw it, the silencer snagging in the robes prescribed for a holy man. Belewa's automatic slammed again, and the last sound Dasheel Umamgi heard was the tinkling of an ejected cartridge case on a desktop.

⚑

No one came in.

Obe Belewa knew they were out there, though, in the hallway, waiting. Waiting to see who would walk out the door of this office. Waiting to see who would be the new leader of the West African Union. He let them wonder. Instead, he sat for a long time in the silent company of the friend who had become an enemy and the ally who had never been a friend.

The flies came after a while, buzzing in through the open patio doors, seeking the freshly spilled blood.

Was this what it had come to? He had dreamed of doing good, of uniting and lifting an entire people out of chaos and degradation. But what good was he doing now, beyond giving the flies fresh meat to raise their maggots in? Where had it all gone bad? What had gone wrong?

Thoughts and memories swirled behind his eyes, and he scrabbled among them, seeking an answer, seeking for someone to accuse: Umamgi, Bey, Sako, the Leopard. And yet, somehow he could not bring himself to lay blame upon any of them. Each had only played out a destined role as the conflict had unfolded. Belewa could not condemn anyone for doing what they had seen as their duty, not even Ambassador Umamgi and Sako Atiba.

Could it be that the dream had not gone wrong, but had in fact been wrong from the beginning?

The day of empires and empire builders is past, General.

Gods! Has it all been for nothing!

The pistol still gripped in Belewa's hand lifted as if of its own volition. The steel of its muzzle, cooled again, felt good pressed against his temple, soothing and simple.

And yet he heard that stern yet gentle voice speak once more. *Out of stub-*

SEA FIGHTER   **413**

bornness and pride, you may allow yourself to slide down into total defeat, taking all that you have built with you. Or you may lift your head again and begin this new and greater battle.

The General lowered the pistol, setting it on the desktop. He was puzzled as to how he had come to aim it at himself. That would have been the act of a coward. And while he was many things, good and bad, Obe Belewa was not a coward.

He got out of his chair and circled around to the body of his chief of staff. Kneeling down stiffly, he brushed the flies from Sako's face and gently closed the lids over the staring eyes. Then, denying himself a limp, he rose and strode to the office door.

He left the gun behind on the desk.

Washington, D.C.   **1534 Hours, Zone Time; September 15, 2007**

"Essentially, Harry, he's put everything we've asked for on the table and then some."

Vavra Bey's matronly features filled the flatscreen of Harrison Van Lynden's videophone. "He has officially acknowledged the Union's military operations against Guinea and has personally accepted responsibility for them. He has also personally guaranteed there will be no further acts of aggression and he is pulling the Union army back from the Guinea border.

"Finally, he has agreed to a full repatriation of all Union refugees in Guinea territory. He has promised a full restoration of property and civil rights and has invited a U.N. observation group in-country to supervise the resettlement program and to monitor the Union side of the border zone. He's giving us everything we've been asking for."

"Well, he's asking for a whale of a lot in return," the Secretary of State replied, frowning. "An immediate lifting of all nonmilitary trade sanctions and a whopping big aid package. We took quite a few casualties during the UN-AFIN operation, Vavra. I can tell you right now we're going to have some Congressmen back here who are going to be asking why we're fighting this guy one day and paying him off the next."

"The same question will no doubt arise within the Security Council, and I will give them the same answer I give you now. If we are to get these refugees resettled, we must first ensure there will be a country to resettle them in. Believe me, it will be far cheaper in lives and money to allow the West African Union to survive than it would to allow that area to backslide into the anarchy it knew in the nineties. We need someone to be in charge there, and General Belewa is our best and only available option."

"That still doesn't get us around the fact that Belewa invaded and took over Sierra Leone to create the West African Union," Van Lynden replied. "That's a fact we can't just sweep under the rug, Vavra."

"I understand this, Harry, but I believe I have a solution. Let's give General Belewa the concessions he asks for, but incorporate a requirement for a U.N.-monitored plebiscite among the former citizens of Sierra Leone on the question of returning to an independent status or remaining as part of the Union. We can give Belewa a broad time frame—say, two years—to stabilize things before mandating the vote. I think the majority of people down there will support the current status quo with the Union. The plebiscite would both legitimize the Belewa government and reintroduce the democratic principle into the region."

"I think you may have something there." Van Lynden tilted his chair back and began to tamp tobacco into his battered rosewood pipe. "The only question is how far we can trust Belewa. This gentleman has proven to be one very tough and resourceful customer. I can't help but wonder if he might be trying to put some kind of move on us. This is an awfully abrupt turnaround for the man."

"I agree," the distant U.N. representative replied over the circuit. "But Belewa knows he must move fast if he's going to stave off an internal collapse of the Union. Also, for what it's worth, my instincts are telling me the man is sincere. I truly believe he is abandoning his aggressive course of action."

"What triggered it, Vavra? Sure, the man's back was against the wall, and the loss of that tanker must have hit him pretty hard, but something else must have happened."

Bey pondered for a moment. "I don't know, Harry. I truly don't know. We understand there has been a major disruption in the relationship between Algeria and the Union. All of the Algerian technicians and advisers have been withdrawn, and the Algerian ambassador has either been recalled or has disappeared. We aren't sure which. We also know that there has been a shake-up in the upper echelons of the Union government. The civilian minister of internal affairs now appears to be Belewa's new second in command. Beyond that, we simply don't know.

"Essentially," she continued, "I think that General Belewa is a good man who may now be on the road to becoming a better one. The kind of leader that very sad portion of the world may need." Bey smiled slightly. "I'd like to think that maybe I had some influence on General Belewa's decision to turn down that road. But no doubt that's only an old woman's vanity."

Van Lynden took a moment to draw the flame of his lighter down into the bowl of his pipe, savoring the first rum-flavored puff. "Who can say? In this great game we play, you can never be sure what card will take the trick in the end. I'll be speaking with the President later this afternoon. I believe you can expect the support of the United States in this matter."

"Thank you, Mr. Secretary. That is good to hear."

"And thank you, Madame Representative. Damn nice piece of statesmanship."

Vavra Bey lowered her eyes modestly and nodded her acknowledgment. The video screen reverted to the State Department net logo a moment later.

The Secretary of State tilted his chair back. Closing his eyes, he drew on his pipe again. It felt good to win one every once in a while. The only problem was that they just kept coming at you.

Van Lynden enjoyed half a dozen more puffs. Then he straightened at his desk once more, knocking the pipe embers out into his ashtray. Returning his attention to the Indonesian Country File he'd been studying when Representative Bey had called, he flipped back the security cover and reread the title:

PIRACY IN THE 21ST CENTURY:
AN ANCIENT THREAT REBORN

Mobile Offshore Base, Floater 1   1921 Hours, Zone Time; October 1, 2007

My Dearest Arkady:

I'm very pleased to hear things are progressing at Jacksonville. I always knew you were a fighter jock at heart, and I'm glad that heart has found a home. I hope you'll be glad for me as well, because I think I've found a new home too.

Remember that last day out on the Seeadler? *(Lord, that seems so long ago now.) We talked about what I was looking for and where I was going. I was a little confused at the time, and I understand why now. I had ideals mixed up with things.*

When I became a naval officer, my focus was on getting myself a ship. Well, eventually I got one, and that was all well and good. But the day loomed when I was going to have to give her back, and I sulked like a kid whose bicycle was being taken away.

However, before I could do anything stupid, I was called away to the Heart of Darkness to fight in an odd little war that nobody else wanted. And while roosting out here on this barge for the past six months, I learned an important truth about myself. It hasn't been the ship that I've craved all this time, it's been the making of a difference.

I like the feel of doing something that matters. I like the thought that by my own small efforts I might be helping steer history onto a better, safer course. Is this vanity or ego? I don't know, but I am stuck with it. It's what I want out of my time in the universe.

I'm a lifer, Arkady. Be it on a bridge or behind a desk, I'm staying and doing the job until I'm old and gray and they throw me out the door.

And where does that leave us, love? As you said, we'll see how it goes. We have our duties to do today and many sweet yesterdays to remember. Tomorrows haven't been promised to us yet, but we will avail ourselves of them if they come along.

Be well. Seek happiness.
Amanda

Amanda paused and reread the letter, then nodded to herself. She was comfortable with the words. Double-tapping the "Send Mail" box on the computer screen, she launched it on its way. Palming a bit of moisture from the corner of her eye, she flipped the laptop shut.

A decisive knock sounded on the module door.

"Enter."

Stone Quillain stepped up into the office, utility clad and packing a back-load of equipment. "We're getting ready to transfer across to the LSD, Skipper," the Marine said, unslinging his seabag and MOLLE harness, "and I figured I'd come by to say so long."

"I'm very glad you did, Stone. I have a couple of things I want to talk to you about before you go."

"Sure thing," he replied, crashing down into the visitor's chair. "Shoot."

"Firstly, I wondered if you could discreetly keep an eye on Commander Lane for me on the crossing to Little Creek. I'll be flying back, and Steamer's taking the loss of Lieutenant Banks pretty heavily."

Quillain nodded. "Already planning on it, Skipper. The Commander's kind of taking the hit on Miss Banks a little harder than average, if you get my meaning."

Amanda nodded. "I surmised as much. The traditional bond of comrade-ship between warriors can become a very strong thing. When the two warriors involved also happen to be man and woman, well, a pretty potent combination can occur."

Quillain shook his head. "That ain't supposed to happen, Skipper. It says so right there in the regs manual."

Amanda smiled an ironic and reminiscent smile. "A lot of things happen in this navy that aren't supposed to. And regulation books don't fight and win wars. People do, with all of their inherent weaknesses and strengths. The system is going to have to live with that fact, at least until we're all replaced by computers and RPVs."

Quillain rolled his eyes. "Amen to that. Now, ma'am, you were sayin' there was something else you needed to talk to me about?"

"That's right. There is. How would you like to come out to Hawaii with me for a while?"

Quillain tilted his head down and lifted an eyebrow. "This isn't some kind of proposition, is it?"

"Well, not quite in that sense." Amanda chuckled. "I've been swapping a few ideas with Admiral MacIntyre and we've decided to keep the Seafighter Task Force together as a littoral-warfare test bed unit for weapons technology and combat doctrine. We'll be taking the Three Little Pigs out to Pearl as our core element. From there, we'll be experimenting with various support and force multipliers for different battlefield environments.

"One of the things we want to try is a composite Force Recon/Marine SOC company, a kind of Seadragon regiment in miniature. We're going to be putting a provisional unit together, and your name came up in reference to the command slot. Interested?"

Quillain grinned. Standing up, he extended his hand across the desk. "I said anywhere and anytime, Skipper. Have the Admiral save me a bunk."

Amanda stood as well, exchanging a strong handclasp. "Welcome aboard again, Stone."

⊗✦

After the big Marine's departure, Amanda brewed herself a cup of tea. Earl Grey at last, thanks to a care package from her father. Taking the steaming mug with her, she went out to sit on the front step of her quarters. Now that she had adapted to it, the lingering heat of the day was a comfortable hug. A Gold Coast sunset flamed the sky, one of the last she would see.

Floater 1 was being stricken, its current mission completed. A big Whidbey Island–class Landing Ship Dock lay close aboard, its deck lights glowing golden in the dusk. The three seafighters had crawled into the commodious womb of its docking well earlier in the afternoon. Now a Marine Sea Stallion skycraned trailers and cargo pallets across from the platform to the amphibious warfare ship's helipad.

Farther out, the silhouettes of a pair of Tribal-class Fleet Ocean tugs could be made out. In another day or two, with the platform emptied and the components uncoupled, they would take up the long tow. First back across the Atlantic to the States for repair and refurbishment, then on to some new crisis point elsewhere in the world.

Soon the sea would roll in to the verdant coast untroubled once more.

Amanda sipped her hot drink and thought about people. The Chief, Danno and the Fryguy, Snowy Banks. Sad thoughts, but good ones. She was proud to have known them all.

She thought also about someone else. A man with whom she had spoken with only once but who had totally dominated her life for half a year. The man who had been her foe through no intent of his or her own.

What kind of man was he, beyond being a skilled and capable warrior? Had he ever wondered about her and who she was? And what were his thoughts?

"Hey, boss ma'am." Christine Rendino ambled up from between the housing units. "Out sitting on the front stoop, huh?"

"That's right. Just enjoying the night airs." Amanda slid over, clearing a space beside her on the step. "Care for some tea?"

"Maybe later." Christine flopped down on the step, bumping shoulders companionably with her friend. "I brought you something," she said, holding up a padded manila envelope. "It came in with the last hard mail shipment."

"What is it?"

"Uh, we're not exactly sure. It's addressed to you, but according to the postmark, it was mailed in Abidjan and there's no return address. FPO security was leery, so they checked it out really well before they cleared it as safe, and I had my antiterror people do the same. There's no explosives or exotic tropical poisons involved, but beyond that, I dunno. Have a look."

Amanda ran a thumbnail under the tape that had been used to reseal the envelope and shook the contents out into her palm.

It was a pendant, a fine braided leather thong with two golden beads and some kind of polished animal's claw centered on it.

"What in the world is this?" Amanda wondered aloud, fingering the curved, ivory-colored shape. "A lion's claw?"

Christine shook her head. "No, it's too small. I asked a couple of guys who know about this stuff, and they say it probably comes from a leopard."

"A leopard."

Amanda Garrett weighed the pendant in her palm for a moment, wondering at the mystery of it. And then she smiled and looped the thong around her neck.

Glossary

Aerostat A blimplike tethered balloon used to carry radar antenna and Elint-gathering systems to high altitude to expand their area of coverage.

Boghammer Generic name for a light, high-speed motor gunboat. Generally an open 30–40-foot Fiberglas hull propelled by powerful outboard motors and armed with an assortment of machine guns and shoulder-fired rocket launchers. The name originates from the Swedish boat-building firm that manufactured a large number of the craft used by the Iranian Revolutionary Guard during the Persian Gulf tanker war of the late 1980s.

Cyclone-Class Coastal Patrol Craft A derivative of the Vosper Thornycroft "Ramadan"-class Fast Attack Craft, twelve of these 170-foot, 35-knot vessels have been commissioned by the United States Navy for littoral patrol work and as a staging vessel for SEAL special naval warfare operations.

Depending on the defense pundit one listens to, the Cyclones are either too large, too small, too lightly armed and vulnerable, or too heavily armed and provocative. The only firm conclusion that can be drawn to date is that there aren't enough of them to go around.

Dash The monetary lubricant that keeps the governmental wheels of many African nations turning. Referred to elsewhere as "squeeze" or "bribery."

Eagle Eye UAV (Unmanned Aerial Vehicle) Built by Boeing Textron, the Eagle Eye reconnaissance drone uses the same tilt-rotor technology developed by Boeing for the V-22 Osprey Verticle Take-off and Landing transport aircraft, permitting it to either maneuver as a conventional aircraft or hover like a helicopter. With a 300-mile radius of operation, the Eagle Eye's dual-mode flight capacity has rendered it of great interest to the Navy, permitting comparatively small surface warships to have an aerial search-and-surveillance capacity.

ECOMOG (Economic Community of West Africa Military Observation Group) A multinational peacekeeping force deployed to Liberia by

ECOWAS. While including military detachments from a number of West African states, it is primarily Nigerian in makeup.

ECOWAS (Economic Community of West African States)   A multinational economic development and security organization that includes in its membership Benin, Burkina Faso, Cape Verde, Côte d'Ivoire, Gambia, Ghana, Guinea, Guinea-Bissau, Liberia, Mali, Mauritania, Niger, Nigeria, Senegal, Sierra Leone, and Togo.

Elint (Electronic Intelligence)   The collection of battlefield intelligence (target location, systems type, nationality, force strength, etc.) via the analysis of emissions produced by radars and other electronic systems.

FALN   A first-generation assault rifle designed by Fabrique Nationale of Belgium. A highly successful weapon firing the 7.62mm NATO round, it can still be found serving in the arsenals of a number of Third World states.

GPU (Global Positioning Unit)   A mobile navigation system that utilizes radio impulses beamed down from an orbital network of satellites. Simple, compact, and extremely accurate, this technology is finding hundreds of uses in both the civil and military arenas. So much so that serious consideration has been given to building a GPU into the stock of every rifle issued by the U.S. Armed Forces.

Hellfire   U.S.-designed heavy antitank missile. A powerful and accurate surface- and air-launched weapon, utilizing either laser or radar guidance. The Hellfire is rapidly finding a second mission with the United States Navy as an anti-small-craft missile.

Humint (Human Intelligence)   The classic art of the spy. The collection of intelligence information by observers operating "on site" inside enemy territory.

Hydra 70   A 2.75-inch folding-fin war rocket. Originally designed as an aircraft-launched air-to-surface weapon, it is also carried as a weapons option by the *Queen of the West*–class seafighter. An unguided projectile, the Hydra is usually fired in salvos from a cluster of launching tubes. Effective and simple, it can be modified in the field to carry any one of a number of different warheads: antipersonnel, antiarmor, incendiary, and high-explosive.

M-2 Browning Heavy Machine Gun   Designed in 1919 by the master gunsmith Dr. John Browning, this 85-pound, .50-caliber weapon has been in continuous production ever since. Like the C-130 Hercules transport aircraft and the K-Bar knife, the only replacement for the "Ma Deuce" is another "Ma Deuce."

M-4 Modular Weapons System The new firearm of choice for the U.S. military's special warfare units. Essentially a short-barreled carbine version of the 5.56mm M-16A2 assault rifle, it comes equipped with a telescoping shoulder stock and the Picatinny Arsenal's "Grab-Tight" rail-mounting system. This latter permits the weapon to be modified to suit the mission requirements and personal preferences of the user. Various handgrips and carrying handles can be installed, and either a 12-gauge riot gun or an M-203 40mm grenade launcher can be mounted beneath the barrel in an over-and-under configuration to augment firepower. It can be equipped with a variety of targeting systems, ranging from simple iron and telescopic sights to lasers, night-bright optics, and thermographic imaging.

Mark 19 Automatic Grenade Launcher Also referred to as the "chunker," the Mark 19 was originally conceived during the Vietnam conflict. In actuality it is a low-velocity, short-ranged automatic cannon firing the same family of 40mm shells as the M203 infantry grenade launcher. Mounted aboard numerous types of helicopters, ground vehicles, and small naval vessels, it can also be found in the heavy-weapons companies of U.S. infantry units, being fired from the same ground tripod as the M2 heavy machine gun.

Marine SOC (Special Operations Capable) A U.S. Marine combat element that has undergone a rigorous enhanced training program, giving it the capacity to function both as a Commando-style Special Forces unit and as a conventional infantry assault force.

Since the Korean conflict, the United States military has fielded a growing number of small elite units to deal with the problems of counterinsurgency, counterterrorism, and Special Warfare. The Army has its Green Berets, its Delta Force, and its Ranger regiment. The Navy has its SEAL (Sea-Air-Land) teams, and even the Air Force has its Air Commando squadrons. To date, the United States Marines have bucked this trend, flatly stating that since the entire Marine Corps is an elite formation, such specialized units are redundant.

MOLLE (Modular Lightweight Load-carriage Equipment) New-gen combination backpack and load-bearing harness issued to U.S. ground forces.

NAVSPECFORCE (U.S. Naval Special Forces)   A unified command exis-
tent in the year 2006 placing all USN/USMC special operations and "silver
bullet" assets (SEAL, SOC Marine, stealth warfare, special recon, intelligence
gathering, etc.) under a single headquarters.

Predator UAV (Unmanned Aerial Vehicle)   A remotely controlled reconnaissance aircraft in use by the United States Armed Forces. Twenty-eight feet in
length and with a forty-nine-foot wingspan, the Predator resembles a small
sailplane with a tail-mounted propeller. Equipped with real-time television
and IR sensors as well as synthetic-aperture ground-search radar, the Predator
can loiter continuously over a patrol zone or specific objective for up to 24
hours, operating at a range of up to 500 miles from its control station.

SINCGARS (Single Channel Ground and Airborne Radio System)   Developed by the U.S. Army and also coming into service with the other
American armed forces, SINCGARS is an integrated family of man- and
vehicle-carried radio systems for tactical battlefield communications. SINC-
GARS is an "Anti-Sigint" technology, encrypting voice- and datalink transmissions via digital scrambling and using "frequency hopping" to render
them difficult to jam or locate via the use of radio direction finding.

Sigint (Signal Intelligence)   The collection of battlefield intelligence via the
interception and decryption of enemy radio and landline communications.

SMAW (Shoulder-launched Multipurpose Assault Weapon)   Designed by the
Israelis and called by them the B-300, the SMAW is a direct descendant of
the World War II bazooka, a lightweight, simple, but powerful shoulder-fired
rocket launcher capable of knocking out bunkers and armored fighting vehicles. Used only by the Marine Corps in U.S. service.

TACNET (Tactical Intelligence Network)   A multisource intelligence-
gathering and analysis system. Utilizing reconnaissance UAVs, remote battlefield sensors, and surface and aerostat-mounted radars as well as various Sigint
and Elint assets, it provides a combat commander with a continuously up-
dated, real-time view of events occurring inside the theater of operations.

The author of *Sea Fighter* may be reached at DDG79@AOL.COM. All criti-
cism and commentary gratefully accepted.